THE
EMPIRE'S
RUIN

ALSO BY BRIAN STAVELEY

The Emperor's Blades
The Providence of Fire
The Last Mortal Bond
Skullsworn

THE
EMPIRE'S
RUIN

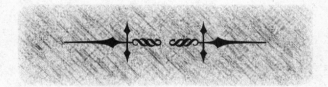

BRIAN
STAVELEY

A TOM DOHERTY ASSOCIATES BOOK

NEW YORK

THE EMPIRE'S RUIN

Copyright © 2021 by Brian Staveley

Maps by Isaac Stewart

A Tor Book
Published by Tom Doherty Associates
120 Broadway
New York, NY 10271

www.tor-forge.com

Tor® is a registered trademark of Macmillan Publishing Group, LLC.

Library of Congress Cataloging-in-Publication Data

Names: Staveley, Brian, author.
Title: The empire's ruin / Brian Staveley.
Description: First edition. | New York : TOR, a Tom Doherty Associates Book, 2021.
Identifiers: LCCN 2021009110 (print) | LCCN 2021009111 (ebook) |
ISBN 9780765389909 (hardcover) | ISBN 9780765389923 (ebook)
Classification: LCC PS3619.T3856 E66 2021 (print) |
LCC PS3619.T3856 (ebook) | DDC 813/.6—dc23
LC record available at https://lccn.loc.gov/2021009110
LC ebook record available at https://lccn.loc.gov/2021009111

Our books may be purchased in bulk for promotional, educational, or business use.
Please contact your local bookseller or the Macmillan Corporate and Premium Sales
Department at 1-800-221-7945, extension 5442, or by email at
MacmillanSpecialMarkets@macmillan.com.

First Edition: July 2021

Printed in the United States of America

0 9 8 7 6 5 4 3 2 1

For Felix, who helped me with the monsters

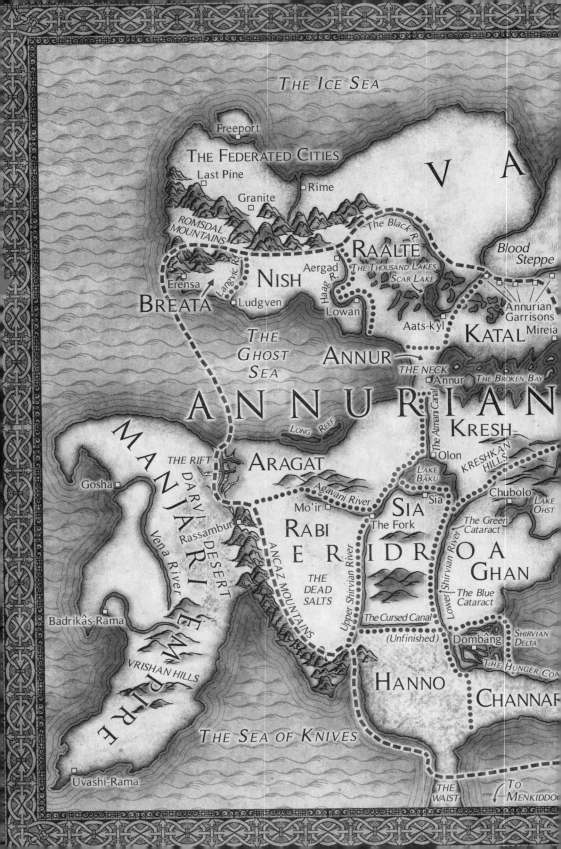

VASH

ANNURIAN EMPIRE

MANJARI EMPIRE

ERIDROA

Dombâng

The Waist

Throne Ships

Solengo

LAND
OF
MENKIDDOC

The Blind

Shorefall

Hamaksha

Kettral Nest

City of Skulls

VOYAGE OF THE *DAYBREAK*, FIRST ADMIRAL JONON LEM JONON COMMANDING

THE
EMPIRE'S
RUIN

1

The bridge was empty.

On the first pass they flew in fast and slow and silent over the wide canal, a smear of darkness across the stars, winging just over the heads of the rotting wooden statues at the top of the Grog Market bridge. Gwenna Sharpe kept her eyes fixed on that bridge, scanning the shadows for her Wingmates— Talal and Qora—who should have been waiting, poised for the extract, just as they'd planned.

"Son of a bitch," she muttered. "Jak, take us around again."

It was supposed to be straightforward. The rain, which had been pelting the city for weeks, flooding the canals, drowning the first floors of the wooden buildings, had broken, if only briefly. For once she could fly without sliding around on the talons, without the fat, warm drops splattering her face, without curtains of rain hazing everything more than a few paces away. Of course, shit went wrong, even on clear nights: a roadblock, an unexpected patrol, some kid awake well past her bedtime who happened to glance out her window and spot two figures—all in black, twin swords sheathed across their backs—and call out to her parents. . . . The world was a mess, even in the best of times, and these were hardly the best of times. A team might be late to an extract for a thousand reasons, and so Gwenna didn't start really worrying until the fourth or fifth pass. By the twelfth she was ready to set the bird down right in the middle of the fucking bridge and go bashing in doors.

"Another go-round?" Quick Jak asked.

The flier sat up on the back of the massive bird, strapped into his saddle, while Gwenna half stood, half hung below, her boots on one of the kettral's extended talons, her harness clipped in high on the creature's leg. The position left her hands free to use a bow or a sword, to light and lob explosives if necessary, to grab a wounded Wingmate and hold on as the bird carried them up and out of danger. Except that there was no one to kill, no one to grab.

She took a deep breath—regretting it the moment the smell of Dombâng, all dead fish, rot, smoke, burned sweet-reed, sewage—clogged her nostrils, and forced herself to go slow, to think the thing through.

"No," she replied after a moment. "Take us up."

"Spiral search?"

Anyone else on Gwenna's perch, anyone not Kettral, wouldn't have been able to hear him. She remembered flying on the talons as a cadet, how the bird's beating wings and the skirling wind scrubbed away all sound. That had been years earlier, though, before her Trial, before she drank from Hull's sacred egg and became stranger, sharper, stronger. Now she could make out his voice just fine, though it sounded far-off and hollow. She could smell him, too, his sweat woven through the miasma from the city below, the acrid soot smeared over his pale face, the damp leather of his saddle; and beneath all that, the too-sweet thread of his worry, which only served to remind her of her own.

"Yeah," she replied. "Tight spiral. But lean west with it."

A moment later, she felt the bird bank.

Over on the other talon, Annick Frencha shifted her posture, twisting casually in her harness as they swung around. If the woman was worried, Gwenna couldn't smell it. She sure as shit couldn't *see* any signs of concern. The sniper hung in her harness easily as a child leaning back in a swing, one hand holding the stave of her bow, the other keeping an arrow nocked to the string. Annick reminded Gwenna of the bow itself: all the slender strength, all the killing—and Annick was nothing if not a killer—folded into a vigilant stillness. She never cheered when her arrows punched home, never pumped her fist, never smiled. While whoever she'd shot was stumbling around, pawing at the baffling shaft, lost in the last moments of dying, Annick was already gone, nocking another arrow, blue eyes scouring the world for something else worth ending. Gwenna had been training, flying, fighting, almost dying alongside the soldier for more than a decade. They'd pissed in the same pots, drunk from the same skins, bled all over the same scraps of ground, and she still wasn't entirely used to the other woman's poise. Just a glance at Annick reminded her of everything she herself was not—not relaxed enough, not calculating enough, not disciplined enough, not cool enough, not fucking *ready* enough. . . .

No surprise that her mop of red hair chose that very moment to come untied. It whipped at her face, tangled in front of her eyes, made itself an unnecessary distraction. Annick didn't have hair—every week she doused her head in a bucket, then shaved it down to the scalp with her belt knife. It made her look like a fifteen-year-old boy, except Gwenna had never met any fifteen-year-old boys who could split a reed with an arrow at a hundred paces.

"If the extract's compromised," the sniper said, "they'll go to ground, make for the secondary tomorrow night."

"Did that extract look compromised to you?"

The sniper kept her eyes on the city below. "There's a lot we can't see from the air."

"Yeah. Two things in particular: Talal and fucking Qora."

"They know the protocol. They'll lie low. Hit the secondary tomorrow."

Gwenna spat into the darkness, watched the wind shred it. "If they're not captured."

"There's no reason to believe they're captured."

"There's no reason to believe they're not."

"They're Kettral."

"Kettral die just like everyone else if you take a sharp piece of steel, put it inside them, and twist it around."

Annick gave an incremental shake of her head. "You want to fly search spirals all night? Dombâng's a big city. Tough to pick two people out of fifty thousand, especially if you don't know where to look."

She was right. Fucking obviously.

When it came to protocol, to doing things by the book, to making the cold, rational call, Annick was never, ever not right. Somehow, though—and Gwenna still spent sleepless nights trying to reason this one out—it was Gwenna herself, not Annick, who had ended up in charge of the Wing. Which meant it was Gwenna, not Annick, who had two missing soldiers, two friends, lost somewhere in the open sewer of a city sprawled out below.

Not that Dombâng looked like a sewer from the air. From the air all you could see was the spangling of red lanterns and cook fires, all those warm human lights and—tonight at least—the greater, cooler brilliance of the stars reflected in the hundreds of canals. A hundred paces up, the warm wet breeze absolved the city of its stench. You could relax a little, flying patrol. No one was likely to stab you while you stood on the talons of the soaring bird. No one was likely to bash you over the head so that they could offer you, alive and squirming, to one of their bloodthirsty gods. At altitude, Gwenna could barely smell the terror soaking the streets and homes below.

Unfortunately, she had two Kettral who weren't *in* the air.

She studied the topography. Jak had them turning slow circles above the tidy wooden tenements of North Point. One block looked more or less like another—tiled roofs, narrow balconies cantilevered out over the canals, each street crooked as a broken leg—except for the dark, ugly scar where Intarra's temple had been torn down by the insurgents. No one had bothered to build anything in its place. They hadn't even cleared away the wreckage.

"Where did you go, Talal?" she muttered to herself. "Where are you hiding?"

No. That was the wrong question.

If the two Kettral were hiding, then they were fine. Sure, Qora had a tendency to stab first and ask questions later, but she was good with her blades—more than good—and Talal would keep her from opening any throats that were better left closed. He'd certainly saved Gwenna from her own idiocy enough times. If they'd gone to ground, as Annick kept saying, then there was nothing to worry about. Which meant Gwenna didn't need to be flying spiral searches or grid searches or any other kind of searches over the entire 'Kent-kissing city. The *danger* was that they'd been captured, and if they'd been captured, there were only two places Dombâng's insurgents would bring them. The Shipwreck was more secure, but that would mean going all the way south over the Spring Bridge, through Goc My's, then doubling back north to Dead Horse Island; a long march with dangerous prisoners in tow. Which left . . .

"Jak," Gwenna said. "Take us to the Baths. Come in from the southeast."

"Against orders," Annick observed. She didn't sound particularly bothered by the fact.

Gwenna shook her head. "Just fucking Frome."

"He *is* the admiral in command of the Dombângan theater."

"Dombâng isn't a theater, it's a cesspool. And Frome's understanding of the place is limited by the fact that he never leaves the 'Kent-kissing ship."

"Nevertheless, the risk to the mission—"

"The risk is for shit. There's one kettral left in the world, and we're on it."

"That's why we have the orders. If the bird is taken—"

"We're a hundred paces up."

"We can't rescue anyone from a hundred paces up."

"So then we'll descend."

"Putting the bird in danger."

"Holy fucking Hull, Annick. It's *all* danger. The *job* is danger." She swept a hand out over the ruddy lights of Dombâng. "Half the people in this city would gut us on sight, and the other half would only hold back in order to feed us to their blood-hungry so-called gods. If we wanted to be safe, we would have taken up brewing or farming or fucking haberdashery."

Annick raised an eyebrow. "Haberdashery?"

"Hat-making. Making hats." Gwenna clenched her jaw, forced herself to shut up. Her anger was just worry. Which didn't make it any less angry. "Look," she went on after a pause. "You're probably right. Talal and Qora are probably lounging in an attic somewhere getting drunk on some local asshole's stash of *quey*. We'll pick them up tomorrow and I'll feel like an idiot for keeping us out here. Fine. It won't be the first time.

"But if they *have* been captured, I want to know it before they're hauled off to the Baths and we never see them again."

"The protocol—"

"Was cooked up by some bureaucrats back in the capital whose idea of 'unacceptable risk' is taking a shit when there's no silk to wipe with."

"Not bureaucrats. The Emperor."

Gwenna shook her head. "The Emperor has amazing eyes and weird scars and an unnecessarily large tower, but she's never been on a bird. She knows fuck-all about flying, fuck-all about combat, fuck-all about Dombâng. She's just scared she's going to lose her last kettral, which is why she has Frome halfway up my ass about it all the time."

The sniper shrugged. "Your Wing, your call."

Gwenna blew out a long, ragged breath. It wouldn't be the first time she'd ignored orders from Admiral Frome. The man was all brass buttons and waxed mustache. Sure, the mission in Dombâng had probably been doomed from the start, but she didn't intend to seal its fate by listening to that fool. She certainly didn't intend to risk the lives of her soldiers for him.

She turned her attention back to the city below.

"Bring us down, Jak, just over the highest houses."

Dombâng was a labyrinth of alleyways, bridges, causeways, docks, and canals—as though the city had been dropped from on high and shattered on the murky surface of the delta—but she'd memorized the map before they arrived, and it was easy to pick out the dark, silted-up expanse of Old Harbor; the mudflats were packed with the shadowy hulks of rotting ships, and there, at the center, the massive, ramshackle Arena where the Dombângans bled for their gods. A few torches burned in the prison yards built up around it. She could just make out the shapes of a half-dozen Worthy up late, training to slice one another into meat.

From Old Harbor, Jak took them northwest past Goc My's plaza with its blank-eyed stone statue, northwest over the old, pillared mansions of First Island, over the sweet-reed barges swinging at anchor in the confluence, and on toward the glittering lights and sweeping rooflines of the Gold Bank. Covering the same route on foot or in one of the swallowtail boats would have been both tedious and dangerous; with the kettral it was a casual matter of relaxing into the harness while the city swept by beneath.

Not that Gwenna was able to relax. Her fingers kept finding their way to the munitions strapped at her belt, testing the wicks, checking to be sure that all the strikers were there. Her eyes ached from the strain of trying to see into every corner, every shadow.

According to her briefings, Dombâng came alive at night, the whole city unfolding into eating and drinking, dancing and lanterns and music. Evidently whoever wrote the briefing had put it together before the revolution chucked everything straight into the shitter.

Dombâng had been a late and reluctant addition to the Annurian Empire, and when the empire started crumbling, Dombâng one of the first cities to reassert its independence. *Most* of the population, at least, had asserted that independence. Plenty of people had been less than enthusiastic about returning to the old ways, the indigenous religion. Unsurprising, really, given that religion's insistence on dragging people out into the delta and leaving them as a sacrifice for the gods. After two hundred years of Annurian rule, plenty of folks had come to enjoy things like trials, and religious tolerance, and trade with the outside world.

All of which meant that Dombâng had fought two wars—one against the Annurian Empire, and one against itself. The first had been bloody enough, but the latter pitted sisters against sisters, children against parents, friends against old friends. That, of course, had been five years earlier. Now, the Annurians were dead—all the soldiers and bureaucrats stationed in the city— along with most of the Dombângans of Annurian descent—merchants with the wrong names, builders with the wrong hair, fishers with the wrong accent or eyes. Some had been burned in their beds, some slaughtered in the Arena, but most were bound and bled, then left in the delta for the gods. Gwenna had never seen those gods, but she'd come across plenty of crocs and snakes and jaguars. The Shirvian delta provided enough ways to die without relying on the divine. Some of the most vicious executions were reserved for the native Dombângans who had dared support the empire—flayings, exposure, painful deaths by serpent or spider. Even five years later, the wounds of the conflict hadn't knit shut. Most people didn't leave their homes at night. Not alone. Not without steel.

Which made scanning the streets and waterways a lot easier. Gwenna was able to check whole plazas at a glance. Her vision, even at night, was owl-keen. From fifty paces up she could make out clothing, faces, the hilts of half-hidden blades. Not for nothing did the Kettral worship Hull, god of the darkness.

A knot of revelers was making its unsteady way through the alleys of the Web. She had Jak double back to check a barge moving west up Cao's Canal. A group of Greenshirts patrolled First Island. No sign of Talal; no sign of Qora.

"Well, fuck," she said, settling deeper into her harness. "Looks like they went to ground after all."

Annick didn't respond. Anyone else might have looked smug or relieved. The sniper didn't appear to be either. She didn't take her eyes off the alleys below.

"Jak," Gwenna said. "Let's check the Baths, then get out of here."

She could just make out the building in the distance, shouldering its way above the other rooftops.

Before the high priests came up with the insane idea to build the Arena, the Purple Baths had been the largest structure in Dombâng—a massive, luxurious, redwood bathhouse thirty paces high and more than a hundred long, sheltering dozens of pools; some intimate, others large enough to float half a dozen boats. For more than a century, it had been the gathering place for the city's rich and powerful, a sanctuary of cool waters and warm sighs. Not anymore. During the Twelve-Day War, the insurgents had seized it and turned it into a military building: part barracks, part training facility, part prison. Some of the drained pools served as sparring arenas, others—their tops covered over with steel grates—cells for the condemned.

Gwenna would have preferred to blow the place wide open when she first showed up, but there was some concern back in the capital that any large-scale, obvious imperial intervention would only alienate the dwindling portion of the populace still torn between the loyalists and the insurgents. So, since arriving in the city, she and her Wing had been working mostly in the shadows—poisoning and sabotaging and assassinating people from rooftops, laying the subtlest finger on the scales in the hope of tipping them back in Annur's favor. The work suited Annick and Talal just fine; it was the kind of thing that snipers and leaches thrived on. Unfortunately, Gwenna wasn't a sniper or a leach. She'd come up through demolitions, and more and more she was starting to think that the only way to deal with Dombâng might be to burn the whole 'Kent-kissing place to the waterline.

Fire—the universal solution.

The soldiers occupying the Baths had made a start on the destruction. All the buildings within a hundred paces had been torn down, wooden frames hacked into firewood, that firewood fed into the huge iron braziers that burned on every side of the massive building. It wasn't the worst defensive position Gwenna had ever seen. Lots of light, even at night. Lots of sentries. Of course, the sentries were all standing *inside* the ring of fires, destroying what little night vision they had. It was stupid, but then, most people were stupid.

Jak circled the bird around the whole place once, twice, three times. Gwenna studied the soldiers below. If the Greenshirts had captured two of the Kettral, the men and women would have been tense, excited, frightened. Instead, they looked half-asleep at their posts, most of them gazing blankly out into the middle distance, dulled by the long night's watch, too fire-blind to notice the huge, manslaughtering hawk turning lazy gyres above them.

"Hold the position, Jak," she said. "We'll loop here a little while longer, make sure these assholes don't show up with our friends, then head for the ship."

Slowly, as the bird banked, she relaxed back into her harness. After more than a decade flying, she'd come to enjoy the motion—the gentle rocking, the slow, smooth beat of the wings. The streets of Dombâng were sticky, hot, miserable, but a hundred paces up the warm breeze feathering her hair felt good. It felt good, too, to be wrong. Talal would rib her about it back at the ship, of course. *I appreciate the thought,* he'd say, *but you worry too much.* She'd tell him the next time he got lost he could go fuck himself. They'd drink a beer, shoot the shit awhile, and that would be that. Another death dodged, another day to wake up and keep fighting.

"All right," she called up finally. "Get us out of here. I want to have time to close my eyes before coming back to pick up these two idiots."

"Sure thing," the flier replied.

Even as he spoke the words, however, the warm southern air turned cold over Gwenna's skin. Her flesh prickled.

"Hold on," she said, then glanced over at the sniper. "Annick, do you . . ." Then trailed off.

Annick raised an eyebrow, but didn't respond.

Gwenna leashed her suddenly pounding heart, marshaled her attention. She recognized this feeling—half readiness, half dread. She'd had it hundreds of times since she drank from Hull's egg. It was a way of knowing, an apprehension bred in the body itself, independent of all the mind's clever methods.

"Hold the position."

She closed her eyes, tried to disentangle the webs of scent and sound, the uncountable strands that made up the world. There was the stench of the outhouses draining straight into the canals, the odor of unwashed bodies, the moldy reek of cloth too long wet, the clean smell of fresh-sawn wood, bright and resinous. She could half follow individual conversations, the voices murmuring in their hundreds and thousands—two men arguing about a fire, a woman hissing something vicious, a commander upbraiding the sentries, and there, teetering on the very edge of her hearing: cursing. Furious, cat-angry, murderous cursing.

". . . will cut open your cock and roast it like a 'Shael-spawned *sausage,* you stupid, skinny, buck-toothed fuck . . ."

Qora.

Gwenna's body went tight, then loose, the way it always did in the moments before a fight.

"They're east," she said grimly. "East-northeast. And captured."

Annick didn't debate the question. She knew that Gwenna's senses were slightly keener than her own. "How do you want to handle it?"

"Jak," Gwenna said, "loop us around half a mile. I want to come in behind them, and fast. Annick, when the time comes, take down whoever's guarding Qora and Talal."

"You sure it's both of them?"

Gwenna breathed in deep through her nose. She wasn't certain, but she didn't need to be certain.

"Just kill whoever needs killing."

She slid the long, smooth cylinder of a smoker free of the holster at her waist.

"We'll hit them in the open area in front of the Baths. Jak, smash and grab. Don't even set the bird down. The smoker will cover our retreat."

"They don't have harnesses," the flier pointed out. "If they're bound, they won't be able to mount up."

"They don't need to mount up. I've got two hands, one for each of them."

"A lot of weight," Annick said, voice flat, factual. "Especially Talal."

Gwenna nodded, rolled her shoulder in its socket, tried to ignore the little click it always did.

Unlike some of the leaches back on the Islands, Talal didn't rely on his arcane power to keep him safe in a fight. He was half a head taller than Gwenna, thick through the shoulders and chest, strong in the legs. On a mission in the Blood Cities two years earlier, she'd watched him seize the tongue of a wagon—a wagon loaded past the boards with bricks—then drag the thing fifty paces to block off the end of a bridge. The bastard was all muscle and scar. Lifting him would be like lifting a sack packed with wet sand, never mind dragging Qora along in her other hand.

She set her boots more firmly on the talon.

"We just need to get clear. I can hold them for a quarter mile, long enough for Jak to land on a rooftop."

"I can carry Qora," Annick said.

Gwenna shook her head. "I need you on that bow."

As plans went, it wasn't the worst one Gwenna had ever cooked up. On the other hand, she'd been the genius behind some pretty piss-poor plans. In this case, at least, they had the advantages of height, surprise, darkness, explosives, and a huge fucking bird.

Everything ought to go all right.

The thought just set her more on edge; *ought* was a word she'd long ago learned to distrust.

Jak brought the bird around, coming in low and hard over the sloping roofs. They were a few hundred paces out when the patrol stepped from the darkness of an alleyway into the ruddy torchlight of the cleared land around the Baths. Ten men—they were all men—moving in a tight knot. Some were looking outward, but most were focused on the two prisoners in their midst. How Qora and Talal had been captured, Gwenna had no idea, but both seemed to have escaped serious injury. They were walking, at least, and while Qora favored her right leg, she was still furiously cursing the soldiers surrounding her.

". . . And *you,* you nutless, gutless fuck, I'm gonna put this hand up your ass, reach all the way up, and rip out your 'Kent-kissing tongue. . . ."

The soldiers outnumbered their prisoners five to one, had them disarmed and bound at the elbows and wrists, but instead of triumph, they smelled of fury and puke-sweet fear. Obviously, the two Kettral had opened some throats on the way to being taken. One of the men prodded Qora with the tip of his spear. Instead of flinching, the woman leaned into the sharp steel. It had to hurt, but Qora was even more pigheaded than Gwenna, which, she had to admit, was saying something.

"You limp-dick piece of shit," the woman snarled. "You don't have the stones to finish it."

It was a stupid gibe. Despite their sun-bleached uniforms, the Dombângans weren't professional soldiers. Most of them were barely more than kids. Probably they'd kicked in a few doors, dragged some terrified families before the high priests. Maybe some of them had a little training with a spear, but they were afraid, and fear made people dangerous, unreliable. It would be easy for one of them to twitch and put that spear right through Qora's ribs. Gwenna willed them to remember that blood was precious in Dombâng, that their gods demanded *living* sacrifices.

Jak trimmed the angle of attack.

"Talal," Gwenna said. *"Qora."* She spoke at a normal volume; the guards wouldn't hear her, but the Kettral would. "Stand by for extract."

Qora was too busy shouting, but the leach started to turn, then stopped himself—no reason to give the guards warning—listened a moment, then nodded.

"Qora," he said. "Smash and grab."

One of the soldiers shoved him forward with the butt of a spear. Talal stumbled, but he had the other woman's attention.

"When?" she demanded.

"In eight," Gwenna replied, pitching her voice over the wind screaming in her ears. "Seven. Six."

Rooftops scraped past just beneath the bird's talons. Alleys, verandas, causeways, docks . . .

"Annick," Gwenna said.

The sniper's blue eyes were black in the darkness. She loosed the first arrow, then two more in quick succession, hands flicking between the quiver and the string, too fast for Gwenna to follow.

"Five," Gwenna said.

The first Greenshirt fell—the group's commander, judging from his uniform—holding his hands to his chest as though in prayer.

Blood sprayed from the throat of a second.

Gwenna lit the smoker. The long fuse hissed, spat sparks.

Another soldier sat down abruptly, reached for the arrow in his eye, then slumped to the side.

"Four."

Panic tore through the Greenshirts like a great wave crashing. Men whirled, brandishing their spears, staring wide-eyed but blind into the night's gulf. Garbled exclamations spilled from half a dozen throats— . . . *attack . . . under cover . . . behind us . . . no!*—the language too broken, too trampled to serve any purpose. One of the soldiers had seized his fallen comrade, was trying to haul him to safety, not realizing the man was already dead. Another broke away, racing for the safety of the Baths. A third stood paralyzed, dark eyes glazed with fire.

"Three."

Talal and Qora, by contrast, stepped into the madness as though it were a dance. The leach lashed out with a foot at the nearest guard, taking him in the side of the knee, buckling the leg. Qora rammed her forehead into another man's nose, smashing it halfway back into his skull. Blood drenched her face when she pulled away, black against her brown skin, but she was grinning as she turned.

"Two," Gwenna said.

The bird's huge wings shifted, beat backward in a great wash of wind. The talons started to swing forward. Gwenna hurled the smoker over the heads of the two Kettral, toward the cordon of sentries posted outside the Baths.

"Starshatter!" Talal bellowed.

She shook her head. "It's just a smoker. Prepare for . . ."

Talal, however, was already moving, hurling himself at Qora. His hands remained tied, but his shoulder took her in the gut, knocking her into a low depression with his own body on top.

The explosion hit Gwenna like a brick wall.

The world blossomed into hard darkness scribbled with fire. Curses and screams slashed the night. Pain flayed her with a thousand blades. For a heartbeat she didn't know where she was, whether standing or swimming or falling. Underwater? No, she could breathe. Back on the Islands? Her trainers were going to be *pissed* if she'd fucked up some exercise. The vets could be unforgiving. . . .

And then, as though in conversation with that first thought, the grim realization: *We* are *the vets now. And this isn't training.*

The rest of the facts came back like a slap as she struggled to right herself, to find some purchase on the empty air. Her hands were empty. Where were her swords? Had she dropped her swords? A moment later, white-hot pain—brighter than the general agony—lanced her shoulder, sliced her across the leg. Her vision narrowed to a tunnel of flame. She gritted her teeth, took oblivion by the throat, forced it back.

Slowly, she growled to herself. *Slowly.*

With blistering hands, she felt for her harness. It was taut around her waist, the tether stretching up and away, still linking her to the bird. She squinted, and the talon came into focus, and there, dangling from her own tether, Annick, also upside down, also struggling to right herself. Grimacing against the pain, Gwenna took hold of the harness strap, dragged herself up, managed to plant her boots on the talon.

The Dawn King was screaming, but they hadn't crashed. Gwenna blinked the haze from her vision. They seemed to be flying rather than falling.

The bird's cry trailed off, and she made out Jak's voice: ". . . hit us."

Presumably that sentence had had a beginning.

"Say again," Gwenna managed.

Something soaked the front of her blacks. She put a hand to it. Oh, right—blood.

"A starshatter," the flier said. "That's what hit us."

"I didn't *throw* a starshatter."

"Not you, them. The insurgents."

Understanding punched her in the gut.

She'd spent the last month supplying Annurian loyalists with Kettral munitions. The point was for them to use the bombs against the bad guys, but people got captured, people switched sides, people panicked and dropped their packs. It wasn't surprising that the Greenshirts had ended up with a starshatter. Shitty, but not surprising.

Her right shoulder blazed. She lifted a hand to the wound, found something hot and jagged lodged in the muscle. Again she almost blacked out, again clamped down on the dizziness and nausea. She could raise her arm, rotate it forward and back. So the muscle wasn't severed, though something was binding in the joint. More carefully, she checked the wound once more.

She couldn't get a good look, but she could feel it well enough—a jagged length of metal about the size of her finger.

"You should leave that in."

Annick had regained her footing over on the other talon. Given the blacks and the lack of light it was impossible to tell if she was wounded, but she looked ready to fight. Which was good, because there was a lot of fighting coming.

Gwenna wrapped her hand around the metal shard.

"Gwenna—"

She didn't hear the rest of Annick's objection because this time, as she ripped the thing from her shoulder, she really did pass out.

For a moment she was floating. Warm salt water buoyed her up. Waves lapped her bare skin, washing her hair against her face. The weightlessness felt good, better than good, as though her land-bound body had been a burden she'd never realized she was carrying, something that had been crushing her little by little, day after day.

I could just stay here, she murmured.

Even as the words left her lips, though, she was waking once more to the horrors of the night, heavy in her harness all over again, spinning like dead weight as the bird hurtled forward through the dark.

"Well, fuck," she muttered to herself, the words chafing over chapped lips.

She dragged in a ragged breath—her lungs felt seared—got a foot on the talon, stopped the spin, hauled herself in once more, checked the puncture in her shoulder. It was bleeding, but she'd spent a lot of her life bleeding. She was conscious. None of her limbs had folded the wrong way. Her heart was getting on with things, banging out the same old angry rhythm, which meant there were no excuses.

"Jak," she asked. "How's the King?"

"Seems all right," the flier replied. He didn't sound hurt, which made sense. He sat on the Dawn King's back. The bird's massive body would have protected him from the blast. "I won't know for sure until we dismount, but he's moving smoothly."

That too made sense. The starshatter hadn't shattered Gwenna or Annick. Whoever detonated the explosive had fucked up—lit it too early or botched the throw. The blast might have enraged the bird, but it wouldn't have knocked him out of the sky. Lucky.

Of course, it *wasn't* fucking lucky that the Greenshirts had a starshatter in the first place. Someone, one of the bastards Gwenna and the rest had come all this 'Kent-kissing way to help, had made a mistake, and now her Wing was paying the price. She let her rage run for a few heartbeats. There was strength in the anger, strength that she badly needed. Then, as she felt her breathing hot and eager between her teeth, she dragged her attention back to the moment. The Dawn King was gliding out over a stretch of dark lagoon. She could hear, somewhere behind them, the kicked hive of the Purple Baths buzzing with shouted orders, questions, cries of pain.

"Take us back around."

She steadied herself against the bird's leg as the flier hauled them into a steep bank. The bathhouse swung back into view, huge as a castle keep, illuminated by the watch fires. Talal and Qora would be on the far side, the eastern side. Or what was left of them. They'd been on the ground, much closer to the point of detonation. Talal had seen the starshatter, tried to get them clear, but the cover had been for shit. How deep was the depression that he'd knocked them into? Gwenna's head throbbed as she tried to remember. She tightened her grip on the harness tether.

"Faster," she called up. Her own voice sounded tight, like a bowstring too short for its straining stave.

"What's the plan?" Jak asked.

"Second verse, same as the first."

"If they have another starshatter . . ."

"We'll be ready this time. Annick, you see someone lighting a fuse—shoot them. Jak, pull up hard if you notice anything—don't wait on my command. Otherwise we're going back in."

She tested her hands. They hurt, but they worked. If the two Kettral were injured or unconscious, she'd need to unclip, dismount, get them to the bird, hold them during takeoff. Her shoulder felt like someone had been going at it with a hatchet for the better part of the night, but that was just too fucking bad. The arm could fall off *after*.

Quick Jak knew his work. He came in low and fast, using the bulk of the bathhouse to hide them until, at the last moment, he pulled the bird up over the roof—so low they skimmed the carved, gilded figures on the eaves. Gwenna caught a glimpse of the serpents and crocs, jaguars and fish with gems for eyes and teeth like knives. The Dombângans set them on their ridge lines to ward off evil spirits. Too bad for them that she and her Wing were a little more solid than spirits. They burst over the roof's peak like the shadow of death itself, and Gwenna got her first view of the chaos in the open space beyond.

Their initial attack, despite its failure, had rocked the Greenshirts. Men and women sprinted in a dozen directions at once, brandishing spears and flat-bows, pointing, shouting, cowering behind dubious cover. The starshatter had ripped a jagged, smoking divot in the soft dirt, and the last shreds of smoke from Gwenna's own munition hung across the mess like a tattered flag.

It took her a moment to flip the scene in her mind, to sort through the chaos and find the ditch where Talal and Qora had taken cover.

Empty.

Stifling a curse, she scanned the open ground. Some of the Greenshirts had spotted the bird. One man raised a finger, started to shout something. His head snapped back, Annick's arrow lodged in his throat. A woman shouldered a flatbow in desperation. The sniper shot her, too. The explosion had obviously hit the Greenshirts just as hard as it had the bird, and unlike the Kettral, they weren't as good at getting hit. Had Talal and Qora escaped in the chaos? Only twenty or thirty paces separated them from the labyrinth of Dombâng. If they'd . . .

No.

Just as she was daring to hope, she spotted them. Some of the Greenshirts, at least, had kept their heads. While most of the Dombângan force milled madly in the open, two men were dragging Qora by her armpits. She slumped, unconscious, or close to it. Talal had managed to regain his feet somehow, but another Greenshirt hauled him by the noose around his neck while two more soldiers followed, spearpoints bloodying his back. Disastrously, the whole group was just a few steps from the doors to the Baths, the angle all wrong, especially given the bird's speed, for any kind of smash and grab. Even as Gwenna opened her mouth to call up to Jak, the bird passed uselessly over them.

"Pull up," Gwenna said, sickness rising in her throat. "We lost them."

"Where?" the flier asked. From the bird's back, he hadn't even been able to see the scene play out.

"Inside the Baths."

She went heavy in her harness as Jak hauled the Dawn King into a steep climb. The ground dwindled below them until the fires were sparks, the Greenshirts so many kicked grubs. A few hundred feet of vertical and they were safe again.

They were safe, while half of the 'Kent-kissing Wing was getting dragged into the Dombângan stronghold to be tortured, imprisoned, interrogated, and then, eventually, if they survived all that, fed to the gods of the delta.

"Orders?" Jak asked.

His voice was ragged. You didn't need to spend a lifetime studying tactics and strategy on the Qirin Islands to recognize the whole thing had turned into a goat fuck.

"Tight circle at three hundred paces."

Annick scanned the madness below, an arrow nocked to her bow.

Gwenna shifted her gaze from the sniper to the Purple Baths. Anywhere else, it would have been an asinine structure to turn into a command center. The Baths were huge, but the massive walls were little more than elaborately carved screens stretching from post to post, the whole structure, like just about everything else in Dombâng, built of wood rather than stone. A determined woman with an ax could have hacked her way inside in a matter of moments, but, of course, the thousands of Greenshirts in and around the Baths would probably object to the hacking. The larger truth was, the Dombângans didn't *need* a normal fortress; the delta was their fortress, hundreds of square miles of muddy, bloody death waiting for anyone who tried to cross it. The Purple Baths weren't built to withstand an attack because they didn't have to.

Gwenna allowed herself a bleak smile, reached for the holster at her belt, pulled free a starshatter.

"Jak, make a saddle run over the Baths."

Annick raised an eyebrow.

"I'm going to blow the roof off," Gwenna explained.

"And then?"

"Then we're going in."

She lit a striker as she said the words, waited for Jak to start the approach run, then touched the flame to the starshatter's fuse. She could feel Annick's eyes on her, but refused to look over. As the sniper had already pointed out, she had orders to avoid the Baths, but she'd been given those orders before Talal and Qora were captured. There were times to lie low, to watch and wait, to play the long game. And then there were times when you needed to light the world on fire and watch it explode.

As the Dawn King swooped up over the roof, she tossed the munition.

It hit just beneath the ridge, rolled a few paces with the slope, then caught on one of the carved wooden figures—something that looked like an eagle or a hawk. Gwenna watched the angry spark burn as the kettral climbed back into the night. She closed her eyes a moment before the explosion—no need to risk her night vision—listened to the detonation tear a hole in the darkness, then opened her eyes again.

She'd never been inside the Purple Baths, but she'd seen rough plans and drawings from some of the loyalist spies. The roof tiles—hard, sunbaked clay—were fixed to a wooden scaffolding spread over the massive, trunk-thick rafters. The starshatter smashed through it all like a great, blazing fist. An entire section of the roof, from one huge beam to the next, folded downward and in, timbers splitting, cracked tiles sliding into the smoke. Screams boiled up from inside—the falling tile and debris would have killed some, injured others, strewn yet more chaos through the already chaotic night. As tactics went, blasting a house-sized hole in the fucking roof was hardly Gwenna's classiest work, but it would have to do. In the wake of the first attack, the Greenshirts were reeling. Given time, however, they would regroup, double or triple the guard, maybe move Talal and Qora somewhere else, somewhere Gwenna couldn't find them or get to them. There was a moment in every fight when you had to strike. She wasn't as ready as she wanted to be, but neither were the bastards down below, and she'd spent most of a lifetime fighting when she wasn't ready.

An ugly win, Hendran wrote in his *Tactics, is still a win.*

"Take us inside, Jak," she growled.

There was a pause.

Then: "The whole bird?"

"They tend to fly better in one piece, so yes."

"It'll be tight."

"Fortunately, you're good at this shit."

Annick shook her head. "Bad extract."

"Maybe we should ask the Greenshirts to take our friends to a nice open field, someplace with flowers and a babbling brook."

"The Emperor—"

"The Emperor can scream at me all she wants when this is over. We're getting Talal and Qora."

"If the bird is trapped—"

"Annick," Gwenna said, shaking her head, "just shoot some motherfuckers, will you?"

The Dawn King banked, came back around, hung for a moment in the hot night air, one heartbeat, then another when she could still stop it, belay her order, call it all back, think up another, better plan. Then time, as it always did, slid past, silent and ungraspable. The bird folded his wings and stooped.

Gwenna tightened her grip on the leather strap holding her to the bird's leg.

There weren't a lot of fliers or birds that she'd trust to pull this off. The gap in the roof was barely larger than the kettral's half-folded wings, which meant they needed to drop through, then pull up before splattering on the floor below. It helped that the hall was huge, easily large enough for the kettral to spread his wings, and it helped that Jak was the best flier she'd ever seen.

Still.

She shielded her eyes as they dove through the opening, plunging from the night's darkness into the flaming chaos of the open space below. The main section of the Baths comprised one huge room, large enough you could almost sail a warship into it without hitting the masts on the ceiling. Untidy rows of cots lined the walls; huge mess tables stood in the middle of the largest of the drained pools; cook fires burned in two dozen places, silting the air with smoke; and everywhere people—there must have been four thousand soldiers crammed into the space—running and shouting, scrambling and seizing their weapons. Which was more or less what you'd expect after blowing the roof off a building and flying a screaming, man-eating bird through the hole. No one was shooting at them yet—probably because no one could quite believe that they were real. Surprise, however, soured faster than milk on a hot day. Not even the weakest soldiers stayed stunned forever.

Gwenna took in the space at a glance. The ends of the hall were there and there, which meant the eastern door, the one through which Talal and Qora had been dragged was . . . *there.*

"I have them," she said, unclipping from her tether while the bird was still dropping.

The kettral pulled up hard at the last moment, legs outstretched in the way of its much smaller brethren when they fell on a hare or squirrel. She leapt from a dozen feet up, hit the ground awkwardly, rolled, and came to her feet with both her short blades drawn. Immediately in front of her stood a man holding the half-eaten wing of some kind of bird. His black beard glistened with grease. Fat dripped down over his fingers. Interrupted in the middle of his dinner, he hadn't even thought to reach for a weapon. Gwenna stabbed him in the gut, one quick stroke, then pulled her sword free before he fell.

"Annick," she said. "Cover me from the bird. Jak, get ready to drag us out of here."

Barely a dozen paces separated her from Talal and Qora. A dozen paces and at least as many Greenshirts. Some she cut down, others she went around. Every heartbeat or so she heard the low thrum of Annick's bowstring followed by the slick whisper of a fletched arrow parting the air. Half the Greenshirts rising to meet her dropped before she could even reach them. Despite the odds, it was barely a fight, and not for the first time a distant part of her murmured that it should not be so easy to kill so many people so quickly.

"Count your fucking blessings, bitch," she muttered, then opened another throat.

Despite his injuries and bonds, Talal reacted better to the attack than the Greenshirts. He managed to crowd into the man holding his noose, then smash his nose with the back of his head. The soldier howled, then dropped the leash as Talal pivoted, kicked him into a shallow, empty pool. One of the other Greenshirts raised his spear, but before he could bring it down, Annick's arrow slid between his teeth, snapping his head backward, kicking up a fountain of blood.

Talal snatched up the spear in his bound hands, ran a third Greenshirt through the stomach, and he was free. Instead of sprinting for the bird, however, he turned.

Qora was still unconscious, slumped on the floor where her captors had dropped her. Talal couldn't hold her *and* the spear, not with his hands bound, but he positioned himself over the body to fend off the regrouping Greenshirts.

A few paces away, Gwenna slashed a woman across the face—the Dombângans were baffled, stumbling about like children, but their numbers seemed never-ending—hamstrung another, then she was there.

Talal looked worse up close. He favored his right leg, and his half-burned-away blacks revealed ugly red weals across his dark skin. One of his eyes had swollen nearly shut, and blood sluiced from his broken nose, staining his teeth red when he grimaced.

"Sorry."

"Save it." Gwenna sliced through the cords holding his wrists. "How busted are you?"

"I'm fine."

Another arrow whispered past. Off to Gwenna's side someone grunted, collapsed.

She risked a glance over her shoulder. The Greenshirts had begun to regroup. Men and women who had been inside the Baths eating or chatting or sleeping when the roof crashed in had snatched up spears and flatbows and formed a rough ring around Talal, Gwenna, and Qora. Another group began to close on the Dawn King. They reeked of terror. One man held his spear before him one-handed, point straight up, as though it weren't a weapon at all, but a torch to force back the darkness. The King screamed his defiance, snatched the man up in his beak, tore him mostly in half, then tossed the broken body aside. The others scrambled back a few steps, stumbling over themselves in an effort to get away from that razor beak, those awful, inhuman eyes, but they didn't break.

Gwenna turned back to find Talal hoisting Qora onto his shoulders. The woman's eyes were swollen nearly shut, her nose broken, her lip split, her brown skin purple with bruises. Talal held the spear in one hand, but he wasn't going to be all that good with it, not while carrying Qora.

"Go," Gwenna said, motioning toward the bird with one hand, parrying a sword thrust with the other, then slicing through the throat of her attacker.

Talal nodded, lurched into motion.

They were halfway to the Dawn King when a crack like the earth shattering brought Gwenna up short.

A roof tile whipped past her, smashing itself to rubble on the floor. Another followed, then another. She sheathed one sword, covered her head with her arm just in time for a tile to gash into her injured shoulder, knocking her to one knee. Pain blazed down her arm, up into her neck. She struggled back to her feet, risked a glance up and found, to her horror, that one of the massive rafters had cracked, was folding slowly in and down, dragging the surrounding ceiling with it. Wood shrieked, twisted past its limits. Tiles fell in a hail, shattering on the deck, staggering to the ground all those they struck.

"Now, Talal," she growled, forging forward.

The falling roof might well kill them all, but it provided an opportunity, a window of madness they could use to escape. Even as she lifted her sword, a tile sliced down through the brow of the nearest Greenshirt, opening his face from the eye's socket to the jaw. He pawed stupidly at the flap of skin, tried to plaster it back in place, then stumbled backward into one of the drained pools. The knot of soldiers that had hemmed her in moments earlier began to dissolve, men and women hurling themselves beneath tables or just crouching in place, arms clutched over their heads. A path to the bird opened. If they could make it, they were free; the larger hole in the roof provided an even better exit than the one she'd originally blown open. The night had become a game of chance, of blind fucking luck.

She'd always hated when it all came down to luck.

Back on the Islands, back when she was a cadet, there'd been an old wrinkled soldier—years past flying missions—named Maxane. She was famous for a siege fifty years earlier, when she'd walked, alone and unarmored, through a withering rain of arrows to set a charge on the fortress gate. Gwenna had heard the story about a hundred times—they all had—but it still made her palms sweat.

Why didn't you run, people asked, half laughing, half baffled.

Maxane always shook her head, frowned as though she'd eaten something sour, gazed out through her milky eyes.

Running's no good. Any archer worth a shit can hit a runner same as a walker.

Gwenna remembered Annick shaking her head. *The odds are better if you're running.*

Odds. Maxane snorted. *Girl, odds are for dice and cards, not livin' and dyin'. Best soldier I ever saw spat his last blood up in Anthera after a little walnut of a farmboy stabbed him with a hayfork. What were the odds? And I've seen my share of idiots live through decisions that should have killed 'em ten times over. Listen to me, girl, and listen good—in the moment, there's just the moment. Just that one thing happenin' that one time. Ain't no* odds. *Either the arrow hits you, or it don't. You die or you don't. That's it.*

As a cadet, Gwenna always found the idea so obviously wrong that it wasn't worth arguing. In the years since, however, she'd come to see the wisdom, if not the logic. You couldn't guard against everything. Maybe not even against most things. When the shit got thick, in the actual moment, as Maxane said, you either died, or you didn't. The notion cradled inside of itself a strange kind of peace, one that dissolved utterly when Gwenna glanced up once more.

In addition to the roof, the whole western wall had begun to give, great posts leaning sickeningly in. The starshatter shouldn't have damaged the wall. Its blast radius was too short to crack the massive trunks. On the other hand, the Purple Baths had been around for hundreds of years. Hundreds of years subjected to steam, heat, rot. It was impossible to know what beetles and termites had been feasting on what posts and for how long, not that it mattered much now. The wall, like soggy paper, flexed inward, beams snapping, blocking their passage to the sky.

At Gwenna's side, Talal stumbled, caught himself, tried to shield Qora's head with one arm while he carried her toward the bird.

Up on the Dawn King's back, Jak shouted something. Gwenna missed the words, but it was obvious he wanted them mounted up already, wanted to get out, but either he didn't see the whole scene or he wasn't thinking clearly. The damaged wall hadn't entirely given way, but a good portion of it—unsupported by the rafters—hung over the space like the ragged jaws of some vast beast, all splinter and stabbing angles, wide as the night itself. Fire licked the wood, found the oil from the broken lanterns, erupted into ribbons of flame. The bird couldn't take off through that.

You die, Maxane said, staring through the cloud of her cataracts, *or you don't.*

It was an ugly situation, made a lot uglier by Gwenna's orders to fly the Dawn King into the Baths in the first place.

For centuries, the kettral—not the order, but the birds themselves—had been the empire's most secret, most dangerous, most vital military asset. They allowed the Annurians to travel faster than anyone else, to attack walls and fortresses from the sky, to wage war in a way that just wasn't possible for lesser nations forced to rely solely on horses, infantry, ships. Those birds had been one of the most disastrous casualties of the civil war. When the Kettral turned on one another in what had to have been the most vicious three days of fighting in human history, most of their mounts were destroyed. Maybe half a dozen fled, scattering along with their masters. Which left Annur with one— the Dawn King.

For five years, Gwenna and her Wing had flown that bird on scores of missions, back and forth across the continents of Vash and Eridroa, from Anthera to the Ancaz Mountains. One bird was a far cry from the several hundred that the Kettral had possessed at the height of their power, but even one was enough to turn certain tides, to alert commanders of impending attacks, to move the best generals to the fronts where they were most needed, to keep the Emperor herself informed of what was happening in all the far-flung corners of her crumbling realm. It was no exaggeration to claim that without the Dawn King Annur might have lost cities, armies, even entire atrepies.

And now Gwenna Sharpe had lost the last bird.

You stupid bitch, hissed a vicious voice in the back of her mind. *You stupid, stupid bitch.*

She shoved the voice down, crushed it, tried to focus on the moment. There would be plenty of time to hate herself later.

"Jak," she shouted, "Annick. Dismount. The King's trapped. Evac on foot."

She scanned the space. The Greenshirts, hundreds and hundreds of them, writhed over one another like grubs or ants, like bees in a hive. Most, panicked by the falling debris and spreading fire, shoved toward the eastern and northern ends of the hall, away from the worst of the danger. Which meant that, if only for a moment, a clear route had opened to the west. Clear of people, at any rate; burning beams and scorched tile continued to rain down.

Two Greenshirts—the only two left, apparently, who still gave a shit about the Kettral in their midst—charged Talal.

As he turned awkwardly to face them, Annick's arrow killed one. Gwenna's belt knife took the other in the neck.

"Go," she said, crowding the leach forward. *"Go!"*

Annick had unclipped herself from the tether, but Jak remained in his saddle on the Dawn King's back. He had a sword out, though there was no one for him to attack. Anger twisted his features.

"I'm not leaving him."

Gwenna bit back a curse. She'd known this was coming. The bird wasn't a pet. He was a soldier, just like the rest of them, and sometimes soldiers got trapped. Sometimes they died. She understood that, everyone else on the Wing understood that, but Jak had raised the King from a fledgling, had trained him to be maybe the greatest bird in the history of the Kettral. He trusted the creature more than he trusted any of the humans on the Wing, which was saying something.

"It's an order, Jak. Dismount. We'll come back for him."

She wasn't sure if that was a lie or not. She'd sure as shit make every effort to recover the bird, but she didn't have high hopes. The Baths were burning, the whole place was falling the fuck down, and the Dawn King was trapped inside of it. The jagged tiles were far too small to do him serious damage, but if the whole 'Shael-spawned *wall* collapsed. . . .

"Jak," she said again, hardening her voice. "Get off the bird now."

"I can fly him out of here."

It was madness, but in the thick of a fight most people went a little bit mad.

The flier's eyes bored into her. "It's not his fault that we're in here. It's yours."

The words landed, a fist to the face. She would have *preferred* an actual fist, but the evening didn't seem to be taking stock of her preferences.

Half a dozen paces distant, a rafter crashed down in a shower of flame and sparks. The end of the great beam caught a pair of fleeing Greenshirts, crumpling one as though he'd been no more than a man made of kindling and twine, shattering the legs of the other, pinning him beneath the smoldering weight. The fire licked at him once, twice, as though uncertain, then all in an awful burst, tore into the man's clothes.

He found Gwenna's eyes, stretched out a bloody hand.

"Please . . ."

She turned away.

"We have to go," Talal said. "If Jak—"

Before he could finish, something struck the flier in the shoulder, knocking him savagely to the side. For a moment, Gwenna thought he'd been shot. Then she saw the slab of jagged tile slide from the bird's folded wings to shatter on the floor. Jak clutched at the reins, failed to keep his seat, then slid, slack and boneless, from the Dawn King's back. Gwenna lunged forward to check his fall, but the man was all muscle. His weight, falling from almost five paces, hammered her to the floor.

The bird, battered from above and hemmed in on all sides by fire, hurled himself into the air. Nowhere to go—just smoke and fire and splintered beams occluding the passage. He beat his wings furiously, kicking up ash and dirt, raising a small storm inside the fire, screamed his frustration, flew the length of the Baths, and alighted once more. The whole thing reminded Gwenna suddenly, absurdly, of far smaller birds, their worlds no larger than the bars of their cage. She'd never imagined a caged kettral, never thought such a thing were even possible. If only she'd been right.

The short flight took only moments, just a few wingbeats, but it put the creature entirely out of reach. Hundreds of Greenshirts crammed the space between Gwenna and the bird. Thousands. The Dawn King might as well have been back on the Islands. He might as well have been on the moon.

Jak shoved himself unsteadily to his feet. The falling tile had torn his ear half off—it dangled by a scrap of skin—and hacked a gouge into his neck, but he didn't seem to notice the wounds. As Gwenna, freed of his weight, struggled to get up, he slid the second sword from the sheath on his back. He reeked of fear, and rage, and desperation.

"Western wall," she said, pointing.

The top half of the wall hung out over the room, swaying with the night wind. The bottom, however, remained more or less intact. Fire wreathed the wide door, but they'd all been burned before. It was still the best way out.

Jak, however, wasn't looking at the door. He was staring the length of the Baths, to where the Dombângans had closed around the Dawn King.

The bird launched himself into the air, raked half a dozen soldiers with his claws, landed, then leapt again. The flier wore a small whistle on a chain around his neck. He lifted it to his lips and blew. The King's head jerked around, his dark eyes swept the Baths, and for a moment Gwenna thought he would come as he had been trained. Not that that would help them much. No one would be cramming the bird through the door, but maybe she could blow open another hole. . . .

She checked her belt for munitions, found a flickwick that might work.

"If I punch out a section of the wall—"

She looked up to find Jak sprinting north, toward the bird.

"Mother. Fucker," she spat, shoving the explosive back into its holster, taking up her second sword once more. "Cover me, Annick."

Just as she moved, however, Talal collapsed, spilling Qora across the floor.

For a moment, the leach lay prone, his face pressed against the ground. Then he staggered to a knee, grabbed the unconscious woman by the arm, hauled her toward him. Blood from the new wound sheeted his face. His pupils pinched tight, refusing to focus.

The Baths had become an oven. Gwenna could feel the heat baking her own blood to her face, singeing her hair and eyebrows, cooking her pale skin pink. Smoke hazed the air, blurred the light, scoured her throat and lungs with every breath. The screams were so loud and so many they had become a kind of silence. Ten paces distant, another beam came down.

"Annick," Gwenna snarled. "Hit Jak with a stunner."

The last thing she needed was another body to carry, but if the sniper could knock him out before he got any farther, Gwenna could get to him. She could save him.

The sniper stabbed the arrow she'd been holding into the wooden floor, plucked a blunt-tipped shaft from the quiver at her back, nocked it to the string, drew, and loosed, all in the time it took Gwenna to exhale.

Too slow.

Three panicked Greenshirts had stumbled behind Jak. The stunner took one of them in the side of the head. He dropped like a sack of grain.

"Again," Gwenna growled, throwing herself into motion.

"No more stunners," Annick replied, voice steady, hard. "We need to evac."

"I'm not leaving him to fight all of Dombâng on his fucking own."

Even as she spoke, a blazing tangle of wreckage fell between her and the flier, forcing her back. For a moment, her world turned a ragged orange-red. Her hair was on fire. She seized a handful in one hand then, hacked down across it with her blade, shearing free a great sizzling nest. The smell made her sick. The whole fucking situation made her sick. Grimly, she raised a hand against the heat, squinted through too-dry eyes, found Jak there, on the wrong side of the wreckage, both blades a blur, fighting for his life and the life of the bird he'd raised since he was a child.

Impossible.

Jak was the best flier she'd ever seen, maybe the best flier in the history of the Eyrie—brilliant and creative in the air, unflinching, utterly calm. On the ground, however, he was a disaster. On the ground, whatever strength he drew on when he sat the saddle on a bird's back evaporated almost entirely. She'd watched him freeze in close-quarters fighting more than once, his great, strong body refusing to execute the orders of his mind. It should have been disqualifying, that panic. It *had* been disqualifying when Jak first tested for the Kettral, but times had changed. Almost all the vets were dead. Gwenna couldn't afford to leave the best flier in the world grounded.

He's fine as long as he stays in the saddle. That's what she'd always told herself. *He's better* than fine up there.

Only he wasn't in the saddle any longer. He was fighting his way down the length of a burning hall, hemmed in on all sides by steel, smoke, and fire.

Each heartbeat she expected the panic to take him, for his body to fold, cringing in on itself. To her shock, however, he fought like a man who had never known fear, never felt those cold talons sliding down his spine, who had never lived anywhere but deep inside the heart of flame and slaughter. He carved into the Dombângans as though they were already meat, hacking through muscle and bone as though his swords weren't swords at all, but a butcher's cleavers. It wasn't bravery so much as madness. In other circumstances Gwenna would have allowed herself a moment of amazement, but there was no time. He was going to get himself killed trying to save a bird that couldn't be saved.

"The wall's coming apart," Talal groaned.

He'd managed to get Qora back onto his shoulders, though the woman's weight had him bent and wavering like an old man.

Gwenna looked up at the structure looming above her. She couldn't say how she knew, not exactly, but all those years of training told her the wall wasn't ready to come down. Not quite, not yet.

"I'm getting Jak," she said. "You start moving."

Down the hall, the flier had become a dream, a nightmare of violence. He slew the Greenshirts even as they tried to flee, forcing his way deeper and deeper. Gwenna could pick out the sound of his breathing, even over the roar of the fire, the jagged shape of his words:

"I'm coming," he panted. "Hold on, King. I'm coming for you."

For two or three scorching seconds, she thought he might actually manage it. The Dombângans, still shocked by the sudden attack and panicked by the blazing hall, scattered before those flashing blades, hurling themselves into the drained pools, diving aside, stumbling backward. Those that held their ground he killed, quickly and viciously. It was easy to forget how large Jak was, how strong, because in all her mission planning she never made use of that strength. Seeing him now wading through the slaughter she was reminded of the man's raw ability.

Ability that meant nothing to a flatbow bolt.

Even as she stared, the flier staggered, twisted back, the shaft jutting from his stomach. Gwenna felt a howl like a spearpoint lodge in her throat. Despite the wound, Jak stayed on his feet, kept lashing out with his blades, forcing himself forward toward the Dawn King.

"I'm coming. . . ."

The words sounded wet, as though the language itself had torn open inside him.

He might have survived the bolts—Kettral healed faster than most people, took fewer infections—but the Greenshirts, sensing weakness, closed in. Jak killed two more before a leaf-shaped spear opened his gut.

The Dawn King heard his scream. The great head snapped around. Fire glazed his black eyes. Jak bellowed again, and from the far end of the Baths the bird answered, the two cries twining around each other, rising in a fever of rage and pain. Then someone slipped behind the flier, hacked down into his neck, and only the bird's scream remained.

Hot blood flecked Gwenna's face, slicked her hands. Ragged breath rasped in her throat. Fire blazed all around her, but she felt ice-cold as the Greenshirts seized the body of the fallen flier, began dragging him away. Kettral didn't die very often. The corpse had become a prize.

Half of her wanted to fight. Fuck that—*all* of her wanted to fight, to hurl herself into the crowd and kill and kill and kill until it was her turn to take a spear in the face or a blade in the kidney. Talal's voice held her back. The leach was calling through the chaos.

". . . He's gone, Gwenna."

She felt like a woman made of granite, as though to turn around and go back would break apart something inside of her, something that could never quite be put right. There were times when it felt like that was all it meant to be a soldier, as though the training and fighting and tactics and strategy were secondary to the ability to break, to be broken, and then to keep going. Jak wasn't the first friend she'd seen die. He wouldn't be the last. There were still the three remaining members of the Wing to think of, and so she turned away from his bloody body, from the Greenshirts, from her own rage, and back toward the people she could still save.

The door blazed, but they could make it.

"Go," she said, waving Talal and Annick forward. *"Go."*

Annick didn't move.

"I have a kill shot on the King," she said, her blue eyes bloody in the firelight, face expressionless. She might have been talking about hunting grouse.

Gwenna hesitated half a heartbeat. As usual, the sniper saw through it all to the frigid, unbeating heart of the disaster. The bird was almost certainly doomed, but they needed a certainty more perfect than *almost*. The only thing worse than letting the King die would be allowing the Dombângans to capture him, to retrain him, to turn him against the empire. It was unlikely, but . . .

"Take the shot," she said.

It seemed impossible that a person could kill something the size of the Dawn King with a slender shaft of steel-tipped wood. In most cases, it *was* impossible. Gwenna had witnessed kettral returning from missions pricked full of arrows, bolts, broken swords, spearheads. All that metal, however, had been in the chest, the wings, the legs.

Annick's arrow leapt from her bow, whistled down the hall, passed through a gout of fire, then plunged, flaming, into the eye of the Dawn King. The bird opened his beak to scream, but the sound spilled out cracked and broken. He flapped desperately, rose a few paces into the air, crashed back to the bathhouse floor, then spread his wings again, baffled as any caged songbird. Annick loosed another arrow. This one caught him in the other eye, burying itself deep in the brain. The last Annurian kettral thrashed, knocked aside dozens of Greenshirts, collapsed onto his side. One wing rowed valiantly, vainly against the air, searching for purchase, then shuddered and stretched out straight, as though it had finally caught the current, as though all it had to do now was glide on the wide-open wind to safety.

"Let's get the fuck out of here," Gwenna hissed, throwing herself into a run toward the door.

She overtook Talal in a few strides, considered taking Qora, then discarded the idea. There were shapes outside, beyond the fire, Greenshirts who had already escaped the blaze, people who would need killing when she came through. She found she was eager to kill someone.

"On me, Annick," she said, grinding out the words. "We need to clear the exit."

The sniper matched her pace as they charged past the leach and his unconscious burden. Halfway to the door, however, Annick paused, turned, began backing up slowly, deliberately, loosing arrows into the madness to cover Talal, who labored on a few paces behind. Gwenna charged through, flame licking her face, her hair. After the fires inside, the hot night air of Dombâng felt cool in her lungs; the breeze washed over her like water. It had begun to rain again, though too lightly to put out the fire.

Three Greenshirts stood outside the door, all armed, their faces painted with shock. One thought to extend his spear. Gwenna hacked the head from the weapon and stabbed the man holding it through the throat. She turned to impale a woman with a mane of black hair, then pivoted to trip the archer, broke his knee with one boot, crushed his throat with the other. Annick stepped out through the door just as the third body hit the wet dirt.

"The canal," Gwenna said, pointing.

Better chances in those winding waterways than on the street, especially at night. They had an unconscious soldier, but Kettral spent half their lives swimming. There would be docks and bridges to hide beneath, boats to steal, dozens of side-canals to slide into. . . .

A sharp crack snapped the riot of sound. She turned, dread opening inside her like a rotten flower, to find the wall coming down in a slow avalanche of flame and burning timber, the doorway, the only passage from the Baths to freedom, caving beneath the weight, and Talal still on the other side of it, running, but four or five paces away.

To a farmer tilling his field, four or five paces was nothing, a matter of a few steps. To a merchant hauling her wares it was even less, the very end of a journey that might have taken days or weeks. To a soldier at the end of a long march, a few more paces were barely worth mentioning. To the Kettral, however, four or five paces, like four or five heartbeats, was an entire world. On one side of those steps waited freedom, even triumph. On the other—an ugly, bloody death.

Talal was on the wrong side.

The knowledge was obvious in his eyes, but he didn't hesitate. Still stumbling forward, he shrugged Qora from his shoulders and, his whole body trembling with the effort, hurled her through the gap. He was strong, stronger than Gwenna, but not *that* strong. The force that carried her through the door was more than mortal; he'd delved into the arcane power of his well, delved deep, in order to throw her to freedom.

Limbs limp, face slack, eyes rolled back in her head, Qora tumbled clear just as the rest of the wall groaned, folded in on itself, splattered sparks across the night, and collapsed.

Bile rose in the back of Gwenna's throat. For a moment she felt as though she was going to fall, but there was no time to fall.

She mastered herself, lunged forward, swung Qora up onto her own shoulders. "We go around, come in through the north . . ."

Even as she was saying it, though, she could see the insurgents spilling into the open space at the northern end of the bathhouse—dozens of them, hundreds. She spun to the south to find the same thing. When the hall caught fire, the women and men inside had fled to the most obvious exits.

"If we go around . . ." she began again, but there was no way to go around, not without passing straight through the mob.

Behind her, to the north, someone shouted. A moment later, a flatbow bolt skittered off the flagstones at her feet.

"We have to leave," said Annick. There was no regret in her voice, no emotion at all.

"I'll go back," Gwenna replied. "You get Qora clear, and I'll go back."

The enemy was still confused, half-panicked. If she could get past the flatbows she could slide through the mob almost unnoticed, get inside. . . .

"Gwenna Sharpe." The sniper's blue eyes blazed with the firelight. "You have no right."

Gwenna stared at her. Annick never spoke like this.

"To fight for our friend?"

"To die before the job is done."

"I'm not going back there to die. . . ."

"Yes, you are. Shit got hard, and you can't face it, and now you want it to be over."

Gwenna's mouth hung open. She tried to object, but found the only word she had was a name:

"Talal—"

"Is a soldier. So are you. This is a hard choice, and you have to make it."

Grief was a jagged bone lodged in her throat. Anything would be better than this. A knife in the eye would be easier. A sword run through her gut would be easier. But no part of the Kettral oath mentioned anything about easy. She ground her teeth together so hard it felt like they were going to break, shrugged Qora up higher on her shoulders, turned away from the fight, and the fire, and her friends—the one dead, the other doomed—and fled into the night.

It took the better part of the night to steal a boat and slip out of Dombâng, and every moment of that night Gwenna felt like a woman being ripped in two. Half of her wanted to go back, hack her way into whatever was left of the bathhouse, then start cutting people apart until she found Talal or died. Half of her—the smarter half, the better half, the half that didn't get her own Wingmates murdered—knew that to return right away would be the worst kind of idiocy.

Jak was dead. The Dawn King was dead. Talal was probably dead. Qora was unconscious, unable to stand or swim, and Annick had only two arrows left. The legions, evidently, had some kind of thing about never leaving men behind. Whole companies had been lost trying to rescue soldiers who were obviously doomed. The Kettral were more ruthless.

Save the ones you can, Hendran wrote. *Leave the ones you can't.*

It made a brutal sense, but as she rowed the stolen boat out through the teetering shacks on the edge of the city, then into the labyrinthine waterway of the delta, she wondered how many friends Hendran had abandoned in burning buildings to die.

Annick spent the journey back to the ship standing on the rails at the swallowtail's bow. Halfway through the night, she killed a twelve-foot croc with one of her remaining arrows. Lucky it was a croc. Everything else in the Shirvian delta was poisonous—the wasps, the spiders, the fucking *frogs*—and arrows and blades—even Kettral blades—didn't work all that well against wasps. In the two months since the warship had dropped anchor at the east end of the delta, the Annurians had lost twenty-eight men—some to disease, some to crocs or *qirna*, some just . . . lost, set out from Dombâng but never returned through the thousand channels to the ship. The Kettral, of course, hadn't had to deal with those particular dangers. They'd had a bird, until Gwenna lost him.

Not lost, she reminded herself. *Slaughtered.*

Over and over again, as she rowed through the long night, she saw the Dawn King struggling, screaming, lashing out with his beak, Jak hacking away with his blades, heedless of the flatbow bolt buried in his guts, Talal falling forward, arms outstretched with the effort of hurling Qora through the gap.

She should have been exhausted by the time they reached the ship—she'd spent the night flying, then fighting, then hauling as hard as she could on the oars—but all she felt when *Anlatun's Lion*—the three-masted flagship of the rump fleet charged with fomenting sedition in Dombâng—finally loomed up out of the dawn mist was a desperate, physical urgency with no focus or aim, as though her own flesh had turned inward to devour itself.

"We get Qora to the surgeon," she said, backing water as the boat knocked up against the *Lion*'s hull, just below the rope ladders. "Get more arrows, more food and water, more explosives, and we go back."

"It's daylight," Annick pointed out, glancing up at the sky.

"Then we'll toss an anchor just outside the city and hide in the fucking rushes until it gets dark," Gwenna snarled. "We're not leaving him there."

Before the sniper could respond, heads appeared over the rail of the ship—Annurian soldiers with flatbows. The *Lion* was anchored far enough from Dombâng that none of the city's fishers or patrols came near it. Still, with twenty-eight dead in two months, no one relaxed, not even on the ship. Frome had a thousand faults, but a lack of caution did not number among them. He had lookouts atop the mast day and night. They would have seen the small boat as it nosed around the last bend, would have recognized what was left of her mop of red hair, but the men staring down at her looked nervous and smelled worse.

"Kettral returning," she shouted up. "Sharpe and Frencha. We've got wounded."

She shipped the oars, and then, without waiting for the reply, hefted Qora up over her shoulders. The motion ripped away one of the woman's bandages. Gwenna could feel the blood—hot and slick—soaking into her blacks.

"I can climb," Qora mumbled.

"You can hold on is what you can do," Gwenna said as she swung onto the rope ladder. Even with the added weight, it only took a few moments to reach the deck. The soldiers stared, baffled as dogs, as she rolled over the rail. Their confusion made sense—there were supposed to be five Kettral returning, flying in on a massive bird, not two and a half in a stolen boat. Still, the lookouts above should have given them enough warning.

"Point those fucking flatbows somewhere else," Gwenna snapped. "You." She stabbed a finger at the nearest man. "Get Qora to the surgeon. You." Pointing to another. "I need rations and a full med kit in the boat. Throw in some rope while you're at it—whatever you have that's light and strong."

"What happened?" one of the soldiers managed. "Where's the bird?"

Gwenna ignored the question, partly because there was no time, partly because she couldn't stomach the answer. Instead, she shoved Qora into his arms—"The surgeon."—then shouldered her way past, toward the forward hatch.

Her own quarters—a tiny space that she shared with Annick—were on the first deck, all the way up in the ship's prow. It only took a few moments to scrub the greased soot from her face, change out of her blacks into local dress, hack off a handful of burned hair, check her blades, then strap a new set of munitions around her waist. She was already headed for the door when Annick entered.

"Frome wants an explanation," the sniper said, filling her quiver as she spoke.

"Frome can fuck himself."

"Frome is the admiral."

"I know what his rank is, Annick. He's going to have to wait. If we want to be in position by nightfall, we need to move now."

With a little luck, Admiral Frome would stay in his cabin stewing over best practices and protocols, waiting for Gwenna to show her face. With a little more luck, he wouldn't realize she was off the ship until she and Annick were halfway back to Dombâng. Of course, if she'd given a little more thought to how the day was going, she might have relied a little less on luck.

She reemerged into the sunlight to find the admiral himself advancing across the deck. Two guards flanked him, each carrying a flatbow. The admiral never went anywhere without his guards.

Gwenna had always thought Frome looked more like a slug than an Annurian military commander. He was slack, short, constantly slick with his own sweat. His brown skin had an unhealthy orange tint, and his eyes bulged from his flat face. He was trying, as he lumbered down the deck, to make up for all of this by walking with his chin high, his lip twisted into the start of a sneer, but Gwenna could smell the uncertainty on him, and the resentment that came with that uncertainty.

"Commander Sharpe," he announced. The man never just *said* anything. He was always announcing or declaiming or proclaiming. "Where do you believe you are going?"

Gwenna glanced over her shoulder at Annick. "I'll deal with this," she murmured. "Get to the boat. Be ready to cast off."

The sniper nodded, slid away toward the rail as Gwenna turned to face the admiral.

"Dombâng," she replied.

He frowned. If frowns had been weapons, Frome would have taken back the city months earlier. "According to the sentries, you have only just returned from Dombâng."

"And I'm going back. I left a soldier there."

"Where is your bird?"

"Dead."

The admiral blinked. "Dead?"

Gwenna strangled her own frustration.

"The mission blew up on us. I lost Jak and the Dawn King. Talal might be dead, might be captive. I'm going back to find out."

"The kettral is *dead*?"

"And Talal will be soon."

"The Emperor, bright be the days of her life . . ." Frome trailed off, licked his lips, picked at the seam of his pants. "The Dawn King," he continued after a moment, "was Annur's only remaining kettral."

"No fucking shit."

He stiffened at the words.

"How did you allow this to transpire?"

"Does it matter?"

Frome drew himself up. "Yes. The way in which you lost one of the empire's most valuable military assets does, in fact, matter." He gestured to the decking beneath his feet. "If *I* were to lose *Anlatun's Lion,* I would most certainly be called to account."

"Well, you're not likely to lose it, are you? Floating out here at anchor while other people do the fighting . . ."

The admiral's face purpled. It was a stupid crack, but the whole situation was stupid. She wasn't going to stand there and debate him while the Greenshirts were torturing Talal.

"You will stand down, Commander Sharpe," Frome said. "You will return to your quarters and write a report of the incident, which you will then present to me before any further steps are taken."

The filing, compiling, and review of reports seemed to constitute the admiral's chief military strategy.

Gwenna tried to shave the edges from her rage. "Admiral. I have a man behind enemy lines. Captured."

"And whose fault is *that*?" Frome demanded. His nostrils flared.

"Mine, sir. Which is why I'm going to set it right."

The admiral shook his head. "We can discuss any further action *after* you file your report. It seems to me, Commander Sharpe, that we have arrived at this pass through too much haste and too little deliberation. These are mistakes I will not allow you to duplicate."

Gwenna forced herself to take one breath, then another, then a third. It was a disaster, she realized, to be having this conversation on the deck rather than in Frome's stateroom. The ship was packed with sailors and soldiers. No one had stopped working, but that work had slowed, as though coiling a rope or scrubbing a section of deck had suddenly become precise tasks requiring patience and perfect concentration. Everyone was listening to the confrontation between the admiral and the Kettral commander, and Frome knew they were listening.

"You're right, sir." She managed to choke out the words, then swallow the bile that came with them. "You're absolutely right. And I will compose a report detailing my role in this disaster as soon as I return."

For a moment she thought he might go for it. He nodded curtly, did something with his lips that on another face might have amounted to a thoughtful frown. Then he glanced over his shoulder, found at least two dozen people within earshot, drew himself up, and shook his head.

"No, Commander Sharpe. I'm afraid not. No. We *have* reports so that, in the event you do *not* return, we will know where to send the next team."

"There is no *next team*. There is one Kettral Wing on this ship—"

"Is there?" Frome raised his brows. "You lost your bird and two of your soldiers. I don't see a Kettral Wing in front of me."

"Things go wrong when you fly missions. It is my job, as the Wing's commander, to fix those things."

As though the arrows in Jak's belly were something that could be fixed. As though the gash opening his neck could be stitched back together. As though the whole night could be put back, blood poured into veins once more, the world unburned, all her mistakes unmade.

Frome shook his head again. "You're the woman who botched the job in the first place. Why would I send you back?"

"Who else are you going to send?"

He waved a vague hand. "I have people in the city."

"You have a network of spies, men and women chosen on the basis of accent, hair color, and skin tone to fit in with the local population. None of them have ever performed a prisoner extract."

The admiral's jaw was so tight it looked ready to crack. "I will not discuss the matter further, Commander, until I have your report."

She opened her mouth, then shut it. It wasn't bad enough she'd lost half her Wing. Now it looked as though, through her own idiocy and impatience, she'd lost the chance to go after the one soldier who was left.

"Sir . . ." she began. Her voice sounded alien in her ears, baffled, pleading. She hated herself for that, but it was just one more drop in an ocean of self-loathing that threatened to drown her. "The space between success and failure will be measured in moments, not days."

She could feel those moments leaking away, like blood from a wound.

She glanced over her shoulder. Annick was nowhere to be seen, which probably meant she was already in the boat. Gwenna measured the distance to the rail, then looked back at Frome. His men carried flatbows, but they weren't likely to use them on her. She might be a fuckup, but she wasn't a traitor.

The admiral made a face that she supposed was meant to look reasonable. "I will send a courier into the city with a message."

"Not good enough, sir," she replied. "I'm sorry."

She brushed past him as he gaped, nodded to the soldiers, crossed the deck in half a dozen strides, vaulted the rail, then dropped into the swallowtail boat below. The craft rocked with the impact. As she'd suspected, Annick was already in the bow, ready to loose the painter. Gwenna lowered herself to the center bench and seized the oars.

It wasn't until she looked up that she realized the magnitude of her mistake, her *latest* mistake. Frome stood at the rail, teeth bared, finger stabbing at Gwenna's face. On either side of him, the guards had leveled their flatbows. They reeked of fear and confusion, but at a distance of three paces, with the high ground and their weapons resting on the ship's rail, they didn't need to be Kettral to hit the mark.

"Gwenna Sharpe!" Frome bellowed. "I *order* you to return to the deck."

She shook her head. "There's no time for this."

The man opened his mouth, froze, found himself with no way to go but forward, and then he said it: "You leave me no choice: for gross dereliction of duty, for insubordination, and for laying hands on an officer, I am relieving you of your post."

When Gwenna was twelve, she'd been shot in the middle of a training exercise down in the south mangroves. The cadet who shot her had used a chisel head rather than a stunner in his haste, and the arrow had punched into her leg just above the knee. She remembered feeling pressure but no pain, looking down, and then staring for a long time at the shaft of wood protruding from her muscle, at the blood seeping from the wound. She knew that she'd been shot, could see plain as sunlight where her skin parted . . . and yet it didn't feel real. The whole moment felt like something dreamed, as though she might close her eyes, then open them again to find herself unscathed.

This was like that.

She understood the words, but couldn't find any way to apply them to herself.

Dereliction of duty . . .

Relieving you of your post . . .

They meant what they meant, but they meant something else as well, something worse. If they were true, then she couldn't go back to Dombâng, couldn't find Talal, couldn't put right even one tiny fragment of what she'd let go so entirely wrong.

And so they couldn't be true.

Out of the corner of her eye, Gwenna saw Annick drop the painter. The sniper didn't reach for her bow, but she didn't need to. Every soldier on the ship had seen her at target practice. Every one of them knew what she was capable of. The men above, the ones at the rail alone, outnumbered Gwenna and Annick four to one. Neither of the Kettral was holding a weapon. And yet the soldiers wore the masks of men expecting to die. They were young, mostly unblooded, far from home in a dangerous place; they'd come to fight traitors and insurgents, not Annur's most legendary warriors. Someone had pissed his pants. The scent hung, hot and acrid, on the still morning air.

"I order you," Frome said again, "to *stand down.*"

He looked ready to hurl himself to the deck of his own ship if she so much as twitched.

"I'm holding oars," Gwenna replied quietly, nodding to her own hands. "Not swords. We're on the same side."

"You will get out of the boat *now,* or I will order my men to shoot."

Gwenna took a slow, steady breath. She could smell Annick, the thin vein of the sniper's anger hammered into that glacial calm. She could smell the terror of the troops, all vinegar and rust. She could smell Frome's rage and frustration, the too-sweet stench of the delta mud, the green of the reeds, the water slopping against the hull of the small boat.

She could probably escape, she and Annick both. They could go over the rail, swim beneath the ship, disappear into the rushes . . . but where would that leave them? Stranded with the spiders, snakes, crocs, jaguars—no boat, no supplies, a dozen miles deep in the delta, a dozen miles from the sea. The fish alone would likely rip them to ribbons, and even if they survived, it would take days to make their way back to Dombâng, days during which Talal might be tortured, might be killed. She imagined him bound to some table, high priests crowded around him, pressing red-hot steel into his flesh, asking over and over again the questions he refused to answer in anything but screams.

Like a woman in a dream, she raised her hands.

None of it felt real, not the sun on her face or the pain blazing in her shoulder, not Frome's wary gaze or the hammering of her own heart. For a moment she thought she might finally wake, discover that Talal was all right after all, that they were all all right. But she did not wake.

Slowly, so as not to spook the soldiers above, she stood, climbed the rope ladder, slid over the rail. The need for haste had passed. Frome would want her to grovel, and so she would grovel, but he would make her wait first. He would make sure every sailor and soldier on the ship *saw* her waiting.

"Bind her," he said, as she stepped onto the deck.

The men hesitated. Judging from the looks on their faces, he might as well have told them to leap into the delta and start swimming.

"It's all right," Gwenna said, putting her wrists together before her.

The words were a lie. Nothing was all right, but this wasn't a situation she could fight her way out of.

After a long pause, one of the soldiers stepped forward, steel shackles in his hands. Not the fault of the soldiers that they served under Frome.

"I'm not going to hurt anyone," she said.

Talal's blood-smeared face filled her memory. Jak's neck opening beneath the blade . . .

Gwenna looked past the men to the admiral. "Are those really necessary?"

He met her eyes, lifted his chin. "Take her to the brig."

"I'm sorry, Commander," the soldier murmured as he clamped the cool steel down around her wrists.

"So am I," she replied. "So am I."

The brig wasn't much to look at, just three tiny chambers deep in the hull. The one into which they'd shoved Gwenna was so small that when she sat with her back against one bulkhead she had to bend her knees. There was no way to stand up or lie down, no way to stretch out. It reminded her of the wooden cages back on the Islands that were used for captivity training. She'd spent a full week in one of those cages once—a week getting rained on and pissed on. Pissing on herself, for that matter. All the cadets had agreed that nothing could be worse than cage week, but what did cadets know? At least you could see the sun from inside the cage. At least you could feel the breeze. At least there were human faces when someone came by to piss on your head. The brig, by contrast, was pitch black, steaming hot, and rank with the twin lingering scents of fear and regret.

Worse, there was nothing to distract her. There was no one to fight, no one to carry, no oars to haul or generals to defy, nothing to do in the darkness but stare into the face of her failure, rehearse again every decision. . . . If she'd followed a different search pattern. If she'd been watching for a starshatter. If she'd chosen to infiltrate the Baths on foot. If she'd kept a hand on Jak. If she'd forced Talal out of the Baths first . . . She stared into those other worlds like a starving woman gazing through the open door of an inn she could never enter.

The ship's bell tolled the watches: morning, noon, dogwatch, night, morning, noon. . . .

No one brought water. Her tongue swelled. The wound at her shoulder throbbed hot, then cold. She found herself pressing at it idly, fingering the swollen tissue just to feel the pain, then forced herself to stop. She listened for Annick's voice, for Frome's, but caught only fragments of either, nothing she could stitch into any kind of meaning. Her muscles cramped, spasmed, pulled so tight it felt as though they were tearing away from the bone. She imagined Talal's body being torn apart, shredded slowly by his torturers as they searched for information.

"I'm sorry," she whispered into the darkness. "Sweet holy Hull, I'm sorry."

The words felt dead on her tongue, rotten. What was it worth, this sorrow of hers? What did it fix?

Nothing. It was worth nothing. It fixed nothing.

Finally, late on the second day, boots sounded in the passage beyond.

Gwenna tried to sit up taller inside the cramped box.

There was a fumbling with the lock, then a feeble gray light that burned in her eyes. She squinted, turned toward the door. She could make out the shapes of two men, soldiers, maybe the same ones who had escorted her down, and beyond them, stiff-backed in the darkness, Admiral Frome.

She opened her mouth to speak, but her tongue was too cracked to manage the words.

"He's dead," Frome said after a long pause. "Your other soldier. The one who was captured."

He didn't use Talal's name.

Gwenna stared at him. Her mind refused the thought. The Dombângans would torture a captured Kettral, but they wouldn't kill him, not yet, not until they'd wrested every piece of intelligence out of him that they could. They'd keep him alive for days, for weeks. . . .

"No," she managed.

The admiral nodded grimly. "The high priests executed him on the steps of the Shipwreck this morning, just after dawn. A strong man, dark brown skin, shaved head, many scars."

He studied her, waiting for some kind of reaction. When she didn't move, he shook his head.

"He's dead, and it is your fault. This mission is over. We are returning to Annur on the next tide where you will answer to the Emperor herself, bright be the days of her life, for all your heinous mistakes."

Gwenna didn't speak. She didn't move. The door to the brig slammed shut.

Something was moving in her lap. Her own hands, she realized. Now that they had nothing to hold—no swords, no explosives, no wounded comrade—they shook. She stared down at them. Even in the dark of the ship's brig she could make them out, though she barely recognized them as her own. She was used to thinking of them as strong hands, but they didn't look strong. Slashed with blood and blackened by fire, trembling in the meager light, they looked like weak, broken creatures, as though they had dragged themselves there all on their own, out of the light, out of the whole wide world to die.

Please, goddess, Ruc begged, blood streaming down his face, sluicing from his chin, draining onto the bridge even as the hot, driving rain washed it away, *help me to love these men.*

The men weren't making it easy.

Two of them held him by the wrists while the third—a bastard the size of a warehouse door—loomed over him, frowning at his own fist.

"Look what you did," he said finally, pointing to a gash along the back of his knuckles.

Ruc tried to focus, to see past the blood and the haze of pain.

"Look!" screamed one of the others, seizing a handful of his hair, dragging his face up, then shoving it forward, until the fist was so close he could have kissed it.

"Your filthy tooth," said the leader, "cut my hand." He cocked his head to the side. "What do you have to say about that?"

"I'm sorry," Ruc murmured without raising his eyes.

Please Eira, Lady of Love, he pleaded. *Help me to be sorry.*

There were priests who claimed that the goddess spoke to them daily, but as Ruc hung there, held up by the hands of these men who hated him, he could hear nothing but the rain drumming on the bridge, on the tiled roofs, on the water, rain so loud it nearly drowned out the sound of people passing a few paces away, of oars creaking in their locks in the canal below, of everything but his own breath rasping painfully in his chest as he struggled to breathe.

Too much rain . . .

The man with the cut knuckles had hit him enough times that his thoughts were beginning to drift. He could feel them floating off, but had no tether to lash them down.

Far too much rain . . .

The hot, wet jiangba season should have ended weeks earlier, around the equinox, but aside from one or two breaks, the storms refused to relent. The sun, which should have been blazing in the sky, was little more than a pale, green-gray disk, like a dream of sun. No fire, no substance.

The rain, on the other hand, was all too real. The rain had weight. Not the individual drops, of course, which splattered harmlessly on the bridges and wooden causeways, drained from the baked-clay tiles of the rooftops, stippled Dombâng's ten thousand canals, but the *idea* of the rain, countless days of it, crouching over the city, pressing down, down, down, gently but unrelentingly, with a billion implacable fingers until even people who had lived their entire lives in the delta, who had seen forty or fifty or seventy rainy seasons, began to go about stooped, hunched, as though the weather were a weight that they bore on their backs.

The canals churned with debris, flooding the decks and markets. First Island was half-underwater. The bridge into the Weir had collapsed. A block of tenements near the east end of the Heights had been washed away, and after years of silting up, Old Harbor looked almost like a harbor again, the Ring of the Worthy standing incongruously at its center, a giant arena awash in the current. Dombâng had grown so large over the centuries that it was easy to forget that the whole place—all the apparatus of bridges and docks and causeways—was built on mudflats and sandbars, but as Ruc struggled to hold on to his thoughts a vision filled him, a vision of Dombâng sinking, all the tiled roofs, each with its carved wooden guardians, sliding beneath the flood until there was nothing left of the ancient city but the wind over the waters.

If only that rain had stopped the fire. . . .

If the rain had stopped the fire, then the Purple Baths wouldn't have burned. If the Baths hadn't burned, there would have been no riots. If there had been no riots, then the man screaming in his face might have passed him by. . . .

"Hey." A quick slap dragged him back to the present. "I'm not finished talking to you, mud sucker. Did I say I was finished talking to you?"

With an effort, Ruc focused on the man's face, watched the black-red heat of slow-building anger baking beneath his features.

"He asked you a question!" screamed one of the others, shaking Ruc by the hair.

"No," Ruc managed. "We're not done talking."

On the other side, the third man remained silent—he hadn't spoken a word since the attack began—but his hands were a vise around Ruc's wrist, and he followed the unfolding violence with disquietingly eager eyes.

Striker, Screamer, and Silence. A grim triumvirate.

"What do you have to say," asked Striker patiently, displaying his bloody knuckles once more, "about what you've done to my fist?"

Ruc struggled to frame a reasonable reply.

"I'm sorry for your fist," he said.

Striker nodded, as though he'd expected the repentance, as though it were only appropriate. Then he frowned again.

"I'm not worried about the scratch," he said with a shrug. "I see worse every day." He stared down at his hands, which were stitched with scar. "What I'm concerned about is disease. I hear you mud suckers carry all kinds of diseases."

Screamer leaned in close. "*I* hear they can't even speak right. Got their own mud sucker babble: *la tra. Chi cho cha.*" He laughed a high, giddy laugh at his own mockery. Then he narrowed his eyes suspiciously. "How in the Three's names did *you* learn to speak so good?"

"I'm not Vuo Ton," Ruc replied. "I live here, in the city."

"Well, I know *that's* a lie," Striker responded, shaking his head.

He hooked a finger, then almost delicately drew back the cuff of Ruc's sodden robe, revealing the tattoos streaking his arm. "Only mud suckers got this crazy ink."

For most of Ruc's life, that ink—slashes of black lines slender as young reeds—had spared him interactions like this. For centuries, the people of Dombâng had held the Vuo Ton in a kind of wary awe. While most of the city's citizens didn't dare set foot into the delta surrounding Dombâng, the Vuo Ton lived their entire lives in that deadly labyrinth of reeds and shifting channels, making their home among the jaguars and crocs, the schools of *qirna,* nests of snakes that could fell a man with a single bite, webs of spiders that laid eggs in the warm flesh of the living. The delta was an easy place to die; city folk gave a wide berth to anyone who managed to survive out there.

They *had,* at least, before the revolution.

One of the consequences of Dombâng's blood-soaked bid for independence was this hatred. Anything different, anything strange, the wrong shade of skin, the wrong texture of hair, the wrong accent . . . *any* of it could see a person beaten, or worse. It had been easy to understand that feeling when it was directed toward the Annurians—after two centuries of occupation, most of Dombâng's population was glad to be rid of the imperial yoke and fiercely jealous of their newfound freedom. That righteous hatred, however, like a river after too many weeks of rain, had strained at its banks, gnawed away at the old levees of human sympathy, until finally the shores burst. When most of the Annurians were finally killed, or driven from the city, or forced into hiding, Dombâng turned on the small Antheran community, then on the Manjari, demanding of each in turn a submission every bit as abject as that to which Dombâng itself had been subjected.

After the worst of the purges, the violence had gradually subsided. People were still murdered, boats were still scuttled, homes were still burned to the waterline for no graver sin than their owners having the wrong eyes or name, but mostly it was possible to move around the city unmolested. Had been, anyway, before someone decided to burn the Purple Baths.

The attack had brought back all the city's savagery in the space of a single night, and this time, it seemed, even the Vuo Ton were not exempt.

Not that he was Vuo Ton.

"I was raised in the delta," he said, "but I chose to live here, in the city."

Screamer glanced at Striker, obviously confused. Vuo Ton never abandoned the delta. The Given Land was as much a part of them as their worship of the Three.

Striker, however, just spat. "Sure. To get close. To blend in. To burn down our buildings when we're asleep."

Most rumor pinned the attack on the Annurians, but the men weren't in the mood to discriminate. Vuo Ton or Annur, *someone* had been bold enough to attack, and Ruc was the person they'd found.

Striker spat again, this time in Ruc's face, then slammed a fist into his gut.

Ruc almost choked on the pain. After a moment, he managed an unsteady breath, then one more, then opened his eyes, made himself look at the son of a bitch who had hit him, *really* look.

Please, goddess, he prayed, *help me to see the man behind the monster.*

They were log drivers—that much was obvious from the tools they'd set aside when the beating began: pike pole, cant hook, a pair of ring dogs. Dangerous work in the best of times, and the height of a too-long rainy season was hardly the best of times. Dombâng relied on lumber felled upstream, well above the delta, then driven down the Shirvian. Without it there could be no boats, no buildings, no bridges, no city at all. Which meant the log drives never stopped, not even for the rain. Men and women died on nearly every drive, caught between the logs and crushed, driven under the surface, held down by the weight of wood until their breath gave out. Sometimes the bodies washed up in the city. More often they were lost, devoured by the millions of things with teeth that lived out in the delta.

Ruc studied Striker's face, tried to look past the violence and rage.

Despite the early hour, the man reeked of *quey*—they all did. They'd obviously been at it all morning. . . .

And then at last, with a flick of her infinite fingers, the goddess opened Ruc's eyes.

"I'm sorry," he said quietly, "for the loss of your friends."

The truth of his guess was clear in Striker's narrowing gaze, in the tightening of Silence's grip, in the way Screamer, who the whole time had been lean-ing so close Ruc could smell the *quey* and sweet-reed mingled on his breath, yanked suddenly back, as though struck.

Understanding is the gateway to love—so ran the Fourth Teaching of Eira—and in that moment Ruc understood a little more of their anger.

"What do you know about our friends?" Striker demanded after a pause.

"Nothing," Ruc replied. Every word hurt, but pain was better than the al-ternative.

Love shuns the easy path, he reminded himself. *She walks on daggers and sleeps on coals. Her strength lies in her surrender.* It had taken him a long time to learn to surrender. Sometimes, as now, he was frightened he had not learned it fully enough.

"I don't know anything about them," he went on, forcing aside his thoughts, "except that they were probably soldiers, and they died defending the Purple Baths, defending Dombâng. The city owes them a debt. We all owe them a debt."

For just a moment he caught a glimpse of the world as it must look to them. While the merchants and priests, shipwrights and seamstresses lived safe be-hind their wooden walls, the log drivers and fishers and soldiers risked every-thing to keep the city alive. Risked anything and, if the reports of the violence at the Baths were to be believed, sometimes lost everything.

Never mind that no one inside Dombâng was safe. Never mind that ever since the revolution those shipwrights and seamstresses could be tied to a bridge piling and left for dead if their neighbors heard them whispering the wrong words, uttering the wrong prayers, questioning the wrong priests. Never mind that even now, years after the execution of the last Annurian le-gionary, people were still dragged from their homes in the middle of the night, hauled into the delta, and abandoned to the beasts—a barkeep maybe, who had once served Annurians with a little too much friendliness; someone who had unwisely taken a soldier as a lover. . . .

Never mind all of that, Ruc told himself. *You cannot hate a person after you see with their eyes.*

Dombângan soldiers had died the night before, died by the score. Maybe childhood friends of the drivers. Maybe lovers. Not just that, but the drivers themselves probably wouldn't live another five years. Running timber down the Shirvian was brutal work. The men beating him bloody would probably find their ends out there—pinned between logs, drowned, shot by Annurian snipers on the bank, bitten by snakes—this season, or the next, or the one af-ter that. The knowledge was built into their bones. Hitting him, hurting him, was a way to remind themselves that they were still alive. Ruc understood better than he cared to admit the fierce vitality burning inside every act of violence.

"A debt," Striker mused, leaning back on his heels.

Ruc nodded. "A debt I can never fully repay, but let me offer this." He nodded weakly toward his sodden clothes. "In the pocket of my *noc* are a few silvers. Take them with my gratitude. Drink a toast for me to your brave, fallen friends."

Not that they looked like they needed more drinks, but it wasn't the role of a priest of Eira to teach another man his needs.

While Striker watched, impassive, Screamer rummaged for the coins. He held them up to the waxy light with a gap-toothed grin.

"Worth a couple bottles, at least."

Ruc could feel the grip on his wrist loosening, and for a moment he dared to hope that that would be the end of it. The men would take the coin, find a tavern, leave him bleeding on the bridge. The beating would be finished. Love would have triumphed over the other, darker thing brewing inside of him, the urge to take them apart limb by bloody limb. . . .

Please, goddess, he murmured. *Let my love for these men shine in my eyes. Let them see it, feel it, and go.*

If love, however, had always triumphed over fear and hatred and despair, there would have been no need for other gods.

"Just a couple coins here," Striker said, swiping the money from Screamer's grip. "You saying the lives of Tall Truc and Pickles were worth no more than a few lousy silvers?"

The glittering silver looked like fish scales in the rain. He tossed it contemptuously over the railing of the bridge.

Screamer frowned, obviously confused.

"If I had more," Ruc replied honestly, "I would have given you more."

Striker shook his head. "All the silver in Basc wouldn't make up for those two."

The man's face didn't change, or his stance, but he was hotter suddenly, even hotter than before. Ruc could see the heat—if seeing was the right word for the way he perceived that red-black burning—baking from his chest, head, skin, until it was a wonder the raindrops didn't sizzle when they struck the man. The goddess of love had given Ruc many gifts, but this ability to see heat came from another, darker, older place. On a cloudy, moonless night, he could track bats by their reddish shapes, watch the dull burning of the rats scavenging in the trash behind the temple, follow the feral cats slinking along the rooftops. In a building with thin walls, he could make out the vague forms of people in other rooms. It was not made for love, this redsight of his, but for hunting, stalking, killing.

As Striker burned, Ruc felt an answering heat rise inside himself, an eagerness, a hunger for violence.

The man drove a fist into his stomach.

Ruc doubled over, tried to cough, but Screamer ripped his head backward.

"You think you can pay for the lives of our friends?" he howled, spittle splattering Ruc's face.

Silence leaned in close, eyes wide as his smile, then shook his head slowly.

He and Screamer still held Ruc by the wrists, but their bodies had shifted. If Ruc dropped to a knee and twisted, he could free his right hand, turn, catch Screamer beneath the elbow, break his arm, throw him. . . .

No, he growled to himself. *Love does not trade in equal coin.* He tried desperately to force down the instinct. *Not hurt for hurt, or rage for rage.*

Please, goddess, he pleaded, closing his eyes against the sight of the log drivers.

In that darkness, however, it wasn't Eira that he found but another goddess entirely, one who had nothing to do with love. She stared at him with her golden eyes, silent as the sun. His whole life, Ruc had never heard her speak, but she didn't need to speak. He could read that unwavering gaze.

These are weak creatures, she said. *Stand, and snuff out their lives.*

Fists rained down on him, pummeling his head, shoulders, ribs.

I did not raise you, those eyes went on, *to cower among the meek beasts of the world.*

Knuckles slammed into his chin, split the inside of his lip. Blood welled in his mouth. The taste made him hungry.

You are a hunter, she insisted. *A predator.*

A vision washed over him that was not a vision but a memory—of racing naked through the rushes, a spear in his hand, running down a jaguar, leaping on the wounded animal, driving the point in at the neck, feeling the hot blood wash over his hands. . . .

He shook his head weakly.

No. I am a priest of Eira.

She bared her teeth. *These three will kill you.*

Then they will kill me, he replied. *Love is not love that answers only to its own voice.*

She watched him a moment longer, lip twisted in disgust, then turned away.

He opened his eyes. Rain and blood smeared his sight, but he could see the people of Dombâng passing back and forth over the bridge just a few paces away, all of them bent to their business against the storm, all of them ignoring the three drivers and the battered man hanging from their grip. In Dombâng, blindness was a shield. To see the violence was to risk being swept up in it.

Ruc wondered if the drivers would kill him. It was slow work, beating a man to death with nothing more than your fists, and they weren't attacking the most lethal spots—the throat, the eyes, the center of the chest. Still, he could feel his ribs flexing beneath every blow. If they kept hitting him, one of those ribs would break, then another, then another. Eventually the jagged edges would lacerate something inside of him—his lungs or liver, maybe—and he would die.

Better, though, to die like a man, than to survive like some mindless beast.

Thank you, Eira, he murmured as Striker sank another blow into his guts. *Thank you, goddess. Thank you for this patience.*

The goddess, as usual, did not respond.

From out of the throng crossing the bridge, however, another voice rose, high and bright and angry, a voice he knew even better than his own.

"Stop it!"

Ruc's stomach sickened.

"Stop right now."

Striding out of the crowd came Bien Qui Nai, priestess of Eira, black hair lacquered to her head by the rain, face streaming, vest drenched, one bare arm extended, as though she could pull Ruc free of the danger with her outstretched hand. No doubt she'd left the temple that morning with a waxed parasol. No doubt she'd seen someone—an orphan, or a beggar, or some old drunk down on his luck—and given it away. She'd spent a lifetime giving things away.

Don't, he tried to say, but the word came out as a mouthful of half-clotted blood.

Screamer narrowed his eyes. Striker paused in his abuse, then turned slowly.

"Let him go," Bien said, shouldering Striker out of the way, then seizing Ruc by the arm, trying to wrest him from Screamer's grip.

She was a full head shorter than the shortest of the men. Striker could have lifted her by the waist and tossed her over the railing into the current below, but for a moment the men just stared. Shock could do that. Ruc had watched mud rats freeze, transfixed by the sight of a snake slithering out from between the rushes. Unfortunately, the divers weren't mud rats, and Bien was no venomous snake.

"It's all right," Ruc managed weakly.

Bien shook her head. "No it is not."

"They lost friends . . ."

"And that gives them the right to seize an innocent man? To beat him unconscious?"

"I'm not unconscious."

Or innocent, he added silently.

Shaking off his surprise at last, Striker took Bien by a shoulder, turned her to face him.

"What's he to you?"

"He is a human being," Bien declared, her voice trembling with outrage.

Ruc couldn't tell if she left out the rest of it—*We share a temple, a god, a past, sometimes a bed*—because it was no business of the drivers', or because she understood that her love for him would only spur them to greater brutality.

Striker laughed. "This is Dombâng. The main thing human beings do in Dombâng is die."

"If he dies, it will be because *you killed him.*"

"So what if we kill him?" Screamer sneered. "The Three will welcome the sacrifice."

Ruc pictured the gods of the delta plucking him from the current, laying his waterlogged body on the mudflats. It was hard to imagine them feeling anything but disgust. Disgust at his unbloodied knuckles, at the lack of flesh clenched between his teeth, at the absence of any sign of struggle, at the obvious fact that he had not fought back.

Bien shook her head. "This is not sacrifice."

"Why not?" Striker asked, his voice suddenly, dangerously quiet.

"What do the gods want with a washed-up corpse?"

"When I was a child," Striker replied, "my father saved his coin for years. Ten years? Twelve? Fifteen? I don't know. He'd been saving since before I was born, skimping on food, wearing the same clothes that were more holes than cloth, and you know why?"

Ruc could guess. All stories had the same ending if you followed them long enough.

"It was so that he could buy a slave," the man continued. "A pale-skinned Annurian boy of fourteen or fifteen. For the price of that slave my father could have rented us new rooms. He could have sent me and my brother to the Annurian school down by the Pot. He could have purchased medicine for the lung rot that was killing my mother, but he didn't. He bought the slave, and then he borrowed a boat, took the slave out into the delta, slit his throat, and rolled him over into the water.

"'The Three will bless us now,' he said. It was the only time in my life I ever saw him smile.

" 'This is a great offering,' he said.

"He spent his fortune to make that sacrifice. Risked being caught and hanged by our Annurian oppressors in order to make that sacrifice." Striker cocked his head to the side, studied Bien through slitted eyes. "Are you saying the gods didn't want it? Are you calling my father a fool?"

"Where is he now?" Ruc asked from between split lips. "Your father?"

Striker shifted his gaze from Bien. "Dead. Crushed on a drive."

"It doesn't sound as though the gods heard his prayers," Bien snapped.

"Maybe that's because," Striker replied, taking her by the throat, "my father didn't sacrifice *enough*."

Ruc felt his own throat tighten as he watched.

His own beating he could endure. Perhaps even his own death, if that was what Eira required. He would not, however, remain kneeling while the men killed Bien. Not even for the goddess of love.

"There's no need . . ." he began quietly.

Screamer cuffed him over the head, but the man looked troubled.

"I don't reckon we've got to beat the girl," he said, then jerked Ruc by the tattooed wrist. "This one's a mud sucker, but she's just . . ."

"She is just *defending* the mud sucker," Striker replied grimly. "Defending him while she mocks my father."

Bien struggled to reply, but the driver had her too tightly by the throat. She managed to drag in half a gasping breath as her brown skin darkened to a sick purple.

"Please don't do that," Ruc murmured. "Like your friend said—she has nothing to do with this."

"She does now." Striker waved a hand at the bridge. "How many people have walked by while we've been here?"

Ruc didn't reply. Screamer was distracted. His grip on Ruc's wrist had loosened. Just behind him, leaning against the railing of the bridge, were the pair of steel ring dogs he'd been carrying, each the length of Ruc's forearm, each ending in a vicious hook. A driver could plunge those hooks a hand deep into green timber. It wasn't hard to imagine what they'd do buried in someone's eye. Not hard at all to imagine the puncture and twist, the spray of hot blood, the dying spasm, then the weight as the body dropped.

And Ruc could do one better than imagining it. He could remember. . . .

"Hundreds of people," Striker went on, answering his own question. "Hundreds have walked by, without a single one sticking their nose in our business."

Bien's eyes bulged. Her lips were beginning to swell. She reached out to paw weakly at Striker's arm, then let her hands fall. She was still conscious, but not for much longer.

Ruc felt old instincts uncoiling inside him, so many snakes stirring after years of hibernation. According to Eira's teachings, he should meet even this violence with compassion and understanding. He could plead for Bien's life, but the faith forbade him raising a hand to save it. Priests had been martyred because they refused to fight back against their attackers. Their forbearance was praised in the commentaries on the Teachings:

Hudebraith understood, as few have understood, that it is a simple thing to love a person who treats you with love. He went further. Even as the Urghul slaughtered his children, he absolved them. As they drove the spikes into his hands, he blessed them. When they leaned close to spit in his face, he inclined his head to kiss them. As they hoisted him above the cold steppe to die, he murmured a prayer for them with his final breath.

The thing was, Hudebraith had been a far better priest than Ruc Lakatur Lan Lac.

He took a breath of his own, dragging it down deep into his battered chest, testing the damage. Pain blazed through his flesh, but beneath the pain, waiting patiently for his command, lay all the old strength and rage. He remembered this feeling well, the stillness before the act, the way he could almost taste what was about to come.

Bien's watering eyes met his, widened slightly. Her lips twitched, but she had no breath left to plead for the lives of the log drivers.

Ruc felt himself smiling, lips twisting back from his blood-smeared teeth.

Sometimes a man needed to be the answer to his own prayers.

Forgive me, goddess, he murmured silently.

Just as he was about to surge to his feet, however, a clamor erupted in the crowd beyond. The people who had been scuttling back and forth across the bridge with quick steps and downcast eyes had begun to slow and cry out. For a moment, Ruc thought someone had noticed them after all, that the citizens of the city, for once in their lives, had caught sight of the unfolding violence and decided not to pass by. Then he realized that no one was pointing in his direction after all, no one was peeling off from the crowd to stop the man who held Bien's neck in his fist. Instead, they were gesturing toward something else, a figure barely glimpsed through the shifting bodies and sheets of rain.

Ruc caught snatches of conversation:

. . . A foreigner . . .

. . . Pale as milk . . .

. . . Annurian . . .

. . . Offer him to the gods. . . .

Silence narrowed his eyes.

Striker frowned, turned to study the gathering crowd, chewed on the inside of his cheek a moment, then, with a gesture so casual it was hard to believe a life had hung in the balance, tossed Bien aside.

Her legs folded beneath her. She sprawled out across the deck like a bundle of wet rags, choking on air like a fish dragged from the current.

"What's going on?" Screamer demanded, craning his neck to see over the throng.

"Something interesting, sounds like," Striker replied. "Maybe some Annurian scum hooked from the water."

Screamer nodded to Ruc. "What about him?"

Striker sucked at something stuck in his teeth, cocked his head to the side, then slammed a final fist into Ruc's gut.

"He's nothing," the man said as Ruc doubled over, puking blood onto the bridge. "Just a filthy mud sucker without any fight in him. Let's go."

And just like that, it was over.

The log drivers hefted their tools and strode off into the crowd, leaving Ruc and Bien huddled at the edge of the bridge. Ten years ago, he might have been surprised. It might have seemed strange that men could forget their murderous intent in the space of a few breaths, distracted by the sight of a crowd and a fragment of chatter. The revolution, however, had been a lesson in the caprice of human violence. Unlike a jaguar, which would stalk its prey until the kill was made or lost, people followed less steady instincts. A man who drew his knife over some imaginary slight might kill with it, or he might not. There were a thousand channels leading to slaughter, and a thousand channels leading away, and as far as Ruc could tell, people floated them at the mercy of currents they barely understood. A creature that killed without reason could forget that killing just as easily.

As the three men disappeared, Ruc felt a quick twist of regret. The ache in his chest was not just pain, but loss. A part of him had wanted to fight, to open up those sons of bitches from throat to gut, to see their insides spilled across the bridge, roped intestines glistening. . . .

He forced the thought savagely aside.

"I am a priest of Eira," he growled to himself, "not a beast of the delta."

Despite the heat he poured into the words, they felt fickle on his tongue, false.

If there is no love in your heart, make it with your hands.

He crossed painfully to Bien, took her head in those hands, shifted her gently so that she leaned against him. He felt the warmth of her soak into him with the blood and the rain.

"They," she said, her voice ragged, "were *such* assholes."

He coughed up a chuckle.

"They were just men."

"What did they want?"

He shook his head. What did men ever want?

"You are also an asshole," she added, glaring at him as her strength returned.

"Because I got hit?"

"Because you didn't run."

He smiled down into her face. "I was practicing loving my enemies."

"An asshole and an idiot."

He shook his head again. "I prayed to the goddess. She sent you."

Bien reached up, took him by the back of the neck, drew his face down to hers, kissed him softly on the lips.

"Truly," he murmured, "the Lady of Love is great."

"We should go back to the temple," she replied, pushing him away at last, rising unsteadily to her feet. "Have someone tend to your wounds."

She touched his split brow, frowned.

"They'll heal." He gestured toward the crowd gathered at the top of the bridge. "I want to see what's happening."

Bien took an unsteady breath. "It's not safe to be out today. After the Baths . . . things are dangerous."

"It's Dombâng."

She hesitated, then nodded.

Ruc was tall, almost a full head taller than most of the people, but he couldn't see much except heads and parasols as he approached the top of the bridge. Two or three hundred people had gathered, but judging from the muttered questions of those around him, most had been drawn in by the simple fact of the crowd itself.

"It's a sympathizer," crowed an old woman to his right. "He helped the imperial bastards attack!"

She was half Ruc's size, couldn't have seen much more than backs and asses, but she waggled an authoritative finger toward the mob. "No end to those rats. Yesterday they hung one from Thum's Bridge." She cackled. "Heard he danced half the morning before quieting down."

Ruc ignored her, threaded his way forward, Bien half a step behind. Finally, near the crown of the bridge, the crowd ended abruptly, as though someone had drawn a line across the decking that no one dared to cross.

On the other side of that line a man had leapt up onto the wide railing. Not Dombângan—that much was obvious at a glance. His skin was far too pale, and his eyes, and his hair, which was brown rather than black, and hung in luxurious waves down his back. He might have been Annurian—the empire counted pale-skinned people among its citizens—but he wasn't a soldier.

An Annurian soldier would have been fighting or cringing or trying to flee; this man stood atop the railing as though he owned it, face split with a smile, arms spread to welcome the crowd. A soldier would have been armed, but the figure at the center of the crowd had no weapons. He was in fact, entirely naked, lean muscles slick with the rain. . . .

No, Ruc realized, not *entirely* naked.

He wore something around his throat, a wide collar cinched tight, the kind of thing a rich woman might purchase for her dog. This man, however, didn't bear himself like a creature collared or kept. If anything, he gazed out over the assembled crowd, the men and women who would in all likelihood tear him apart, as though *they* in some obscure way already belonged to *him*.

Having achieved his perch above the rushing water, the pale-skinned foreigner spread his arms, fixed his gaze on the crowd, then said nothing, as though his naked, well-muscled presence were the only message necessary.

People in Dombâng were used to seeing human skin. Bathing was a daily ritual almost as important as eating. Public bathhouses dotted the city. Kids swam naked in the canals, and fishers thought nothing about stripping their clothes after a day's labor, then scrubbing clean in the current. From any deck or dock at almost any time of day, you could probably find someone in some state of undress, and yet there was something different about this man, something flagrant. He wore his nakedness like a statement, a challenge.

"Oh my . . ." Bien murmured as she ran her gaze over his body.

"Love of the flesh is a shallow love. . . ." Ruc said, quoting from the Fifth Teaching.

She glanced over at him. "Remind me of that the next time you come scratching at my door." When she turned back to the foreigner, however, her face darkened. "People aren't going to put up with him standing there for long."

It was true.

For the moment, the crowd didn't move beyond gawking and muttering. The sight was so strange, so incongruous, so unexpected, that the man had, for the moment, failed to ignite the distrust and rage of the people staring at him. He might have been some exotic animal—a bear, or a moose—rather than a human being. The fact that he was naked and silent only reinforced the impression, but he did not remain silent for long.

Even as Ruc studied him, the morning gongs began tolling through the city, first just one bronze, then ten, then hundreds, until the sodden air shook with the sound. It drowned out the rain on the bridge, the surging of the current below, the voices of the individuals in the crowd. The stranger tilted back his head as though he were basking in the noise. The thick rope looped around his neck seemed to twitch, as though it were alive. Then, when the sky finally shivered itself still, he began to speak.

"Hail, people of Dombâng."

"Hail?" Ruc shook his head. "Who says *hail*?"

"Dead men in books," Bien replied.

"And evidently the people wherever he comes from."

She frowned. "What accent is that?"

Again, Ruc shook his head. The words were clear enough, but the syllables drained strangely from one into the next, as though poured from vessel to vessel.

"Hail," the man continued, "my brethren in faith! Hail, tenders of the ancient flame!"

He smiled as he spoke, ran his gaze over the crowd with the ease of a speaker confident of his reception.

"Hail, worshippers of the Three!"

An uneasy ripple ran through the crowd. Dombâng had rebelled against imperial control just five years earlier over that exact worship. In most corners of the empire, Annur allowed the local religious traditions, even encouraged them. At least that was what the sailors had insisted, when sailors were still welcome in the city. Ruc had never set foot outside of the delta, but those men talked about shrines on Basc to the twin gods of storm, idols carved into the stone of the Broken Bay, temples grown from living trees near the mouth of the Baivel River where villagers laid offerings to the spirits of the wood. They weren't Annurian gods, these forest spirits and stone idols, but the empire tolerated them. Legionaries didn't smash the statues and burn the shrines. They didn't hang people for murmuring the sacred names.

"Why," Ruc had asked a priest once—a priest of *Eira*—when he was younger and dumber, still just a child struggling to stitch together a world that seemed broken into opposing halves, "do the Annurians let the Bascans have their gods, and the Breatans, and the Raaltans, but not the people of Dombâng? Why do they hate the Three?"

"Because," the man said, setting a kindly hand on his shoulder, "to worship the Three, one must become a murderer."

That single sentence, offered so casually, had been a cold knife sliding through Ruc's guts.

It only confirmed what he knew already, but the protest rose in him anyway, like some kind of reflex.

"It's not murder. It's *sacrifice*."

"There is nothing sacred," the priest replied gravely, "in dragging the sick or orphaned or drunk into the delta and leaving them to die."

"That has nothing to do with the Three. The Three don't *want* sick people or kids. They want warriors to hunt, to fight."

The priest shook his head, regarded Ruc with sad eyes. "You were too long among the Vuo Ton, my child. Their faith, like the old faith of this city, is no faith at all, but hatred, violence, blood. Moreover, all of it is based on a lie. The Three are not real. Kem Anh, Sinn, Hang Loc—they're just names people gave a long time ago to the worst sides of themselves, the ugly parts, their desire to hurt, to humiliate, to murder."

You're wrong, Ruc wanted to say. *They're not just names, and they're not ugly. They're so beautiful that it hurts to look at them.*

But if he said that, the priest might ask more, might ask how he was so certain, and Ruc had no words to frame the answers. All he had were his memories, hundreds of them, thousands, of Kem Anh's golden eyes as she held him at her breast; of Hang Loc cracking a snake's skull, peeling back the scales, plucking out the tenderest portion—the eyes—then popping them one by one into Ruc's tiny, eager mouth; of the two of them kneeling in the soft mud to plant river violets in the skulls; of the rise and fall of their bodies as he slept between them, warmed by the heat of their flesh.

You're wrong, he wanted to say.

But, of course, the priest was not wrong. Alongside the memories of flowers and warmth and light stalked the other memories, the indelible visions of the things those gods had done, that they had taught *him* to do, that drove him from the delta in the first place. He felt his face hot with sunlight and splattered blood, his fingers tight around the knife. . . .

"It is love that makes us human, son," the priest said.

And Ruc, child of the city and the delta both, had doubted those words almost as much as he believed them.

The priest died a few years after that conversation, which was probably lucky for him. The revolution turned the old world on its head. What had been profane for two hundred years became sacred once more, while the sacred became unsayable. If the priest had lived, if he had dared to spread his message in the streets of Dombâng after the overthrow of the empire, he would have been torn to pieces by an angry mob for his blasphemy, emissary of love or not. Eira's temple and her priests had weathered the uprising and its aftermath in large part by avoiding all talk of Annur, of the larger pantheon of Annurian gods, and of the Three. It was a wise strategy for any foreigner who had survived the purges and wanted to keep surviving.

Evidently no one had informed the naked man atop the bridge.

"Dombâng alone," he continued, "among all the cities of this land, remembers something of the old ways, the ways of tooth and fist, flower and bone."

That earned him a little wary applause. It was a tricky situation. No one wanted to be seen supporting a foreigner, but, on the other hand, this particular foreigner seemed to be praising both the Three and the virtue of those who worshipped them. It could be wise to support such a declaration, to be *seen* supporting it. Even as they stared, however, most of the people in the crowd slid expressions of neutral disinterest down over their faces like masks. The high priests of the city had spies on every street, and even if they hadn't, the revolution taught one lesson above all others: your neighbors are always watching.

"Dombâng alone remembers the rhythms of the land and the truth of the testing. It is here still, if only faintly."

Bien shook her head. "Don't say *faintly*," she murmured.

"Probably don't say anything," Ruc added.

"I, Valaka Jarva, *rashkta-bhura* of the *hoti* of the armorers, beloved of the Lord and proud bearer of his *axoch*"—here he touched with two fingers the strange collar circling his throat—"am come before you with a greeting, a reminder, and a warning." He spread his arms as though inviting the whole of Dombâng into his embrace. "The greeting is this: hail. Hail from he who holds us in his fist, who dreams the world into being. Hail from the First, your once and future Lord."

Mutters and questions rippled through the crowd. The man spoke clearly enough, but half the words were nonsense. *Rashkta-bhura? Axoch?*

"What," someone demanded finally, "is a *hoti*?"

The man's smile grew.

"I was told you had forgotten, and so my reminder: you have lived before, people of Dombâng. You have lived and lost a thousand thousand lives. You have lived and you have forgotten, but the Lord will open your minds. He will fill you with the truth of what you have been and what you will be, and when you see, you people of Dombâng, you keepers of the old ways, you will join us in serving his great and holy purpose."

The mutters rose to growls of displeasure.

More voices and louder sprouted from the mob, like traitor's heart flowers after a hard rain.

"Fuck your great and noble truth."

". . . Annurian pig . . ."

"Dombâng bows before none but the Three!"

The messenger—Valaka Jarva—nodded as though he had expected this outburst, as though all the men and women gathered on the bridge were children bent on some small folly. He raised a hand.

"The Three are worthy of your worship, but they are not all. The Lord is of the Three and also above them, beyond them. It is for this that he is called the First. Your gods are to him as the moon beside the sun. He is coming, people of Dombâng, and you will see that he is like to those that you revere, but stronger, faster, wiser, *more.*"

Bien took Ruc by the elbow. "We need to get him out of here."

Ruc glanced down at her. "How do you plan to do that?"

"I don't know," she replied, shoving her way forward through the press of the crowd, "but he's about ten sentences away from having his tongue nailed to that railing."

All things considered, ending up with a nail through the tongue seemed like an optimistic outcome for the messenger. Ruc had seen men and women flayed during the Annurian purges, lashed to bridge pilings and left for the floods, cut into dozens of pieces and used as chum for the croc hunters. Things could go a lot worse than losing a tongue. They could, and, judging from the shifting temper of the crowd, they were about to.

Ruc and Bien weren't the only people pushing toward the railing. The human bodies on the bridge might all have been part of one great snake, twisting tighter and tighter around its quarry. The only reason the idiot was still up there at all was that, despite the mounting outrage, no one had yet gathered the courage to strike the first blow. The restraint of the mob would last until it didn't. When it collapsed, it would collapse utterly.

"Move," Bien shouted as she shoved her way forward. "Get out of the way."

A short, wiry man—a fisher, judging from his clothes—shot her an irritated glance. "Wait your turn. We all want a piece of the bastard."

Not all of us, Ruc thought grimly, lifting the fisher as gently as he could, wincing at the pain in his ribs, then setting him aside.

"Hey!" Bien shouted when she was just a few paces away. *"Hey!"*

She waved her hands over her head.

Valaka Jarva turned, met her gaze, nodded to her as though she were some petitioner come to beg a favor. He seemed oblivious to the fury burning through the crowd, as though his own violent demise were a possibility he'd never bothered considering.

"Get down," Bien shouted, pointing toward the bridge. "They're going to kill you."

Ruc stifled a curse, took Bien by the shoulder. "There's no way to do this," he said, careful to keep his voice low. "It's too late. You've already saved one idiot today."

She shoved his hand away. *"Love the meek. . . ."*

"He's not all that fucking meek. He's been standing naked on a railing shouting at anyone who will listen that he serves the world's greatest and most holy purpose."

"Love those on whom the world heaps hatred, the outcast and the shunned. . . ."

"*Shunning* is a colossal understatement for what these people are about to do to him. And to you, too, if you're helping him when they take him down."

He'd almost seen her killed once that morning. He wasn't ready to see it again.

The bridge shook beneath the weight of the stamping feet. Hundreds of angry voices carved their fury on the stormy sky. A forest of raised fists had grown up around Ruc and Bien, all clenched to bursting. When he ran his gaze over the crowd, he almost couldn't see the faces for the rage-red heat burning from the skin.

Bien rounded on him. Tears stood in her eyes.

"What will we be," she demanded, "if we don't try to help this man?"

There were hundreds of possible answers, thousands. *We'll be alive,* Ruc wanted to say. *We'll be servants of Eira instead of food for the fish.*

It was impossible to rescue every single person. Tens of thousands had died during the revolution while Ruc and Bien did nothing to save them. In the delta, he had learned one lesson very early: there was a time to fight, and a time to flee. A rush wren felt no shame taking to the air at the passage of a snake. Even a croc would retreat at the sight of a jaguar. Bred into the flesh of every bird and beast was a single, simple unalterable law: *survive.* No animal would risk its life for an unknown creature, but then, that was Bien's point: she was not an animal, and despite his childhood, neither was Ruc.

"Finally," the messenger declared, "my warning." His gaze went stern. "If you insist on your forgetting, if you smear mud over your eyes, if you turn your backs on the truth . . ." He took a deep breath, seemed to fill with fury and regret, then shook his head. "If you deny him, he will destroy you all and utterly. He will take you apart as he has taken apart so many and so much greater than you, and you will wake in your next lives as grubs and worms, the meanest creatures ever to creep in terror through the wide spaces of the world."

Even as the messenger finished speaking, a massive man surged forward out of the crowd—Striker, Ruc realized—his eyes on the stranger, lips twisted into a vicious smile. With a desperate cry, Bien hurled herself in front of him. The chaos saved her. In the crush and rain and swelling sound, no one could tell what she was trying to do. She might as well have been just one more citizen driven forward by righteous rage. The thought that she might be shielding the stranger with her body would have seemed insane.

Striker didn't even glance down at her—another stroke of luck—just cursed and shoved her roughly aside. Bien fell, but instead of giving up, she wrapped herself around his leg like a child looking for a ride, indifferent to the fact that this was the man who had strangled her nearly to death not much earlier.

It might have been the dumbest, bravest thing that Ruc had ever seen; Eira seized him by the throat, the grip of love's goddess stronger than any need for survival.

He shrugged off the people pressing in around him, shucked away his own pain, ducked under Striker's extended weapon, and, with the fury of the crowd pelting down around him, hurled himself at the man on the railing of the bridge. The priests of Eira knew nothing of hunting, nothing of tracking, or stalking, or leaping, but Ruc had not been raised from an infant by the priests of Eira.

He hit the man with his shoulder, knocking the wind from him, folding him neatly in half, then wrapped him close in his arms as they fell away from the murderous mob into the churning current below.

5

"Sweet Eira's mercy," Bien breathed, rushing to Ruc's side as he kicked open the door to her room.

Bloody light from the red-scale lantern washed her face. Fear twisted her features, fear and anger. For a moment she stood there, frozen. Then relief washed over her like a wave.

"You're alive," she said, reaching up to touch his face, as though to reassure herself.

"I'm alive," he agreed.

Alive was about the best he could say for his battered state. His body throbbed. The echoes of Striker's fists ached in his face and chest. The ribs on his left side twinged whenever he twisted, and blood dripped from the gash across his forehead and his split lip.

"I just came back for a lantern when it got too dark," Bien went on. "I've been out looking for you all day."

"I'm sorry," Ruc replied, lowering the unconscious messenger as gently as he could onto the bed. "Seemed like a good idea not to be found."

"How'd you get him back here without anyone seeing you? The city's a kicked termite nest right now. People are everywhere, most of them eager to kill something."

"It was slow work. Drifted down past the Fish Market hidden in some flotsam, but Cao's was too busy east of that to risk it. Swam north instead, hid out until dusk in the wreckage of Intarra's temple, then floated east in the shadow of a patrol boat."

"A patrol boat?" Bien's eyes widened. "If they'd caught you with *him,* you'd be locked in the Shipwreck or the Baths."

He put a hand on her shoulder. "The Baths burned, remember? And they didn't catch me. Anyway, I'm not the one you should be worried about."

He gestured toward the bed.

Valaka Jarva's skin had gone waxen, yellow rather than tan. Whoever he was, he didn't look good. The collar had chafed his neck an ugly red, and his lips had gone a livid shade of blue. They twitched for a moment, as though he were trying to talk, then fell still.

"What happened to him?"

Ruc grimaced. "One of the sawed-off pilings from the old bridge was just beneath the water. When I knocked him off the railing, he landed on it. I landed on him."

He lifted the messenger slightly. Bien gasped. The rotted end of the piling had torn into the man's back, shredding skin and breaking ribs. Finger-long splinters of dark wood protruded from the wound, which was already soaking the bedding with blood. For most of the day he'd been unconscious, muttering fragments of what sounded like warning or prophecy in a language Ruc didn't recognize.

"We have to clean it . . ." Ruc began, but Bien was already moving, scooping her ewer and washbowl from the bedside table, then crossing to the bed.

She plunged her facecloth into the water. "Roll him over."

The messenger let out a faint groan as Ruc dragged him onto his stomach, reached weakly for something, then subsided. The wound was vicious enough, but the real danger lay in it souring. The canals to the west, where the Shirvian first flowed into Dombâng, were clean enough, but the mid-city channels bred flies and disease. Despite the gashes in his own skin, Ruc wasn't worried for himself. He had never in his life taken sick—another inexplicable gift, like the redsight, of his childhood in the delta. Untended, however, the messenger would almost surely die. He might die even if they tended him.

Bien had pulled a stool alongside the bed, sat crouched over the wound. She spread it open with one hand while pulling free the largest of the splinters with the other. Blood and pus smeared her fingers. She wiped them absently on the bedsheets and went on about her work. As a priestess of Eira, she'd spent half her childhood tending to the city's sick and injured. Her voice was calm, focused when she spoke.

"I need white *quey*. From the infirmary. And slick-reed."

Ruc nodded, took one more glance at the inexplicable man they'd rescued from the mob, then slipped out the door.

Eira's temple was part of a larger compound built in a rough rectangle, with the refectory, sleeping quarters, infirmary, and the temple itself forming the four sides. Ghostblossom vines climbed dark teak walls; the evening flowers were just starting to open, spilling their perfume into the hot, thick air. Two young acolytes were lighting the red-scale lanterns hanging from the long lines overhead. The dried, gutted bodies of the fish glowed a soft orange-red, as though they'd acquired in death a heat they'd lacked while still alive. Dangling from their lines, mouths agape, they might have been finning their way straight up through the murky air to join the stars.

Ruc strode across the courtyard, trying to hurry without seeming to.

He'd just reached the infirmary when a familiar shape stepped from the door—Old Uyen, leaning heavily on his cane. He paused at the sight of Ruc, studied him with half-blind, milky eyes, then smiled.

"Hello, son."

Uyen called everyone *son,* but to Ruc the word carried more than a casual warmth. Ruc had been twelve when he abandoned the delta to come to a strange city where he knew no one and nothing. Everything he'd learned out among the rushes—to hunt, to hide, to stalk, to kill—was useless in Dombâng. The buildings were too high and too close, the reek of too many people packed together made it hard to breathe. There were days that he felt the city might crush him. Even now, fifteen years later, he could remember standing motionless as a stunned burrow rat, convinced that his chest would collapse beneath the weight of the place. Somehow, in those moments, it always seemed to be Uyen who found him, Uyen who led him up to the roof of the dormitory, where the air was cleaner, the walls less close, Uyen who would light a pipe and sit with him in silence until the panic passed, Uyen who never asked any questions, who seemed to understand that some terrors could not be talked away, only outlasted. By the age of twelve, Ruc had reconciled himself to the fact that he had no true parents, none he would ever meet, at least. Still, he felt a moment of peace every time Uyen looked at him, saw him, smiled, and called him *son.*

"Hello, Father," he said, pausing a few feet from the infirmary.

"A strange day."

Ruc kept his face still, his body relaxed. He would trust Uyen with any secret, but the courtyard was hardly the place for the sharing of secrets. Eira's temple was one of the safest places in the city. That did not mean it was safe.

"I heard some talk of a crazy man," Ruc said carefully. "Naked, over the Spring Bridge." He hesitated. "Heard he was killed, knocked into the river and drowned."

"I heard that, too," Uyen replied. "That was *one* of the stories. I also heard that the Vuo Ton took him." He paused for a long moment, gazed at Ruc with those worn-down eyes. "Or someone who *looked* like the Vuo Ton, who had the tattoos. Spirited him away into the delta."

Ruc stifled a curse. The whole thing had happened so fast—barely a heartbeat between when he hit the man and when they'd plunged beneath the water—the scene on the bridge had been so chaotic, the rain blinding. . . . It hadn't seemed unreasonable to hope people might miss the tattoos snaking out from beneath the cuffs of his robe.

"Most people," Uyen went on mildly, "don't believe the thing about the Vuo Ton."

"What would the Vuo Ton want with some crazed fool?"

"Indeed. I suspect the poor man was killed, just as the others were."

Ruc felt his pulse quicken. "Others?"

The priest nodded gravely. "There were at least a dozen, maybe more, all over the city. One at the Arena. One at the Purple Baths. Mad Trent's Mountain. Goc My's. The Grog Market."

"What did they want?"

"They all had the same message: hail. Someone named the Lord or the First. Join his ranks. A great and holy purpose . . ."

"And they were all killed?"

Uyen nodded once more. "Fear fills Dombâng, especially after this violence at the Purple Baths. One could almost wish that the man from the Spring Bridge *had* been rescued by the Vuo Ton." He eyed Ruc shrewdly. "Or by one who looks like the Vuo Ton."

Ruc put a gentle hand on Uyen's shoulder. "Best not to spread that story, Father."

The priest smiled. "Of course not, my son."

It didn't take long to slip into the infirmary and retrieve the *quey* and slick-reed, but by the time he'd returned to Bien's room she was already waiting impatiently, one of her clean tunics pressed to the messenger's wound.

"You walk all the way to the Grog Market for the *quey*?"

He passed her the jar and the small pot. "I didn't want to draw attention. People are already talking about what happened on the bridge. Some are saying the messenger was taken by the Vuo Ton."

She glanced up at him sharply.

"It's just a rumor," Ruc said. "Still, I didn't feel like adding to it by racing back and forth."

"One of the disadvantages, I guess, to having your skin slashed with ink."

Blood and pus welled in the wound the moment she pulled back the makeshift bandage. She uncorked the *quey,* doused a cloth with the liquor, then pressed it to the shredded flesh. The messenger writhed at the touch—*quey* burned even worse in a wound than it did on the tongue—then cried out a few words.

Bien glanced up at Ruc. "What was that?"

"I don't know. He's been trying to talk on and off all day." He looked out the narrow window into the night. Sacrificial fires, large and small, burned on a hundred rooftops. "I spoke to Uyen. He said there were messengers all over the city, a dozen or more."

"I know." Bien dabbed more *quey* onto the wound, then set the bottle aside. "I heard people talking when I was out looking for you. Rumor has it the Greenshirts snatched one before the people could tear her fully apart. She died before the high priests could put her to the question."

"That must have displeased the high priests."

"Not as much as foreigners showing up in the city to blaspheme the Three."

"Would we call it blasphemy?"

Bien glanced up at him. "*One is coming like those you revere, but stronger, faster?* Yeah, I'm pretty sure we'd call it blasphemy."

The slick-reed was already prepared, sliced down the middle into long, flat strips. Bien took one up, laid the wet, fleshy side against the messenger's shredded skin. With any luck, that and the *quey* would keep the wound from turning sour. She worked confidently, quickly. When she'd plastered it with the leaves, she pressed her blood-soaked tunic atop it, then wrapped the whole thing in a fresh shirt.

"Your belt," she said, holding out a hand. "You sit him up, while I wrap it around the bandage."

Ruc slipped the belt from his waist, passed it to Bien, then took the messenger by the shoulders. He tried to be gentle, but as he lifted, a scream spilled from the man's lips, a wordless, animal cry that lasted half a heartbeat before Ruc could get a hand clamped over his mouth. Bien slipped the belt deftly around the messenger's torso, cinched it tight. He thrashed, but Ruc held him in place until it was finished, then laid him back gently against the bed.

The man murmured a few words, then subsided against the gory sheets.

Ruc studied him a moment, then turned to Bien.

"What are people saying about the Baths?"

"People are saying it was Annur."

Ruc frowned. "Annur?"

"Huge empire? Just to the north? Occupied Dombâng for two hundred years . . ."

He ignored the sarcasm. "Attacked the Baths with *what*?"

"One of those giant birds they have. Keppral. Kestrel. Whatever."

Ruc shook his head. "People in this city are always talking about kettral. Whenever a cloud crosses the moon, someone's convinced the Annurians are back."

"Yes. Well. This was a very convincing cloud. The high priests had the charred remains dragged out of the wreckage, hauled over the Arena, displayed in the pit for everyone to see."

"Did you see them?"

She stared at him like he'd gone mad. "I was looking for *you,* asshole. Even if I wasn't, you know I don't go to the Arena. But Chui went. A few of the others. They said the claws were as long as paddles."

"Were there any other attacks?"

Bien shook her head. "Just the Baths. Burned it to the ground, more or less."

"Did the priests get any captives?"

"One. They're saying they're going to execute him on the steps of the Ship-wreck tomorrow at dawn." Her face hardened. "If I hadn't been searching for you, I would have gone tonight, offered to sit with him."

"I'm glad you didn't. Kindness has become a dangerous game in this city."

"It is not a game," she replied. "Regardless of his crimes, he must be terrified."

Ruc decided to sidestep the argument. "Was he wearing one of these collars?"

He gestured to the strange, snakelike thing coiled around the messenger's neck.

She shook her head. "Not that I heard. But it can't be coincidence, can it? The Annurians burn down the Purple Baths and then, the very next morning, these naked fools show up talking about an attacking army."

"Not much of an army—a few soldiers burning down the Baths."

"The Baths were a major barracks for the Greenshirts."

"Still seems vaguely half-assed. The Annurians conquered the world with good planning, not casual arson."

"Maybe they're desperate. Maybe the plan went wrong."

He nodded. "Maybe."

As Bien opened her mouth to reply, the messenger spasmed, tried to sit, fell back, but seized her by the wrist. His eyes were open, glassy but commanding.

"You must *prepare,*" he groaned.

Bien glanced over at Ruc, then back at the messenger.

"Prepare for *what*?"

"The Lord. You must *join* with him, with his people, his host. . . ."

Ruc shook his head. "Who is the Lord?"

"The First. I told you. I have poured the truth like honey into your ears, but you refuse to hear."

It didn't sound like honey to Ruc. It sounded like something barbed, something spiked and violent.

Sweat drenched the messenger's brow. He looked even paler than he had that morning on the bridge.

"Yeah," Ruc replied. "We heard. Great and holy purpose, all that. But *who is he*?"

"Our source and our scourge. The one who comes to break you, then see you made anew."

"It's talk like this," Bien added sternly, "that almost got you murdered back there on the bridge."

"Murder." The man shook his head weakly. "What do I care for my murder? What is this one life set in the scales against all that I have been, all I will become?"

Ruc shouldered aside his frustration.

"You said he has a host. . . ."

"Not a host. *The* host. A great army of his people."

"Fine. Where are they coming from? How many people?"

"All of them."

"All?"

"Every woman, man, and child of every *hoti*. The *andara-bhura,* the *rashkta-bhura,* the *shava-bhura, all . . .*"

The words trailed off, bubbling into blood.

Bien shook her head. "We don't know what any of that means."

"Doesn't matter," Ruc said. "No army is going to make it ten paces into the delta."

Faith filled the messenger's gaze. "The Lord is already *in* the delta. Even as we speak, he comes for your gods."

"We worship Eira, the Lady of Love," Bien said, not taking her eyes from the man. "The Three are not our gods."

She glanced over at Ruc. He nodded slowly, but at the same time memory flooded him—riding on Hang Loc's huge shoulders, playing slap-hands with Kem Anh, feasting on the fish they ripped from the river's gleam. Bien was right—they weren't his gods.

To Ruc Lakatur Lan Lac, they were something far more intimate than gods.

"What do you mean," he asked carefully, "when you say he comes for them?"

The man nodded eagerly. "He comes to accept their submission, their fealty."

Ruc tried to imagine Kem Anh submitting to anything. His mind balked at the thought. He could, if he worked very hard, just barely imagine something killing her—Sinn had been killed, after all, whatever the high priests and people of Dombâng believed—but the notion that anyone could force her to *submit* . . .

"If he is real, this Lord of yours, and he is really in the delta, then he is already dead."

The man shook his head with an awful vigor. "He is not dead. If he were dead, I would know it. I would *feel* it."

Bien frowned. "Feel it. How?"

He gestured to his collar. Ruc had taken that collar for snakeskin or some other kind of scaled hide. As he leaned closer, however, he realized there was more to it than skin. It was thicker than a belt, almost round in cross section, as though someone had taken an actual snake, hacked off the head and tail, then stitched the ends back together to form a ring. He reached out a finger to touch it, but the messenger recoiled, bared bloody teeth.

As Ruc watched, the collar convulsed. A ripple ran under the scaled skin, as though the thing were alive and tightening, then fell still.

No one spoke. Overhead, a moth, trapped inside the lantern, battered the dried skin with its meager wings.

"What is that?" Bien asked finally, her dark eyes fixed on the collar.

"It is my *axoch*."

"And what," Ruc demanded quietly, "is an *axoch*?"

"A mark of favor," the messenger replied, pride ringing in his voice, "in the eyes of the Lord."

"Is it . . ." Bien hesitated, struggling to frame the question, "alive?"

"As long as I am alive, it is alive. It is my strength that feeds it."

Ruc studied the coiled flesh with disgust. The delta was home to dozens of creatures that infested living bodies: gut flies and summer worms, meat puppeteers and eye wasps. They were horrifying, ghastly, and yet their grisly burrowing and hatching had always seemed natural to Ruc. Like all the delta's other beasts, they too needed to eat, to breed. This thing around the messenger's neck, on the other hand, this *axoch*, was anything but natural, not a living creature at all, but a twisted mockery of one.

"What did you mean you would *feel* it if your lord were dead?" Ruc asked.

The man raised a finger to stroke the scales of the *axoch*. Sweat drenched his brow, his skin was sickly sallow in the lamplight, but his smile was that of a saint contemplating his god.

"This joins me to him," he replied. "Allows me to feel his grace and his displeasure." A shadow passed over his features at the word *displeasure,* then fled. "I can feel him now."

Bien glanced over at Ruc. He shook his head.

"And what is it, exactly, that you feel?"

"His might." The man shuddered, his eyes rolled back in his head. "I can feel him, racing through the rushes, I can feel the blood slamming in his veins. He is eager. He is hunting."

"Hunting what?"

"Your gods."

The words sent a chill through Ruc.

Bien frowned. "I thought you said he wanted the Three for allies."

The messenger shook himself free of whatever vision had possessed him, fixed his feverish gaze on Bien. "He has no allies. He is the *First*. Your gods will bow before him, or he will break them apart. Even now he pursues . . ."

The *axoch* twitched.

The man's eyes widened.

"I'm sorry, my Lord," he murmured. "I was told to spread the word, the tale of your glory. . . ."

The collar writhed, then began to tighten. Veins throbbed in the messenger's neck. His face began to purple.

He raised a hand to the *axoch,* then yanked it back as though scalded.

"I'm sorry, my Lord . . ." he gargled, the words thick, wet. "Kill me quickly. . . . Close this unworthy throat. . . ."

"What's happening?" Ruc demanded.

"It's choking him," Bien snapped. She tried to slide a hand inside the collar, but there was no space.

The messenger's eyes bulged, watered.

Ruc snatched his belt knife from its sheath.

"Hold him," he growled.

Bien threw herself on the messenger, pinning him against the bed.

The man opened his mouth, but managed to hack up only a few mangled syllables. With the last of his strength he tried to force Bien back, but she bore down with all her weight, arms clasped tight around his shoulders. Ruc went to work with the knife, but the messenger was thrashing, and the *axoch* was tough as twenty-year-old choke vine. He might have been able to hack through it with a hatchet, but the knife, despite its keen edge, just scratched uselessly at the scales.

"Hurry," Bien hissed.

Ruc sawed harder.

The man began to spasm, and the knife slipped, slashing down into his shoulder.

"He's *dying,*" Bien said.

Ruc shook his head, sat back, breath ragged in his lungs. A purple tongue lolled between the messenger's swollen lips. His hands had stopped twitching at his side. The *axoch* twisted, tightened further, until it was half-buried in the flesh of the neck, then went still.

"Not dying," Ruc murmured. "He's dead."

6

"The men you lost," the Emperor said, "I remember them. Five years ago they helped to save Annur. They were good soldiers."

Gwenna nodded, mute. The Emperor watched her with those burning eyes.

They sat in a small room. The floor was slate, the walls paneled wood. A single wide window behind the woman's head opened onto a garden. From where Gwenna sat, there was no visible hint that they were inside the Dawn Palace—no gleaming regalia, no gold, no ostentatious statuary. From this small room, she couldn't see the towers soaring above, or the miles of red walls circling the fortress, or the hundreds of structures—temples, armories, scriptoria, banquet halls, libraries, kitchens, laundries, audience chambers, baths—that packed those walls. If she had awoken here, her memory scrubbed, she might have believed they were anywhere, a small, neat room in an unremarkable house somewhere between Sia and Freeport.

She had not, however, just awoken, and her memory was all too whole.

It had taken more than a week to reach the capital, more than a week with her wrists and ankles shackled, locked inside the dark box of the brig, more than a week during which she'd spoken to no one, not even the soldier who brought her food and lugged off the bucket filled with her piss and shit. The man had tried to engage her, explaining how Frome had pulled everyone, the whole Annurian presence out of the delta. She hadn't bothered replying. Talking, like fighting, was only worth the effort when it could accomplish something, change something, fix something, and there was no way to fix what she'd done.

"My condolences," the Emperor continued, "for your loss."

Gwenna nodded again. Condolences. Just another kind of talk, worth even less than the rest.

"You also lost one of Annur's most critical military assets." She paused, shook her head. "No. None of this is quite right, is it? You didn't *lose* them— not your friends and not your bird. You flew them into a fortress controlled by people who have sworn to destroy Annur, a fortress you had specific orders to avoid. You flew them in, you lost a fight, and you left them there. Some dead, some alive."

Gwenna's shame boiled instantly into rage. The Emperor hadn't been at the Baths when it all went down. The Emperor hadn't witnessed the Greenshirts hacking Quick Jak to pieces. The fucking Emperor had never been faced with decisions that she had to make *right now,* between one heartbeat and the next.

She opened her mouth to say as much, but the woman forestalled her with a single raised finger. She was not large, Adare hui'Malkeenian. She lacked Gwenna's muscle, Gwenna's training, Gwenna's weapons. If it came to a fight, Gwenna could murder her a hundred times over in a hundred different ways, even with her hands shackled behind her back, as they were. None of that mattered. Not here, not under the circumstances. That raised finger was enough to invalidate any objection or defense, and despite her fury, Gwenna had no defense.

Adare glanced down at the parchment on the table before her. She tapped a finger at the looping script.

"Admiral Frome says you've been reckless since you arrived in the delta. That you regularly ignored or subverted his orders."

On this, at least, Gwenna had to speak.

"I failed at the Baths," she said. "I failed both my team and my empire, and I accept whatever punishment you see fit. You should know, however, that Admiral Frome is an idiot. His orders have done more damage to the Annurian cause in Dombâng than all the local priests and Greenshirts combined."

To Gwenna's shock, the Emperor nodded. "Frome is a fool."

"Then what the fuck was he doing commanding the operation?"

"Dombâng was the least damaging place for him to be."

"The least damaging place would have been digging latrines."

The Emperor chuckled grimly. "Frome's family estates cover a quarter of Raalte and feed half a million people. My people. His sister has a web of alliances spanning the northern atrepies, from Katal to Nish. His brother just married into one of the oldest families in Sia. If Annur is going to survive, I need the admiral's family to be cooperative, compliant. Which means giving them things they believe that they want."

"An admiralty?"

Adare nodded. "In this case, yes."

"And Annurian soldiers pay the price."

"Someone always pays, Commander Sharpe. But I had hoped *you* might mitigate Frome's idiocy. Instead you have added to it."

Gwenna's shame was a fire. A scream rose inside her, sharp as a knife. She refused to let it out. For the thousandth time she imagined Talal executed on the steps of the Shipwreck. She imagined his head and Jak's and even the Dawn King's mounted on stakes, paraded around the Arena, while their bodies were tossed into the canal.

The irons bit into her wrists. She ached from straining against them. If only there were someone to *fight*. . . .

"What's happened to Annick and Qora?"

"I haven't held them responsible for this debacle."

"Where are they?"

The Emperor shook her head. "I won't have you haring off after them."

"I'm not haring anywhere. I've been in a brig, then a fucking cell." She met the other woman's blazing gaze. "I need to know that Qora's all right."

"According to Frome, she'll make a full recovery." The Emperor looked back at the paper before her, studied it a long time, then brushed it aside and returned her gaze to Gwenna. "Why did you go into the Baths?"

"The locals had two of my soldiers."

"Why did you not fall back, regroup, request support from Frome?"

"Battles happen fast. There's not always time to regroup. Do you remember the fight for Andt-Kyl? The fight for Annur? You weren't actually *out* there, but you saw how they went. You're not stupid. Soldiers aren't bureaucrats. We don't have days and days to haggle over our decisions. Most of the time we have one breath, one heartbeat, one glance to *make the fucking call,* and the people who don't do that, who can't? You know what happens to them? They *die.*"

The Emperor's face was a mask. "Gambler's folly."

"What does that mean?"

"Do you play dice, Commander Sharpe?"

"Who has time to play dice when Annur's in flames?"

The Emperor snorted. "The irony is that you would have done both Annur and your Wingmates less harm playing dice than flying our last kettral into a heavily fortified position. You may also have picked up a basic lesson in probability and decision-making."

"You weren't there. . . ."

"I did not *need* to be there." She shook her head. "There are winning bets, Commander Sharpe, and there are smart bets."

"Winning is winning. The rest is just theories."

"Well, you didn't win, did you?"

Adare's eyes bored into her, then she blew out an exasperated breath.

"You're like a drunken dice player, Sharpe. You've had enough dumb luck to win big on some very bad bets—Andt-Kyl, Annur—and because you won a few purses calling snake eyes you've forgotten a basic truth—when you roll the bones, seven comes up more than two. Only kids, drunks, and idiots think otherwise."

Kids, drunks, and idiots.

Gwenna stared down the words. She wasn't drunk and she sure as shit wasn't a kid anymore. . . .

She thought of all the blades that had missed her by inches, all the arrows that had whistled past her head, all the spears and crossbow bolts that hadn't hit her. Some of that had been skill, sure—training, tactics, strategy, whatever. But plenty of it had been dumb fucking luck.

"It was a mistake," she growled, "to take the bird into the Baths."

The words tasted like ash.

"A realization," the Emperor replied, "that comes weeks too late."

Before she understood what she was doing, Gwenna had surged from her seat. Her hands were still shackled behind her, but she loomed over the table, over the absolute ruler of all Annur.

"Jak and Talal were my friends, you miserable bitch. *I* fucked up. *I* let them die. I don't need you to lecture me about what's too fucking late."

Adare leaned slowly back in her chair, her eyes ablaze. Gwenna could smell wariness on her, but no real fear.

A light breeze slid through the open window. It smelled of wet dirt, cut grass.

"Do you know why I chose to hold this audience here?" Adare asked finally. "In this room? Alone?"

"Because you have a thing for me?"

"Because," the Emperor replied grimly, "I knew you would respond this way. And because if you had done so in front of the entire court, I would have been forced to have you executed."

"So have me executed."

"You are not listening, Gwenna." It was *Gwenna* now, she noted bleakly. *Gwenna.* Not *Commander Sharpe.* "We are having this conversation in private precisely because I do *not* want you dead."

Gwenna studied her. "Then what?"

"Sit down."

Gwenna hesitated, found her legs trembling beneath her, sat heavily. The Emperor rose, crossed to the window, gazed out onto the garden beyond. She spoke without turning.

"From the reports I've read, you were never the best choice to command your Wing. My understanding is that you simply . . . assumed the role after your former commander—my brother—disappeared."

Gwenna didn't reply. Adare continued.

"Annick Frencha will lead . . . what is left of the Wing henceforward. Her service record is impeccable, even by your own account."

The words were an obscure kind of relief, like the lancing of an abscess long infected and festering.

"Annick's brilliant," Gwenna said. "She'll be a perfect Wing leader."

"She'd better be," the Emperor replied, "given that she'll be working without a bird or a full Wing." She shook her head. "I would cut off my right arm to have the Kettral back at full strength. I could do so much with just ten Wings. With *five* . . ."

She trailed off, turned back to Gwenna, examined her with those burning eyes.

"Someday I might forgive you for losing me three of my last, best Kettral. Three *and* the bird."

Gwenna shook her head numbly. "Two. Talal and Quick Jak."

The Emperor pointed a long finger at Gwenna. "Three including you. I am stripping you of your rank. Removing you from the order entirely, in fact."

The air in the room felt thin, unbreathable, as it did when flying a bird at altitude. Gwenna's chair remained planted firmly on the floor, but she felt as though she might fall out of it. The sunlight pouring through the window was too bright. The day was cool, far cooler than Dombâng, but she was sweating through her blacks.

The Emperor narrowed her eyes.

"Are you all right?"

"Yes," Gwenna replied, fighting down the nausea in her gut. "I'm fine."

Her whole life long, that was the answer she'd given. She might be sick or shot, pushed past the point of exhaustion, but she could always keep going—a little further, a little longer—and so if anyone ever asked *Are you all right?* that was always the answer: *I'm fine.*

She'd never wondered, never even dared to imagine what it might be like to stop being fine.

There were places in the world where disgraced warriors impaled themselves on their swords. She imagined walking out of the room when the audience was over, walking out of the Dawn Palace, out of the whole 'Kent-kissing city, walking until she found someplace quiet and alone, maybe a bluff overlooking the sea, waves scraping the rocks below, gulls circling. . . . She'd been cut enough times that it was easy to imagine the way the steel would feel pressed against her ribs, the cool, precise edge of it, the readiness. What she couldn't imagine was how *she* would feel. Would her hands shake? Would she hate herself less or more as the blade sank home? She wondered what Talal and Annick would say. It was hard to know whether dying now would be brave or cowardly. All the old scales of strength and honor lay in wreckage around her.

"I understand," she said, her voice brittle. "Am I dismissed?"

Adare laughed at that, a rich laugh of true amusement.

"Not even remotely."

"If I'm not Kettral anymore—"

"Millions of Annurians are not Kettral, Gwenna. I rule them, too."

"What do you want from me?"

A long pause. Then: "I want you to go on a voyage."

Gwenna tried to parse the words. "Exile."

"Not exile." Adare drummed her fingers on the polished table. "Something else." She studied Gwenna with those unquenchable eyes. "I need more kettral. Annur needs more kettral."

"Sigrid, Newt, and the Flea are training the new cadets as fast as they can. Which isn't very fast."

"Not the soldiers. The birds. What makes the Kettral the Kettral has always been the birds."

"Well, there aren't any more. The King was the last one, and I lost him."

The Emperor shook her head. She looked tired, suddenly, and older than her twenty-eight years. "Half a decade ago there were, what? Hundreds?"

"Three hundred and forty."

"It doesn't seem possible."

"That's what happens when there's a war."

A bright-plumed bird alighted on the sill, cocked its head, surveyed the inhabitants of the room, then disappeared in a spasm of wings.

After a long pause, the Emperor shifted in her chair. "What if there were more?"

"More wars?"

"More birds."

"There are no more birds."

The Emperor pursed her lips. "Don't be so certain."

The leaden weight settled tighter around Gwenna's heart. The Eyrie had torn itself apart five years earlier in a brief, savage civil war—just one more casualty in the broader crumbling of the empire. According to most accounts, all the kettral had been destroyed in the violence, but there were rumors that a few Wings had escaped, skipped out on Annur altogether. It wasn't impossible that some of the men and women who had trained Gwenna herself might have gone rogue or mercenary.

"You want me to go after them," she said. "You want me to kill the traitors and bring back the birds."

She had no idea how to feel about that. She didn't want to kill any more kettral, not the birds or the people flying them. On the other hand, the Emperor seemed to be offering her a purpose. Rogue Wings were a horrifying prospect, but one that meant there was work to do, work she was capable of. It meant the empire still needed her. That she could still be redeemed.

Adare, however, shook her head.

"I don't know where the surviving Wings are or even *if* they are. Besides, I don't want one or two birds back. I want dozens, hundreds."

"There aren't dozens."

"There may be."

Gwenna stared at her. "Where?"

For the first time, the Emperor seemed hesitant. Beneath the delicate scent of her perfume, a whiff of uncertainty asserted itself. The woman lifted a hand, set it on the codex in front of her. The book had been there all along, but until now Gwenna had paid it no mind. It was bound in leather, finely tooled. The ends of the pages may have been gilded once, or maybe that was just dust. It didn't sparkle in the sunlight. It looked dull as dirt.

"This is the Itzal Codex," the Emperor said. "It was penned before the Csestriim wars."

The words soaked into Gwenna slowly.

"That would make it . . . what? Ten thousand years old?"

"Older."

She tried to wrap her mind around the time frame, failed. How many generations was ten thousand years? She imagined her parents and her parents' parents and the men and women before them, stretching back and back and back, past the founding of Annur, past the reign of the Atmani, past the first tribes and kingdoms, earlier than that, to when the very first humans fought a war for survival against the immortal, inhuman Csestriim. . . .

"This particular text," the Emperor went on, oblivious to Gwenna's sudden vertigo, "is a copy of a copy of a copy. How many times removed from the original manuscript, I have no idea."

She traced the binding with a fingernail.

Gwenna dragged her attention back to the present.

"What's it about?"

"Magnetism. Animal migration. The author—one of the Csestriim—had a theory about the way in which birds find their courses across vast bodies of water."

Animal migration . . . Birds . . .

Understanding backhanded Gwenna across the face.

"You think you know where they came from. The kettral."

The Emperor nodded. "They aren't indigenous to the Qirin Islands."

"Nothing's indigenous to the Islands. There are kettral skeletons to the east, over on Baliin, but the colonies there died out thousands of years ago."

"According to this text, they aren't native to Baliin, either."

Gwenna considered this. She'd always been more interested in explosives and swordplay than the tedium of Kettral history, but she was certain that all her lessons as a cadet had agreed on one fact: the birds originated on Baliin.

"Where?"

Her mind filled with the vision of some remote coast, uncounted miles from all human settlement, teeming with massive birds.

"The place names in this book," the Emperor was saying, "are almost entirely unfamiliar. Most of them exist in no other extant text."

"But there's something," Gwenna said. "You know something."

Instead of responding, the Emperor flipped open the cover, opened to a spot marked with a long blue ribbon. A map, a very detailed map, sprawled across the two facing pages. The Kettral were the best cartographers in the world—one of the advantages of being able to map everything from the back of a flying bird—but none of the maps rolled up in the Eyrie's chart room compared to this. Even after dozens of copies, the degree of detail was remarkable. It showed what looked like an island. An island with ranges of ice-rimed mountains and intricately braided rivers, something that might have been desert sands, thick forest. No, Gwenna realized after a moment, not an island, but an entire *land*.

"Here," the Emperor said, indicating with a flick of her finger a point at the southern tip.

Gwenna ran through the maps in her head—dozens of them, hundreds—maps she'd memorized as a Kettral cadet. She didn't have the best memory for all the intricacies, but the shape didn't look familiar.

"Where is that?"

The Emperor looked at her, then past her, face carefully blank.

"Menkiddoc."

Gwenna frowned. For a few moments, she struggled once again to compare the lines on the page with the maps in her memory. The Kettral had charted the northeastern coast of the continent, but they'd been hamstrung in their efforts by the fact that the birds couldn't fly south through the equatorial heat. There was nothing of strategic importance in Menkiddoc to merit a major effort—no potential allies or threats, no trading partners, barely any settlement at all. Which meant that unlike the precise, detailed, regularly up-dated maps of Eridroa and Vash to which Gwenna and every other cadet had grown accustomed, the few maps of Menkiddoc back at the Eyrie weren't really maps at all—little more than tentative, meandering scrawls of coastline unfurnished with detail, a coastline that vanished into the emptiness of the page a few hundred miles south of the Waist.

She looked up. "Didn't another emperor—Anlatun?—send an expedition to Menkiddoc?"

"He sent three," Adare replied. "None of them returned."

"So where'd this map come from?"

"The Csestriim."

"The Csestriim?"

Adare nodded.

"We wiped out the Csestriim thousands of years ago. Lots of thousands."

"As I told you—this is a very old book. My chief historian has traced the map's provenance back to the first century of the Csestriim wars. He assures me it is authentic."

As Gwenna stared, Adare reached up, tugged twice on a length of silken rope hanging from the ceiling. Somewhere beyond the wooden door a bell chimed, the bright sound muffled by the distance, probably inaudible to any ears but her own.

She shifted her gaze back to the map, studied the coastline and contours.

"Does your chief historian say anything," she asked carefully, "about why the people who go there never come back?"

According to what she remembered of her history, some early explorers—dating back to the Atmani and before—had ventured into the continent. They were searching for the usual—gold or timber, rock to be quarried, ore to be mined, slaves to be locked in chains and hauled back to the north. Most of those expeditions, like Anlatun's much later, had vanished. The few people who returned came back broken. They spoke of a cursed continent, a whole land blighted by sickness and disease, a place where the very dirt turned to rot beneath your feet, where there were no beasts but monsters, where just breathing the air or drinking the water could drive a person mad.

"Sailors," the Emperor replied, "have vivid imaginations. I've read accounts of the first people to set foot on Jakarian and the Skull. They claimed that the earth came alive at night to devour men whole." She shook her head. "Ants, as it turned out. Dangerous ants—camp too close to one of their mounds and they'll sting you to death and eat you—but still just ants."

Gwenna frowned. "But people settled on Jakarian and the Skull eventually. No one lives in Menkiddoc."

"In fact, they do. There are small towns along the northwest coast, whaling villages that trade with the Manjari."

That was news to Gwenna, but then, the northwest coast of Menkiddoc wasn't on the Kettral map.

"Villages. Are they part of some larger political force?"

The Emperor shook her head. "Not that I know of. I don't have any intelligence from south of the Waist." A flicker of irritation crossed her features. "My point is that the stories are wrong. People do live there. The monsters described in those early accounts are, without a doubt, nothing more than strange and unusual species. Sickness afflicted those early explorations, but there is sickness everywhere. People are afraid of unfamiliar places. That doesn't mean the whole continent is cursed."

As she finished speaking, there was a knock at the door.

"Enter," Adare said.

The slab of bloodwood swung open, and an old man stepped inside.

"Gwenna," the Emperor said. "This is Kiel, my historian."

Kiel bowed to Adare, then to Gwenna.

Gwenna studied the old man. No, she realized at once—not old. There was no gray in his black hair, and his skin was unlined by sun or weather. What she'd mistaken for age in those first moments was, instead, breakage. The historian might have been barely into his fourth decade, but it looked as though most of the bones in his body had been snapped, then forced to heal at awkward angles. His nose was crooked, as was his jaw. His knuckles were more swollen than Gwenna's own, the long fingers bent, as though they'd been shattered over and over. He stooped, carrying his right shoulder ahead of the left, and limped slightly when he moved. Altogether, it gave him the air of a man more than twice his age, but his voice, when he spoke, was filled with a quiet confidence, and his eyes were keen.

"Gwenna Sharpe. It is a pleasure. Your actions occupy many pages of my account of Annur's recent history."

"My actions."

Kiel nodded. "The defense of Andt-Kyl against the Urghul. Wresting the Kettral back from Jakob Rallen. Your rescue of Valyn hui'Malkeenian and his companions. Your involvement in the defeat of Balendin Ainhoa, just beyond the gates of this city . . ."

For a moment she was speechless. She recognized the fights, of course. She could remember every preparation she'd made for the defense of Andt-Kyl, the placement of each barricade, the rigging of the bridges, the deployment of every one of those loggers. She *had* defeated Rallen, *had* rescued Valyn from the Urghul, *had* brought down Balendin. . . . And yet when the historian talked about it, none of it sounded real. Or if it was real, it sounded like something that had happened to someone else, some Kettral legend to whom she had no relation.

She glanced down at her hands. They'd stopped shaking, but she could feel the fear threaded into her flesh, the uncertainty and doubt. She poured that doubt into the forge of her rage, stoked the fire higher.

I did those things, she told herself. *I was a good soldier.*

She looked up from her hands, met Kiel's eyes.

"Sounds like you've been listening to too many stories."

He raised a brow. "Listening to stories is the work of a historian."

"Is it?" Gwenna asked. "Is that how you came up with this horseshit about some birds at the ass end of Menkiddoc?"

All her life, her anger had been a kind of secret weapon, one she could rely on even when her bombs and blades had been stripped away. Now, though, as she reached for it, she found it slipping from her grasp. Even when she managed the crack at Kiel, the edge in her voice sounded brittle.

"In part," the man replied, unruffled by her gibe.

In that moment she realized something strange about him—he didn't smell. Or rather, he smelled of all the things she'd expect of a historian—ink and dust, glue and the musty odor of old pages—but nothing else. There was no hope on him. No fear. No eagerness. Not a whiff of lust or impatience or anticipation or distaste or . . . *anything.* Since drinking the egg of the slarn, she'd grown so accustomed to smelling the emotions of others that the absence made her skin crawl. Even Kettral had emotions, though kept sharply in check. *Everyone* had emotions, except . . .

"Are you a monk?" she asked.

Adare shifted in her seat. The motion was almost imperceptible, but Gwenna recognized a retreat when she saw one.

Kiel just raised his brows. "Why do you ask?"

"Her brother," Gwenna said, nodding toward the Emperor. "Kaden. He was trained by monks. You remind me of him."

In fact, Kiel looked nothing like Kaden. Kaden's eyes had burned like Adare's. He'd been young, and strong, where Kiel was broken a hundred times over. Gwenna herself had been young at the time, unaccustomed to her new powers, but she still remembered the strangeness of Kaden's scent, the way there seemed to be no *person* beneath the robes, no heat behind the fire of those eyes. Kiel was like that, only . . . *more.* She might as well have been facing a statue.

"Keenly observed," the historian replied with a nod. "I spent some . . . considerable time among an order kindred to Kaden's own."

"Strange place for a historian, out there at the edge of everything."

"Centers are defined by edges."

"Whatever the fuck that means."

Kiel laughed. It was a perfectly normal laugh, exactly the kind of thing she might have heard on any street in Annur, utterly unremarkable, completely forgettable. Except that normal laughter had a smell that went with it, or a range of smells—astringent for mockery; sickly sweet for nerves; rough and tannic for true, unrestrained joy. . . . The historian smelled vaguely like a book. Nothing more.

He nodded, then gestured to the map spread open before Adare.

"Take these kettral. Though they are at the world's edge, they have the power to change everything."

"These *hypothetical* kettral," Gwenna reminded him. "Kettral that are probably nothing but bones by now, nothing but fossils. If all of them didn't migrate north in the first place . . ." She ran straight into the fact the way a woman stumbling through the dark might run into a stone wall.

"He's wrong," she said.

Adare raised a single imperial eyebrow.

"Or the codex is wrong, or the translators are wrong, or the fucking map is wrong."

"The map," Kiel interjected quietly, "is accurate."

"Maybe. Maybe not. All I know is that *someone* made a mistake. The birds didn't migrate from some mountain range in the south of Menkiddoc. They couldn't have, not even by accident. They can't cross the equator any more than they can the poles. Can't get within five hundred miles of it. It's too hot. Their physiology breaks down."

The realization filled her with fury. No kettral meant no mission. No mission meant nothing for her to do but leave, walk out of the palace . . .

"Not birds," the historian said calmly, cutting into her thoughts. "Eggs. The Csestriim who compiled this treatise brought back hundreds of them."

Gwenna's fingers twitched. She clenched them into a fist.

"Why?" she asked.

"To study."

"Why?"

"It is what they do." He made a wry face. "What they did."

"And these eggs gave rise to the entire kettral population of the northern hemisphere."

He nodded.

Gwenna took a deep breath, held it for a long time, then blew it out, shifted her gaze to Adare. "And you want me to go."

The Emperor nodded.

"After I botched everything in Dombâng. After I lost a bird and got half my Wing killed."

Another nod.

Gwenna stared at her, struggled for the right word, managed it at last. "*Why?*"

"You know the birds. Where they nest. How they behave."

"I came up through *demolitions*. You need a flier for this. Someone like Quick Jak."

The Emperor's eyes were twin pyres. It was strange to find such ferocious flames so silent. "Quick Jak is dead," she replied. "What I have left is you."

Outside the window a young man had inched into view—a laborer on his hands and knees, wooden bucket at his side. He was scrubbing the flagstones of the garden path with a rough brush, one at a time. The Dawn Palace was filled with such paths, hundreds of them, thousands. Gwenna tried briefly to calculate the number of stones, then gave up.

"So I take a ship down the coast of Menkiddoc," she said, "pick a spot on the coast, land, start hiking, start looking for mountains that look like," she waved a hand at the codex, "this."

"Kiel will accompany you."

Gwenna blinked. "How the fuck is a crippled historian going to help?"

"I assure you," the man replied. "I am less infirm than this body suggests."

"I don't *care* how infirm you are. It doesn't help us find the birds."

"You are traveling," the Emperor said, an edge in her voice, "to shores no Annurian has ever visited. We know these lands only from ancient accounts, accounts that Kiel understands better than anyone else."

Outside, the young man straightened, knuckled his back, then bent again to his task. He scrubbed in simple, scrupulous circles, careful in his work as though each flagstone were the last, the only, as though it would not be dirty again in a matter of days. She tried to imagine spending the rest of her life scrubbing, or mending, or building.

"It will take time," she said. "Annur could be in shambles when we finally get back."

"Annur," the Emperor replied, "is already in shambles." Her voice was stone-steady, but again, for just a moment, Gwenna could smell the desperation, the urgency beneath the perfume. In some ways, Adare's life had been harder than Gwenna's: she'd seen a father murdered, a brother killed, and another vanished into the vast frozen north. They were, none of them, ready for this shit.

The Emperor closed her eyes, briefly extinguishing the flame, then opened them again. "My younger brothers used to play a game with the ocean, down by the docks. When the tide was out, they would light a small fire on the narrow strip of beach inside the fortress. Then they would build a wall of sand and stones around it—three feet high, sometimes. Maybe five. Once, they ordered their Aedolians to help, and managed to put together a wall as high as a grown man." She paused, stared back at the memory. "Do you want to guess how many times the wall kept out the coming tide?"

Gwenna snorted. For half a heartbeat she didn't quite hate this woman. "Those boys always did love lost causes."

Adare's face hardened. Suddenly, she was all emperor once again. "I do not. What I have been doing is not working. What *we* have been doing is not working. There might be no more birds left in the southern hemisphere. You might die trying to find these mountains; drowned, diseased, slaughtered by whoever it is that lives on that side of the globe. Maybe there *are* monsters that inhabit the continent; maybe they'll kill you. Maybe you will go mad. But the alternative is sitting on the beach as night clamps down, the clouds roll in, and we all watch, helpless, as the waves chew through the wall and put out the fire."

7

He'd been seven when they did it. Or maybe six. Shit, maybe he'd been eight. There'd been no one to tell him his age—that was for sure. No mother or father. No sisters or brothers. It was a wonder he remembered his own name—Akiil. Maybe he'd had another one once, a family name—plenty of people did—but if so, he'd forgotten it. What he *hadn't* forgotten was the branding.

It was the soldiers who caught him stealing—him and Skinny Quinn and Butt Boy, not twenty years between the three of them—the soldiers who locked them up, and then the same soldiers who, the next day, dragged them along with half a dozen other thieves—some blubbering, some begging, some just stumbling along dumbly like animals bound for the slaughter—out into the massive open square before the Dawn Palace. You had to give it to the Annurian legions—they had a system for everything, including the branding of children.

A dozen men set up a loose perimeter to hold back the gawkers—even at dawn the plaza at the eastern end of Anlatun's Way was thronging with people hurrying about their business—while three or four others dragged out a table from the guardhouse, then kindled a fire in the neat stone pit built for just that purpose. They worked with the disinterested boredom of men doing an unpleasant task at an early hour. Akiil had expected sneering, taunting, a few extra blows before the branding itself, but the soldiers might as well have been stacking wood or digging ditches. Looking back on it, a little cruelty would have been nice, actually, a kind of acknowledgement that he and the other thieves kneeling on the stone were, in fact, people—*bad* people, sure, morally corrupt, a poison to the order of the empire, but still *people,* not just so much meat to be processed.

"I'll remember this," Skinny Quinn hissed at a man guarding them. "I remember everything. I'll remember your stupid, ugly face and when I'm older, when I'm older . . ."

Akiil couldn't recall what it was she'd said she'd do when she was older. She was the one with the perfect memory.

He *did* recall trembling as the sergeant in charge laid the cool brands in the fire, then sat down behind the table to flip through a sheaf of papers, remembered hating himself for that trembling. What he *wanted* to do was sneer as the soldiers seized him by the armpits, offer some kind of clever gibe to show Butt Boy and Quinn he wasn't afraid, then to stare the man branding him square in the face, to hold that bastard's gaze without flinching. It didn't happen that way. By the time they dragged him forward he was screaming, kicking, thrashing like an alley cat, trying to bite the hands holding him. He managed to land one good kick to the side of someone's knee, but it didn't matter.

They forced him to his knees before the table. Behind him he could hear Butt Boy shouting—*It's fast, Aki! It'll be over so fast!*—and Quinn's furious cursing. Then a huge man with breath that smelled like rot leaned against his skinny back, pinning him down, all that weight against his child's frame, while another took him by the wrist, yanked his arm out straight.

"Please," he begged, shame and terror flooding him. "Please, I won't do it anymore. Not ever again. I'm sorry. I'm *sorry*!"

"Good," the sergeant replied. Then: "In the name of Sanlitun hui'Malkeenian, Emperor of all Annur, bright be the days of his life, I administer this justice."

He lifted the glowing iron from the fire and pressed it into Akiil's skin.

The pain felt like dying, like something no one could possibly survive, certainly not a child of seven or eight. It went on for a lifetime while he screamed and screamed and tried to pull away. He could hear the sizzling of his skin, smell the flesh beneath blackening to char . . . and then suddenly it was over. The soldiers hoisted him up, hauled him clear, tossed him onto the broad flagstones.

He lay there for a long time, moaning, curled in on himself like some dying creature as his mind swam slowly free. He'd bitten a chunk from his bottom lip, shat himself. He was curled in a puddle of his own watery shit. He remembered the others then, raised his head to see Quinn forced down over the table, her arm yanked out. They locked eyes. He opened his mouth to shout some kind of courage, anything at all to help her through the red wall of pain, but no sound came, nothing but a slobbery mewling which had shamed him then, and for which he'd never quite forgiven himself.

The brand didn't hurt anymore. It hadn't hurt for years. He traced the circle absently, running his fingers over the slick, glabrous curves: the rising sun of Annur burned into his brown skin. It had always seemed to him like a strange decision, branding thieves with the seal of the imperial family, like forcing whores to wear corsets cut from the flag. If Akiil had been in charge he would have saved the emblems of empire for the really *noble* shit—prows of ships, tops of towers, shining shields of the Aedolian Guard. . . . No need to have his family's crest tattooed on the dick of every drunk.

On the other hand, having no family and no crest, the question had never vexed him all that much. The Emperor was the Emperor, which meant he—or *she,* now—could do any stupid thing she wanted, and anyway, it wasn't as though Akiil himself was about to go down in the chronicles as a maker of brilliant decisions. The stealing—sure. He'd been a kid—stupid, desperate, and starving. What else was he going to do? The stealing had made sense at the time.

What *didn't* make sense was what he was preparing to do now, all these long years later.

"An icicle," Yerrin announced.

Akiil had no idea what that meant. The morning was hot and humid. He'd already sweated through his robe. There were no icicles, but then, a lucid conversational style had never ranked high on the list of Yerrin's charms. No one lived fifty years alone in a cave without ending up a little strange.

Akiil patted the old man gently on the shoulder.

"No icicles here, Yerrin."

"There," said the monk, pointing up. "An icicle."

"Ah." Akiil followed Yerrin's gaze up and up and up some more, to the very top of the tower of Intarra's Spear. Much like Yerrin himself, the icicle comparison was at once perfect and ludicrous. Back at the monastery, icicles had formed beneath the eaves of the refectory, growing one drip at a time all winter long until they were thicker than Akiil's arm. Intarra's Spear did, in fact, look like an inverted icicle, something poured rather than built. Dawn gleamed off its smooth surface, scattering light across the city.

So . . . sure, Yerrin, like an upside down icicle—if icicles were thousands of paces high.

Intarra's Spear stood taller than any structure Akiil had ever seen, taller than some *mountains* he'd come across—and he'd lived a good portion of his life near the top of a 'Kent-kissing mountain. According to Kaden, it took a fit person an entire day to climb from the base to the tower's top, and that was barely stopping to rest or piss or eat. The structure made something deep inside of Akiil cringe. It looked . . . impossible, the girth too slender to support the height, the glassine walls too delicate not to shatter. Kaden said it wasn't the work of the Malkeenians, and he ought to have known, given that he was a Malkeenian. Lots of people thought it was a Csestriim relic, but the Csestriim had been dead for, oh, ten thousand years, so it wasn't as though there were any left to ask. Whatever the case, one of Kaden's great-great-great ancestors had been bright enough to claim the thing for the Malkeenians, plop a palace beneath it, ring the whole massive complex in blood-colored walls, then sit back on the throne while people came from across Vash and Eridroa to stare in awe.

Yerrin didn't seem to be feeling the awe.

The monk was looking down—all talk of icicles forgotten—his bald, spotted pate furrowed. After a moment he knelt on the flagstones, brushed something gently aside with his finger.

"I'm sorry, my friends," he said. "Your beautiful home, and I have crushed it."

It took Akiil a moment to see the ants milling about in disarray. Evidently Yerrin's bare foot had scuffed aside a tiny hill between the flagstones. Slowly, he began reassembling the grains of sand.

Not for the first time, Akiil found himself envying the elderly monk. Barely twenty paces distant loomed the crenelated red walls of the Dawn Palace, ten times Akiil's height and allegedly washed in the blood of Annur's foes. Before the walls, at stiff attention, stood a full Annurian legion, a forest of pole arms in their hands. Behind the walls, Intarra's Spear stabbed into the sky. He and Yerrin were standing a few dozen paces away from the center of the empire, the center of the whole 'Kent-kissing *world,* and the old man was fretting over an anthill.

Akiil had a cool head—something he'd earned as a thief in the Perfumed Quarter, practiced as a Shin monk, and nearly perfected trying to keep himself and Yerrin alive traveling the thousands of miles from the Bone Mountains to the capital. He had a way to stand, a way to look or not look, a way to move. He had a face he used for dangerous situations—the one he wore now—half a grin, half a smirk. It was a face that irritated some people, charmed others, and fooled almost everyone. Yerrin, though—he didn't *need* a face. The ant fascination wasn't an act. He just didn't care all that much about the greatest fortification in the known world.

Of course, Yerrin wasn't going inside in a few days. Yerrin wasn't going to have to talk his way past a thousand soldiers, and ministers, and Aedolians. Yerrin wasn't about to run a con on the 'Shael-spawned Emperor of Annur.

Akiil turned away from the palace, back toward the older monk.

"I'm going to check out the other gates. Do you remember how to get back to the inn?"

"The inn," Yerrin replied, not looking up from the ants. "It is beyond time, beyond death, beside the sky."

It took Akiil a moment to unpack this.

"Yes. Follow Anlatun's Way west past the water clock and the cemetery. You'll see it on top of the hill."

Yerrin nodded, as though Akiil had spoken his own words back to him. "Beside the sky."

He made no move to depart. If the guards didn't move him along, it was possible he'd still be kneeling there when Akiil finished his examination of the palace.

In truth, that examination was just a way of stalling. He wasn't going to storm the 'Kent-kissing thing. He wasn't planning to climb the walls. When the time came, he was going to walk up to the front gate and present himself, just like any other petitioner. Still, old habits died hard.

He ran a hand over his brand again. The woman sitting on the Unhewn Throne, he reminded himself, was Kaden's sister. *Your Radiance,* he would say. *I was friends at the monastery with your brother,* dear *friends. . . .* Of course, Kaden was years dead, and for all Akiil knew, Adare was the one who'd killed him. Didn't seem like very sisterly behavior, but the annals of history made growing up in a great family sound even more dangerous than trying to survive in the slums. Adare might well agree to see him, smile when he told her that he'd known Kaden, then have his arms torn off, his balls stuffed in his mouth, and his body thrown to the pigs.

Were there pigs inside the Dawn Palace? One of a million questions about the place to which he had no answer.

Not for the first time, he considered abandoning the whole idea. Other people found a way through the world without relying on thievery and tricks. *Work,* they called it. Akiil was young—twenty-three or twenty-four, maybe— strong, smart, quick. He should have been better at work.

It wasn't that he hadn't given it a shot. Back in the Bend, after the monastery burned, he'd briefly earned enough coin to take care of Yerrin by loading and unloading the harbor ships. After a couple months, he quit. He told Yerrin it was because the overseer beat him, which was, on the one hand, true, and on the other hand, utterly irrelevant. He'd had worse beatings from his masters at the monastery—far worse. The truth was, he couldn't bring himself to stare down a lifetime moving crates from one place to another, then putting other crates back where the first ones had been.

He might have managed it, before the slaughter at the monastery. Ten years among the monks had started to instill in him the strange joy of rising early, working hard, of denying the pleasures of the flesh. If the soldiers hadn't come and killed everyone he knew, maybe he would have eventually become the kind of man who could find peace in a life of daily labor, some freedom in the bearing of weight across the shoulders. But the soldiers *had* come, and they had taught a lesson of their own, a lesson different from that of the Shin, one articulated with bloody blades: *You could die tomorrow. If you want something, take it now.*

What, exactly, he wanted, or why he wanted it? Well, those were trickier questions, ones he'd somehow managed to avoid.

He'd never imagined, during his long years with the Shin, that a monk's training might be useful for anyone other than a monk. The endless days of sitting, running, building, painting, watching, thinking, *not* thinking, had seemed more or less perfectly useless for anyone who didn't live on the edge of a cliff near the top of a mountain.

Wrong.

He discovered quickly that all those frigid years weren't wasted after all. Monastic discipline, as it turned out, was the perfect foundation for a life of crime. Oh sure, the monks hadn't taught him shit about coins or cons, lying or locks, but those were just the details. Anyone with half a brain could learn to pick a lock, and he remembered most of the skills from his childhood. What the Shin had given him was something deeper, better—patience, fortitude, and best of all, *vision*. He'd had good instincts as a child, but they'd been no more than that—wordless gut impressions that sometimes turned out to be wrong. Now, however, with barely a glance, he could tell if a man was eager or frightened, lying or honestly confused. He could read faces like most people read books, and not just faces, but the whole *world*. All those days spent in meditation had left him with a memory to rival Skinny Quinn. He could remember a scene—the inside of a tavern, the sprawling paths on a map, the faces of an entire crew of sailors—almost as easily as breathing, could pick out and study any little detail at will. Which was handy because it was the details, after all, that ended up fucking you.

The details, or, you know, the drinking.

Drinking had ended his crime spree back in the Bend.

After one particularly satisfying score—an Antheran merchant's daughter had a taste for diamonds—he'd spent half the night in the Whale's Head. There'd been no rum back at Ashk'lan, no alcohol of any kind, and as it turned out, rum had a way of dissolving Shin discipline. By midnight the boasts had begun to spill out of him, and by morning he found himself locked in a cell in the local prison, one finger broken, half his clothes gone. Escaping—after he'd sobered up enough to contemplate escape—was a dicey matter of slowing his breathing to the point where the guards believed him dead, then making a break for it when they'd carted him outside the walls. He should have counted himself lucky that he'd been able to find Yerrin and get out of the city alive, should have quit then and for good.

He didn't, of course.

As they made their way west—short hops on coastal boats, then a long trek the length of Katal—he moved from one mark to the next, stealing from mayors and merchants, sailors, soldiers, seamstresses, anyone with two coins to rub together and not enough wit to keep them safe. Another man with Akiil's skills, a more prudent man, might have built up a small fortune quickly, then retired. Instead, Akiil found himself blowing his coin on ale, plum wine, and black rum, waking up bleary-eyed most mornings, his head splitting, his mouth tasting like a mouse had crawled in, taken a shit, then died. Didn't seem like much of a life, actually, when he paused to consider it, so he didn't pause. Didn't consider.

Of course, there was a big difference between swindling a few rich merchants on the empire's edge and coming to the very heart of Annur to take down the Emperor herself. A little voice inside his head, the voice that had kept him alive for the past twenty-something years, whispered that this was stupid, stupid and unnecessary. The Emperor would have guards, hundreds of guards. Just getting to her meant stepping through those massive gates into a fortress that could transform, with the closing of a door, into another prison. It meant promising something he had no ability to deliver to a woman who could have men executed with a flick of her little finger. And for what?

Gold.

Sure. Piles of gold. Piles and *piles*. Hills of gleaming gold, heaped up deep as cow shit.

The gold would be great. He could buy more wine. He could buy a little house for Yerrin, something with a garden, a place where the old monk could tend his plants and insects without getting trampled by every passing wagon. Gold meant pleasure, and safety, and power. Gold meant not having to look over his shoulder, not having to palm every meal in the markets, being able to wake up each morning without wondering where he would sleep.

In truth, though, he didn't give much of a shit about the gold.

"So," he muttered to himself, gazing up at the walls. "Why are you here?"

He fingered his brand again. For half a heartbeat he felt all over the soldier's hand clamped around his wrist, the scream spilling like vomit from his throat, the smell of the glowing iron searing his flesh. . . .

Slowly, deliberately, he tightened the belt around his robe, then exhaled.

Fear is blindness, he reminded himself. *Calmness, sight.*

An old Shin aphorism.

They might have been poor as dirt, those monks who'd trained him, but they knew how to still the body, smooth the agitation from the mind, move beyond the animal instincts of freezing and flight. He took another breath, held it for a matter of heartbeats, let all his fear and doubt soak into it, then blew it out slowly. When it was gone from him, he felt light, empty, ready. They could have done great things, the Shin. A shame they'd never bothered to try.

8

"I have to go to the delta," Ruc said.

Bien didn't respond. She might as well have been sitting alone on the roof of the dormitory. Instead of glancing over at him, she kept her eyes fixed on the flame fisher working the canal, her face just barely lifted from the darkness by the light blazing in the iron basket hanging from the boat's prow. Ruc watched her silently until she shifted and her hair slipped forward, a black curtain obscuring her face. He let out a long, quiet breath, then turned to follow her gaze.

The fisher tossed a split log into his swaying basket. Sparks splattered, hissed into nonexistence on the glassy water. Ruc couldn't see the fish rising stupidly to the light—the water was black except where the flames glazed it—but according to the fishers, the red-scales and ploutfish took the blazing basket for the moon. That desire to swim to the moon, of course, he had never understood.

"Why?" Bien said finally.

Ruc had touched ice only once, years earlier, in the mansion of an Annurian merchant, a devotee of Eira who had invited several priests to perform a ceremony in her home. He had gone along to swing the censer and to sing, and when it was over, the merchant had given him a glass of squeezed juice poured over ice. It was a luxury beyond his childhood imagining, that draught of coolness in a world where everything else was hot. And yet, something about those clear shards made him uneasy. He drained the glass, stared at the ice, then gingerly took one of the fragments on his tongue. The cold ached in his mouth. In a way he could not explain, it felt dangerous.

Bien's *why* reminded him of that ice.

"The messenger," he said finally.

They'd managed to smuggle the dead man out of Bien's room in the middle of the night almost a week earlier. By the time they did, the *axoch* had already begun to wither around his neck. It felt wrong to slosh the body into the canal, but the man's spirit was gone, and neither Ruc nor Bien could think of any other choice. The crematorium was at the far eastern end of the city, and if they'd been discovered lugging the corpse, the Greenshirts would not have been understanding.

"He was a madman," Bien said.

"He did not speak like a madman," Ruc pointed out. "And there were more of them. All with the same message."

"They'd hardly be the first cult in the city. PureBlood. The Sons of Cao. Jem Von and her followers. The Threefold Truth. If I wandered down to the Weir right now I'd find some poor fool standing on a bridge prophesying a flood or a plague or a rain of blood. Half the people in Dombâng believe we're days away from some kind of apocalypse. All this rain isn't helping."

"He wasn't *from* Dombâng."

"All lands have their false prophets."

"And that thing around his neck?" Ruc forced himself to remember the twisting, tightening noose of flesh. "The *axoch*?"

"I don't *know,* Ruc."

"What if there *is* some kind of army bearing down on Dombâng?"

"Dombâng just defeated the most powerful empire in the world. If this . . . Lord—I detest that name, by the way. I feel like I'm choking on my own spit every time I say it. Anyway, if he turns out to be real, if he actually *has* an army, he'll die in the delta like everyone else. Just like you said."

"That wasn't quite right, though, was it?" He hesitated. "Not everyone dies in the delta."

Her lips tightened. "Most people do. We weren't all raised by the Vuo Ton."

The words were soft, almost gentle, but Ruc could hear the echo of a warning behind them.

He turned away, looked back out over the canal.

Behind the fisher, ranked along the rails of the boat, perched the cormorants, heads like weapons, hooked beaks stiletto sharp. As Ruc watched, one of them plunged into the water. He counted his heartbeats while it stayed down. *Eight . . . Nine . . . Ten . . .* As he reached *fifteen* the bird surfaced a few paces from where it had entered, head and back slick with the water's black. A silvery fish tail—coin-bright in the firelight—twitched in its beak, then vanished.

Bien turned to watch him with silent eyes.

"You haven't been to the delta in what? Fifteen years?"

He nodded.

"And now you want to go back."

"I'm not sure *want* is the right word. . . ." He wasn't sure there *was* a word for the storm churning inside him.

"You said you'd chosen Dombâng. Chosen Eira."

Chosen me, she didn't add.

"I'm not planning to stay there. I'll go, find the Vuo Ton. If there's anything . . . strange moving through the channels, anything worth seeing, they'll have seen it."

She watched him awhile, then for the second time asked, "Why?"

The easy answer dangled like bait: *Maybe I can learn something that can protect the temple, something that can protect you.*

It wasn't untrue, but it wasn't everything either. Another answer loomed behind it, something darker, more dangerous, far harder to name.

He stared into the night. "The delta used to be my home."

"You said you'd given it up."

He shook his head slightly. "The past has barbs, Bien. You know that as well as I do. It's like a fishhook. You can't just give it up."

†

In the dark hour before dawn, the city was still mostly asleep. The rain had finally stopped, though the air was heavy as a water-soaked blanket. Smoke from a few clay chimneys—the homes of fishers or laborers up early, getting ready to go about their work—rose reluctantly, smudged a handful of stars, lost its heat, then settled, feathering the water of the canal. If the breeze didn't pick up by dawn, that smoke would thicken, fed by a hundred thousand fires, choking the streets and waterways, blanketing the city in a hot, itchy haze until it was impossible to make out more than vague shapes in the gray. For now, though, as Ruc paddled along Cao's Canal—east past the looming bulk of the Shipwreck, then south—the air remained mostly clear, rinsed by the storms. The day had yet to shrug on its bronze mantle of heat. The paddle felt light in his hands, and the canoe carved a silent passage through the star-slicked water, leaping forward at each stroke as though eager to be free of the city.

As he reached the last shacks, a man's voice, low and gravelly, drifted out over the water, rising and falling with the melody of an old Dombângan love song.

"No more," swore the fisher, "I'll stay here no more."
And he folded his nets, and he settled his oars,
"For my love loves another,
   "Ah-lu, and ah-lay,
   "Ah-lu, and alack, and ah-lay."

And he followed the current right out of the city,
And he didn't look back for love or for pity.
"For my love loves another," he sang as he rowed,
  "Ah-lu, and alack, and ah-lay."

A year and a day and his boat drifted back,
  Ah-lu, and ah-lay,
  Ah-lu and alack,
The hull, it was empty, the fisher was gone,
Slipped into the delta along with his song,
  Ah-lu, and alack, and ah-lay.

The final strains faded to silence behind him.

Ruc adjusted his grip on the paddle, stabbed it down into the murky black, dragged the slender craft forward.

He must have been a mile outside Dombâng when dawn began to dissolve the night's dark. Black bled into purple, which drained to bloody red, then pink. In the east, stars dwindled, lost in the broader wash of light. Blueheads tested the silence with their clipped, high-pitched song—*twee-wit-wit, twee-wit-wit*. Then the gorzles joined in, then the reed wrens and mud wrens, then, lower and slower, the sad notes of the burnbreasts: *too true, too true*. Ruc caught glimpses of the birds flitting through the reeds to either side of the channel, flashes of blue and green and black. He paused in his paddling, let memory slide over him along with the sound. . . .

He was some young age to which he had never learned to put a number—five? seven?—standing still among the rushes, his arms outstretched. This was before his time with the Vuo Ton, when all he knew of the world he'd learned from the brutal, beautiful creatures that the people of the delta worshipped as gods. He didn't think of them as gods. At that age, he knew neither the word nor the concept. He knew only that they had raised him, protected him, trained him. . . .

He had been standing there a long time, since before dawn. His eyes itched and his shoulders ached with the strain of keeping his hands out, but he didn't move. He breathed only through his nose. When his bladder began to strain he let it go, ignoring the warmth as it drained down his naked leg. He tried to imagine himself a tree, rooted, patient. The sun crept up the sky.

Various birds came and went, perched on his shoulders, his wrists, even his ear, but it wasn't until nearly noon that the burnbreast finally alighted on his finger. He could see it out of the corner of his eye, all twitch and stillness, head cocked to the side, black eye like a wet stone lodged in its head, feathers of its breast shimmering red-orange to glossy black and back again. At that age, Ruc had not learned to make fire—*they* had not needed fire any more than they did language—but he had seen the smoldering of trees struck by lightning, the way the hot light lived in the wood, the red-black heat pouring from the embers. Those trees he could not touch, but the bird . . .

The trap of his hand snapped shut, snaring the scaly leg. A spasm of wings as the creature raked desperately at the air, then the sharp beak stabbing down into the meat between his thumb and the forefinger. He made a hood of his other hand, slipped it over the bird's head, covering the eyes until it quieted to a hot, feathered tremble. He could feel the heart through the chest, small and impossibly fast, battering out its terror. He brought the bird close to his face and cooed to it: *too true, too true.* They weren't words to him then, just sounds. He waited for the creature to go totally still, then snapped its neck.

He wore the feathers in his long black hair for weeks, along with the scabs on the back of his hand.

Now, sitting still in the center of the canoe, gazing out into the rushes, he tried to think how long it had been since he'd killed something. Eira's Teachings laid down no prohibition on the slaughter of animals. People needed to live, after all, even those who had sworn allegiance to a goddess. The other priests gutted fish and hacked the heads from chickens daily, and yet since Ruc had left the delta, left it for the last time, he couldn't remember taking a single life, nothing aside from insects. Strange, when he paused to think about it; he had been so good at it, once.

Before the sluggish current could take the hull and bear him back toward the city, he slid his paddle into the water once more. His shoulders ached, and his hands had already begun to blister, but he found himself enjoying the pain as it settled into his skin. He shifted on the hard bench; his skin had grown soft, but his body remembered. Each year, just before the start of the rainy season, the Vuo Ton held a boat race. Three years in a row he had won it, won as a boy against women and men twice and three times his age. The thought brought an unexpected smile to his lips, one that lingered as he paddled deeper into the shade of the overhanging reeds.

The Shirvian delta was one enormous maze, a rough triangle more than fifty miles to a side, the whole thing webbed by a hundred thousand channels, some wide enough for a three-masted sailing rig, some of them hip-narrow and winding, barely a few inches deep. Straight-line travel was impossible. The sun helped, where you could see the sun, but in most places the reeds and rushes—twice or three times the height of a grown man—arched overhead, filtering the light to a vague, diffuse green that seemed to come from all directions at once. A handful of *cang* trees grew on the few true islands, but even if you managed to find one and climb it, managed to take a bearing by the sun or stars, as soon as you climbed down, the rushes would close around you once more.

Fishers had been found dead in their boats barely a thousand paces from Dombâng, close enough that they must have seen the smoke, caught the choking scent, heard the city's gongs sounding the hours, close enough that if they'd dared to climb free of their boats and make a break for it, braving the mudbanks and swimming the channels, they might have survived. Most didn't dare. They'd been raised, after all, on tales of flailing swimmers stripped to the bone by schools of *qirna,* of arms ripped off by crocs, of snakes and spiders. Everyone knew how it went—the quick nip at the calf, then the twitch, cramp, spasm of muscles closing and refusing to open, the shaking and then the rictus stillness and staring eyes, last breath stoppered in the lungs. Given those dangers, most chose the dubious safety of their boats, shouting for help, and then, when shouting took too much strength, waiting and hoping, then giving up on that hope by slow degrees as day after day the heat ground down, until eventually there was nothing left but the rustling of the rushes, just the delta muttering in a language no one understood.

That, Ruc reminded himself as the canoe nosed up a narrow watery passage, *would be good to avoid.*

There were, of course, ways to navigate the delta. The Vuo Ton would never have survived out among the rushes for so many generations if there hadn't been. Ruc had learned early to read the river's flow in the swirl of the current, to know which channels would branch out and which would clamp down around him. The breeze offered its own clues, as did the fish finning beneath the surface, as did the birds. Someone with the knack could weave all the signs together—if the blueheads were winging a certain way, that meant a hatch of bo flies, which meant fast-moving water. Find that water and you could divide the world roughly into halves—west and east—because no matter how the channels twisted and turned, the fast water, the true current, never actually doubled back on itself. As you moved west the reeds changed, growing taller and greener. Or, in the colorless night, you could taste the water for some hint of the sea's salt. Among the Vuo Ton, the most skilled navigators were respected almost as much as the fiercest fighters, but even the children could make their way—indirectly, with much second-guessing and backtracking— from one shabby island to the next.

Ruc found the first without much trouble, a crescent-shaped rise the Vuo Ton called Feast of Rats. He didn't recognize any of the channels leading away, but picked a course vaguely southwest, held to it as best he could, caught a lucky glimpse through the bars of the reeds of a marsh hawk circling, followed the creature west to Old Grave. From there, a broad channel—so wide and slow it almost looked like a long pond—opened up most of the way to Four Feathers. From there . . .

Gradually, like a man sliding into a cool bath, he let himself slip back into the delta, allowed the hum and chitter to close over him, sank into the warm, muddy reek, the hot green-brown haze. Ten thousand fragments of sun shattered silently over and over again on the *water's* top. He hadn't realized, or had known once but then forgotten, how much of himself he'd packed away—half a lifetime—crammed inside some wooden crate in his mind, then shoved ungently out of sight. It surprised him how easily it all came back, like a hawk to its master's call—the paddle strokes, the casual balance of the slender craft, the sense for the best passage through the screens of reeds. He'd lived in the city so long he'd almost come to believe all the most histrionic tales of the delta, but of course it wasn't so bad. He'd survived out here as a *child,* for Eira's sake, had made necklaces of snake fangs. . . .

And then, as though the warm echo of his own pride had summoned the creature, he felt the cool scales coiling at his ankle.

He froze at the top of the stroke. Water dripped from the tip of the paddle blade, each drop marking a fickle circle on the surface, a path that would fade long before he could ever follow it back.

Slowly, he lowered his gaze to the hull of the boat, to where the snake, banded in red and yellow, lay half in cool shadow while the other half looped lazily around his leg.

Dancemaster.

That was what the Vuo Ton called them, for the way their bite made a person jerk and writhe as though to the beat of some cruel, uncompromising tune. The Dombângan name was simpler: *twelve breaths.* That was what you had, more or less, once those fangs sank home.

Ruc's heart tripped, then stumbled unsteadily forward.

Eira have mercy . . . he began silently, then stopped himself.

He didn't doubt the power of the goddess. He'd witnessed a thousand times over love's power to transform a person, make them into something stronger, brighter, better. Here, though, miles beyond Dombâng's last ramshackle habitation, there were no people to transform. The beasts of the delta obeyed older, darker, bloodier gods than love.

Ruc studied the snake's red eyes as it spiraled up his leg. It must have come in over the canoe's stern—the dancemaster could climb as easily as it could swim—drawn by the splash and movement of the hull. The forked tongue flicked out, tasting the air. Muscle flexed beneath the wet scale and, without seeming to move, the snake slid higher, raising its head until it came almost level with Ruc's own, staring at him across the narrow gap.

Caught in the silent current, the boat turned, began to drift backward.

Slowly, ever so slowly, Ruc uncurled the fingers of one hand from the paddle.

As a child, he would have laughed at the snake. Kem Anh and Hang Loc had worn them in the way the women of Dombâng wore bracelets and arm rings, and Ruc himself used to play games with the creatures, seeing if he could snatch them by the necks before they sank those fangs into his arm. He'd had no idea then that those bites—which burned like embers stitched under his skin—would have killed another person, had never learned later why he was safe from the venom, and did not know now, as he gazed at the pointed head, whether, after all these years away, his protection still held. It would be madness to trust in it, which left just one question: how fast was he, after half a life as a priest of Eira?

Delta silence roared in his ears.

He measured the distance from the snake's head to his face, from his hand to the snake's head. Not close enough. If he was going to have any chance at all, he needed to draw it off. His chest ached with the effort of doling out his breaths, as though he'd been bitten already.

Slowly as a reed floating on the water's top, he shifted his free hand, drawing it back toward him until it hung even with the dancemaster's head. Like Ruc himself, the snake could see heat. The warmth of his body had it intrigued, but plenty of things in the delta were warm. It wouldn't strike until there was motion.

He tucked aside all the stories he'd heard—of people clawing at their own throats, of eyes bulging with the lack of breath—and tried to remember his sun-bright, naked days playing with the snakes. They tended to strike high, not at where their prey was but where it *would* be when startled into flight. Ruc pressed the pad of his thumb against his middle finger, felt the tension creep up his arm to his shoulder, then, all in one motion, snapped, dropped the hand, looped in underneath, swept up, and caught the striking serpent just behind the head.

For a shard of a heartbeat he thought he'd pulled it off.

Then the dancemaster twisted in his grip, doubled back on itself, sank fangs deep into his wrist.

Ruc dropped the paddle, seized the snake with both hands, wrung hard until he felt the spine beneath the coiled muscle snap.

Too late.

He'd grabbed the creature too far behind the head, left it enough room for it to bury one final bite. The dead, red eyes gazed at him. He tossed the body in the bottom of the boat—no need to chum the water for some other eager predator—and raised his hand to study the wound.

Two drops of blood welled at the puncture. He didn't bother slicing it or trying to suck out the venom. It was too far inside him already. He could feel it, like barbed, white-hot wire threaded into his vein, dragged deeper and deeper with each spasm of his heart. He tried to remember how many breaths he'd taken—three? Four? The delta air clogged in his lungs, suddenly too hot, as though he'd plunged his head into a boiling pot and tried breathing the steam. Around him, the reeds shifted, swayed, wavered. A breeze? Or his vision, already fraying?

He put an unsteady hand on the rail of the boat, stared into the reed-sliced sunlight, waited for his body to start that last awful dance.

Instead, the fiery spike that had been driving up his arm slowed, then stopped. After another dozen agonizing breaths, it began to fade from a blaze to a vicious itch, then a vague tingle, until all that remained was a deep ache at the site of the puncture and a hand's span upward toward his elbow.

He lifted the limb, turned it over, stared awhile at the twin drops of blood, drops that were clotting already, clotting, as they always had, far faster than human blood should clot.

He closed his eyes. The sounds of the delta swaddled him—water lap and bird chirp and the low drone of ten million tiny insects.

So.

Fifteen years away had changed nothing. Turning his back on that sun-green world of mud and blood and death had changed nothing. Denying the gods of the Vuo Ton had changed nothing. Eira had not remade him in her image. Despite the years of prayer and penance, it was all still there, the redsight and the memory, the strength, the ability to survive what no one should survive. He was still what he had always been.

Whatever that was.

9

Gwenna felt, during the ride to the western port of Pirat, as though she were moving underwater, or into an unrelenting wind. It was no fault of the weather. The air was clear and crisp. Sun shone on the towns and wide fields outside Annur. In fact, she, Kiel, and the two legionaries charged with guarding them made good time. The short imperial flag carried by Cho Lu ensured that all traffic on the wide boulevard—farmers with their carts, merchants with their wagons, women and men going about their business—moved smartly aside to stand on the verge of the road until Gwenna and the others passed. They were able to trot the flats and mild downhills, keep their horses to a brisk walk on the ups. Compared to some of the treks Gwenna had been on it was relaxed, even casual. And yet, it was a struggle just staying on the fucking horse.

She couldn't say exactly what she wanted to do instead. Stop? Turn around? Dismount and start fucking running? Sleep? It was insanity—the small part of her mind not bent to the struggle recognized that. There was no reason not to carry on, nothing impeding her, and yet just sitting in that saddle took an effort of will equal to any she'd ever felt when fighting for her life.

Cho Lu and Pattick only made it worse. They might have been a couple years older than her—twenty-three or twenty-four, maybe—but they looked young. She caught the glances they shot at her when they thought she wasn't looking. Even with her eyes closed, she could smell the awe on them, the marvel, the excitement. She hadn't come flat out and told the two legionaries that she was Kettral—that she *had been* Kettral—but they weren't fucking blind. They could see the blacks and the twin blades—there'd been no reason to discard the weapons she'd spent a lifetime learning to fight with. They could see her scars.

The legionaries had probably never met one of the Kettral before, but they knew the stories. *Some* of the stories, anyway, the ones where the empire's greatest warriors swam oceans, razed fortresses, fought on in the face of horrific wounds, saved people, won everything in the final moment, triumphed.

Obviously they'd never heard the ones where Kettral died pointlessly because their commanders fucked up.

Halfway through the first day, Cho Lu couldn't restrain himself any longer. Reining his horse in a little, he fell back beside Gwenna.

"I just want to say," he murmured, "that it's an honor to be riding with you, Commander. For me and Pattick both."

Gwenna turned to look at him.

He looked vaguely Dombângan—straight black hair, brown skin, brown eyes.

"I've spent the last two months," Gwenna said, "killing people with names like yours, Cho Lu. People who look a lot like you."

The words were cruel, unnecessary. The Annurian legions were home to soldiers from all over Vash and Eridroa. Cho Lu's family might have been Dombângan—his father or his mother, or one of *their* parents. Didn't mean he was any less loyal to the empire. Still, if a little nastiness meant he'd stop looking at her with all that 'Shael-spawned admiration, she was willing to pay the price.

The legionary looked momentarily taken aback, then he smiled, shook his head. "I know about the trouble down in Dombâng."

"Trouble?" Gwenna shook her head. "It's been a half-decade fucking massacre, one that started with thousands of legionaries hacked up and chucked in the canals."

He nodded resolutely. "We all heard when it happened. My grandfather was Dombângan, but he moved to Annur eighty years ago. My parents grew up in the Silk Quarter, and so did I." He rolled up his sleeve to show her the rough tattoo of the Annurian sun inked into his muscular forearm. "There's not a man in the legions more loyal than I am."

"It's the truth," Pattick added.

He'd dropped back beside them while they were talking. Unlike Cho Lu, Pattick was almost as pale as Gwenna herself. His hair was brown rather than red, but freckles spattered his cheeks and forehead. He didn't have his friend's good looks or easy smile, was, in fact, more than a little ugly, his chin and ears too large, his green eyes too close together. Like Cho Lu, however, he had the physique of a soldier.

"Back when that Dombângan nastiness first happened," he went on, "there were a few men in the company who went after Cho Lu."

"Back when it first happened," Gwenna said, "the two of you were what? Fourteen?"

"Sixteen." Cho Lu grinned.

"A year too young for the legions," she pointed out.

His grin widened. "We lied."

Not that Gwenna was one to judge. She'd been a cadet at eight, had been blowing things up since the age of ten.

"So what happened," she asked, "when your brothers in arms came after you?"

Cho Lu shrugged. "I had to . . . reeducate a few of them. Remind them that the oaths we take are more important than the names our parents gave us."

"And how did they take to this reeducation?"

"Scorch still has the scar over his eyebrow, and Farrel's fingers healed a little crooked, but they got the message. Fought shoulder to shoulder for another five years. Until now, actually. We were the ones who put down the Anklishan Rebellion. We were the ones that burned Setje's bandits straight out of Raalte."

For a moment, his smile was almost cocky. Then he remembered who he was talking to, and the pride slid from his face, replaced by that 'Kent-kissing awe again.

"Of course," he went on, "I'm sure all that's nothing, kids' stuff next to whatever the Kettral have been up to."

The Kettral, she wanted to tell him, *have been having their asses handed to them. We're practically extinct. The birds are gone, and the few soldiers who survived the civil war are mostly too old or too injured to fight.*

Instead she looked him in the eye, said nothing, then rode on in what she hoped was a pointed silence.

Not pointed enough, evidently.

After pacing her for a quarter mile or so, Cho Lu spoke again.

"I get it. Of course we know you can't talk about . . . whatever it is you've been doing. But maybe you can settle an argument Pattick and I have been having."

Pattick looked uncomfortable, but Gwenna could smell the eagerness on him, too, the curiosity.

"Probably not," she replied.

Cho Lu laughed as though she'd cracked the best joke of his life. *"Probably not!"* He glanced over at Pattick. *"Probably not,* she says." He shook his head, then went on as though she hadn't spoken. "So, here's the question, right? Can Kettral breathe underwater?"

"No." Maybe that would be the end of it.

The two legionaries exchanged a glance. Cho Lu didn't look remotely convinced.

"Is it true you can see in the dark?"

That one *was* true, but there was no reason to feed their obsession.

"No."

"Do you feel pain?"

She almost choked. Since the slaughter at the Baths, her pain had been almost constant. She'd thought, for the first few days, that it was the result of the shrapnel she'd ripped from her shoulder, along with the other cuts and bruises she'd picked up fighting her way free. Her skin had stitched itself shut just as it always did. The bruises had faded. But she still felt as though there was an iron fist wrapped around her heart, long thorns driving into her brain, a pile of bricks on her chest, making it hard to breathe.

"Yes," she managed grimly. "We feel pain."

Pattick looked slightly disappointed. Cho Lu, however, just winked at her. "Understood, sir. We don't expect you to reveal your secrets."

"I don't have any secrets."

A lie, of course, but there was truth behind it. The secrets she had weren't the kind either of the legionaries wanted to hear.

"About the birds . . ." Cho Lu began.

"About shutting your mouth," Gwenna said before he could continue, "and letting me ride in peace."

Pattick looked chastened, but Cho Lu just smiled. "Of course, Commander. Just an honor to ride at your side, sir."

An honor. As though she were some kind of fucking hero.

†

If they'd pressed hard, they could have reached Pirat in a single day. According to the Emperor, however, the ship wouldn't be provisioned and ready to sail for two, and so they stopped at a small inn frequented by travelers between the western port and the capital. Cho Lu went about acquiring rooms while Pattick saw to the stabling of the horses, which left Gwenna alone with Kiel in the private dining room the innkeeper had fallen over herself to provide them with. The woman brought food—quail, figs, goat cheese, sliced firefruit—along with a bottle of wine.

Gwenna ignored it all. Her stomach was a knot. Any time she put food in her mouth it tasted like ash. She had dreams where she was choking to death, and when she looked at the figs she could imagine them swelling in her mouth, lodged in her throat, blocking the air as she clawed at her neck. . . .

"You should eat," Kiel said.

"I don't think the Emperor would have sent me on this mission if I didn't know how to feed myself."

The historian shrugged, twisted one of the legs from the quail, stripped the meat from the bone with his teeth. Gwenna watched him chew.

She didn't want to be there, in that room. She wanted to be away already, on board the ship. She wanted to be fighting someone, killing someone. She clenched her fist, felt her anger rise. She couldn't put anything right sitting in a private dining room watching the historian eat his quail, but her room wasn't ready, and if she went out to the common room, Pattick and Cho Lu would be waiting with their wide eyes and their questions. She forced herself to pick up a slice of firefruit, forced herself to chew and swallow it. If she was going to fight, she needed to stay strong, and besides, she had questions for the imperial historian.

"What don't I know?" she asked, studying him.

Kiel paused in his chewing, raised an eyebrow. "The list, I would imagine, is long."

It was a good joke, but he didn't smell like a man who'd just made a joke. He smelled like a fucking stone.

"Are you a leach?" she pressed.

The question would have provoked some kind of reaction from almost anyone. The Kettral worked with leaches, but everyone else in Annur burned them or hanged them or drowned them. Kiel should have been shocked, angry. Instead, he looked mildly intrigued.

"Why do you ask that?"

Gwenna hesitated. She couldn't answer honestly without revealing a secret of her own. No one outside the Kettral knew about the Trial, the slarn, the eggs, and the heightened senses they conferred.

"I'm good at reading people. What's your well?"

The historian shook his head. "I'm not a leach."

"You're not just a historian."

"No one is just anything."

It was hard to know what to say to that. Gwenna herself *was* just a soldier. Or she had been, until the Emperor stripped her of her rank.

"Why are you on this mission?"

"As the Emperor said—for my knowledge of Menkiddoc. Among other things."

"Your knowledge of Menkiddoc comes from a pile of books that are thousands of years out of date."

"Some of it."

"You're working with a Csestriim map and a Csestriim text when the Csestriim have been extinct for how long now?"

"Roughly ten thousand years."

"Right. Ten thousand years. If I planned an invasion of Eridroa with a Csestriim map, I'd be mighty fucking dismayed to find an entire empire already here."

"The coastlines did not die with the Csestriim, though some have shifted. New mountains did not spring from the ground in the last ten thousand years."

"You're not coming along to show us the coastlines and mountains. That's what maps are for."

"There is more to Menkiddoc than what appears on the maps."

The words were mild enough. He chose a fig from the platter, chewed thoughtfully. He didn't look like a man discussing a lost continent. He didn't look like a man discussing much of anything at all. Thing was, Gwenna didn't trust the way he looked.

"You've been there," she said at last.

It was the only explanation that made sense.

The historian nodded. "A long time ago."

Gwenna gestured to his crooked nose, crooked jaw, crooked fingers. "Is that where you got all this?"

"My injuries?" The historian studied his own hands. "No. Most of those came much later."

"What were you doing there?"

"Studying."

"Studying what?"

"History."

She frowned. "I thought historians were interested in people. Why go to a place where there aren't any?"

"It was not always as empty as it is now."

"It's been uninhabited as long as Annur's been around, as long as people have been writing history."

"People," Kiel replied, "have not been writing history very long."

The words sat between them while the historian returned his attention to the quail. Gwenna watched as he used a fork and knife to carve into the breast. She'd been eating meat her entire life—fish, mutton, pork, beef, venison, whatever she could trap or Annick could shoot—and yet suddenly the sight of the historian stripping the meat from the skeleton beneath made her think of Talal standing in the doorway to the Baths, blood pouring from his wounds, his skin charred, as though he'd been roasted on a spit.

She turned away, gazed out the small window. The road to the west was wide and spear-straight, stabbing through the low hills and villages toward the distant glimmer of the sea. The sun setting on the water looked like fire, then like blood.

"So what's in Menkiddoc?" she asked finally.

"Monsters," Kiel replied evenly. "Sickness. Madness."

Gwenna turned to stare at him. "According to the Emperor, that's all just horseshit and stories."

"People wouldn't tell stories," the historian replied, "if those stories didn't mean anything."

She grappled with that a moment. "And you've told the Emperor this? She didn't believe you?"

He shook his head.

"You didn't tell her?" Gwenna pressed, surprise warring with her confusion.

"I did not."

"You understand that's treason?"

"Treason?" He mulled the word as he poured tea into a cup, spooned in honey, swirled it around. "It seems to me more treasonous to deny the empire a tool of which it has such dire need."

"The birds."

He inclined his head. "The birds."

"Knowing the dangers makes the mission *more* likely to succeed, not less."

"Which is why I am telling you. Why I will tell the commander of the expedition when we have set to sea."

"Telling me and the commander, but not the Emperor." She shook her head. "Why?"

The historian took a small sip of his tea, savored it a moment, then set down the cup. "Adare hui'Malkeenian is a capable ruler, but she is cautious. It is already a risk, sending one of her most valuable ships, one of her best admirals, one of her last Kettral—"

"I'm not Kettral."

He nodded in acquiescence. "All the same. She is risking much on a report that, as you point out, may be ten millennia out of date. If she knew the dangers of the continent, I suspect she would never have committed to the expedition."

The whole conversation made Gwenna's head spin. The historian was telling her things that could easily see him beheaded, and he was doing so casually, over tea, figs, and roasted quail. Hiding the truth about Menkiddoc from the Emperor—if it even *was* the truth, if he wasn't as mad as all the explorers in the stories—was bad enough, but he was going beyond that. This broken, keen-eyed, odorless man seemed to have his own interest and agenda in the expedition, interest he was willing to pursue at the risk of the Emperor's displeasure and his own life.

"Why do you care about this?"

He looked at her, pursed his lips, took another sip of his tea, frowned, spooned a little more honey into the steaming cup, then stirred, gazing down into the cloudy liquid.

"A historian's work is easier when there is order in the world. If Annur crumbles, my task will be that much more difficult."

"I thought historians were supposed to chronicle events, not take part in them."

He slipped the spoon from the cup, set it on the table, tested the tea again, smiled. "Anyone close enough to chronicle a thing accurately is inevitably a part of it."

"If I told Adare, she would kill you."

"She might," he agreed. "Although I doubt it. We're all working toward the same end, you, and she, and I." He shrugged. "Besides. I do not believe you'll tell her."

"You don't know shit about me."

"On the contrary. I know a great deal about you. Your activities comprise four hundred and thirteen pages of my chronicle. More or less."

Gwenna raised her brows. "Four hundred and thirteen?"

"More or less."

"So what did you learn, writing those four hundred and thirteen pages?"

He offered her a mild smile. "I learned that you are the kind of woman who, given your current situation, needs a voyage, a mission."

She shifted in her chair. "Who the fuck needs a trip to the other side of the world?"

"Those who have lost their way on this side."

The room felt suddenly tight, too small, airless. Gwenna shoved back from the table, stood unsteadily, her legs weak beneath her, turned away from the historian, crossed to the window. She put her hands on the sill, held them there until she was sure they wouldn't shake. Outside, the last light of the sun glazed the windows in the building opposite, slicked the small fishing pond with gold. She dragged in a deep breath of the cool evening air, held it a moment, breathed out, then in again. She turned back, finally, to find Kiel watching her over the rim of his teacup.

"Tell me about Menkiddoc," she said.

"What do you want to know?"

"Why no one lives there. Why anyone who's ever come back says that it's cursed."

"Cursed." The historian furrowed his brow. "Not the right word, but not altogether wrong. It might be more accurate to say that the land of Menkiddoc—the vast majority of it, at least—is sick. Sick with a disease that afflicts all living things."

"Fatal?"

"It doesn't kill so much as it . . . twists."

"There's quite a bit of dying in the stories I've heard."

"Twist a thing hard enough, and sometimes it dies." He shrugged. "In many cases, however, the disease is content to simply . . . deform."

"The monsters—"

"Normal beasts warped into something new."

"What *kind* of something new?"

The historian shook his head again. "I have seen spiders the size of full-grown pigs, tigers with eight legs, plants that prey on blood and flesh."

Gwenna rolled her eyes. "Your stories are worse than the ones I used to hear from the drunks back at Mankers."

"Perhaps some of the drunks in Mankers traveled to Menkiddoc. Perhaps that is why they became drunks."

There was no levity in the historian's voice, no wounded pride. He provided the inventory of Menkiddoc's horrors in the way another man might recount the contents of his morning meal.

"People don't go to Menkiddoc."

"People go everywhere," Kiel countered. "It is one of the fascinating, inexplicable things about people. Bring word of an island of fire lost in a poisonous sea and someone will build a ship to sail there, just to stare into the combustion with their own eyes as they burn."

Gwenna wanted to argue with the man, but it was true enough. She'd known a Kettral once—a sniper—who'd insisted on climbing the highest peak in the Bone Mountains. He could have taken his bird straight to the summit, but that wasn't the point. He lost two fingers and an ear to frostbite, but came back satisfied.

"Adare said there were people living there. On the northwestern coast."

The historian nodded. "Maybe a few thousand, scattered between a dozen villages."

"And this . . . disease—why doesn't it twist *them*?"

"The disease isn't everywhere. It has spread over time, but there are still areas—around the coasts, high in the mountains—where the land remains untouched."

"How much land?"

"I haven't made a study. Maybe ten percent of the total area is clean."

"Meaning," Gwenna said, "a continent five times the size of Eridroa is almost entirely . . . what?"

"Corrupted," Kiel suggested. "Polluted. Rotten."

Rotten.

It was, she realized, how *she* felt, how she'd felt since Frome tossed her in the brig. Not rotten as some figure of speech, but literally rotten, like a fruit left too long in the hot summer sun, all the parts that had held her together slackening, what should have been strong inside her—her heart, her muscle, her mind—softening to mush. She dragged herself from the thought, looked across the table at Kiel once more.

"Why are you going back?"

"The Emperor asked me to."

"Horseshit. You made this happen. You brought her the map. You gave her the codex. You could have arranged it so that the expedition went without you. We'd have come back with the birds. Or not. You could have stayed here, safe."

The historian studied her. "Does Annur appear safe to you?"

"Safer than the place with the pig spiders. Fewer monsters here. Less madness."

"A thing I have learned about both monsters and madness," he replied, "is that they range more widely than people are willing to believe."

✝

The *Daybreak* was unquestionably majestic—a massive, triple-masted vessel with high castles at the prow and stern. Everything above the waterline was oiled, polished, gilded. Morning light gleamed on the glass of the cabin windows—there were three decks of them in the sterncastle. Even from where she stood, at the crest of a small hill above the harbor, Gwenna could see that every line was coiled, every stitch of rigging stretched taut. The neatly reefed sails glowed pristine white, as though they'd never been unfurled. At the prow, a female figure surged from the bowsprit. In her outstretched hand she held a sword—bronze or leafed with gold. The weapon was flawless, utterly unblemished by actual battle.

"There she is!" Pattick declared. "The most magnificent ship in the western fleet!"

"The most expensive, anyway," Gwenna muttered.

The young man wilted slightly.

"What's wrong with her?" he asked.

"She draws too much water, for one thing."

It was obvious from the shape of the hull and all that wooden weight piled up above the waterline.

"What does that mean?"

"It means we're more likely to hit shit. To run aground on reefs or rocks. To rip the polished bottom out. To sink."

Pattick frowned, but Cho Lu shook his head.

"The *Daybreak* is famous. She's patrolled the coast of Breata and Nish for twenty-five years. Keeps the Manjari dogs in their place."

"The Treaty of Gosha keeps the Manjari away," Gwenna replied. "And the coast of Breata and Nish is well-charted deep water. We don't know how deep the water is where we're going. The one map we have doesn't provide depths, currents, reefs—none of it."

Pattick shook his head.

"If she's the wrong ship for the mission, why did the Emperor choose her?" He sounded torn, as though the thought that the Emperor might disagree with one of the Kettral had never occurred to him.

"I wouldn't blame the Emperor," Gwenna replied. "I suspect she let Jonon choose his vessel."

The legionaries exchanged a baffled glance.

"Jonon?" Pattick asked after a pause.

"First Admiral Jonon lem Jonon," Gwenna said. "The commander, not just of that glittering trinket, but of the entire western fleet. The leader of this glorious expedition."

┼

Jonon lem Jonon looked as though he'd been born with the title, uniform, and bearing of First Admiral. He stood atop the sterncastle, hands clasped behind his back, chin high, gazing the length of the *Daybreak*'s bustling deck. His uniform was spotless, gold braid radiant, hat canted at just the right angle. He was taller than Gwenna by a head, built of muscles she could see through the cut of the cloth, and, though it vexed her that the thought even crossed her mind, almost sculpturally beautiful. His skin was a dark, burnished brown, his hair and close-cropped beard rust-red, his eyes as green as her own. He must have been older than her, maybe into his early forties, but his face showed none of the wear and tear so common among the Kettral—no scars, no torn-off ears, no broken nose. All of his teeth were straight, white, and gleaming.

Usually, she'd take a man like that for some court peacock rather than a real soldier, but even a full ocean away, she'd heard the stories: Jonon refusing to surrender during the Battle of Erensa, Jonon swimming five miles to shore after his ship had been sunk, Jonon requisitioning a fishing boat, rowing *back* out to the enemy vessel under cover of night, freeing his men from the brig, killing the Manjari captain, seizing the vessel for his own. If even a quarter of it was even a little bit true, the man was a legend, the kind of soldier even Kettral might admire.

That admiration did not seem to work both ways. His expression, as he studied Gwenna, was level enough, a neutral mask of command, but beneath it she could smell the man's contempt.

"First Admiral," she said, saluting. "Gwenna Sharpe."

The gesture felt odd. Kettral didn't salute, but the navy placed greater weight on forms and decorum.

Jonon ran his eyes from her brow to her boots and back. "Of course. The former Kettral."

He leaned just slightly on the word *former,* but Gwenna could feel the heat rising to her cheeks—a curse of her pale skin.

She gave a tight nod, saluted again because why the fuck not.

"The Emperor has placed me under your direct command."

"Everyone aboard this ship," Jonon replied mildly, "is under my direct command."

Gwenna cast an eye over the deck. The men she could see were about equally divided between sailors and what looked like legionaries or marines.

"May I ask how many men you have?"

Jonon pursed his lips, studied her a moment, then nodded. "The *Daybreak* is crewed by seventy-eight men and a dozen officers, the pick of the western fleet. In addition, we carry a full legionary company, decorated men, all of them."

Decorated had a dangerously confident ring to it. Pattick and Cho Lu seemed capable, despite their youth, but holding a tower fort somewhere or hunting down a few dozen bandits was a far cry from exploring the interior of an unknown continent—a fucking *diseased* continent—with no backup or resupply, thousands of miles from everyone and everything they'd ever known.

"This," he went on, "brings me to a vexing point." Once again he ran his eyes over Gwenna. "These decorated men are, of course, *men*. As are my sailors."

"I won't hold it against them, sir." She knew she shouldn't be saying the words, but somehow couldn't call them back. "I've known a number of men who proved to be excellent soldiers."

"And from what I've heard," he replied, "you got them killed."

The words were delivered with no particular venom. They landed like a fist. Gwenna clamped her mouth shut, as much to keep down the rising nausea as to stop talking.

The First Admiral put a hand on her shoulder. "Let me be perfectly clear. Whatever you used to be—Kettral, a Wing commander, an expert in demolitions—you are not any longer. Your rank and command were forfeit to your failure. If you had been one of my sailors, I would have seen you whipped bloody, then abandoned, destitute and naked, in the nearest port of call."

He paused, waited for Gwenna to reply. She ground her teeth together so hard that they ached. When no response was forthcoming, the man continued.

"The Emperor, however, bright be the days of her life, has chosen the path of mercy over the path of justice, and so here you are."

Gwenna felt the quick fuse of her anger burning, burning, hot and awful through the flesh of her body. When it reached her heart, however, nothing exploded. Instead, she felt massively, almost impossibly heavy. He wasn't wrong. She was here because she'd fucked up, and bad. She almost wished that someone *had* whipped her bloody.

"I serve the Emperor and the empire," she said quietly. "Like you."

Jonon nodded. "I believe that this is what you've tried to do, but trying to do a thing is not the same as succeeding at it. You should know that I have been forced to set aside a separate cabin for you, a cabin that might otherwise have been used to store supplies, weapons, food, things that might keep the men on this ship alive if we come to a dire pass."

"There's no need, sir. I'll take a hammock among the sailors and soldiers. The Kettral don't separate women from the men."

"The Kettral are dead."

Gwenna choked down a retort. This, too, was true, or close enough.

"All the same, sir. I don't need a separate cabin. I've spent my life living and training among men."

"I don't care how you have spent your life. My crew have *not* spent their lives sailing with women. Most of them are good men. Some are not. In either case, I will not allow you to become a distraction, an impediment to order, or an incitement to misconduct."

"Is *misconduct* your word for *rape*?"

Gwenna turned from the First Admiral to look the length of the ship. The deck was awash in sailors, men scrubbing and hauling and lifting and stowing. Some were spindle-thin, others large enough to toss around the hogsheads of water and black rum. A few of them glanced up, caught her eye. It wasn't lost on anyone that she would be the only woman on the ship. She watched the way they moved, the way they carried themselves. She drew in a deep breath, sorted through the various scents: curiosity, determination, lust, anger. A lot of women would be afraid, she realized. A lot of women would accept Jonon's private cabin and be grateful. She tried to imagine being afraid of these men, found that she couldn't. Perhaps it was a failure of imagination.

"You will confine yourself," Jonon replied, "to your cabin and the officer's mess. If you come above, you are restricted to the deck of this castle. If you

disobey, you will be whipped, as would anyone else on this ship. Do you understand?"

She turned to the First Admiral, took a deep breath, nodded. "Yes, sir. I
understand."

10

For thousands of years, the people of Dombâng had been sinking tarred posts in the mud, bracing them against the current, trying to climb above the level of the highest flood, struggling to engineer some fixity into the river's flux, as though if they could only dig deeper or build higher or timber over more of the shifting, watery acres they would finally be safe.

Foolish. That was the Vuo Ton assessment of this strange faith in the immutable.

When the Shirvian flooded, there was no holding it back, not with a hundred thousand wooden posts, not with all the dykes and bridges and levees in the world. You couldn't trammel a river inside its channels any more than you could hold water in an open hand. The whole notion of the city was flawed, and at the bottom of that notion were all the buildings. Maybe somewhere else, somewhere far away, where the ground was more rock than mud, where rivers remained in their stony courses and hills didn't shift between one day and the next—maybe *there* it might make sense to lay a foundation and build atop it. In the labyrinth of the Given Land, however, what a person needed was something that could shift with the current and rise with the flood. Not a building, but a boat.

And so the Vuo Ton had built an entire village out of boats, a village that moved with the seasons and the currents, dropping anchor for a week or a month until the time came to move on.

It took Ruc nearly three days to find the place.

He'd paddled south of White Rock first, then checked the shallows to the west, then angled north, working against the current until he hit Obi's Bivouac. There was a pattern to the yearly Vuo Ton migration, but a pattern wasn't the same thing as a map. When there was no sign of them in the crescent lake by the bivouac, he felt unease settle on him, like a fly he couldn't quite reach to kill or brush away.

The words of the collared messenger bubbled up in his mind: *They are already* in *the delta.*

As the day waned and night came on, he paddled deeper and deeper into the reeds, into the sluggish eddies where even the Vuo Ton never ventured. He should have died half a dozen times over. A red dreamer dropped onto the nape of his neck just past dusk, burying its fangs into his skin. He snatched the spider off, crushed it in his palm, then waited, tense and shuddering, until the poison dissolved in his veins. Around midnight, he paddled directly through a ghostfinger web, earning himself a dozen excruciating bites. Not long after that, something fast and cool plunged a fangful of venom into his wrist, then slipped over the side of the boat with a gentle plop before he could get a good look at it. In each case, he felt the poison knife into him, burning, boiling, carving its way toward his heart for the space of a few breaths until something else, something strong and cool, rose up to gentle the venom.

A gift, the Vuo Ton had called it, gazing at him with envy and awe. *A gift from the gods.*

Never mind that Ruc had never asked for their gifts. Never mind that he'd spent the last fifteen years trying to deny them. Evidently, there were some things that, once given, could not be given back.

Finally, just before the morning of the third day, when dawn began to plaster the eastern sky with a vague, thick light, he broke from the reeds into a wide, cleared space to find the village of the Vuo Ton.

He paused, shipped his paddle across the rails, let the canoe slide into the predawn quiet as he studied the place that could have been his home.

Unlike the Dombângan boatbuilders and shipwrights, the Vuo Ton constructed their craft almost entirely from the tall delta rushes. As Ruc sat there in the silence, sweat slicking his back and chest, the last of the water dripping from his paddle's blade, it all came back to him—slicing those rushes with his machete, gathering them into bundles as thick as his arm or leg or whole body, binding the bundles every foot with twine, loading them onto a raft, then poling them back to the village where the weavers lashed them together to form the bases of their floating platforms or the frames of the huts that sat atop them.

Although *huts,* he was reminded as he studied the structures, didn't really do justice to the work of the weavers. While the homes of the Vuo Ton were small and simple, there was nothing slipshod about them. In fact, the clean lines of the bundled reeds, the meticulously woven screens that served as walls, the stylized knots of the lashings, were far more elegant than the mad, ramshackle city blocks of Dombâng, all that creaking, half-rotting wood cantilevered out over the canals.

The village never took quite the same form twice, but the Vuo Ton tended to moor their rafts—eighty or ninety of them, all told—in a circle, anchoring them around a wide inner pool in much the way Dombângans built their stilt houses around plazas or courtyards. Tethered to the outside of the ring, where they could be easily cut loose if they caught fire, floated the cooking rafts, the tops of the reed bundles coated with baked clay. As Ruc watched, he caught a glimpse of children moving over the rafts in the gray, watery light, but no one kindling the ovens or fire pits. There was no smoke at all, he realized, not the vaguest thread from a morning lantern, nor any scent of it on the light breeze.

Even in the depths of the Wallow, the Vuo Ton were hiding.

As he tied off his canoe, the children were already racing away over the tethered rafts, chasing their own high voices into the village as they spilled the story that *someone*—a man with the inked arms of the Vuo Ton, but without the tattoos on his face—had just paddled out of the reeds, come see, come *see*! Other children arrived first, wide-eyed, pointing. By the time Ruc had stepped out of his canoe onto the long, empty raft that served as a dock, the older inhabitants of the village began to appear, men and women that he recognized, and who, judging from the looks in their eyes, recognized him in turn.

A few smiled, or even raised a hand in greeting. There was Troc, Ruc's old fishing companion, his huge body finally grown into his huge ears, a wide smile splitting his massive face. And beside him, barely half Troc's size, her black hair shaved down to the scalp, Lien Mac. She'd been the best tracker among the village children—aside from Ruc himself—had once followed a jaguar half a dozen miles through the thorny darong of the northern delta. She watched him now with dark, unreadable eyes, then nodded incrementally in greeting.

Most were not so friendly. Women and men who years before had hosted him at their rafts studied him with mute contempt. No one drew a knife or spear, no one pointed a bow at him, no one so much as raised an accusatory finger, but he could hear the mutters passed back and forth like counterfeit coin. Then, cutting through those mutters, approaching unseen through the crowd, an angry voice, one that Ruc recognized all too well, though it had grown deeper and rougher.

"See that the sentries are staked out in the sun for their lapse. If it had been another attack . . ."

The man erupted from the group, caught sight of Ruc, and stopped abruptly.

Off in the reeds, the gorzles made that cry of theirs that sounded like children weeping.

"Boa," Ruc said, inclining his head.

The man did not nod in response. He studied Ruc, dark eyes glittering in the scarred wreckage of his face. He twirled a short spear idly between his fingers.

"*Kha Lu,*" he replied finally. His voice was suddenly quiet, stone calm, almost indifferent, but his lip twisted as he said the words.

Ruc shook his head. "My name is not Kha Lu."

Boa raised the ruin of an eyebrow. "This is what we called you, was it not? *Chosen of the Gods?*"

"It has been a long time since anyone called me that."

Dozens of people looked on, silent, just as they'd looked on fifteen years earlier whenever Ruc and Boa fought.

"Why have you come back?" the man demanded finally. "We have built no bathhouses in your absence. We have stuffed no mattresses, not even for the chosen of the gods."

"I did not go to Dombâng for the bathhouses," Ruc replied, "and I did not come back to trade insults with you. We are no longer children."

Boa opened his mouth to respond, then shook his head, spat into the still water. The ripples spread out and away, dissolving into the reeds. "Why are you here?"

Ruc held the man's glare for a moment, then ran his eyes over the assembled Vuo Ton. "I must speak with the Witness. There may be a threat to the Given Land."

To his surprise, Boa barked an angry laugh. "There *may* be? Why do you think we are here, anchored in the Wallow?"

Ruc forced down a dozen questions. A public interrogation on the docks of the village was unlikely to go well. He put on his meekness as though it were a robe.

"Will you take me to the Witness?"

The corner of Boa's lip turned up. "You would rather speak to a corpse than a warrior?"

Ruc felt a blade of sorrow laid against his heart. "He is dead?"

The Vuo Ton's leader had been old when Ruc quit the village for the final time, his brown skin creased and weathered, joints arthritic—and yet there had been so much life in his single remaining eye.

"Near enough," Boa replied indifferently. "A matter of weeks. Maybe a season."

"I must speak with him."

"Such urgency. Tell me, when did you become so concerned for this land that you abandoned?"

"I followed my own channel."

"You *fled*."

Fury's heat bathed Boa's face a bloody red. Ruc felt an answering anger rise in his own chest.

Please, goddess, help me to love this man.

The goddess was silent. Out in the rushes, the gorzles sobbed their song.

Suddenly, standing there on the sunbaked raft, Ruc felt as though he hadn't been paddling out into the watery labyrinth at all, but *back* into his own past. Days and nights breathing in the green, humid heat, sliding between the spears of the reeds, listening to the sounds of living things and dying things and the silence of the dead, feeling all over again the snake's poison burning in his veins, the sunlight slashed across his skin, the ache of his muscles, the beauty and the strain of the place—just three days of that and he could feel the old instincts hatching inside him like eggs, the fanged and clawed parts of himself flexing, testing their strength, straining toward the light and the heat, toward all the old needs of meat and blood and hunger.

"Fled?" he asked quietly, raising his brows. "No."

Boa's lip twisted. "Look at you." He gestured. "Soft shoulders. Blistered palms. You went to the city because you were soft."

Ruc raised his hand, displaying the double-puncture of the snake bite.

The Vuo Ton were too stoic to truly gasp, but a quick intake of breath—like the lick of wind on still water—rippled through the crowd.

"Dancemaster," Ruc said simply.

Boa tried to sneer. "So you have grown slow and stupid as well as soft."

"I am alive," Ruc replied. He smiled—not a kind smile. "Perhaps you have forgotten that I was *raised* by your gods, raised from a baby, and though I worship a different mistress now, I have not forgotten the things they taught me."

"Haven't you?" Boa spat.

His voice was just as angry, just as combative as before, but there was another note now lurking deep beneath the surface—the old hurt bafflement, huge and toothed as a hundred-year croc. A priest of Eira hearing that note, recognizing the confusion and pain behind it, would have tried to find a way to make peace. That's what Bien would have done. That's what Ruc would have done, in another place, on another day.

But they were in this place, on this day. Despite his prayers, he could not find Eira's voice in his heart.

"I will speak to the Witness now."

Boa hesitated, then stepped out of the way, made a mockery of a Dombângan bow. "Go. Speak. You will find him rotting in the westernmost raft.

While you trade tales of your greatness, the rest of us will keep the village safe."

†

Back in Dombâng, the high priests of the Three lived aloof from the people they led—all but Vang Vo, who refused to leave the Arena—cloistered behind the high walls of the temple compound, attended by ranks of the faithful, emerging to ladle out their sermons of civic pride and defiance, then disappearing again through their teak gates. There was no teak and there were no gates in the village of the Vuo Ton. The hut of the Witness floated at the western end of the village, unmarked by any crest or heraldry. It might have belonged to anyone—a young family, a weaver, a fisher—save for the spill of delta violets tumbling in a purple riot from the clay pots by the door.

Ruc stood awhile in silence, gathering his thoughts, then crossed the short plank. He tapped once at the hollow wooden knocker.

Warm silence seeped from between the bundled reeds.

He tapped again, waited, then lifted the leather thong from its hook, pulled open the door, and stepped inside.

A welter of smells washed over him: broth and sweat, piss from an unemptied pot, sweet pipe smoke and something rich and thick and wrong that Ruc could describe only as sickness. Darkness hung in the room like a wet, heavy garment pinned from the rafters to dry. He could make out the clay jars just inside, fishing spears propped against the wall, some vague forms deeper in the gloom that might have been baskets, and there, lying on a mattress against the far wall, curled up on itself like a child, the red-black smolder of someone sleeping.

Behind him, the door whispered shut.

Ruc waited a moment for his eyes to adjust, then moved forward to kneel at the side of the mattress.

Beneath the baking heat—too *much* heat, a fever beyond the glow of normal human flesh—he could see the old man's face, the lid closed over his good eye, the gouged-out emptiness of the other socket gazing blindly up. His mouth hung open, a string of spittle draining from his lips. Ruc found a rough cloth folded over the rim of a ewer at the edge of the bed, wiped it gently away.

"Witness," he murmured.

The old man frowned, jerked in his sleep, murmured something incomprehensible.

"Witness," Ruc said again quietly, laying a hand across the burning forehead. "I've come back."

That one eye twitched, fluttered open, scoured the darkness for a few desperate heartbeats, then came to rest on Ruc.

"Ah," he said, his voice a husk. "Kha Lu." He offered up an emaciated smile. "You took your time in returning. If you had dallied longer . . ." A rough, wet cough took him by the chest, shook him a moment, then tossed him back against the mattress. He gestured weakly for the cloth in Ruc's hand, spat into it, closed his eyes, took a long, ragged breath, then tried again. "You almost missed me."

Ruc eased himself from his crouch down into a cross-legged seat beside the thin mattress.

He had sat enough vigils, in his years as a servant of Eira, to understand that the needs of the dying were as various as their faces. Some insisted on jesting their way into the grave, others on a blind, furious denial. The Witness of the Vuo Ton had never been one for turning away from a hard truth.

"What can I do?" Ruc asked simply. He tested the ewer with a hand—full, or nearly so. The bowl beside it, however, was half-empty, some cool broth pooled at the bottom. "Can I get you food? Fish? Sweet-reed?"

The old man pursed his lips as though he were going to spit. "Pipe," he said, gesturing feebly toward a shelf on the wall of the hut.

"The smoke will hurt your lungs."

"When you are dying, Kha Lu, everything hurts. Give me the pipe."

Ruc nodded, lifted the polished pipe down from the shelf.

"Reed," the Witness said weakly, "in the bowl. Ember in the pot."

It took just a few moments to fill the pipe. With a pair of wooden tongs, Ruc lifted a glowing shard from the sand inside the clay pot, lit the reed, lifted it to his lips, dragged in the sweet, acrid smoke, then passed it to the old man.

The Witness drew a shallow breath on the pipe, blew a faint cloud of smoke, managed something that might have been a smile, then turned his head toward Ruc, his good eye narrowing shrewdly in the gloom.

"You got fat."

Ruc choked back a laugh.

"I'm the leanest priest in the temple."

"Priests." The Witness fluttered a dismissive hand. "They're all fat. Lighting candles and singing songs does not carve the softness from a man."

With unexpected deftness, he spun the pipe in his hands, jabbed Ruc between the ribs with the stem.

"Fat and slow."

For a moment, his eye glittered with delight. In a whole lifetime, it was one of the few attacks he'd managed to slip past Ruc's guard. Even as a child, *especially* as a child, Ruc had been faster, gifted with some preternatural ability to see the movement before it unspooled, to anticipate the lunge of a human with the same ease that he did the striking of a snake. That had never stopped the Witness from stabbing at him when he wasn't looking—over meals, while swimming, from the back of the canoe. Evidently dying had not denied him the twin joys of struggle and pride.

Then, between one creaking breath and the next, his gaze darkened.

"You need to be better than this, Kha Lu."

Ruc shook his head. "I left that title when I left the delta."

The Witness hacked up something that might have been a cough or a laugh. "The favor of the gods is not something you can slip on and off like a vest."

"I haven't seen Kem Anh or Hang Loc in almost twenty years."

"And this new goddess of yours—Eira. When did you last see *her*?"

"Eira doesn't stalk the delta," Ruc began. "Her power doesn't come from—"

Before he could finish, the Witness caught him by the wrist, twisted his arm with a feverish strength, pulled the hand close to study the twin scabs left by the snakebite, grunted, his suspicion confirmed.

"How long ago?"

"Three days ago. Around noon."

"If you were anyone else, you would have begun to rot by now."

Ruc nodded again.

"And I will wager you can still see through reeds, through walls."

"Just heat," Ruc replied quietly.

The Witness was the only person with whom he'd ever shared the secret.

"*This* is power," the old man growled. "*These* are the gifts you were given by the gods. These are the gifts that are needed *now*, Kha Lu."

"Needed for what?" Ruc asked warily, though he could already make out the vague shape of the looming answer.

"Something has come to the delta," the Witness replied. "Something new."

"I know. The messengers came to the city as well."

The old man frowned. "I would not call them messengers, but perhaps I am wrong. Perhaps I am too old and stupid to understand the message."

"The one I spoke to rambled on about someone called the first, or the lord."

"These did not speak at all," the Witness replied. "I don't believe they are capable of speech."

Ruc stared. "They were people, right? Beautiful. Naked. Wearing collars?"

The old man shook his head grimly. "They are not people, and they are certainly not beautiful. I would try to explain, but it will be easier if you see for yourself." With a grimace, he levered himself onto one elbow. "Help me up."

✝

The delta was home to dozens of species of bats: reed bats and river bats, red bats and long-haired bats, tiny furred bats the size of your thumb, double-fanged bats, blood bats, and plenty of others to which Ruc had never learned to put a name. At dusk they rose from the rushes to sweep the sky in great, dark clouds, hazing the sun's last rays, so dense, sometimes, they almost blotted out the rising moon. To Ruc's eyes, their warm, furred flight left red slices across the black, scrawls and scribbles of drained-off heat, a vast, fast-fading map of their passage. His whole life he'd enjoyed watching them, first as a child, then later on the roof of Eira's temple, lying alone or with Bien gathered in his arms, tracing the shape of their hunt with his gaze.

None of that prepared him for what hung shackled from a pair of thick wooden posts in a watery clearing a few hundred paces from the village.

Three canoes of the Vuo Ton floated in a loose ring around it, two warriors in each, all armed with short bows or spears. Even when Ruc's canoe nosed out of the reeds into the open space, none of them shifted their eyes from the posts or the creature suspended between them. They might not have been men and women at all, but wooden figures, like those the Dombângans carved into the ends of their ridgepoles to ward off ill luck and evil spirits; though had that been their job, judging from the thing hanging in their midst, they had already failed, and badly.

A tall, lean woman that Ruc didn't recognize spoke without turning. "It lives still."

"Some of us are harder to kill than others, Lu Cao," the old man replied from his seat in the bow of Ruc's canoe.

Lu Cao flicked a glance his way.

"Your pardon, Witness. I was expecting Boa."

"I expect he is off checking his traps."

She nodded, shifted her full attention back to the creature.

The Witness turned to Ruc, narrowed his eye.

"So. This is not what you spoke of when you mentioned a messenger."

Ruc shook his head slowly, unable to rip his gaze from the sight before him.

The thing might have been a bat, except that the largest bat Ruc had ever seen was the size of his hand. This one was taller than him, taller than any person he'd ever seen, nine feet, maybe ten. The Vuo Ton had pinioned it, wings half-spread, between the two posts, driving steel spikes through the skeletal, almost human limbs that supported those wings. The clawed legs had been fixed likewise to the posts, and the creature strained furiously against this vicious, four-point crucifixion, ropy muscles in the dark-furred body twisting and spasming. The face was something harvested from nightmare: slick, hideously flattened, glistening, as though all the hair had been seared off. It panted through gaping nostrils that might have been bored with an auger straight back into its skull, worked fangs the size of hooked human fingers. Then, all at once, it fell still, watching Ruc with dark, alien eyes.

It pried open that slavering mouth, slowly this time, and Ruc felt—*felt* rather than heard—a sound like a needle sliding into his ear, pitched too high to make out, ice-hot, shaped like things breaking. He almost went for his knife. A quick vision skittered through him—plunging the blade into the thing's chest, twisting and ripping, shredding it until no threat remained. With a shudder, he forced himself to remain still.

"What is it?" he asked.

"An abomination," the Vuo Ton woman spat.

"It is a riddle," the Witness replied quietly. "Posed to us by the world."

"Where did it come from?"

"Boa captured it."

"Can it fly?"

The old man nodded. "It could before Boa shattered its wing." He gestured to a point low on the limb where the bone stood brutally out of joint. "We are lucky to have this one."

Ruc turned to stare at the old man. *"This one?"*

"There were almost a dozen," the woman said. "They attacked the village."

The Witness nodded. "They killed nearly thirty of the people. Not since the frog plague have we lost so many so quickly."

"How?" Ruc demanded.

The Vuo Ton were strong, skilled hunters, capable of taking down crocs and jaguars. The delta was their home. Even the children could survive for days with little more than a knife and barbed spear. The frog plague was one thing—no one could fight a plague—but these . . .

"They attacked before moonrise on a cloudy night," the Witness replied. "We heard the sound first. That . . . screaming. Then they were seizing people. Most they carried up into the sky, higher than the circling of a marsh hawk, then dropped them. Some they killed with those fangs. Their bite carries a kind of poison.

"We took up spears. . . ." He shook his head, and when he spoke again, his voice was thick with self-contempt. "I have grown old and slow."

"You killed one of them," the woman said.

The Witness shook his head. "Too little," he replied, "and too late." His eye went distant. "Boa rallied the people, got them inside their homes, forced the *khuan*—"

"*Khuan?*"

"It is what we call them."

Ruc frowned. *Khuan* were imaginary monsters from the firelight tales the Vuo Ton whispered to their children.

"The *khuan* in the stories are like lizards. And they're *stories*."

"The name is a reminder," the Witness replied wearily, "that we may be wrong about our monsters." He shook his head. "Out of the air, the *khuan* are less dangerous."

The woman grunted as though someone had punched her in the gut.

"Still dangerous," the old man acknowledged. "They killed several of us inside the huts, but the fight was more even. Eventually, we drove them back, bleeding and broken, an offering to the Given Land."

"Except for this one."

"I hoped I might learn something from it."

"What have you learned?"

The old man shook his head slowly.

By the time Ruc had paddled the quarter mile back to the village, the Witness was so weak he could barely sit up in the bow of the canoe. Whatever stubborn defiance had dragged him from his hut in the first place seemed to have melted beneath the blazing sun. He hunched forward, elbows on his withered knees, coughing so violently Ruc could see his ribs jerk beneath his vest.

"I will walk," he insisted when Ruc tied off the canoe to the side of his raft, but for the few strides between the canoe and the hut, Ruc supported almost all of his meager weight.

Back in the dimness of his home, he subsided onto the reed mattress, covered his face with his gnarled hands, weathered another savage bout of hacking, rolled weakly onto his side, spat into a bowl, then lay back, breath whistling in his chest.

"Now you see, Kha Lu, why the gods have called you back."

Ruc hesitated.

All the old arguments rose up like bile in his throat.

They're not gods and they didn't call me. The things you worship are worse than the khuan. *You'll never be free of monsters as long as you live in the Given Land.*

At the same time, though, he could feel his own eagerness stirring. What would it be like to fight those creatures, to test himself against them, to feel the claws in his flesh while he drove home the killing stroke. . . .

"You defeated them," he said, shoving aside the vision. "You didn't need me."

"This is only—" Another cough flecked his lips with blood. "—the start of something."

"You don't know that."

"An army," the Witness whispered. "Your messenger said an *army*."

Ruc shook his head. "I learned a long time ago not to believe a thing just because someone says the words."

The old man fixed him with a glittering eye. "Then why did you come back?"

The answer rose in him unbidden: *to fight.*

He tried to picture the statue of Eira. He tried to imagine Bien's face, her fierce, kind eyes, but in the moment all he could remember was Boa glaring at him, gaze alight with hatred.

I could take him apart, Ruc thought. *Even now, even like this, I could slaughter him.*

He blinked, stared hard at the light slicing through the gaps in the walls of the hut.

"Kem Anh chose you," the Witness murmured. "She fed you at her breast. She and Hang Loc wove their gifts into your blood and bone. Raised you as though you were their child."

"I am *not* their child," Ruc replied, more violently than he'd intended. "And despite the years I spent here, I am not your child either."

The Witness didn't flinch. "We do not choose what we are, Kha Lu."

"I did," he replied. "I still do. Every day I choose to give myself as a servant to Eira."

"Then why, when I look at you, do I see a warrior of the Given Land?"

"Because you're a stubborn old man who doesn't listen, even when he's dying."

To Ruc's surprise, the Witness smiled, a crooked, spittle-wet grin revealing cracked, yellowing teeth. "Do you think I choose to be dying?" He raised a weak, trembling hand to his ruined socket. "Do you think I choose to have only one eye? Did I choose to be born in the Given Land in this time? Did I choose to find you on that riverbank? Did I choose this pride for you that floods my heart?" He shook his head. "This choosing, Kha Lu—it is an illusion."

Ruc blew out a ragged, angry breath.

"What do you want me to do? The *khuan* are gone, dead. You won."

The words tasted bitter.

"There will be more, and worse."

"And if there are? I haven't held a spear in years. I've swum maybe a dozen paces."

"What happened to the dancemaster that struck you?"

"I killed it."

"With what?"

Ruc hesitated, then held up his right hand, flexed the fingers slowly.

The Witness smiled, nodded.

"No," Ruc said, shaking his head, denying his own hunger more than the old man's hope. "You're forgetting that it *bit* me first. If I'd been anyone else, I'd be dead."

"But you are not anyone else, Kha Lu. You are yourself."

The hut had grown darker. Clouds must have snuffed the sun, blotting the light that, a few minutes earlier, had knifed through the gaps in the walls. Thunder grumbled somewhere off to the west, and moments later the patter of rain started on the roof and the raft beyond.

"What about your gods?" Ruc asked. "They're the ones who have guarded the Vuo Ton and the Given Land since . . . what? The dawn of time?"

The face of the Witness darkened. "Boa went to see the gods. After the attack."

"And?"

"They were not there."

"That's because they're unreliable." All the old memories, churned up like muddy water. "They range all over the Given Land. They could have been fucking on some mudbank in the southern shallows or hunting at the edge of the salts."

"Boa thought the same thing. He waited on their island, at the wall of skulls."

"For how long?"

"Thirty days."

"One moon. Most Vuo Ton go their entire *lives* without seeing their gods."

It was true enough, but Ruc could feel uneasiness coiled like a snake in his gut.

"Most Vuo Ton do not go to that island," the Witness replied. "On the times I have gone, I have sat vigil no more than two days, three at the longest."

"Maybe they don't like Boa as much as they like you."

The old man closed his eye. "This rivalry between you. You must let it go."

"I let it go fifteen years ago. I quit the Given Land."

"And now that you've come back, you will need to work together. He is not a bad man, Kha Lu. Only proud. It is a hard thing for one as fierce as him

always to be second-strongest, second-fastest, second in the eyes of his people
and his gods."

"I saw the eyes of the people when I stepped out of my canoe. I'm not winning any prizes with the Vuo Ton."

"If you find the gods . . ."

"I don't know *how* to find the gods. . . ."

"Then they will find you."

Ruc shook his head. "I spent three days looking for this village, three days
searching this whole quarter of the Given Land. If they wanted to see me, they
would have seen me."

The Witness grimaced. "It is this that frightens me."

"You don't need to be frightened. Not for Kem Anh and Hang Loc. You've
seen them fight."

Another memory—a still-shuddering heart ripped free of a chest and held
up to sunlight, Hang Loc's roar . . . Ruc felt the glee and the sickness roll over
him just as they had when he was a child. . . .

The Witness, oblivious, raised a hand to his missing eye. "I have *fought*
them," he reminded him.

"So you know they'd open those bat things up the same way you'd filet a
fish. They're unkillable."

"Your mother and father killed one."

"My mother and father . . ." Ruc trailed off, shaking his head, staring into
the gloom. "*You* were my father. There's a priest at the temple, Old Uyen. *He*
was my father. I've had half a dozen mothers and fathers. And sure, those
animals you call your gods were my mother and father. . . ."

"You still insist on calling them animals."

"I lived with them. I know the truth."

"Don't confuse truth with the masks it wears."

Ruc shook his head again, suddenly weary. The weight of two days paddling through the rushes settled in his shoulders, over his back. It had been
folly to come back. Even if the dead messenger was right, even if an army was
about to descend on the delta, even if the *khuan* were some kind of vanguard
to that army—what was he going to do about it? Boa led the Vuo Ton now, led
them, if the few stories he'd heard were true, better than Ruc would. If a war
was coming, there would be work for the priests of Eira, houses to rebuild,
hungry mouths to feed, orphans to take in. The whole point of leaving the delta
in the first place was to choose something better than the bloody tooth and
claw of the Vuo Ton and their gods.

Ruc took the Witness's pipe, filled it, lit it once more with the ember, passed
it to the old man.

"I love you," he said.

After the bestial heat that had been building inside him, the words were cool relief.

The Witness didn't raise the pipe to his lips. "It is not your love that we need."

Ruc leaned forward, kissed him gently on the forehead. "Then speak to Boa. I am a priest of Eira now, and love is what I have to give."

11

To her horror, Gwenna found that she liked her cabin. No. *Liked* was the wrong word. There was nothing to like about the dim chamber—three paces long and two wide, the ceiling barely higher than her head—but she found that she preferred it to anywhere else on the ship. Jonon lem Jonon had obviously aimed to make her a sort of prisoner before the expedition even began, and yet she found that she preferred to remain alone belowdecks. The headaches persisted, and the weight that seemed to be crushing her heart, and that sensation low her in chest, the constant gnawing, as though some clawed, jawed emptiness were inside her, eating her alive. And the anger, the slow-boiling fury at Jonon lem Jonon, at Adare, at the Dombângans, at herself, at the world. It was all still there, but in the dimness of her cabin there was no need to hide any of it.

She might have spent the entire passage to the southern tip of Menkiddoc in that cabin had the imperial historian not come for her. Two or three days into the voyage—she hadn't been keeping track—he knocked at her door. She considered not responding, just sitting there until the historian—she could smell the ink on him—went away. Except he wouldn't go away. For some reason she felt sure of that. If she tried to ignore him, he would wait, and the whole thing would take longer, and so, after the third knock, she levered herself to her feet and opened the door.

"What?"

Kiel studied her in the dimness.

"May I come in?"

Gwenna waved an indifferent hand. "There's not much *in,* but have at it."

The historian stepped through the door, closed it behind him, and leaned against the wall. The *Daybreak* was rolling gently with the even swells, and Kiel shifted with them almost as easily as Gwenna herself.

"According to my sources," the historian said, "you were eighteen when you held Andt-Kyl against the Urghul."

Gwenna shook her head. "It was Ran il·Tornja who held it."

"Il Tornja did not arrive until well after the fighting had begun. Until then, you were in charge. With nothing more than a few hundred untrained loggers you held back the entire Urghul nation."

She looked him in the eye. "Do you know what happened to most of those loggers?" Memory washed over her—the small islands aflame, bridges burning, Urghul everywhere, howling in their horrible language. "They died. A lot of them got shot. The Urghul are brutal with their bows." Her voice was conversational but she could hear the breakage inside it, as though if she spoke too loud or too fast it might shatter. "A lot of them got speared. There was one old bastard—I couldn't get him to leave his house, to retreat across the river. The Urghul tied his arms and legs to horses and tore him apart. You want to know what I did when that happened?"

The historian didn't reply so she answered for him. "Nothing."

Finally he spoke. "The battle at Andt-Kyl was a victory."

"Not for the people who ended up with a half foot of Urghul steel through the throat."

"There are casualties in every battle."

"Spoken like a fucking historian," Gwenna spat. "Like an ink-fingered bastard who never got out from behind his desk to see the hacked-up bodies."

She was trembling suddenly, her heart racing, breath burning in her chest.

"I have seen my share of hacked-up bodies," the historian replied quietly. He glanced down at his gnarled hands. "Some of them I hacked apart myself."

Gwenna stared at him, at the scar lacing his skin. She might not know shit about the man, but it was obvious—obvious if she'd bothered to look past her rage—that he hadn't spent his life behind a desk.

"Who the fuck are you?" she asked wearily, the fire going out of her.

He shook his head. "That is not the right question."

"I'll ask whatever questions I want."

He ignored her. "The right question is, who are *you*?"

"You know who I am."

"I thought I did. I've certainly written enough about you, Gwenna Sharpe. I thought I understood some things."

"Yeah? Like what?"

"I thought, for instance, that you were a woman who would never let herself rot in a ship's cabin."

"Fuck off."

"I thought you were a woman that the world couldn't break. You might die, of course. Fail. You might fail spectacularly. But I never expected you to quit." He cocked his head to the side. "I will admit, I am surprised."

"I didn't quit," she snarled. "I was stripped of my rank by the Emperor her-self. I'm not Kettral anymore."

"The world is filled with people who are not Kettral. The vast majority of them manage not to cower day and night inside an unlit room."

"I'm not cowering, you son of a bitch. Jonon forbid me the run of the ship."

"I suppose, then, that there's nothing you can do." He shrugged, turned toward the door.

"We're on a ship in the middle of the Ghost Sea—there's nothing *to* do."

Kiel pursed his lips, squinted into the gloom. "There is a passage I will have to revise."

"What are you talking about?"

He glanced up into the corner of the room, quoting from some text in his memory. *"Gwenna Sharpe was hardly the most skilled among the Kettral. Her own Wing included stronger fighters, more proficient archers, superior tacticians. What set Sharpe apart, what made her the Wing's true commander, was her un-conquerable heart."*

She stared after him as the door closed.

Her unconquerable heart.

She closed her eyes, felt that heart working away inside of her—the beat staggered, staggering—like something captive, something already defeated.

What set Sharpe apart was her unconquerable heart.

Had that ever been true? She remembered standing on the barricades at Andt-Kyl, screaming her defiance as the Urghul came on, diving into the river to break up the log jam, even when she thought it would mean her death. She remembered how it felt, the exhilaration and terror, the grim determination girding her. She *remembered* it all, but when she looked inside herself for those old emotions she found only scraps, fragments, just a pile of busted, rusting, useless detritus. The woman that the historian described in his book was a stranger.

The question was, what would that stranger do?

Slowly, she stripped off her wool coat, then lowered her body to the floor. Everything ached—her knees, her shoulders, as though every injury, every slice and puncture and torn muscle she'd ever encountered in her life had returned at once to plague her. She lay on her stomach, face pressed against the boards. What she wanted to do was to keep lying there, but that wasn't what the woman in Kiel's story would do. Even trapped in her cabin, that miserable bitch would have been training. And so, slowly, achingly, Gwenna pressed her palms against the floor, raised her body into a plank. The woman in Kiel's histories had done this often, had once held the position for a count of ten thousand.

Trembling, tears standing in her eyes, Gwenna Sharpe began counting.

†

The training didn't make her feel any better, but at least it was something she could blame for the pain. The ache of muscles forced past the point of exhaustion was a feeling she recognized, a feeling that, if she pushed herself hard enough, could shoulder aside the other, deeper, newer pain for which she had no excuse or explanation.

Running and swimming were out, obviously, which meant thousands of push-ups. Thousands of sit-ups. Holding plank while she counted and counted and counted. At first, she stayed inside her cabin, but the space was too small for proper training and so, after a few days, she made her way up onto the deck of the sterncastle.

She'd almost forgotten the brilliance of the sun, and for a while she stood there blinking while the salt wind ripped at her hair. She took a deep breath, sucked in the sea air, and for just a moment, a sliver of a heartbeat, felt like herself again, like a person who could find joy in the rolling of the hull beneath her feet, in the strength of her own body. Then she looked down the deck and noticed Cho Lu. It wasn't his fault that his grandfather had come to Annur from Dombâng—wasn't his grandfather's fault, for that matter—but he reminded her of the city, of the people she'd killed there, of the people who she'd left to die. All over again, more viciously, the weight clamped down around her. She'd already turned back toward the hatch, was about to retreat to her cabin, when the voice of the First Admiral brought her up short.

"If you were one of my officers, I'd have you whipped for appearing on deck in this condition."

His voice was level, sober, but at first the words didn't make sense. What condition was he talking about? Then she looked down at herself, at the wrinkled blacks she'd been wearing since the ship set sail, at her hands, which were seamed with grime. She hadn't bathed. She'd told herself that the reason was that Jonon had forbidden her the run of the ship, but the truth was that it had seemed pointless. She wasn't going to fix anything that was broken by scrubbing her fucking face, and so she hadn't bothered.

She forced herself to straighten, then turned slowly to face Jonon lem Jonon.

All over again, she was struck by the fact that he didn't look like an admiral so much as a masker who had rehearsed for many days to play the part of one—the polished buttons, the golden braid, the carefully brushed uniform, the close-cropped hair, the square jaw, the gleaming white teeth. Only the scorn twisting his mouth seemed out of place.

"I'm sorry, sir," she said. "I've been training. . . ."

She trailed off. It sounded ridiculous.

"Training."

The word came out flat, emotionless, but contempt wafted off of him.

The other officers and sailors on the deck went about their duties, but she could feel their eyes on her. The weight of those stares made her want to fold in on herself.

Kiel spoke from behind her. "I've heard it said that Kettral are twice as strong as normal men."

What the fuck was he doing? It wasn't true, for one thing, and the words were perfectly crafted to chafe against Jonon's pride.

"I'm not Kettral," she said, "and I'm not a man."

"Nonetheless," the historian continued. "I am curious."

She shook her head, the motion almost reflexive.

Jonon, however, was studying her. "It might be useful," he mused, "to put to rest once and for all the legend of the invincible Kettral."

"The Kettral aren't invincible."

"I know that," he replied. "But there are souls on this ship who were raised on stories of the empire's unstoppable warriors. It could be salutary for them to see the truth." He considered a moment, then turned, pointed to a young, bare-chested sailor who was coiling rope a few paces away, his eyes studiously focused on the task.

"Raban," the admiral said. "Come here."

The man dropped the rope, snapped to attention.

He was wire-thin, but she could see the muscle corded beneath his skin, the strength in his ropey forearms, the muscles of his back carving a V down to his thin waist. If ever a man had been born to scramble around in the rigging, Raban was it.

"What do you say to a contest, Raban?" the admiral asked.

Raban blinked.

"As you will, sir," he replied, offering a rough bow.

"A race." Jonon pointed to the mast behind him. "To the top. You against the"—he gestured to Gwenna—"whatever it is that she is now."

The men on the deck of the sterncastle had given up even the pretense of work. Most of them were watching the admiral, shooting the occasional glance at Gwenna. Even the sailors and soldiers amidships had noticed that something was unfolding in the stern, had paused in their labors to take stock of it.

"There's no need—" Gwenna began.

Jonon silenced her with a raised hand.

"You and Raban will race to the top of the mast. If he wins, I will double his wages for the journey."

Raban's eyes went wide as plates. The admiral had offered him a small fortune, just for climbing.

"If you win, Gwenna Sharpe, I will open to you the freedom of the ship."

She didn't want the freedom of the ship. She didn't even want to be on the deck, with everyone watching her, but it was obvious that Jonon didn't much care what she wanted. He smiled at her, and in that moment he smelled of nothing but satisfaction.

The sailor shot her a wary glance, then turned back to Jonon. "The rules, sir?"

Jonon shook his head. "There are no rules."

Which made it, Gwenna reflected briefly, a lot like life.

The rising sun glinted off the admiral's brass.

"Go," he said.

Raban darted for the ratlines stretching up from the deck. He was swinging up into them before Gwenna had even moved. For a few heartbeats she almost *didn't* move. She felt heavy, dull, unready. Racing to the top of the rigging wasn't going to change anything. It wasn't going to make Jonon or any of the others respect her. It wasn't going to make her respect herself. Then she caught a scrap of conversation from down the deck, just a handful of words— . . . *bitch is pretty, but she's no fucking soldier . . .* —and, if only for a few moments, she was the soldier from the historian's chronicles once more.

She went up the underside of the lines, hand over hand, not bothering with her feet. It was harder that way, obviously, but it was also faster, and by the time she reached the first yard Raban was almost within reach. He glanced down as she slithered past the yard, shock painted on his face, then threw himself into the climb with renewed fervor.

The deck of the *Daybreak* had erupted into a cacophony of taunts and cheers. It reminded her of the arena back on the Islands, how all the Kettral would gather at the end of the day to watch the cadets beat each other bloody. There was a knack Gwenna had developed early to ignore the noise, blotting it out, focusing only on the fight at hand, and as she climbed now she found the sound falling away, as though if she only went fast enough, high enough, she could win free of it. Her shoulders and forearms blazing, she dragged herself higher into the rigging, the deck dropping away beneath her, the ship shrinking, the great ocean widening on every side.

Halfway to the third yard, maybe five paces from the top of the mast, she drew even with Raban's feet. He felt her coming, set himself, then lashed out with a heel. It caught her a glancing blow on the side of the head, not enough to stun her or knock her out, but the sailor was only getting started. As she clung to the lines, he kicked down at her over and over again. His aim wasn't great—most of the attacks landed on her ears or shoulders—but after a few attempts he connected square in the center of her face. She felt her nose crunch, the hot gush of blood explode down over her mouth, then the pain.

That pain unlatched something inside of her.

The next time Raban struck, she reached up and caught him by the ankle. She should have done it earlier, but her mind hadn't been working right. The sailor jerked, tried to rip his limb free, but she had him, and she wasn't letting go. Hauling on his leg with one hand, the rigging with the other, she pulled herself up, caught the rope belt cinched around his waist, twisted until she was facing away from his body, reached up blind with the other hand, grabbed the belt, then let her legs swing free.

Raban strangled a groan. The belt was tight enough that, instead of slipping, it was gouging into his stomach. He was also holding both of them now, his weight and hers suspended from weary arms. As she hung there, Gwenna looked down. They were high enough that the cant of the ship carried them out well over the rail. Falling now would mean a long drop into the blue-gray chop. It was the kind of fall a very lucky person might survive. She wasn't feeling particularly lucky.

"I can't . . ." Raban gasped.

His breath failed before the sentence ended. Gwenna could feel him slipping, his pride and determination evaporating into panic.

Tightening her grip, she swung her legs up, up until she was upside down. She caught the sailor around the throat with the back of one bent knee, completed the triangle with the other, and squeezed. As Raban jerked and clawed at her, she shoved away from him. For a moment, as she shifted her grip from his belt back to the rigging, she was suspended only by her legs locked around his neck. Then she had the ratlines in her hands and it was over. He'd begun to spasm, to sag away from the ropes. She could let him go now, and he'd drop, probably break his back on the yard below, and crash into the water. Or she could hold the triangle as he fell and break his neck.

Both good options.

The deck below had become one enormous roar.

Between the sails and the rigging, the men probably couldn't see exactly what was happening, but they could tell that the two were grappling, that the race was a race no longer, but a fight for survival. What they didn't know was that the fight was already over. Gwenna smelled it as Raban's bladder gave way, smelled the panic pouring out of him. The twin scents reminded her of her days in the brig of *Anlatun's Lion* during the voyage back from Dombâng, and suddenly the desire to win went out of her, scrubbed away by disgust.

She reached out, snagged Raban by the belt once more, then loosened her legs. Unanchored from his neck, her legs dropped. Then Raban did. His weight hit her at the same time as her own, almost ripping her shoulder from its socket. She grimaced, hung by one hand from the rigging, held the young man limp above the gnashing waves with the other. Everything seemed to pause there, the ship heeled over at the end of its roll, the mast leaning out over the ocean, Gwenna dangling from the rigging, Raban from her burning hands. Then the world slid into motion once more, the mast righted itself, the sailor and Gwenna swung back toward the lines. She established her feet and gave him a shake.

"Wake up."

He twitched, arms jerking like a puppet's. Then his eyes snapped open.

"Where?" he asked, staring about himself, baffled. "What?"

"Hold on," Gwenna said.

More out of instinct than any conscious thought the young sailor grabbed the rigging.

"Now climb," she said.

She watched the understanding flood back into his brain along with the blood.

"The race—" he began.

"Is over," she replied. "You won." She nodded toward the top of the mast. "Go finish it."

He stared at her, horror and confusion warring in his face. "Why?"

"Fucked if I know." She was suddenly, profoundly weary. Everything hurt, her shoulders, the shredded skin of her hands. "Just go."

Some of the men on the deck below might have seen what happened, glimpsed it throught the spread acres of sail, but it had been fast, maybe too fast to follow. To most of them it would have looked like a ferocious struggle, one from which Raban had emerged victorious. Jonon's point would be proven—the fabled Kettral weren't any more special than common sailors—and maybe the admiral would leave her alone.

As Raban climbed the last few paces to the top of the mast, Gwenna hooked an arm around the rigging and stared out toward the horizon. After so many days in the dimness of her cabin, the world was dizzyingly wide, the sky too bright, the sea too dark. She stared at it as the ship swayed back and forth, back and forth, stared and stared, was still staring when the mast and flag of the Manjari ship climbed up over the rim of the world.

12

"You are a Shin monk."

Yumel, appointments minister of the first rank, did not laugh when he said this. He didn't look capable of laughter, or any other expression for that matter. Everything about him was gray—his face, his thin, receding hair, his teeth. Akiil had the feeling that if he'd shown up claiming to be the Blank God himself the man would have had the same reaction.

"The last of the Shin monks of Ashk'lan," Akiil replied.

The minister didn't blink. For all Akiil knew, it was precisely this ability—to not blink when accosted with preposterous claims—that had seen him raised to the first rank. The appointments ministers of the third and second rank had certainly been far less circumspect in their disbelief. The appointment minister of the fourth rank had almost choked on his tea.

"The last of the Shin monks of Ashk'lan," Yumel said. Even his words sounded gray.

"And a friend of the Emperor, Kaden hui'Malkeenian."

Yumel stared at his hands, as though deeply embarrassed.

"Adare hui'Malkeenian, bright be the days of her life, is the Emperor of Annur."

"I'm aware of that," Akiil said. "I've come to speak to her about her brother. I have a message from him."

"Kaden hui'Malkeenian was laid in his tomb five years ago."

Akiil smiled genially. "It's an old message."

The minister frowned, studied the ledger before him. The room was immaculate. There was nothing to look at except the bloodwood walls, the small window opening onto a maple tree, the desk, the ledger, and Yumel himself. Maybe, instead of his circumspection, the man had been raised to the first rank for his ability to stall. It was possible that his function was to so thoroughly bore petitioners that they gave up and went away without ever troubling the Emperor.

"May I trust," the minister asked at last, "that the Emperor is familiar with your name?"

"Kaden may have mentioned me."

It seemed unlikely. Akiil had been at the ass end of the world when the empire began to tear itself apart, but from the rumors he'd heard, Kaden and Adare had been on opposite sides of that rift. According to the stories, Adare came back to the capital to make common cause with her brother only as the empire tumbled headlong into war. It was hard to imagine that conversation—or any of those that had followed—containing much about Akiil. *I had this friend at the monastery. Used to steal shit in the Perfumed Quarter when he was a kid. Pretty good juggler . . .* The more he thought about it, the less likely it seemed.

Yumel turned a page of the ledger, then another page, then another, then shook his head slowly. "You will understand, of course, that the Emperor, bright be the days of her life, has myriad responsibilities."

"I have something that can help her with those."

Brightened wasn't quite the word, but the appointments minister of the first rank turned marginally less gray.

"Gifts," he said, "you may leave with me. I offer you my absolute assurance that I will see them brought before the Emperor."

Akiil shook his head, tapped gently at his own temple. "The gift is in here."

"A message." Yumel darkened once more. "From Kaden hui'Malkeenian."

"A message and an offer."

"An offer. Very generous, I am certain. May I inquire after the nature of this offer?"

Akiil hesitated. He'd planned to save this part for the Emperor herself, but if he never got to speak with her, there was no point saving it.

"I know about the *kenta*."

Back at Ashk'lan, one of Akiil's teachers had forced him to paint leaves for months on end. *Thousands* of leaves. Every time he finished a painting, the monk would say, "Do you see now? There is no such thing as leaves? There is only *this* leaf. And *this* leaf. And *this*."

It made Akiil want to punch him in the neck, but the monk didn't seem to notice.

When they were finally finished with leaves, he was assigned to watch snow melt.

"The world is change," the monk said, sitting beside him. "See the change, and you see the world."

Now, sitting across the immaculately polished desk, Akiil watched the appointments minister, first rank as though he were snow.

Yumel's face didn't move. Akiil might as well have announced that he knew about apples. There was nothing but the same gray boredom in the minister's eyes, and yet, *something* had changed. There was the tapping of the finger. It was quick, silent, barely a motion at all, but that finger had lain perfectly still before Akiil mentioned the *kenta*. Yumel was breathing faster, too—not much faster, but faster. His pupils had dilated.

Akiil smiled. "So you know about the *kenta*. Which means the Emperor told you about them. She asked you to look out for someone like me."

"*Kenta*," the man said, shaking his head. "I am afraid I do not know the term."

"Yes, you do."

Akiil winked.

Yumel closed his ledger, set down his quill.

"What would you say to the Emperor, bright be the days of her life, about these *kenta*? In the unlikely event that you were honored with an audience."

Akiil smiled.

"In that *unlikely* event, I would tell her that I can use them. That no one else can. And that I can teach her to do the same."

†

Back at the monastery, Kaden had talked at length about the Hall of a Thousand Trees—its size and beauty, history and magnificence. To Akiil, an orphan who'd lived half his life in the slums and half in the stony nowhere of Ashk'lan, it had sounded like a place straight out of myth or legend. And so the fact that he wasn't escorted there was a little irritating.

Shouldn't have worn the robe, he thought. *Should have stolen something fancy.*

Not only, in fact, was he not being led to anything that looked like the Hall of a Thousand Trees, the Aedolian Guardsmen at his shoulders—stone-faced soldiers built more on the scale of armored bears rather than men—seemed to be taking the most obscure passages they could find, guiding him through a labyrinth of courtyards and corridors, outside, then inside, then outside again, twisting and turning past temples and graceful halls, across bridges and beneath them, to a nondescript wooden door in an unremarkable stone wall in an utterly unimpressive long, low building that looked vaguely like a stable.

"This?" Akiil asked, raising a brow.

The smaller of the two guardsmen—*smaller* being a very relative term—didn't reply. Instead, he knocked three times, paused, then a fourth. The door swung open. Two more Aedolians waited in the chamber beyond, hands on the pommels of their swords.

"Hello," Akiil said, nodding to each in turn. "Hello."

One of the men, his face grim as an undertaker's, gestured with a gauntleted hand. "Undress."

Akiil raised his brows. "Excuse me?"

"Remove your robe, or it will be removed."

Kaden had mentioned nothing about being forced to strip in some obscure room for a group of nameless soldiers, but then, as the son of the Emperor, Kaden presumably hadn't been the one doing the stripping. For a moment the cold hand of Akiil's childhood reached out to seize him. He'd had friends back in the Quarter who'd disappeared into rooms like this and come out broken. Some hadn't come out at all.

He took a steady breath, slowed his breathing, his heart.

To see the world, you must look past your own mind.

There was no lust in the faces of the soldiers, none of the eagerness or shame he might have seen if they'd brought him to the small room in order to rape him. Instead, they wore the hard gazes of men who distrusted everything, including Akiil. Especially Akiil. The leader held himself back, hand still resting on his sword, as though he half expected an attack.

Akiil allowed himself a smile.

"Of course," he said, pulling the rough robe up over his head, holding it out to the man. "I promise I didn't bring anything sharp."

Evidently, the Aedolian didn't think much of his promise.

As Akiil waited naked at the center of the knot of men, the soldier went over every inch of the fabric, taking special care to probe the seams, the hem, the doubled fabric where the hood met the shoulders. When he was finally satisfied he handed it back, waited for Akiil to dress once more, then opened a door on the far side of the room.

Akiil stepped past him, conscious of the man's stare, into a walled garden. Unlike almost everything else about the Dawn Palace, the scale of the space was human. A small brook flowed in from beneath one wall, meandered in a lazy arc, then flowed out beneath another. Flowering ivy climbed low trellises. A maple with sun-bright orange leaves cast a light, dappled shade. There were no soldiers or flags. No statuary. No courtiers or palace guards or gongs. Nothing, in other words, that Akiil had expected. Instead, a ramshackle wooden table stood on crushed stone in a small clearing, the kind of workmanlike surface he remembered from back at Ashk'lan, a place for puttering or potting. Everything in the garden was natural, normal.

Except, of course, for the woman standing behind that table.

"Kneel," growled one of the Aedolians. His gauntleted hand closed around Akiil's shoulder, crushing it, forcing him down.

The stone dug into his knees. Half a pace in front of him, the ants had made three small hills. He watched as they dragged the body of a dead spider toward their home. If the Emperor or her thugs thought to put him off balance by making him kneel and wait, they'd made a mistake. He'd spent days at Ashk'lan, weeks, *months* kneeling in the snow, or the rain, or the vicious autumn wind, freezing his balls off, studying the migration of the birds or the shapes of the clouds or the incremental erosion of the rocks. Not that he'd ever been able to see the rocks erode. Still . . . if this was a waiting game, he was prepared to wait for a very long time.

"You knew my brother," the Emperor said at last.

She sounded distracted, indifferent, as though she'd barely noticed his arrival. It was an act, of course. An excellent act, but then, he hadn't come expecting amateurs.

Akiil nodded, kept his eyes on the ground.

"Tell me about him."

A test. Tattered robes weren't hard to come by, and it was no secret that the heir to the Unhewn Throne had trained among the Shin. Akiil would have been shocked if he were the first one who'd come to the palace claiming to have known the Emperor's brother. The fact that he was telling the truth didn't make his story any more plausible. There was a lesson in there, he thought, about the relative value of stories and truth.

"He didn't like jam," he said finally.

"I thought all you monks ate was tubers and gruel."

Akiil nodded. "The Shin were great ones for tubers. Also gruel. But every year in late summer, way down in the valleys, the bruiseberries ripened. Hue and a few of the others used to make jam. Not very good jam, mind you, but better than anything else at Ashk'lan. I stole the whole pot once, hid it in my room. . . ."

"I am waiting," the Emperor said, "to hear what this has to do with my brother."

"Kaden hated it. Something about the texture. Didn't like the way it stuck to his fingers. I told him he was insane to pass up the only tasty thing in that 'Shael-spawned place, but he never liked being told things."

The Emperor didn't respond. Somewhere deep in the palace a gong began tolling out the midmorning hour. Only when it was finished, when the last reverberations had died away, did Adare speak again.

"I expected you to choose as your proof some grander secret. Some greater revelation."

Akiil shrugged. He tried to, anyway. It was hard to shrug with the Aedolian grinding his shoulder to mush.

"The mind knows nothing," he replied. It was an old Shin aphorism, one that always annoyed him. Which wasn't to say it couldn't be useful now. "Truth lives in the hands, in the eyes, on the tongue."

The Emperor snorted. "Certainly sounds like my brother's type of bullshit."

"We were raised, Your Radiance, by the same order of bullshitters."

Adare's laughter was grim.

"Leave us, Hugel, Brant."

"Your Radiance—" protested the guardsman.

The Emperor cut him off. "If everyone is doing their jobs, he has been searched a dozen times since he set foot inside the palace."

"They were admirably thorough," Akiil added.

Hugel's—or maybe it was Brant's—voice came out a rumble. "Some men do not need weapons to kill."

"If he murders me, I expect you to exact some terrible vengeance. Until he does, I expect you to obey my orders."

The iron hand disappeared from Akiil's shoulder.

"Apologies, Your Radiance. We will be just beyond the door."

The footsteps retreated. The wooden door swung shut with a faint thud. A latch fell into place.

Akiil remained on his knees, eyes downcast. Kaden had never insisted on his imperial prerogatives, but Kaden had been raised by monks. Adare had grown up here, inside the palace, waited on by a thousand servants and slaves. For all he knew, he might have joined those abject ranks the moment he walked through the gate.

"Akiil, no family name, of the Perfumed Quarter of Annur," the Emperor said.

So Kaden *had* mentioned him. That made things easier.

"Your Radiance."

"You may stand."

He straightened up slowly, ignoring the pain where the crushed stone had gouged into his knees, raised his eyes to meet those of the Emperor, produced his most winning smile.

Adare hui'Malkeenian did not smile back. Her face—all hard planes and angles—didn't seem built for smiles. She stood beside the table, the stem of a single white orchid in her fingers, a vase filled with flowers before her, but she wasn't looking at the orchid or the vase. She was looking at Akiil, and her eyes were on fire.

He'd expected this, of course. The burning eyes were the Malkeenian birthright, proof of the family's descent from the Lady of Light, the goddess Intarra herself. Kaden's eyes had burned, too—a fact that Akiil had always found vexingly ostentatious—but where Kaden's gaze had reminded him of campfires or lanterns, the blaze in Adare's irises was both brighter and colder.

A whirl of delicate scar cascaded down her face, a labyrinth of dozens of interweaving lines falling from her hairline into the collar of her robe. Her arms and hands were likewise marked. Akiil had heard this story all the way back in the Bend—how she'd raised a spear to call down the lightning, how, instead of killing her, it left her with this tracery of beautiful, inscrutable scar. Unlike her brother, Adare claimed to be Intarra's prophet. Akiil knew a man back in the Quarter once—Drunk Tym—who'd claimed to be a prophet. This woman was nothing like Drunk Tym. She studied him with those shifting, burning eyes the way a butcher might size up a hog.

"My brother did mention you," she said at last.

"We were close."

"He said you were a thief and a liar raised by cutthroats and whores."

Akiil spread his hands. "I *requested,* as soon as I was old enough to frame the words, a suite of private rooms in this very palace." He put on his best perplexed frown. "I can only assume my request was somehow mislaid."

The Emperor raised an eyebrow, then turned her attention to the orchid in her hands. "Perhaps you believe," she mused, trimming the stem with a small, bone-handled knife, "that your purported friendship with my brother allows you to take liberties with me."

"I believe," Akiil replied, "that you'll never learn what I can teach you as long as you insist on being an emperor and a prophet."

"I am hardly going to become a monk."

"What you need to become is nothing."

A light breeze feathered the leaves of the maple. Adare trimmed the stem of the flower, tested it in the vase, then trimmed it again.

"Do you know what I tell my ministers," she asked finally, "when they rise to the first rank?"

"Congratulations?"

The Emperor shook her head, chose a bloodred lily, considered it from one angle, then another.

"I tell them not to waste my time. If they can't make a point in fewer than five sentences, then they are not worthy of the post." She held the lily against the nuns' blossom, narrowed her eyes, frowned, discarded it. "You have spoken sixteen."

Akiil nodded, held up five fingers, lowered the first.

"The *kenta* are gates built thousands of years ago by the Csestriim to let a person cross half the world in a single step."

"I'm aware of that," Adare replied. "Every Malkeenian emperor before me used them to hold Annur together."

Her face remained still, indifferent, but Akiil could hear the frustration in her voice, flecks of rust on a fine steel blade.

He nodded again, lowered another finger for each sentence that he spoke.

"A traveler through the *kenta* passes, between her origin and her destination, through nothing.

"Nothing is the territory of the Blank God.

"To pass the *kenta* safely, you must carry nothingness inside you.

"An emperor and a prophet are the opposite of nothing."

That, at least, was the theory.

Akiil had never seen a *kenta*. The monks never talked about them, but he had learned early in life to ferret out the best secrets, and in this case he'd had an advantage; Kaden, after all, was sent to the monastery, like his father and his grandfather and all the rest of them, to learn to use the ancient gates. Akiil would have known a lot more if there had actually *been* a *kenta* at Ashk'lan. He'd have known a lot more if soldiers hadn't come and slaughtered everyone who could have taught him. He'd have known a lot more if someone had bothered writing this shit down instead of passing it along in 'Kent-kissing riddles from one generation to the next for hundreds or thousands of years, but they hadn't and he didn't. The whole situation was less than ideal, but he'd spent a lifetime making the most of lousy situations. The Emperor didn't know what he didn't know, and he intended to keep it that way.

"Are you here to teach me Csestriim history?" Adare asked.

"I am here because I can teach you to use the *kenta*."

The fire shifted in her eyes as she watched him.

"How?" she asked finally.

Instead of replying, he stepped forward, took the vase off the table.

"A beautiful arrangement," he said, considering it. "As though these exact flowers were meant to be here, together, in just this way."

"Szi szian," the Emperor replied.

Akiil shook his head, admitting his ignorance.

"Right place," Adare said. "It's an old phrase."

"What does it have to do with flowers?"

"There is beauty in a system—a painting, a government, a flower arrangement—in which the place of everything seems necessary, inevitable."

"Spoken like a woman whose own place is atop the throne."

"I believe in order. In the beauty of order."

"Do you know what the Blank God has to say about beauty? About order?"

The Emperor watched him with those burning eyes, but didn't reply.

Akiil upended the vase, scattering the flowers across the crushed stone. With the bare sole of his foot, he ground the petals into the rock, then shook the last drops of water from the vase.

"Nothing," he said, setting the vessel back on the table.

"That was a ghost orchid." The Emperor's voice was mild, but he could hear the anger beneath it. "It blooms only once every four or five years. That single flower was worth a hundred Annurian suns."

"And do you know," Akiil asked, "how many Annurian suns will purchase you passage through the *kenta*?"

The Emperor's jaw tightened. "I am beginning to suspect the answer is none."

"Some things can't be purchased."

"Does that mean you'll be providing this instruction for free?"

"The Blank God has no interest in coins or titles." Akiil slid on the mask of his smile. "I, alas, am made of far weaker stuff."

✝

All around him the monastery blazed. Flames chewed through the wooden roofs of the buildings, hurled a garish light across the night sky. Armored men with massive swords stalked through the stone buildings, blood darkening their blades. There should have been screaming, terror, fighting or flight, but the monks did not die as other people died. They went silently, steel passing through them as though they were already gone.

A dream, Akiil tried to plead. *This is a dream.*

No, Akiil.

He looked down to find Scial Nin, the abbot of Ashk'lan, kneeling at his feet. Soot smeared the old man's face. Blood caked his wrinkles.

This is not *a dream, is it?* the abbot asked. *This is what actually happened.* He lifted a hand to touch the sword buried in his chest.

Akiil, as he did every time, followed that blade, followed it back and back, followed it for what seemed like forever, dread mounting inside him, until he found the handle clutched in his own hand. Instead of his robe, he wore a suit of gleaming steel, as though he weren't a monk at all, as though he never had been.

You killed me, Nin said.

I'm sorry, Akiil whispered. *I didn't mean to. I killed the soldier, stole his armor. . . . I was going to look for Kaden. . . .*

But who did you find instead?

The words leaked out of him. *I found you.*

And when the other soldiers saw you, when your disguise worked, when they took you for one of their own, when they told you to murder me, what did you do?

Akiil felt the dream seize him, force the words free. *I killed you.*

Scial Nin nodded, then smiled, as though Akiil were a child who had solved a particularly tricky riddle.

They were going to kill you anyway, Akiil protested. Tears burned down his cheeks. *It was going to happen.*

It was, the abbot agreed equably.

And if I didn't do it, they would have known. They would have slaughtered me, too.

Nin nodded again. *They would have.*

I didn't have a choice.

No? Nin raised his eyebrows. *What about dying? That's what the rest of us did. You could have died.*

Shit yes, you could have. A new voice cut in, bright and angry. Akiil looked over to find Skinny Quinn bleeding out through a gash across her throat. That was wrong. She wasn't usually part of the dream, not *this* dream anyway. He had other nightmares about her—her and Runt and Butt Boy—but there she was, small inside her monk's robe, kneeling on the cold stone as a place she'd never seen burned to the ground around her. Despite the wound she kept speaking, blood frothing from the cut. *You could have fucking died, Akiil. That's what the rest of us did.*

We died, Runt agreed. He sat a few paces away, cradling his guts in his hands.

We died, Butt Boy said, brow furrowing, as though the notion confused him. He lay in a spreading puddle of blood. *But you didn't. You escaped the Quarter. You escaped Ashk'lan. You always escape, Akiil.*

Somehow, impossibly, Butt Boy levered himself up. Quinn had risen, too, and Runt, and Scial Nin, all of them hacked half apart, gushing blood from their wounds, but moving forward, reaching for him. He tried to turn, but his stolen armor was too heavy, too stiff, as though all the joints had rusted shut.

You always escape, they chanted, eyes blazing with fire and accusation.

Scial Nin pulled the sword from his guts—somehow Akiil had lost hold of it—turned the bloody weapon in his hands, then handed it to Skinny Quinn.

That's the thing about you, Akiil, she growled, setting the blade to his throat. *You always fucking escape.*

Then, with a vicious thrust, she forced the hot steel home.

13

After a hot, hazy sunrise, the green-gray clouds began to pile up. Ruc had been paddling all night, since leaving the village of the Vuo Ton. He'd been hoping to reach Dombâng before the storm, but the delta had a way of rotting hopes. The pressure mounted until it felt like an effort just to breathe. Then, sometime around noon, a blade of lightning slashed the belly of the sky and the storm came down, rain as thick and green as the reeds.

Water sloshed in the hull of the wooden canoe. Again and again he paused, bailed out the blood-warm rain, waited for a momentary break in the torrent to test the flavor and flow of the channel, started paddling again. If he hadn't spent half his life in the delta, he would have ended up utterly lost. As it was, night bruised the roiling clouds as he slid back into the city, and the rain had still not slackened. That had to be the reason, he told himself, for the lack of people on the docks and causeways, the near-complete absence of boats in the canals.

As he forged deeper into the city, however—threading his way beneath the arcing bridges, between the wooden tenements that leaned over the narrow back channels—a cool unease coiled around his heart. Even through the monsoon, Dombângans lit their lanterns by the hundreds and thousands, and yet in half a mile he'd seen only a handful, smears of bloody light behind a curtain of rain. Likewise, there weren't enough fishing craft. At dusk, the plout-fish boats should have been coming in and the eel netters heading out. Fishers might grumble about the rain, but they didn't let it stop them. If they quit working for the monsoon, half of Dombâng would starve, and yet Ruc had passed no more than a dozen. Up on the decks and the bridges he could make out just a few figures, hunched and furtive, their heat steaming red as they scuttled through the deluge and gathering darkness. The scene reminded him of the worst months following the revolution, when whole quarters of the city had seemed barren and lifeless for days on end.

Except that the revolution was long over. The Annurians had been defeated.

All the reports said they lacked both the will and the wealth to fight, even for a prize as rich as Dombâng. Warily, Ruc scanned the skies, followed the red streaks of a few birds searching for less sodden roosts. Nothing nearly as large as the *khuan* the Vuo Ton had captured, but an itch was growing between his shoulder blades all the same. Maybe an attack had already come and gone. Maybe no one was outside because the *khuan* had already swarmed the city, hauling people screaming into the sky, dropping them to their deaths on the sharp-peaked, tiled roofs. He considered stopping, asking a few questions, but that would only delay his return to the temple.

Grimly, he paddled faster.

The usual motley collection of boats bobbed at the temple docks. He nosed the canoe in among them, leaped out, tossed the painter around the cleat, mounted the tall stairs up from the dock two at a time, crossed the temple square at a light jog, ignoring the water dripping from his vest and *noc,* then shouldered his way into the dormitory. He took the empty hallway at a tense trot, stopped in front of Bien's door, raised his hand, knocked more roughly than he'd intended. Silence. The doors in the temple were built of solid teak, but he could usually see a haze of heat through them if someone was inside. He knocked again, then flipped open the latch.

The neatly made bed was empty, the lamp unlit.

She is Eira's servant, he reminded himself. *The goddess will watch over her.*

The words were easy enough to rehearse, but he had trouble holding on to the thought, as though his faith had been slicked with oil. Eira was a far more powerful goddess than the bloody creatures that had raised him. Her touch extended to all corners of the world, to the deepest eddies of every human heart, and yet Bien did not live in all corners of the world. She lived here, in Dombâng, and if danger came, it wasn't clear how the goddess would stop it.

He shoved the thought aside. If he was going to have a crisis of faith, he could do it later, after finding Bien. There was still the temple proper to check, along with the refectory. Maybe the city felt strange because the high priests had imposed a curfew. After the attack on the Purple Baths, they'd want to crack down on the worst of the riots and violence.

The thought did nothing to reassure him.

Back down the hallway, down the stairs, through the door. The rain fell like arrows in the courtyard, splattering on the stones. He could make out the heat of a few people, more yellow than red, hunched against the storm as they hurried between buildings. He ignored them, turned instead onto the covered walkway leading to the temple.

Only when he'd shoved the door open did he allow himself to pause. He'd half expected to find the nave packed with huddled, frightened families, people sheltering from the unrest outside. Instead, a few score of Eira's faithful sat scattered among the dozens of wooden pews, heads bowed mildly in prayer. Someone was singing in the clerestory—a deep, smooth man's voice that Ruc took for either Ma Moa or Chiem—moving through the simple melody of an old hymn. In the rafters high above, about half of the 214 lamps were lit. Ruc knew the number because when he first emerged from the delta it had been one of his jobs to light them every evening, climbing through the vaulted beams with a pot of embers and the metal tongs. Now, as he looked up, he could just make out Diemba dangling easily from a hand and a crooked knee while he reached down to kindle another wick.

Ruc took a deep breath.

The boy was up there lighting lamps, just as he did every other night. The usual priests prayed from the usual pews. There was no disaster. No calamity.

He dropped his gaze from the ceiling to the far end of the nave, where a huge bloodwood statue of Eira—four-armed, flanked by her carved wolves—watched over the faithful. A handful of people knelt on the floor before her, but Bien, if she'd come to the temple at all, wouldn't be there. She'd never liked the massive statue.

"Looks like an emperor," she'd complained one night, studying her goddess with a critical eye. "Or a general. One of those shitty statues the Annurians put all over the city." She shook her head. "So big. Too big."

"She's a goddess," Ruc remembered pointing out.

"She doesn't look like a goddess. She looks like architecture."

The idol that Bien preferred was barely the size of her hand, tucked away in one of the small, private side chapels that opened off the nave. A screen of carved teak shielded the space, but even from across the temple, Ruc could see the heat of someone kneeling there. He reached it in a few dozen strides, slid sideways through the gap between the wood and the wall, and there she was, back to him, black hair still wet with the rain, kneeling before her goddess, head bowed, hands clasped.

Relief washed through him.

Thank you, Eira, he murmured, shifting his gaze from the woman he loved to the small sculpture set into a niche in the wall. Unlike the massive statue at the head of the nave, this one was carved from ivory, though the white had yellowed over the years while overfond hands of the faithful had smoothed away any features. The wolves and the *avesh* were vague forms at the feet of the goddess, the killdeer nothing more than a lump on her shoulder. Her torch and her sword and her jug of wine had become more or less interchangeable in her three hands, while her fourth arm was broken off at the elbow, though time had sanded away the roughest edges of the damage. Her face was a smooth blank—there was no way to know if she'd ever had eyes or a mouth—but for just a moment, Ruc had the sense that she was watching him.

He felt suddenly that he should have washed before entering the temple, scrubbed the delta strangeness from his skin. Coming back so quickly, coming here, seemed like some kind of betrayal.

"Bien," he said quietly.

She didn't move, but a sharpening of her stillness told him she'd discarded her prayer.

After a moment she replied, just as quietly: "Asshole."

"I'm sorry."

"One day, you said. One day and *maybe* a night."

"It took longer than I expected to find them."

"Do you know what it means," she demanded, rising to her feet, turning to face him, her brown face glowing with the light of the lamps, "when people are in the delta longer than expected?"

"It means that there's even more going on than we realized."

She ignored him. "It *means* that those people are *dead*."

To punctuate the last word, she stabbed him in the chest with a finger.

She tried to, at any rate.

Out in the reeds, when something came at you that fast you dodged it, or you blocked it, or you killed it, and for just a fragment of a heartbeat some old instinct took hold of him. Before he knew what he was doing, he'd caught her wrist as if it were the body of a striking snake.

It wasn't a rough grip. It couldn't have been painful, but she fell suddenly silent, staring at the place where their bodies met. He'd held her before, of course. Hundreds of times. Thousands. He'd cradled the spot where her skull met her nape as he pulled her close for a kiss, slid his thumb along her cheekbone, gathered her tight in his arms as she drove her nails into his back, even held her by the wrists, pinning them on the mattress above her head as her lips cracked open, spilling a moan. None of that was like this. He'd never touched her like this.

He let her hand drop.

"I'm sorry," he said, though just what he was sorry for he couldn't say. Not the action itself, which was harmless. No—the regret was for something else, something inside, an awful eagerness threaded into his flesh before he'd even learned to speak.

When he first arrived at the temple, fifteen years earlier, he'd repeated the same prayer over and over, thousands of times a day. *Please, Eira, don't let me be like them.* The words were a barricade against a childhood stalking, hunting, killing, feasting. *Please, goddess. . . .*

For years now, he'd thought Eira had answered his prayers.

He took a step back.

Like a dance partner matching his movement, Bien stepped in, gathered him close, pressed her face to his soaking chest.

"I was about to take a boat and come after you."

He pulled her in even tighter. "Promise you won't ever do that."

"Follow you?"

"Into the delta."

"Nope."

Her hair smelled like incense and rain.

"You won't follow me?"

"I won't promise."

"People die in the delta."

"People die here," she shot back. "The riots are worse. They've been worse every night since the Purple Baths."

Frowning, Ruc disentangled himself from her embrace.

"They're still saying that was the Annurians?"

She nodded. "They killed the captured soldier—the Kettral—the morning you left."

"Have there been any other attacks? On the channel ships? Or the Causeway?"

His mind filled with visions of the *khuan,* leathery wings battering the sky as they hauled people from decks and bridges. . . .

She shook her head, then studied him with narrowed eyes. "What did you find out there?"

He hesitated. When he'd left the delta for Dombâng, he'd closed the doors of his childhood behind him. Tried to, at least. Bien knew that he'd grown up among the Vuo Ton, of course, but he'd never offered details and he'd certainly never told her about his time *before* the Vuo Ton, those wordless early years hunting the delta with Kem Anh and Hang Loc. He'd never told her, and she'd never asked.

She's not asking now, he reminded himself. Still, it felt dangerous to talk about anything beyond the city's reach, as though language itself were another muddy channel that might drag him out and away.

"Things are . . . not right."

She rolled her eyes. "That's not an answer."

He took a deep breath. "Something attacked the Vuo Ton."

"Annur?" she asked, eyes widening.

"I don't think so. There were things . . ." All over again he saw the captured monster straining against the nails, those snapping fangs, the hooks at the ends of the spasming wings. "The Vuo Ton call them *khuan*. They look like bats, if bats were twice the size of you."

Skepticism and horror warred in Bien's face. "Bat people?"

"They aren't people." He tried not to think of the thing's inhuman shriek.

She shook her head. "First the Annurians. Then the messengers. Then the bats."

"They're not bats."

"Whatever. The man in my room? The dead one? He wasn't lying. Something is happening."

Ruc nodded, tried to fit the pieces together, failed. The weight of the last four days settled into his limbs. He glanced over his shoulder, through the carved screen. Whatever horrors were unfolding out in the world, the temple remained peaceful enough, a quiet eddy in the roiling current. He turned back to the ivory statue.

Forgive me, goddess, for doubting your power.

The idol stared back at him, blank-faced, silent.

For a moment, he tried to match her eyeless stare, then gave up, lowered himself to the floor with a groan.

"You're soaked," Bien said, studying him for the first time. "And you're soaking my favorite prayer rug."

"Eira will forgive me," Ruc replied, lying back, weariness washing through him.

"It's not Eira you should be worried about." The words were tart, but she sat beside him all the same, took his hand in her own, flipped it over to study the line of blisters that had burst across his palm. "I have tougher hands from scrubbing pots after neighborhood dinner. You might have been some feral Vuo Ton child fifteen years ago, but you got soft."

He closed his eyes. "That's what the Witness said."

"The Witness?" He could hear the tension in her voice, the eagerness to know straining against the refusal to ask.

"One of the Vuo Ton," he replied. "It doesn't matter."

For a while she didn't respond.

Lines of song filtered through the screen, punctuated by faint, angry shouts from beyond the walls; someone in the street maybe, or down in the canal. Ruc couldn't make out the words, but people were always shouting near the east end of the Serpentine. When the temple was built after the Annurian invasion, two hundred years earlier, that quarter of Dombâng had been stately and sedate. The intervening centuries, however, saw the money move west, upstream, where the water was still largely unsullied by the city's refuse. The old mansions and graceful homes that once surrounded the temple fell into disrepair. Fishmongers and beggars took over the bridges. Verandas became taverns from which drunks pissed into the canal. Usually the racket didn't bother him. Serving Eira meant dredging up some love in your heart for all people. Even the loud ones. Even the drunks.

"You know," Bien said, "that you don't need to hide your life from me. Whatever you were before you came here, whatever you did, I'm not afraid of it."

For the thousandth time, he tried to imagine telling her.

I was raised by the gods of the delta, except they're not gods. They're predators. And what they want isn't worship, but blood and struggle and death. . . .

Bien would still love him if she knew the story—would probably love him more, as she did all broken, baffled people—but he didn't want to see his childhood reflected back every time he looked in her eyes.

"It's bad for us," he said, shifting the subject, "if the Annurians are actually back. Bad for the temple."

"Eira's not an Annurian goddess," Bien objected. "She's bigger than that. Older. Older than any empire."

"Doesn't change the fact that it was Annurians who built this place. Annurians who burned down all the old shrines to the Three."

"*We* didn't do that. All the priests of Eira have ever done is help. Clothe people, feed them, listen to them. That's why we've survived when all the other temples were torn down."

"Given a choice between remembering a kindness and feeding a hate, which do you think they'll choose?"

Bien had just opened her mouth to protest when a scream from outside sliced through her words.

Screams had a shape just as light did a color or music pitch. Before he'd ever had words for the notion, Ruc could tell which birds were shrieking with rage as predators invaded their nests, which were hoisting their hunting cries into the air, and which were dying, their broken bodies caught inside some predator's jaws. People were more or less the same. There were the bright, light screams of children thrilled by acrobats or jugglers, or the shrieks of young women and men courting in canal boats, feigning terror when the hulls tipped. Then there were the darker, graver shouts of the injured—a carpenter fallen from the ladder, a fisher with a hook lodged deep in the flesh. What he heard now was worse—the red, dark scream of terror, just outside in the street and growing louder as, at the far end of the nave, the temple doors crashed open.

Bien's head snapped around.

"*. . . Murderers!*" Someone was sobbing, voice teetering on the edge of reason. "You're all *murderers*. He never hurt you. Never threatened you. Loi never hurt *anyone* . . ."

The name hit Ruc like a fistful of knuckles. Of all Eira's priests, fat, friendly Loi had been the most gentle, the most devoted. If he never got out of bed before noon, that was because he stayed up half the night poling the cramped channels of the Weir, doling out food to the orphans, setting their broken bones and bandaging the worst of their gashes. Every day for thirty years he'd traversed the most dangerous parts of the city unmolested, guarded by the invisible hand of the goddess or his own radiating goodness, and now . . .

". . . You killed him. You *slaughtered* him—"

The voice—so churned up with hysteria that Ruc couldn't recognize the speaker—spiked in a wordless scream, then collapsed into silence.

"Loi . . ." Bien murmured.

"Not just Loi," Ruc replied. Even through the screen, he could see the heat of the bodies pouring in at the far end of the nave. "They've come for everyone."

Her eyes widened and then, between one breath and the next, hardened. "Then what are we still doing in here?"

Before Ruc could object, she rose to her feet, turned, and slipped out through the gap in the screen.

He followed just a few steps behind, stepping from the privacy of the side chapel into a bath of blood.

More than fifty men had flooded into the temple, all dressed in *noc* skirts and vests—the ancient style of Dombâng—all carrying bronze weapons: knives, swords, sickles, spears. The metal gleamed like false gold in the lamplight. It was weaker than steel, but no one in the church of Eira carried steel, not anything more formidable than a belt knife. Like the temple in which they lived and worshipped, the priests and priestesses of Eira were not prepared for defense. Defense was incommensurate with love.

Open hearts. Open doors.

That openess was going to get them all killed.

The attackers had spread out through the nave, overturning pews, smashing lanterns, knocking askew the sconces of candles, hacking at the elaborate carvings with their blades. Across the way, they were dragging a young priest—Hoan—into one of the small side chapels. He struggled weakly, but blood ran from a nasty gash along his hairline, and he looked dazed. He was still wearing his shirt, but his pants were a tangled ruin around his ankles. When he tripped, one of the men slammed the butt of a spear up between his legs. Ruc could barely hear his scream over the din.

"Stop it!" Bien shouted. She'd raced to the center of the nave, planted herself athwart the main aisle, arms outstretched. In the madness, no one seemed to have noticed her. *"Leave him alone!"*

For a moment, Ruc thought she was talking about Hoan. Then he realized she was looking toward the entrance to the temple. His stomach shriveled as he followed her gaze.

A few paces inside the wide doors, standing up against the wall, stood a wide wooden offertory. People without the time or inclination to pray would often enter the temple all the same, just for a few moments, to kneel on the floor, drop a coin or two through the slot in the huge wooden chest, and murmur a prayer to the painting of the goddess hanging above.

Two men had Old Uyen backed up against the box. One held a broad-bladed spear casually in his hand while the other pressed the flat of an ax head up into the priest's throat. Eira stared down from the painting overhead, her dark eyes somber.

Ruc was halfway across the open space before he realized he'd moved.

"Knees," growled the man with the ax, pointing to the ground.

Uyen shook his head. "What are you doing, child?"

Ax cuffed him across the face, hard enough to split open his cheek. "On your knees, Annurian," he growled, then shoved the old man down, knocking askew the candles set at either end of the offertory.

Uyen crumpled, steadied himself with a hand, then looked up at his assailant with dark, watery eyes. "I am no Annurian. My father was Dombângan, a fisher. And my father's father. I was raised in this city."

Flame licked at the silk hangings flanking the painting.

"Then you are a traitor," Ax replied with a shrug.

The other man, the one with the spear, placed the blade of his weapon against Uyen's stomach.

"I love this city," the priest protested. "I love her people."

"You are a traitor and a worshipper of idols."

Uyen shook his head. "Love is no idol." He put a gnarled hand around the shaft of the spear, gently, as though he were taking the wrist of a wayward child. "She is the light in dark places, the melody threading the notes."

But there was no melody inside the church; the notes of evening song had come unstrung, replaced by smashing, screaming, and the eager, crackling growl of fire, which had caught in half a dozen places. Ruc could feel it on the back of his neck, on his cheeks. Vaguely, he was aware that the wooden arches overhead were ghostly with smoke. The canvas of the painting above Uyen's head had begun to burn, small flames lapping at the figures of the wolves that prowled at the feet of the goddess, chewing through the *avesh* where it gnawed at its young, licking at Eira's feet as she stared out at the violence.

Ruc stood just two or three paces from the old priest and his attackers, but could find no strength to draw closer. It wasn't fear that held him back. Or rather, he could feel the fear boiling inside of him, but not of the men with the weapons. If he took another step, he would strip away the ax and spear. The Witness's taunts of softness aside, he would seize that bronze and use it to open those men, one and then the other, from their bellies to their throats. Despite the long passage of the years, he remembered all too well how it felt to kill a thing, the perfect, crystalline thrill of it. He knew precisely what it would be like—the struggle, the bright denial in the eyes of the men, the triumph raging in his veins—but this time Uyen would be watching, old gentle Uyen, who had taught him what it was to be human, forced to witness his savagery.

"Let him *go,*" shouted Bien, forcing her way past Ruc as he stood there, mute.

She had no weapon. Her hands were clenched into fists at her sides. She was not a small woman, but Ruc had never seen her throw a punch.

He reached out a hand to pull her back, but too late, too slow, as though he were moving underwater.

Spear had already turned to face her while Ax glanced over his shoulder. He smiled a brown, broken smile.

"Hello," he said, stretching out a welcoming hand, as though he intended to help her aboard a boat.

"Let him go," Bien said again.

Ax raised his brows. "This old goat? I suppose we could let him go. He's too feeble to interest the Three." He smiled even wider. "You, on the other hand, will make a beautiful sacrifice. You might even join the ranks of the Worthy."

"Fine," she replied, straightening her shoulders, standing to her full height. "I will be your sacrifice. Leave Uyen and take me."

"Take you?" Spear chuckled through his mustache. "*Take* you." He glanced over at his companion. "What do you think? I suppose we *could* take her before we give her to the Three. They won't mind a little blood on her thighs. Just like a sauce for them."

Hate took Ruc by the throat, dragged him forward. Flame gnawed at the wooden pillars, chewed through the pews, but the heat of the fire was cool beside the burning in his veins. The screams had faded to a vague din. The ache in his arms and shoulders was gone. He reached out to seize a chest-high candelabra, heedless of the sparks scattering across the floor, of the burning candles rolling beneath the pews. The church was burning already; he couldn't stop that. The iron was hot in his palm. The heat felt right.

"Look at yourselves," Old Uyen was pleading. "Look inside yourselves. You do not want—"

With a casual, backhanded swipe, Ax smashed the blunt head of his weapon into the priest's temple.

"*Stop!*" Bien screamed, but it was too late to stop.

Uyen raised a trembling hand, but his attacker flipped the ax deftly in the air, caught the shaft, then buried the bronze blade in the priest's skull.

Bien hurled herself forward, but Ruc, finding his speed finally, caught her by the robe, yanked her back. She hit him in the side of the head—the lashing out of a baffled, panicked creature—but he barely noticed the blow. With one arm, he slid her behind him.

"Run," he said, swinging the candelabra between himself and the men with the weapons. He couldn't save Uyen anymore. He couldn't save Hoan. He couldn't save the temple or the people inside it, but maybe he could still save Bien. "I love you," he said, then shoved her back up the nave. The press of bodies was less up there. With a little luck, she could escape through one of the smaller doors, either into the temple plaza or out toward the dormitory.

He didn't dare turn to see which direction she chose.

The two men hesitated a moment, surprised by the unexpected resistance.

They shared a glance, then Ax let out an ugly chuckle. "I guess we finally found one willing to fight."

Spear looked at him with dead eyes, but said nothing.

Without a word, both men began to close. The spear tip burned in the firelight while the bronze head of the ax dripped blood. The man holding it grinned, as though the whole scene of slaughter was a show held for his entertainment. Spear was smiling too, but his eyes were empty, hollow.

Ruc swung the candelabra in a tight arc in front of him. The thing had no sharpened edges, no pointed ends, but it was heavy enough to snap a limb or stave in a skull. He took half a step forward, knocked aside the spearhead.

Above Uyen's crumpled corpse, flames wreathed the body of Eira, blackened her arms, devoured her face. There was no time to contemplate the immolation of a goddess.

Spear lunged. Ruc knocked aside the shaft, stepped clear of a looping blow of the ax.

The man holding it coughed up a laugh. "Fights about like you'd expect from an Annurian whore."

He'd aimed for scorn, but surprise flecked his voice, surprise and the beginnings of fear. He hadn't expected anyone to fight back, not like this, anyway.

Somewhere else, somewhere nearby, people were dying. Ruc shoved the thought from his mind, tested his weapon. It was too heavy. All that weight was good for crushing or breaking, but it made him slow. He wondered if Bien had escaped the temple complex. Once she was out the door, the shortest path was across the courtyard, through the refectory, down two dozen stairs to the docks. How much time had passed? He had no idea.

"On the other hand," Spear said, gritting his teeth as he prodded cautiously at Ruc, "he's strong, young. Could be good for the Worthy. Better than anyone else in this place." He met Ruc's eyes and raised an eyebrow. "What do you think, traitor? Want to serve a *real* god?"

"They aren't gods," Ruc replied grimly. "They are animals."

"What do you know, Annurian bitch?"

"I know," Ruc replied, raising his arm so that his sleeve fell back, revealing the lines of ink snaking along his forearm, "because I have seen them."

Ax's eyes widened. Spear's did not.

"Ink is cheap," he said, voice flat.

"Not this ink." Ruc nodded toward his skin. "This arm I earned for killing a croc. This arm, for a jaguar."

He wasn't trying to convince them of anything—people who slaughtered priests and burned down churches were long beyond convincing—but every moment the conversation dragged on was another step toward safety for Bien. More than a dozen boats waited at the docks. If she could just get into one of them . . .

The two men had begun to split apart, coming at him from the sides. Ruc tossed the candelabra aside.

"Giving up?" Ax demanded.

Ruc shook his head. "No. I'd just rather do this with my hands. I want to feel it when I take you apart."

Ax feinted low, then came in high and hard. Ruc slipped under the blow, slammed his fist into the man's side, felt one or two ribs snap beneath his knuckles. Ax staggered back, but Spear lunged into the gap, thrusting wildly with his weapon. Ruc caught the shaft, held it a hand's breadth from his chest as the man holding the other end tried to drive the bright head forward. For the first time something moved in those dead eyes—confusion molting into fear.

Ruc smiled.

Not much of a fight, but he could feel the joy rising inside him all the same, the *rightness* of being faster and stronger. . . .

Then the world collapsed atop him.

An awful weight—hard, heavy, hot—slammed into his shoulders, snapping his head forward, folding his legs, smashing him into the floor. He groped for something to hold on to, something he could use to pull himself up, found the corner of the pew, hauled on it, lost his grip, found his face pressed back against the smooth floor. One of the beams . . . gnawed through by fire, it must have fallen, struck him . . . Darkness seeped in at the edges of his vision while the center of his sight whirled in a vision of screaming and flame. Again, he tried to right himself, but the temple felt like it was tilting on some inexplicable axis, the floor tipping him off and down.

He knew that this was dangerous, that he needed to get up, but the knowledge was small and far-off, like a rumor of war in another country. His body was too heavy. He struggled to sit, to lunge to his feet, but his limbs didn't work right. Urgency leaked out of him. He kept trying, more out of stubbornness than anything else, and at last managed to roll to his knees. The world had dimmed to a smudge of fire and shadow. The lights were like nails driven through his eyes and into his brain. Two figures loomed over him, men with weapons, tall, bold, like guardians of something sacred. He felt like he should know them, but couldn't haul the names to mind. Where *was* he? Why was everything burning? Who was the woman behind them with four arms and a body of flame?

"This place is coming apart," muttered one of the men, the one holding the ax. He was bent over, free hand pressed to his side.

The other just nodded, then prodded Ruc in the ribs with the tip of the spear.

"You want to take him? Give him to the Worthy?"

The man with the ax hesitated, spat, then shook his head.

"Too weak," he said.

Ruc almost laughed. Bien had told him that, too.

Bien.

The name cut through his mind's hot fog.

The men before him were not gods, not even false gods. They'd come to break things, to terrify and kill. They'd done all of that, and Ruc hadn't stopped them. The memory was a stone on his chest. Bien, though—he remembered finally—Bien had escaped.

She'd escaped, so why was she standing behind these two? Ruc squinted, blinked. Or was that the burning visage of Eira? His vision was too blurred to be sure.

"No," he said, shaking his head, trying to will her away. She should have been outside, down by the canal, *across* the canal, somewhere safe, somewhere free. Only there *was* nowhere safe in Dombâng, not anymore, and she was standing just a few paces behind the killers, the men with weapons, the ones who wanted to rape her and feed her to the delta. She was standing there, back-lit by the burning church, face streaked with sweat and blood, black hair soaked and glistening as though ablaze.

"*No!*" he groaned, trying to drag himself up.

He got one foot beneath him, then lost his balance, crashed to the side.

"Doesn't know when to stay down," observed Ax. "Might be good in the Arena. Maybe we ought to tie him up. Bring him with us."

"No time," replied the other. He stepped forward, laid the point of his spear against Ruc's throat. "City's filled with traitors and heretics. We'll find some-one else for the Worthy, someone tougher than a priest of love."

Ruc ignored the words, ignored the spear, ignored the man holding it. He stared past them all, at Bien. He could see clearly now that it *was* Bien.

Please, Eira, he pleaded. *Make her run.*

Eira didn't answer. Her eyes stared blankly from the blackened painting. Bien's eyes, however, were fixed on Ruc.

Her robe had caught fire, but she didn't seem to notice. As he watched, she raised her hands. Her lips pulled back to reveal her teeth. She was snarling something to herself, something Ruc couldn't hear over the roar of the fire, the same words over and over: *All of them. All of them.* That's what it sounded like, anyway, though the syllables made no sense.

Confusion creased Ax's face. He began to turn, aware, finally, that some-one stood behind him. Too late.

Bien clenched her right hand into a fist, and the man's head—like too-ripe fruit caught beneath a wagon's heavy wheel—exploded into pulp and bone, drenching Ruc, spattering Bien's face. The body swayed a moment, then fell, blood spraying in great gouts from the neck. Bien screamed, closed her other hand, and the other man's skull erupted. When Ruc finally struggled to his feet, she was still screaming, trembling, her arms spread wide, hands balled into fists, as though she was holding something precious inside them, some-thing she refused to relinquish.

14

"We have to go back," Bien said.

Ruc shook his head. The motion almost made him vomit. "If anyone survived, the mob took them."

"Not to look for survivors. To see to the dead."

"One thing about being dead is that the living can't help you."

It was an open question, in fact, whether the living could do all that much to help the *living*.

He couldn't remember much about the night before—a lot of fire and screaming, blood, the statue of Eira engulfed in flame. He couldn't remember how he'd picked up the savage bruise on the back of his head or the throbbing pain in his neck and shoulders, or escaped from the temple, or found his way to Li Ren's tiny shack, but one thing was clear: he and Bien had escaped alone. They hadn't brought anyone else.

Just outside the door of the shack, Li Ren hunched over a small, smoky cook fire, stirring something in a black iron pot that smelled of eel, salt, and sweet-reed. Ruc had known her for the better part of a decade, ever since he'd spent a month tending to her after she broke her leg. The old woman—she'd been old even then—was a storehouse of tales and stories, most of them probably invented, but entertaining all the same. Even after she'd healed, he'd made a point of visiting her once or twice a season. He couldn't remember making the decision, but it made sense that they'd come here after they escaped from the temple. As much sense as anything else.

"Our friends deserve better. So does our goddess."

Fire flared in Ruc's memory.

"I watched the goddess burn."

She looked over at him sharply. "I thought you said you didn't remember anything." An urgency he didn't understand prowled beneath the surface of the words.

"I remember her face. I remember watching her eyes turn to ash."

Bien studied him a moment, as though waiting for him to say more. When he did not, her shoulders relaxed a fraction. She nodded. "That was just an image. Eira's not like the Three. She doesn't live inside some idol. She lives in what we feel, what we do. And what I'm going to do is go back."

Ruc closed his eyes against the sunlight filtering through the cracks in Li Ren's hut. Maybe it was safe. The murderous mob was almost certainly gone. The residents of the eastern Serpentine would have picked through the rubble already, dragging out anything of value. As long as they had the gold, the glass, the brass, they weren't likely to care who came looking for the bodies. As for the Greenshirts—they didn't have enough soldiers to patrol every burned-out ruin in the city. So what if a couple of Eira's priests had survived the slaughter? It wasn't as though he and Bien were in any position to mount a counterrevolution.

"Are you coming with me?" she asked, studying him.

There was an ache in her voice, a need he wasn't accustomed to hearing.

He sat up, leaned forward. His split lip cracked open when he kissed her. He ignored the salt taste of his blood, and so did she.

"Of course I'll come," he said quietly, after he'd finally pulled away.

"Not before you eat." Li Ren turned in the doorway, waved her wooden spoon in admonition. "And not until you promise to come back when you've finished."

"Thank you," Ruc said. "For everything. We'll come back, at least for tonight."

Bien nodded. "We've got nowhere else to go."

†

A drunk was pissing on the smoldering wall. Urine hissed, ghosted upward in fetid steam.

"Stop it," Ruc said, his voice rougher than he'd intended.

The drunk looked over, frowned, narrowed his eyes as though trying to decide how seriously he needed to take this order. The truth was, probably not all that seriously. Ruc's head still throbbed. He'd walked the quarter mile from Li Ren's shack to the temple without help from Bien, but whatever had left the massive lump on the back of his head had drained away most of his strength. The man seemed to sense his exhaustion.

"Fuck're you?"

"I am a . . ." Ruc began.

Bien silenced him with a hand on the arm. She shot a significant glance at the street beyond, where people went about their business, all of them trying a little too hard not to look at the burned temple, not to look at the people standing near it.

"We had friends who lived here," Bien replied.

"Friends!" The drunk cackled. "Hah. You want to loot the place, you're too late. S'all gone. Picked over."

Rage washed through Ruc, like a hot spring storm blowing up out of a clear sky. He suddenly wanted to hit the man, to shove his leering face into the ashes, to knock him down, start kicking him. . . .

He closed his eyes.

I am a servant of the goddess of love. I am a priest of Eira.

He didn't feel like a priest. He barely felt like a man. Standing was hard. Thinking was hard. When he moved too quickly, the world reeled.

"Did anyone survive?"

It took him a moment to realize the words were his own.

"Hah," the drunken man replied again. He retied the rough cord he was using for a belt, then nodded toward the wreckage. "What d'you think?"

The temple was a ruin, the lineaments of the graceful nave lost in the jumble of snapped beams and shattered glass. The roof had burned away or collapsed, leaving a few charred pillars to stab the sky. The northern and western walls still stood, though they leaned precariously inward. To the south and east there was only wreckage: smashed statuary, twisted lintels, all the polished teak burned to a shapeless slag. The place reeked of torched oil and an awful, almost-sweet smell that could only be human flesh.

Bien, who had been gnawing at her lip since they first arrived, abruptly doubled over, puked into the dirt, straightened, wiped her mouth with the edge of her sleeve, and pointed.

At first it just looked like more destruction. Then he saw. When the wall had slumped sideways, one of the tall, graceful windows had clamped shut. Clamped shut on someone who'd been trying to climb out. There was an arm—brown flesh charred black—fingers twisted into claws. There was a head, the hair singed away, the mouth locked in an open scream. It was impossible to know whether it was a man or a woman, whether the collapse had killed them or just held them there for the fire.

A delta vulture alighted on the wall just above the corpse. The bird turned its head one way, then the other. The brown-black feathers were mangy, matted, missing in places, the black eyes wary in the tight pink featherless skin of the face. But the beak—it looked like an artifact, something precious to someone, kept meticulously polished and ready for the moment it might be needed.

Ruc turned from the bird back to the drunk. "It's time for you to go," he said.

"Or?" the man demanded, swaying on his feet.

"It's time for you to go," Ruc said again.

He didn't raise his voice or change his posture, but something in his eyes made the other man blink, then take a step back. He ran an unsteady gaze over Ruc, seemed to pause at the sight of the tattoos snaking out of his shirt cuffs, then hocked a glob of phlegm into the ash.

"Good luck with your friends," he said, then turned to stagger unsteadily back toward the street.

For a while Ruc and Bien stood there, staring silently at the wreckage. The rest of the compound had survived. Beyond the burned temple, the dormitory still stood, and the refectory and infirmary, smeared black with soot, but otherwise untouched. No one moved across the plaza, however. The doors were all still, the windows silent.

"We need to finish burning the bodies," Bien said at last.

"The crematorium . . ." Ruc glanced to the east.

"No one will take them to the crematorium."

Ruc nodded slowly. There were people out on the street, a few dozen paces distant. The leaning walls obscured him and Bien from most of the eyes, but anyone who bothered to really look could see them clearly enough. Not that there was anything to be done for it. They had come to do a job. The sooner they finished it and got back to Li Ren's shack, the better.

"I'll bring the bodies."

Bien nodded, then gestured to the labyrinth of shattered timber. "I'll re-kindle a fire with what's left of this."

Ruc had heard that in other parts of the world, where the dirt was dirt rather than layers of mud, people laid their dead in holes in the ground. It seemed like a disgusting, degrading custom. In Dombâng, bodies were always burned—the rich on pyres behind the walls of their own courtyards, every-one else in the massive crematorium on Rat Island. Instead of putrefying into a sack of rotting organs, the body became heat, flame, fine white ash.

But not the bodies in what was left of Eira's temple.

Some were nearly untouched—a dent in the skull or a slit between the ribs, a smear of blood seared black, eyes wide and lifeless. These were the heaviest, but the easiest. They looked like the people they'd been. Ruc was able, as he carried them to Bien's pyre, to imagine them alive. He apologized to them silently, bid them farewell, committed them by name into the arms of the goddess.

Most of the corpses, though, were blackened, withered, desiccated, half-chewed-through by the fire. Their limbs broke when he tried to lift them. The eyes had melted away. The skin sloughed off when he gripped it, leaving his hands covered in a black, greasy char. A day earlier they had been his family, his friends: Old Uyen, and Hoan, and Chi Hi, and Ran. Now it was impossible to tell one from the other. They felt loathsome, like things that had never been human, and Ruc hated himself for this loathing. He wanted to dive into the canal and scrub himself clean, but the priests and priestesses of Eira had not taught him to scrub off the last remains of the people he'd loved. Instead, one by one, whole or in grisly pieces, he carried the bodies to the fire, finished what the attackers began.

When it was over, he stood beside Bien, staring into the blaze. She'd been working at least as hard as he had, dragging broken beams to the pile, keeping it high enough, hot enough to do its purifying work. Her face was streaked with soot, sweat, tears, her right hand bruised and bleeding. Two fingernails on the left had torn away. Ruc wanted to put an arm around her, but he reeked of charnel. He settled for a hand on the shoulder instead. She leaned into him, as though she couldn't hold herself up.

"We should go," he said at last. "It's not safe here."

"It's not safe anywhere."

Fire licked up around the last of the corpses. Heat chivvied the sparks aloft, where they glowed against the wan sky, then failed.

"They might come back."

She shook her head. "No one's coming back. They did what they came to do."

Ruc squeezed his eyes shut. Visions flickered across the backs of his lids—priests begging; walls aflame; weapons bright in the firelight. His head ached. He couldn't string the memories together. He remembered sitting in the small chapel with Bien before it all started, remembered the doors bursting open, remembered Old Uyen pressed up against the altar. The rest was chaos or darkness.

"How did we escape?"

Bien shifted away. He opened his eyes to find her staring at him, her gaze black, bleak.

"You don't remember."

"I remember shouting, fighting." He hesitated. "Someone with a scar and a mustache." The face was there, leering and immediate, then gone. "Did I have a weapon?"

"You had a candelabra."

His hand remembered better than his mind—the weight of the thing, the heat emanating from the metal.

"I fought our way free with a candlestick?"

Bien hesitated, looked past him, then nodded. "Yes. You saved us."

Something about that wasn't right, but he couldn't remember what.

"There's more," he said slowly.

Someone he'd abandoned? The thought sickened him. He'd abandoned everyone, evidently. Everyone but Bien.

"No," she said. "You fought them off. You saved me."

The silence was a wedge driven between them. Ruc's pulse pounded in his head. His legs felt like water. A few feet in front of him, fire chewed at the bones.

"Why didn't I save anyone else?"

"You tried." Tears stood in her eyes. "There were too many."

"You're leaving something out."

In all the years he'd known her, Bien had never lied to him, not that he was aware of. He'd never heard her lie to anyone. Which meant she was protecting him from something he'd done, or, more likely, something he'd failed to do. His mind was a sieve.

"I need to know."

He closed his eyes again, but all he found were other, older memories:

Kem Anh teaching him to plunge his stiffened fingers into the eyes of a croc, to dig deep, searching for the brain. Hang Loc showing him how to hold the throat of a wounded jaguar just so, squeezing, squeezing, his own sun-darkened, mud-slicked body pressed down into the hot fur until the beast's thrashing weakened, then ceased.

What if he hadn't put that behind him? What if, in the moment of truth, he'd forgotten all Eira's lessons, lapsed back into the old animal savagery?

He met Bien's gaze. "Whatever it is. Whatever I did. I need to know."

She exhaled—a long, shuddering breath.

"We ran," she said.

He wasn't sure whether he wanted to believe that or not. Running was the coward's path, but better a coward than a killer. He studied Bien for a long moment, trying to read her eyes, then nodded, exhausted. It made sense. There had been dozens of men in the temple, armed men. If he'd fought, he would have died, regardless of his childhood. He must have run. That's why he was there, tending the fire, while the others lay unmade inside the wreckage left by the blaze.

"You saved me," Bien said, putting a hand on his arm. "You held off those two while I fled. . . ."

Those two . . .

Ruc opened his eyes, stared into the fire's heart until they burned. He could almost hold the memory—two men, both armed, sneering, backlit by flame. . . .

"They murdered Uyen—"

"Don't think about it." Bien's voice was thin, as though someone were strangling her.

"They murdered Uyen. I went after them with the candelabra but something hit me. . . ."

He raised a hand to the back of his head, pressed hard against the scabbed-over egg, let the pain fill him, then let go. The relief was a kind of clarity. He stared at the fire before him as it leaped and hissed.

"We should go," Bien said.

"I can almost remember. . . ."

"We should go. . . ."

It was a plea this time. He'd never heard her plead.

In the funeral pyre, a thick beam, chewed through by the heat, folded on itself, collapsed in a red mess and a splatter of sparks . . . and suddenly he could see it all over again: the heads of his attackers exploding in a bloody pulp, the bodies dropping, Bien standing just behind them, hands balled into fists, her face a mask.

The vision threatened to unstring his legs.

"You're a leach," he said, turning to stare at her. "Sweet Eira's mercy, you're a leach."

Tears carved down her sooty face. She reached out for him. Unthinking, he moved to block.

She flinched, let her hand drop.

"I'm sorry," he said, stepping forward.

Mute, she shook her head and moved back, refused to meet his eyes.

"Did you know?" he asked, his voice a husk. "Before last night?"

She nodded.

"For how long?"

"I didn't *want* this," she whispered. "I never use the power."

"But for how long?"

She stared into the fire as though the answer to his question raged in the flames. "Since I was eight."

She sat down abruptly, as though someone had hacked her legs from beneath her. Ash billowed up in a quiet cloud, settled on her black hair, turning it gray, as though she'd become an old woman in the space of a few moments.

Slowly, he lowered himself beside her.

"It's all right," he said. The words sounded useless, stupid.

She shook her head. "There is nothing right about it."

"Like you said—you never use the power."

"I used it last night."

"Used it to save people. To save *me*."

She shook her head again. "Doesn't matter. *A leach is a twisted creature, polluted and unnatural . . .*"

"Who cares about the Annurian penal code? The empire isn't even *here* anymore."

"It's not just Annurians," she replied dully, "and you know it. *Burn them, break them, bury them all, for every living leach is an affront to the beauty and the courage of the Three.*"

How much time, he wondered, had she spent studying the statutes? How much time lacerating herself with the condemnation of poets and statesmen and playwrights? He imagined her still awake when the rest of the priests were long asleep, poring over old tomes, committing to memory the language of her own self-loathing.

"*Love is not earned,*" he quoted. "*Love exists beyond all limit and precondition. It is given absolutely, or it is not love. It is given with no thought of merit or blame—*"

She cut him off with a sob. "There's nothing in the Fourth Teaching, Ruc, about leaches. There's nothing in *any* of the Teachings about leaches."

"You think I need a Teaching to love you?"

He shifted closer. The worst thing was that she looked just like herself. Her eyes were red from the crying and the smoke; her face smeared with soot and ash; she was gaunt, exhausted; but for all that, she looked like the woman he had held so many times. She glanced over at him.

"What are you going to do with me?" she asked quietly, the question bright as a new-sharpened knife.

He just stared, unable to respond.

"We kill leaches, right?" she pressed. "Drown them or burn them before they make the world worse, before they hurt anyone else?" She tilted back her chin, exposing her neck. "I'd rather you do it than someone else."

She was trembling like someone diseased. Blood pulsed in the vein running up the side of her neck. Her breathing snagged.

There was an ache inside of him worse than the bruising of his ribs or the throbbing in his temples, a horrible soreness, as though some crucial organ—one he hadn't even realized he possessed—had been crushed. He wanted to hold her, to comfort her, to tell her all would be well, but that was a lie. The whole world had been knocked askew, and that question—*What are you going to do with me?*—severed the last threads holding it together. What did she think of him, if she believed he could turn on her, hurt her?

For a while, he could only sit there stupidly, like a slaughtered ox, bloodless, lifeless, but not quite able to fall.

"I'm not going to do anything to you," he said finally.

He reached out, wrapped an arm around her shoulder. She trembled herself still, then shifted away. There were only a few inches between them, but she felt suddenly, utterly out of reach.

"Then what?" she asked quietly.

Ruc shook his head, tried to imagine a day beyond this day, then a day beyond that. The last of the corpses smoldered on the fire. Behind him, a hot wind scraped through the ruins of the temple walls. Eira had never lived inside the temple; her home was the human heart, but when he stared into his own heart he found only anger and doubt, agony and ash.

"We keep going," he said.

"Going toward what?"

"I don't know," he said, getting painfully to his feet, reaching out a hand to help her up. "But we can't stay here."

✝

It was midafternoon before they left the temple. Half a day hauling corpses to the fire had done nothing for Ruc's aching head or unsteady legs, and the stench of charred flesh lingering at the back of his throat made him want to vomit. His vision was still blurry at the edges, his memories imperfect, except for the one he kept seeing over and over: the heads of two men crushed to pulp, Bien standing behind them, eyes closed, fists clenched, face drenched with blood.

"How are you?" he asked, putting a hand on the small of her back, as though that small gesture might support her for the quarter-mile walk.

She glanced over at him. She'd stopped crying, but her face was just a mask of bravery, ready to shatter.

"I don't know."

"You were right," he said. "It was right for us to go back."

She shook her head. "Was it? I wanted to show everyone the power of love, but what did we show them, really? Just two filthy people throwing bodies on a fire."

"*Love takes a million forms.*"

"Is one of them shattering skulls?"

He stopped, caught her by the shoulder, pulled her out of the flow and press of the crowd into the shade of a wide awning.

"I saw your face," she said, staring at him, then past him, "when you remembered."

"It doesn't matter."

"I'm a *leach,*" she hissed.

The words were quiet, and the street abuzz, but if anyone had heard . . .

He dragged her into the opening of a narrow alley even as he tried to remember where it let out. No one had stopped. The porters labored on, bent-backed beneath their loads. Fishers hauled woven baskets brimming with their catch. Old folks loitered as they did every day in the eddies of the human current. It seemed as though the slaughter at the temple should have scribed a deeper mark into the world, but of course it had not. Death happened all the time. Tragedy was always unfolding somewhere.

"I'm a leach," Bien said again, her voice withered almost to silence.

"Stop saying that," Ruc murmured.

She shrugged, stared down at the dried blood, the grime and char coating her hands. "It's true."

"Only a part of the truth." He took her by the shoulders. "You're also a priest, a friend, a scholar, a lover."

"My temple is burned along with my friends. My scholarship didn't stop it, and my lover"—she raised her eyes to his—"is looking at me like I'm a stranger. A monster."

Suddenly, Ruc didn't know what to do with his face. It felt like any expression he tried would be unnatural. For just a moment he envied the small ivory statue of Eira her featureless visage. Where was it now? Probably shattered by the heat.

He shook his head. "You're not a monster." The words felt rotten on his tongue.

Bien shrugged again.

He forged ahead. "This is the first time you've used your power in what . . . ?"

"Sixteen years," Bien replied, the defeat heavy in her voice.

"Sixteen years. That's the proof. We can *choose* what we want to be."

"I used to think that, too."

"It's true."

She smiled sadly. "Only part of the truth."

In that heartbeat he was a boy again, naked and baffled, standing on the sandy bank of the channel, Kem Anh's warm, strong arm draped across his chest. All over again, he felt the eagerness and disgust of his childhood twisting like twin snakes around his heart.

"I was born in Eira's temple," he said finally, quietly. "My mother bore me there, nursed me there, and left me there."

Bien looked over at him sharply, her own grief occluded for just a moment. Never, in all their years together, had he talked about this.

He gestured to an old fishing trap leaning against a wall. The two of them sat.

"I was born in the building that burned last night."

"But the delta . . ." she protested.

"A man, the Witness, a leader among the Vuo Ton, came for me when I was just a year old."

"Why?"

He took a deep breath, exhaled wearily. Once he told this story, there would be no untelling it.

"The Three are real," he said quietly.

Bien began to shake her head, but he held up a hand to forestall the words. "But there are only two of them now: Hang Loc and Kem Anh."

"What about Sinn?"

"My parents killed him."

And there it was, the start of his life's story.

He was surprised, once he began, at how easy it was to keep going, as though the history had been alive inside him all along, trapped and struggling to escape. Like one channel draining into another, the tale of Sinn's death led to Ruc's upbringing by the gods of the delta, which led to his rejection of them, to his life with the Vuo Ton, to his decision to leave the reeds and rushes altogether and return to the place of his birth. He told her everything, everything except the reason he left the delta gods in the first place.

When he was finally done, he waited for the regret to overtake him. All these years he'd held his bloody secrets so close. Surely there was a price to be paid for the revelation. To his surprise, all he felt was relief.

He put on something he hoped was a smile. "I didn't want you thinking you were the only one with an exciting secret."

Bien stared at him, her face caught in an expression he couldn't read.

"You . . ." She shook her head, laid a hand on his chest, not to push him back, but as though testing if he were real. "*Raised* by the Three?"

"Two," he reminded her.

For a moment her mouth hung agape. "You must be even more broken than I am."

The laugher poured out of him. Despite the night's slaughter and the day's grim work, he couldn't help it. After all these years, he'd finally told Bien the truth and she was still there, sitting right beside him. Looking horrified, it was true, but beneath the horror there was something else, some kind of . . . hope?

"We're all broken, Bien." He wrapped an arm around her shoulder, pulling her close. "If we weren't, why would anyone need the love of the goddess?"

"Sure," she replied, resting her head on his shoulder. "Right. But you and I? We're a pretty special kind of broken."

For a long time they sat in stillness, in silence, each savoring in their own way the weightlessness of honesty. Then, as clouds scudded in and the sky darkened, Ruc felt their predicament settle over them once more.

"We can't stay in Dombâng."

Bien tensed.

"We talked about this before," she replied after a pause. "During the revolution."

"This is worse than the revolution."

She shook her head. "No. It's the same. More murders. More terror. They just never came for *us*."

"Now they have."

That ugly fact sat between them, grim and unmoving.

"It's a big world," Ruc went on after a pause. "We could go somewhere else."

Bien stared off over the rooftops, as though she could see past the city to what lay beyond.

"Leaving Dombâng," she said finally, "means abandoning the people of Dombâng."

Ruc raised an eyebrow. "The same people who slaughtered Loi and Old Uyen and Hoan?"

Bien gritted her teeth. "Even them."

"That's a radical interpretation of the teachings."

"The teachings are radical. *Love those who cut you. Mend those who mock you. Heal those who harm you. . . .*"

"What if this city's beyond healing?"

Bien rummaged in the folds of her robe, withdrew a small statue. So it hadn't shattered after all.

"The *avesh*," she said, running a finger over the smoothed form at the feet of the goddess, "is a loathsome creature. Every litter, it devours its kits until one day it grows too old, and they rip it apart." She shook her head, stared at that ivory figure. "And yet it appears in every painting of Eira, every statue, to remind us that her love extends even to the hideous things of the world. Especially to them."

"The *avesh* is a myth."

Bien met his eyes. "Until today, I thought the Three were myths."

"They are monsters," Ruc replied, "who rip men and women open for their own amusement." He gestured back toward the ruins of the temple. "And the people who follow them are no different."

"It is our work to *help* them be different."

"We can't help them if we're dead."

"We could go underground. Carry on the ministry in secret."

He shook his head. "Underground where?"

"I don't know. But that's what the worshippers of the Three did, right? For two hundred years while the Annurians burned their shrines."

"And while we're ministering in secret we'll be paying tithes to the high priests, paying taxes to fund the Greenshirts, going to the markets with fake smiles on our faces, nodding when people talk about the glory of the Three." He shook his head. "When do we become complicit?"

"People need an alternative, Ruc! What's going on here—it's a *sickness*. The Three are disgusting—" She stopped abruptly, as though someone had snatched the words from her open mouth. "I'm sorry."

"Don't be. I agree with you. It's why I left."

"But they were your family."

He gazed down at his filthy hands. The twin puncture of the dancemaster's bite was just visible beneath the grime.

Bien took the hand, pressed it between her own.

He tried to imagine the lands beyond Dombâng, beyond the delta—miles of solid dirt, hundreds of miles, *thousands,* so much land that you could walk for months and not get to the end of it. It was tempting to think that if they left, went to the other end of the world, that he could finally escape. Tempting and foolish. Despite the char covering him, he could see his own heat shifting and burning beneath. There was no escaping what Kem Anh and Hang Loc had made him. If he turned to run, it would hunt him down. The only choice was to face it, day in and day out, to stare squarely at the beast prowling inside him, to hold that animal gaze until it turned away.

"The Vuo Ton," he said finally, raising his eyes to Bien's.

"What about them?"

"That's where we need to go."

Her eyes widened, but instead of objecting she nodded slowly. "This wave of hatred won't last forever. Things in the city will stabilize, and then we can come back. And while we're out there, we can bring the teachings of Eira. . . ."

"The Vuo Ton have less than no interest in the teachings of Eira," Ruc said. He grimaced. "In fact, you will not be allowed to speak at all."

"Because I'm a woman."

He stared at her, momentarily baffled. "No. Because you're weak." He shook his head, struggling for the right words. "Because they *think* you're weak. Among the Vuo Ton, a voice must be earned."

"How?"

"By killing."

She flinched at the word, and her gaze went distant. "Then I will remain silent."

He started to respond, then paused. The question of her speech or silence paled beside the greater issue of their survival. "So you'll go?"

The thought of Bien in the delta filled him with a vague dread, but the idea of staying in the city was worse.

"I don't see," she replied bleakly, "that we have any choice."

He nodded slowly, studying her face. He'd been expecting, he realized, more of a fight.

"Come on." It took all his strength to stand up. "We need to eat."

She rose beside him. He took her hand in his. For the first time that he could remember, the first time in all the years he'd known her, she allowed herself to be led.

✝

Li Ren looked up as they approached. She was sitting on her battered stool, stirring whatever was in that iron pot with her wide wooden spoon. Her face cracked into a hundred wrinkles as she smiled, revealing her few remaining teeth.

"You came back for supper."

Ruc nodded. "We did. Thank you."

"A shame," the old woman murmured, lowering her eyes to the steaming pot. "A shame."

Shame. Something in the word, in the way it seemed to catch between her teeth, made Ruc pull up short. Too late. Even as he paused, armed men burst from inside the shack, two, four, ten of them, some carrying spears, others flatbows.

"Them," Li Ren said, leveling her spoon at Ruc and Bien without looking up from her stew.

The wooden spoon dripped into the mud.

Ruc spun around, grabbed Bien's arm. Half a dozen paces across the street and they could duck into the mouth of an alley, if they sprinted. . . .

"You run, you die." The voice sliced through his thoughts like a falling blade. "Nican isn't much with a flatbow, but I promise he can hit you at this distance."

The man sounded relaxed, even amused.

Bien said nothing, didn't move or raise her hands, just stood there, head bowed.

Ruc turned back to face their assailants.

The bowmen were sighting down the stocks of their weapons, fingers hovering above the triggers while the men with the spears trotted out to either side, flanking them. The soldier who had spoken stood at the center of the group—a short young man, his head shaved down to his scalp. He hadn't bothered to draw the sword at his waist, but then, he didn't really need to.

"I am Gao Ji, commander of the Sixteenth, and I am taking you into my custody."

Ruc held up his hands. "There's no need for that, Commander. We've broken no laws."

"Broken no laws?" Ji raised an eyebrow. "What about preaching Annurian heresy in the streets of Dombâng?"

"Love is no heresy," Bien hissed.

The soldier chuckled. "Love is fine. Love is great. Who doesn't love love?" He cast his eyes around the rutted roadway as though expecting someone to answer, but in the space of a dozen heartbeats the street had emptied as people slid into alleyways or retreated behind doors. Ruc caught a glimpse of eyes peering out of a second-story window; then the shutter slammed shut. "The trouble," Ji went on, "isn't with love. It's with this false goddess of yours." He shook his head. "The only gods are the Three. The rest are nothing more than idols, propped up by the Annurians to make us weak."

"You're wrong," Ruc said.

Ji pursed his lips. "Regarding what, exactly, am I wrong?"

"You're wrong about Eira and the Three," Ruc replied. "And you're wrong to be chasing us instead of the bastards who burned our temple and killed our friends."

Beside him, Bien was trembling, and for a moment he wondered if she might do it again, ball her hands into fists and unleash the vicious power that had always been there, waiting in her veins. He found himself praying she did not, even if it meant their escape. A glance over, however, was all it took to see that she was defeated. The fear and defiance that illuminated her face the night before had vanished, scrubbed away utterly, as though the emotions had been nothing more than so much splattered mud.

Ji nodded thoughtfully. "I've been wrong before. I might be wrong now. But a man has to act on the truth as he understands it."

Behind the screen of soldiers, Li Ren had gone back to stirring her pot.

"Why?" Ruc asked, shifting his gaze to her. "Why did you give us to them? I was never anything but kind to you."

The old woman paused, looked up, met his gaze without flinching. "It's true, and for that I'm sorry. But times are hard, and kindness don't fill pots. The men here, they brought gold."

As though that settled the matter, she went back to stirring. Ruc stared at her, waited for the fury to wash over him. All he found was sorrow. So Li Ren had betrayed them. What did it matter? The whole city had betrayed them, watched and done nothing as the temple burned, and the priests along with it. The rot in Dombâng ran a lot deeper than one old woman trying to fill her pot. It ran deeper than a Greenshirt commander who had never seen the gods he worshipped.

He turned his attention back to Gao Ji.

"Are you going to kill us?" he asked, stepping forward, trying to put his body between Bien and the nearest of the flatbows. "Murder us the way you murdered everyone else at the temple?"

"I wasn't at the temple," the man replied mildly. "I don't like mobs and I don't like idiots. The people who killed your friends were both."

"You didn't stop them."

Ji shrugged. "The Sixteenth patrols the whole eastern end of the Serpentine. We can't be everywhere."

People had died the night before, died in terrified agony, and all this man could muster was this logistical platitude. *We can't be everywhere....*

Ruc moved forward.

"Nic," Ji said. "If he takes another step, shoot him in the chest."

Ruc matched the man's stare. "You're going to kill us anyway."

"I was hoping I wouldn't have to."

"Then why all this?" Bien asked, gesturing. "The bows, the spears?"

"When word of your temple's burning reached Vang Vo, she sent orders that I should look for survivors." Ji smiled. "The Three appreciate survivors. You could serve a more elevated end than bleeding out in the mud of the Serpentine."

"The Worthy," Ruc murmured.

Bien twitched, as though bitten by something venomous.

The soldier smiled. "Indeed. I have no idea whether you *are* worthy, of course, but there's only one way to find out, and the bronze blades tell no lies."

15

At first Gwenna wasn't *sure* it was a ship. She'd caught just a flicker at the edge of her vision, a glimpse of something that might have been a flag, gone as soon as she really looked. The sailor in the raven's nest hadn't cried out, and he was holding a long lens. On the other hand, like everyone else on the ship, everyone except Gwenna, he'd probably been watching Raban as the sailor climbed the final few paces to the top of the mast. Her heart thudding inside her, Gwenna fixed her gaze on the razor's edge of the horizon and waited. It might not have been a flag at all, she told herself. It might have been a cloud, a swell, a gull darting down to take a fish. It might have been a phantasm of her busted imagination. Hull knew she'd been walking the world for weeks in dread of her own shadow.

There *shouldn't* have been a ship. Not out there. Not if the *Daybreak* was following the course she thought it was following. The Treaty of Gosha had put an end to naval warfare between Annur and the Manjari, and part of that treaty stipulated that no Annurian vessel of any sort was to travel west of Cape Arin. They were *way* west of Cape Arin, out into waters the Manjari had no reason to patrol. The thought had been that by swinging wide enough west, they could avoid the coastal traffic—merchant and military—altogether.

Gwenna gazed into the blue until her eyes hurt. If the *Daybreak* was discovered this far into Manjari waters, it could start a war.

She'd half convinced herself that she'd imagined the shred of flag when she saw it again, a little higher this time, a little clearer, stabbing into the sky, then gone.

She slid down the lines so fast that she was forced to let go a few paces from the ship's deck. She hit hard, grimaced at the pain lancing through her knees, then straightened.

Jonon lem Jonon studied her, his face unreadable. It wasn't clear whether he'd been able to see the fight that transpired in the rigging, and at the moment it didn't much matter, not with a fucking Manjari vessel hoving up over the horizon.

"There is a ship," she managed. She was still breathless from the climb, from the fight, and the words came out ragged. "To the west."

Jonon's lip turned up. "Already you are making excuses for your loss."

"It's not an excuse, it's a ship flying Manjari colors, and it's getting closer."

"I have a man aloft," the admiral said, indicating the raven's nest with a raised finger. "A man with a long lens. A man whose only job it is to watch the horizon."

"The horizon's a circle. He can't watch all of it at the same time."

"We are well west of the Manjari shipping lanes."

"Sometimes ships don't stay in their lanes."

"The Manjari do. They travel from Freeport to Gosha, from Gosha to Uvashi-Rama. Sometimes they trade in the smaller villages along the Sea of Knives. There is nothing to the west but open ocean and the benighted north-western tip of Menkiddoc. There is no reason—"

The cry from the raven's nest sliced through his words.

"Flag! Flag to the west!"

Jonon's face hardened. For half a heartbeat Gwenna thought he was going to hit her.

She'd known, of course, that it was a mistake to be right. Worse, she was right out *here*, on the deck, in front of the first mate and however many sailors. A man like Jonon lem Jonon wasn't accustomed to being wrong.

To his credit, he pivoted immediately to face the situation. However much Gwenna might hate him, he'd risen to his rank honestly, through years of capable command.

"Stations, please, Rahood," he said, his jaw tight. "All hands."

Half the sailors had already paused in their work to watch the race to the mast top. They'd heard the cry from the raven's nest, and so by the time Rahood—the first mate—thundered out the order, many of them were already moving. Jonon had run station drills every day since leaving port—it had been impossible not to hear them, even cloistered in her cabin—and the sailors and soldiers took up their positions with admirable efficiency. The legionaries—Gwenna could make out both Pattick and Cho Lu—formed a line to the great chests at the center of the deck where the boarding pikes were stored, began distributing the weapons. Sailors swarmed aloft, flatbows in their hands.

She found her own hands aching for her blades. The twin swords were in her cabin, stowed in the sea chest along with her munitions, but it would take only moments to dart below and retrieve them. After that she could find a position amidships, or maybe atop the forward castle. Maybe in the rigging.

It didn't really matter. What mattered was that after weeks mostly confined to cabins and brigs, weeks shut up in the dark spaces of her own mind, weeks chewing through her mistakes while she was awake, and nightmares every night of Talal and Jak dying over and over and over, after weeks of being able to do precisely nothing, finally she could fight someone, stab something, kill someone.

She was baring her teeth, she realized, in an expression that might have been a snarl or a smile.

"*Two* ships!" bellowed the lookout. "*Two ships.* Both Manjari!"

A babble of curses and questions washed the deck.

Jonon, his jaw tight, stepped into the rigging, extended a hand. Rahood passed him a long lens.

"Anything out here," the admiral said as he scanned the horizon, "anything moving from that quarter, is coming from Menkiddoc."

It was still strange to hear people mentioning the continent so casually. Until Kiel's discovery of the map, no one in Annur had even known that the north-western tip of the continent was out there, almost a thousand miles west of the Manjari empire. The thought lodged like a broken bone in Gwenna's mind.

"What would the Manjari be doing in Menkiddoc?" Rahood asked.

"Let's hope they're trading," the admiral replied grimly.

"Why?"

"Because it's easier to sink merchant ships than naval ones."

That the ships would need to be sunk was not in question. If they returned to Badrikas-Rama with word of an Annurian naval vessel several days' sail past the line of the Treaty of Gosha, it would mean war. Strange that the fates of empires could hinge on the vagaries of the wind, but there it was.

"Throne ships!" The sailor in the raven's nest stabbed a finger, as though that would help the others to see.

Jonon dropped down out of the rigging, slammed the long lens closed. His face was a wall.

"So," he said. "It would appear as though the easy option has just been denied us."

Throne ships were the pride of the Manjari Navy. They were just barely smaller than the *Daybreak,* but plenty large enough to attack it. Worse, they were faster and more maneuverable. And there were two of them.

"We'll run with the wind," the admiral said. "They're still on the horizon. We can stay ahead of them until dark, then double back. They'll find it more difficult to coordinate by moonlight."

The first mate nodded, but Kiel was staring up at the sails. He shifted his gaze to the horizon, closed his eyes for a moment, then shook his head. "No."

He said it with the confidence of a man who'd been commanding sailing vessels his entire life. Another piece to the puzzle, but one Gwenna didn't have time, just at the moment, to fiddle into place.

"What do you mean," Jonon asked, his voice quiet, dangerous, "*no?*"

"The angles are wrong," Kiel replied. "The wind is wrong. They'll catch us when the sun is still two hands above the horizon."

"You are a historian."

Kiel nodded. "Among other things."

"What's the defense?" Gwenna asked.

Jonon didn't bother looking at her. "You will clear the deck. Both of you."

"If you're going to fight," she began, "you're going to need every soldier."

"You keep forgetting that you are *not* a soldier. Neither is this bureaucrat. You will go below and you will stay there, or I will have my men drag you to the brig."

Before Gwenna could reply, she felt Kiel's hand on her shoulder.

"Come, Commander Sharpe," he said quietly.

She knocked the hand aside. "I'm not a commander."

Kiel followed her down the three ladders of the sterncastle to the main deck, through the door, down the short passageway, then down another ladder to the lower deck. Outside her cabin he paused.

He was still standing there when she reemerged, as though he'd known all along she didn't plan to stay put.

"Where are you going?"

"Forward," she snapped, buckling the munitions belt around her waist. It held three starshatters, a few smokers, and two flickwicks. She already had her swords sheathed across her back. Normally, the familiar weight of steel and explosives would have steadied her. In the moment, however, all the straps felt too tight, as though they were constricting her breathing, cutting off her blood. "To the fight."

Judging from the smell of him, the historian shared none of her eagerness. She could hear his heart measuring the blood in slow, steady beats.

"You don't need to come," she said, not looking back over her shoulder.

"If I'm to write an account of this expedition," he replied, "I will need to watch the battle."

Gwenna shook her head. "I'll save you the trouble. The Manjari are going to catch us, flank us, rain down arrows, throw grapples, then try to board."

"And in the face of this attack, you intend to . . ."

Gwenna ignored the hanging question. She felt light-headed, close to passing out. Her heart clenched inside her, as though it were ready to burst.

"Can you fight?" she demanded.

"I can," he replied, matching her pace down the cramped corridor.

"What's your weapon?"

"I am proficient in a variety of weapons."

Gwenna forced down the obvious questions about historians and weapons proficiency. There would be time enough to interrogate the man after the battle was finished, provided he was still alive to interrogate.

"Great," she said simply. "We'll find something for you in the forecastle."

"You will need to stay out of Jonon's sight."

"Jonon can throw me in the brig when this is over."

"If he sees you he will be distracted. We cannot have him distracted."

"What the fuck is it about this ship," Gwenna growled, "that I'm such a big distraction?"

"The admiral does not have your discipline."

"Is that a joke?"

"It is not."

"If I had more discipline, I'd be back in my cabin, obeying orders."

"There is discipline, and then there is discipline."

"Doesn't matter," Gwenna replied, shaking her head. "Pretty soon, we're going to be swimming in smoke, fire, arrows, bodies, and blood. Jonon won't be able to see farther than the Manjari trying to scale his castle. Until then, I'll wear a fucking helmet."

In the short dash—galley, crew's mess, bunks—Gwenna dodged around one sailor and plowed straight through another, but most everyone else was above, footsteps pounding, pounding, pounding, as though the deck had become one great wooden drum. She hadn't been out of the stern since setting foot on the vessel, but the layout was standard for a Dominion-class warship, and the ladder to the forecastle was obvious. She took the rungs two at a time, up one level, two, three, out of darkness into the afternoon sun spangling the waves.

The castle was a scene of controlled chaos. Second Mate Pool Hent stood near the center, bellowing orders to the sailors swarming the rigging above. Hent was as small as Rahood was massive—a stooped, bowlegged man with a knack for carving ivory. He'd always struck Gwenna as someone who would look more at home on his own small fishing boat than on the huge Annurian vessel, but as the Manjari ships bore down she saw how he'd earned his rank. His orders were crisp, clear, decisive. When one of the sailors above bungled a line, he swarmed into the rigging, growling something about fixing the 'Kent-kissing thing his own fucking self.

At the same time, what looked like a quarter company of soldiers had taken to the small deck. Some of the men carried boarding pikes, others bows and flatbows. Their commander, a soldier Gwenna barely recognized, was chivvy-ing them into place to port and starboard, alternating archers with polearms. It wasn't the worst deployment, but "not the worst" wasn't going to get them through the coming bloodbath. For a moment she had a vision of them all dead, bodies torn apart and scattered about the deck, sightless eyes staring at the sky. She squeezed her own eyes shut, forced the carnage to the side of her mind, made herself focus on the tactics of what was about to happen.

There were three ways to attack another ship: burn it, ram it, or board it. The *Daybreak* didn't have a ram; she was designed for burning or boarding, and her two castles had been built accordingly: high, thick-walled, and, aside from the stern, almost entirely windowless. The top deck of the forecastle stood about fifteen feet above the main deck, and maybe another six or seven above the waterline. The castle itself was built of wood sheathed with copper. The weight of the metal made the *Daybreak* unstable in high seas, but it didn't burn when people tried to light it on fire. Chest-high walls punctuated by ar-row loops guarded the crew. The main defensive idea was pretty straightfor-ward: use the high ground to rain down all manner of suffering on whatever miserable idiot approached. At first glance, it didn't seem so different from defending a tower on land.

Which was why Gwenna dearly wished that the company commander had taken more than one 'Kent-kissing glance.

Holding a ship's castle *wasn't* the same as holding some stone tower over a mountain pass. For one thing, the other ship had a castle, too, one they could sail right alongside your own. The towers on the two Manjari throne ships were about the same height as those on the *Daybreak,* which meant the legionaries would be fighting men at their own eye level across a treacherous gap. An-other problem was the masts. The Manjari would have men aloft, men with bows, men with even more height than those in the castles. Walls provided no cover against arrows loosed from above. Most dangerously, everything *inside* the castle's walls was wood. The metal skin would keep off the worst of the burning arrows, but the decks, the walls, the ladders, everything they were standing on and hiding behind would burn if the fire found it.

A few strides took her across the deck.

The legionary captain was a gray-haired, grizzled man of around forty. Scars crisscrossed his face, and he was missing a finger and a half on his left hand, all of which Gwenna took for good signs. He'd seen fighting, which meant he understood the stakes.

"Sir," she said, pitching her voice above the din. "My name is Gwenna Sharpe."

He turned, blinked, then shook his head. "You're not supposed to be here."

"Neither are those Manjari ships."

The man snorted, glanced over his shoulder toward the sterncastle, where Jonon was pacing back and forth across the narrow deck.

"I'm not here to fuck with your command, sir," she said. "I just want to help."

"You're Kettral."

"Not anymore."

"You remember how to swing those swords?" He nodded to the twin blades sheathed across Gwenna's back.

"You don't need more swords right now. You need water."

He shook his head, gestured to the wet wood beneath their feet. "The deck's been doused. We're ready."

"No. You're not. The incoming arrows will have heads wrapped in pitch-soaked rags, just like ours. A skim of water over the boards won't put them out. You need more."

The commander sucked at his teeth.

Gwenna took a deep breath. One of the first, most important lessons she'd learned back on the Islands had been patience. Well, she'd been supposed to learn it, anyway.

With demolitions, the patience came naturally; it was stupid to blow a bridge before the enemy had committed to crossing it. She'd been able to see that when she was six. It was harder to use the same wisdom in a fight—she always wanted to wade in with her blades swinging instead of waiting for the opening—but eventually she'd sort of figured out the trick. Talking to other people, though, trying to convince *them* of things—that was where she still struggled. Especially talking to other people while two Manjari throne ships angled in for an attack. She wanted to seize the captain by the throat and slam his head against a wall until he understood. Instead, she exhaled slowly.

"What's your name, sir?"

"Aron Dough."

"Dough? Like the stuff bread is made out of?"

"Don't bother with the jokes. I've heard 'em all."

"Dough, I'm not trying to be a burr in your asshole." She leaned in, careful to keep her voice private. It wasn't hard, with all the chaos surrounding them. "I'm not trying to pull rank in front of your men. I don't even *have* a fucking rank anymore, as I'm sure you've heard. What I do have is over fifteen years' experience in Kettral demolitions. I've blown up bridges, buildings, barges, temples, towers, fucking *trees*. I've spent *years* of my life studying how things burn and how to make them burn faster. That's why I'm asking you to have your men get more water. If they don't, this castle is going to burn, and we're going to burn along with it."

The dead bodies rose in her vision once more. Once more she shoved them aside.

Dough grimaced, then spat onto the deck.

Gwenna shook her head. "That's a start, but it's not going to get the job done."

The man looked at her, caught the joke, then broke into a grim chuckle. "The admiral will have me whipped bloody for listening to you."

"Who says you're listening to me?" She took a step back, raised her hands. "This water thing is your idea."

He looked out over the waves to where the two Manjari vessels were bearing down on them, glanced back to the sterncastle, then met Gwenna's eyes and nodded.

"How much water?"

"Fill every bucket you have. When you run out of buckets, start filling boots."

As Dough called out the orders, Gwenna crossed to the wall. Kiel was already there, gazing out over the waves. He'd found a bow somewhere, though he hadn't bothered to string it. Instead, he was watching the enemy ships.

"How intriguing," he murmured.

"Intriguing." Gwenna stared at him. "Not the word I would have chosen."

Back on the Islands, the cadets had spent most of their precious free time at a beach over on the eastern side of Qarsh where the waves were biggest. It was possible, if you waited for the right moment, then swam very fast toward the shore, to catch those waves, to ride them on your stomach as they hurtled toward the sand. She hadn't surfed a wave like that in years, but she remembered the sensation, the frantic paddling, then the water rising up from below, lifting, lifting, then shoving you inexorably forward, the quick spike of fear when you realized it had you, that there was no way out, followed by the rush of the speed. She felt that same rush as she stood there watching the foe come on, buoyed up and carried onward by the momentum of events.

Of course, she remembered too the way those rides sometimes ended. Sometimes the wave overtook you. Maybe you didn't paddle fast enough. Maybe you didn't hold your body just right. Maybe you just had bad fucking luck. Whatever the case, she'd never forgotten that awful feeling of her body slowing, getting dragged back into the shadow of the breaker, then that whole awful wall of water closing over her head, crushing her, grinding down, down, down into the airless, directionless dark. She could feel that weight above her as she stood atop the castle, suspended, ready to fall. . . .

The Manjari vessels were less than a mile off, close enough that she could see the tigers on the bowsprits, the individual sailors clambering through the rigging, racing around the decks, readying their own castles for their attack. That there *would* be an attack she didn't have any doubt. Jonon had been running with the wind, trying to give his own men time to prepare, but the Manjari ships, though slightly smaller, were sleeker, faster. They were going to catch the *Daybreak,* and soon.

She turned to consider the situation atop the castle. Dough's men had dug up half a dozen empty hogsheads, arrayed them near the center of the space, then started a bucket line down to the pumps. The commander himself was walking the wall, speaking quietly with the soldiers, checking weapons, cracking jokes.

"Dough," she shouted, crossing to him. He turned. "I need two of your men."

"For what?"

"A boarding party."

He stared at her.

"We got barely enough people to hold *this* ship, let alone take one of theirs."

"I'm not going to take it. I'm going to sink it."

"With a three-person boarding party?"

"Yes."

The man shook his head. "I know you're Kettral, but that's insane."

Insane.

She considered the word a moment, wondered if he was right. The desire to fight—the *need*—was a blaze inside her, hot and implacable, gnawing through every thought, every other emotion. It wasn't rational—that much was obvious—but then, with the Manjari attack drawing closer every breath, maybe it was the right insanity for the moment. Either way, she was boarding one of those ships.

"I need . . ." she said, casting about the deck, "*them.*"

Cho Lu and Pattick stood in the bucket line a few paces away, ferrying water up from the pump. Pattick looked serious, intent. Cho Lu was taunting the others to work faster, but she could hear the nerves in his voice. When he saw her pointing, he passed the bucket to the next man, grabbed Pattick, dragged him out of the line.

"You looking for us, Commander?" he shouted.

She shook her head. "I'm not your commander."

"You board one of those ships with two men," Dough growled, low enough that the legionaries wouldn't hear, "and you're going to die. All of you."

The fire in the Purple Baths raged through her mind, the vision of Quick

Jak hacking his way into the throng of Greenshirts, of the sword slicing down into the back of his neck.

The two young men joined them, chests heaving, eyes bright.

"What's the plan?" Cho Lu demanded, looking from Gwenna to Dough, then back again to Gwenna. "You've got a plan, right?"

Gwenna imagined him falling from the rigging, his lean body shattered on the deck of the ship below. She imagined Pattick's ugly face torn open by a flatbow bolt.

"No," she said, turning away from the legionaries, from the trust in those wide-eyed faces. "I'm going alone."

"Going where?" Cho Lu called as she stepped into the rigging.

She ignored him, but Aron Dough did not. "She's going to board one of the thrones. Alone. Some crazy plan to get herself killed."

A crazy plan to get herself killed sounded more or less right, but at least it would be just *her* doing the dying.

"Hold the ship," she shouted without looking down. As though it were her order to give.

"Wait!" Cho Lu shouted, but she didn't wait.

Waiting was too close to thinking, and she didn't want to think.

She pulled herself into the ratlines, rope chafing her already shredded palms. The pain was good. It kept her in the present, kept her from thinking of the dead bodies she'd left behind her, or the ones that lay ahead.

A light wind threaded the rigging, drawing the ship over the lazy swells. The lean didn't feel like much down on the deck, but halfway up the mast she found herself ten paces out over the ocean. The yards were aswarm with sailors, some prepared to pile on more sail or trim it as Jonon demanded, others armed with flatbows. A few glanced over as she passed, shock scrawled across their faces; most were too focused on the approaching vessels to notice.

As she climbed, she studied the scene. The Manjari ships had split. The quicker of the two was almost even with the *Daybreak,* but a quarter mile distant and carving through the water under full sail. Naval tactics had never been Gwenna's strength, but the play seemed obvious. The lead ship would overtake them, turn hard, cut across the *Daybreak*'s bow, leaving Jonon with a choice. He could ram the other vessel, crippling both, or he could turn with her, spilling speed and wind at the same time. Unless he was a madman, he'd turn, at which point the second ship would close while her sister, lagging back, approached from the other side. The Annurian vessel would be caught between them, cinched tight with grapples, and then things would get ugly. Against one ship, the *Daybreak* could hold her own. Flanked, she'd be fighting for her life.

Gwenna ran a sweat-slicked hand over the munitions at her belt, checked her strikers, then reached back to pat the handles of her swords. The waiting was the worst. The world felt too close, too bright, too real. She should have been rehearsing her plan—if you could call a single, simple thought built atop a wobbly tower of luck a *plan*—working through the contingencies, considering variations and escape routes, but she didn't want to rehearse. Something like this—it came down to training and luck. Either she'd catch a stray arrow in the gut or she wouldn't. Either she'd carve her way into the hold of the other ship, or she'd be cut down. No way to know without going for it.

Her smile felt like a snarl.

"Commander! Commander! *Sir!*"

She didn't realize until the fourth time that someone was calling out to her.

"Commander!"

She glanced down between her legs, felt her heart clench.

Twenty feet below, the two legionaries were ascending through the rigging. Cho Lu moved nimbly up the ratlines, but Pattick was awkward, white-knuckled and gray-faced. A wave of rage washed over her.

"Go back," she said, stabbing a finger toward the deck.

Pattick paused. Cho Lu did not. "You're going to blow up the ship, right?"

She hadn't told him that. She hadn't told him anything. Still, the kid wasn't stupid. He'd obviously grown up on tales of Kettral derring-do, and a lot of those tales involved explosives. What the fuck else could one woman do, alone on an enemy vessel?

"I don't need you here," she shouted down at him. "I don't want you. You're better off below."

"Dough left the decision to us," Cho Lu replied.

"Well I'm not. Go back to the deck. That's an order."

The legionary shot her a wide, rueful grin. "Like you keep saying, sir. You're not our commander."

"You fucking idiots. I'm probably going to die over there."

Cho Lu nodded. "That happens in war sometimes. If you're going to blow up that ship, you'll need someone to watch your back. Now. What's the plan?"

Before she could reply, the *Daybreak* heaved over to port. The mast swung through its arc, then dipped toward the swells. Gwenna tossed an elbow around one of the ratlines, twisting with the motion. As she'd expected, the faster of the two Manjari ships was moving to block their escape. The sudden turn slowed both vessels, and the enemy wasted no time in closing the distance. The soldiers on the far ship readied their grapples and pikes, even a few wooden ladders, while around to port, the other vessel approached.

There was no time to argue with the legionaries, even if she'd known how to convince them. It was wrong to bring them. She felt that wrongness like a jagged stone settled in her gut, but there was no way to force them to return to the deck and no time even if there had been a way. They were grown men, Annurian soldiers. They had their own decisions to make just as she had hers.

"We're going after this one," she said, pointing.

Pattick stared. "How?"

"The footrope." She drew her knife and pointed to the line running taut beneath the yard. The sailors stood on it when they were setting or reefing the sails, but no one was on it at the moment.

The legionary shook his head. "It doesn't . . ." He gestured. "It just goes to the end of the yard."

Gwenna flashed him a feral smile. "That's because I haven't cut it yet."

She reached up and began sawing through the rope where it was tied off close to the mast. When only a few strands remained, she sheathed the blade, glanced down.

Directly below her, Kiel was at work with his bow. He looked like a man taking target practice out in the field behind his farm, aiming and loosing, aiming and loosing with an almost hypnotic regularity. When a Manjari arrow sprouted from the deck at his feet, he didn't blink, didn't hesitate, didn't retreat. For a historian, he showed as much composure as the most hardened Kettral.

The other Annurians didn't share his calm. Though they held their formation well enough, she could smell fear oozing up through the eagerness. Even the greenest among them could do the math: two Manjari ships to one Annurian. There was a hinge in every battle when the waiting was finally over and people started to die, and they had reached it. As she watched, another volley of arrows hit with a sound like hail on the deck. Like hail, except that this hail left one man screaming. The poor fucker—one of the unlucky four dozen stationed amidships—was splayed across the deck, the wooden shaft buried in his gut.

"No!" he sobbed over and over. "No. No. No." As if that one little word could somehow unmake all the sad facts of the world.

Gwenna closed her eyes, clamped off the organs of pity and mercy, tossed the dying man's cries onto the fire of her anger. More people were going to die before this was over, more people and more painfully. She'd tried to get Cho Lu and Pattick to back off, but they'd refused and so she was going to use them. Use them up if necessary.

"I'll swing over," she said. "I'll lash the end of this line"—she nodded to the footrope—"to their rigging."

Pattick's eyes were wide. He seemed to realize that these might be the last few moments of his life.

"Then—"

Before she could finish the thought, the two ships came together with a vicious jolt that almost ripped her from the rigging. The *Daybreak* shuddered as though feverish, straining against the vessel pressed against her flank. The hulls scraped, wood and steel grinding against wood and steel, while Manjari grappling hooks clattered onto the deck. Both ships still had sail aloft, and though they'd spilled most of their wind, the breeze hauled on the masts, dragging them awkwardly through the waves. Things were breaking down below. Wood groaned and splintered, lines snapped, the metal sheathing of the castles screamed as shattered spars dragged across it. The Manjari and Annurian officers were all hurling orders, not that the orders mattered. The fight would boil down to two things: fire and blood.

An arrow whistled past, maybe two paces from Gwenna's head.

The throne ship was also a three-master, the foremost of which had drawn alongside the *Daybreak*'s own. Like the Annurians, the Manjari had dozens of archers aloft. Mostly, they were shooting down into the forward castle, raining arrows on the soldiers. A few, however, had focused on the Annurian marksmen, and one man with tattooed hands was lowering his flatbow at Gwenna. He narrowed his eyes, steadied his weapon against the yardarm, and loosed. The bolt hissed by, a few feet from her face. It was a difficult shot. Both ships were pitching with the wind and the waves. She could probably hang there all morning without him hitting her. As long as the mast stayed up, hers was just about the safest spot on the whole ship.

But she hadn't climbed all the way up there to stay safe.

She slipped a striker from her belt, then scraped a flame from its tip. The fire blazed with something like her own eagerness.

"Is that . . ." Cho Lu trailed off, his eyes wide.

"A smoker," she replied, putting the flame to the fuse of one of the munitions still strapped to her belt.

The smoker hissed, then began billowing green-gray smoke. In the space of a few heartbeats it swallowed her, swallowed the rigging, blotted out the decks of the ships below, smudged the sun. Of the Manjari vessel, she could see nothing. Pattick and Cho Lu were shadows hanging from the ratlines below. Somewhere to her right, another flatbow bolt whined past.

"This smoke," she said. "It's made to burn, to taste bad, to make you feel like you're choking."

Even as she spoke she could taste the acrid tongue forcing its way down into her lungs. Pattick coughed. His breathing came faster, shallower.

"You're not choking. It just feels that way. They're designed to make people panic. Don't. Breathe normally."

She could hardly blame them for failing to follow the advice. Inside the cloud it was easy to lose track of up and down. When the mast dipped, it felt as though she was plummeting, and when it rose again a wash of vertigo swept over her. Far below, men were shouting, screaming. Some were screams of fury or encouragement. Others held nothing but agony. The ships were screaming, too, copper plating shrieking as the hulls ground against each other. Wrapped in the cloud of smoke it was easy to imagine those hulls buckling, water folding over the *Daybreak* and her attackers as they slipped—still locked in a fatal embrace—beneath the waves.

A flatbow bolt jerked her back to the present.

It tore through her blacks, ripped a chunk from her thigh, then clattered down through the rigging, its deadly speed spent.

She cursed, pressed her fingers to the wound. Trivial. The bolt had missed the bone, the artery, and most of the muscle. Still, it hurt like fuck. She ground her nails in deeper, harvesting the pain.

"I'm going," she announced, not bothering to look down at Pattick or Cho Lu, half hoping they weren't there, that they'd already retreated.

She wrapped a hand around the end of the footline, gave a strong tug to snap the last few strands, clamped her belt knife between her teeth, let go of the mast, and dropped. For half a heartbeat she plummeted straight down, out of the cloud of smoke and into daylight. The world was fire, blood, sunlight shattered across the waves, and flashing steel. Her stomach clenched as she dropped toward the deck.

Then the line went taut—burning across her palm, wrenching her shoulder—and she was swinging out and across the narrow, grinding gap between the two vessels. She caught a glimpse of the soldiers fighting below, going hand to hand at the rails amidships, stabbing one another with boarding pikes, brandishing cutlasses, hauling on the grapples to drag the vessels even closer. One man had slipped into the space between the hulls. He screamed horribly as the vessels shifted, then went limp. She didn't see what happened next because she was already swinging through the bottom of her arc and up again into the Manjari rigging.

When she reached the still point at the top of her swing, she shot out a hand and grabbed the footline at the end of the Manjari yard. For a moment she hung there, one hand wrapped around each line, the muscles of her arms and shoulders straining, feet dangling in the bright air, smoke trailing behind her.

A chorus of alarmed shouts erupted from the Manjari archers, but the smoke, which had trailed behind during the swing, closed around her once more, billowing from her belt. Arrows flitted past—one clattered off the wood a few feet from her hand.

With a grunt, she flung out a leg, caught the same footline she was holding, then dragged herself over until she could hook an elbow and knee around it, freeing up her hands to make her own line fast. Her trainers had stressed knots with a fervor she'd found inexplicable at the time. Kettral cadets were forever tying knots—at night, underwater, upside down, at night *and* underwater— thousands and thousands of repetitions, until their skin blistered and broke. Now, as Gwenna hung there with the bitter end of the rope in her hands, her fingers remembered. She stared at them as they wove the knot out of nothing, and then it was done, one more link shackling the two vessels together.

Just as she finished the knot, the world shuddered. The groaning and grind-ing, almost deafening before, redoubled. She realized dimly that the other Manjari ship must have come in hard against the *Daybreak*'s starboard side.

She considered shouting over to Cho Lu and Pattick, but they wouldn't hear her above the din. They'd either follow her, or they wouldn't. She hoped they wouldn't.

She started moving along beneath the Manjari footline, hanging from her hands and her heels. Like her fingers, the rest of her body remembered what to do, and so she let it take over, dragging her along the line one pace at a time.

Fifteen feet along she encountered the first Manjari. He was standing on the same rope she was dangling beneath. She could see him looming above her, but he was looking out, not down, sighting his flatbow along the length of the yard. With a movement so simple it felt like reflex she slipped the knife from between her teeth, then slashed the tendons in his heels—one first, then the other.

The man screamed, swayed, lost his feet, dropped his flatbow, collapsed onto the yard, clinging to it as the ship quaked. For a few heartbeats, he held himself there, draped over the wood while he pleaded in his own language. Gwenna didn't understand all of it—it had been a while since she'd studied Manjari—but she heard the words for *mercy* and *life,* then over and over again, *sorry* with something that sounded like a name.

Her forearms burning, she hauled herself up, stabbed him in the stomach. Hot blood gushed across her face, drenched her hand.

"That's for Talal, you son of a bitch," she snarled.

A part of her knew that it made no sense. The Manjari had nothing to do with Talal's death. The poor fool pouring his blood all over her had been a continent away when everything went to shit in the Purple Baths. Didn't matter. What mattered was that after weeks she was fighting again, doing what she'd actually been trained to do. She couldn't put right what had happened back in Dombâng, but she could still save the *Daybreak*.

The sailor's eyes fixed on her. He stared, reached out a perplexed hand to touch her hair, then slid from the yard like a rag slipping from a clothesline, tumbling silently past her into the smoke. Normal people would never have been able to pick it out from the madness, but because she was not a normal person she heard his body break against the deck below. She was moving again before she thought of moving, the bloody blade clenched between her teeth, though she didn't remember biting down.

As she reached the mast, one of the munitions on her belt rattled free. She lashed out with a hand, but it tumbled through her grip, falling to clatter on the deck below. For a moment she stared at it, numb. Then the ship shifted again, she tipped with it, swung herself upright, and seized the mast.

At her waist, the smoker that had covered the madness of her attack had hissed down to the bottom of its charred husk. The breeze was already shredding the smoke, tearing it into streamers and tatters, then lifting it away. She caught a glimpse of Pattick and Cho Lu. They'd both reached the yard of the Manjari ship, but Pattick's tunic seemed to be stuck on something. He was clinging onto the line with one hand, tearing at the fabric with the other. The sail above him blazed, rained down bits of flaming canvas.

Gwenna turned away—there was no helping him—moved onto the ratlines running the length of the mast, pulled a starshatter from her belt, lit it, dropped it.

As she watched it tumble end-over-end into the fire and fury below, Adare's words snagged like a hook in her memory—*There are winning bets, and there are smart bets.* Gwenna shoved the memory aside. The Emperor didn't know shit about explosives, didn't know shit about battles, or killing, or dying. The blast wouldn't reach her, sixty feet up. It would, however, shred everything around it on the deck below, clearing a passage through the assembled soldiers. It would also crack the base of the mast, but Gwenna was gambling on the tangle of stays, shrouds, braces, and ratlines to keep the thing upright long enough for her and the legionaries to get to the deck.

The explosion ripped the air in half, spraying a great flower of flame into the air. She felt the heat wash up around her. The mast bucked, shuddered, swayed, leaned precariously to the side, then hung drunkenly in place.

She glanced up. Pattick and Cho Lu had managed to hold on.

"Down," she said, stabbing a finger toward the wreckage of the deck below. "Get down!"

Another impact jolted the ship. Lines snapped. The mast juddered beneath her, began to list even further. A body plunged past, arms windmilling. Above, a series of quick explosions detonated. No, not explosions—those were the yards cracking under the strain.

She loosened her grip and started sliding. After the race against Raban her palms were raw meat, but her palms didn't matter. Winning was all that mattered. When she was a dozen feet above the deck, she leaped, hit weird, slipped in the blood, and went down. Bodies lay splayed all around her, bodies and parts of bodies—a leg a few inches from her face, shredded just above the knee; a hand curled on itself like some small, terrified animal. . . . Several paces beyond them, a man was dragging himself forward on his elbows while blood drained from a ragged hole in his gut. Demolitions could be beautiful. Gwenna had always marveled at the vast architecture of force folded silently into a slender metal tube. It was always the aftermath that got ugly.

Something crashed to the deck behind her. She spun to find Cho Lu standing unsteadily, one hand on his head, the other on the pommel of his sheathed sword. A moment later, Pattick dropped down beside him. Red smeared both men, whether their own blood or someone else's Gwenna couldn't tell. They were both able to stay upright, though, which was more than she could say for the mast. The explosion had sheared through the base, knocking the top length off a ragged stump about knee-high. It careened above them, swinging farther and farther out each time the hull rocked. In another battle, dismasting the vessel would have been enough; the *Daybreak* might have been able to break away, escape or outmaneuver the crippled ship. In this fight, however, there would be no escape. No maneuvering. All three hulls were locked together, and they were going to stay there until someone surrendered or sank.

"I'm going below," Gwenna growled. "Stay here. Make sure no one comes down after me."

The starshatter had cleared the space with indifferent efficiency, shredding wood and rope and flesh alike, punching holes in the walls, buckling the decking, setting just about everything aflame.

"Keep your heads down," she continued. "No one on the *Daybreak* knows it's you over here. Neither do the Manjari. If they figure out what happened, they'll try to take back this castle. Don't let them."

Pattick nodded. His eyes were wide, but he had his sword out.

Cho Lu pointed at the wounded sailors huddled against the walls, the ones not quite finished off by the starshatter.

"What about them?"

"Kill them."

"But they're . . ." He gestured. "They're . . ."

She made herself say the words. "They're the sons of bitches who ran us down and tried to sink us."

They didn't look like sons of bitches. No one looked like a son of a bitch when they were dying. However cruel they'd been, however vicious or sadistic, backstabbing or bigoted, death had the trick of draining all that away. The men on the deck looked like children. Some were frightened, some defiant; all of them baffled by the twin inexplicable facts of life and death. Whatever they'd done, it was hard to hate them.

Kettral, however, spent a lifetime training to do hard things.

"Kill them," she repeated, "then hold this castle."

She tossed open what was left of the hatch, stepped down onto the ladder, descended from light into darkness.

It took four more ladders to reach the ship's hold. The hull shuddered and lurched against the *Daybreak,* but the sounds of battle were muted, even to her ears. She'd encountered no one since descending—in a fight like this, there was nothing to do belowdecks but hide.

Hide or blow the whole fucking thing up.

She made her way through the darkness, stepping carefully over the ship's ribs, moving forward until she reached the middle of the vessel. She knelt, unspooled an extended fuse—half a dozen feet long—from a pouch at her side, twined it around the short fuse of the remaining starshatter, laid the munition against the hull—the side away from the *Daybreak*—then rolled a pair of barrels on top to ensure the force of the explosion blew outward. She paused when the charges were set. The long fuse would give her time to get out of the hold, probably enough time to get back up to the top of the castle, but she'd still be on the ship when the starshatters exploded. So would Cho Lu and Pattick.

"Told them they shouldn't come after me," she muttered.

The words meant nothing, changed nothing.

She shook her head, struck a flame, touched it to the fuse, started running.

She burst into the light just as the explosion ripped through the hull. The whole ship bucked like some great beast awaking from a lifelong sleep to find itself dying. It yawed wildly toward the *Daybreak,* trembled, then crashed back to windward.

The two legionaries were huddled behind the wall of the castle, their blades out, washed with blood. Those Manjari who had been alive when Gwenna went below were dead.

Cho Lu stared at her as the ship shook and began to list. "Was that . . ."

She nodded.

"Did it work?" Pattick asked quietly.

Another nod. The sound of the explosion had told her everything she needed to know.

"We have to get back to the *Daybreak*."

"How?" Pattick asked.

She considered the options, then pointed to the midships, where the vessels were locked together. "There."

Cho Lu shook his head. "I was hoping you wouldn't say that."

The midships were awash in carnage. It was impossible to piece together exactly what had happened there, but the general picture was clear enough—the Manjari had tried to board, the Annurians had held them back, and scores of men had been butchered in the process. Bodies littered the decks of both ships. The dead dramatically outnumbered the living. Which was why that was the spot. They might get shot by archers on either side, might get stabbed trying to make the crossing, or crushed between the two vessels, but with the mast broken above, they couldn't go back over the footlines, and the walls of the castles were canted too far back to even consider the leap.

She tried to sort through the chaos. A knot of Annurian soldiers, fifteen or twenty, stood bunched up by the rail, pikes thrust out to hold the Manjari at bay. Aron Dough stood at the center of the formation—when or why he'd left the forward castle she had no idea—one boot on the rail, his bloody brow furrowed with concentration, like a man trying to figure out the answer to a particularly vexing riddle, as he ran a Manjari sailor through with his spear. He twisted the weapon, ripped it out, raised his eyes, and somehow, improbably, found Gwenna. The smile that rose to his face was so genuine and out of place that she almost laughed.

"Come on!" he bellowed, waving. "We'll clear a path through the bastards for you!"

She nodded, then her eye caught something in the Manjari scrum, something she'd seen without realizing it. One of the soldiers, a tall, thin man toward the back, held something, something short and cylindrical, something with a burning fuse.

"Holy Hull," she murmured.

The luck was almost too good to be true. Somehow the man had picked up her dropped starshatter—not the one that had blown up the mast, but the one that had slipped from her belt just before that. He was staring at it as though he had no idea what it was, because, of course, he had no idea what it was. The Kettral were the only ones with explosives. Even Annurian soldiers wouldn't recognize a starshatter. Now, if he just held it a moment longer, Dough wouldn't need to clear a path at all; the explosive would sort that out for him.

She grinned, feeling something like her old confidence come over her once more. It was going to work. They'd boarded the ship, sunk it, and now they were going to get back, all three of them.

"Fuck your gambler's folly," she muttered at Adare, then turned to Cho Lu and Pattick. "Let's go."

When she turned back, however, horror slid a cold sword through her guts. The man with the starshatter wasn't just holding it. He had it drawn back, arm cocked behind his head. Through dumb luck or some kind of animal instinct, he knew that it was dangerous.

As she stared, too far distant to do a 'Kent-kissing thing to stop it, he hurled the tube.

It seemed to float through the fire and smoke between the ships, like something weightless, harmless, without significance or heft, like a feather or scrap of cloud. Then it dropped. Even with her senses, she didn't hear it hit the deck, but she heard what happened after. Everyone on all three ships must have heard it, a sound like the sky being cracked apart as the bodies, bodies of Annurian sailors and soldiers, bodies of the men she'd been trying to protect, blossomed into blood and screaming and shattered, splintered bone.

16

Even by the impermanent standards of Dombâng, the Arena had always reminded Ruc more of a wreck or ruin than a religious structure. Not surprising, he supposed, given that it was half-built from the cadaverous hulks of ships silted into the mud of what had once been Old Harbor. The former harbor was the only place large enough to hold such a colossal edifice, but for eight decades, ever since the dredging of New Harbor in the north, the people of Dombâng had used the fetid, open flats as a dumping ground for their rubbish, building small mountains of food scraps and fish bones, clothes worn and shredded past all repair, rotted baskets and rusted shards, fishing nets too hopelessly snagged to disentangle, the cast-off wreckage of uncounted lives piled up nearly as high as the ships that had waited year after year for repairs that never came, mud piling up around them, cementing the listing hulls forever into place.

After the revolution, the high priests had hired thousands of Dombângans to cart away the trash. Lumber, however, even old lumber, was too valuable to waste, especially since the Annurian blockade, and so the nine towers that anchored the rough walls of the Arena were actually nine stranded ships, decks long ago scavenged of anything valuable, glass chiseled out, rigging cut away, yards sawed off, masts chopped down. They reminded Ruc of the carcasses of great, half-butchered beasts. High wooden walls linked the hulls into a rough oval. On the inside, those walls stepped down in graduated benches—seating for tens of thousands—until they reached the round of the pit. Pressed up against the outside of the walls, as though in weariness or supplication, leaned a mad ramshackle of storage sheds and dormitories, kitchens, privies, warehouses, training yards, and all the rest of the apparatus necessary to the housing and training of the warriors who came, however briefly, to live there. Because the bulk of those warriors came unwillingly, another, lower wall had been built around all of that.

The whole place reeked of mortality. Ruc could smell the decay from a hundred paces out, even as he stepped onto the low wooden causeway leading across the mudflats: a temple to death built from rotten ships on ground still choked with buried trash.

Mortality, of course, was the point.

Death is worship, the high priests claimed. *Sacrifice brings glory to the gods.* They weren't entirely wrong.

Kem Anh and Hang Loc bathed in slaughter as naturally as snakes basking in afternoon sun, and yet Ruc couldn't imagine either of them anywhere near the Arena. Death in the delta was a different thing—hot and bright, awful but beautiful, all feathers and rippling fur, scales and roaring and gleaming. Of course, most people in Dombâng didn't know that. The Arena was the closest they came to the wordless contests of will unfolding every moment out in the rushes. And so, despite the miasma of decay that hung over the place, the Arena was a source of civic pride. There were no guards demanding coin at the massive wooden gates, and those gates were never closed. The meanest beggar could enter any time, day or night, sleep in the rickety wooden stands between training bouts and fights, live an entire life there and never be asked to leave. Blood and struggle were birthrights in Dombâng. Violence was sacred; the only tithe was devotion.

Halfway along the causeway Bien stopped, staring hard at the Arena. Ruc paused. He would have touched her, put a hand on her shoulder, but his wrists, like hers, had been bound behind him.

"Let's go," grumbled one of the Greenshirts, gouging Ruc in the back with the butt of his spear.

Ruc stumbled forward, but Bien didn't move.

"They burned our temple," she marveled quietly, "but kept this place."

"Not where you thought you were going to die?" a second soldier asked, chuckling.

"Some of the Worthy survive," Ruc observed grimly. "That's the whole point. If they didn't, there'd be no one to send to your gods."

"*Some* of them survive," the Greenshirt agreed genially, then laughed again. "But I'm not putting my coin on the two of you."

He punctuated the sentiment with another jab to the back, and the whole small procession lurched into motion once more.

Two hundred paces farther on, the causeway passed beneath a wooden arch, plunging from the sickly light of the day into gloom. Judging from the madness of beams and braces high overhead, they had entered beneath a large section of stands. The causeway ran straight another dozen paces, then climbed in a wide flight of stairs toward a mouth of daylight. The Greenshirts, however, guided Ruc and Bien off the main thoroughfare and onto a narrow gangplank branching off to the right, one with a worn wooden railing to either side. This they followed through the shadows to a spiral stair leading up, up, up, then out finally onto a ship's slightly canted deck, up near the prow.

A few paces away stood a stump as wide as Ruc's waist—one of the masts, presumably, before someone hacked it down for timber. Beyond that, built along the inside rail, ran a long gallery covered with a tent of fluttering silk. Golden censers hung from golden chains, wafting threads of sweet-smelling smoke that masked the reek of the harbor mud. Ewers of cold water and plum wine waited on ornately carved tables. All for the city's good and great, who required someplace a little more opulent from which to applaud the slaughter than the hard wooden benches of the surrounding stands. During the high holy days the gallery would be full, but those were still months off. Today there were only a dozen people sitting there, women in brocaded vests, hair piled atop their heads, men in their *nocs* leaning forward, pointing down into the Arena.

The rest of the stands weren't close to filled either, but even the practice duels of the Worthy could draw a crowd of hundreds or even thousands. Today the gamblers and gawkers had come in about equal measure. Some reclined on the wooden benches, while others stood, screaming encouragement or invective at the figures sweating and bleeding down below.

From the ship's deck, the two men looked tiny as household idols. Furious idols. Ruc paused, watching as a tall warrior with a huge sword advanced on a smaller, faster opponent. The smaller man moved like a whirlwind, lashing out with a pair of bronze daggers. The metal flashed in the sunlight. Those weapons would be blunted, but even a blunt length of bronze could maim or kill. The dagger-fighter seemed to be getting the better of the contest, striking at the knees and elbows. Each time he landed a blow, he tipped back his head and crowed.

"Rooster," said the Greenshirt approvingly. "If you're lucky, he'll be the one to kill you."

"Why would that be lucky?" Ruc asked.

"If any of this lot survive, it'll be him. Not a bad thing for you, heretic, killed in the pit by a future high priest. There's honor in it."

Bien shook her head slowly, as though she were struggling to wake from a feverish dream. "There's no honor in murder."

It was impossible to know whether the murder she imagined was one wrought by or upon her.

The Greenshirt just laughed. "Not an attitude that's going to get you far in here."

A few of the men and women in the gallery had turned at the sound of their voices. Even in the brutal years after the revolution, some people had grown so rich and comfortable that novelty was the only luxury left to them. Evidently, he and Bien had just become that novelty.

". . . newest Worthy . . ." one of the women murmured.

"They don't look like much."

"He's tall, good reach, might be strong."

"She'll die on the first day."

Bien twitched at the remark, but didn't look up.

Ruc matched gazes with the assembled aristocrats. An old man, fingers aglitter with rings, studied him the way a shipwright might consider a newly built ship. A few seats farther on, a woman winked, then blew him a kiss.

"Come on," said the Greenshirt. "No time for dawdling, lover boy."

The soldier pointed with his spear toward the end of the deck, well beyond the opulent gallery, almost all the way in the ship's stern, where a solitary woman gazed down at the fight below. She wore the bloodred robe of Dombâng's high priests, but the hood was thrown back, revealing her beaked nose, hooded eyes, the web of scar marring her cheek. He'd seen her before, preaching in the city, but never up close. Standing there at the rail of the ship she reminded him of a bird of prey. There were half a dozen high priests in Dombâng, but the Arena belonged to Vang Vo, and so, in a way, did the rest of the priests.

It hadn't always been that way. After the Annurians were driven from the city, after the last fires were put out and the final, straggling ranks of the occupying bureaucrats and legionaries fed to the delta, the oldest families of Dombâng, those with the names and the wealth and the history, seized control. They donned the robes of priests, decorated themselves in the raiment of the old ways, called themselves by the old titles, took control of what had been Annurian property and wealth—all for the good of the city, of course—and in those first months the people of Dombâng were so flushed with victory, so thrilled at having finally overthrown the imperial yoke, that they didn't notice what was happening. Didn't notice, or didn't care. If the new high priests were really just the city's richest citizens in different clothes, what did it matter? Annur had been vanquished. The legions were gone. The old faith could flourish once more.

That flourishing was one of the uglier periods of Dombângan history.

During the centuries of Annurian rule, imperial troops had driven the religion underground. The only ceremonies were held in secret; forbidden prayers whispered furtively in the dark. Priests of the Three, or those suspected of being priests, were beheaded each week on the steps of the Shipwreck. Without any guidance in their faith, the people of Dombâng lost track of the old ways. Sacrifice came to mean nothing more than killing. A fish could be a sacrifice, or a snake. A cock was a decent offering and a pig an opulent one.

Humans, of course, were the greatest sacrifice of all.

Unlike the Vuo Ton, who sent only their finest warriors to face their gods, the citizens of Dombâng were not so scrupulous. What mattered, they told themselves, was the simple fact of the death, and so drunks were snatched from the streets and docks, along with rotweed addicts, the very ill, the very poor, orphans too small to fight back or too slow to run. . . . Every night saw someone taken, drugged, bound, and abandoned in the delta to die. The Annurians outlawed the practice, but laws were weak things when set against hope and fear and faith, and when Annur was finally driven out, Dombâng erupted in a weeks-long orgy of slaughter. In the rough days of the early purges, that violence had been enough. If it didn't sate the gods of the delta, at least it appeased the rage of the people who worshipped them.

It might have gone on like that a long time, had it not been for Vang Vo.

She was an unlikely challenger of the new order. She came from Sunrise, the slum at the city's easterly, downstream edge, where even the fast water reeked of shit and rotten food. She had no manor, no family pedigree, no gold to support a private army, but she had three things that the new high priests lacked: ferocity, knowledge of the delta, and an unquenchable faith in the Three.

Before the war, Vo had been a croc wrangler. She caught and killed the beasts when they slipped into the city's canals, or worked for the sweet-reed farmers at the fringes, clearing their crop before harvest twice a year. It was a common occupation in Dombâng, and a deadly one. Most wranglers didn't reach thirty. Some never made it out of their teens. Vo was forty when the revolution against Annur finally erupted, and during the long battle for independence she seemed to be everywhere—burning buildings, ambushing patrols, poling out into the delta in her swallowtail boat with nothing more than a hand brace and saw to hole the Annurian ships. There were no ranks during the revolution, but she quickly became a hero of the resistance. Babies were named for her. People whispered her exploits on the bridges and in the taverns. Most didn't know what she looked like, but everyone knew what she'd done.

Then, when it was all over, just as the Annurian oppressors were being fed to the delta, Vang Vo disappeared.

Some people said she'd died during the final battle. Others insisted they'd seen her take that swallowtail of hers out into the watery labyrinth, poling it all alone into the reeds. Either way, she was gone, a fact that suited the new high priests just fine. Heroes were invaluable during a revolution, but when the revolution was won they could be inconvenient, especially for whoever ended up on top. The priests erected a small wooden statue to the woman just north of Thum's Bridge, praised her bravery, her nobility, said a few words about how she'd been the best of them, and then proceeded to forget all about her. She might have stayed forgotten, too, or nearly so, except for the fact that after a full month alone in the delta, Vang Vo returned.

She poled her narrow boat through the water gate, up Cao's Canal, and past the Heights, tied off to a piling beneath Thum's Bridge, got out, walked into the tiny square, unsheathed a machete—the kind the reed farmers used to harvest their crop—and proceeded to chop down the statue of herself. When it fell, she looped a rope around the wooden neck and dragged it—by now with a large crowd following her—to the center of the bridge. Then she heaved it over the side into the canal.

Right there, at the top of the bridge's span, as the current carried off the monument to her greatness, she preached her first sermon.

The Three, she said, were not interested in statues.

They were not interested in gold or jewels.

She knew this because she had gone deep into the delta, beached her keel on a sandbank, built a huge fire and tended it day and night until they came. They were gorgeous, she said, more beautiful than any painting or carving could possibly convey, and what they wanted was not faith or prayers. They scorned the gory sacrifices ordered by the new high priests. To cripple any-one—a helpless child or an Annurian legionary—and leave them in the delta was as useless to the gods as it was cruel. What the gods wanted was not a bloody, fish-gnawed flank of meat, but a *fight*.

And so Vang Vo, all alone on that sandbank in the middle of the delta, remembering what the Vuo Ton had never forgotten, fought her gods.

That was how she lost her right hand—twisted off at the wrist—although as she spoke she changed her mind. It wasn't *lost,* she said, shaking her head, but *traded,* traded for wisdom, and part of that wisdom was this: Dombâng must change. The gods wanted no more waterlogged bodies clogging the chan-nels of the delta. And they were less than pleased by those in the comfortable halls of power who invoked their names without ever setting foot in the reeds, where blood ran hot in the water.

Not that any of that came as a surprise to Ruc. He could have preached the thing himself, had he been so inclined. To the masses of Dombâng, however, Vang Vo's claims were a revelation. Hardship and struggle, formerly marks of failure, became the new yardstick for piety. Suddenly, it wasn't necessary to trade one set of impossibly rich overlords for another. After the Sermon on the Bridge, *anyone* brave or insane enough to step into the delta could lay an equal claim to the faith.

The self-proclaimed high priests were less thrilled. They held a hasty and secret confabulation, named Vang Vo a heretic and a traitor, and placed a bounty on her head. It proved a poor decision. Everyone knew where she was, of course—living out of her swallowtail beneath Thum's Bridge—but no one made any attempt to claim the bounty. The high priests might have killed her then, but they were too frightened by the mass of the faithful encamped on the bridge above—hundreds and then thousands who came to listen to her preach, hundreds and then thousands who had begun to call her the one *true* high priest.

There might have been a civil war, except that, with the Annurians gone, Vo was no longer interested in war. Instead, she offered the high priests a challenge they couldn't refuse: she would guarantee their safe conduct to Thum's Bridge where she would meet them to determine whose faith was the most pure, the most true. They would put their piety to the test in the old way—a fight to the death. None of the high priests wanted to fight a croc wrangler, of course, but Vo added one detail to make the offer more tantalizing. As three was a sacred number to the gods of the delta, they could fight her in groups of three.

There were nine high priests at the time.

In three fights over three days, she killed them all.

When it was done, the people lifted her up on their shoulders and proclaimed her the *new* high priest of all Dombâng. She refused the honor, or most of it, at least. She would accept the role, but only on the condition that others could rise to the position in the same way that she had—by entering the delta, facing the Three, taking their wounds, and returning. And so that the gods would not find their supplicants weak and wanting, Vang Vo insisted on overseeing a series of sanctified fights, duels to the death that would determine who had earned that sacred right.

And so the Arena was built.

In the intervening years, dozens of warriors—trained and blooded in that Arena—went to face their gods. Six had emerged. Most of these new priests turned their attention to the governance of the city, to the necessary questions of defense, infrastructure, taxation, trade. Vang Vo, however, continued to involve herself only with the Arena. She lived inside the hulk of one of the abandoned ships. Every day she made the rounds of the training yards. For every fight, whether training or sacred, she took her place at the stern of the wooden ship where Ruc and Bien stood. And it was Vang Vo who made the final decision regarding all those conscripted to the ranks of the Worthy.

As Ruc and Bien approached, however, she didn't take her eyes from the fight.

Out in the ring, the larger man was staggering, sweeping his sword in wild, desperate arcs. The people on the benches screamed their eagerness, demanded to see him beaten, broken, finished, though it wasn't clear that they hated anything about him aside from his weakness. One clean blow would have put him down, but Rooster refused. Instead, he danced around his opponent, flapped his elbows, crowed louder and louder.

Finally Vang Vo spoke.

"Who are these two?"

Gao Ji stepped forward. "Survivors from the Annurian temple, High Priestess."

"It wasn't an Annurian temple," Ruc said. "It was a temple to Eira, to the goddess of love."

"She did a shitty job defending it." Vo didn't take her eyes from the fight as she spoke. "For a goddess."

"Defense is not Eira's way."

"Why would you worship a goddess who refuses to defend you?"

"Her gifts are of a different order."

Vo snorted. "Sounds like you ought to rethink your faith."

"It was rethinking my faith," Ruc replied, "that led me to Eira's temple in the first place."

The woman turned to face them at last. She ran her eyes over Ruc, pausing on the tattoos snaking down his arms, then looked up at his face, her gaze frank, appraising.

"Vuo Ton ink."

Ruc nodded.

"On a love priest."

Another nod.

"There's a story there."

"There are stories everywhere."

"This one I need to know."

"Are you in the habit of getting everything you want?"

Gao Ji surged forward, biting off a curse as he brought the blade of his spear up to Ruc's throat.

"Apologies, High Priestess. Allow me to open the throat of this heretic."

Vang Vo studied Ruc a moment, then shook her head. The spear vanished as quickly as it had appeared.

"I keep going looking for the village of the Vuo Ton," the priestess said. "I never find it."

"They don't like to be found."

"No shit." She narrowed her eyes. "Where is it?"

"It moves," Ruc replied. "With the rains. With the season."

"Can you show me?"

"Not a chance," he lied. "I left the delta fifteen years ago."

Vang Vo sucked at something in her teeth, then shook her head.

"I tell the Greenshirts to bring them to me—the Vuo Ton who come to the city." She frowned. "They barely talk, even the ones who know the language."

"Why would they?"

"We serve the same gods. They could teach us. They remember things we've forgotten."

"They don't want to be polluted."

She laughed. "Polluted by a croc wrangler?"

"Polluted by a priestess of Dombâng. Worship in this city is sick, twisted. For hundreds of years you were dumping kids with slit throats into the canals."

Vo nodded thoughtfully. "That was wrong. We stopped it. Your people had the right of it all along."

"They are not my people."

"You were raised by them," she said, gesturing to the ink corded around his wrists.

"And I left."

"Why?"

"Because I wanted something more than blood, and struggle, and suffering."

Because, he didn't add, *I was afraid of what I might become. What I was already becoming.*

The high priestess offered a surprising smile. "And did you leave them behind?"

"The Vuo Ton?"

"The blood and struggle. The suffering."

Ruc hesitated.

"You can't, you know," the woman went on after a pause. "There's no way to get free of it. It's part of us."

"An ugly part."

"Doesn't have to be." Her gaze went distant. "You haven't seen them. I'm not much with words, but I don't think there *are* words for our gods."

"Of course there are. *Bestial, brutal, savage, merciless.*"

"Merciless," Vo mused, raising her right arm to study the stump. The wound had not been clean. The pocked, scarred brown skin looked like so much melted wax dripped down over the bone's end. "But when our fight was over, they left me alive."

"Watch a cat play with a mouse sometime. Seeing the thing struggle is part of the cat's fun."

Vo lowered her ruined wrist, shifted her shrewd gaze to Ruc. "Huh," she said.

"What?"

"Looks like I was wrong."

Ruc blinked. "Didn't take much to convince you."

"Not about the gods," she said. "About you. You *have* seen them."

His memories surged against their shackles—Kem Anh floating on her back with Ruc in the sun-spangled water, Hang Loc with his huge hands tending to the delta violets planted in the skulls of the vanquished, the two of them tossing Ruc back and forth through a warm evening rain as he laughed and laughed and laughed. . . .

"I've seen them slaughter people."

"The Vuo Ton won't tell me shit, but I always thought their warriors went willingly. That's what people always said." She frowned. "That's why *I* went, after the revolution."

"People do all sorts of things willingly. They gamble away fortunes and drink themselves to death. They betray their friends and family. They steal. They rape. They kill."

"Hardly the fault of the gods."

"What are the gods for, if not to help us be better?"

"Better," Vo mused. "There's a word slick as an eel." She ran her eyes over his body once more. "Has serving Eira made you better?"

"It has," he replied without hesitation.

They locked gazes. Then she shrugged. "Maybe. We'll see. The Arena has a way of clarifying these things."

She shifted her gaze to Bien. "What about you?"

Bien didn't move, didn't reply, kept her eyes fixed on the deck of the ship.

Vo frowned. "Whoever you are, you seem a lot less promising than your friend."

Gao Ji shifted uneasily. "Perhaps I was wrong to bring her, High Priestess." He glanced at Bien. "She may have nothing to offer the Three."

"Well shit, Gao. You dragged her all the way here. Besides . . ." Vang Vo took Bien by the chin, tilted her head back, stared down into her face. "Everyone has something to offer."

"She's not a fighter," the man protested, carried away by his own self-castigation.

"You were in the temple when it burned?" Vo asked.

Bien refused to reply, refused to meet her eyes.

"We were," Ruc said.

Vo nodded. "Then she's something better than a fighter." She looked over at the captain. "She's a survivor."

"I won't do it," Bien said, her voice raw but firm.

Vo turned back to her. "Won't do what?"

"I won't serve the Three. I'll never kneel before them."

The priestess nodded again. "Good. Too many people want to kneel. Not enough know how to stand."

A roar went up from the crowd. Ruc glanced down into the pit. The huge swordsman was stumbling forward, but the Rooster caught him in one arm, kept him from falling, spat in his face. Then, with the blunted bronze tip of his dagger, he dragged a furrow through the soft flesh of the cheek. The larger man made a sound, half roar, half cry, the anguish and rage swallowed up in the larger noise.

Vang Vo ignored it, shifting her attention from Bien to Ruc.

"I went into your temple once. Saw a statue of your goddess. Not what I expected. Those wolves. All those arms. The fire and the sword. The *avesh*, chomping on its kits." She shook her head. "What does it mean?"

"Symbols," Ruc replied, "for the different types of love."

"What are the different types of love?"

He hesitated. He hadn't expected this line of questioning from the priestess.

"The scholars disagree—"

Bien cut him off. "Romantic love, familial love, love of friends and country-men, universal love."

Ruc glanced over at her. She was worrying the inside of her cheek with her teeth. He'd never seen her do that before. She'd always been so sure, so confident. Now it looked as though she was trying to devour herself by incre-mental degrees. For all that, though, she had raised her eyes for the first time since their capture, and she met Vang Vo's stare without looking away.

The priestess pursed her lips. "What about the rest?"

"What do you mean, the rest?"

Vo shrugged. "What about love of self? Love of sun on your face? What about love for . . ." She frowned, searching for the word. ". . . doomed things? For things that won't last?"

It was hard to know whether the woman was mocking them or not. Her voice was level. The questions seemed serious, but Ruc couldn't imagine a croc wrangler taking a true interest in the finer distinctions of Eiran theology.

"The point," Bien said, "is that love is the *opposite* of what happens here."

Down in the pit, the larger man had finally fallen. Rooster cocked back a foot, then kicked him in the jaw.

"You know," Vo replied, "I loved the crocs." She grinned at the memory. It was the first time she'd fully smiled since they emerged onto the deck, and Ruc realized that one of her front teeth was broken. "The ones I was hired to kill, I mean."

"Then why did you kill them?" Bien demanded.

The priestess shrugged. "That was the job. Didn't stop me loving them."

"It wasn't love."

"No?" Vo raised her brows. "That feeling, like something's squeezing your heart a little bit tighter than normal? The eagerness. The way, when you really get into it, you lose track of where your body starts and the croc's begins. The way you know in your bones what it wants, what it needs, what it fears. That . . . hollowness when it's over."

She was looking out over the Arena, not at the fight winding up below, but beyond the rough stands and the tiled rooftops of Dombâng to the green-gray smudge where the sky met the reeds.

"Bloodlust," Bien said. "Not love."

The priestess blinked, as though she'd forgotten Bien was there, then refocused on her. "You're pretty quick to tell another woman what she loves."

"You can feed me pig shit, but I won't call it pudding."

To Ruc's surprise, Vang Vo laughed, snorting through her nose. "You make that one up yourself?"

Bien shook her head grimly. "One of the priests in my temple used to say it. One of the priests your men murdered yesterday."

Vo let go of her laugh with visible regret. "They weren't my men, girl. It was a mob."

"One you did nothing to stop."

"There's a lot going on in the city right now. Annurian attacks on the Purple Baths. All this idiotic chatter about some army marching on Dombâng . . ."

"It's not just chatter," Ruc said quietly. "It's not a normal army. And it's not marching. At least not all of it."

Vang Vo turned to him slowly.

"What are you talking about?"

He hadn't intended to tell the high priestess about the *khuan* or their attack on the village of the Vuo Ton. When the Greenshirts seized him and Bien, his first thought had been to flee, his second to resist. Now that he was here, however, standing on the deck of the ship, confronted with the most powerful woman in Dombâng, it occurred to him that there could be a better course than mindless resistance. The information he'd gathered in the delta was valuable. Valuable things could be traded.

"I just returned from the delta," he replied evenly. "From the Vuo Ton."

"Thought you said you hadn't been back in fifteen years."

"I lied."

The woman narrowed her eyes. "And what did you find there?"

He shook his head. "Before I tell you, I want your vow, sworn on the names of the Three, to let us go."

"To let you go."

"Bien's not a warrior. There's no point forcing her to fight in the pit. All she can do down there is die."

He felt Bien stiffen beside him, but ignored her, kept his eyes on Vang Vo instead.

"Release us," he continued, "and I'll tell you what's coming. You have plenty of Worthy already. You don't need two more."

The high priestess studied him awhile, then turned away to gaze out over the swaying reeds once more.

"No," she said finally. The word was a spear driven into the deck between them.

"It's not an unreasonable trade," Ruc pointed out.

"Reasonable trades," Vo replied, still not looking at him, "are for fishmongers and merchants. I am neither."

"You're a high priest of Dombâng. It's your job to keep the people safe."

"If it were my job to keep them safe, I have chosen a strange way to do it." She gestured toward the open space of the Arena. Rooster had stepped up onto the defeated warrior's back, placed one foot between the shoulder blades, settled the other at the base of the head, grinding the man's face into the sand. The crowd roared. After a time, he finally dismounted down, like some merchant prince alighting from a palanquin. His bow was disdainful, sardonic, but no one in the crowd seemed to mind. People were shouting, stomping furiously, bellowing their approbation. Some—unwilling to wait the necessary months until the sacred fights—were screaming for more blood, for a sacrifice right then and there. The fallen man was trying to rise, or maybe just to drag himself free of his own pain. The Rooster turned back, kicked him savagely in the ribs, spat on him once more, then strolled away toward the gate in the far wall.

"Not a lot of safety down there," Vang Vo observed. "Even less out in the delta." She shook her head. "It might be the work of the Greenshirts to keep people safe, or the builders, or the doctors. *My* work is larger than that."

"Opening throats for your bloodthirsty gods?" Bien demanded. She seemed unable to tear her gaze away from the broken, crawling warrior.

"Showing people that survival is not the same thing as life."

"You won't be able to show them anything," Ruc ground out, "if the army of this . . . First takes Dombâng."

"We are preparing."

"You can't prepare if you don't know what's coming."

"Preparation isn't about sharpening spears and testing bowstrings. It's here that you need to be ready," she said, tapping him gently on the chest. "And here." Two fingertips laid against his forehead. She shook her head. "I will not trade away my faith or the faith of the people for a few scraps of the enemy's battle plan." Once again she squinted toward the horizon. "If there *is* even an enemy."

"There is," Ruc said. "I can promise you that. There's an army, and it's coming."

Vang Vo nodded thoughtfully. "In that case, you will be glad to have been trained here, by the best warriors in Dombâng, at the city's expense."

17

The air in the small room was hot, still. There was a table with a chipped ewer of water but no cups, two chairs, one of which was missing a seat, and a stool. Sunlight lanced through cracks in the walls, illuminating motes of dust. After their meeting with Vang Vo, Gao Ji had escorted them here, to a wooden chamber buried deep inside the belly of one of the abandoned ships, shoved them inside, then locked the door. There'd been no explanation about what to expect next, or how long they might have to wait for it. Bien paced back and forth several times, as though measuring the length of the room, then sat on the stool. Ruc remained standing.

"I'm sorry," he said, after the footsteps had retreated down the corridor outside.

Bien snorted. "For burning down our temple and murdering our friends?"

"For not getting us out of the city when we had the chance." He shook his head. "I shouldn't have trusted Li Ren. Should have taken us straight to the delta . . ."

As he was speaking, Bien rose abruptly from the stool, crossed the small room, took him firmly by the shirt with both hands.

"If you continue talking about me," she said, voice deceptively mild, "as though I were a small child or a delicate trinket to be transported from one place to the next with no volition of my own, joining the Worthy is going to be the least of your problems."

Her hesitation from earlier had vanished. Her gaze was dark, fierce, sober, brave, her face inches from his own.

"In that case," he replied after a long pause, "*I'd* like to be the trinket. You have my full permission to transport me out of here."

"You're not pretty enough to be a trinket."

"Hasn't stopped you from keeping me all these years."

He could feel the heat of her fists against his chest, her breath warm on his face. It didn't matter. She might as well have been on the other side of the delta.

Bien seemed to feel the same distance in the same moment. She loosened her grip on the front of his shirt, smoothed down the fabric, then turned away.

"We can't stay here."

"I think most prisoners feel that way."

"This isn't a prison," she said, testing the latch on the door, then running her fingers over the rusting strap hinges. "It's a slaughterhouse. You saw that Rooster person down in the pit earlier. There will be dozens like him. If we don't escape, we die."

Ruc watched as she probed the hinges, the boards of the door, the frame, the latch again, the hinges again, testing the unyielding iron and wood over and over.

"It's not dying I'm worried about," he said quietly.

"That seems short-sighted."

"It's killing."

Bien went still. She didn't turn.

Her voice when she spoke was barely a whisper. "We don't have to kill."

"That's what they brought us here to do."

"Then we *refuse*."

He considered that. The histories of the order were filled with tales of men and women martyred in far-off lands, the words of the goddess on their lips even as the steel slid between their ribs or the fire lapped at their naked flesh. *You are beautiful,* St. Henseln told the Edish as they staked him down to the ice, slit his skin, and left him for the great white bears. *There is more to you and better*—the ivory piercing him, pinning him—*than this act of violence. I see it shining in your faces, blazing in your eyes.*

Unlike Henseln, however, Ruc was no saint.

Alone, he might have managed the sacrifice. He'd spent half a lifetime starving the instincts of his youth, bridling the violence, learning to find something more in life than the raw, bloody struggle. Without Bien, he might have found a way to bow his head when he was brought among the Worthy, to accept the blows, the broken bones, his own bloody end as it closed down around him. He might have gone to his grave with bravery and grace, faithful to the goddess who had raised him up and saved him from the swamps.

Or maybe that was just a story he told himself.

In truth, he hadn't buried the past nearly as deeply as he'd hoped. Returning to the delta had dredged up all the old bones. It had felt good to be out among the rushes, paddling the narrow boat, watching the crocs sliding through the silty water. Eira help him, it had felt good to kill the snake. A snake wasn't a person, of course—Eira held no prohibition against the killing of animals—but he knew how easily that hot, red eagerness could slide into evil. When the men came to burn the temple, when they bared their blades and began hacking down his friends, a part of him had been glad.

"You're right," he said. "We need to escape."

Bien shook her head. "This ship may be a hundred years old, but the door is solid."

"Can you . . ." Ruc hesitated. He wasn't even sure of the right words.

Bien's shoulders slumped. "I don't want to do that," she murmured, not looking at him. "I don't want to *be* that."

He nodded. "All right."

Despite the fact that he'd been the one asking, it was almost a relief to hear her refuse. The thought of her giving up a fight she'd been waging her entire life, giving it up just because he'd asked, sickened him almost as much as the idea of his own eroding faith. As long as she stayed strong, he could lean on her.

She didn't look strong.

"It's awful," she said quietly, "to have this thing inside you, this *terrible* thing."

"I know."

"I tell myself that I can ignore it, defeat it, that it doesn't have to be a part of me, but that doesn't make it go away."

He nodded, mute.

Bien blew out a weary breath.

"It doesn't matter what I want, does it?"

"Yes," Ruc replied. "It does."

He stepped behind her, wrapped an arm around her waist, pressed his lips into her dark hair. It reeked of smoke and blood, but beneath it all he could still smell *her,* the woman who, as much as Eira herself, had saved him from the delta.

"There will be other opportunities to escape," he said quietly. "Other ways."

She slipped free of his encircling arm. "Or there won't." Her face hardened.

"Bien—"

"If I do this," she said, staring at the door, "then at least the . . . whatever it is inside me . . . it doesn't have to be *all* evil."

"You aren't evil, Bien."

"The Teachings tell us to love everyone, even those who hate us. What did I do when those men came for you? I killed them. Two men, utterly defenseless, and I shattered their skulls."

Ruc stared at her. He could still see the blood-slicked bronze of the weapons. "They weren't defenseless."

She met his gaze without flinching. "Against me they were."

Before he could reply, she turned away from him, pressed her hand against the lock, and closed her eyes.

It felt suddenly hot in the small chamber, close, as though the air had grown too thick to breathe.

Bien's jaw tightened, the muscles in her cheek clenched, the cords of her neck strained beneath the skin. The heat radiating from her face deepened from yellow into baking reddish-black. Sweat slicked her brow, as though she weren't just standing there but laboring beneath a crushing load. An anguished moan slipped from between her gritted teeth.

Nothing happened.

He'd half expected some unseen force to rip the door from its hinges. Instead, she let out a desperate, shuddering breath, then slumped against the wall. The raging heat beneath her skin faded to a bruised yellow. Ruc caught her as she tottered backward.

"Bien—"

She raised a feeble hand. "I'm all right."

He lowered her gently onto the stool, took the ewer from the table, lifted it to her lips. She took a shallow sip, then another, then motioned it away.

"Too bad," she managed, "that the door isn't made out of human skulls."

Her face was so bleak that it took Ruc a moment to realize she was joking. "What happened?"

"I don't know." She stared down at her empty hands, as though the answer had been there before she lost her hold on it. "I've only used my power"—she shuddered—"a few times before. Never on purpose."

"And this time?"

"I tried to concentrate, to feel something like what I felt the other night, back at the temple." She closed her eyes. "I . . . *reached* for it, for the power . . ." She shook her head in frustration. "I don't have the words for any of this. It was like trying to breathe in a place with no air, or to suck water through a reed, but the reed was blocked. . . ."

She trailed off.

Ruc glanced around the dark, cramped room, turned back to Bien. "What is your well?"

It felt strange to ask the question out loud, almost like asking *How many people have you murdered?* Her eyes snapped open. She stared at him a moment, as though the words made no sense, then shook her head. "I don't know."

"You don't know?"

Every story about a leach—from bridge market gossip to the elaborate plays of the city maskers—led, at some point, to the question of wells. Every leach had one, some aspect of the world from which they drew their power. As far as Ruc understood, a well could be anything—stone or salt, wood or water. There were even tales of leaches who drained power from more obscure sources—dreams, pain, the fear of their foes. It was hard to know what to believe, in part because leaches hid their abilities, in part because they were killed as soon as those abilities were discovered. Very occasionally, a leach ended up imprisoned—there were infusions that could blunt their power—but the alternatives—lynching, burning, drowning—were safer. Safer and, to a blood-hungry mob, far more satisfying.

Still, for all the obscurity in the stories, Ruc had always believed that a leach would know her *own* well.

Bien, however, just shook her head.

"I haven't been experimenting with it," she snapped. "I've spent all this time trying to *deny* it."

Ruc frowned, glanced around the room once more—wooden walls, wooden ceiling and floor, wooden table, wooden stool. "I guess it's not wood."

Bien managed a chuckle. "Or it *is* wood, and I just don't know how to use it. Or I can only use it when I'm not trying. Or when I'm angry . . ." She scrubbed her face with her hands. "If I have to be some twisted perversion of nature, I'd at least like to be *good* at it." She looked up at him. "I'm sorry, Ruc. I can't get us out."

He crossed the small space, knelt down before her, took her shirt in his hands. "If you continue talking about me as though I were a small child or delicate trinket to be transported from once place to the next . . ."

"All right," she said, laughing in spite of herself. "*All right.* It's cruel to use a woman's own words against her."

He started to reply, then stopped. Boots were approaching down the corridor outside. Bien's laughter evaporated. She met his eyes for a moment, then they both rose to face whatever was coming next. Ruc braced himself for more Greenshirts, more prodding with spears, more abuse, but when the door finally swung open—after what seemed like a protracted battle with the lock and latch—the man standing in the frame didn't have a spear and he certainly didn't look like a soldier. He was two heads shorter than Ruc, at least twenty years older, and built like an ill-stuffed sack of grain, the kind of person who would have drawn no attention whatsoever working a booth in one of the markets or drinking late in a tavern. Standing there, however, deep in the hulk of the rotting ship, he seemed utterly out of place, even more so given the four liveried guards looming in the passageway behind him.

He held up a mutilated hand—two fingers had been torn away long ago—in a strange sort of greeting, then scrubbed the sweat from his brow with the palm.

"Apologies! A thousand apologies!" He glanced around the room, ran his fingers through his scraggly hair. "No food," he exclaimed, shaking his head, "warm water, a day in darkness. This is a—" He paused, tutted his dissatisfaction as he searched for the word. "—a *travesty*. A *miscarriage* of the respect owed to the newest members of our . . . hallowed ranks." He shook his head even more vigorously. "I tell that woman over and over that this is no way to introduce our newest warriors to the . . . the valor, and brilliance, and the . . . the *sublimity* of struggle."

Bien studied him. "Who are you?"

"Ha!" the man exclaimed. "Of course! *My* manners, too—deplorable and only growing worse. I am your trainer, and my name, my *name*"—he sketched a small bow—"is Goatface."

Ruc stared.

There were dozens of trainers in the Arena, dozens of trainers for hundreds of Worthy, but only a few were household names: the Nun, Small Cao, Trun Le . . . and Goatface. Those four had been responsible for training the only warriors to triumph in the Arena, survive the delta, and rise to the rank of high priest. They were nearly as legendary as Vang Vo herself. Every year during the high holy days, as the Worthy hacked one another apart on the hot sand, the streets of Dombâng were abuzz with stories of the trainers, of their brilliance and brutality.

Goatface looked neither brutal nor brilliant. The most Ruc could say for him was that he'd come by his name honestly: his tiny eyes were set too wide in a too-narrow face that tapered into the gray-black of a withered little triangular beard. The notion that he had trained some of the most savage, most feared of Dombâng's Worthy seemed almost laughably implausible. The hard-eyed men behind him weren't laughing, however, and neither, for all his regretful muttering, was Goatface.

"Come," the trainer said, gesturing them through the door into the corridor beyond. "*Come.* Enough . . . enough . . . *languishing* in this darkness. Allow me to show you to the yard."

"The yard?" Bien asked.

Goatface pressed the heel of his hand to his forehead, as though something inside his skull pained him.

"Did she not *explain* to you? Has no one explained to you?"

"It's been explained," Ruc replied, "that we're being conscripted into the ranks of the Worthy. Beyond that . . ."

The trainer shook his head. "I should be accustomed to such . . . such . . . *indecorousness* by now. Some come within these walls willingly, of course, and they, *they* are treated on their first day as honored guests. The—what word did you use?—the *conscripted,* on the other hand, are shown no such honor. *Toss them in darkness, then give them to Goatface.*" He looked ready to spit, then gestured them even more urgently into the shadowy passageway. "Allow me to make what paltry amends I may."

Bien and Ruc followed him out the open door. The guards stepped back against the wall, allowed them to pass, then formed up again behind them— four men, two armed with loaded flatbows, two with spears. No wonder Goat-face seemed unconcerned that they might try to fight their way free.

"So," Bien said, as they descended a steep, creaking stair. "You will be our trainer?"

Goatface nodded his head without glancing back. "Of course! Few of the others will work with . . ." He hemmed for a moment, suddenly awkward, then heaved up a shrug. "Forgive the hideous nomenclature, but few of the other trainers will work with the chum."

"Chum?" Ruc asked, raising a brow.

"A disgusting slur, of course, but it is, regrettably, *regrettably,* the term down in the yard for those who arrive here . . . not of their own choice. Those who show the least promise."

"Why *chum*?" Bien demanded, a note in her voice that might have been fear or anger or both.

The trainer shook his head. "Those who *choose* the path of the Worthy spend years in preparation before they step through these gates—sword work, spear work, knife work—honing their bodies and their minds in order to be worthy of our gods. They believe,"—he glanced back, concern in his dark eyes—"falsely, mind you—they believe *falsely*—that your lack of preparation will render you easy targets, that you will be cut apart in the ring as if you were . . . well . . . chum."

Behind them, one of the guards made a sound that might have been a cough or a chuckle.

"Not to fear!" Goatface continued. "As your trainer, I can promise you this—if you *do* prove . . . *foreordained* to die in the Arena, I will teach you to die gloriously and with honor."

"How comforting," Ruc muttered.

Bien walked in grim silence at his side.

The passage led them out through a door carved in the sloping hull of the ship and into a warren of wooden structures built beneath the stands of the Arena, a dim labyrinth that managed to seem both cramped and never-ending. For the most part they walked on wooden planks raised a few inches above the mud. Occasionally there were no planks. When Ruc looked up he could make out scaffolding in the gloom above, and beyond that, blades of light slicing through the gaps of the Arena seating. The boots of the people walking or stomping above rumbled like thunder.

Goatface spoke effortlessly over the noise.

"Storerooms," he said, gesturing vaguely to locked doors. "Guards' quarters. Food. Weapons. The Arena is a . . . city within a city. A veritable *metropolis* unto itself."

The trainer seemed always to be searching for the right word, gesturing with the three fingers of his mangled hand, squinting at nothing in particular as though the choicest phrase was lurking somewhere nearby, always just out of sight.

"How many Worthy are there?" Ruc asked.

"The number varies from year to year. On this *particular* year, you will be pleased to hear, the Arena houses ninety-two."

Why he should be pleased to hear that, Ruc had no idea. Ninety-two warriors, all intent on Bien's slaughter and his own. The full weight of what faced them settled down on him like lead.

After what seemed like a long time they reached a door. Goatface stopped before it, rummaged around inside his tunic, emerged with a heavy steel key, and slid it into the lock. When it turned, he leaned his stooped shoulder against the weight until it swung ponderously open. Noise washed over them—grunting, shouting, the hollow *thwock* of wooden training weapons and the louder crash of bronze against bronze. Ruc raised a hand to shade his eyes from the rich, late-day light.

The space was huge, almost as large as the pit at the center of the Arena, though rectangular rather than circular. The wall through which they had entered was the outside of the Arena itself. On the other three sides of the yard stood wooden buildings of two or three stories. Just beyond them loomed a second wooden wall at least ten paces high. Ruc caught a glimpse of guards moving back and forth atop it, polished helms and weapons flashing in the sun.

It was the warriors ankle-deep in the churned-up mud of the yard itself, however, that drew his attention.

At a glance, it seemed as though every one of Dombâng's ninety-two Worthy was packed into the yard. Some lounged around the perimeter, chatting, checking weapons, drinking from ladles and gourds, heckling. One man sat on a log, blood sheeting down his face, while another stitched shut a gash across his forehead. In a far corner, half a dozen men and women trained with a variety of stone and iron weights, tossing them back and forth, lifting them from the ground or pressing them over their heads, sweat-slick muscles bulging with the strain. Two or three people were running the perimeter. Most of Dombâng's Worthy, however, were busy with the furious, holy work of battering one another into the sodden dirt.

Some fought with wooden swords or staves, others with their bare hands. Ruc watched as the largest man he'd ever seen attacked a woman half his size, roaring as he closed in, swinging his fists. The woman ducked the first blow, but instead of retreating, slid close to the giant, reached up to put a hand on his shoulder, the movement incongruously graceful, as though she were preparing to dance, then leapt up, wrapping her legs around his waist, locking her heels behind him. The man bellowed, tried to strike down at her, but she was too close, her arms hooked up behind his shoulders, face pressed against his chest, looking for all the world like a newborn reed squirrel clinging to its mother's chest. Her opponent battered at her back, but the angle was wrong, robbing him of most of his power, and after a few heartbeats he gave up, cursed, then hurled himself down atop the woman. If the ground had been hard, the force of the blow might have broken her back. As it was, however, the two of them hit the mud with a soft squelch. The man grinned a vicious, broken-toothed grin, grunted, ground his body down hard. The sheer weight of it looked debilitating, but the woman unhooked her legs, shifted her hands, and when the huge man reared up to consider the damage he'd wrought, she struck, snake quick, rolling back onto her shoulders, hauling him close with one arm, then tossing her legs around the giant's neck. The man bellowed, thrashed, but she tightened her thighs. He managed to rise to one knee, struggled to get his other leg beneath him as his eyes bulged and lips turned purple, then collapsed into the mud. The woman held the choke for another heartbeat or three, then rolled off, stood up, spat out something that might have been mud or blood or both, and kicked the unconscious man casually in the gut.

"Welcome," Goatface announced grandly, sweeping a scarred hand over the yard. "*Welcome*. This place is now your home. *More* than your home. It is a . . . a *sanctuary*."

"Sanctuary?" Bien asked, her voice thick with disgust.

"Indeed," the trainer nodded. "*Indeed*. The work we do here is sacred work. This space is a sacred space."

Unbidden, the memory of Eira's temple filled Ruc's mind—the soft light of the white lanterns, the smell of incense and flowering night blossom, the voices twined in hymn and prayer, the polished wood, the tapestries and statuary, the wooden boards of the floor worn smooth as glass. . . . It was a place—

had been before it burned—that raised people out of the mundane, that made them kinder, gentler, better. *That* had been sacred. The yard of the Worthy was a kennel for animals, a filthy, fenced-in scrap of land where people became beasts.

"I don't need to tell you, I'm sure," Goatface continued, smiling his yellow grin, "that at this point any . . . how shall I put it . . . *changes of heart,* any second-guessing of the providence that brought you here, well it's all . . . what's the phrase? *Strongly discouraged.* It would be imprudent, now that you have joined us, to try to leave these walls."

"Imprudent," Bien observed, "seems like a dramatic understatement."

There were stories of Worthy who fled. They never made it far. The city's worship of the men and women who joined the bloody ranks had a dark side: a collective fury against any apostates who attempted to escape. Ruc had seen the bodies—everyone who lived in Dombâng had seen the bodies—strung up from the bridges or lashed to pilings. Sometimes the Arena guards hunted them down. More often, the people of the city took the execution onto themselves. Love might be a simple, sustaining meal, but hatred was a delicacy.

"Not that you would *desire* to leave, of course!" Goatface smiled, spread his arms wide, gestured with his hacked-up hand as though presenting them with a palace. "This is your home now, and these . . . *exquisite* warriors are your family."

That family appeared to have finally noticed the new arrivals. The warriors closest to Ruc and Bien turned first, hard eyes narrowing. Slowly, however, word traveled around the open space of the yard. The fighters paused in their conversations, left off their sparring, slung weapons over scarred shoulders. Gradually, a thick silence settled.

"What's happening?" Bien murmured.

Ruc started to put a steadying hand on her shoulder, then stopped himself. In a place like this, kindness meant weakness.

Goatface hemmed for a moment. "It is a . . . tradition. A . . . how shall I put it? A *ceremony* of *welcome.*"

"Doesn't look all that welcoming," Ruc observed.

All eyes were fixed on them now. Some of the Worthy were grinning as though they'd been let in on a cruel joke. Others hefted their wooden weapons. Still others just watched, as though they were waiting for Ruc and Bien to break and run. Then, gradually, they began to move, stepping forward or shifting back, until they formed two lines, roughly a pace apart, with an open channel running down the center.

"The Way of Kings," Goatface said, gesturing.

"Dombâng doesn't *have* kings," Bien pointed out.

"Indeed." The trainer beamed. "Indeed."

The nearest of the warriors, a short man with an ugly scar dragging his lower lip down toward his chin, struck his shield with his training sword— once, then again, then again. A few at a time, the others began to join him— pounding fists against chests, blades against blades, the butts of spears onto the few patches of solid ground—until the whole yard was one slow, rolling, percussive heartbeat.

Goatface smiled encouragingly as he gestured Ruc and Bien forward. He might have been inviting them to step onto a well-appointed pleasure barge.

"You will want to move with some . . . *alacrity*," he suggested. "But do not run. Runners are punished."

"Any other suggestions?" Ruc asked.

"Upright. Try to remain *upright*."

It proved even more difficult than Ruc expected.

"Stay behind me," he murmured to Bien as they approached the gauntlet. Most of the blows would come from the front, and he was larger. No one would be trying to kill them. If all the Worthy died on the day they arrived, there wouldn't be anyone left to fight in the Arena, no one to go into the delta to face the gods. The gauntlet couldn't be more than fifty paces long. He took a deep breath, lowered his chin, raised his arms to shield his face, and stepped forward.

The wooden sword took him squarely across the ribs, knocking half the air from his chest.

Move with some alacrity, he reminded himself.

For just a moment, the words struck him as funny. He stifled a laugh, stuffed down the pain, and forced his way forward.

Sound closed around him like a fist. People were still drumming their weapons, but they were shouting now, too, screaming, leaning in as they attacked to bellow in his face. Blows fell like rain across his shoulders and back, cracked against his shins, lashed his stomach. Something horribly heavy battered down into his elbow, knocking his arm askew. He caught a glimpse of reaching hands, howling mouths, tried to get his arm back up, felt some wooden weapon break across his skull, knocking him sideways. A triumphant roar rolled over him.

Clutching hands, some trying to shove him back on course, others trying to drag him down.

Ringing like a bronze gong in his ears, in his skull.

Remain upright, he reminded himself grimly. *Remain upright.*

Someone stumbled against him, cried out. *Bien.* He tried to stretch a hand back for her, to provide some kind of shelter, but something smashed into his forearm.

"Move! *Move,* you idiot!" Bien's voice, angry, desperate.

He'd stopped, he realized. In trying to help her, he was slowing them both, giving the people to either side a second shot, and a third, and a fourth.

This is how it starts, he realized, forcing himself grimly into motion once more. *The first thing they teach you here is to leave the ones you love.*

Love.

What would Eira ask of a man in the middle of a gauntlet?

He thought for a fragment of a moment about dropping to his knees, letting them martyr him before he became what he would become. But if he stopped, he would block Bien's passage.

What did the Teachings say?

He tried to remember them, to find some message, some lesson he could cling to, but the pain had driven from his mind everything but a single thought—*survive*—and so he lurched forward into the storm of fists and whips and wooden swords, into that rain of human rage.

"Chum," chanted a bearded man, striking him across the knees with a long staff. "Chum!"

The others joined in.

"Chum! Chum! Chum! Chum! Chum!"

A gorgeous woman with her black hair in braids leaned in, screamed, spat in his face, reeled out of the way, and then there she was again, not just her, but three of her, blurry around the edges, red-lipped and vicious.

Remain upright, Ruc reminded himself, shoving the woman out of the way with one hand and lumbering on.

Whether Bien was following or not, he had no idea. Two or three times he started to turn, but there was no space, no air, no way to go but forward.

The hardest blow was almost the last, a skull-ringing crack across the back of his head. He stumbled forward, darkness fringing his vision, dropped to one knee, forced himself back up, back into the screaming, felt a fist to his ribs, something that might have been a stave across his lower back and then, abruptly, he was free. For a few furious heartbeats he struggled on through the mud, thrusting with his hands, trying to drive away his attackers, flinching from blows that had suddenly stopped falling. He was shouting, he realized, roaring like some mindless animal, thrashing in the filth, his eyes half-shut, lips drawn back in a snarl.

He took hold of himself, shut his mouth, straightened from his hunted crouch just in time for Bien—bleeding, screaming, weeping, clawing with her hands at empty air—to barrel into him. He caught her, hesitated, then wrapped his arms around her.

It would be seen as weakness, but they weren't animals.

Not yet.

"It's over," he said, pulling her against him. She felt so small. Too small. "It's over, Bien."

She let him hold her for a moment, then pulled away. Blood streaked her face. Her right eye was already starting to swell.

She shook her head. "No, it's not. It's not over at all. This is just the beginning."

18

The sinking Manjari ship had disgorged all manner of detritus: shattered decking, broken spars and yards, tangles of rigging, bobbing barrels. The wreckage stretched away from the *Daybreak*'s stern like a ragged wooden road leading across the water toward the horizon. Beside that road and on it the bodies floated, scores and scores of bodies, arms slack, heads lolling, like men who had grown tired trying to follow the path to its end, who had lain down awhile to rest. Gwenna watched as a corpse in a Manjari uniform rolled slowly with the waves: faceup, facedown, faceup. When she caught a glimpse of his expression he looked almost relaxed, lazy.

She envied him. The only way she could keep her hands from trembling was by clutching tight to the ship's rail.

She'd managed to sink an entire enemy vessel more or less by herself. She'd also dropped her starshatter. She'd dropped it, a Manjari sailor had picked it up, and then used it to kill dozens of Annurians on the deck of the *Daybreak*. She thought of Aron Dough, the legionary commander, his smile when he saw her on the other ship, the way he'd gestured her onward, promising to clear a path to safety. She'd barely even known the man, but he'd been there, spear in hand, risking his life to see her safe back on the ship, and now he was dead. She felt as though someone had cut a long slice from her throat to her belt, opened her up, scraped out everything inside, every human organ, and replaced it all with stones. Just breathing was hard. Standing was hard. She wanted to be gone, but she was on a ship in the middle of the ocean. There was nowhere to go.

"We let them drown."

The words jolted her from her thoughts. Pattick stood at her shoulder. Fire had seared his pale face, burning his eyebrows half away.

No, she wanted to say. *They didn't drown. They were torn apart by the starshatter. By* my *starshatter.*

But he wasn't talking about the Annurians. He was looking over the rail at the Manjari bodies in their wake.

She nodded silently.

It was one of the more cold-blooded decisions she'd ever seen. After the fight, after one of the Manjari ships had sunk and the other had been taken, Jonon circled back through the wreckage. Scores of men—those still alive when their ship slid beneath the waves—remained on the surface, some clutching to bits of flotsam, others swimming desperately after the *Daybreak,* pleading in their own tongue. The First Admiral watched from atop the sterncastle with hooded eyes. He rescued the surviving Manjari captain; tossed him a rope and hauled him aboard. The rest—all the soldiers and sailors of the sunken vessel—he ignored.

The wind had dropped just after the battle, which meant that for a long time the *Daybreak* drifted among the desperate. Gwenna heard them splashing, begging, clawing at the hull. A kinder captain would have dragged them from the water, clapped them in irons, and loaded them aboard the captured Manjari ship. A crueler captain might have ordered them shot where they swam. Jonon did neither. He went about the business of seeing to his own injured and dead, ordered the fires on the *Daybreak* quenched and the wreckage cleared as though they were in port back in Annur, utterly ignoring the pleading, cursing, sobbing from the waves below. Gradually the cries grew weaker, fewer, more hopeless. Most of the men accomplished their final slide beneath the water silently, the last of their strength drained away. It was a mercy when the wind finally picked up, the *Daybreak* leaned over with the breeze, and sailed away.

"This was a battle," Gwenna said. "People die in battle."

The words were hollow, rote. They'd left the drowned Manjari behind, but at her back, stacked like cordwood, lay the bodies and the parts of bodies of the Annurian soldiers who had been ripped to ribbons on the deck of the *Daybreak,* men dead because one of their own, a woman trained to know better, had let a live explosive fall from her belt into the hands of the enemy. She could smell the carnage, the blood and charred meat, the piss and shit spilling from the ripped-open skin.

At least the dead were silent.

She listened, as the sun sank over the starboard bow, to the voices of the sailors and soldiers who had lost only a finger, or a hand, or an eye, or an arm. Some moaned, some prayed. Some were too weak to do anything but pant. The sounds of suffering rose and fell like waves laving the hull. Every so often a scream stabbed through the low drone of misery—someone going beneath the surgeon's knife, someone dying, someone afraid to die. Two-thirds of the crew of the *Daybreak* was wounded. Maybe half of those would die, either quickly, bleeding out on the surgeon's table, or slowly, victims of the rot and disease that preyed on broken bodies.

"We won, though, right?" Pattick asked.

"Sure."

She supposed that they had, in spite of it all. Sometimes victory looked like that—no flags, no speeches, no laughter—just a lot of people baffled to find the violence over and themselves still alive.

She heard boots approaching from behind, felt the vibration in the deck. Rahood—she knew him by his smell: pipe smoke and a hint of rum. She'd expected him to come, had been waiting for it. She turned away from the rail to face the man.

A gash ran down the side of the first mate's face, and the ends of his long black braids were singed. Someone had hacked a fair-sized piece of fabric out of his tunic, although he seemed to have avoided any further injury. The massive hand resting on the pommel of his cutlass certainly looked like it worked well enough. In the other, he held a pair of manacles.

He held them out. "Admiral Jonon requires you on the sterncastle."

Gwenna glanced at the irons. "In those?"

The first mate nodded silently.

The manacles were a thousand times lighter than the gazes that settled on her as she walked the length of the ship, her hands bound before her. No one shouted or threw anything. No one said a 'Kent-kissing word. Most of them probably had no idea that half the slaughter amidships was her fault. A few, though, would have put the pieces together—Kettral, explosion, death. She could smell their anger, hot on the warm wind.

How many men died, she wondered, *because I let that starshatter drop? Fifteen? Twenty? Thirty?*

Somehow it didn't matter that she'd managed to sink the Manjari vessel. She should have done it without dropping the starshatter. That was what all the years of training were for, after all—learning not to make stupid fucking mistakes. Sure, battle was chaotic. Things happened that you just couldn't plan for. Losing a starshatter wasn't one of them.

She'd hated herself for the disaster at the Purple Baths, but in the long weeks following she'd managed to transmute that hatred into rage. Rage at Frome, at Adare hui'Malkeenian, at the city of Dombâng, at herself, at Jonon lem Jonon. Yes, she'd fucked up. Yes, she'd lost the bird. Yes, Talal and Quick Jak were dead. But no, *no,* that did not mean she was ready to stop fighting. Things were hard, shitty, ugly, but if she'd learned one thing in her two and a half decades it was that when things got hard you had to *keep going.* Keep running, keep swimming, keep hauling, keep fighting. That refusal to quit had saved her dozens of times over, seen her through the grimmest fixes. All her life she'd worn her stubbornness like a talisman, one that could rescue her and her people from anything.

Or not. Not this time.

As she walked the length of the *Daybreak*'s deck, she made herself look at the dead. The bodies pressed close, as though huddling against some cold that only they could feel. Some—those whose faces had been spared by the explosion—gazed blankly at the sky. She was tempted to look up along with them, to search for whatever it was they saw up there in all that wide blue nothing.

When she finally reached the top of the sterncastle, she found Jonon lem Jonon gazing out over the deck. His uniform was singed. Blood seeped from a nasty slice to his shoulder. His right pant leg, torn half off, flapped in the breeze. Either he wasn't the kind of commander to hide behind his men, or the battle had offered nowhere to hide. Probably both. It would have been easier to hate him if he'd been cowardly or incompetent. Instead she was left hating him for no better reason than that he'd hated her first.

She kept her back straight, her eyes forward, as she mounted the steps to the castle's top.

Rahood stopped her a few paces from the First Admiral, who turned slowly, ran his eyes over her, then spat off the stern.

"Did I or did I not," he began quietly, "order you to remain in your cabin during the engagement?"

Gwenna exhaled slowly.

"You did, sir."

"And you disobeyed this order."

"I thought—"

"You are not aboard this vessel to think."

Blood pounded in Gwenna's temples.

"We were losing the fight."

"Is that what you believe?" He waited, then shook his head slowly. "No. We were not losing. A boarding party had already reached the Manjari ship that you took it upon yourself to sink. The men slaughtered by *your* munition were about to join them. We would have taken two ships rather than one, and with fewer losses."

She stared at him. "I saw no boarding party, sir."

"Of course you didn't. They were not meant to be seen."

Her head swam. From up on the mast, she'd had a view of the decks of both ships. She hadn't noticed a boarding party, but then again she'd been looking through fire and smoke. . . .

"I'm ashamed, sir, for the casualties to our crew."

"*Our* crew?" His green eyes blazed.

There was almost no warning before his hand whipped around.

Of course, *almost* no warning was not the same as none. Gwenna never intended to defend herself. She would gladly have let the blow land, but a lifetime of training didn't just evaporate with a few failures. Her body took over before she could stop it. She caught the admiral's wrist when the open palm was still inches from her face, twisted, pivoted, brought the arm up behind his back, forced it to the breaking point, then pulled herself up short. No one moved. She stared at her own hand clenched around the admiral's wrist. It wasn't trembling. It looked strong, certain, as though it belonged to some other woman altogether.

Then she felt the warm steel press slowly against her neck.

"Release him," said Rahood quietly.

For a moment, she didn't know how. Those fingers she didn't recognize were curling tighter, tighter. Then Jonon turned, wrenched himself free, and the hand was her own once more. She let it fall.

The first mate kept his blade at her throat while Jonon studied her with those piercing eyes. The hate was there, just as it had been the first time they met, but she saw something beneath it now, too, a wariness, a caution. Not long ago that might have made her proud. He understood, finally, that she was dangerous, and yet not dangerous in the way of a soldier serving her empire. More like a wild beast: thoughtless, red-toothed, rabid.

"The Emperor," the admiral began, "bright be the days of her life, insists you be a party to this expedition, and unlike you, I obey my orders." He shook his head. "But that does not mean I need to look at you, or let you murder any more of my men." He waved a hand at Rahood. "Get her off of my fucking deck."

Gwenna spent the first day in the brig with the ghost of Sad Tym.

Tym was one of the first Kettral she'd ever met. He was there to greet the new cadets when, wide-eyed and unsteady, they first stepped off the boat. It wasn't, she learned later, any formal duty, nothing anyone had ordered him to do. Hull knew he had other responsibilities. He was one of the Eyrie's most respected commanders, had flown hundreds of missions before Gwenna ever showed up. Probably he should have been off somewhere going over tactics or readying weapons, but there he was, reclining in a canvas chair he'd lugged out to the dock just for that purpose, a bottle of black rum on the boards at his side, and a wide grin on his tan, scarred face.

"Welcome to Qarsh, you poor miserable runts," he bellowed as the sailors made fast the ship and the first of the new class disembarked. "I'd offer you rum—" He paused, hoisted the bottle to his lips, took a good slug, set it back on the dock. "—but I'm told it's bad form to give liquor to kids before they turn ten." He shrugged, took another swig. "Anyway, most of you pitiable idiots will be thinking of quitting by the end of the day. By the end of the week at least. I'm out here to tell you one thing—everyone feels that way when they first get here. We all did, no matter what horseshit the other trainers tell you. I'm out here to give you one piece of advice." He met Gwenna's eye at that moment, winked. "Don't give up."

Tym was *called* Sad Tym as a joke. On an island where most of the men and women were scarred, driven, angry, obsessed, even murderous, Tym was almost constantly laughing. Unlike most of the soldiers, who wore their blacks everywhere, Tym preferred the ludicrous grass skirts he'd picked up on some mission somewhere. He organized the only races and games on the island, and somehow managed to keep them almost lighthearted, despite the fact they were being played by the deadliest warriors in the world. More than once he'd swum out in the sound in the middle of the night, treading water for hours, waiting to flip the boatloads of cadets rowing back drunk from a night on Hook. Gwenna had no idea when he found time to prep for his missions, but every one was a success. He picked up a scar here, a bruise there, but he came back from every single sortie laughing.

Until he didn't.

Gwenna was fourteen at the time. No one worried much when Tym's bird was a day overdue. The world was a big place. Kettral were delayed all the time for all manner of reasons. When a week passed with no word, however, people started to wonder, then mutter. At ten days, there was talk of sending another bird in pursuit. Pretty much every Wing on the Islands was willing. Even the vets who'd hated Tym's games were chafing to go after him, but before the Eyrie could put anyone aloft, Tym returned. Just Tym, flying in the saddle of his kettral where his flier should have been. He'd lost a hand and the better part of his blood.

"They're dead," he said when he slid off the bird's back. His eyes were blank. "My Wing's dead."

Tym didn't last much longer. The next day, one of the cadets assigned to clean his bunkhouse found him hanging from the rafters. There was an empty bottle of rum on the table. The bedding on all of the bunks was askew, as though he'd spent the night sleeping in the cots of his dead companions.

Gwenna had felt nothing but rage at his suicide. Wasn't he the son of a bitch who had been there the first day, who had greeted them when they got off the ship with his grinning insistence that they not give up? Well? What was looping a rope around your neck and dangling from the roof but giving the fuck up? The rage had faded over the years, but she'd never really forgiven him. It was a weak way to go. Cowardly. Feeble.

Nothing had changed her mind, but for the first time she felt like she understood why he'd done it.

It wasn't guilt. Not exactly. She'd felt guilt before. A person could survive guilt, could soldier through it, could live with it on her shoulders. What she understood, as she hunched in the blackness of the brig, arms wrapped around her knees, staring into the darkness, was that a person might tie that knot not because she wanted to die, but because she felt dead already. All alone, without Jonon, or Cho Lu, or Kiel, or Adare, or some mad fucking battle to distract her, Gwenna could feel herself rotting, as though all the organs inside her were putrefying slowly. Her skin might hold her together for a while, but for what? Sooner or later she would burst. Better, maybe, to just have it over. Braver.

She was still grappling with Tym's ghost when the door to the brig clattered open.

She raised her head in time to see a man shoved roughly through the opening. He tripped over her empty bowl, stumbled forward, obviously blind in the darkness, drove the toe of a boot into Gwenna's side, then fell forward with a curse.

Another distraction.

She watched him reach out, grope, find the wall, turn himself until his back was against it. He moved cautiously, as though he'd been hurt over and over. When he was leaning back against the wall, he took a shallow breath, pressed a hand to his ribs, testing them, took another breath, then nodded. It was a private motion, some kind of reassurance meant only for himself. Finally he narrowed his eyes and spoke.

"*Teja vad masta, sanghat nirhat?*"

A long, thick silence followed.

"*Sanghat nirhat?*" he asked again. The question held a bite of command, and this time Gwenna recognized the language.

"I don't speak Manjari."

"Ah." A pause. "My apologies." The words sounded strange in his mouth, stiff, like leather that hadn't been broken in. "I expected you were one of my men."

"Not men. And not yours."

He leaned forward slightly, eyes on a point just to the left of her head. He couldn't see her in the darkness, but she could make out his features well enough—thin face, long black hair, long mustache that dropped past his chin in the classic style of Manjari nobility. His left eye was swollen shut, bruises marred the whole side of his face, his nose looked broken, and he smelled of blood. Wariness, too, and fear, but that fear was held tightly in check, despite the circumstances.

"You are the woman."

"I'm *a* woman anyway."

"The woman who boarded my ship. Who sank it."

Anger edged his words. She wondered vaguely if he would come after her, despite his injuries. She wondered if she'd do anything about it if he did.

"You're the captain," she replied.

"Bhuma Dhar. I was captain of the *Ashwaya*." He raised both hands, palms in, ducked his face between them three times in a gesture Gwenna didn't recognize.

"What's that?"

He looked up sharply. "You can see me?"

It was a tactical error, revealing that, but she found she didn't care much about tactics. "Yes. What's that gesture?"

"It is my shame."

"Looks like you're washing your face."

"Shame is not blood, to be washed away so easily."

Gwenna didn't have a response to that, and for a while the two of them sat in silence as waves laved the hull. Bhuma Dhar settled back against the bulkhead, his hands folded in his lap. He didn't look like he was about to attack.

"Your men," Gwenna said after a long silence. "Did Jonon rescue anyone else?"

She hadn't seen it, but then, she hadn't seen everything.

"Many lived through the explosion and the sinking." Dhar shook his head. "Your admiral pulled only me and my first mate from the sea."

Again, he made that strange gesture with his head and his hands.

Gwenna imagined the waterlogged bodies slipping below the surface, then sinking down out of the light, slow as snowflakes.

"I'm sorry."

Dhar shook his head. "The shame is not yours."

"I'm the one who blew up your fucking ship."

"You are an Annurian soldier. It was your *davi* to attack. It was my *davi* to defend."

"*Davi?*"

"Duty, but stronger."

Gwenna choked up a painful laugh. "People haven't had a very high opinion of my *davi* recently."

The captain squinted into the darkness. "You are being punished."

She didn't reply.

"Why?" the captain asked.

Gwenna hesitated. Bhuma Dhar was the enemy. He had ordered an attack on the *Daybreak*. Just because he was locked in the brig with her didn't mean he'd stopped being dangerous. On the other hand, the story had to be pretty obvious already and she was too exhausted to lie.

"I dropped an explosive. One of your soldiers picked it up, threw it aboard the *Daybreak*. Dozens of Annurians died." She shook her head. "You're not the only one who knows something about shame."

"And yet, you sunk my ship."

"By disobeying the admiral's direct order."

"What was his order?"

"To stay out of the way."

Dhar frowned. "This is a foolish order. If you had not sunk the *Ashwaya*, we would have had victory."

She shook her head. "There was a boarding party on your ship, one I didn't know about, didn't see."

"If there was," the captain replied slowly, "I, too, did not see it. Either way, you sank the ship."

"That's not how it works."

"It?"

"Armies. Battles. Command. It doesn't matter whether Jonon's boarding party was there or not. Doesn't matter if I sank the ship or not. You can't have every fucking soldier going by her gut, making shit up as she goes along. People die when that happens. People who didn't need to die."

"*Need to die.*" He smoothed his long mustache. "This is true of all of us, no? We need to die? My sailors are dead. My first mate is dead. Your admiral killed him, just as he will kill me when he is finished with his questions."

"What questions?"

"Why we attacked. Why we are here."

Gwenna felt the barest prick of curiosity's pin.

"Why *are* you here? There's nothing out this far from shore."

"Except you."

"You couldn't have known we'd be here. *We* barely knew we'd be here."

Suspicion wafted off the man—the dusty, too-sweet smell of an orange or lemon just starting to rot. "You will forgive me if I do not believe that."

"Why wouldn't you believe it?"

"An Annurian warship in Manjari waters? You did not arrive here through an error in navigation." He shook his head. "No. You may not follow orders, but your admiral does."

She leaned back against the bulkhead, weariness washing through her. "We thought we were going around. We didn't expect to run into anyone this far from the coast."

A pause. Then Dhar nodded slowly. "This, I believe."

"If you believed it, you could have hailed us before attacking."

"I believe it *now*," the captain amended. "When I gave the order to attack, I was certain it was this ship that had been sinking our vessels."

It took a moment for the words to make sense. "Sinking your vessels?"

Instead of replying, Dhar fell silent. The beasts of history, language, loyalty, and war crouched between them, fangs bared. Nothing about the situation made sense. Adare hadn't moved on the Manjari, not that Gwenna had heard. And why in Hull's name would she? Annur was coming apart at the seams. Bandits roamed the roads a hundred miles outside the capital. The Emperor didn't have enough soldiers to hold her own land, let alone send ships into the unmapped void of the western ocean. Not that Gwenna was about to explain any of that to Bhuma Dhar. If he didn't know about Annur's weakness, she didn't intend to be the one to tell him.

After a while, however, the Manjari captain shifted.

"Almost a year ago," he said quietly, "our trading ships began disappearing."

"Maybe no one was sinking them. Did you consider that?"

Dhar nodded. "This was my first thought. The ocean is the ocean. There are storms. Ships sink. Men die." He paused. "But not this many."

An obscure dread dragged a nail down the nape of Gwenna's neck. "How many?"

"In the past year, twenty-nine vessels have gone missing."

She shook her head, grappled with the number. *Twenty-nine.* Dhar was right. No storm accounted for that many losses, especially not spread over a year.

"Six months ago," Dhar continued, "a ship limped into Badrikas-Rama, badly damaged. The captain reported an attack by Annurian vessels."

"That makes no sense. Even if we *were* out here attacking you, we'd hardly be flying the fucking sunburst while we did it."

"The attacking vessels bore no flags, but as a child the captain apprenticed to a shipwright. He recognized the design of the ships." The man stared into the darkness for a while, then went on. "Two months after that, another trader returned, also badly damaged, also telling tales of an Annurian attack. *For Intarra.* It was these words he heard shouted from the deck of the vessel. *For Intarra.*"

Gwenna's head ached, a spike of pain just behind her eyes. "Why are you telling me this? If you think we've been sinking your ships, why are you telling me anything at all?"

"I believe this vessel and the sailors on it are innocent of these attacks."

She struggled to make sense of that. "You just got done telling me it was the Annurians."

"Not you. Not this ship."

"How do you know?"

He hesitated. "The eyes of your sailors."

"What's wrong with their eyes?"

"When I was taken aboard, they stared at me. Their eyes were the eyes of men who had never seen a Manjari captain. I heard them talking as I was dragged to the brig. They were not the words of men who had been sinking our ships." After a pause he went on. "Your admiral as well. His questions are not the questions of a man who has been preying on our traders."

Even as he spoke, a new thought occurred to her. "None of this explains why you're out *here*," she said. "We must be, what? Hundreds of miles from the coastal shipping lanes?"

Dhar nodded. "Manjari trade extends beyond our western shore."

"To *where*?"

"There are settlements along the northwestern horn of Menkiddoc, small villages on the coast."

Kiel's account from the inn came back to her. "So people keep telling me."

The captain cocked his head to the side. "What people?"

"It doesn't matter. Settlements, you were saying."

"The people came from our empire, originally. Before it was an empire. There was a . . . what is the word? A great emigration. West and south. The people of these villages share similar languages with us, customs."

"What do they have to trade?"

"Whale oil. Fruit. *Gabhya.*"

Gwenna frowned at the unfamiliar word. "*Gabhya?*"

"Twisted beasts from deeper into the continent."

She felt a new unease, cold as late-autumn rain, settle into her skin.

"What kind of twisted beasts?"

"There are all manner."

"Monsters," she said quietly.

"Indeed."

"And you . . . buy them?"

"Only the very, very wealthy. Many go to the family of the Empress."

Gwenna struggled to make sense of it. "What does the Manjari Emperor want with monsters out of Menkiddoc?"

"Owning one is a sign of power, of wealth. You have seen the imperial crest?"

She ransacked her memory, came up with something that might have been a winged lion. "No . . ."

"It was a *gabhya*. Brought to the Empress as a pet centuries ago. The bones are interred in the labyrinth beneath the citadel in Badrikas-Rama."

"There's a labyrinth?" She shook her head. "Actually, forget the labyrinth. Why doesn't anyone in Annur know this? About the *gabhya*?"

Dhar did something with his shoulders that might have been a shrug. "A mountain range and a desert stand between our two lands. No trade. No trust."

"What about those villages on Menkiddoc? *They* could be taking your ships."

"It is one of the things I was sent to investigate." He frowned. "But they have no unity. No navy."

"Maybe they want one. Maybe they're stealing it one ship at a time."

"If so, your admiral would do well to be cautious. He lacks the men to fully crew this ship and the one he has taken."

He lacks the men.

At these words, she saw the starshatter explode all over again, saw the center of the *Daybreak* erupt in a fountain of blood and flame. Twenty-one killed, eight more who wouldn't last the week, and at least another dozen injured. The memory scrubbed away any interest she'd had in Menkiddoc. Her lungs felt too small, as though someone had wrapped a fist around each of them and begun to squeeze.

"You should be telling Jonon this," she managed finally. "Not me."

"Your admiral? I have told him. He does not believe me."

"Then I certainly can't help you."

"I will be dead soon," he replied. "If you know the truth, it might survive."

A sick laugh rattled out of her. "You picked the wrong woman for keeping things alive."

The captain cocked his head to one side. "You are Kettral. Is this correct?"

She shook her head. "No."

"A woman on an Annurian vessel crewed and captained by men. A woman with your skill and bravery . . ."

Bravery.

The word made her sick.

Dhar, however, extended one upraised palm, then laid his other hand atop it, the palm also facing up.

"What the fuck is that?" she asked.

"*Rasa,*" the man said. "A gesture of respect between soldiers."

"I'm not a soldier. I'm not Kettral." She closed her eyes, tried as hard as she could to wake up into some world where she could breathe. After a while she opened them. The darkness was still there, the stench of the brig, the reek of her own blood. This was the world. There was no other. She closed her eyes again, leaned her head against the boards. "I'm nothing."

"You will pardon me," the captain replied, "if I do not believe this."

19

"You haven't puked on yourself yet. That's a good sign."

Ruc looked up. The motion made his head swim, but after a heartbeat or two he was able to focus on the figure standing above him. Tall, bare-chested, well-muscled—the man would have drawn attention anywhere just for his physique, but it was the deep brown of his skin—almost black—that made Ruc stare.

"You're Bascan," he said.

Five years earlier, it wouldn't have been strange. A whole quarter of Dombâng—Little Basc—had been given over to a population of immigrants from the distant island. They'd been bankers and merchants, mostly, had for centuries played a crucial role in the city's economic life. Then came the revolution. Most of the Bascans were foresighted enough to get out before the worst of the purges began. Extended families, clans, entire blocks disappeared over-night, loaded all their belongings onto ships, hauled anchor, and set sail for their homeland before the Annurian blockade could drop into place. They were the lucky ones.

Those who remained—too stubborn, some of them, or too poor to afford an oceangoing passage—were trapped in the city as the empire tried to starve it out. As hunger took hold, Dombâng had begun to devour itself. Most of the Annurian soldiers and bureaucrats were already dead, but people needed a target for their fear and their rage, and so they turned on these men and women who had lived peacefully among them for so long. After all, hadn't most of the Bascans slipped away in the night like thieves? Didn't that prove that they were in league with the empire?

The slaughter was quick, and it was ugly. The remaining population—maybe a thousand or so—were hauled from their homes, dragged out into the delta, hamstrung, and abandoned. Good, upstanding Dombângans—those with straight hair, skin of the right color brown, accents untrammeled by for-eign parentage—laid claim to the empty houses, and between one rainstorm and the next the Bascan population of the city was erased.

Except, it seemed, for the man now crouching in front of Ruc. New cuts and bruises stitched his skin, dozens of them, the purple-red weals laid over as many or more much older scars. It was the body, Ruc thought, of a man accustomed to violence. His voice, however, was calm, quiet, his eyes sober.

"How do you feel?"

"About the way you'd expect," Ruc replied, "after being beaten repeatedly with swords and sticks."

Something that might almost have been a smile creased the man's face, then vanished as he turned to Bien.

"What about you?"

"I'm fine," Bien said. She didn't look up.

"Are you nauseous?"

"Yes, I'm fucking nauseous," she snarled. "Last night I watched my friends murdered, today we buried the bodies, and now I'm here. This whole *place,*" she said, casting an arm out toward the yard, "makes me nauseous."

If the stranger was taken aback by the outburst, he didn't show it. Instead, he raised a hand.

"Focus on my finger."

Bien glared at him.

"Look at my finger," he said again. "Follow it with your eyes."

"Why?"

"You took some good blows to the head. Both of you. This is a way to see if your brain is bruised."

"What are you," Ruc asked, "some kind of surgeon? The doctor?"

That hint of a smile again, as though the notion were amusing. "There *are* surgeons here," the man replied, "but I'm not one of them. I'm a prisoner, like you." He gestured down to where a skull-sized iron ball lay on the ground, chained to a manacle around his ankle. "My name is Talal."

Ruc studied the man's wounds. "You're new here, too."

Talal nodded. "I walked that same gauntlet yesterday."

"Yesterday?" Ruc squinted through his pain. Talal's cuts and gashes looked older than a day. More like a week. Most had already stitched shut.

The other man followed his gaze, shrugged. "I guess they went easy on me."

"Why are you helping us?" Bien asked warily.

"As I said, we're all prisoners here. Like the two of you, I came . . . unwillingly. Surviving a place like this will be easier as a team."

"A team?" Bien shook her head. "You don't even know us. We could be anyone. We could be murderers."

Talal chuckled, glanced back over his shoulder at the yard. Most of the Worthy had already gone back to their training, the new arrivals evidently forgotten. Just a few paces away, one man was hammering another into the mud with a short club.

"Given where we are," he replied after a pause, "I was sort of *hoping* you might be murderers."

The words were light, and he delivered them with an easy smile, but something about that level gaze gave Ruc the impression that Talal—whoever he was—saw more than he was letting on.

"Follow the finger." He gestured once more to his hand.

He had Bien perform the simple task, then Ruc, then put them through half a dozen more drills before he was convinced that they'd escaped without any damage to the brain.

"You're lucky," he said, sitting back on his heels. "From what I hear, the man before me suffered a broken skull. Doesn't remember his own name."

"You've got a strange definition of lucky," Ruc said.

Talal laughed.

Bien gestured to the iron ball and chain. "What did you do to earn that?"

"What did he *do*?" While they were talking, Goatface had approached on surprisingly quiet feet. The trainer rested a casual hand on Talal's shoulder—a strangely paternal gesture. "*What did he do?* He flew a massive bird into the Purple Baths, set fire to that . . . venerable structure, then slaughtered *dozens* of our Greenshirts in his effort to escape."

Bien, who had been leaning forward wearily on her knees, jerked back as though burned.

"Not dozens," Talal demurred quietly.

"*Dozens.*" Goatface sounded almost proud. "I was . . . vouchsafed this information by Vang Vo herself!"

"Kettral," Ruc said quietly.

He glanced around the yard. How many people had seen them talking to the Annurian? What price would they pay for that conversation in the coming days and weeks?

"But the high priests cut his throat on the steps of the Shipwreck," Bien said. "A 'message to the meddling imperial dogs.'"

She glared at the Kettral who, for his part, looked almost apologetic.

"They cut *someone's* throat," Goatface said, "just not *his* throat." He clapped the soldier more vigorously on the shoulder, as though to indicate his continued corporeal existence. "The rest of his . . . what are they called? Team? Band? Assemblage?"

"Wing," Talal replied quietly.

"The rest of his Wing fought their way out of the Baths and vanished."

The Kettral shook his head. "Not all of them."

"So who did the high priests execute?" Bien asked.

"Some . . . unfortunate hauled up from the prisons." Goatface shrugged at their surprise. "A fiction our priests deemed necessary. People already whisper of the Kettral. After the Baths, the priests thought it wise to ensure those whispers grew no louder."

Bien, open-mouthed, shook her head. "And so they staged it. They executed an innocent man."

"Oh, hardly innocent."

Ruc shook his head. "Why are you telling *us*?"

Goatface spread his arms wide, as though preparing for an embrace. "Because you are among the Worthy now! If you ever leave this place, it will be for the delta. If you survive the . . . what is the best word? *Rigors* of the delta, you will be raised to the priesthood when you return. Speaking here is like speaking among the dead." He beamed, as though the sentiment ought to comfort them.

"It doesn't make sense," Ruc said. "If the priests are so afraid of the Kettral, why didn't they kill him for real?"

Talal smiled, but made no effort to join the conversation.

"They were going to," Goatface winked, "until Vo demanded him."

Bien shook her head. "Why would Vang Vo want one of the Kettral among the Worthy?" She stole another glance at the man.

"She wants him among the Worthy," Goatface replied, "to . . . adjudicate his worth."

"I'd have thought she'd be frightened by the idea of an Annurian facing the Three."

"Vang Vo?" The trainer's bushy eyebrows climbed his forehead. *"Frightened?"*

"Put off, then," Ruc said.

"Unbelievers are regularly . . . encouraged to join the Worthy."

"Because no one ever expects them to survive. Most are just common soldiers. One of the Kettral, though . . ."

Goatface shrugged again.

"Annurian. Dombângan. Doesn't matter to Vo. Some of the other high priests were less than . . . exuberant about the idea, but all that matters to Vang Vo is the fight, the faith."

"Which is it?" Bien demanded.

"In here," the trainer replied brightly, "the distinction between the two is academic."

Ruc nodded slowly. Already the conversation had gone on too long. No wonder the Annurian had approached them looking for an alliance. Everyone else in the yard was probably already plotting to kill him.

"Thank you," Ruc said carefully, nodding to the soldier as he rose gingerly to his feet, "for checking on us. I guess we'll see you around the yard."

"See him around the yard!" Goatface slapped his thigh. "Your interactions with our fine Annurian friend will be a great deal more . . . intimate than that."

"What do you mean?" Bien asked.

Goatface blinked at her, as though he didn't understand the question, then pressed the heel of his hand firmly against his forehead. "Of *course*. The two of you, devotees of such a . . . pacific goddess will not be aware of the intricacies of our worship. Talal is your *third*."

"Third?" Bien asked.

The trainer nodded. "As the gods of the delta are three, so with the Worthy. Over the months to come you will train beside him, spar beside him, eat beside him, guard his back as he guards yours. When the holy days come, you will stand beside him in the Arena, and if you survive, it is with him that you will go into the delta to face your gods."

Ruc had known, of course, in the back of his mind, that the Worthy always fought in groups of three. In all the madness of their capture, however, followed by the forced march to the Arena, it had not occurred to him to wonder about the person he and Bien would be grouped with.

"Why the three of *us*?" he asked warily. "Why not someone else?"

"Why . . ." Goatface mused, stroking his scraggly beard. "*Why* is a question . . . beyond my ken. The Worthy are grouped in the order they arrive, but as to *why* you arrived at the times you did?" He shook his head regretfully. "Fate? The hand of some . . . providence beyond mortal comprehension. Perhaps the Three can answer when you face them. Perhaps they have a more . . . *profound* plan."

"Unlikely," Ruc replied grimly.

Talal studied him a moment, then shrugged. "Relying on plans hasn't worked out so well for me lately."

Goatface laughed, then quickly sobered. "If you will allow me to offer some modest counsel."

"In a matter of months, we're going to be fighting for our lives in the Arena," Ruc replied. "You're our trainer. I'm hoping for a little bit more than modest counsel."

"Quite so." Goatface nodded. "*Quite* so. Well then, my first and best advice is this: *embrace* one another. You did not choose to come together, but here you are. Your choices now are between cooperation and . . . well . . . annihilation." He stood up, clapped his hands together, nodded brusquely as though that were a vexing question settled. "Now then. Talal. Will you be so kind as to show our newest recruits around the premises? I would do so my-self, but regrettably, *regrettably,* I must attend yet another . . . confabulation with Small Cao and the Nun in which we argue endlessly over the proper length of the ritual blades."

When the trainer had trudged off across the yard—he moved more like some kind of crab than a man—Talal turned to Ruc and Bien. For what felt like a long time, the three stood silently, measuring one another.

"Well," the Kettral said finally. "Given the choices, I'm inclined to lean to-ward cooperation rather than the alternative."

To Ruc's surprise, Bien exploded into laughter. It was a laughter just on the edge of hysteria, true, but any mirth was better than the weight of despair he'd felt settling over himself.

In a way, being linked to the Kettral was almost preposterously good luck. Most of the Worthy were religious fanatics, men and women who had joined up willingly, exactly the kind of people who had burned down Eira's tem-ple and slaughtered her priests. The thought of fighting beside them kindled a slow, hot fury inside him, one that if it caught would prove impossible to quench. Talal might have torched the Purple Baths, had proven himself a foe to the entire city, but he seemed to hold no antipathy for the servants of Eira. Better yet, if the stories Ruc had heard were any indication, the man was probably one of the deadliest people in the yard. It wouldn't hurt to have him at their side when the time came to trade the wooden training weapons for bright bronze.

On the other hand, the identity of the Annurian made him a target. There would be those among the Worthy convinced—despite the sanction of Vang Vo—that the simple fact of the foreigner's presence in the training yard was a sacrilege. Some would wait for the high holy days to try to plant a blade in his neck. Others might not. Worthy died in training all the time. Unless Ruc had vastly underestimated the charity of his fellow Dombângans, it would be days not weeks before someone arranged an "accident." And if a couple of heretical Eiran priests also died in the process, well, so much the better to purify the ranks of the Worthy.

As he stared out over the yard, half a dozen warriors broke away from a larger group, and then, as though summoned by his bleak thoughts, began to approach, sauntering through the mud, practice weapons swinging loosely in their hands. Ruc couldn't hear what they were saying, but it wasn't hard to make out the ugly laughter. It took him a moment to recognize the man at the front—Rooster, the same warrior he had watched from the deck of the ship, the one who had so viciously taken apart his opponent as the crowd roared its approval.

Up close, the man was both smaller and more striking. A strip of dark hair—spiked with some kind of lacquer or animal fat and glistening in the sun—ran down the center of his shaved scalp. Around his neck he wore the sun-bleached skull of a rooster, and at his wrists and ankles, bracelets with silver bells that tinkled softly as he walked. There seemed to be no fat on him at all, only cords of muscle stringing his compact frame. He bore no signs of his earlier combat in the Arena; in fact, his brown skin shone as though he had just oiled himself after a long bath. He wore the expression of an artist well satisfied with his day's work.

At his side strode a tall, lean woman. Like Rooster, she went shirtless in the heat of the day. A dozen necklaces of small, threaded vertebrae hung over her flat chest, rattling as she moved. The lobes of her ears were plugged with small circles of bone. Her eyes might have been carved from bone, too, for all the emotion they showed.

The Worthy behind them were a rougher lot, a walking collection of scar and scowl, crushed ears and chipped teeth, sunken knuckles and sneers. One man was the size of a barn door. Ruc barely glanced at him. It was obvious that wherever Rooster and the woman led, the rest would follow. Unfortunately, the two were leading them directly toward Ruc, Bien, and Talal.

"I guess beating us bloody wasn't enough for the first day," Ruc muttered.

Talal glanced over his shoulder. "There are rules about violence in the yard."

"Rules!" Bien almost choked on the word. "All I've *seen* since stepping into this love-forsaken place is violence."

"Well." The Kettral shrugged. "There's violence, and then there's violence."

Exactly what that meant, Ruc wasn't sure, but there was no time to ask. Rooster was bearing down as though he planned to walk right through them. As he approached, however, he smiled and spread his arms. Ruc took a step back, but the man caught him up in a rough embrace, held him in those vise-like arms a moment, then pulled away and kissed him, first on one cheek, then the other, then the lips.

"Welcome!" he declared, releasing Ruc finally, then bestowing the same treatment on Bien.

She tried to hold him off, to push him away, but her hands might as well have been the flapping of a thrush's wings for all he noticed them.

"Welcome!" he said again, when he had finished kissing her. "I wanted to be the first to greet you after the gauntlet, but it seems our Annurian companion has beaten me to the punch." He paused, then winked at Talal. "A figure of speech, of course."

The Kettral didn't respond. His face betrayed nothing, and, to Ruc's surprise, his temperature didn't rise. People talked about men and women who were cool under pressure, but Talal was quite literally cool. Judging from the soft yellow glow bathing his skin, he might have been sleeping, rather than facing down one of the yard's more dangerous fighters.

Rooster held his gaze for a moment, then turned back to Ruc.

"I'm told," he said, tapping with one finger at the lobe of his ear, "that you and your companion come to us from a slightly different religious tradition."

"We are priests of Eira," Bien said, stepping forward defiantly.

"Eira!" Rooster raised his eyebrows, then turned to the warriors behind him. "Gentlemen!" He inclined his head toward the woman with the neck-lace of vertebrae. "Gentlemen *and,* naturally, Snakebones. The rumors are true! We have among us today a pair of citizens who have dedicated their lives to love."

He lingered on the last syllable, drawing it out, as though savoring the taste.

The men growled their lewd appreciation, while the woman he had called Snakebones stepped forward.

"Love," she purred, studying Ruc. "Not enough love in this camp, if you ask me."

She reached out, ran a hand over Ruc's chest, then, whip-quick, snaked it down the front of his pants, squeezed his cock and balls appraisingly. His body reacted before his brain. As she was withdrawing the hand, he lashed out, caught her wrist, twisted, wrapped the arm up behind her body. The attack should have been incapacitating. She should have ended up doubled over, her hand cranked up behind her head, her shoulder straining at the socket. Instead, with a sick snap, that shoulder actually popped from the socket, and in a quarter heartbeat his leverage was lost. The woman whipped around, snatched back her arm. With her other palm, she slammed the shoulder back into place. Ruc had treated people with dislocated joints before, had seen them pass out from the pain. Snakebones didn't pass out. She only grinned at him, white teeth flashing beneath those emotionless eyes.

Rooster crowed a long, joyful laugh. "Lesson number one, love boy!" He draped a casual arm over his companion's shoulders. "We don't call her Snake-bones because of those necklaces. It's because she's not put together like the rest of us. Writhes like a snake in a fight."

"Fighting's not the only time," the woman added. She turned to Bien, ran a tongue over her teeth. "What about you, sweetheart? Are you friendlier than your man?"

Bien's jaw was tight, her eyes wide, her hands clenched into fists at her sides. "Less so."

Rooster shook his head. "I was given to understand that you Eira-huggers loved *everyone.* Part of the faith."

"My faith suffered," Bien replied grimly, "when my temple burned."

"A shame." Rooster frowned. "In here, a little love goes a long way. Share it with the right person—it might even mean the difference between living and dying."

"The only way anyone lives through this place," Ruc said, "is fighting."

"To be sure," Rooster agreed. "To be sure. But we've got some time before the killing begins in earnest. I guess it's up to you how you spend the last months of your lives." He waggled a cautionary finger. "Or *if* you do. There aren't a lot of folks in here willing to extend the hand of friendship to a pair of Annurian whores."

"Annurian whores," Ruc repeated. "Doesn't sound very friendly."

Rooster shrugged. "I've got nothing against whores."

"What about Annurians?" Talal asked mildly—the first words he'd spoken since the others approached.

Snakebones spat in the dirt. Rooster met the man's gaze, then turned back to Ruc.

"Choose your friends wisely," he said.

Ruc nodded. "I intend to."

Rooster laughed, pursed his lips, blew Ruc a kiss, another to Bien, then turned on his heels. Snakebones lingered a moment longer, a smile playing on her lips, then followed.

Only when the group had disappeared into one of the buildings fronting the yard did Talal speak.

"If you'd been friendlier, Rooster would have taken you under his wing. Rooster and Snakebones both. There are almost a dozen Worthy here with their protection."

"I'm not sure," Ruc replied, "that I'd enjoy what happens underneath that wing."

"Did they make the same offer to you?" Bien asked.

Talal shook his head slowly. "I'm almost surprised no one's tried to kill me yet." He glanced over at them. "I can't promise to provide Rooster's level of protection. On the other hand, I'm not looking for that level of . . . affection either."

Ruc exhaled. He felt suddenly exhausted. "You're getting the raw end of the deal. Doesn't really matter how much we watch out for you. We're not soldiers."

"Priests," the Kettral replied. "I know." He glanced from Ruc to Bien, then shifted his gaze out over the yard. For a while the three of them stood in silence, watching a dozen skirmishes unfold across the mud. Then Talal spoke again. "You move pretty fast for a priest."

It was a casual comment, but Ruc felt himself tense.

"Not that fast. She was out of my grip in half a heartbeat."

Talal shrugged. "You couldn't know her joints don't stay put."

"But Ruc's right," Bien said. "We're not like the others here. We didn't train for this. We're not ready for the fighting, for the killing."

The Kettral kept his eyes on the combat unfolding in the middle distance. "A thing I've found about killing," he said quietly, "is that all the training in the world doesn't always make you ready."

"Is that supposed to be reassuring?" Ruc asked.

"Maybe. Some of the readiest killers I've encountered had almost no training at all."

20

"Ruc, Bien," Goatface said, "meet Mouse, Monster, and Stupid."

Despite the names, it was impossible to tell at a glance which was which. A huge man—large to the point of fat—sat at the rickety wooden table inside the common room of Goatface's barracks, gnawing on a chicken wing. Beside him, a woman was drinking from a glass bottle. Ruc took it for water at first, then noticed the dead snake coiled at the bottom. A moment later, he caught a whiff of the eye-watering reek bleeding from the neck. It was early to be drinking *quey*—barely dawn, in fact—but she didn't look drunk as she studied Ruc and Bien. Furious, but not drunk. The third character was lying on a bench along the wall, a straw hat tucked down over his face, asleep, or just too bored by the introductions to bother looking up. Talal stood by the window, staring out into the yard. Evidently he already knew everyone.

"Colorful names," Ruc observed.

The fat man grunted into his chicken something that could have been a chuckle or maybe just a grunt. The woman took a slug of her *quey,* then shook her head.

"We didn't all have a nice pair of parents to name us."

"What Monster means to say," Goatface interjected, "is that the three of them hail from Sunrise. They grew up orphans, then survived as criminals, venturing into the richer parts of the city to murder and to steal until nine months ago, when fate brought them to me."

"Fate!" The big man laughed, then went back to gnawing on his chicken.

"Yeah," Monster muttered. "If by *fate* you mean an idiot in a swallowtail who managed to get his fucking boat stuck in the middle of the fucking canal right in the middle of our fucking escape."

"Fate," the big man said again, as though that settled it.

The woman shook her head. "Fuck you, Mouse." She glared at him awhile, then shook her head again, took another pull on her *quey.*

"The warrior on the bench," Goatface said, pointing to the reclining figure, "is Stupid."

Stupid didn't move. It wasn't clear whether or not Stupid was even breathing.

"For the . . . *preponderance* of the year," the trainer went on, "the three of them have constituted my entire stable."

"I thought there were more," Ruc said. "A dozen or so Worthy for each trainer."

"Usually, there are," Goatface replied. "This year has been . . . *inauspicious.*"

"Inauspicious!" Mouse spat out a bit of gristle with the word. "Ha!"

"Goats had another three," Monster growled. "'Til Rooster and Snakebones took 'em apart."

The trainer pulled a melancholy face. "Regrettable. Deplorable, really. I did everything I could for them, but they lacked a certain . . ."

"They lacked everything," Monster cut in. "Those fucking idiots couldn't pour water out of a boot. Thought ending up with the Worthy would make them famous—like you lot, probably. What do you figure, Mouse—these bastards gonna last the week?"

Ruc felt Bien stiffen beside him.

"We'll aim at getting through the day, for now," she replied.

"Not good enough," Monster growled, narrowing her eyes over the top of her bottle.

"Why do you care?" Bien demanded. "If we can't fight, it just means we're less likely to kill you when the time comes."

Monster shook her head. "You don't get how it works in here."

"What Monster means to intimate," Goatface interjected, "is that while we—all of us inhabiting the yard—are gathered in common cause, joined in the worship of our gods, there are certain . . . terrestrial concerns, even in a sacred space such as this."

"I think we encountered some of those concerns already," Ruc said. "There was a small welcoming committee."

"The Nun's got nine," the woman said, ignoring him, holding up nine fingers. "Small Cao's got twelve. Rooster's got . . ."

"Rooster's not a trainer," Ruc pointed out.

"Look who knows so fucking much." Monster rolled her eyes. "Been here a day and ready to start lecturing us poor fucks already." She shook her head, disgusted. "Of course he's not a fucking trainer. Technically he and Snakebones belong to Other Dao."

"Other," Mouse chuckled.

"He's *called* Other Dao," Monster went on, "because there's already a trainer named Dao. I'll let you guess who's the less impressive of the two. Point is, Rooster and Snakebones don't *need* a trainer. . . ."

Goatface tutted. "Even such . . . accomplished pugilists could benefit from the right guiding hand."

"Yeah. Well. Other Dao's not the right fucking hand, is he?" She shook her head, answering her own question. "Which means Rooster's pretty much in charge of that stable. Him and Snakebones and Toad. And they've got a dozen others, not to mention *another* dozen loyal fuckboys and girls plucked from the other stables."

"Why do the numbers matter?" Bien asked. "I thought high holy day fights were always three against three."

"Bitch, that's if you *make* it to the high holy days. Lots of ways to get cut apart in here before the real celebration even begins."

Goatface nodded. "There is a certain . . . vigorous rivalry between the fighters of the different trainers. . . ."

"Vigorous." Mouse nodded.

"Vigorous," Monster elaborated, "is Goatface's colorful way of saying that on any given day you might get a shiv in the back."

"It is for this reason," the trainer said, "that I counsel you toward unity." He made a gesture circling the small room. "Think of your three as your family, and the others under my care as your clan. Two days ago Monster, Mouse, and Stupid were only three. Now you are six."

He beamed.

Monster did not.

"And if you idiots get killed nice and quickly," she said, "we can get back to being three."

Ruc shook his head. "I thought you *wanted* more people."

"The *right* people maybe," Monster replied. "But an Annurian war machine and two priests of whatever-the-fuck are definitely *not* the right people." She shook her head. "After Rooster shredded Goat's last three, the rest of the camp pretty much wrote us off. There were bigger rivalries. We were nothing, an afterthought. No one was coming after us because no one *cared* about us."

Mouse shook his head almost mournfully.

"Then," Monster went on, jerking a thumb at Talal, "*that* fucking asshole showed up, fresh from his performance at the Purple Baths."

The Kettral didn't respond. He didn't even turn.

"Now *you* fuckshits are here, and suddenly every motherfucker in the camp's interested in us again. Suddenly everyone's talking about knocking Goatface's squad back down a few pegs."

The trainer spread his hands. "The others are intrigued. There is a . . . *mystique* to new arrivals."

"Mystique," Mouse said, shaking his head gravely, as though the word augured nothing but ill.

"We don't *want* fucking mystique," Monster said. "In our line of work, we want the exact fucking *opposite* of mystique, whatever that is."

"Obscurity," murmured Stupid from beneath the hat. His voice was rich, deep, and mellow. "Insignificance. Anonymity."

Monster nodded, pointed a finger at the supine man to indicate her agreement. "That. What he said. Where we come from, there's a *value* to anonymity."

"You are no longer where you come from," Goatface observed. "When you entered this yard, you became . . . paladins of the faith, men and women worthy of your gods."

"Worthy." Mouse sucked at something stuck between his teeth. "Worthy." For a paladin of the faith, he didn't sound as though he found much value in the word.

Before anyone could say anything else, a savage pounding rattled the barracks door. As Goatface was still rising to his feet, the latch shot up and the door clattered open. Ruc half expected to see Rooster and Snakebones framed there, naked bronze in hand and to 'Shael with whatever rules were supposed to govern the yard. Instead, he found himself staring at three Arena guardsmen.

No, he realized, as they bulled forward into the room, not three—*five*. Two carried loaded flatbows at their shoulders and two wielded spears; they spread out through the room, but most of their attention seemed focused on Talal. The Kettral, for his part, hadn't bothered turning from the window.

The last of the guardsmen—a captain with his rank stitched on his shoulders—bore an unsheathed sword in one hand and a glass bottle with a corked top in the other. He was older and heavier than the others. His stomach strained against the front of his tunic, and sweat matted his hair, despite the early hour.

"We're here for the leach," he said grimly.

Ruc went instantly, feverishly cold. He had no idea how these men had ferreted out the truth. It didn't matter. There was only one way out of the barracks, *zero* ways out of the larger compound, and the soldiers hadn't brought all those weapons just for show. Out of the corner of his eye he saw Bien stiffen. He didn't dare look over at her, but he shifted in his seat. The men with the flatbows were still looking at Talal, which made sense; it was impossible to say how the Annurian might try to turn the situation to his advantage. Their distraction also gave Ruc a chance. It had been a long time since he'd stalked jaguars, but he was sure he could get to the captain, knock the sword out of his hand, crush his throat. No . . . that was the wrong play. If they were going to have any chance, he needed to kill the bowmen first. He measured the distance in his mind, tensed for the strike. Maybe the others would follow his lead. They were prisoners as much as he and Bien, after all.

And then what? Even if they managed to kill the five guardsmen, they'd still be trapped inside the yard, penned in by a wall more than four times Ruc's height. It would be a simple matter for the dozens of remaining guardsmen to lock down the whole place, wait for reinforcement from the Greenshirts, then come in and take their bloody revenge.

We're going to die here, he realized. *Today. Right now.*

The only remaining question was how many of the guards he could take with him.

He felt Bien's hand settle on his arm.

He turned to find her eyes on his—wide and frightened, but unflinching. She gave a tiny shake of her head.

The gesture was, in its own way, sharper than any blade, a reminder of how far he'd fallen in the short time since the burning of the temple. He'd spent fifteen years trying to wipe clean the bloody stains of his youth, starving the part of himself that had grown up only to stalk and to slaughter. He thought he'd made himself into something better than a delta beast.

Wrong. All of it, wrong.

It was one thing to endure a few taunts and curses, to hold back his savagery for the occasional beating. When it came down to it, however, when his own survival and Bien's were on the line, his faith in Eira evaporated like so much water spilled on a dock on a hot day. All over again, he was ready to rip and to rend, to shatter bones, to go after the soft flesh of the throat. . . .

He took a deep breath, closed his eyes, tried to find inside of himself some fragment of love for these men who had come with their bows and their spears. What was it he'd insisted to the old Witness of the Vuo Ton?

I am a priest of Eira now, and love is what I have to give.

All he felt was a dark rage burning in his veins.

"Ah!"

Ruc opened his eyes to find Goatface had risen fully from his seat. He lifted his shirt to scratch absently at his hairy belly, all the while beaming at the guards. He didn't seem in the least discomfited by the talk of a leach in his midst.

"A visit from the . . . *intrepid* Captain Gon."

The captain turned to the trainer. "My men told me he was out of the barracks this morning."

"Obviously," Goatface replied, "he did not go far."

"It's your job to keep an eye on this son of a bitch."

Goatface pursed his lips, stroked his scraggly beard. "No, Captain. I'm afraid you're laboring under a . . . misapprehension. *Your* job is keeping the Worthy contained, yours and that of the other guards who so diligently patrol the yard. *My* job is to ready them for the . . . exigencies of faith."

"What," Monster asked quietly, "the fuck?"

Ruc might have asked the same question, though the answer was quickly becoming clear. The guards hadn't come for Bien at all; they'd come for Talal. He felt his gut unclench, the black, hopeless rage drain slowly from his heart.

"I'm not a leach," the Kettral said mildly, turning from the window at last. "As I've told you twice now already."

The men with the crossbows and spears didn't look remotely reassured. They watched the soldier as though he were a particularly venomous snake poised to strike.

"Then you won't mind drinking this," the captain said grimly, holding out the bottle.

Adamanth, Ruc realized.

In the rare instances that a leach was brought to trial, they were invariably dosed with adamanth. Evidently the strong, dark infusion did something to block them from their powers.

"I mind," the Annurian said, ignoring the flatbows pointed at his chest as he crossed the small room, "because it tastes like piss." He took the bottle from the captain's hand, tossed it back in a quick swig, grimaced, passed the bottle back. "It's a myth, you know, that the Kettral use leaches."

"The high priests think differently."

"The high priests have spent as much time around the Kettral as I have around the Three."

Captain Gon gritted his teeth, unable to tell, evidently, if this comment crossed the line into blasphemy.

"As long as you're here," he growled finally, "you drink."

The Annurian just shrugged.

When the guards had left, Goatface lowered himself back into his chair with an audible grunt. For a few moments, no one said anything.

Then Monster exploded. "You're a fucking *leach*?"

Talal shook his head wearily. "As I keep telling everyone, no. The Kettral hate leaches as much as anyone else."

Mouse looked wary, and Monster was halfway out of her seat. Even Stupid had tipped back his straw hat to follow the action. Bien was staring at the soldier, her eyes wide, lips cracked, as though she were about to scream.

"I apologize," Goatface said, "for not informing the rest of you earlier. It has been an . . . eventful several days."

"You can take your apology and stuff it up your dickhole," Monster spat. "This, *this* is *exactly* the kind of shit we don't need."

Talal met her fury with his own level gaze. "They're afraid," he said. "The priests. The guards. They've never captured one of us before. If someone told them I could grow a second head they'd believe it."

"That's exactly the *problem*." As she talked, she sketched her anger in the air with an agitated hand. "We're trying to get everyone in here to think we're . . . What's the fucking word, Stupid?"

"Insignificant," Stupid suggested. "Pedestrian."

"*Insignificant*. I don't give a runny shit if you're a leach or not. The issue is that *they*"—she stabbed a finger toward the window, toward the yard beyond—"will believe it. Which means they're going to come after you. Which means they're going to come after *us*."

Despite the gravity of the situation, Ruc felt light, almost buoyant. They hadn't come for Bien after all. He'd managed to avoid, for another day at least, unleashing the predator straining inside of him.

"Look," he said. "Maybe Rooster will rip us to shreds, too. Maybe we'll be gone in a week, and you'll be insignificant all over again."

Goatface shook his head gravely. "It would not reflect well on me if you were gone in a week. Not well at all. Not when I have already lost a three this season. I will have to . . . redouble my efforts."

"Well, fuck," Monster said, rolling her eyes.

"Redouble *what* efforts?" Bien asked.

"Your training," the man replied. "Perhaps you have forgotten, overwhelmed as you are by the new sights and sounds, but I am your trainer."

In a way, Ruc *had* forgotten. Nothing about the man suggested that he knew anything about fighting, or killing, or survival. Hardly a wonder that he'd already lost half of his fighters. Hardly a comfort for those who had come to replace them.

"Now that we are back up to six," Goatface proclaimed, "I believe that a boat ride may be appropriate."

Ruc glanced at the others, but they looked as baffled as he was.

Monster slugged back another gulp of *quey,* studying the trainer as she swallowed. "A boat ride sounds suspiciously fucking pleasant."

"Pleasant?" Goatface took some time to consider the word. "Yes. Well. I suppose it depends on your feelings regarding boats."

"What kind of boat?" Ruc asked warily.

"Perhaps it will be easiest to show you."

✝

"These," Goatface said, gesturing to the hulls knocking gently against the dock, "are the funeral skiffs."

The boats were as beautiful as they were grim: slim-waisted, tapered to a high prow at stem and stern, lacquered black, upholstered in black crushed velvet beneath black canvas canopies. Bronze oarlocks and fittings gleamed in the morning sunlight.

"If you have the . . . profound honor," the trainer went on, "to fall in the Arena during the contests of the high holy days, your body will be cleaned, carried to these docks, laid in one of these hulls, then rowed into the delta, where it will be burned on a sacred island."

"Some fucking honor," Monster muttered. "Tossed in the delta and torched." Stupid shrugged. "An improvement on rotting in a stagnant backwater."

"Is it?" the woman demanded. "Dead is fucking dead."

"Dead," Mouse agreed, as though the word needed saying one final time. Ruc ignored the exchange.

"We're taking one of these now?" he asked, trying to keep his voice level, even bored as he studied the boats, then glanced over his shoulder.

Goatface had warned them as they left the yard about trying to escape.

"Some Worthy," he'd said, producing the key from the thong inside his shirt, "when leaving the yard for the first time have made a . . . how should I put it . . . a series of reckless and unfortunate decisions."

"Which one do you want to be?" Monster asked, turning to Ruc. "I'd take Reckless. Your girl's got Unfortunate scribbled all over her, but it's up to you two."

Bien didn't reply. She was staring at the heavy wooden door, the straps of iron banding it, the massive apparatus of the lock itself.

"We've been here one day," Ruc said, raising his hands. "No one wants to get reckless."

"Disappointing," the woman muttered.

Goatface shook his head. "A very *prudent* choice, in fact."

He gestured to the guards walking the wall overhead. They weren't Green-shirts. The Arena had its own dedicated patrol, every man armed with a loaded flatbow and a sword, all of them focused like circling hawks on the warriors below.

"It is a great honor to serve in the Arena," Goatface continued. "Vang Vo chooses only the most . . . scrupulously devout, the most meticulously trained." He waved cheerfully up at the guardsmen. None returned the gesture. Goatface shrugged, turned his attention back to Ruc and the others.

"Do you know what happens to the men on duty if one or more of the Worthy escape?"

"I'm willing to bet it's not a hand job from the high priestess," Monster replied.

"Indeed." Goatface nodded. "Indeed it is not. When the last Worthy escaped the men on duty were given one day to find her. When they failed, they were stripped . . . of both their rank and their garments, taken a small way out into the delta, tied to posts which were sunk in the mud until only their noses were above the water, sliced at the armpits and thighs, and left for the schools of *qirna*."

Bien stared at the man, aghast.

Goatface caught her expression and nodded once more. "It has made the others . . . what is the phrase? *Exceedingly zealous* in their work. They have been known to kill entirely innocent Worthy for the sin of looking with too much longing at the world beyond these walls. Isn't that right, Cho Min?"

Ruc turned to find a complement of a dozen guardsmen approaching from across the yard. The man at the head of the column—Cho Min, presumably—nodded curtly, his face flat and expressionless as a brick wall.

"Cho Min and these others will accompany us," Goatface said. "Not to worry. It is a purely . . . prophylactic measure taken whenever the Worthy venture outside the yard."

"A lot of loaded flatbows for a prophylactic," Talal observed.

"Yes. Well. Cho Min is nothing if not thorough."

"What happened to her?" Ruc asked as Goatface fit his key into the lock, then shouldered the heavy door open.

"To whom?"

"The Worthy. The one who escaped."

"Oh, her. She was caught hiding in an attic over on the Gold Coast," Goatface replied genially, "hauled into the square, then torn apart by the . . . more *devout* of Dombâng's citizenry."

Which should have made for a compelling cautionary tale, but as Ruc stood there on the docks studying the funeral skiffs, he couldn't help but consider the possibilities. Unlike that nameless Worthy, if he and Bien were able to make it out of the yard, make it into one of these boats, or *any* boat, for that matter, they wouldn't be forced to hide in attics. A small head start and they would be gone into the delta, where none of the Dombângans dared follow.

At the moment, unfortunately, the guards didn't look inclined to offer that head start.

Cho Min had his men deployed in a loose net around them, four out ahead, at the end of the dock itself, the rest blocking any passage onto the mud flats flanking those docks. They carried their flatbows at the shoulder, aiming down the stocks as though ready to loose at the first sign of flight. It made Ruc queasy just watching them. An overreaction, the barest twitch of a finger, and someone, maybe all of them, were dead. Any escape was going to have to wait.

"Yes," Goatface said, turning to Ruc, "and no." It took him a moment to realize the trainer was answering his earlier question. "We *are* taking one, but not in the . . . most traditional manner." He gestured to the nearest of the boats. "If the six of you would be so obliging as to lift it from the water."

"Lift," Mouse repeated, as though he'd seen this coming from the moment they set foot on the docks.

Goatface nodded encouragingly. "Lift."

The boat was three times as long as Ruc was tall, but narrow and cunningly built. Once the six of them managed to arrange themselves on the dock, they were able to haul it from the water without too much effort, Stupid giving instructions, Monster cursing the entire time. When they went to set it down on the dock, however, Goatface shook his head.

"No! Oh *no,* my fine warriors. You would damage the keel! And besides, we haven't even begun."

As Ruc and the others held the hull in place, uncertain what to do next, Goatface took hold of the rail, made a surprisingly nimble leap, and vaulted into the boat. Bien and Stupid staggered beneath the additional weight. Mouse grunted with the strain, and for a moment Ruc felt the boat slipping from his grasp. Before he could drop it, however, all the old reflexes snapped into place—as a child with the Vuo Ton he had spent endless days in and out of dugout canoes, hauling them, flipping them, righting them—and he shifted his weight, slid a thigh underneath the slick hull, adjusted his grip, and felt the boat steady. When he looked down the hull, he saw Talal, Mouse, and Monster similarly braced, bodies bent with the strain as Stupid and Bien regained their footing.

"Now," Goatface continued, opening a red parasol, propping it against the rail, fidgeting with it a moment, adjusting it so that it more thoroughly blocked the sun, then settling himself onto one of the seats. "To the Arena!"

"This has to be a fucking joke," Monster muttered.

The trainer shook his head. "While I appreciate a hearty jest as much as the next person, I assure you that I am in earnest."

"It would be easier to carry," Ruc pointed out, "if we flipped it over."

Goatface laughed. "I have many goals as your trainer. Among them, however, I regret to say that I do not include your *ease.*"

Monster shook his head regretfully. "Ease."

"The longer we stand here arguing," Bien growled, "the longer we have to hold the boat. Let's just get it to the Arena."

Ruc nodded, shifted his grip so that he could hold one of the thwarts instead of the rail, waited for the others to get similarly situated, then began walking.

They carried the funeral skiff the length of the dock, across the wide landing fronting the Arena, in through the wide gates, down a long corridor, then back out through a smaller doorway into the sunlight, onto the damp sand of the pit itself. The stands loomed above them in a rough oval, blocking out all but a disk of smoky sky above. The wooden benches were mostly empty save for a few drunks, a few orphans, a few gamblers scouting the warriors, hoping to get an edge in the betting of the high holy days.

"So this is where it happens," Bien breathed quietly.

They'd seen it from above. It was different standing on the dirt. It felt, Ruc thought, as though they were being swallowed by the place.

"An arena," Goatface agreed, "*sanctified* by the blood of the brave."

Ruc tried to imagine what it would feel like to fight in that captive space, to fight to the death with ten thousand people screaming, leaning out of the stands, hurling curses and encouragement, pounding thunder from the wooden boards beneath their heels. It was one thing to wrestle crocs and stalk jaguars in the solitude of the delta, another to do your struggling, killing, and dying with all those eyes fixed on you.

"Is it sanctified enough," Monster demanded, cutting through his thoughts, "to put this fucking boat down?"

"Down?" Goatface sounded genuinely baffled. "*Down?* My dear Monster . . . we are going *up!*"

He looked like some debauched emperor, half-reclined against the thwart, lazing in the shade of his parasol, a finger extended toward the top of the stands.

"Up," said Mouse.

"Fuck," said Monster.

The short man smiled pleasantly down from the comfort of the boat. "Indeed."

Goatface wasn't the only trainer who had brought his warriors out of the yard. The pit—fifty paces across at the center—was more than large enough to accommodate the fifteen or twenty Worthy who were stretching and warming up in the shadow of the stands, along with their trainers, and at least as many Arena guards, flatbows at the ready. None of them, however, had thought to bring a funeral skiff, which left them free to watch with a mixture of curiosity, amusement, and contempt as Goatface's team attempted to get the boat out of the pit and up into the stands.

The trouble was the eight-foot wooden wall ringing the pit. For obvious reasons, there were no steps leading up from the sand, which meant lifting the skiff. . . .

"Vang Vo will be very displeased," Goatface observed, "if the keel of her boat is damaged."

"Then maybe we should have left the 'Kent-kissing thing in the water," Monster snapped.

"We need someone up top," Bien said. "At least two people."

Ruc nodded. "You and Stupid. You're the shortest. You won't be doing any good down here."

"We're also the weakest," Bien pointed out.

"I resent that," Stupid said mildly.

"Go," Talal put in. "Once we tip it up, we'll have most of the weight on our end. You'll just have to steady it."

The Kettral didn't raise his voice, but there was a note there that Ruc hadn't heard before—not urgency, exactly, but something that, coming from another person, might have been a command.

"The four of you are good to hold the boat?" Bien asked.

"Good," Mouse confirmed.

"Speak for yourself, fat man," Monster muttered.

Stupid laced his fingers together, Bien stepped into his cupped hands, and he boosted her up. From the top, she reached down to grab his wrist, and with a little scrabbling he was over.

By that point, the other Worthy had become fully absorbed in the spectacle. As Ruc and the others struggled to lift the boat above their heads, the abuse began.

"This is what it's going to look like on the holy days," someone joked. "These Annurian whores scrambling over each other to get out."

Ruc ignored the gibe.

Monster did not. "What it's going to look like," she shouted over her shoulder, "is me shoving this skiff up your puckered fucking asshole."

The crack earned her a wave of derisive laughter.

"It's your own ass you ought to be looking out for," someone shouted. "You keep waggling it around the yard, one of these days we're gonna test it out, see if it's as tight as it looks."

The woman half turned, her lips twisted with fury.

"In the Arena," Goatface observed calmly, invisible as an oracle in the boat above their heads, "your opponents will try to unsettle you, to provoke you."

"It's working," Monster growled.

"And when we get finished with you," the heckling continued, "we're moving right on to the one with the mud sucker ink."

"Bet mud isn't the only thing he sucks."

Do not measure scorn for scorn or hate for hate, Ruc told himself, straining beneath the weight of the boat. *Who makes their heart a home for bile and rage is never clean, never free.* The last fifteen years it had been those words, those and the other Teachings, that he had leaned on in the roughest quarters of Dombâng, reciting them in his mind whenever he was cursed, or mocked, or spat upon. He remembered his amazement at discovering, for the first time, that they were true, that they *worked,* that the world was a brighter, better place when he looked at it through the twin lenses of love and forgiveness.

Lenses that had cracked when Eira's temple burned.

He could still recite the words, still remember every teaching, still believe intellectually in the message of the goddess. It was the *feel* of her truth that had vanished. He tried to put away his rage only to find it stuck to him, lodged in his soul like a burr in good silk. What he wanted to do was to drop the boat, round on the other Worthy, and bury his fist in their faces over and over until they stopped talking. The urgency of the desire frightened him.

"If," Goatface continued mildly from above, "you want to provide your foes with a gift, you will allow yourself to be goaded."

Ruc took a deep breath, felt the rage fill the air inside his lungs, then blew it out slowly.

"Just lift the boat," he growled, straining beneath the weight.

"Lift," Mouse agreed.

"All right, you ungoadable shitheads," Monster snapped. "I'm fucking lifting."

Talal, for his part, remained silent, the muscles of his back and shoulders flexing as he drove the bow of the boat upward toward the top of the wall.

"Forward," Bien called down. "You have to come forward." Then, after a couple of laborious steps: "I've got it!"

It didn't feel like she had it. It felt, if anything, as though the hull were growing heavier. It was one thing to hold the boat at shoulder height, quite another to steady it high overhead. Ruc could hear Monster muttering a string of curses just behind him, and beyond her, down by the end of the boat, Mouse's labored breathing.

"We need someone else up here," Bien said, her voice tight with strain. "Quick."

"Talal . . ." Ruc began.

"Go," the Kettral said.

"Go," Mouse agreed.

"Can the three of you . . ."

"Just get the fuck up there, lover man," Monster spat.

The hull sagged when Ruc released his hold. Mouse groaned and Talal gave a quick, involuntary grunt. Monster, for a miraculous few heartbeats, quit her cursing.

Ruc lingered just long enough to make sure they weren't going to drop it, then took two quick strides toward the wall, leapt, caught the top, and vaulted himself over. Bien and Stupid were leaning out over the sand, hands on the rail of the boat, trying to lift it and guide it forward all at the same time. Ruc slid between them, found purchase just under the front deck, and lifted. It felt as though his shoulder might pop from its socket, but then Bien and Stupid were able to adjust their hold and the weight became bearable once more. Gradually, step by laborious step, they moved the boat up until it was Monster's turn to climb the wall, then Talal's, and finally, when almost the whole hull had slid over the top of the wall, Mouse's.

The huge man, as it turned out, was better at lifting than climbing. He'd held the stern of the boat all alone, sweat streaming down his forehead, eyes squeezed tight against the strain, as Talal scampered up to join the others. The wall, however, seemed likely to defeat him. He'd taken hold of the top easily enough—he could reach the full distance without even jumping—but couldn't pull his weight up. After a couple of aborted pull-ups, he tried walking his feet up, then heaving a leg over as Monster had done—to no avail.

"Any week now, you fucking anchor," Monster shouted.

"Anchor?" Mouse protested, straining yet again to drag himself up.

"He needs help," Bien said.

"We all need fucking help," Monster shot back. "Unless you grow some muscle, we're not holding this boat just four of us."

Bien hesitated, then nodded. "I'll go. I'm the weakest."

"There seems to be a gap," Stupid managed, "in the logic there."

Bien, however, had already slipped out from beneath the hull. The skiff dipped a little without her support, but it wasn't like losing Mouse or Talal. Ruc gritted his teeth, pushed a little harder, and the boat steadied as Bien dropped into the pit. How she planned to hoist a man three times her weight over the obstacle Ruc had no idea. The answer, as it turned out, was that she didn't. Instead of trying to lift Mouse up, she dropped to all fours next to the wall. Ruc could just glimpse her over the edge, knees and hands buried in the wet sand.

The Worthy of the other trainers whooped with delight.

"At least the Annurians know how to kneel!"

"Take her, fat man. Take her!"

Bien ignored them.

"Stand on my back," she said. Her breathing was labored but her voice was steady.

"Stand?" Mouse asked, staring down at her with obvious dismay.

"You won't break me."

"We'll fucking see about that," Monster muttered.

Mouse continued to hesitate.

"In the Arena," Goatface observed mildly from his swaying perch, "what separates the living from the dead is often not skill, but the ability to make a quick decision."

"Go!" Bien growled.

Mouse grimaced, put a massive foot on her lowered shoulders, closed his eyes, then stepped up.

She let out a low, choked, involuntary groan, but managed somehow not to collapse. The step put Mouse barely a couple of feet above the level of the sand, but it proved enough. With a furious heave the man dragged himself upward, managed to hold for a moment, his arms bent, his boots scrabbling. Bien staggered up, threw herself against the wall, cried out as one thrashing foot took her in the side of the head, braced her back against the planks, caught Mouse's foot as it swung wildly, and planted it firmly on her slender shoulder.

"Stop kicking," she shouted. *"Stop kicking!"*

"Sorry," Mouse panted.

"Don't be sorry, just *climb.*"

For his perch on her shoulders, the man was able to throw a leg over the top of the wall, and then, as Bien turned around and pushed with her hands against his other foot, to drag himself over.

It took him a moment to straighten himself out. Then he reached down, caught Bien's outstretched hand, and plucked her up as though she weighed no more than the clothes on her back.

"In the event that the two of you have finished with the acrobatics . . ." Stupid suggested.

Mouse turned, caught the stern of the skiff, and suddenly the weight was manageable once more.

Bien was shaking. Monster panted like a woman who'd just paddled the circumference of the city. Mouse's face had gone from pale brown to angry purple. Only the Kettral looked strong. He looked, in fact, as though he could go on carrying the boat all day.

Which proved fortunate, as that was just what Goatface expected them to do.

As the trainer sat in the hull sipping his wine and enjoying the shade of his parasol, they carried the funeral skiff to the top of the Arena, across a section of seating, down the next long flight of stairs, across the bottom, up again, across, down, across, up. . . .

"I had a reason for choosing this *particular* boat," Goatface told them after some time had passed. "It is, after all, a *funeral* skiff. This hull is what awaits on the high holy days for all those who lag in the . . . *diligence* of their training."

"Forget about the high holy days," Stupid replied. "You might be packing me into it this afternoon if we keep carrying the 'Kent-kissing thing around in this heat."

Goatface chuckled. "I find that . . . improbable. Another purpose of this exercise is to remind you that your bodies, even those of you who are new to the Arena, are far stronger than you realize. Remember this, when you are fighting in the ring."

"Remember that I carried a fucking boat on my back for half a day?" Monster demanded.

"Remember that when you thought you could not go on, you went on. Remember that when you thought you would fall, you stood."

"Or," Monster said grimly, "we could just put you and it down."

"You are correct, naturally," Goatface replied. "You don't have to do this. The six of you could decide to lower the skiff right now. I certainly couldn't stop you." He paused to let that sink in, then continued. "I will point out, however, that I am not the only . . . *observer* here."

Ruc managed to lift his head enough to steal a look down into the pit. There were, if anything, more Worthy gathered than there had been in the morning. They had come for their own training, but many of them were stealing glances up into the stands, following the strange progress of Goatface's Worthy. Sometime around the middle of the morning, Ruc realized, they had stopped laughing.

"If you put the boat down now," Goatface said, "you will be the Worthy who put down the boat."

"Fucking obviously," Monster muttered. Some of the heat, however, had faded from her voice.

"If, on the other hand, you bear up under this burden, you will be known as the Worthy who, all through the crushing heat of the day, carried on their backs this vessel of death, who from sunrise to sunset, refused to put it down. They will face you in the Arena soon enough, these foes of yours. What do you want them to learn about you today? That you cannot be broken? Or that halfway through, you put down your burden?"

A silence stretched, thick and hot.

Then Bien hacked up something that might have been phlegm or blood before managing two words: "Fuck. That."

Stupid coughed a chuckle. "Barely a day, Monster, and your foul mouth is rubbing off on the priests."

"I assume this means," Ruc said, shifting the weight on his shoulders, trying to find some position where the agony was a little less, "that we're not putting it down."

"Not," Mouse agreed.

Talal snorted.

"The decision is, of course, all yours," Goatface announced from above.

"I hate you all," Monster said, adjusting her grip on the hull, then lifting it just a little bit higher.

21

"That," Akiil said, studying the curve of the weapon in the bloodwood cradle, "looks like a very expensive sword."

"Priceless," Adare replied.

He glanced over his shoulder, toward the spiral staircase that climbed through the floor, twisted three times, and disappeared through the ceiling.

"Hugel and Brandt must be slipping, leaving you alone in a room with me and a sword."

Room. Sword.

The words were almost laughably inadequate.

The space in which he stood—an entire circular floor of Intarra's Spear—was hardly a *room*. It was at least the size of the whole dormitory back at Ashk'lan, and seemed even larger because, instead of being walled off into tiny cells, the floor was open, an undivided expanse ringed by twenty-foot walls of glass.

Or whatever impossible, ancient, possibly Csestriim substance it was that passed for glass.

They'd climbed barely a fraction of the tower's height, but even that fraction lifted them into what felt like another world. The myriad buildings of the palace complex sprawled far below—a city inside the larger city—and beyond its walls, the labyrinth of Annur's streets and canals. To the west, the sword-straight avenue of Anlatun's Way plunged through the heart of the capital, wide flagstones illuminated by a thousand burning braziers. To the east, ships rocked at anchor, lanterns swinging from their sterns. Akiil turned, gazed out to the south, followed the streets with his eyes—along Tailor's Row, over the Duck Bridge, through the Flower Market and the Wool Market, under Rishinira's Gate, over Dead Man's Canal, and *there* . . .

Even from the Spear's height, the Perfumed Quarter looked different from the rest of Annur. Worse. A smudge across the city's flank. No blazing braziers. No temple fires kept always burning. No torchlit mansions. What lights he could make out were dim, furtive, hooded lanterns and barely cracked shutters. Tallow was expensive. Oil was expensive. With the nearest forests hacked back further and further every year, even wood cost more coin than most people in Annur's most desperate neighborhood could afford. No one lived long in the Quarter without getting used to the darkness.

A knot tightened beneath his ribs. He took a deep breath, set about unraveling it.

"Have you been back?"

He glanced over to find Adare just at his shoulder. Silken slippers; he hadn't heard her following him across the polished floor.

"Back?"

She gestured. "To your former neighborhood."

"Why would I go back?"

"People tend to."

He forced down a vision of Skinny Quinn's bleeding face, her arm reaching out to claim him. The dreams had been coming more often, almost every night. The only way to hold them off seemed to be drinking half a bottle of black rum before turning in. The liquor offered at least a few hours of blank oblivion before the abbot he'd murdered and the friends he'd abandoned rose up again.

He cobbled together a laugh. "Not people from the Quarter." Before she could ask him anything else, he turned away from the glass wall and the city beyond, back toward the riches of the lamplit room. "What's the point of having all this stuff," he asked, "if you have to hike up five hundred stairs just to see it?"

Stuff, like *room,* was not the right word.

The great, soaring space was filled with treasure, hoard, plunder.

The gorgeous sword was only one of a hundred pieces. Ancient vases sat atop ancient plinths. Rings, necklaces, and bracelets lay across rich velvet. An inscrutable mechanical instrument the size of a wheelbarrow crouched on a long bloodwood table, all lenses, and springs, and polished gears. Something like a huge bronze bowl—large enough to boil half a dozen humans—hung from massive hooks set into the ceiling. There was a collection of skulls in a glass case. A rack of spears. Glass spheres filled with liquids that might have been wine, or vinegar, or blood.

"Protection," Adare replied.

"Sure," he agreed. "It's safer up here." They'd passed through three guardhouses—one at the base of the Spear and two during the climb. "But the whole point of *having* expensive shit is to show it off."

He reached out for a ring that might have been carved from glacial ice.

Adare's voice snapped like a whip. "Don't."

He glanced over, offered a winning smile. "If I was going to steal it, I'd be a lot sneakier."

She shook her head. "If you stole it you would die."

"I get it. It's yours. No need for the threats."

"It is a fact, not a threat. The last man to wear that ring went mad. He raved for a period of weeks, even after taking it off, then clawed out his own eyes, drove his fingers straight into his brain, and kept gouging until he collapsed."

Akiil blinked.

She offered him a chilly smile. "I'm afraid you misunderstood me. It is not the artifacts that need protection from the thieves. . . ."

Gingerly, he withdrew his hand.

"So," he said, looking around slowly. "This is leach stuff, then."

"Csestriim," she replied. "Some of it almost certainly crafted by Csestriim leaches. The rest the result of other knowledge and processes long since lost."

"Where did it come from?"

"The collection was acquired by my father, and his father, and all the rest of them back to Terial hui'Malkeenian."

"How do you know that it's Csestriim? Most of it's pretty shiny. Nothing looks like—what?—ten thousand years old."

"The Dawn Palace houses over a hundred historians and scholars of Csestriim antiquity."

Over a hundred.

The decadence made him momentarily dizzy. Somehow, that single figure drove home the Emperor's wealth more than the palace and guards, more than all the fine furnishings, more than Intarra's Spear itself. There was a point, after all, to having guards. A point to all the servants. A point to the gardeners and cooks and carpenters and all the rest. But a hundred people—*over* a hundred people—whose only work was to sit and read, maybe jot the occasional note, all of them clothed and housed and fed within the walls of the Dawn Palace. . . .

"That's a lot of people," he replied, "to study a race we wiped out millennia ago."

He almost missed it.

Adare's expression didn't change. She didn't flinch or recoil. She didn't move at all. And yet there was *something,* some reaction too fast and fleeting for his conscious mind to follow. . . .

He closed his eyes, summoned the image back to mind.

"What are you doing?" she asked.

"Looking at something," he said, scrutinizing the *saama'an* of her face. Perfect memory had uses other than monastic study.

"Looking at what?"

"You."

He let the memory move forward slowly, dragged it back, set it into motion again. Three times he went through the vision until finally . . .

. . . *A race we wiped out millennia ago.*

There—a minute dilation of her pupils, the flutter of the pulse in the vein at her neck.

"Oh," he said, smiling, opening his eyes. "I see."

Adare's pupils blazed. "What is it, exactly, that you see?"

"The Csestriim *aren't* actually dead. Not all of them, anyway."

She hid her reaction well, but this time he was ready for it.

"The Csestriim are gone," she replied—he let the lie go for the moment—"but their artifacts are not."

"What does this one do?" he asked, turning to the geared mechanism.

"I was hoping you could tell me."

He couldn't help his laughter. "You have over a hundred—what did you call them?—*historians and scholars of Csestriim antiquity* and you're asking a thief from the Quarter?"

"Have you not been trying to convince me for weeks now that you are no longer a thief? That you have cut yourself free of your past?"

He tried to imagine that, being cut free, the weightlessness of a life with no memories, no doubts, no regrets, no one left behind. . . .

He realized Adare was studying him.

"What I said," he replied, dragging himself back to the moment, "is that I can teach you to use the *kenta.*"

"The *kenta* were made by the Csestriim. As were the things here. There may be a link between them."

"Maybe." He nodded. "Sure." He eyed her slyly. "What *about* those Csestriim? The living ones, I mean. Why don't you ask them?"

Again, that almost invisible flicker of recognition.

"I have told you that there are no living Csestriim."

"You did tell me that." He winked. "It was a lie, but you *did* say it."

The Emperor took a slow breath. Her eyes burned so brightly it was amazing her face didn't catch fire. "Would I be asking you the questions if I already knew the answers?"

So. Whatever her relationship to any surviving Csestriim, clearly it left something to be desired. In time, he might be able to ferret out the truth, but she clearly had no intention of sharing it with him willingly.

He spread his arms in invitation. "What do you want to know?"

"Did the monks ever mention the other artifacts?"

He shook his head. "I think you're confused. The Shin didn't care about the Csestriim. They didn't care about the wars or the fortresses or the artifacts."

"They cared about the *kenta*."

"No. The *Malkeenians* cared about the *kenta,* so they sent their heirs to the Shin. All the Shin cared about was learning to snuff out the self."

Adare grimaced. "You're proving less useful than I'd hoped."

"I didn't promise to teach you about any of this shit," Akiil replied. "I didn't even know it existed. What I told you, that first day in the garden, was that I could train you to use the gates."

"For a fee."

"Even monks have to eat."

"With what I have paid you already, you could feed an entire monastery."

"And I am grateful."

"I am not. Since you arrived, you have peddled me nothing but nonsense. I have spent every morning since the new moon sitting like a stone—"

He shook his head. "No. You sit like an Emperor. If you could sit like a stone, you wouldn't need me."

"I grow less convinced every day that I *do* need you."

"Look." He held up his hands in a placating gesture. "I get it. I spent a decade with the Shin. *Watch the snow melt, Akiil. Watch the ice drip. Run up that mountain. Akiil, why don't you take this ladle and empty the river.* It all feels like horseshit if you don't understand the point."

Adare's voice was dangerously calm when she replied. "Then why don't you tell me the point?"

He shook his head. "That'll just make it harder. I tell you what the exercises are for, and you'll start focusing on your goal, on your *desire*—and *poof.*"

"Poof."

"Exactly."

She watched him. "I'm not sure you appreciate the precariousness of your position."

Akiil spent a moment trying to decide whether she'd really said that.

It seemed as though she had.

He smiled at her.

"When I was young, really young, five or six, we had a little gang. Horan, Skinny Quinn, Runt, Butt Boy, and me. Raced around the Quarter stealing shit, hawking it in the market, sleeping like puppies in a washed-out part of the bank beneath Lover's Bridge. *One day,* we told each other, *we'll steal enough coin to buy a house, something outside the Quarter, maybe even a place with glass in the windows.*"

He shrugged.

"As you can probably guess, we did not. By the time I was eight, Horan had been knifed in a brawl. The Captain scooped up Skinny Quinn and Runt, started selling them for five coppers a fuck. When Butt Boy tried to break them out, a pair of the Captain's men caught him, took turns beating him with sticks until his face was mush, then fed what was left of him to the Captain's hogs. I watched the whole thing from behind a wagon. The beating, I mean. Not the bit with the hogs. I even thought about charging in bravely to save him. Then I thought better of it.

"Things seemed safer out in Ashk'lan. The monks would hit you, starve you, make you run naked through the snow, but they didn't kill you. *This is better,* I thought. *It's boring here, but it's safe.* Then a bunch of men dressed exactly like your Aedolian Guard showed up and killed everyone."

"Those were not Aedolians," Adare replied, voice tight. "Not true Aedolians."

"I didn't spend a lot of time pondering the truth of their Aedolianness."

"And the moral of this plaintive tale?"

"That maybe, Your Shiny, Sparkling Radiance, when it comes to the precariousness of life, you should not be the one giving the lectures."

Most people would have been discomfited by the account of rape and slaughter. Adare just snorted.

"I would be delighted to listen to a lecture," she replied, "on the use of the 'Kent-kissing *kenta.*"

"That's not how it works."

She leaned toward him, eyes ablaze. "I do not have ten years to spend sitting atop mountains listening to the wind. I do not have ten years to ladle water out of rivers or watch ice drip. I do not have five years. I might not have one year. Whatever the Shin did, whatever their method, *I do not care.* Annur is staggering. . . ." She trailed off, shook her head, as though dismissing everything she'd just said. "Let me put this in language that will matter to you. If you want more gold, you will explain to me something useful, something I can understand. There will be no mention of stones, or stillness, or empty vessels. If you cannot do this, we are finished."

Her eyes blazed so bright he half expected to feel the heat on his face. After matching that gaze for a full breath—long enough to show her he wasn't impressed, not so long that she'd take it for defiance—he turned away, back toward the city, toward the blighted streets of the Perfumed Quarter.

It wasn't a bad offer. It was true enough what she'd said about having given him enough coin to feed a monastery. With that gold he could buy a small cottage somewhere, a farmhouse, a little place on the ocean, complete with a dock and a boat. There would be enough left over to live for years, him and Yerrin both, especially if they were frugal. And anyway, he'd *done* what he came to do, hadn't he? He'd returned to Annur, talked his way into an audience with the Emperor, and tricked her out of her gold. All that was left was to nod, apologize, and explain that the Shin path was the only path he knew. A handful of words and it would be over. Victory for the orphaned kid from the Quarter.

It didn't feel like victory. It didn't feel like anything.

"Did Kaden ever talk to you about the *vaniate*?" he asked, not looking away from the stars gleaming beyond the glass wall.

"No," Adare said after a pause. Then, "Why don't you assume Kaden never talked to me about anything."

"It's a Csestriim word. It means *emptiness*. Or *nothingness*."

When he turned to face Adare, he could see the tightness in her jaw. "I just finished telling you that I do not have time to contemplate a sermon on empty pots."

"Not pots," he replied. "People."

Adare narrowed her eyes. "Meaning what?"

"What is a person?" Akiil asked. When she didn't reply, he gestured to his body. "Not this. Not the legs and the head and all the rest of it. You see a few bodies rotting in canals and you know that the body has nothing to do with the person who used to live inside it." He shook his head. "The person is all the *other* stuff—all the thoughts, and memories, and emotions. The *vaniate* is what you end up in when you get rid of those."

"Get rid of them," Adare repeated.

Akiil nodded, plastered on his most confident smile.

The tricky truth of the matter was that he didn't *really* know. A few of his teachers had mentioned the *vaniate,* and he'd spent days and days arguing about it with Kaden, but he wasn't lying when he told Adare that the Shin method was long on sitting and short on any kind of explanation. He'd certainly never managed the trance himself. At least he didn't think he had. Would you know if you'd managed to scrub out your self? Yerrin was the only monk left alive, and Yerrin was even worse at explaining things than the others had been.

Not that he intended to tell Adare any of that.

"The *vaniate* is the trance that remains," he said instead, "when you have extinguished everything that makes you who you are."

She frowned. "If I had no thoughts, how would I act? If I had no memories, how would I reach the *kenta*? If I had no emotions, why would I bother doing anything at all?"

Akiil aimed for something like the quiet sternness of Scial Nin. "Every novice asks these questions."

"I am not a novice. I am the Emperor of Annur and the prophet of Intarra."

This was safer ground. The nuances of the *vaniate* eluded him, but he was more or less certain that insisting on titles wasn't part of it.

"The Blank God cares nothing for words."

"Does he not?" Adare asked. She cocked her head to the side, considered him with those burning eyes, then nodded. "Perhaps you're right."

He started to smile.

"Enough words, then," she went on. "I think it is time for a demonstration." She met his brittle smile with one of her own. "I think it is time for you to *show* me how a student of the Shin monks can pass through the gates."

22

Five days after the battle, Gwenna and Bhuma Dhar were hauled out of the brig onto the deck of the *Daybreak*.

She squinted at the too-bright sun, the waves so blue they burned her eyes, the green . . .

"Land," she murmured as the coastline resolved in her vision.

She hadn't expected to see land again, she realized. Hadn't expected to see anything.

Every day, legionaries had come for the Manjari captain, hauling him out of the brig, then returning him later with a new complement of gashes and bruises.

"Your admiral is zealous in his pursuit of the truth," he remarked after the third day.

"So tell him the truth."

"I have. Men with this hunger do not want to believe. As long as he thinks I am lying, he has something to strive for."

Jonon hadn't broken the Manjari captain, despite the burns, the bruises to his face and body, the dislocated fingers that Gwenna had reset one by one, but Dhar had begun to smell of resignation. He expected to die aboard the ship, and soon, that much was obvious. Every day he ate less, said less, and so she spoke less in turn. It was a species of relief to be locked away with someone else who had also moved beyond hope.

The anger that had sustained her since the Purple Baths had vanished, snuffed out as surely as yesterday's flame. Darkness yawned in its place, a wide, blank, black expanse with no name or limit. After the battle, she'd tried to return to her exercises, managing half a dozen push-ups before she sank to the damp decking and stopped. The muscles of her arms and shoulders felt like mud, but the muscles weren't the problem. She'd pushed her body past the point of failure plenty of times—in training, in war—but as she lay there on the rough wood, she found nothing inside herself capable of pushing. In place of the old stubbornness there was only pain and regret, and when she tried to lean on them, they folded beneath her.

The nights were worse. When she was awake, she wanted nothing more than to tumble into oblivion, but her snatches of sleep offered up the same dream over and over:

Talal's face, just as it had been in the Purple Baths, streaked with blood and sweat. All over again, she watched his features strain as he used the last of his strength to heave Qora through the collapsing door. Screaming, Gwenna forced her way back through that door only to find herself on the deck of the *Daybreak,* with Talal sprawled out dead before her, his arm torn off at the shoulder by the force of an explosion. A few paces away, Jak hunched over the stump of a shattered leg.

Need to find the artery, he muttered. *Need to stop the blood.*

He looked up, met Gwenna's eyes.

Do you have a bandage?

Every time, instead of a bandage, she handed him a starshatter, its fuse already lit.

What's this? he asked, face quizzical.

No, she tried to shout. *Get rid of it! Throw it overboard!*

But the words congealed like day-old grease in her throat, and, every time, Jak smiled his thanks at her, pressed the bomb to his ruined leg, relief flooding his features, as though he'd known all along that she would be there, that she'd save him.

The explosion itself offered the barest moment of respite, jolting her from the dream's daylight into the rolling darkness of the brig. Sweating, she'd drag in a harried breath, and for just a moment she'd start to relax, realizing it was all just a dream. Then memory would wrap a fist around her guts and twist: the dream was wrong in the details, but the details didn't matter. Talal was dead. Quick Jak was dead. All those Annurian sailors . . .

The weight felt like water, like fathoms of ocean piled on top of her, crushing the air from her lungs, squeezing her heart until she thought it would burst. The world was too tight, too small. Her hands trembled as she stared at nothing, stared into the nothing for hours sometimes, from one watch to the next. Darkness was the only consolation. It absolved her from putting on any kind of face for Bhuma Dhar, absolved her from doing anything at all. Not that there was anything to do. Nothing but sit and rot.

After days of that, it hurt to be dragged back out into the sun, forced to see that the world was still there, bright and waiting, as though it expected something.

She stared through the haze of her sun-blindness toward the shore.

They were in a harbor, she realized, sheltered from the sea beyond by a craggy headland thirty or forty paces high. In the lee of that headland, stacked in concentric terraces up the rocky hillside, stood a village. Two hundred homes, maybe three, most built of wooden posts and thatched with palm leaves, roofs overhanging to provide outdoor shelter when the storms came. If the details were slightly strange—the ends of posts carved into wooden ornaments, bouquets of brightly colored flowers pinned up above doorways to flutter in the wind—it still looked like a normal enough town, the kind of place she might have stumbled across anywhere in southern Eridroa. Nothing, at first glance, to raise the small hairs on the back of her neck, and yet she could feel those hairs standing on end.

You're a fool, she told herself wearily. *A fool and now*—she glanced down at her trembling hands—*a coward, evidently.*

She found herself baffled by the fear. Of course she'd been afraid hundreds of times before, *thousands* of times. You'd have to be insane to go through Kettral training—let alone war—without feeling fear. And yet, always before there had been a *reason* for the fear, some danger or threat to which she could put a name, some problem she could go about solving. Not any longer. No foe prowled the deck of the *Daybreak.* The day was warm, calm, the offshore breeze soft in her hair. And yet she felt the terror like a claw around her throat.

Something in the village, she told herself desperately, scouring the shore.

A thin stream of water split the town, tumbling down the slope from the land to the east. It wasn't much—so narrow Gwenna could have leaped over it with a running start—but the inhabitants had made the most of the current, digging pools into the hillside to catch the flow—for washing, probably, or bathing. There was even a small waterwheel near the bottom spinning noisily away, though its purpose wasn't immediately obvious. Down at the water, two docks extended into the harbor, each larger than Gwenna would have expected for such a small town. Evidence of trade with the large Manjari ships, maybe, although there were no ships other than the *Daybreak* in the small harbor. No ships, no boats, nothing at all that looked like it could float.

That *was* strange.

She turned her attention back to the town. Not only were there no boats, there seemed to be no people, either. All the signs of human habitation remained. Large clay water pots sat beside the doors, ladles hanging from the lips. Tidy earthen ovens squatted beneath the overhanging roofs, pots and pans stacked atop them. Hammers hung neatly beneath the eaves of an open-walled structure that could only be a forge. The village didn't look abandoned. All signs pointed to people, but there were no people. The only living things were a few gulls perched on the eaves, and a solitary pig wandering between the cottages, rooting at the dirt, snorting disconsolately.

The locals might have been hiding—a foreign warship hung at anchor in their harbor, after all—but when Gwenna closed her eyes to focus she heard nothing. Oh, there was the knocking about and shouting of Jonon's sailors and soldiers going through their duties on the deck of the *Daybreak*, but beneath all that she could find no hint of whispered voices, no footfalls on the village paths, no muffled sobs. She drew a deep breath in through her nose, braced herself for the reek of rotting bodies, then exhaled slowly. The only rot she smelled was faint, vegetal. Squash, maybe, or manioc. A whiff of salted fish drifted over from the drying racks down by the harbor, but it felt old, faint, mostly scoured away by the wind, as though no fish had hung there for days, maybe even weeks. For a moment, the wind shifted and she caught the copper sent of blood. Then it shifted back and the scent vanished.

"Something is wrong here," she whispered.

Bhuma Dhar nodded at her side. "Indeed."

The words earned each of them a cuff alongside the head.

Gwenna half turned to find the man who'd struck her—one of the two legionaries responsible for dragging her out of the brig—with his hand still raised.

"Keep talking to each other," he said. "See what happens."

He wore a smile that she recognized. People decided to become soldiers for a hundred different reasons: to serve their empire; for a handful of coin; to escape something or somewhere; because their friends signed on; to spite a father or a mother; to please a father or mother; for the misguided notion it might make them famous. . . . Some, however, joined up for the simple joy of inflicting pain. Back on the Islands, Gwenna had learned to recognize them. There was a gleam to the eye, an eagerness, a hunger you learned to pick out in the way they leaned toward any scene of violence, and often, as now, there was a hook at the edge of the smile.

"What do you want with us?" Gwenna asked quietly.

"What do *I* want?" The legionary tapped a finger on his bottom lip, looked her up and down, leaned in so close she could have torn off his ear with her teeth, then smelled her hair, her neck.

"Chent," said the other soldier. There was a warning in his tone, but Gwenna could smell the lust on him, too, cloying and sick. "Admiral said bring 'em, not sniff 'em."

Chent fingered her hair, then pulled away. Like Gwenna, he was pale-skinned, one of only a few men in the crew who shared her complexion. He stared at her with blue eyes that might have been the mirror of her own, ran a tongue over his lips, smiled wider, then shrugged. "Today, it's not a question of what *I* want." He gestured toward the shore. "Jonon sent for the two of you."

It was not Jonon, however, who met them at the dock, but the Emperor's historian. Gwenna hadn't seen him since the battle. Something had torn a gouge across his cheek, but aside from that he appeared none the worse for the encounter. He watched silently as Gwenna, Dhar, and the two legionaries disembarked from the boat.

"More torture?" Dhar asked, gazing around at the village.

"Not today," Kiel replied. "Not from me."

Chent put the tip of his naked cutlass against Gwenna's lower back. "Up," he said, gesturing with his free hand toward the stone steps snaking up the hillside. "Don't want to keep the admiral waiting."

"I'll take them from here," Kiel said.

The legionary narrowed his eyes. "Angling for some time alone with the lady, old man?"

"Jonon wants every soldier going through the houses looking for people."

"No people here," scoffed the other soldier. "None alive, anyway."

"The orders are not mine," Kiel replied evenly. "If you come with us, you can explain to the admiral why you chose to disobey them."

Chent shifted his gaze from Kiel to Gwenna. "She's shifty, this one. Squirmy. What if she runs off on you?"

"If she runs," the other legionary said, "we get to chase her."

The historian raised his brows, ran his eyes over the empty town, the rocky headland. "To where would she run?"

"I'm not running," Gwenna said.

Not long ago, listening to three men talk about her as though she were a stray dog would have led her to hit someone, maybe several someones. As she stood there on the shifting dock, she half expected the anger to come. It did not. All she wanted was for this to be over—whatever *this* was—so she could go back to the brig, back to the darkness.

Chent patted her on the shoulder, gave a little squeeze, then turned away.

"Come on, Lurie," he said to the other legionary. "Let's see if there's anything in this dung heap worth taking."

As the two soldiers broke off to search the homes, Kiel led Gwenna and Dhar along a path verging the harbor. Sunlight jeweled the harbor waves. It was hot, Gwenna realized, almost as hot as it had been back in Dombâng. She'd done nothing but sit in the boat and already she was sweating beneath her blacks.

Twenty paces on, they came to a large, unwalled building with a half-built boat sitting in a cradle at the center. Adzes, axes, chisels all hung neatly from hooks in the low rafters. Only one tool lay out of place—a large hammer, incongruously dropped or tossed in the sawdust.

Dhar stepped from the path into the shade, crossed to the unfinished vessel, ran a hand along the lapstrake planking.

"This is the labor of many days. Not a thing a person would walk away from."

Gwenna nodded, nudged the sawdust near the hammer with her boot. It was dark, clotted with dried blood. "Maybe they didn't walk."

The Manjari captain turned warily.

"It's all right," Gwenna said. "This happened a while ago. Maybe three weeks or so."

Dhar raised his eyebrows.

She gestured at the tools. "It's been about three weeks since those were oiled. Give or take."

"How do you know?" the captain asked.

"The rust." The barest haze of brown smudged the steel. "It's about right for three weeks unoiled out in the salt air."

Evidently there was some stubborn, stupid part of her mind that still thought it was Kettral.

"What is this place?" she asked, turning in a slow circle, taking in the town all over again.

"Solengo," Dhar replied. "One of the larger towns on Menkiddoc's northwestern coast."

Gwenna glanced over at Kiel. "What does Jonon lem Jonon want with Solengo?"

"It would appear," the historian said, "that our admiral's curiosity has been whetted by tales of missing ships."

"Not tales," Dhar replied. "Truth."

Kiel nodded, cast a significant glance around the empty harbor, the empty homes. "So it appears. Jonon has questions for you. For both of you."

"You might as well toss me back in the brig," Gwenna said. "I don't know shit about any of it."

"You knew," the historian pointed out, "that the inhabitants had been gone about three weeks."

"Or not. They might have different steel here. Or different oil. I really have no fucking idea how long they've been gone."

"The admiral will be disappointed to hear that. I suggested to him that your perspective might be valuable."

She stared at him.

"I don't know shit about Menkiddoc," she said. "Or Solengo, or any of it, and you know that."

Kiel nodded.

"So why the fuck am I out here?"

"Because I want this mission to succeed. It is more likely to succeed if you are involved."

Gwenna was shocked to feel the tears welling in her eyes. She turned, scrubbed them away with a cuff. "Maybe you haven't been paying attention to what's been happening to missions when I get involved."

Out of the corner of her eye she saw him shrug. "I'm certain the First Admiral will return you to the brig when he has asked his questions."

"What of the homes?" Dhar asked.

"See for yourself," Kiel replied, gesturing to a cluster of wooden houses across the path from the boathouse.

Gwenna half expected something to attack her as she put a hand on the door's latch. Solengo had offered nothing but sunlight and a warm breeze, but she still couldn't shake the sense of impending disaster. She reached up for one of her swords, closed her fingers around empty air, felt the absence like a staff to the chest.

The historian noticed the motion. "It seems quite safe."

"Nothing's safe," Gwenna replied, pushing open the door.

Despite her foreboding, nothing erupted screaming from the shadows. Inside the house she found a neatly made bed, two feather-stuffed pillows propped at the head. A table with an oil lamp sat across the room, a wooden chest beneath it. When she flipped open the lid she found it brimming with neatly folded clothes. Clay pots waited by the door. Dried herbs and flowers hung from the beams overhead. A meticulously woven carpet sprawled across the floor. A box of pungent-smelling herbs sat on a shelf beside a scroll inked in some language she didn't recognize.

She stood alone in the center of the dim space, rotated slowly, running her gaze around the room. Something twitched in the corner, and she spun, fists raised, to find a rat staring back at her, teeth bared, black eyes gleaming.

"Fuck you, too," she muttered.

Her heart scrabbled inside her chest like an animal caught in a trap.

She took a deep breath, closed her eyes. She could smell the damp thatch overhead, the pipe leaf in the jar on the shelf, even the faded scent of the flowers on the table. Underneath all that lurked the sea and salt, the dirt. Outside the door, the rest of the men were banging around, exploring the other houses one by one. By the sound of it, they hadn't found anything more interesting. Empty houses, no people . . .

"It's like they all just got up one morning and walked out," Dhar murmured.

Gwenna shook her head. "The hammer at the boathouse. The blood. A few people fought, but most were caught totally unaware. The question is, what happened to them?"

"That question has a part of an answer," Kiel replied.

He was standing by the open doorway, half in light, half in shadow.

"You have found people?" Dhar asked, turning.

"In a manner of speaking. We have found bodies. Twenty-two of them in the town square."

Gwenna shuddered at the word *bodies,* seeing in a flash the carnage of the *Daybreak*'s deck after the battle. She forced herself to stare at the historian, to focus on the moment.

"You didn't say anything about bodies."

"I am telling you now."

"You should have told us when we stepped off the fucking boat."

Kiel studied her as though she were a text in a strange language, a look in his eyes that was almost concern. Almost, but not quite.

"A few extra moments will make no difference," he replied finally.

"What happened to them?" Dhar asked.

"It is best that you see for yourself."

Gwenna's legs ached as they climbed the wide stone steps leading up through the village. She didn't realize how stiff she'd grown, locked in the narrow space of the brig. The simple work of walking hurt, each step a twist of the tendons, a spike through the hips and knees.

She glanced over at Kiel, an ugly new thought hatching inside her.

"What about the . . . sickness you described? The pollution of Menkiddoc? Could it have spread here, caused this?"

Kiel shook his head. "We would feel it."

"You can *feel* it?"

He nodded.

Dread unfolded inside her.

"What does it feel like?"

"At first, drunkenness without the confusion, a kind of confidence, strength, euphoria. Some explorers record a heightened sexual arousal, or a desire to sprint for miles and miles. Others, those with more education, might hurl themselves into elaborate mathematical proofs, convinced that they may finally apprehend truths that have eluded them for a lifetime."

"What about the insanity? What about the monsters?"

"Those," Kiel replied quietly, "come later."

"You are speaking," Dhar said, "of the *yakshma.*"

The historian nodded, as though he recognized the word. Gwenna just shook her head. "The what?"

"The *yakshma*. It is the . . . breakage of this land. The sickness. It is from the *yakshma* that the *gabbya* come."

Gwenna studied the captain. "What do you know about it?"

He shook his head. "Only that. Menkiddoc is sick. To stray from this coast is to invite disaster."

Before Gwenna could reply, the stone stairs leveled off. Kiel led them between two buildings into the central square of Solengo. The villagers had obviously taken pride in their town. Shopfronts with awnings of palm fronds opened onto the plaza. Halved trunks of trees carved into wooden benches sat in the shade. The whole space was cleverly cobbled in patterns of black and white stone, unfolding circles that reminded Gwenna of waves on still water. A stream was channeled through the center, spanned by a graceful wooden bridge. It wasn't hard to imagine kids splashing in the water while their parents leaned on the railing to chat. It seemed like a nice place to grow up, a nice place to live.

Except for the bodies hanging from the walls.

Bhuma Dhar muttered something beneath his breath, a curse or maybe a prayer.

Gwenna stopped, stared blankly at the carnage.

More than twenty bodies had been stripped naked, then tied to the walls of the surrounding buildings. . . .

No, she realized as she studied them, not tied. Their arms were stretched above them and nailed into the wood. They gave the impression of men and women reaching for something forever beyond their grasp. Her stomach clenched, trying to vomit, but nothing came up.

"They don't smell," she murmured.

She should have smelled them the moment she set foot on the dock. The square had become a small charnel yard. She should have smelled it from the fucking ship.

"That's because they are not rotting." Kiel gestured to the nearest corpse. "The blood has been drained away. All of it."

Gwenna crossed to the body. The historian was right. His flesh was sunken, shriveled, the brown skin dry as leather to the touch. Flies buzzed around what was left of his eyes, but aside from that, there was no sign of putrefaction. He reminded her of the herbs hung up to dry from the rafters of the houses below.

It was only when she drew close that she noticed the sun.

That's what the wound was shaped like, at least—a sun the width of her two palms side by side picked out in the skin across the dead man's chest. It looked like the work of some mad tattoo artist, as though someone had plunged needles into the dark skin over and over. . . . No, she realized, reaching out to run her hand over the punctures. Not needles, but hooks, each one embedded in the surface, stretching the skin and the muscle beneath.

At the center of the sun, right below the sternum, was a puncture. Gwenna pressed the ends together with her thumbs. The skin was stiff, but with enough pressure it yielded, opening like an angry mouth. She slid a finger inside, in, and in, until she was touching something that might have been the heart. When she pulled her finger out, it was clean save for a few brown flakes that seemed more rust than blood. Something had opened the man's chest, then drained the blood directly from his heart.

She stared at the shape of the sun. The scar tugged at her memory, like something she'd seen. . . .

"Why is she not shackled?"

The words knocked aside her thoughts. She turned to find Jonon striding across the square toward her, that beautiful face of his hard.

"I can vouch for her behavior," Kiel replied mildly.

Jonon shook his head. "My orders stand, regardless of your whims, historian."

Kiel nodded. "I apologize, First Admiral. I wanted to bring them as quickly as possible."

The admiral looked as though he might say something more, then turned abruptly from Kiel to Bhuma Dhar.

"What do you know about this?"

The Manjari captain shook his head. "Only those truths I have told you already. Our ships have not returned. Something is amiss here."

Jonon snorted, gestured to the silent, gaping bodies. "I didn't need to drag you out of the brig to learn that something is amiss. What else."

"Nothing," Dhar replied. "I was bound here when you encountered the *Ashwaya* and sank it."

"But your people trade here."

"All accounts describe these as peaceful, prospering villages."

"Well, they're not prospering now."

Jonon turned to Gwenna.

"The historian says the Kettral know something about this part of Menkiddoc."

She kept her face still.

The historian, she thought, *is lying.*

"A little. Not much."

"Local rivalries?" Jonon demanded. "Wars?"

Gwenna shook her head, recited back what she'd learned from Kiel and Dhar. "They're whaling villages. They trade with the Manjari. That's it."

"What about religion?" he pressed. "This could be some sort of sacrifice. Not the first place beyond the bounds of the empire where heathens like to open each other up for their gods." He gestured to the sun. "Looks like some kind of symbol."

Gwenna turned back to the body and the realization slapped her. "It's not a symbol," she said. "And it wasn't put there by a person."

Jonon studied her, then gestured mutely to the nails pounded through the dead man's wrists.

She nodded. "Sure. Someone nailed him up there, but this." She pointed to the wound. "I've seen it before, or something like it. It wasn't made by a knife or a spear. It looks like the bite of a lamprey."

"Lamprey." Jonon shook his head, then spoke slowly, as though explaining something to an idiot. "Lamprey live in the water. The largest are the length of my arm. They do not feast directly from the heart."

"*Gabhya,*" Dhar said quietly, not taking his eyes from the dead man. He made a gesture with his right hand, a sort of circle in the air.

Gwenna nodded. "You know the stories about Menkiddoc. About the monsters."

"I've been on ships since I was a boy," Jonon replied. "One thing I learned early was not to believe the stories."

"They are the truth," Kiel said. "Or there is truth inside them."

The admiral turned back to Bhuma Dhar. "Would you care to revise your tale of peaceful, prospering villages?"

Dhar shook his head. "The sickness is farther south. The journey of a week, perhaps. There should be no *gabhya* here."

Gwenna turned back to study the corpse. The man's lips were thin, flesh-less, drawn back from the teeth in what might have been a scream. His fingers were half clenched, as though straining to reach the nails driven through the wrists. She squinted. It was hard to see—the brown of the old blood was almost the same brown as the skin—but the wounds from those wrists had bled, bled a lot, streaming down the upraised arms, down the torso, and legs, to puddle on the ground. The cobblestones were stained with it. She knelt, scrubbed it between her fingers. It might have been dust.

"These people were alive when they were nailed up," she said quietly.

"Many *gabhya* are attracted to blood," Kiel suggested.

"So there was a fight," Jonon said. "These were the losers. The winners hammered them up to make an example. The monsters smelled the blood and came."

"Maybe," Gwenna said. The sun wasn't just warm, it was hot, relentless. As she straightened, she wavered on her feet. "Or maybe they weren't just found by the *gabhya*. Maybe they were *fed* to them."

For a few moments, even Jonon said nothing. Wind skirled through the square, lifting the hair of the dead, spinning dried leaves in tiny whirlwinds, then dropping them. Gwenna turned away from the body, but the vision was already in her mind, the man screaming, struggling as the nails went in, lashing out with his feet over and over until pain and exhaustion drained his strength. She imagined him hanging there, unable even to scream as whatever it was came on.

23

For half an afternoon back in Solengo—breathing the salt air, bathed in the sunshine, studying the aftermath of the massacre—Gwenna had almost felt like Kettral again, a woman with a job to do and the skills to do it. She'd tried to take that feeling with her when Jonon stuffed her back into the brig, and for the rest of the day she'd peppered Bhuma Dhar with questions:

Had he seen any *gabhya* that could suck the blood from a person's heart?

No.

Had he *heard* of any?

He'd heard all kinds of things.

Did the Manjari traffic in large *gabhya*?

No.

But maybe someone had decided to try?

Maybe.

Maybe something had gone wrong?

Maybe.

But that didn't explain the fucking nails pinning the people to the walls.

No. It did not.

What about the inhabitants of Solengo? Did Dhar know anything about them?

Not really.

Did *they* keep *gabhya*?

He didn't know.

What about the other villages in Menkiddoc?

He didn't know.

Were they empty too?

He didn't know.

After the twentieth or thirtieth thing he didn't know, Gwenna leaned back against the bulkhead and lapsed into silence. It was hopeless, of course, trying to solve the mystery of Solengo from the confinement of the brig, and that hopelessness soaked into her slowly, like a cold rain, merging with the sodden dread she'd felt ever since the sea battle, ever since the Purple Baths. In the space of a watch or two, whatever life she'd experienced back in the village faded. In the darkness of the brig, her memories closed in once more, circling like beasts.

Maybe the real mistake, the parent of all the others, was joining the Kettral in the first place. She could have stayed on her father's farm, spent her life raising cattle, splitting firewood, baking bread. She'd probably have fucked that up, too—she'd never been any good with animals or cooking—but when you botched the bread no one died. No one had their head hacked off if the cows weren't milked on time. If you were a little late getting the firewood under cover, no one had their legs blown from their bodies.

The only interruption to her thoughts was the arrival of the soldiers every morning. They brought a bucket of food, hauled away a different one sloshing with shit and piss. Sometimes they took Dhar with them.

Evidently Jonon had decided not to kill him. Not yet.

"The mystery is larger than Solengo," the Manjari captain said one day after the guards stuffed him back in the brig. "There are other villages, also empty. Your admiral believes the Manjari may be involved."

"Are they?"

The question rose more out of habit than anything else. It was the kind of thing she would have asked when she was Kettral, when she was a Wing commander, the kind of thing she would have asked when there was something she could do about the answer.

"No," Dhar replied. "I have told him this, but he does not believe me."

He squinted toward her in the darkness.

"The Kettral know nothing of this continent?"

"No," she replied.

"I am surprised that you have not flown those birds of yours south, to explore."

She almost choked on the bitterness of her own laugh. Even the Manjari, it seemed, believed the myths of the invincible Kettral. She wanted to tell him they weren't her birds, there weren't any left, and even if there had been, they couldn't fly through the equatorial heat. That, though, would have been treason, or something close to it, so she just shook her head.

"The Kettral are a military force, not a bunch of cartographers."

"Knowledge of terrain is important in any military contest."

"Annur's not fighting anyone in Menkiddoc. There's no one down there to fight."

"Not long ago," he replied thoughtfully, "I would have agreed."

She opened her mouth to argue—to tell him that emptying out a village was a far cry from threatening an empire, to point out that even monsters died if you lit them on fire or put a solid length of steel through the middle part—then she closed it without replying. It didn't matter. Even if there was something stirring in Menkiddoc, even if it eventually threatened Annur, she was locked in the brig of a ship headed to the wrong end of the world. The thought should have made her angry. Instead she felt an obscure species of relief—not that she wouldn't have to face whatever it was, but that at least locked away she couldn't make any more mistakes.

†

Gwenna stared down at her legs sprawled across the deck of the brig. She prodded one thigh with a finger. The muscle was softer than it had been, slacker, as though it weren't muscle at all, but just so much sodden grain stuffed into her pants. After more than a month aboard the *Daybreak,* she'd gone from a warrior to a passenger, a passenger to a prisoner, a prisoner to . . . she searched for the right word. Not a foe. Foes were dangerous. Foes bore watching. She, on the other hand, had been deposited back in the brig and forgotten.

Ballast, she decided finally, considering the dead weight of her body. She had become ballast.

She shifted her leg, just to make sure she still could. Her knee ached with the movement. Strange that her body hurt more after disuse than it had after the nastiest training. Sometimes, when she closed her eyes, she imagined her flesh rotting, the ligaments and tendons decomposing slowly. After weeks in the tropical heat, weeks with no baths or wash water, weeks pissing and shitting in a pot, bleeding into her blacks when the time came, sweating through the grime and crusted blood, she certainly *smelled* like something rotten. She could hear the guards gagging their disgust when they opened the door to shove in food or remove the shit pail. It should have shamed her. It *would* have shamed Gwenna the warrior, or Gwenna the passenger, or even Gwenna the prisoner, but ballast didn't feel shame.

If only she could have said the same about her other emotions.

Ever since the Purple Baths she'd expected the grief to come, and at first she'd mistaken the pain in her limbs and joints, the knotting of her guts, the obsessive poring over her memories for that grief. As the long, hot days ground past, however, she realized that she was wrong. She'd felt grief before. It burned, painful as fire or salt water in a wound, but that burning cleaned and clarified. Grief was something a woman could pass through and emerge from better, stronger, wiser. Instead of grief, what she felt during the weeks in the brig was nausea, dizziness—even in calm seas—flashes of stabbing panic, and dread, always the dread, nameless, faceless, breathless, crouching beside her in the darkness, dragging fingers through her tangled hair, whispering wordlessly in her ear.

There was nothing clarifying about any of it.

Her mind had become a swamp, and each day she sank further below the murky surface.

She would have preferred to be alone, but whenever she looked up, Dhar was there, sitting barely a pace away, sometimes asleep, sometimes alert, sometimes moving his lips in silent prayer, always smelling of cold resolve.

What he was resolved to do, Gwenna had no idea. Maybe it was as simple as not cracking, not abandoning his oaths to his empress. Not losing his pride.

A few months earlier those would have struck her as sensible goals. Now, she couldn't see the point in them. Cracked or not, proud or not, Dhar was still in the brig, just like her. However hard he held to his oaths, his ship was still at the bottom of the ocean, littered with the bones of the men under his command. Whatever stories he was telling himself were just that—stories. The truth was the wooden cube of their confinement, the stench, the uselessness.

Hendran had penned an entire chapter on captivity—how to stay sane, gain intelligence, eventually break free. His first instruction was simple: *Find something useful to do, then do it.*

There'd been a Kettral commander a century before Gwenna's time who'd spent eight years in an Antheran prison. By the time he finally escaped, he'd learned half a dozen languages from his fellow prisoners, languages that he taught at the Eyrie for the rest of his life.

When the panic didn't have her by the throat, Gwenna tried to work on her Manjari with Dhar, reviewing the few phrases she knew, adding gradually to her vocabulary.

"What's the word for *fear*?" she asked one day.

"There are many words," Dhar replied. "As there are many kinds of fear." He paused, waiting for her to respond. When she did not, he shrugged. "*Daksha*—the fear of bodily injury. *Veksha*—the fear one feels for others. *Bhakshma*—the fear that gives focus. *Bhikshma*—the fear that steals all thought. *Yajusha*—the . . ." He grappled for the translation. "The pure fear."

"Pure?"

"A fear with no . . . source. No cause or object."

Gwenna repeated the word quietly. *"Yajusha."*

It didn't sound like the word for an emotion. It sounded like the name of a monster.

Dhar picked something from his teeth with a fish bone, stared into the darkness near where her head was.

"I have watched men go mad inside my brig," he said finally.

"Yeah? What happened to them?"

"One sailor tried to punch through the bulkhead. He broke all the bones in his hands and wrists. Another hanged himself with his belt."

Gwenna tried to imagine it—looping her belt around her neck, pulling it tight, watching her vision constrict, then go black. . . .

"There's nothing in here," she said finally, "to attach a belt to."

Dhar stared blankly into the corner of the brig where she sat.

"The stillness is difficult for you."

"The stillness?"

The captain nodded. "You are trained to struggle, to fight. Here there is no one to fight. Nothing to struggle against. And so you turn your training on yourself."

"I'm good at killing things," she replied. "If I wanted to kill myself, I'd be dead."

He nodded again, but there was no agreement in it. "The Manjari have two words for dead. There is the dead of corpses—people, animals, all of it. We call that *martya*. And then there is the dead of those who go on living and breathing but as husks or shells. This we call *vadhra*."

Gwenna stared at him awhile, then closed her eyes.

"I think I'm done learning your language for today."

┼

For today.

Those were the words she'd said, but one day bled into the next, several days became a week, and gradually she realized she'd quit. It was amazing how easy it was, after a lifetime of *not* quitting, to just let go. She abandoned the language lessons first, then stopped bothering to wash her face and hands with the bucket of salt water they were given once a week, then stopped bothering to get up at all.

Each day, Dhar sat across from her in the brig. She could smell his concern souring into disgust. She tried to care, couldn't. For the first time in her life, she felt herself getting fat. It seemed impossible, given the diet of warm ale, stale bread, and salt fish, but then, she'd never been so sedentary. At night she'd prod at the flesh over her ribs with a kind of morbid fascination, test the weakness of muscles going gradually slack, thinking all the time, *So this is what it's like.*

Shocking how easy it was. How sickeningly close to pleasant. What the fuck had she been doing getting up all those mornings in the blue-black dark, swimming across the 'Kent-kissing sound, running laps around Qarsh? The world was filled with people who never ran a step in their lives, who never pushed themselves, never risked anything, never failed. Why couldn't she be one of them? She hated herself, but there was a richness to the loathing, as though it were some kind of too-sweet syrup she couldn't stop pouring down her throat.

Two or three times, Dhar offered to teach her more of his language. She declined.

She already had the only two words she needed:

Yajusha—fear, pure fear, the fear that held her by the throat almost every waking moment—and *vadhra,* the word that meant death.

24

The night was still and hot, heavy with rain that refused to fall and the greasy smoke from Dombâng's uncountable cook fires. Ruc could smell the last of the congee—fish broth laced with hot peppers and roasted sweet-reed—cooling in the massive pots set at the north end of the yard. He'd managed to eat some, but another day of Goatface's unrelenting training had left his stomach a clenched, angry fist. It would be hours, probably past the midnight gong, before his body finally relaxed enough to finish the covered bowl he'd carried back to his room. In the meantime, he should have been sleeping. Resting, at least. Off his feet, letting his body recover before the rigors of the next day. Bien had collapsed onto her cot with her food half-chewed. Monster, Mouse, and Stupid were still awake when he left the bunkhouse, but he didn't expect them to be up when he returned. Even Talal, who endured the daily training better than the rest of them, had been stretching quietly on the floor in a corner of the common room.

Sleeping and stretching, though, weren't going to get any of them out of the Arena. After the initial brutality of the Way of Kings, no one had attacked them, but he'd seen Rooster and Snakebones eyeing them from across the yard. Watching. Waiting for their chance. Which might have been an argument for remaining with the others back at Goatface's barracks. The problem was, while that might keep him alive for the night, it was hardly a long-term survival strategy. Sooner or later, someone would catch him and Bien unaware. Even if they made it all the way to the high holy days, the chances of surviving them were miserable. If they wanted to live, they needed to escape, and so, instead of sleeping or stretching with the others, Ruc was out in the yard, walking a slow perimeter around the open space, studying the shape of his prison.

By night, it looked almost cheerful. No one was cursing or bellowing, and the man who'd spent the afternoon screaming beneath the surgeon's knife had finally fallen silent, whether resting or dead, Ruc couldn't say. It was too dark to see the churned-up mud, the brown blood splattered across the walls of the buildings, the piles of slop outside the kitchens that no one had yet bothered lugging to the top of the wall to toss into the canal below. The windows of the bunkhouses glowed with the lamplight within, and atop the walls dozens of red-scale lanterns danced in the warm, northerly breeze.

Ruc paused in his circuit to study the top of that wall. The guards couldn't see him where he stood, of that he was reasonably sure, but even without the light he could follow their heat as they paced their rounds or kept watch from the wooden towers. Thirty-six of them. He'd expected the number to go down at night, but in fact, the opposite was true. Daytime saw only two dozen, but evidently day wasn't the most tempting window for escapes. The wall itself wasn't particularly high—about ten paces—but it was utterly featureless and canted slightly inward, so that the top overhung the base by a full pace. With the right tools and half a night unobserved, it would be possible to climb out. The guards at the top, however, looked disinclined to give anyone half a night.

"The latrines are a better bet."

Startled, Ruc rounded on the speaker, ducking his head and raising his fists.

Talal nodded thoughtfully. "Definitely faster than most priests I've met."

Ruc straightened, lowered his hands. "How many priests *have* you met?"

"Not many. Still . . ."

"I'd say you're sneakier than most Kettral I've met, but I haven't met any Kettral, and I imagine you're all pretty fucking sneaky."

The soldier smiled. "Sneaking, swimming, stabbing—those are pretty much the main qualifications."

"What about flying those birds?"

"I mostly just hang on underneath and try not to die." He paused, then cast a meaningful eye around the empty yard. "Speaking of not dying, you sure it's a good idea to be out here alone?"

"I'm not alone. You're here. Though I couldn't say why."

"Trying to make sure one of my only friends in Dombâng doesn't accidentally trip and fall on a sword while taking the night air."

Ruc raised his brows. "Are we friends?"

"You haven't tried to kill me yet." He shrugged. "That'll have to do for now."

A litany of curses erupted from one of the bunkhouses a few dozen paces to the north. Wood scraped against wood, something that sounded like crockery crashed against something that sounded like a wall, and a moment later a man careened through the open door into the yard. It took him a moment to stumble to his feet—he was either drunk or stunned—then he started to barge back in, paused for a moment swaying on the threshold, evidently thought better of it, and staggered off toward the mess hall.

"Why *are* you here?" Ruc asked.

"Same reason as you." The Kettral nodded toward the perimeter of the yard. "Walls. Men on top of them who don't want me leaving." He hefted the iron ball in the crook of his arm. "This thing."

"Not here in the yard. Here in Dombâng."

"Ah."

"Why did you burn down the Purple Baths?"

Talal shook his head wearily. "You have no idea how many people asked me that in the days after I was captured."

"What did you tell them?"

"That the Baths weren't a target. My Wing hit the Baths *after* I was captured—to get me out. They went there because of me."

A cloud of something that might have been weariness or regret moved across his features.

"Doesn't explain what you were doing in Dombâng in the first place."

The soldier locked eyes with him. "Are you accustomed to getting explanations for everything?"

Ruc thought back to the *axoch* strangling the foreign messenger on Bien's bed, to the hideous creature the Vuo Ton had nailed to the posts out in the Wallow. He heard again the voice of the old Witness in his ears: *Boa went to see the gods. They were not there.*

He shook his head. "It's been a while, actually, since I've had a good explanation."

Talal gave him a half smile and a nod. "I know the feeling." After a pause, he gestured to the tattoos snaking Ruc's arms.

"Vuo Ton work, right?"

Ruc blinked, then studied the man warily. "How do you know about the Vuo Ton?"

"Read about them before the mission. Read everything we had on the history of Dombâng."

"I suppose it's pointless to ask you about that mission all over again."

"Probably."

"We don't seem to trust each other very much. For friends."

The Kettral considered him awhile, then nodded, as though to himself. "We were arming and training the local insurgency. Training, mostly."

"Insurgency?" Ruc frowned. "It was the local insurgency that overthrew your empire in the first place."

Talal gave him a lopsided grin. "The insurgency changes when the regime does. We were working with Annurian loyalists."

"Where were you finding them? Rotting in the bellies of crocs?"

"Your high priests . . ."

"They're not my priests," Ruc reminded him.

The soldier nodded. "Dombâng's high priests were thorough in their purges, but it's impossible to clean out a city this size. Same way that the worship of the Three survived two hundred years of occupation, there are plenty of imperial sympathizers now. They've been forced into hiding, sure, but it was our job to find them, give them the skills they needed in order to resist."

"What does this have to do with the Vuo Ton?"

"That's where we started. Thought, given their . . . tenuous relationship to Dombâng, that they might make a nice spearhead for the movement. We visited them to find out."

Ruc stared.

The Kettral looked almost apologetic. "They're much easier to find from the air."

It took a moment to imagine that. It was the labyrinth of the Shirvian delta that had kept Dombâng safe from the outside world for so many centuries, and the same labyrinth that had hidden the Vuo Ton from the citizens of Dombâng. The ten thousand branching channels were nearly impassable, impossible to navigate for anyone not raised among them. The thought that someone might not *have* to navigate them had never crossed Ruc's mind. Talal's casual talk about flying in to visit the Vuo Ton felt, in a way he couldn't quite describe, like a violation.

"How long does it take," he asked, "to get from one side of the delta to the other with one of those birds?"

"Depends on how fast you're flying. Took us weeks to find the Vuo Ton— even from the air you can't see through the reeds—but if you were going straight across? Maybe a portion of a morning."

Ruc let the words sink in. *A portion of a morning.* If he'd asked the same question to anyone in Dombâng, the answer would have been: *never.* Forget about making it to the other side, most of them would have died within sight of the city.

An unexpected vertigo washed over him. He'd thought about the outside world before, of course. Prior to the revolution, sailors had come and gone every day bearing tales of far-flung ports, cities with strange names: Ganaboa, Sarai Pol, Mireia. He knew that the Annurian Empire was huge, and that there were lands *beyond* that empire. And yet, when he thought about *his* world, it was the delta that filled his mind. Dombâng sat at its center, and beyond that, the reeds stretching away in all directions. He'd traveled several times to the end of those reeds—more to establish that they *had* an end than anything else—set foot on the solid bank, gazed up at the massive trees . . . then turned around and went back. Everything beyond remained a thin, vague rim.

Until now.

He tried to see the delta as Talal saw it: a tiny patch of brown and green, just so much mud. The Shirvian could flood all of it, submerge every island, drown every living thing, and there would be people, thousands of people, millions, who would never even know. It was hard, for a moment, to understand why any of it mattered—the Arena, the revolution, the high holy days, the Three, even his own survival.

A portion of a morning.

He shook his head, trying to clear it. "Why do you care what happens in Dombâng? Why does Annur care?"

"It's a strategic port. A crucial link between river trade on the Shirvian and the oceangoing vessels of the Iron Sea." He shrugged. "And revolutions are dangerous to an empire. One people seize their freedom, and suddenly you've got a dozen states and cities remembering their ancestral pride, clamoring for their own liberation. Doing more than clamoring, sometimes."

"And you," Ruc said quietly, "the Kettral—you're the ones who discourage them from clamoring."

Talal didn't flinch. "Discourage them or kill them."

A bat knifed through the night—just a small, ordinary swamp bat—so close Ruc could have snatched it from the air.

"You ever wonder if you're on the wrong side?"

"Anyone who doesn't shouldn't be given a blade in the first place."

"But here you are."

Talal nodded.

"Why?"

"You already asked that," the soldier pointed out.

"I was asking about the Kettral before. Now I'm asking about you."

The soldier studied Ruc awhile, then shifted his gaze to the lanterns burning atop the walls, or perhaps the men walking between those lanterns, or maybe to the smoke-smudged stars trembling in the sky beyond.

"Seemed like the right thing to do," he said finally.

"Murdering people who don't agree with you? Killing them for wanting to be free?"

"It was that freedom," Talal observed quietly, "that led to the burning of your temple. To the slaughter of your fellow priests. For two hundred years, Annur stopped things like that from happening."

"It was Annur being here for two hundred years that fueled the hate that made them want to kill us in the first place."

"Maybe. Maybe not. Human sacrifice has been happening in this delta a long time. At least a thousand years before Annur showed up."

"Before Annur showed up," Ruc replied grimly, "it was different. Men and women went willingly to face their gods. The chance to die in the delta was a coveted honor awarded only to the fastest, the bravest. It went wrong when your empire drove the worship underground. *That* was when people started plucking orphans and drunks off the streets. The last two hundred years were a perversion, one brought on by the empire itself."

Talal nodded as though he'd considered this argument. As though he'd heard it all before.

"Every people has a story of their golden age. How it was different. Better. More noble. It's funny how those golden ages are always in the past, always eclipsed by some more recent catastrophe. *You* think Dombâng was better two hundred years ago, but go back two hundred years, and I promise you, the people then were just like us. They were angry, confused, afraid. And *they* thought that they'd already missed it, some golden age that took place two hundred years before *them,* or five hundred, or a thousand. . . ." He turned from the stars to look at Ruc. "Instead of worshipping the past, I'd like to work on the present."

"By murdering people."

"Some people need murdering."

It was chilling, the calm with which he said those words. There was no anger to them, no boasting. If anything, he sounded regretful, as though he would have preferred it were not the case.

"Not a sentiment," Ruc replied, "that my goddess would agree with."

"Not your goddess, maybe. What about you?"

"I am a priest of love."

"A priest of love who seems pretty invested in defending the worship of the Three." He nodded again to Ruc's tattoos. "A priest of love with Vuo Ton ink. A priest of love with reactions I haven't seen outside the Kettral. *Better* than I've seen from some Kettral . . ."

Ruc met the man's stare. "What were you before you became a soldier?"

"I've always been a soldier."

"Well. I haven't always been a priest."

"I guessed as much."

"But like you said—the past is past. I'm a priest now."

"No," Talal replied soberly. "You're a prisoner, just like I am. And every day we stay in here we're more likely to become corpses."

Ruc started to nod, then paused. He narrowed his eyes. "*Why* are you a prisoner?"

Talal raised his eyebrows, hefted the iron ball.

"No. If the Kettral can find the Vuo Ton, fly their bird right to them, they can pluck you out of here. Why hasn't anyone come for you?"

The soldier hesitated, then shook his head. "We don't have the birds."

"You had the birds to attack the Purple Baths."

"Bird. Singular. He died in the attack."

"And that's it? There aren't any others?"

"Not . . . readily available."

Ruc shook his head. It seemed vastly improbable. "I thought you had a whole winged army. . . ." He stopped abruptly. "What about bats?"

"Bats?" Talal asked mildly. The words were mild, at least, but the heat of his face raised just slightly, yellow baking briefly into orange before it faded.

"So you already know about them."

The soldier raised an eyebrow. "Seems like you have a sixth sense to match your unexpected reflexes."

"Are they yours?"

Talal shook his head slowly. "No. We don't know what they are."

"But you've seen them?"

Another nod. "Half a dozen attacked our bird about a month back. We thought they might be something from the delta."

"They're not."

Talal considered this. "Where did you see them?"

"They went after the Vuo Ton."

"How'd that go?"

"They killed about a dozen people before the Vuo Ton rallied." Ruc studied the other man. "You're sure they're not some kind of . . ." He groped for the right words. ". . . secret breed created by Annur?"

This time, the Kettral actually seemed to consider the question. "I guess it's not impossible," he conceded. "The Annurian military is complex. Lots of branches. Lots of commanders. Lots of secret projects." He shook his head. "Still. Not much gets kept from the Kettral. It's unlikely we'd be running this mission without knowing about another imperial op unfolding in the same place at the same time."

"What about the First?" Ruc asked.

Talal looked at him blankly. "The first what?" His confusion seemed genuine.

It took Ruc a moment to reassemble the timeline. It all seemed like a lifetime ago, but the attack on the Purple Baths had happened *before* the day when the man appeared on the bridge.

"You didn't hear about the messengers."

"Everyone's been generous with the questions but no one's bent over backward to tell me what's going on. Not when I was back in the Shipwreck, and not here. I've heard some chatter in the yard about an attacking army. Just assumed that was us."

It took some time to explain—the naked man, his ranting, the *axoch* around his neck, the strange warnings about the First and his army. Talal listened in silence, scarred face unreadable. When Ruc finished the tale, the other man remained still, staring out into the dark.

"So," Ruc ventured at last. "They weren't on your side?"

The soldier shook his head slowly.

"What about the collar? The *axoch*?"

"It reminds me of something I heard of once. . . ." He seemed about to go on. Then something in his eyes, something that had opened slowly over the course of their conversation, swung silently closed. "We need to get out of here."

"You want to explain to me what it means?"

"I don't know what it means."

"But you have some idea."

"My idea," Talal said, "is simple. Something bad is coming, and when it arrives, we don't want to be locked inside a pen."

25

There was a ziggurat.

Despite Kiel's claim that all of Menkiddoc south of Solengo was consumed by the sickness, right there, at the tip of the southernmost cape of the entire continent, at the edge of a high plateau looking out over the sea, someone had built a fucking ziggurat.

Gwenna stared up at it, eyes aching from the sunlight, muscles and joints throbbing from the unaccustomed movement, heart thudding stupidly with the simple exertion of dragging herself up on deck. It had been more than a month since Solengo. More than a month of lying in the darkness listening to the prayers of Bhuma Dhar and the silent, plaintive keening of her own regret. More than a month during which her daily activity consisted of hoisting herself up to shit into a wooden barrel. More than a month of her body and mind turning slowly to sludge.

It hurt to be dragged back out. The air—chilly here, so far south of the equator—burned in her lungs. The wind cut through her filthy blacks, lashed her face with her sour-smelling hair. Even the sounds hurt. Everything was too loud—the soldiers shouting back and forth as they set up a perimeter around the stone quays, the seabirds shrieking as they quit their craggy nests to circle overhead, Jonon's Annurian flag snapping at every gust. It was too much. The whole world had become too much.

Not to mention the 'Kent-kissing ziggurat.

The thing had obviously been built to command a view of the entire cape. It stood maybe a quarter mile distant and a hundred paces above, at the edge of a tableland that dropped in precipitous cliffs down to a quarter-mile skirt of land wedged between their base and the lapping waves. Packed into that quarter mile and running four times that distance along the base of the cliffs—improbably, impossibly, given what Kiel had claimed about southern Menkiddoc—sat what Gwenna could only describe as a city.

The *Daybreak* had thrown anchor in a harbor shielded by a long break-water. Fronting that harbor ran a broad, cobbled street. Just on the other side of that street, Jonon had set up a command tent in a broad open space, a market most likely, complete with wooden booths, naked poles at the corners of each where the merchants would have stretched canvas to keep off the sun. Farther back lurked a row of long, windowless buildings that could only be warehouses, and behind them, a riot of streets and neighborhoods, thousands of wooden buildings—two stories, three, even four—some crouched against storms blowing in off the sea, some leaning bravely, drunkenly out over the roads. Gwenna compared it to other cities she'd seen; smaller than Annur, certainly, far smaller, but still large enough to accommodate tens of thousands of people.

Except that there were no people.

It wasn't just that she couldn't see them; she couldn't smell them, either. No human sweat, no scent of cook fires or grilling meat, no reek of latrines, nothing that would indicate any recent habitation.

She was staring blankly over the space, trying to make sense of it, when Chent and Lurie—the same men who had dragged her and Dhar out of the brig, then rowed them across the harbor—prodded her forward.

"Enough gaping. Jonon wants you."

As though summoned by his name, the admiral swept aside the flap of his command tent and stepped out. Sunlight gleamed on his brass, on the handle of his cutlass, on the gold thread of the Annurian sun stitched into his uniform. The image of the dauntless commander was marred only by his frown, a frown he directed at Kiel as the historian followed him out of the tent.

". . . saying this was built *after* your map," the admiral demanded.

Kiel nodded. "The map is over ten thousand years old."

"What about that thing?" Jonon pointed up at the ziggurat. "Some kind of Csestriim ruin?"

"It is hardly a ruin," Kiel replied. "And the Csestriim generally had little interest in monolithic structures for their own sake."

"Well, someone was interested. Interested enough to haul several hundred thousand tons of rock to the edge of a cliff and stack it up. Any idea who?"

"No. Perhaps when we explore the city more will become clear. . . ."

Jonon's frown deepened. "When I was ordered to bring a historian on this expedition, I dared to hope that he might provide some useful history. It seems I was too optimistic."

"To my knowledge," Kiel said, "there has never been a human exploration this far south."

The admiral turned. He ran a brief, disgusted glance over Gwenna, then focused on Bhuma Dhar.

"What about the Manjari? Anything in your histories about this?"

Dhar frowned. "No. There is mention in the chronicles of a great famine many centuries back. Perhaps two millennia. An exodus. Solengo and the other villages along that coast date from that period, but I have never read of such a place as this."

"And the Kettral?"

Gwenna shook her head, mute.

Her head ached, as though her brain had swollen inside her skull. Not for the first time since leaving the ship, she wondered if she was dreaming. What, after all, were the chances that they had actually arrived at the cape on Kiel's map? What were the chances that Jonon lem Jonon had allowed her and Dhar out of the brig? The questions made her dizzy, panicked, and for a dozen hard, hammering heartbeats she waited to wake again to the damp, fetid dark. It felt wrong that she couldn't wake up. Terrifying.

"No sign of anyone, sir."

Gwenna turned to find Cho Lu trotting up, half a dozen legionaries—Pattick included—behind him. They'd come in from the south, from farther down the shore. All had weapons ready to hand. They smelled like men expecting to be attacked, men who didn't expect to survive.

"What about bodies?" Jonon asked, gazing past the soldier out over the wood-shingled roofs. "Like in Solengo."

Cho Lu shook his head.

"What *did* you find, soldier?"

"It's . . ." Cho Lu glanced over his shoulder, as though to assure himself that the city was still there. "It's just like you'd expect—"

"I did *not* expect this."

"No, sir. Sorry, sir. I just mean, it's like any other city, more or less. Houses. Shops. Waterwheels by the streams. A tannery. A shipyard. Just like any other city, except there's no one here."

He glanced over, gave a start as he noticed the prisoners, then looked away. He'd locked eyes with Gwenna for less than a heartbeat, but she'd seen everything she'd needed to see: confusion then recognition, shock then embarrassment, disgust curdling into pity. The Kettral hero he'd thought he was meeting back in Annur had revealed herself to be no more than this—a useless, filthy creature with no blades and no spine. He'd made the mistake of thinking her unbreakable. Well, now he'd learned.

Pattick let his gaze linger longer. Unlike Cho Lu, his confusion shaded into anger, as though she'd betrayed him somehow. For a moment, she felt a faint, answering anger of her own. She hadn't promised the soldier anything. It wasn't her fault he'd made up a story about her that turned out not to be true.

If he'd believed her when they left Annur, if he'd never followed her onto Bhuma Dhar's ship, if, if, if . . .

Her anger drained away like water into dry sand.

"Any sign of violence?" Jonon asked after a long pause. "Any indication of a fight?"

Cho Lu shook his head. "None." He opened his mouth once more, then hesitated.

"Out with it, soldier."

"Well, we didn't go in every structure, sir, not even close, but it feels different from that other town, Solengo. There's nothing . . . abandoned here. No grain in the jars. No water in the jugs. Not even any clothes folded away. Hardly any tools in the workshops. At the shipyard, for instance—there were a couple of hammers, a few chisels, but most of the stuff was just . . . gone. As though when they left they took everything with them. I . . ." He shook his head, as though to rid it of some awful vision. "I don't like it, sir."

"We're not here to like things," Jonon said grimly. "We're here to do a job."

"What kind of people abandon an entire city?" Pattick murmured. He didn't seem to be posing the question to anyone in particular, gazing out over the houses as he spoke, but the admiral responded.

"Desperate ones." He turned his green gaze toward the cliff. "Perhaps there are more answers above. Did you find the base of that thing?"

Gwenna squinted, confused. The base of the cliffs seemed more than obvious, but then she saw it: a gradual ramp had been carved into the cliff's face, climbing at a grade that would have been manageable to a wagon, switching back seven or eight times before it reached the level of the plateau above.

"We did, sir," Cho Lu replied. "I left four men at its foot."

Jonon nodded, as though that were the first reasonable thing he'd heard all day.

"We have to go inland after the birds anyway, and I'm not leaving this city at my back until I know for certain that it is empty. We'll spend the afternoon scouting while the others unload the *Daybreak*. From the top of that ziggurat we'll be able to see more. Maybe from up there something about this place will start making sense."

Cho Lu looked doubtful, as though he'd already given up on the very notion of sense.

"What do you want to do with these two, sir?" Chent asked, gouging Gwenna in the ribs with the butt of his spear.

Jonon ran a cool eye over the prisoners. "Bring them."

Chent smelled momentarily disappointed, as though he'd been hoping for some time alone with her, out of sight of the admiral. If it came to it, if he tried to rape her, she wondered what she would do. The man was obviously strong, but she'd killed plenty of strong men; it was a question of will rather than ability. She searched inside herself for some of the old stubbornness, the old resistance. It felt like standing on the edge of a deep well looking down, down, down. She could see nothing in the darkness, no gleam of sunlight on the water, no bottom at all.

"You heard him," Chent said, driving the spear's butt into her back. "We're all going."

And so the admiral, the imperial historian, a Manjari captain, two dozen soldiers, and a woman who had once been Kettral made their way from the docks inland, then up, toward the heart of a city that was on no map, told of in no human chronicle.

The ramp proved more than wide enough for a wagon, maybe four paces from the cliff on one side to the abyss on the other. Despite a lifetime hanging from the talons of birds, however, Gwenna found herself hugging the rock wall, her breath shallow in her chest. As they climbed, the wind picked up, keening over the stone, tugging at her hair and clothes, threatening to strip her from the path entirely. She tried closing her eyes, trailing a hand along the wall, but that just made her feel worse, as though she were already falling. In the end, she kept her gaze on the cut stone directly in front of her, refusing to look up or out or down.

It was Pattick's voice, finally, that broke her from her concentration.

"Sweet Intarra's light," he murmured.

She looked up to see that the column had stopped. Pattick stood just at her side, a hand on his sword, gaping. "All that down below—it wasn't even half of it."

From the harbor, they'd seen only the ziggurat. The angle had been wrong to make out the other buildings on the plateau, the *thousands* of other buildings, all built of stone rather than wood, blocks upon blocks upon blocks of them. The scale shifted in her mind. *This* was the city. The ramshackle structures below were just some kind of slum, like so much driftwood tossed up at the base of the cliffs.

For a moment Jonon didn't speak. He just glared at the place as though it had delivered him a personal affront. Only when the soldiers started to shift nervously did he turn to face them.

"If someone were going to attack us, they would have done it there." He pointed back the way they had come. "On the ramp. That was the natural point of defense."

This observation seemed to breathe some confidence back into the men. It was self-evidently true, for one thing. And the admiral was still the admiral—focused, stern, dismissive—despite the strangeness of the surroundings. A few nodded. Most loosened their grip on their swords and spears. One man elbowed his companion in the ribs.

"Scared of a bunch of empty houses?"

Gwenna didn't share their confidence, and whatever relief she'd felt about reaching the top of the plateau vanished as they pressed deeper into the city.

There were no bodies. The streets were wide, empty, open to the sky. Though she scanned the windows and doors of the buildings they passed, there was no sign of ambush, no rustling of some hidden army massing for an attack. And yet she felt her hackles rising. Every time she glanced over her shoulder she expected to find eyes upon her. The wind keened through the streets, kicking up dust and tattered leaves, but in the moments that it dropped, she thought she heard scuttling, shuffling, as though something furtive were following. Beneath the smell of the soldiers—leather, and sweat, and oiled steel—beneath her own reek, she was almost certain she caught a whiff of something else, warm and feral.

She glanced over at Dhar.

"Do you hear anything?"

The Manjari captain closed his eyes for a moment, then shook his head. "Only the wind."

Gwenna looked up the column. Despite Jonon's words, the animal wariness of the men had reasserted itself. They walked with drawn blades and half-leveled spears. Even the admiral had a hand on the hilt of his sword. Only Kiel seemed unconcerned by the strange city spread out around them. The historian moved with that strange gait of his, awkward but strong at the same time, studying the place with the kind of dry interest most people reserved for books.

Most of the construction proved more or less familiar—limestone blocks fitted and mortared, slate roofs, wooden doors hung on steel hinges, shutters over the windows to keep out the worst of the wind and weather. And yet the total effect was somehow strangely alienating, as though every angle had been knocked just a few degrees awry.

Then, at the end of a broad avenue, they reached the first square, the first pit, and the first statue.

Though Jonon had given no command, everyone stopped. It was hard to know where to look first. At the center of the square the ground simply . . . opened. It looked like a great well, thirty paces across, had been bored into the flagstones. At the center of that well, sunken down inside it, evidently hewn from the bedrock itself, stood some kind of stone structure, its flat roof coming just flush with the flags of the square where the soldiers stood. The lines of the building reminded Gwenna vaguely of something sacred, a shrine, a temple, but it had no windows or glass, no openings at all, save for what looked like a heavily fortified door deep at the bottom of the well. She stepped as close as she dared, peered over the edge into the darkness, but there was nothing else down there, just the temple, the flat open space ringing it on every side, and the sheer walls of the pit, all carved from the same stone.

Atop the temple, however, stood the statue.

It loomed over them, five paces high at least. Gwenna stared up at the thing, trying to make sense of the strangely jointed limbs, the impossibly limber spine, the eyes. Her first thought was that the sculptor had been a madman, someone who'd rendered his nightmares in stone.

Dhar, however, frowned, then stepped forward.

"*Gabhya,*" he said after a pause.

Jonon turned to him. "You have seen one of these before?"

The captain shook his head slowly. "But I have witnessed smaller specimens. This has the same . . . wrongness to it."

That wrongness extended beyond all the limbs, all the eyes. There was something obscene about the figure, twisted, almost nauseating. For the second time, Gwenna had the horrible feeling that she was dreaming.

"Why is it up on a pedestal?" Pattick murmured.

The admiral glanced over at him, then nodded. "Why, indeed. Historian?"

Kiel gazed up at the sculpture, his eyes blank with the reflected sky. After a moment's pause, he gestured across the gap to the roof of the temple and the statue's base. "It has a name."

Gwenna hadn't noticed the letters carved into the circular plinth. If they *were,* in fact, letters. The script looked more like splattered blood—all slashes and accents—than text.

"Can you read that?" the admiral asked.

Kiel shook his head. "Not yet. I may be able to learn it if we find more samples."

"Do you want to write it down?"

"There is no need," the historian replied mildly.

No one seemed to want to get too close to the edge of the well. Gwenna didn't blame them. A strange, cold . . . wrongness to which she couldn't put a name wafted up out of the depths, as though the stone itself were rotting. Some of the soldiers eyed the pit warily. Other seemed more worried about the tight alleyways and empty buildings at their back; they turned in slow circles as though uncertain where to look. Several had looped around to the other side of the square.

"Sir!" Chent called suddenly. He was gesturing out toward the temple, to something on the roof occluded by the statue. "There's a . . . some kind of door."

More like a trapdoor, Gwenna saw when she'd joined the others, broad and heavy, banded with steel, set flush into the flat stone.

"How do you get to the 'Kent-kissing thing?" Lurie muttered.

"There." Cho Lu pointed to the side of the square. A long wooden plank hung against the wall of one of the buildings. Metal brackets had been set into its ends, at right angles to the plank itself.

Cho Lu gestured to the brackets, then to two holes drilled into the stone at the lip of the well.

"These fit into those. It's a bridge."

"A drawbridge," Jonon corrected him. He studied the building at the center of the pit. "For some kind of prison."

"Strange place for a prison," Pattick said, "out here for everyone to see."

The admiral shook his head. "The seeing would have been the point. Whatever happened down there"—he pointed into the shadowy depths—"it was meant to be observed."

Whatever the place had been, it wasn't the only one.

They worked their way deeper into the city, navigating by the top of the ziggurat, which loomed over even the tallest buildings. In some places the roads ran straight, in others they bent unpredictably, almost pointlessly, as though the builders had shied away from some obstacle that had long since eroded. Deep ravines scored the plateau—streams running along the bottom—and in places they were forced to cross stone bridges that looked too slender to support their own weight. The city was marvelously intact, but the layout of the place felt . . . shattered, carved up, as though it were actually a score of different cities forced uneasily together.

A few hundred paces farther along, they reached another square, another pit, another sunken prison or temple or whatever it was, another statue looming over the flat roof. This one reminded Gwenna vaguely of a bear. If bears had eight limbs and walked upright.

"It's like they worshipped these things," Cho Lu said, shaking his head.

A few of the legionaries shot wary glances at Dhar.

"The Manjari," he said quietly, "have never worshipped monsters. The statues in our cities are of generals, patriots, lawmakers."

"That thing," Jonon said, leaning hard on the second word, "does not look like a giver of laws."

The soldiers had grown openly agitated, checking over their shoulders every other breath, overgripping their swords, tapping at the triggers of their flatbows. Gwenna closed her eyes, tried to listen. The patter she'd heard had vanished, but she could still smell something out there. It was tricky to decipher the scent, but she could make out dirt, blood, hair. . . . For half a heartbeat she thought she heard panting. Then the wind kicked up and it was gone.

Jonon turned to face his men, putting his back to the pit, as though indifferent to whatever might lie in wait there.

"We have come to a new land, and so, of course, there are new creatures. A traveler from afar who arrived in Annur, or the foothills of the Romsdals, say, would be amazed by the sight of a moose, a porcupine, even something as simple and natural as a beaver. These creatures"—he raised a finger toward the statue—"these . . . *gabhya*—if they are real at all—will seem strange to us. This is a reason for vigilance, not fear. The world is brimming with beasts, but one thing links them all—if you put a sword in them, they bleed, and when they bleed enough, they die. Remember that you were brought on this expedition, all of you, because you are skilled at putting swords into things."

As speeches went, it wasn't bad. It raised a cheer from the men. Cho Lu nodded, as though the comparison between an eight-legged bear and a beaver were reassuring. Gwenna could smell the wariness on him all the same, the wariness on all of them.

They passed three more wells and statues before they reached the city's inner wall—some enormous ant thing, maybe a bat, and a tree. That last was almost comforting until Gwenna realized there were thousands of mouths where the leaves should have been.

She shifted toward Kiel. "It affects the plants, too?"

The historian nodded. "All living things."

"So the sickness is here?" Gwenna glanced over her shoulder once again. "In this city?"

"No. As I said, you would feel it."

"You said a lot of things. One of them was that no one lived down here."

"I said I was not aware of any human habitation this far south."

It felt like an extremely thin hair to split, but Gwenna let it go. "What does it feel like?"

"Good," Kiel replied. He narrowed his brows. "Too good."

Gwenna tried to imagine feeling *too good*. She failed.

The world still felt painfully bright, shockingly cold. The fear still prowled inside her, black-eyed and sharp-beaked, tugging at the sinew of her chest. And yet, a strange thing about that fear—though it was no less intense than what had attacked her inside the brig, it felt easier to bear out here, in this strange city, where they were almost certainly being stalked by . . . something. At least there was a *reason* to be afraid. At least the jagged pieces of her own emotion fit, for once, with actual danger in the actual world. She was a lot more likely to die, of course, maybe ripped apart by some nameless monster, but she wasn't quite as insane. Somehow, it felt like a reasonable trade-off.

As she tried to sort through her emotions, Cho Lu came trotting back to the column, his face grave.

"There's a wall, sir."

Jonon nodded. "Makes sense. A central fortification around the ziggurat."

Cho Lu shook his head. A chill crept up Gwenna's spine.

"This wall, sir. It's backward."

They rounded one last corner, and Gwenna was able to see for herself. The structure looked normal enough at the base: massive blocks of mortared limestone curving away in both directions, obviously strong enough to withstand all but the most protracted assault. As Jonon said, a wall deep inside a city wasn't all that bizarre—plenty of cities had old fortifications crumbling away inside their neighborhoods, scarred reminders of invasions that had taken place decades or centuries earlier. This wall, however . . . Cho Lu was right. The walk at the top was completely open to attack from where Gwenna stood because the parapets had been built on the far side.

"This wasn't built to keep people out," she murmured. Wind keened through the empty streets. Her fingers itched all over again for her absent blades. "It was put here to keep something *in*."

✝

There was no gate.

Instead, after following the wall for maybe a third of its circuit, they found a stone staircase—wide enough that ten people could have climbed abreast, the treads shallow, steps long, the whole thing ceremonial rather than functional—ascending to its top. At the base of the stairs, as though they'd been frozen in the process of marching down and out into the large, open square, stood two columns of statues. More *gabhya,* although this time what drew Gwenna's eye wasn't the gaping mouths or too-many limbs or the wrongness of the twisted flesh rendered in stone, but the skulls at each statue's base, human skulls, thousands and thousands of skulls.

She'd seen plenty of bones in her life, strewed around old battlefields mostly, some with gobbets of flesh and scraps of skin still clinging to them. These were nothing like those. They were neatly stacked in rings around each statue. All had been scrubbed clean, but the interiors were packed with dirt.

Some kind of flowering vine spilled from the eyes, tumbling in graceful, leafy, verdant curls to the stones below.

Gwenna looked over at Kiel.

The historian still didn't smell like anything, and yet there was something in his posture as he gazed on those piles, some faint shift she could neither identify nor describe. He'd seen skulls stacked up like that before, or—more likely—read about them somewhere. He recognized them, at any rate.

"Was this . . ." Pattick trailed off, staring at the skulls.

"Sacrifice," Jonon replied grimly. "Human sacrifice. They could build, the people who made this place, but make no mistake about it—they were savages all the same."

Gwenna expected the admiral to send a team of legionaries to scout the steps. Instead, after a last, derisive glance at the *gabhya* and the skulls heaped beneath them, he mounted the stairs himself, hand on the pommel of his undrawn sword, gaze fixed on the top of the wall. The soldiers watched for a few moments in mute amazement, then scrambled to follow him, their own weapons at the ready.

Kiel still hadn't moved.

"You know what happened here," Gwenna said quietly.

"People died."

"But you know *why* they died. Who killed them."

"On the contrary, I am as shocked by the existence of this city as anyone. Like you, I am struggling to . . . gain my footing."

"You don't look like a man who's struggling."

"I've found that people often do not look like what they are." He held her gaze for a heartbeat or two. "Wouldn't you agree?"

Before she could reply, he turned to follow the others, hunching slightly as he climbed the steps, leaving Gwenna alone with the stone monsters and the dead.

For a mad moment, she considered running. Chent and Lurie had gone ahead with the others, distracted from their charge by the horrors of the place. She could bolt from the square in a matter of moments, lose herself in the city, get free of Jonon, and Kiel, and all of it. . . .

And then what? The *Daybreak* was the only way back. The *Daybreak,* or a trek through thousands of miles of Menkiddoc, straight through whatever sickness plagued the interior of the continent, through whatever poison had created the *gabhya.* Unless there was a boat. She'd seen nothing in the harbor, but Cho Lu had mentioned a shipyard. If she could find a small craft, something nearly finished, forgotten when the inhabitants fled, she might just manage to pilot it back to Annur.

Without charts? whispered a grim voice in the back of her head. *Without supplies?*

There'd been a time she would have strangled that voice and started running. Now, however, when she tried to imagine sailing away, the horror of spending months in a boat alone unfolded like the horizon. It wasn't impossible, but it felt impossible.

Bhuma Dhar's words came back to her: *The stillness is difficult for you, and so you turn your training on yourself.*

At least here, in this land of bones and *gabhya,* there might be something to distract her from herself. Something to fight. Something to loathe that wasn't named Gwenna Sharpe.

She forced her body into motion. Moving hurt, but then, staying still hurt. It all fucking hurt. Slowly, like some beast tamed and brought to heel, she followed her captors up the wide steps.

At the top of the wall she stopped, transfixed by the sight that had brought everyone else up short. It was like the wells they'd encountered earlier—a great hole bored into the plateau—except larger, a hundred times larger, a thousand, a huge pit carved from the bedrock, and there, rising from its center, hewn from the same unbroken stone, the ziggurat. A stone walkway, held up by a dozen or so heavy arches, stabbed inward from the wall, spear-straight, stretching all the way to the first level of the stepped pyramid. It was wide enough that even a drunkard might stagger across without falling, but it had no wall or balustrade, nothing at all to block the view down into the wilderness below.

Wilderness.

It seemed a strange way to describe the expanse of land at the heart of such a large city, but she could think of no other. Unlike the earlier wells, which had been nothing but barren rock, this one comprised a madness of leaf and thorn spreading from the wall itself to the angled planes of the ziggurat, so thick in places it looked almost impenetrable. Most of the trees she didn't recognize. Some were thick, fat, bulging, as though grown from flesh, not wood. Some had leaves that glittered like spear blades as they sliced the air. Others seemed to strain with their branches toward the stone walkway, as though they could feel the people standing there, as though they wanted to hold them, harm them.

"What *is* this?" Pattick asked, staring.

Kiel stepped out onto the bridge, then pointed down at the inside of the wall. The stone had been slashed over and over. Gwenna imagined something with more claws than brains trying repeatedly to escape. "A pen, like the others."

"A pen for what?" Chent demanded.

"For the *gabhya*," Jonon replied.

Gwenna could smell them now even more powerfully than she had at the wells, the bile and living rot, although the scent was faint, scrubbed away, as though the monsters had been gone for weeks or even months.

"It doesn't make sense," Cho Lu said. "Back there . . ." He gestured toward the city behind them. "All those statues . . . it was like they worshipped them."

"It's one thing to worship monsters," Kiel observed. "Another to have them living among you."

"So what happened," Pattick asked, gazing the length of the bridge to where the ziggurat rose from the tangle of vegetation, "out there?"

Jonon nodded, as though the question weren't a question at all, but a personal challenge. "That is what I intend to learn."

Instead of providing answers, however, the ziggurat raised more questions. Chief among them was why the builders hadn't bothered with any defenses. The walls of the massive pyramid sloped up so gradually that Gwenna could have scrambled up them barely using her hands. There was no need for anything living in the pit below to hurl itself against the unyielding outer walls. A creature that was hungry, or angry, or eager for freedom had only to climb the sloping walls of the ziggurat, then follow the stone walkway back to the outer wall, then down the stairs into the city. And yet, no claw marks marred the stone. Instead, lines and lines and lines of script, carved in what looked like the same language from the plinths in the city beyond, circled the massive structure, coiling up from the base, winding around and around, climbing toward the summit.

"Can you read it now?" Jonon asked, turning to Kiel.

"I can understand something of the syntax, the morphology. This word, for instance . . ." The historian pointed to an angry trio of slashes that looked no different from any of the rest. "Generally appears in proximity to these . . ." A gouge and a wide sweep.

"What does it say?"

The historian shook his head. "Language doesn't work like that. I can see the patterns, but I need a referent to decipher them."

"A referent." The admiral's flat voice belied the smell of his impatience.

"This text could be anything," Kiel replied. "A historical account. A prayer. A list of the citizens of the city, although the syntax suggests otherwise."

"I think it's safe to say," Jonon replied, gazing up the steps leading to the top of the ziggurat, "that it's not an invitation."

"Did you expect one?"

He grunted. "Chent, Lurie, Vessik. In front. Cho Lu, Pattick. To the rear, eyes on that pit. If anything comes out, shoot it."

The two legionaries raised their flatbows, took up a position in back of the group. Gwenna could hear their hearts smashing out a rough rhythm.

By the time they reached the ziggurat's top, Gwenna was sore, out of breath, her whole body bowstring tight. With the exception of Intarra's Spear, the stone monolith was the largest structure she'd ever seen. It felt more like a feature of the landscape than something built by human hands, and from the summit she could see the entire city sprawled out below: the wide circular canyon at the base—like a moat filled with warped trees; the wall surrounding it; the twisting streets; the squares with their wells; the canyons riving the plateau; then the abrupt end to the west and south, where the tableland plunged in cliffs down to the sea. To the north, beyond the last of the buildings, farmland stretched all the way to a line of low hills, fields demarcated by stone walls, crossroads punctuated by clusters of cottages and barns. Those fields made the whole place seem almost normal. Whoever had lived here, they still needed to eat. No doubt farmers had followed the sky and the rhythms of the seasons just as they did everywhere else, fretting over too little rain, or too much. At harvest time the wide roads would have been choked with wagons piled high with grain or maize, the markets loud with the clamor of barter. . . .

Then she remembered the ziggurat beneath her feet.

She wasn't sure what she'd expected from the summit. A temple, maybe. Maybe a tomb. Certainly not a garden.

Unlike the riot of vegetation filling the canyon below, the flat space at the top of the ziggurat—a space the size of a small muster field—grew lush with resinous trees, swards of open grass, and cascades of flowers. The builders must have buried the summit paces deep in dirt for so much greenery to flourish. Near the center stood another pile of skulls. These, however, were far from human.

Some looked feline, as though they'd belonged to tigers or lions. There were a few that might have been bears, a bunch more with massive tusks and fangs—boars, maybe, or crocodiles, though the climate didn't seem right for crocs. And then there were the inexplicable ones, those with six eye sockets, or two mouths, or single horns protruding from the foreheads. Some of those skulls were the size of Gwenna's torso. One was large enough that she could have crawled inside the razor-toothed mouth and fallen asleep.

"More *gabhya*," Dhar murmured.

Jonon turned to him. "It would appear that humans were not the only sacrifice."

"But if the humans were killed by the monsters," Cho Lu said, shaking his head, "then what killed the monsters? What kind of people are capable of killing something like *that*?" He pointed to a skull near the base. It was the size of a small cart—four eye sockets, fangs the length of Gwenna's forearms, horns sweeping up and out. . . .

"Not people," Kiel said quietly.

All eyes turned to him.

"This is the work," he went on after a pause, "of the Nevariim."

For a full five heartbeats, no one spoke. The soldiers smelled baffled. Chent's face was twisted halfway to a laugh that died before it left his lips. Jonon smelled of steel and doubt, all of it edged with anger. Here was a man, Gwenna thought, who was not used to being uncertain.

"Do not toy with me, historian."

"I am not."

"The Nevariim are a myth, a story for children."

"And where," Kiel asked, "do you think the stories come from?"

"Wait," Pattick cut in. "*Hold* on. In the stories, the Nevariim are *good*. They're gorgeous, brave, kind, all the rest of it. They don't have"—he gestured—"stacks of human skulls. Or *any* skulls. Skulls aren't a *thing* in the stories."

"The stories are wrong," Kiel said mildly. "Or warped, at the very least. The human accounts are based on the Csestriim accounts, many of which are fragmentary, or altogether lost."

"But somehow you alone know the truth," Gwenna said, staring at the man.

"Not quite alone."

"But you know it. That's what you're saying."

Kiel nodded. "It is a historian's labor to sift truth from fiction."

"And the truth," Jonon demanded, "is what?"

"Complicated."

"Uncomplicate it."

"The Nevariim were beasts. Though shaped like us, they were not like us. They lived for two things—to mate, and to hunt. They nearly took over this world before the Csestriim rallied and destroyed them."

Jonon repeated the words. "The Csestriim destroyed them. The childhood stories my sailors are so quick to relate all agree on that fact. Fantasy or not—the Nevariim are gone."

"As I said before," Kiel replied, picking one of the smaller skulls from the pile, lifting it down, studying the jutting fangs as he gazed into those flowering eyes, "the stories are often wrong."

"So you're claiming this whole city, the entire place, was populated by a lost tribe of the Nevariim?"

The historian shook his head. "No. The skulls below, the ones piled outside the wall at the base of the statues, those were human. *Everything* outside that wall was built to accommodate humans. The Nevariim hated buildings, roofs, enclosed spaces. They would have lived here," he gestured to the sward of grass around them, "where they could smell the wind and feel the sun on their skin." He nodded, as though the whole mad theory made perfect sense. "This would explain, too, why the beasts penned in the canyon below never attempted to scale the ziggurat walls or cross the bridge. They dared not venture so close to their predators."

"Predators?" Cho Lu shook his head, baffled. "The Nevariim? Why are you calling them predators?"

"That is what they were. It is *all* that they were." Then he smiled, as though at some private error of little consequence. "It would seem my tenses are incorrect. I should say: it is what they *are*."

26

In a way, the pain to which Ruc woke was different than it had been the day before—a gash across the knuckles and a vicious bruise to the ribs instead of a headache and a dislocated finger. In a way it was exactly the same—the marrow-deep weariness of a body pushed to the edge of endurance, then left to tighten overnight. Every part of him felt like rawhide about to snap.

Warm, weak sunlight drained through the open window. For a while, he lay motionless, staring at it, trying not to breathe too deeply. What he wanted to do was close his eyes, fall back into oblivion, and wake up in a week. What he wanted, though, didn't figure into it.

He closed his eyes, took hold of the sheet, shifted it aside, then dragged himself upright. A muscle somewhere deep in his back started to spasm. It felt as though the tendons were tearing away from the bone. He drew in a deep breath, then another, then another, until the agony subsided into a dull, grinding pain. When he opened his eyes, he found Talal standing in the doorway.

"I'm headed over to the mess hall with Bien," the Kettral said. "And Monster, Mouse, and Stupid. You want anything?"

Ruc nodded, then immediately regretted the motion.

Talal had his own share of bruises and lacerations, including one sloppily stitched gash behind the ear. Despite the injuries, however, he looked fresh, almost rested as he took a seat on the stool, then set his iron ball on the table beside him.

"You could have the grace to at least *look* a little miserable," Ruc said.

The Kettral smiled, poured water from the earthenware crock into a cup, handed it over.

"I puked during last night's run, if that's any consolation."

"Not really."

Ruc took a sip of water. It felt like life, trickling down the back of his throat. "What time is it?"

"The dawn gong rang a while back."

Ruc blinked. "And we're not outside sweating and bleeding on things? Goatface must be losing his touch."

"He's a good trainer. He understands that all the work is useless without some rest."

"Rest!" the trainer declared, entering the room with a flourish, as though summoned by the sound of his name. "Glorious rest! Rest is—" He paused, stared up at the ceiling as though the words were flies buzzing around the beams. "—water for the parched; broth for the famished." He shook his head, brow wrinkling with vexation. "No. No," he muttered. "Too obvious, too . . . trite. *Rest,*" he tried again, raising a finger in declamation, "is the cool air in which the steel is tempered."

He raised an eyebrow, waited expectantly.

"Very nice," Ruc said after a pause.

Talal nodded his agreement. "Vivid."

Goatface beamed. "Of course, the cool air is nothing without the fire and the hammer." He gestured with his folded parasol to the door. "Time to work, my . . . *indefatigable* charges!"

"I promise you," Ruc said. "I'm very fatiguable."

The trainer laughed, as though this were a wonderful joke that they shared. "Nonsense. Too much modesty is . . . unbecoming in a warrior."

Before Ruc could object, the trainer turned on his heel and vanished through the doorway.

Talal shook his head. "So much for the cool air of rest."

The phrase *fire and hammer* proved all too apt. After a week of cloud, the sun had finally managed to burn through. It blazed down pitilessly on the yard, gleamed off the steel of the guards' spears, baking what had been mud to a hot, uneven clay. As for the hammering, Goatface had chosen this of all days to practice shield work. The standard shields of the Worthy weren't particularly large—oval, about the size of Ruc's torso. Fashioned of wood and bronze, they weighed maybe fifteen pounds, which didn't seem like all that much until you were forced to hold the 'Kent-kissing thing in front of your face for half the day while Mouse pounded on it with a club.

Goatface had them arranged by threes—Talal, Bien, and Ruc standing shoulder to shoulder facing Monster, Mouse, and Stupid. The trainer himself reclined in his strange wooden folding chair, red parasol shading him from the worst of the sun, a sweating crock of water in his free hand. He nodded contentedly as they traded blows.

"Strike! Block!" he chanted. "Strike! Block!"

Ruc wondered how many times he had struck and blocked. Five thousand?

Ten? The shoulder of his shield arm felt about ready to rip from its socket. His clubbing arm didn't feel much better; the weapon might as well have been made of lead. Sweat poured down his bare chest, soaked his *noc,* splattered on the hot clay. Two or three times Mouse had battered his shield hard enough to knock the bronze rim back into his face. One eye had swollen half-shut. His nose was bleeding. Maybe broken. There was no way to know without stopping. Goatface didn't look as though he had any intention of stopping.

"What is the *point* of this?" Monster demanded finally. She kept battering away at Talal's shield, panting out the words in between her own blocks. "We're not . . . fucking . . . learning . . . anything."

"You are learning to strike," Goatface replied cheerfully. "And to block."

"Fighting's . . . not dancing. No one takes . . . fucking . . . turns."

"True," Goatface said. "True. If I had ten years to lavish on your training, I would instruct you in all manner of feints and misdirections, a thousand canny tactics to . . . baffle and disconcert your foes."

"Instead . . ." Monster panted. "We get . . . strike . . ." Ruc swung his club, was vaguely aware of Bien at his side, doing the same thing. "Block . . ." Mouse's weapon smashed into the shield. "Strike . . . fucking . . . block."

"Indeed!"

"We are going to die," Monster spat.

Mouse echoed her: "Die." He sounded resigned.

"Perhaps," Goatface agreed. "And yet, I have made something of an . . . informal study of the fights in the Arena . . . Don't slacken just because I'm talking! Keep up the tempo! Strike! Block! Strike! Block!" When they'd resumed the battery to his satisfaction, he continued. "When one of the Worthy dies, I ask myself, '*Why* did they die?'

"*Occasionally,* they die because their foe unleashes a sequence of true tactical genius, a never-before-seen sword form, an incomparable feat of agility with a spear. There are moments of genuine brilliance in the Arena. . . ." He shook his head sorrowfully. "Generally, however, not. What I have learned, watching men and women fight for their lives, is that they tend to die for two reasons. They are frightened, or they are tired. I have watched how, in the hot sun, as the fight drags on, warriors gradually let their shields droop, how they are slower to strike back after they have been attacked, how their weariness is their undoing.

"I cannot make you into blade masters in a matter of months. It is best that we acknowledge an awkward truth—you are thieves and priests. Aside from our resident Kettral, of course. Some of you display some measure of raw talent, some . . . less so, but there is not enough time to develop even the talent you have. I cannot give you a lifetime of martial skill, but I can promise you this . . . in the heat of the day, when you are tired and frightened, and ten thousand people are screaming for your demise—your shield will not drop."

Evidently parched from this extended speech, Goatface took a long drink from his crock of water, then went back to counting out the agonizing rhythm. "Strike! Block! Strike! Block!"

✝

Only when the sun had sagged behind the western wall did Goatface allow them to stop. As they hunched over, hands on knees, spitting into the mud, chests heaving, he clapped his hands as though delighted to introduce them to another wonderful experience.

"It is time," he announced, "*past* time, really, that you are introduced to the . . . formalities of the sacred contests." He cast an eye over them. "You have all *witnessed* a fight, at the very least. Have you not?"

Bien straightened up, knuckling her back. "Not," she replied wearily.

"That is . . . unfortunate," the trainer said, brow furrowed. "Most unfortunate." He tugged on his scraggly beard. "Where to begin?"

"How about with the weapons?" Bien asked. "I've seen all kinds of stuff in here. What will we be fighting with?"

"That, regrettably, is not as simple a question as it might appear."

"There's a choice," Ruc asked, "right?" Like Bien, he had never attended a fight. He'd come to Dombâng, after all, in order to escape the violence of the delta. Still, it was impossible to live in the city, especially during the frenzy of the high holy days, without learning something of the bloodletting that went on.

Goatface corrected him. "There is a *series* of choices. The contest begins . . ." He stopped himself. "No. This will not do. Come with me."

A dozen guards stood outside the armory. Four more with loaded flatbows watched from atop the roof. Goatface waved to them as though they were old friends, produced a key from the thong around his neck, turned it in the lock, folded his parasol, then led the six of them inside. The afternoon sun poured through the open doorway behind them, glinting off the racks of weapons standing against the wall. Goatface crossed to them.

"Spear," he said, lifting free a slender fishing spear, then tossing it onto a huge wooden table at the center of the room. "Net," he went on, moving down the wall. "Grapple and line. Dagger and shield, ring dogs, sickles."

One by one, the weapons clattered into a gleaming pile. When the trainer had made a circuit of the room, he returned to the table and sorted them out.

"This is what you will be faced with, a table much like this one at the very center of the pit. You will be . . . invited to choose from these weapons."

"Well," Monster said, "given that I'm awful at handling half that shit, I choose the spear."

"Regrettably, that choice may not be yours to make."

"Tell me what I'm not fucking understanding about the words *choose from these weapons*."

Goatface frowned. "I was under the impression that you had in the past attended the contests of the high holy days."

"Attended them, yes. Sucked down two bottles of *quey* by noontime—also yes. Forgive me if my memory's hazy."

"There's only one of each weapon," Stupid said. "You pick, they pick, you pick, they pick. . . ."

"Indeed," Goatface said. "The threes alternate in their choice of weapons. If the other three chooses first, and if they choose the spear, the spear is no longer an option."

"But we haven't trained with most of this," Bien protested. "What even *is* that thing?"

"This," Goatface said, hoisting a three-pronged bronze hook about the size of his hand, "is a grapple." There was a slender rope, maybe eight feet long, knotted through an eye at its base. "This is the line. Surely you have seen others training with them in the yard? It is an ancient weapon, from the days when Dombângan pirates raided oceangoing vessels near the delta's mouth."

"What do you do with it?"

"That depends," the trainer replied, "on your level of skill."

"Why don't we assume zero," Bien said, "since I'm not an ancient pirate."

Ruc shook his head, crossed to the table, hefted one of the short, curved blades, hooked like the moon. "Sickles?"

"Another . . . venerable weapon of Dombâng," Goatface said. "Adapted from the tool so favored by the sweet-reed harvesters."

"When were you going to train us in all this?" Ruc demanded. "You've had us handling the spear, the sword, the shield. . . ."

"When was I going to train *you*?" Goatface blinked, obviously confused. "Never."

A hot, humid silence swelled to fill the room.

"I told you he was a shit trainer," Monster said finally.

"Monster, Mouse, and Stupid," Goatface replied mildly, "were here for half a year before you arrived. They have received instruction in all of these weapons."

"What about us?" Bien demanded.

"There isn't time," the trainer replied. "You arrived with no martial training whatsoever. I will consider it a triumph if you are able to acquit yourself well with the simplest of these weapons . . . the spear or the sword."

"I might not *get* a spear or a sword," Bien growled.

"Of course you will." He gestured to the table. "If they choose the spear first, you choose the sword. If they choose the sword, you choose the spear."

"That's fine for me," Bien said. "What about Ruc? What about Talal?"

Goatface turned to study the soldier. "I have a suspicion that our resident Kettral is . . . more than capable with any weapon on this table. Am I correct?"

Talal shrugged. "I'll make do."

Monster cackled. "I've seen a lot of cocky bastards in my life," she said, "but you're really resetting the fucking bar."

The ghost of a smile crossed the soldier's lips.

"What?" Monster demanded.

"Nothing. I had a friend, a Kettral flier—cockiest bastard I've ever met. He'd be proud."

"What happened to him?"

The smile disappeared. "He died holding a bridge."

"Against who?"

"Half the Urghul nation."

"Fortunately," Goatface said, "you will not be required to face a nation, whole or fractional, Urghul or otherwise." He gestured to Ruc with the bronze grapple. "As for our second priest, I would be greatly surprised if he never learned to use a knife or a net during his time with the Vuo Ton."

"I've been away from the Vuo Ton more than fifteen years. If you want me to fight with the net, why haven't I been training with the net?"

Goatface blinked. "Have I not explained this adequately?"

"Evidently not."

"One of the Worthy from the other three may choose the net before you. Rather than belabor your . . . preexisting skills, I chose to instruct you in weapons less familiar to you. Now you have choices."

Ruc nodded grudgingly. "Still. If I *do* end up fighting with the net, it would be nice to have one or two days to brush the dust off."

"I had intended," the trainer replied, looking mildly affronted, "to give you several weeks of . . . review. There is ample time yet before the fights of the high holy days."

"I don't know if you remember," Bien cut in, "but we're not warriors, not soldiers. We're priests of Eira."

Goatface frowned, raised a finger. "No. You *were* priests of Eira, once upon a time. Now you are killers. The only remaining question is whether you are capable in your new calling."

✝

"Have you . . ." Ruc hesitated, unsure how to frame the question. "Have you tried again?"

Bien closed her eyes, nodded wearily. After spending most of the day in the blazing sun striking and blocking at Goatface's command Ruc's arms felt ready to fall off. Bien looked half a step from collapse.

"Every night," she said. "After training. When everyone's asleep." She shook her head. "The only thing worse than being a leach is being a *useless* leach."

Ruc grimaced, glanced over his shoulder. The shaded corner behind the storage shed was the safest, most private space he'd found in the yard. Which didn't mean it was either safe or private. If anyone heard her talking about leaches, about the fact that *she* was a leach, she was dead.

He would have preferred to talk in the barracks, but there was always someone else *in* the barracks. Goatface set a relentless training schedule. Every single day he had Bien, Ruc, and his other four Worthy running, wrestling, or sparring from before dawn until after dark. By the time they stumbled through the mess hall and returned to the barracks no one was much inclined to go for a stroll. Talal shared a tiny room with Ruc and Bien—each three was expected to live together just as they would fight and probably die together—which left the gap between the storage shed and the mess hall.

"If you think back to the temple," he said, "to the night it burned—"

"We've been *over* this—" She cut herself off, scrubbed her face with a grimy hand. "I'm sorry, Ruc. It's just, it doesn't help. You asking me to remember it again and again. I can see them dying. I can *feel* them dying. But it doesn't get me any closer to knowing what I did."

He opened his mouth, then shut it before he could make things worse. The sad truth was that he had absolutely no idea how to help her. If she'd asked him for advice on her knife work or spear technique, he would have stayed up all night every night teaching her what he knew. But she didn't need advice on knives or spears. She had Goatface for that. What she needed was the power bred into her flesh. More than any weapons work, it was *that* that would save her, maybe save them both, and he could do nothing but look on uselessly, day after day, as she struggled.

"I need to tell him," Bien said.

The heat radiating from her face deepened from yellow into orange.

"Tell what to who?" Ruc asked, though he could already see the shape of the answer.

"The Kettral. Talal. He's a leach."

"He says he's not."

"That's what we all say. It's the only way to stay alive. But they bring him the adamanth every day. They make him drink it."

Ruc shook his head. "They're spooked. Look at that iron ball they've got shackled to his leg. They've never captured a Kettral before."

"But if he *is* a leach," Bien said, "then he can teach me."

"And if you're wrong, he'll tell Goatface. Goatface will tell the guards. Your throat will be cut, your heart carved out, and you'll be tossed into the delta for the crocs."

Bien didn't flinch. "Not necessarily. Talal is rational enough to see that my power is . . ." She searched for the word. ". . . an asset. Even if he's *not* a leach."

"You have no idea how rational he is. We know precisely one thing about him—he's Kettral. Which means he is a killer." Ruc thought back to his conversation with the man out in the yard. What was it he'd said? *Some people need murdering.* "A ruthless killer."

She met his eyes defiantly. "He's been nothing but kind to us since we arrived."

"He has no other *choice.* Monster, Mouse, and Stupid spend most of every day hoping he'll die so that they can go back to not being noticed, and everyone else in here wants to be the one to do him in. Talal's trying to stay alive, just like we are."

"Right. So don't you think that he'll see *this*"—she gestured vaguely to herself—"as a way to stay alive? You know the stories even better than I do. The Kettral use leaches."

"Sure. I've heard plenty of stories, usually from sailors on their second or third bottle of *quey.* I spent the better part of one night listening to a man tell me how the Emperor of Annur—not the woman, the other one—was actually the god of pain."

She shook her head. "You're smart enough to sort the crazy from the rest."

"And I'm telling you this sounds crazy. Right now your secret is safe."

"*Safe?*" She stared at him, agog, then gestured madly to the walls behind them, to the churned-up mud leading out into the yard. "Nothing about this is *safe.* Every day we stay here is a day someone might knife us, or choke us, or bash in our skulls, and if we make it, if we somehow *survive* all the way to the high holy days, the big prize is that we get to fight for our lives over and over until someone kills us."

"Or we kill them."

"Ruc." She placed a hand on his chest, either to steady herself or hold back his words. "You've seen me out there every day. We've been here for what feels like forever and I can barely swing a sword. Goatface tied both Monster's hands behind her back and she *still* managed to choke me out with her legs. If I don't figure out how to use this . . . *thing* inside me then we're stuck here. And if we're stuck here, I'm going to die and you're going to murder people trying to save me."

He took her hand, held it against him. It seemed like a long time since they'd touched each other. For a while they didn't move. After the endless running and sparring, it felt good to be still, her hand on his chest, his own holding it close.

Every part of him ached. Goatface had seen to that. Some days what the trainer demanded of them felt impossible, and yet he could feel himself growing stronger as some long-dormant thing inside him asserted itself once more. How, he wondered bleakly, must the whole ordeal feel to Bien? She hadn't been raised in the delta by gods and Vuo Ton. She had no inexplicable speed or strength running through her veins. She was relying day after day on nothing more than her own bravery, stubbornness, hope, staying on her feet long after Ruc expected her to fall. How long could she keep up the pace without breaking?

He lifted her hand to his lips, kissed it. "All right."

"All right, what?"

"Tell him."

She withdrew her hand slowly. Her dark eyes were grave. "I wasn't asking your permission."

"I know that."

"Do you?"

She hugged her arms to herself, as though she'd caught a chill.

"Bien." He struggled for words to frame the feelings churning within him. "I don't know how to do this."

A small, bitter laugh forced its way through her lips. "How to join a group of murdering religious fanatics?"

He shook his head. "How to be afraid for you."

"It doesn't help," she said quietly.

"I know." He exhaled unsteadily. "I know it doesn't, and I'm sorry. It feels like someone lifted my heart out of my chest"—he forced down the memory of Hang Loc doing just that to some hapless warrior of the Vuo Ton—"and hung it, still beating, around my neck. Every time you fall down, every time you get hit, every time you get cut"—he reached out, traced a shallow slice down the side of her cheek—"it's like a blow right to that naked heart."

"That's romantic," she replied, "and poetic. But do you know what it feels like to *me*?" She worried her lip with her teeth before continuing. "It feels like I need to protect myself *and* you at the same time. I can't just deal with my own exhaustion and pain, I need to worry about *your* heart, too. I need to worry about whatever my failures are doing to it."

Ruc started to respond, then stopped himself. Whatever she needed from him in that moment, it wasn't more words.

Bien watched, waited for an objection, and then, when none was forthcoming, softened. "I worry about you, too, you know. It's just that, you looking at me every moment like I'm made of porcelain makes me feel even more like I'm about to break."

"You don't need me to tell you you're not going to break."

"No," she agreed with a sad little smile. "I need to look in your eyes and see that you believe it."

Ruc hesitated, then opened his arms.

Bien hesitated, then stepped into them.

An embrace, like thousands they'd shared over the years. Like those, and not like them at all.

27

The First Admiral was a puckered asshole, but he knew how to lead soldiers. A lot of commanders would have retreated to the ship for the night rather than setting up camp within the walls of a foreign city, a city almost certainly hostile, even if it appeared empty, a city bristling with statues of monsters and stacked with the skulls of the dead. A ship at anchor in the harbor was far easier to defend than a barricade erected in a city square. It was hard to sneak up on someone in a ship. Hard to surround and slaughter them. Gwenna herself would have been tempted to fall back to the *Daybreak* for the night. Jonon, however, was thinking beyond the night.

The mission, after all, wasn't to find some ziggurat piled with skulls, poke around awhile, then go home. It was to journey inland, to the mountains on the horizon, to find the kettral and their nests—provided that both still existed after so many thousands of years—plunder the eggs, and bring them back. Which meant Jonon and all the rest of them were going to spend days if not weeks in the strange land. By establishing camp on the shore that first night, he was making a statement—*Whatever challenges await us here, we are equal to them.* Just as important, the work of building the barricades—dragging beds and tables and chairs from the homes, stacking them athwart the streets, setting torches alight around the perimeter, establishing guards and snipers— gave the soldiers something to do, something to take their minds off the rumors that threatened to spread like plague through the crew.

Monsters. Skulls. Sickness. Sacrifice.

Nevariim.

In a strange way, that last revelation was the least threatening. Kiel had spoken about the Nevariim as though they were real, real as the stone of the city streets or the sky above, as though they might at any moment stride naked and gorgeous from the surrounding forests, gleaming swords in their hands. To Gwenna, however, the word still sounded like something out of a fireside story. She remembered her father sitting by the cozy blaze in the cabin where she grew up, unspooling soldiers' tales of the legendary warriors. In the way of stories, they were all different but all the same: two or three Nevariim holding a pass or a gate or a bridge against hundreds and hundreds of Csestriim. Despite being wounded over and over—punched full of arrows, slashed with swords, burned with flaming oil—they kept fighting and fighting toward one of only two possible ends: triumph, or a heroic death surrounded by mountains of the enemy slain.

It was all a batch of horseshit. She'd learned that later. That just wasn't how war worked, Nevariim or not.

A few soldiers—properly trained and heavily armed—might hold a perfect defensive position against a superior foe for some length of time. Half a day. Maybe, with great luck and bravery, if the opposing numbers weren't too great, a day. No one could stand in the middle of a bridge against an army and survive. Gwenna'd had a friend who'd tried just that; he'd ended up skewered on a forest of Urghul spears. Or Quick Jak. The flier's attempt to carve his way the length of the Purple Baths would have been an exploit worthy of the Nevariim, except Jak hadn't made it the length of the Baths. He'd managed maybe twenty paces before the Dombângans hacked him apart. Not surprising. That was what happened when you fought a battle against long odds—not glory, but blood, suffering, failure, death. For all her wide-eyed childhood fascination, the stories of the Nevariim were just that—stories.

On the other hand, *someone* had built the city. Actually, more like tens of thousands of someones, judging by the size of the place. Whether or not Kiel was correct about a cadre of immortals dwelling at the top of the ziggurat, real, actual *people* had lived in all those houses, and not long ago, either. That thought—not the myths of the Nevariim—had Gwenna glancing over her shoulder and listening to the wind for the rest of the day. The place *seemed* empty. Certainly, the bulk of the population had vanished, but she'd never heard of a city emptying out entirely. There were always the old, the sick, and the young, those too green or feeble to leave their houses, even their beds, let alone to abandon everything. Even if everyone else had quit the city, what had happened to them?

That part of the mystery, at least, was solved by nightfall.

The sun was just bloodying the western waves when Jonon's last patrol came jogging back toward the makeshift palisade, weapons out, faces grim. Vessik had the command, and after dismissing his soldiers to their evening posts, he approached Jonon's large tent at the center of the camp. Gwenna was not allowed inside, of course; there was no brig onshore, but she remained a prisoner all the same, under the watchful guard of a pair of nervous-looking legionaries, close enough to the admiral's tent that he could summon her if he had any need. Which, so far, he had not.

Gwenna closed her eyes as Vessik slipped through the canvas flap, and sorted through the night's ten thousand sounds—wind scraping over the slate roofs, the rasp of stone sliding across steel, the uneasy jokes and hollow boasting of the soldiers, the clank of spoons against pots, crackling of fires, rustling of bedding spread on the chill ground—and found the voices of Jonon and Vessik.

". . . Bones, sir," the legionary was saying. "Must have been hundreds of skeletons, maybe thousands."

"A grave?" Jonon asked.

"Not a grave, sir. Not even skeletons, now I think of it. Just bones. All of them near the bridge, as though they'd been thrown off."

So. Vessik had been given the unenviable assignment of exploring the wilderness ringing the ziggurat. No wonder he sounded rattled.

"Why didn't we see them when we crossed?"

"The trees, sir. The leaves. It was only when we went down there. . . ." He trailed off, lost in the memory, then went on. "It was like the folks they'd belonged to had been ripped apart."

"How long ago?"

"I . . . don't know, sir."

"Was there flesh on the bones? Skin?"

"No, sir. They were clean, sir. Like they'd been there some time. And . . ."

"Say it, soldier."

"A lot of the bones, sir . . . they had marks."

"Marks?"

"Tooth marks, looked like. Like they'd been gnawed."

Gwenna could picture the man making the sign of the Annurian sun over his heart, a ward against the darkness of the alien night.

"I took the teeth, sir, like you said I should if we found anything. The back teeth from a dozen different skulls."

There was a sound like dice rattling across a wooden table.

"Ground down," Jonon said after a pause. "All of them. These people killed their old before they left."

Vessik's voice was thick with what sounded like nausea. "Didn't just kill them, sir. *Fed* them to . . . something. To those monsters."

"Or the monsters found the corpses later and fed," the admiral replied. "It doesn't matter."

"But what kind of people, sir," the legionary asked, "slaughter their mothers and fathers?"

"The world is a dark place, soldier. We have been blessed to live under the light of Annur, but that light does not reach everywhere. The lands beyond our borders are peopled with savages, brutes, men and women little better than dogs. They look like us—arms, legs, noses in the centers of their faces—but never make the mistake of believing that they *are* like us."

"Never, sir."

"If there ever comes a moment, Vessik, when you doubt our purpose here, remember those bones, remember the way the savages who built this place fed their elders to the beasts."

"Yes, sir."

There was a long pause, followed by a clacking, as though Jonon were rolling the teeth in the palm of his hand. Then he spoke again.

"Do you know what we're doing here, Vessik, in this darkest corner of a dark world?"

The legionary hesitated. "Looking for birds, sir? The big ones?"

"Yes, Vessik, and no. The birds are only a means."

"A means, sir?"

"They are a tool."

"A weapon, sir?"

"Better than a weapon. Brighter. Each one is a torch, as I am a torch. As you are a torch. We are here, Vessik, to bring light."

"How do we do that, sir? Bring light?"

Gwenna could imagine the set of Jonon's jaw, his level gaze fixed on the soldier. "By never compromising what we know to be right."

The legionary exited the tent looking shaken but resolved. For a moment, as the flap swung shut behind him, he stood there, staring out over the camp, the dozens of cook fires reflected in his eyes. They'd brought light to the city, that was true enough, but it seemed a small thing compared to the darkness pressing in against it from every side, compared to the great cold gulf Gwenna felt yawning inside herself. She shivered, pulled her coat tighter around her shoulders.

A few moments later Jonon emerged from the tent.

"Sharpe."

Her guards fell over themselves in their haste to drag her to her feet.

The admiral pointed. "Inside."

There was almost nothing inside the tent—a folding camp table illuminated by a pair of lanterns, Kiel's map at the center, a pitcher of water and a wooden cup beside it. A cot in the corner—the admiral's presumably—barely thicker than the bedrolls used by the soldiers outside. A banner with the Annurian sunburst hung from one wall. There were no chairs, not even one for Jonon.

Gwenna stood while the admiral crossed to the table, poured into his cup, sipped the water, and stared at the map. What he wanted with her she had no idea, nor did she have the energy to guess.

"You were in Dombâng," he said finally, not looking up from the map.

She nodded. "Yes."

"Yes, *sir*," he corrected her absently.

"Yes, sir."

"How are their forces deployed?"

She blinked. If anything, she'd expected to be dressed down once more for her failures, not consulted on a matter of military intelligence.

"They aren't. Sir. The whole city is surrounded by the Shirvian delta. It's a huge swamp."

"Armies can fight in swamps."

"Not this one. You try to deploy there, half your men will be dead by night-fall, the other half by morning."

"But the delta does not stretch across the entire Waist."

"Not even close."

"How would the city respond to an army marching north through the Waist?"

Gwenna shook her head. "They might not even notice it. I guess some of the loggers from up the Shirvian might bring word, but we've got soldiers up there whose job it is to kill those loggers."

Jonon looked up at her sharply. "How many legions?"

She shook her head. "Just one, last I heard. It's possible that Adare's—"

"You will refer to the Emperor," he said grimly, "bright be the days of her life, as *Her Radiance,* or I will have your tongue."

"It's possible that Her Radiance—or one of her generals—has pulled that legion. I think she's given up on Dombâng, letting it go its own way."

"Because of your failure."

Gwenna nodded mutely.

"So nothing—no military force—stands between this continent and the empire."

"There are the Waist tribes."

Jonon waved a dismissive hand. "Gibbering apes, I'm told. A few naked, pitiful creatures with weapons that aren't worth the word."

"Those pitiful creatures," Gwenna replied, "have remained stubbornly un-conquered for centuries. Anlatun lost ten legions in the Waist."

"Don't lecture me on Anlatun's misguided military adventures. The Waist tribes can harry an army, but can they stop one?"

Gwenna studied the man. "You think that's where they've gone," she said, nodding toward the wall of the tent, to the great empty city lying beyond. "You think whoever lived here is marching on Annur."

"I do."

She tried to imagine it—an entire city, an entire *people* walking out of their lives to cross half the world. . . .

"Why Annur?"

"It is the only place that makes sense."

"The empire is what, two thousand miles distant?"

"More."

She shook her head. "How would they even know about it, let alone decide to go there?"

"I don't know," Jonon admitted. His own ignorance seemed to gall him. "But we are standing, right now, at the southern tip of the continent. To the west and east there is only ocean. Which leaves north."

"There's a lot of *north* between here and the Waist."

"The center of Menkiddoc, almost the whole interior if the historian is to be believed, is poisoned, uninhabitable. And there is Solengo to consider. There, like here, the human sacrifice. There, like here, the evidence of *gabhya,* the vanished population."

"Solengo's not exactly on the way to Annur."

"It is for anyone traveling by ship. A fleet might stop there to top off their water and stores."

Wind tugged at the walls of the tent, as though hungry to rip the canvas from the frame. Gwenna had always hated tents. They gave the illusion of safety—walls, a roof, a cradle for the lantern's light—but anyone with a knife, anything with claws, could slice through the canvas with a casual swipe. Worse, you couldn't see it coming. She'd always preferred to bivouac in her bedroll. It was colder, wetter, but at least you felt like what you were: not the lord of some fake chamber; just another naked creature in the night.

A gust ripped open the flap of the door, and she caught a snatch of sound—the fragment of a curse somewhere off toward the northern edge of the camp.

She half turned, hesitated.

Jonon narrowed his eyes. "What?"

"Something . . ." She shook her head. "Something is happening outside."

For once, the admiral didn't question her. Instead, he dropped a hand to the pommel of his sword, crossed the tent in a handful of steps, and thrust his way into the dark. Gwenna followed him, her hands aching for the handles of her own absent blades.

The camp reeked of confusion and alarm. Soldiers halfway through their meals surged to their feet, spilling bread and soup as they reached for weapons. The shouting was getting closer, voices resolving out of the wind and darkness.

"... Stop it, you miserable little—"

"Hold it. *Hold it!*"

"My *finger*! My fucking *finger*!"

The smell of blood thickened on the cold wind.

From behind one of the fires stumbled a handful of legionaries. One of them—Lurie—clutched a blood-soaked hand to his chest, while the others grappled with some half-naked creature, all rags, and filth, and skin, and tangled hair. Firelight smeared off a gleam of bloody teeth, wide, panicked eyes as the thing thrashed, lashed out with its heels at every step, making a noise halfway between a snarl and a scream.

Gwenna squinted as the men hauled it closer.

Not it, she realized. *Her.*

The creature wasn't a creature at all, but a girl, maybe eight or nine years old, judging by her size.

As Gwenna stared, she spat a spray of blood, blood and something else. A chunk rolled across the cobbles, came to rest a few paces from the fire. A finger. Half of one, at least. Lurie's, presumably. After the initial shock, the man's rage shouldered aside his pain, and he closed on the struggling girl, his sword raised.

"Stop."

Jonon's voice sliced through the night.

The legionary turned. "Little savage bitch bit my finger, sir. Bit it clean off."

"See the surgeon. Even small wounds can fester strangely in foreign lands."

The soldier looked ready to object, saw Jonon's face, thought better of it. Reeking of pain and rage he strode off into the camp.

The girl, in the meantime, hadn't stopped thrashing. The remaining soldiers had her by the wrists—one to each arm—but that didn't stop her from flipping her entire body upside down, lashing out at their faces with her bare feet, writhing so violently she looked likely to rip her shoulders from their sockets. The girl was less than half their size, but she fought with a strength that belied her skinny frame, battling so furiously that she seemed on the verge of breaking free. Only when Jonon stepped close, laid the naked point of his sword against her neck, did she fall instantly, tremblingly still, wide eyes fixed on that length of gleaming steel.

"Bind her wrists," Jonon said.

Those wrists were sickeningly thin—a little skin wrapped around a twig of bone. The girl's face, likewise, bore the signs of hunger, if not starvation.

The high bones of her cheeks looked ready to punch through the last shreds of flesh; her lips were withered, cracked. It was a miracle that she could stand, let alone harry three hale Annurian soldiers, but Gwenna knew the strength that fear could lend a body, and the girl was most definitely afraid.

She tried to hide the fact, baring her teeth as the cord pulled tight around her wrists, staring up at Jonon with brazen defiance. It was a good act, especially for a nine-year-old, but it was only an act. She reeked of terror.

"Where did you find her?" the admiral asked.

"She found us," one of the soldiers replied. "Tried to sneak off with a ration of salt pork. Stole it from right over the fire. Had some kind of creature with her."

"What kind of creature?"

"Didn't get a good look. Monkey, maybe. Lots of teeth."

"Did you kill it?"

"No, sir." The soldier ducked his head. "It escaped, sir. Fast, it was."

"This was in the northern quarter of the camp?"

"Yes, sir."

Jonon nodded. "The sentries there will stay at their posts, unrelieved, until dawn. Bring their rations for the girl. I won't have her starving to death before I can wring some answers out of her."

"Whatever answers you get, sir, they won't be in our tongue. She started gibbering her crazy babble when we first grabbed her. Sounded like a pair of crows, sir, fighting over a dead dog."

"What would you expect," the admiral asked coldly, "of a child raised thousands of miles from the empire's light?"

"Of course, sir. Just saying, sir. Someone will have to learn that babble."

Jonon nodded, stared at the girl awhile longer, then turned to Gwenna with a thin, joyless smile. "I believe I know just the person."

Gwenna stared at him, a new horror unfolding inside her. She shook her head. "I don't . . . I'm no good with kids."

"As far as I can tell," the admiral replied, "you are no good with anything. You lost your bird, abandoned your men, and allowed my soldiers to be blown up. You were never meant to be Kettral. Perhaps you will prove a more capable nursemaid."

He spat into his hand, scrubbed his palm roughly against the girl's face. There was, Gwenna realized, pale skin beneath all that grime.

"She shares your complexion," the admiral went on. "If you had given yourself to a more appropriate pursuit—marriage, housekeeping, child-rearing—she could be your daughter."

"She can't . . ." Gwenna began, scrambling for some way to deny the girl.

"We're about to march into the mountains. She'll slow us down. Better to leave her on the ship until we get back."

She wasn't frightened of the child's strength or ferocity. Sure, the girl might try to bite off her finger or rake out her eyes, but that much she could handle, even without her swords. It was everything that lay *beneath* that brittle defiance that filled her with horror—all that fear, confusion, bafflement. It was too much. Gwenna could just manage, from sunrise to sunset, to hold her own horrors at bay. She had nothing left to take on some . . . some *child*.

"Inside this skull," Jonon said, tapping ungently against the girl's temple, "is knowledge that I need, that the *empire* needs. If I could crack it open with a hammer and extract it, I would. Minds, however, do not work that way. It would take weeks to break her, maybe months. Weeks and months on top of that to learn her language. I will not waste valuable days because you've grown indifferent to the orders of your emperor and the welfare of your people."

"But if she tries to run—"

Now Jonon's smile had teeth. "I think she will find that difficult with the two of you chained ankle to ankle."

"And if she refuses to talk?"

"If your maternal skills prove as wanting as your martial ones," the admiral replied, "and she hasn't yielded anything useful by the time we return to the *Daybreak,* we'll try a different method."

"What method?"

"The one with the cutting, and the screaming, and the blood."

28

"Gwenna," Gwenna said, touching her own chest. "Gwenna. Gwenna."

She pointed to the girl. The girl tried to bite off her finger.

Gwenna slapped her on the ear. The girl made a sound like a growl, bared her teeth, then retreated to the end of the length of chain linking them. It was not a long chain.

Jonon's blacksmith had hammered shut the shackle around her ankle the night before, linked it to the chain, then pinned that chain to the smaller shackle around the girl's ankle. Stretched out all the way it left maybe two paces between them. Enough to use the privy without pissing on each other. Enough to sleep on separate bedrolls, only the girl didn't have a bedroll, and Gwenna couldn't sleep.

She spent the night awake, listening to the girl's breathing, to her heartbeat, to the terrified half cries and protestations she muttered in her sleep. For a small child, she took up a lot of room, kicking and sprawling, as though she were fighting something, or fleeing, then whimpering, curling in on herself, hiding from whatever monsters stalked her dreams.

"Fuck," Gwenna muttered to herself, dread folding over her as she stared at the girl's filthy features.

Being locked in the brig with Bhuma Dhar had been bad enough, but at least they hadn't been chained together.

No, she thought, tracing the cool steel links with a finger. The chain wasn't the problem.

Bhuma Dhar had been a grown man and a naval captain, equal to his fate in all the ways that mattered. He might have *preferred* to share the long, dark weeks with a more talkative prisoner, someone who wasn't lost in the labyrinth of her own emotions, but he didn't *need* her. He'd made a few salvos when she stopped talking, tried asking questions, then gave up, retreated into his sleep and his prayers, left her to rot. Which was just what she'd wanted.

Now, though, Dhar was back in the brig, and she was here, on the soil of a foreign continent, chained to this fucking *child*. She considered ignoring her as she'd eventually ignored Dhar, spent half the night telling herself to put the girl out of her mind entirely, but the girl was nothing like Dhar. She was obviously baffled, and terrified, and utterly alone, and so, when the sun rose, Gwenna tried talking.

"My name is Gwenna," she said again, pointing at herself. "Gwenna."

The girl didn't turn. She had her legs pulled up to her chest, arms wrapped tight around them, face buried in her knees. She was crying. Crying silently and motionlessly, but Gwenna could smell the tears.

"My name is Gwenna," she said again. "Gwenna Sharpe."

She felt, for some vicious reason to which she could not put a name, as though she were lying.

┼

Every day the camp came alive before dawn. The men busied themselves with the eternal work of soldiers in the field—pissing and shitting, washing if they'd camped near water, checking weapons as they bolted down a cold morning ration of salt cod and water. The jokers joked, the malcontents grumbled, some few remained silent, staring mutely into their cups or stealing glances toward the horizon where Kiel's promised mountains jutted up, still small as broken teeth.

They were moving every morning before full sunup. For the first two days, they marched along a wide dirt track through open farmland. Stone walls carved the dirt into neat parcels, but the fields, fallow at least a season, had gone to seed. The stone cottages that they passed were all empty, just like the houses in the city. According to the soldiers Jonon dispatched to search them, the inhabitants had left behind almost everything large—chairs, tables, cast-iron pots—and taken whatever a person might carry—blankets, knives, small tools.

Rat—Gwenna had decided to call the girl *Rat* because she was small and vicious, and because rats had seemed to be the only creatures left in the city—stared at the cottages with a kind of mute rage, as though the inhabitant of every single one had personally betrayed her.

"Gone," Gwenna tried halfway through the first day, gesturing toward the fields, then the city behind them. "People gone."

The girl refused to look at her.

Midmorning on the third day they came to a place where the land folded into low, treeless hills. The road straggled on a few more miles, threading between boulders, skirting exposed rocky ledges, turning to a dirt track, then petering out entirely. The occasional cottage dotted the gray-green hills, but these were squat, windowless—shelter for crofters caught out in the storm rather than proper dwellings.

Jonon set an exacting pace, close to thirty miles a day, as far as Gwenna could judge. Her legs throbbed. Her shoulders ached from lugging her pack. After a night sleeping on the chill ground, her back hardened into a solid knot and refused to let go. Blisters rose on her heels, burst, cracked, then bled. For all of that, however, the marching was the easy part. She didn't have to think to march, didn't have to hope to march, didn't have to believe in anything to march. It was easier, actually, not thinking or hoping, just putting one bloody foot ahead of the next, over and over until someone told her to stop.

She might well have spent all day walking, all night unconscious in her bedroll, were it not for Rat.

Somehow, implausibly, the girl managed to keep pace, matching Gwenna step for sullen step. There was an uncanny, almost unnatural resilience to her young body. Whenever Gwenna tried to talk, however, she turned her face away, retreated to the end of the chain.

"Jonon is going to hurt you," Gwenna told her. It was late in the fourth day, and she'd long ago given up on simple phrases, basic lessons. She wanted to give up on the whole fucking enterprise, but the thought of the girl strapped to the surgeon's table while Jonon tried to cut or burn some truth out of her twisted Gwenna's stomach to the point of nausea. And so she kept trying.

"Hurt you," she said again, making a stabbing motion at the girl. "He is going to *fuck you up*."

Rat looked away, off over the empty hills.

"She doesn't understand."

Gwenna glanced back to find the historian walking quietly at her shoulder. For all his brokenness, he moved easily, almost silently over the uneven ground.

"No shit," she replied wearily. "You're welcome to give it a try."

Kiel shook his head. "In this, Jonon chose well. The girl is more likely to trust you."

"Because I'm a woman?" Gwenna demanded wearily. "Because I'm the right age to be her fucking mother? I'm *not* her mother."

"Because you are trustworthy," the historian replied.

Before she could think of anything to say to that, the man moved on up the column, leaving her chained to the girl and somehow, at the same time, alone.

Later that afternoon, one of the soldiers brought down a deer, and that night Pattick came by with a cut of meat for Gwenna and Rat.

"Here," he said awkwardly, offering it up, still sizzling from the spit.

"Thanks," Gwenna said.

The legionary stood there a moment longer, as though he wanted to say something, then turned abruptly and walked back to his fire. Gwenna watched him go. It was hard to believe that he'd followed her onto an enemy vessel just months before.

She was still watching him when Rat came at her with the knife.

Where the girl picked it up, Gwenna had no fucking idea, not that it mattered. In the space of a heartbeat, Rat leapt across the space between them, silent as a shadow, hacking down.

Gwenna was saved by the Flea. Not the actual man, obviously; he was thousands and thousands of miles away, back on the Islands, training Kettral cadets, utterly oblivious to the fact that she was at the ass end of Menkiddoc, chained to some savage child. But the Flea had been in charge of knife-fighting when Gwenna herself was a cadet, and he had taken the training seriously. It was impossible to forget the endless drills—fighting with one knife or two knives, on foot or in the water; against one foe, or two, or three; against dogs; against soldiers wearing plate armor, or chain, or none; fighting with double-sided daggers, stilettos, filleting knives; and yes, fighting with no knife, empty-handed, against someone else who held the weapon. Without thinking, she knocked the attack aside, caught the girl's wrist, twisted just *so,* and the blade clattered to the dirt. It was over in a quarter heartbeat. Rat stared at her, teeth bared, eyes brimming with tears.

"Don't," Gwenna said, picking up the blade.

The girl looked ready to die. Nine years old, chained to some bitch she'd never met, forced to walk thirty miles a day, and still defiant.

"Oh, fuck it," Gwenna muttered. "Fine. Have another shot."

She tossed the knife into the dirt at Rat's feet. The girl stared at it. Gwenna could smell the anger on her, the hunger, the hesitation.

"Go ahead," she said, gesturing. "You stab me, you win."

Rat was fast. Very fast. Faster than any kid had a right to be. But Rat hadn't spent an entire childhood drilling against the Flea.

She came in hard and low, Gwenna twisted, hacked down into her arm, knocked the knife free.

"Again," she said, tossing it to the girl.

This time, Rat didn't hesitate.

Again and again she attacked, and again and again Gwenna disarmed her. It wasn't training. There was nothing playful in the motions. Rat attacked with everything she had, aiming for Gwenna's chest, or face, or neck, aiming every time to maim or to kill. One missed block, one ill-timed grab, and the girl would be on top of her, opening a nice wide hole in her skin. The Emperor's words floated through Gwenna's mind for the thousandth time—all that about smart bets, and winning bets, and gambler's folly. This was obviously the stupidest of stupid bets—nothing to win and a whole life to lose—but she found she didn't give a shit. Rat's attacks blotted out, if only for a few moments, all the rest of it—the doubt, the despair, the million-toothed dread burrowing constantly through her guts. Her whole world narrowed to that weaving knifepoint. It was almost like being back on the Islands—the rhythm of attack and defense, the heat rising through her muscles, the readiness. . . .

"Look," she said, snatching the blade again. This time she didn't give it back. Instead she raised it overhead, point angled down, the most basic threatening posture.

"You're quick, but you need to learn to lie."

She feinted with the knife, then slapped the girl across the cheek with her free hand.

Rat recoiled, face twisted with fury.

"See," Gwenna said. "You don't need to speak in order to lie." She leaned slightly to the right, gave just a twitch of her right hand, then, when Rat turned to defend, tapped her ungently on the temple with the pommel of the knife.

"If you're defending," Gwenna went on, "you need to see three things at once. The knife." She pointed to the fire-licked blade. "The hand." To her own hand. "And the body." To the center of her chest. "Any one of these can lie. The knife can point down, but the hand"—she gave a quick flick, reversing the blade—"can trick you. Or the knife and the hand can lead one direction"—she reached out with her arm—"while the body breaks the other way. Any one can lie, any *two* can lie, but if you learn to see the knife, the hand, and the body all at the same time . . . then you're looking at the truth.

"If you're attacking? Well, you need to learn to obscure that truth."

She handed the blade back.

"Go again."

This time, however, Rat did not go. She crouched, staring at Gwenna from behind her nest of tangled hair. Then she glanced down at the weapon.

"Knife," she said.

"The point is, the knife is the least important part of . . ."

Gwenna trailed off, staring. "Well I'll be shipped to 'Shael," she muttered. "Yes. That's the knife."

So much for *Hello, my name is* . . .

"Hand," Rat said, raising her hand.

Gwenna nodded.

"Body." She pointed to her chest.

"That's your body," Gwenna agreed.

"Knife," the girl said, pointing to Gwenna's body. "Gwenna body."

Gwenna's grin was so sharp and shocking it hurt. "That's right, you miserable little shit. Put the knife in Gwenna's body."

And the girl came on again.

†

Gwenna had been so wrapped up with Rat's training, not to mention the exhaustion of the march, that she'd forgotten all about the words of the soldier who'd first captured the child: *Had some kind of creature with her. Monkey, maybe. Lots of teeth.*

Then, on the fifth day, as they were passing through a copse of trees, the 'Kent-kissing thing attacked.

Pattick had dropped back with some dried meat for Gwenna and Rat. Every day he came, sometimes twice a day. Ostensibly he was there to check over the chain and shackles, to make sure the two prisoners weren't contriving some kind of escape, but he seemed more concerned with Rat's diet—the girl was still incredibly thin—with *Gwenna's* fucking diet, for that matter. It was ludicrous, having the legionary clucking over them as though he were their mother, but Rat hadn't tried to murder *him* yet, which was saying something, and Gwenna wasn't about to deny the girl the extra rations.

The young soldier had just finished his cursory inspection of the restraints, was straightening up, when he jerked back with a strangled cry.

Gwenna's first thought was that he'd been shot.

Her body responded for her, one hand shooting out to drag the soldier down, the other hauling Rat behind her with the length of chain. The girl hissed, yanked back, but even after two months of doing nothing, Gwenna was stronger. Not that she had much of a plan beyond getting them to ground. The nearest cover—a long, rotting log—lay a few paces distant.

Should have gone for that. The thought was savage, lacerating. *You fucked it up again, you stupid bitch.*

"Shit," Pattick managed.

"Where are you hit?"

"No." He shook his head, wiped something foul-smelling from his face. "It's *shit*."

Gwenna stared at him, opened her mouth to reply, then felt her own head snap back. The smell came a moment later—rotten and foul—then the taste of it splattered across her teeth, over her tongue. She gagged, spat, gagged again, half puked, dragged herself back to her feet, scanned the surrounding trees.

It took her only a moment to find it.

Maybe ten paces away, high up on a tree limb, crouched . . . something.

It was the size of a bear cub—gray-haired, pointy-eared, with hands that looked almost human. It might have been cute—huge eyes set wide in the fuzzy head—were it not for the teeth. Those teeth—at least a dozen of them, gleaming, stiletto-sharp, at least as long as Gwenna's thumb—looked as though they belonged to some other creature altogether—a barracuda or shark maybe, something that survived by ripping and rending flesh.

As she stared, the thing reached back, shat into its hand, and let fly another volley, although this time, Gwenna managed to dodge.

Several of the soldiers had taken hasty aim with their flatbows. Rat let out a desperate shriek, hurled herself at the nearest of them, tripped over the chain, and fell.

"Kill it," Jonon commanded.

Three bowstrings loosed at once, but the creature was fast, *too* fast. It moved like something out of a dream, something not quite subject to the normal laws of the world. Two of the flatbow bolts sailed through the space where it had crouched. The third, it snatched from the air, snapped in half, hurled to the ground.

It bared its teeth, hissed at the soldiers.

"Yutaka!" Rat shouted. She made a flinging gesture with one hand.

The creature glared at her with those too-large eyes, gnashed the teeth, and then, before anyone could take another shot, fled into the trees, swinging nimbly from one branch to the next until the shadows swallowed it.

By the time Gwenna had untangled herself and Rat from the chain, Jonon loomed above them. He glared down at the girl.

"What was that thing?"

Rat stumbled to her feet, flashed her teeth, as though she were no more human than the creature in the trees.

Jonon took her by the hair, lifted her onto her toes.

"What was it?"

"She doesn't understand you," Gwenna said.

The admiral didn't take his eyes from the girl. "She understands enough. *Yutraga?* Is that what you called it? What is a yutraga?"

Rat gave a wordless snarl. Jonon hoisted her higher, until Gwenna expected the hair to rip from her scalp. Then Kiel was there.

"That," the historian said mildly, "was a *gabhya*."

Jonon hesitated a moment, then dropped Rat as though she were a filthy rag, turned to face Kiel.

"How do you know?"

"There is a wrongness to the way they are made. A shape nature would never have created."

"A *gabhya*," Jonon mused, turning to gaze into the trees.

"An *avesh,* to be precise," Kiel added. "At the very least, it fits the descriptions."

The admiral reeked of disbelief. "The mythical creatures that eat their kits?"

"Most myth has a grounding in fact."

"What did it want with the girl?"

"I don't know."

Jonon rounded on Gwenna. "You will learn what it is, how she knows of it, what it wanted. You will learn what she meant by that word."

Gwenna opened her mouth to explain how ludicrous that was, to tell him she'd only barely established any kind of communication at all with the girl, that Rat spent most of the time trying to kill her, that even if they could speak the same language, she wasn't likely to spill her secrets. Then she saw the girl out of the corner of her eye, tensing as though she were about to hurl herself at the admiral.

"Yes, sir," Gwenna said, putting a hand on Rat's shoulder, clamping down so that she couldn't move. "As fast as I can, sir."

✝

Gwenna had learned precisely nothing about the *avesh* by the time they reached the foothills of the mountains, but the long days were not without progress. The girl had more or less gotten the hang of a dozen attacks, along with a working knowledge of the words *yes, no, me, you, stab, piss, blood, shit, fuck,* and, oddly, *sun, moon,* and *rain.* Though she'd staunchly refused to give her true name—despite Gwenna's growing certainty that she understood the question—she responded to the name Gwenna had given her—*Rat*—and she knew those of Kiel, Pattick—who brought them food every night—along with a few of the legionaries. It was hardly a vocabulary for nuanced discussion.

"Rat," Gwenna said one evening as they trained. "You need to keep your elbow in." She pointed. "Your elbow."

The girl glowered. "Fuck you. Fuck Gwenna."

"You're the one who's gonna get fucked if your elbow keeps sloshing around."

"No."

"Yes," Gwenna replied.

"No."

"Yes."

Rat lunged with the knife. Gwenna pivoted, tripped the girl, came down hard with a knee in the center of her back.

"Shit," Rat said. "Shit. Shit. Shit. Fuck. Shit. Moon."

Maybe she hadn't quite mastered a few of the words.

"You also need to keep your body upright," Gwenna said, dragging the girl back to her feet. She demonstrated. "Don't hunch over. Lead with the knife, not your face."

Rat narrowed her eyes, emulated the posture. This part was new. When they first began training, the girl had slashed at her with every opportunity, a wild thing bent only on killing. Now, almost a week later, she still seemed to want to kill Gwenna, but she had grown more patient. When there was something to learn, she put down the knife and listened. She'd mostly stopped trying to slit Gwenna's throat while the older woman was asleep or eating or taking a piss. Mostly.

"The moon," Gwenna said, taking advantage of the moment, "is up there." She pointed toward the bright coin hanging just above the northern peaks.

Rat glared at it. "Shit moon."

"Yeah," Gwenna replied. "Kettral feel the same way. It's easier to sneak up on people when there's no moon."

"People," Rat repeated, brow furrowing.

"People." Gwenna made a sweeping motion to include herself and Rat. She pointed toward the other fires of the camp, where the legionaries were bedding down for the night. "People. People. People. All of these are people."

"People," the girl murmured. There was something new in her voice, a note Gwenna hadn't heard before. She looked back over her shoulder, toward the empty lands through which they had traveled. "People," she said again, the word little more than a whisper. "No people."

Gwenna took a deep breath. "No. No people." She hesitated. "Where did they go?"

Rat looked back at her, confusion, grief, and anger warring across her features.

"Your people," Gwenna said. "Rat's people?" She held out an empty hand, shook her head. "Where?"

"Fuck people," the girl said, her face hardening. She threw herself at Gwenna, everything she'd learned in the last week utterly forgotten, scrubbed out. Gwenna kicked the knife to the dirt, caught the girl by the shoulders, grappled her close, where she couldn't do any damage with her flailing fists. "Fuck people," Rat screamed. "Fuck people. *Fuck people.* Fuck, fuck, fuck. Fuck Gwenna Sharpe."

"Yeah," Gwenna muttered, holding the girl against her. "You're right about that, kid. Fuck people. And fuck Gwenna Sharpe."

†

"You are training the girl to use a knife."

Jonon stared at her over his camp table. It wasn't a question. The wonder was it had taken this long for someone to tell him.

Gwenna nodded. "It was the only way to get her to talk."

"And what has she said?" He turned his attention to Rat, who was glaring at the admiral through her hair, hands clenching and unclenching, as though her fingers were hungry for the handle of the small blade.

"That her people are gone."

"Do not attempt to jest with me."

"I'm not jesting, sir. It's been barely a week. She doesn't have the words yet, but she's learning."

"According to Chent and Vessik, what she is learning is how to cut people apart with a dagger. Once again, you have placed my men and this mission in danger by indulging your own idiocy."

"The danger of a chained-up nine-year-old girl?"

Gwenna was surprised to hear a note of contempt in her voice. It had been a long time since she'd felt contempt for anyone but herself.

"A girl with a knife can slit a throat as well as any Annurian soldier."

"It's *my* throat she's been trying to slit."

"And have you considered that this expedition may suffer if she succeeds? You were sent here, sent by the Emperor herself, bright be the days of her life. You were sent because, despite your many and manifest failures, you alone have experience in dealing with the birds we have come to seek."

"Kiel's book—"

"The historian's book is just that. A *book*. Many thousands of years out of date. You have handled these birds, fed them, studied them, flown them. Your knowledge may still prove necessary, prove crucial. *You* will never fly again, but your fellows, the rest of your Wing—those you didn't get killed—*they* stand to gain if we succeed here. If we come away with eggs, one day *they* may have birds once again, but you are not thinking of them, are you? You think your life is your own, to throw away if you want for the chance to play soldier with this stinking brute of a girl." He stared at her with those deep green eyes. "Your selfishness astounds me. This is why your men died. Because of your selfishness."

And all over again she saw it, Quick Jak wading into the flames, Quick Jak fighting what seemed like the entire city of Dombâng, Quick Jak hacked down like some dead tree fallen across a path. Talal shouting for her to go, go, go. Talal gone, everything that he was, all the steadiness and laughter, snuffed out. As she stared at the memory, the sick, decaying flower of her shame blossomed inside her. The doubt, which for a day or two she'd managed to elbow to the edges of her thought, closed down around her once more. The fear surged, that nameless, reasonless, implacable fear—*yajusha*—etching like acid into her gut. The world seemed impossibly far off, a land that she would never return to.

"Fuck sir."

Gwenna's mind reeled as she struggled to make sense of the words, to pin them to a source.

"Fuck you. Fuck sir."

It was Rat, she realized, glaring at Jonon, shaking her head, pointing a skinny finger at the admiral.

"So this is the imperial light," Jonon said, lip twisting as he studied Gwenna, "that you have kindled in her savage heart."

"She's learning," Gwenna said. "Every day she learns more words."

The admiral reeked of disgust, but for a while he studied them in silence.

"You will hand over the knife," he said finally. "I won't have you killed until I'm certain to have no more use of you."

Like a woman moving in a dream, Gwenna slid the dagger from her belt, passed it to the admiral.

"Now get out," Jonon said, turning away.

The night was cold. A glacier-honed wind sliced down from the high peaks, carving into her. She felt like the deer the soldiers had killed days earlier—gutted, opened.

Rat tugged at the chain joining them.

Gwenna turned to stare at the girl.

"No knife," Rat said, her eyes intent. "Body. Hand." She took Gwenna's wrist, made as though to twist it. "Body," she said, hurling herself at Gwenna, seizing her awkwardly around the waist. "Hand." She drove her bony knuckles into Gwenna's kidney, hit her again and again and again, punctuating each punch with the same word. "Hand, hand, hand."

Gwenna twisted free before she realized what she was doing, caught the skinny wrist, jerked it up behind the girl's back.

"Yes," Rat said, craning her neck to look up at her. Her bright eyes brimmed with moonlight. "Yes."

"You want to learn hand-to-hand?"

"Hand-to-hand," the girl said. "Yes."

Gwenna shook her head. "You don't know when to quit, girl."

"No quit," Rat replied, voice fierce. "Hand-to-hand. Fuck quit."

✝

By the time they reached the foot of the mountains, Rat had more or less gotten the hang of half a dozen wrist locks. Gwenna tried to start out with the grappling basics—establishing, escaping, and passing a guard—but the girl's legs were too short, and she was too light to control the fight with her weight. The wrist locks made more sense, even if they were trickier and less crippling than a good choke. Rat muttered to herself as they fought, sometimes in Annurian, sometimes in her own language, the same furious syllables over and over and over as she twisted Gwenna's wrists into positions just a degree or two from breaking. Every night she wanted to train, regardless of the miles they'd covered, regardless of the exhaustion Gwenna could read in her eyes, smell on her skin and in her tangled hair. It was a way to stay warm, anyway, as they followed a valley up into the peaks and the nights went from chill to cold, a way to avoid thinking, feeling, and so Gwenna didn't stop her. Sometimes they fought all the way until the camp's second watch, rehearsing the same positions over and over.

Once, Rat fell asleep in the middle of a bout; the girl had gone after Gwenna's right hand, found herself—for the thousandth time—caught, turned, wrapped up, her back to Gwenna's chest, Gwenna's elbow around her neck. At first, when she went still, Gwenna thought she'd sunk the choke too deep. Then she realized the girl on top of her wasn't passed out; she was asleep, snoring, her head tipped back into the crook of Gwenna's neck. Gwenna craned her neck to look at her. The girl's mouth hung open, lips twitching through a few silent syllables. In that moment, her face lit by the pale moon, she looked even younger than her years. Her small hands, which had been trying to pry away the older woman's arm, had closed gently around it, pulling it close, as though it were a blanket. Gwenna let her own head drop back against the stony ground, listened to the girl breathe, stared up at the stars.

"I can't take care of you," she murmured.

The world's cold seeped up into her back. Rat's small breaths steamed the night air.

"I can't protect you."

The girl turned in her sleep. The chain linking their ankles clinked quietly. She burrowed her face deeper into Gwenna's neck.

"Shit," Gwenna said, staring up into the cavern of the night. "Shit. Shit. Shit. Fuck. Shit. Moon."

29

Ruc studied Talal from across the small bunkroom that the two of them shared with Bien. The flame from the single lantern licked the warm night air. He wondered if he could kill the man if the next few moments went wrong. Almost certainly not, he was forced to admit. Despite the chain and iron ball, the Kettral was quite obviously one of the deadliest people Ruc had ever met. He tried, during Goatface's training, to hide the full extent of his strength and speed, but Ruc had sparred with enough people back in the delta to size up an opponent and he didn't care for his chances going toe-to-toe with the soldier. Not just that, but he actually liked the man. Talal didn't seem like a heartless killer, despite what Ruc had argued to Bien. He was quiet, thoughtful, tough—exactly the kind of ally they needed if they were going to escape.

Provided that he *was,* in fact, an ally. They were about to find out, and fast.

"Is it really true," Bien asked casually, "that the Kettral don't use leaches?"

She was putting on a better act than Ruc had expected. There wasn't much call for lying and dissembling among the priests of Eira, but then—she wasn't just a priest. It stood to reason that she could perform her own innocence. Ruc wondered how many times she had lied to him, hiding this secret part of her as they walked the streets of Dombâng, or chatted in the markets, or lay together in bed, their naked limbs tangled.

Talal nodded, didn't look up from his soup. "There are hundreds of myths." He blew the steam from the spoonful, sipped it, grimaced. "I've also heard that we can breathe water and fly."

He sounded indifferent, even bored, but the yellow heat radiating from his face darkened for a moment into orange. Not that that proved anything. Body heat fluctuated with a hundred factors. It could have been a lie . . . or the soup.

"The guards, though," Bien said. "Every morning with the . . . what is it they make you drink?"

"Adamanth."

She nodded. "Right. The adamanth. The guards seem pretty concerned."

The soldier took another sip of his soup, nodded as he swallowed. "Pride."

"Pride?" Bien blinked. Her confusion didn't seem feigned.

Talal nodded. "The Purple Baths was one of only two command centers in the city. It served as barracks for thousands of troops, at least half of which were there when my Wing attacked. No one—not the high priests, not the Greenshirts, not the Arena guards—wants to believe that five Annurian soldiers could have destroyed it with nothing more than blades and bows."

"Blades, bows, and a *preposterously* large hawk," Ruc pointed out.

"Sure, the bird gave us an edge, but the ground wasn't right for kettral. It *might* have killed a dozen Greenshirts before we brought it down."

Bien stared at him. "You killed your own bird?"

The Kettral looked out the open window awhile, then turned his gaze back to her. "We couldn't get him out, and we couldn't leave him for the priests."

Ruc was struck all over again by the realization that beneath Talal's easy smile and offers of camaraderie ran a vein of cold iron. He might talk about friendships and alliances, would probably do his best to keep them alive as long as they were fellow prisoners in the yard, but if the moment ever came when he was forced to choose between their lives and his own, he wouldn't hesitate.

"The point is," Talal went on, "no one wants to believe that it only took five of us to bust into the barracks, kill a couple dozen Greenshirts, then burn the place down. It's easier to think there was something else to the story, some sick, twisted, mystical power." He shook his head. "All the adamanth and hand-wringing about whether or not I'm a leach? It's just a way to save face. Believe me—if I were a 'Kent-kissing leach, I would have burned the place from five hundred paces up and flown home."

Ruc studied the man from his post by the window. He didn't look like he was lying. He looked like a prisoner who was sick of answering the same ridiculous questions over and over, who'd had a long day out in the hot sun, who just wanted to sit and enjoy his soup. More than that—his story made sense. If he were a leach there wouldn't have been any need to infiltrate the Purple Baths. In fact, if the empire really did have leaches at its disposal, the Dombângan revolution never would have succeeded in the first place. He opened his mouth to change the topic, to ask about one of Goatface's spear drills, but Bien was already talking, almost vomiting into the momentary silence the words that could end their lives:

"I am." The shifting light of the lantern painted shadows across her horrified face. "I'm a leach."

Talal's spoon stopped halfway to his mouth. He held it there a moment, then put it back in the bowl. Somewhere outside in the vast night, a dusk owl loosed its screech.

"That," the Kettral said quietly, "is the most interesting thing I've heard all day."

His voice was flat, emotionless, almost the same voice he'd used when he talked about killing his bird.

His soldier's voice, Ruc thought. *His true voice.*

Bien stared at him, lips parted, brown eyes defiant.

"Why are you telling me this?"

"Because I think you can help. Because I think you're a leach, too."

"After everything I just told you?"

Bien nodded. "Yes."

The man stared at her.

Ruc slid forward another step, just behind Talal's chair, brought his knife up beneath his chin. He expected the soldier to curse, recoil, or lash out. Instead, he remained perfectly, preternaturally still.

"You don't need to kill me," Talal said quietly.

Bien leapt to her feet, her eyes wide.

"What are you *doing*?" she demanded.

"He's protecting you," Talal said calmly.

"*Stop it,* Ruc. He's on our side."

Talal gave an incremental shake of his head, careful not to open his throat on the blade. "He doesn't know that."

"No," Ruc agreed. "I don't know that."

"I respect the play," Talal said, "but it's unnecessary. Bien is right."

She shifted her gaze from Ruc to the Kettral. "I am?"

"We do use leaches, and I'm one of them."

The lantern's wick hissed, just at the edge of hearing. When Talal swallowed, Ruc could feel the bronze blade scrape against his stubble.

"Then why," Ruc asked finally, "didn't you do what you said? Burn down the Baths from the back of your bird without ever landing?"

"The same reason I didn't burn all the Greenshirts to cinders when they attacked me." With one slow hand, he gestured to his body. "The same reason I have all these scars."

"Which is?"

"I'm weak."

Ruc coughed up a chuckle at that. "My bet is you're the deadliest person in here."

"I'm weak as a *leach*."

"There are different strengths?" Bien asked.

Talal nodded. "As in everything."

Another silence, shattered by a burst of raucous laughter from somewhere across the yard. Someone belted out a few lines of an old Dombângan drinking song, then was shouted down.

"You can put away the knife, Ruc," Bien said. "Please."

He shook his head. "I think I'll hold on to it for now."

"He *said* he's a leach," she protested. "Just like me."

"He is nothing like you, Bien. He's an Annurian soldier."

"Even Annurian soldiers tell the truth sometimes," Talal observed quietly.

Ruc shook his head. "Did you see any marsh rats when you were out in the delta?"

"I was too busy keeping an eye out for the snakes and spiders."

"The marsh rat," Ruc said, "has a problem. It likes to eat birds—blue-headed vultures, spadebeaks—but it's a *rat*. It can't even get close to them. So do you know what it does?"

"I have a feeling you're about to tell me."

"It pretends to be dead. It shits out something that smells like rotting carrion, then lies there until the birds come to pick at the carcass. Then it rips out their throats and devours them."

"If you're comparing me to a shitting rat," Talal said, "I'm not flattered."

"You ought to be. Everyone talks about crocs and jaguars, *qirna* and snakes, but kill for kill, the marsh rat is the most deadly predator in the delta."

"Listen to yourself," Bien hissed. "You sound *insane*. Put *down* the *knife*."

Ruc met her eyes. "He's faster than me, Bien. Stronger. This whole thing, claiming to be a leach—it could be an act, a way to appear weak. He only said it when he had the blade at his throat. If I put down the knife, there's nothing I can do to stop him if he decides to turn on us. Nothing you can do, either."

"So . . . what?" she demanded. "You walk around everywhere holding that knife to his neck?"

"It would look strange," Talal agreed.

The other alternative, of course, didn't need to be spoken. With a quick snick of the wrist Ruc could open the soldier's throat. Goatface wouldn't be pleased, but Talal wouldn't be the first person to die in the yard. Bien's secret would be safe. She might not learn to use her skills, but they could find another way to escape. For a moment, he thought he could feel Kem Anh's eyes on him, the weight of her golden gaze, patient, measuring, waiting for him to finish the kill.

"You are a *priest* of *Eira*," Bien growled.

"Am I?" he asked. "The temple is burned. The others are dead. We're training *right now* to fight to the death for the greater glory of the Three." He nodded toward the window. "If we want to survive in here, we can't be what we were."

Bien shook her head, crossed to him slowly, put a hand on his wrist. "You are a priest of Eira," she said again. Her voice was softer this time, but no less firm.

He met her eyes. "Maybe. But he's not. He's Kettral."

"And he has his own choice to make," Bien said.

"That choice might be to betray you."

She nodded. "Then he betrays me."

"And you die."

"And I die."

They stood there for what felt like a long time, gazes locked, her hand on his wrist. Talal was silent, motionless. One of the most dangerous soldiers in the world, and he might as well have vanished. There was only Bien, the heat of her skin, the depth of those brown eyes, the faith she had in him, in Talal, in all of them—that unreasoning, unreasonable faith—drawing him back from the teetering brink.

He nodded finally, lowered the knife.

She smiled wearily.

Talal glanced over his shoulder at Ruc. "Are we good?"

For a simple question, it felt strained to bursting.

"You tell me," Ruc replied. "I'm the one who put a knife to your throat."

The soldier shrugged. "It's not the putting that matters so much as the cutting." He raised a hand to rub the stubble at his neck. "No damage done."

Ruc studied him. "Not all damage draws blood."

"Still. There's something strangely reassuring about knowing you had the chance to kill me but didn't."

"You're *both* insane," Bien said, shaking her head in disbelief.

Talal raised an eyebrow. "You were the one who thought it was a good idea to tell an enemy soldier you were a leach."

She glared at him. "Was it?"

"Let's find out." The soldier rose to his feet, crossed to the window, glanced outside, then pulled closed the wooden shutters. He opened the door, scanned the common room, then closed it behind him. Despite those precautions, he still lowered his voice when he spoke. "Tell me about the first time you used your power."

Bien shook her head, as though to deny the truth of the story she was about to relate, then began.

"I was eight. One of my jobs at the temple was watching the babies."

Talal shook his head. "Babies?"

"People came to worship sometimes, to pray or speak with the priests, and they had no place to leave their kids. I would watch the babies for them." She smiled at the memory. "I liked that job." The smile darkened, then disappeared. "One day we were down at the docks. Normally I wouldn't have gone down there, but it was so hot and I only had the two kids with me. The older one—she was maybe three—got a nasty splinter stuck in her foot. It took me a while to get it out—she kept squirming—and when I finally looked up, the smaller one was gone." She stared into memory's dark well. "I never heard her fall into the water—didn't even hear the splash. She was too young to swim. Too young to do anything but float. When I finally found her, she was bobbing beneath the surface maybe a dozen paces away, facedown.

"Normally I would have jumped up, dove into the water after her, but I had the other girl in my lap, holding me down, and without thinking I threw out a hand toward the baby and . . ." For two or three breaths she searched for the words. "The current stopped. Everything stopped—the water and whatever junk was floating on top of it. And the baby. And then I lifted her out of the water." Tears streaked her cheeks. "Not with my hand. She was almost to the middle of the canal. I lifted her out with"—she shut her eyes—"that power. *My* power . . ."

A moth gyred toward the flame, then away, then closer. Ruc found himself following it, as though it were the path of the creature's flight and not Bien's revelations that truly mattered. For the moth, he supposed, it was.

"What about the older girl?" Talal asked. "Did she notice?"

Bien nodded, then shook her head. "I don't know. The baby looked dead when I set her down on the dock. I was hunched over her, trying to clear out her lungs, trying to get her to breathe again. The other girl was only two or three. I don't think she understood what was happening." She dragged in a deep, unsteady breath. "I tried to tell myself that it was the goddess working through me, that it was *Eira* who saved the baby. But it wasn't. When it happened again, I knew."

"When did it happen again?"

"A couple of weeks later. I was over in the Weir bringing food to the orphanage when some drunk started pawing at one of the boys. I asked him to stop, to go away. He wouldn't. He knocked the basket out of my hands, turned back to the boy—just a *little* boy—had his hands all over him. . . ." Bien shuddered. "I shouted at him, shouted for someone to help, but no one helped. Finally I shoved him. . . ." She trailed off, caught in the unyielding talons of her memory.

"You defended the kid," Ruc said gently.

She rounded on him, her face crumpling. "I threw a man across the *street,* Ruc. I threw him so hard that something crunched when he hit the wall." Her lips moved silently, helplessly. She raised a hand, as though there were something to grasp, then let it fall. "There was blood," she went on finally. "His head sat on his neck the wrong way. He didn't move."

Ruc put a hand on her shoulder. Whether it steadied her or weighed her down, he couldn't say.

"What did you do?" Talal asked.

"I ran," Bien whispered.

"And after that? How many times did you use it?"

"*Never,*" she replied, then closed her eyes against the truth. "No. That's a lie." She glanced up at Ruc. "I used it once more, just before we were captured. When the men came to burn our temple."

"What did you do to them?"

Bien buried her face in her hands. Her voice was choked when she responded. "I murdered them."

"It wasn't murder," Ruc said grimly. "*They* were the murderers."

He saw again Old Uyen, cloudy eyes blank, the axe lodged in his skull.

"*Love those who loathe you,*" Bien replied—a line from the Tenth Teaching. "*Love your worst foe as you would your own child.*"

"How did you kill them?" Talal pressed.

"I reached out. I crushed their skulls."

The Kettral nodded, calm as a man listening to a story about laundry or fishing.

"Do you know what your well is?"

Bien raised her eyes. Her face was smeared with tears.

She shook her head. "I never thought about it. I tried not to think about *any* of it."

"A lot of leaches have that response." Frustration flashed across the soldier's face. "The world would be so much safer if we trained these children instead of telling them that they're monsters—"

Bien stared at him as though he were insane.

"I crushed the skulls of two men, broke them open like they were rotting fruit. That *is* monstrous."

Talal shrugged. "It's unusual. Most of the leaches I knew back on the Islands would have cut off their own arms for that kind of strength and precision. And I'm talking about *trained* leaches, men and women who had been studying for years. You're powerful, Bien."

"I don't want to be powerful."

"What do you want to be?"

"I want to be good."

"They're not incompatible."

She shook her head helplessly. "I can't even control it. . . ."

"I can teach you. The first step, though, is figuring out your well."

Bien studied him warily. "What could it be?"

"Almost anything. Salt. Blood. Some kind of animal species. Pain. Fear."

"Fear?" Bien's eyes widened.

"Some leaches draw their strength from emotion." His voice was bleak. "It's a dangerous, unpredictable well."

"You've fought them," Ruc said.

Talal nodded. "One. He almost killed me several times. He killed people I cared about."

"I don't want to be like that," Bien said.

"So don't be. I've known plenty of leaches who weren't twisted by their power, but you have to understand the danger."

"What danger?"

"Leaches become attached to their wells. Some people would say we become dependent. Most of us feel naked without our power. Afraid. Paranoid. Frightened people do desperate things, sometimes horrible things."

"I don't feel desperate for my well," Bien said. "I don't even know what it is."

Talal nodded. "You've resisted it almost entirely, so you haven't come to rely on it."

"But I can't resist anymore," she replied, voice trembling.

"Probably not. Not if you want to survive this place. Not if you want to escape."

Ruc shifted his gaze from Bien to the soldier. "What's *your* well?" he asked.

Talal pursed his lips, exhaled slowly. "There are only four people living who know the answer to that question."

"I take it this is the paranoia you just mentioned?"

"It's not unjustified."

"That's what the paranoid tend to say."

Talal snorted a half laugh. "Everyone wants to kill leaches. We have only two defenses: secrecy and the power itself. No leach shares their well if they don't have to. It's too easy to get cut off from it, to be attacked when you're weak."

"But the adamanth," Bien protested. "You're cut off from your well all the time in here."

"I don't plan to be in here forever."

"And you think what?" she asked. "If we escape, we're suddenly going to turn on you? What about working together? What about being allies?"

"I've had allies before. Doesn't always work out."

"You're asking a lot," Ruc said. "To know Bien's well without sharing your own."

"I'm not the one asking," Talal reminded him. He turned to Bien. "I was sitting here eating soup when you told me you were a leach. You want help. I'll try to give it. To do that, I need to know certain things about you, about your power and how it works. That's just the way it is. Or if you've changed your mind, say the word and I'll go back to my soup, and none of this ever happened."

So much, Ruc thought grimly, *for mutual trust.*

Beneath all the talk of friendship and alliances, the man was an Annurian soldier trained to hunt and to kill. If he helped Bien, it would be for his own reasons.

"All right," Bien said.

Talal raised his brows. "All right, what?"

"I don't care what your well is. I just want to learn."

The soldier watched her a moment, then nodded.

"Keep in mind, I can't do anything like what you're capable of."

"How do you know what I'm capable of?"

"Crushing a skull, let alone two at once—most second- or third-year cadets on the Islands wouldn't be able to manage that much."

Ruc stared out the window into the night. Somewhere beyond the yard's wooden wall, across the mudflats, a group of what sounded like very drunken revelers were singing raucously and out of tune. Ruc felt a sudden, powerful craving for a slug of Monster's *quey.*

"So," Bien asked. "How do we figure out my well?"

"It's something that was on the dock that day, when you first used your power. And in the Weir. And in the temple."

Bien stared down at her hands. "That could be anything. Wood. Air. Water . . ."

"It's daunting, but with the right method it's possible to sort through the possibilities more quickly than you'd think." He cocked his head to the side. "Can you feel your power now?"

She stared at the Kettral for eight or ten heartbeats, then shook her head. "I don't . . . How do I know if I can feel it? What does it feel like?"

Talal chuckled.

"What?"

"The Kettral trainers have been asking cadets—ones with the power—

exactly this question for hundreds of years. They've got all the answers in a massive codex back on the Islands."

"What do they say?" Bien asked.

He shrugged. "They all say something different. It's like sun on your eyelids. Like the feeling of dreaming but knowing you're dreaming. Like voices you hear on the other side of a wall or a door, when you can follow the sense of the conversation without actually making out the words. . . ."

"I don't feel any of that."

"The codex runs to about six hundred pages."

"And your cadets," Bien asked. "They just . . . know?"

"Most of them." Talal frowned, studied her from across the table. "Some people, though, are so filled with self-loathing that their minds refuse the knowledge."

"I'm not refusing anything."

"It's not something you mean to do. It just happens. Like breathing."

"But I've used . . . whatever it is."

"Reflexively. Mostly in self-preservation. Or the preservation of others." He shook his head. "You need to control it. To direct it."

"So what do I do?"

The leach hesitated, then stood up, took his chair, planted it half a pace away from Bien.

"Turn toward me," he said.

Bien stared at him. "What are we doing?"

"Something I saw back on the Islands. I don't know if it will work, not with the adamanth. But there's no harm in trying."

"Trying *what*?"

He sat down with his elbows on his knees, leaned forward, opened his hands in the space between them.

"Sometimes leaches describe their power as a kind of vibration. Not a sound, but something you feel in the flesh. Some wells seem to . . . resonate with one another. No one understands why." He gestured. "Take my hands."

Bien glanced up at Ruc. For a moment, he didn't know what to do with his face. Whatever road they were about to tread, it was one he could never follow. In the past, whenever he'd thought about time he'd imagined it as a delta channel, the current stretching off and away into the future, carrying the world along with it. In that moment, however, standing awkwardly to the side of the room, he realized the vision was wrong. Time was a knife, or an ax, or a sickle, something with a blade, anyway, always carving its silent slices, severing this moment from the one before, unmooring people from what they'd been and believed in, from whatever it was they thought they'd known. He managed a nod, and Bien turned back to Talal, stretched out her hands. They were scabbed, Ruc realized, nicked and scratched with a dozen cuts from the unrelenting training. The soldier took them in his own, the motion surprisingly gentle.

"Close your eyes," he said quietly. "Rest your forehead against mine."

Hesitantly, Bien leaned forward until her brow touched his just at the hairline. Ruc shifted, glanced toward the window. It was closed, just as Talal had left it.

"I'm going to delve into my well," the soldier said.

"I thought you were cut off from it," Bien protested.

"Not exactly. I can feel it, even with the adamanth—I just can't *draw* from it. Does that make any sense?"

"Not at all."

Talal chuckled, and a moment later Bien was laughing with him, their heads still pressed together.

"Focus," the soldier chided her.

"Focus on what?"

"On the places we're touching."

Bien's laughter subsided. Ruc could just make out the sliver of an expression, the tightening of her lips as she tried to concentrate. Her face was warmer than it had been—her whole body was warmer—as though she'd been running laps around the yard.

"I can feel your skin," she said. "Your scars."

Talal gave a slight shake of his head. "Ignore the scars. Go deeper."

"I don't know what that means."

"Yes," he said quietly. "You do."

For a long time, they sat like that, eyes closed, her brow resting against his. Ruc expected the Kettral to say something else, to continue with the instruction, but he didn't speak. The only movement was the slow rise and fall of his chest, the flutter of Bien's black hair as it tangled with her breath. She was breathing more heavily now, clutching Talal's hands, the skin tight around her knuckles. Her lips twitched, as though she wanted to whisper something but couldn't arrive at the words. Somewhere outside, one of the guards began tolling the midnight gong, but the two figures didn't move. They might have been painted there, save for the heat baking off of them—smoldering red instead of the usual orange and yellow. Ruc felt suddenly that he should look away, that this was a private communion not meant for his eyes, but there was nowhere else to look—three bunks, a stretch of wall, a closed window, a closed door—and so he was still watching Bien when she jerked, gave a small cry, half terror, half delight, and yanked her hands back.

Time's bright knife parted the past from the future.

She was staring at Talal.

When he smiled at her, she shook her head, then smiled back.

"Yes?" he asked.

She nodded uncertainly. "Maybe?"

They looked like two people who had known each other a very long time, friends maybe, or lovers, or family, sharing a secret that was all their own.

30

"Tell me again," Akiil said, turning from the window back to the dim room, "about the *vaniate*."

As usual, Yerrin sat on the floor of the small garret. Over the weeks since they'd arrived in Annur, the monk had managed to befriend a small squirrel living in the space between the walls, coaxing it farther and farther into the room each day with trails of nuts pilfered from the kitchens below. As Akiil watched, the tiny creature perched on the man's knee, holding a sliver of walnut in its paws.

"She prefers acorns," Yerrin said, almost accusingly.

Akiil nodded wearily. If he could have chosen another monk to teach him the greatest secrets of the Shin, he would have. Unfortunately, all the other monks were dead.

"I know that I can't want things," Akiil said. "I know that desire gets in the way of the *vaniate*."

Yerrin sniffed. "You think too much about the *vaniate*."

Akiil resisted the urge to strangle the old man.

The other monks at Ashk'lan had devoted their lives to achieving the mystical trance, the annihilation of self, the perfect union with the Blank God that would bring absolute peace, absolute stillness. Akiil had told the Emperor that much of the truth, at least. Yerrin was the only Shin monk who didn't seem to give one watery shit for the *vaniate*.

"There are men outside right now, Yerrin," Akiil said. "The Emperor's men. Large, humorless men with swords and spears. . . ."

He'd already done everything he could to stall.

First, he'd told Adare that he needed to purge his body of all impurities.

Next, he'd claimed that the *kenta* wouldn't admit someone who had engaged in sexual acts within the moon; the leftover desire, he'd claimed, clung to the body like oil.

Then he'd said he was too sick to enter the necessary trance. . . .

For almost a month, he'd managed to string her along, presenting himself at the Dawn Palace each morning, teaching her "lessons" that mixed a handful of Shin teachings together with a bushel of bullshit. The genius of the con was that no one in the world could contradict him. Only the Shin and the Csestriim could use the gates, which meant that whatever yarn Akiil decided to spin, whatever imagined bits of the Blank God's wisdom he managed to drum up—well, Adare could believe him or not, but she couldn't very well check on his story.

Except, of course, by tossing him through the 'Kent-kissing gate.

That had always been the danger, the reason he should have walked away when she first offered to cut him loose. The Emperor was playing at a disadvantage, not having known the Shin, but she hadn't managed to hold on to the most precarious seat in the world by letting people lie to her indefinitely. It was built into the bones of the scheme that sooner or later Akiil would have a choice: step through the *kenta* or run away.

He'd been avoiding that unpleasant fact, but there was no avoiding it any longer.

He glanced through the narrow gap in the shutters of his room. Six men stood on the street outside, hands resting casually on the pommels of their swords. Six men, not two.

The Emperor, of course, had been having him trailed since the very first day. She'd tried to get him to stay inside the Dawn Palace itself, but Akiil had demurred, and—because she was shrewd enough to realize she could learn more about him by having him followed as he wandered free—she'd allowed him to go. For weeks, he'd been playing a kind of cat-and-mouse game with her spies. Every afternoon he led them directly back to his inn, let them get comfortable, and then, when it was dark, slipped out through his window, climbed a dozen feet to the eaves, then set off over the rooftops. There wasn't anywhere in particular that he wanted to go, but he liked going, liked knowing that, despite the men loitering on the street or in the common room below, he was still free. Some nights he would range for miles, leaping from roof to roof, slipping down into the alleys, then climbing up into the warm night air once more. Oddly, it wasn't so different from running the cliffs around Ashk'lan—tile and slate beneath his bare feet rather than clean white granite, but the feeling of space was the same, of solitude and danger and freedom.

Freedom that, if the men in the street were any indication, Adare intended to forcibly curtail.

He blew out an irritated breath, turned away from the window. He'd hidden most of Adare's gold—the fee she'd paid him for her "training" when he first arrived—beneath the furthest floorboard, the one crammed in the angle where the roof met the floor. After some sweating and cursing, working at the gap with his belt knife, he popped the board up, reached in, and scooped out the leather purse. It was stippled with mouse shit and smelled vaguely of piss and mold. When he upended the contents on the bed, however, the coins gleamed in the light of the lantern, a fortune large enough to buy a small farm.

Not that he wanted a fucking farm.

Yerrin glanced over, squinted at the gold.

"Not acorns," he said after a moment.

"Better than acorns, old man."

The monk shook his head. "The squirrel prefers acorns."

"The squirrel is going to have to get used to disappointment. We're leaving."

"It looks to me," Yerrin said, nodding toward the pile of coin, "as though you are *taking*."

"Taking the coin, leaving the city. It's not safe here anymore."

The vexing thing was that he'd come so *close*.

Kaden had achieved the *vaniate*—Adare had revealed that much—and Akiil had spent more time at Ashk'lan than Kaden. They'd run the same mountains, stared into the same rivers, slept in the same cells, suffered under the same teachers. . . . Which meant he *had* to be close. Since arriving in Annur, he'd gone hammer and tongs at the old Shin exercises, meditating on the rooftops whenever he wasn't "teaching" the Emperor or exploring the city. Sometimes he could feel something inside his mind, a kernel or a seed, smooth, dark, and empty. Whenever he reached out to grasp it, though, it slipped away. If just one other monk had survived—Scial Nin, or Huy Heng, or Rampuri Tan—*one* person to teach him the last few lessons . . .

Instead, he had Yerrin.

Wringing the secrets of the *vaniate* out of the old monk was like wringing water from a 'Kent-kissing rock.

Don't bother, Yerrin had told him once.

Another time: *You can't do it.*

"Did you see those men outside the window?" Akiil asked.

"Men?" Yerrin asked. He didn't sound particularly interested.

"The ones with the swords. The Emperor's soldiers."

"The Emperor does not have soldiers."

"I assure you she does."

"No one has soldiers."

"I am looking at them right now. They are standing directly outside the door to our inn."

Yerrin shook his head, stroked the squirrel gently along the length of its back. "It is not our inn. We do not have an inn."

Akiil started to respond, then clamped his mouth shut, sucked a long breath in through his nose, held it in his lungs. It was impossible to argue with Yerrin; he'd learned that years earlier. It wasn't that you couldn't *win* an argument against the other monk; there was never even an argument to be had. Fighting with him felt like planting your feet for a tug-of-war, bracing your back, tightening your grip, then hurling yourself backward to the ground when you discovered no one holding the other end of the rope.

"Regardless," Akiil replied finally, "those men, the ones outside, are going to take me to the Dawn Palace tomorrow morning. They are going to lead me to the *kenta,* and they are going to shove me through it."

Yerrin looked up at him with an expression of mild, benign interest, as though waiting for the good part of the story.

"If I can't master the *vaniate* between now and then," Akiil went on, "I will die."

"Oh!" The monk smiled. "Yes. You will die." He nodded something that might have been encouragement, then went back to stroking the squirrel with a gentle finger.

"I appreciate the confidence."

"I will die," Yerrin went on. He nodded toward the nibbling creature. "She will die."

"I'd prefer to wait a little while."

"So wait a little while."

Akiil shook his head. "Why have I been taking care of you all these years?"

He didn't expect Yerrin to answer, partly because the monk almost never responded to questions, and partly because Akiil didn't quite know the answer himself. 'Shael knew life would have been *easier* without the monk. Yerrin slowed him down, ate his food, refused to blend in to any city or town. Without Yerrin he could have reached Annur months faster, *years* faster. He certainly would have gotten laid more often along the way. Instead, he'd found himself babysitting an old man with half a mind.

The best explanation he could offer himself was that it felt like a debt. Which was strange, because Akiil had more or less made a career skipping out on debts. And yet, whenever he thought of abandoning the old man, just putting a small pile of coin in his gnarled hands and leaving him in some village square, the memory of Ashk'lan filled his mind, of the monastery aflame, dead monks scattered like leaves across the courtyard. Some of them had been surprised, but most had had time to understand what was coming. Some had gathered on the cliff's edge, sitting in silence as they awaited their slaughter. None had tried to hide or run. None but Akiil.

The memory still filled him with fury. Living a life of quiet contemplation was all well and good, but when men came with fire and steel to annihilate your entire world it was time to do something other than fucking sit there. He'd been the smart one, the sane one, the only one who'd deserved to get away. If he'd killed the abbot in the process, well, the old man was going to be killed anyway, murdered by the Aedolians, just like the rest of them. There'd been no way for Akiil to save him. No way for him to save any of them. . . .

He shoved the memory aside.

"Can you just tell me what you do," he asked wearily, "when you want to enter the trance?"

Yerrin shook his head, tickled the squirrel's white belly. "I don't."

"Don't go into the *vaniate*?"

"Don't do anything."

Akiil bit down on his impatience.

"I don't know what that means."

The monk's face brightened. "That's good. That's right."

"What's right?"

"Know less. Know nothing."

"I'm *trying*," Akiil growled.

The monk shrugged, fed the squirrel another nut. "Stop trying."

Akiil started to respond, then stopped himself. The squirrel made a sound that might have been happiness or hunger, gratitude or greed. Seemed like they should have been easier to tell apart. While Yerrin shelled another walnut, Akiil slipped a few coins into the hem of his robe, then filled two separate purses, each with half of what remained. Two coins he left out on the bedside table.

"I'm going away for a while," he said.

Yerrin looked up, smiled. "No you're not."

Akiil had no idea how to explain the situation, so he didn't bother trying.

"You can use the coins to buy food. The Emperor will send people for you. She'll ask you questions, but she won't hurt you."

He didn't *think* she would hurt him, at least. Adare could be ruthless—that much was obvious—but she was smart enough to see there was nothing to be gained from torturing a senile old man. She'd ask her questions, try to figure out where Akiil had gone, maybe try to learn something about the *vaniate* from Yerrin himself, and then, when she'd failed at all that, she'd let him go. Akiil would pick him up and they'd slip out of the city, alive, well, and quite a bit richer than the day they'd come. He'd conned the Emperor of the Annur and gotten away with it. Escaped.

Just like he always fucking escaped.

31

For days they followed the valley up and up. The plunging river at its center ran blue-white, ice-cold, and tasted of frost and stone. The last traces of human habitation had vanished days earlier, leaving them to thread their way between the moss-covered trunks of massive, ancient trees. Like so much else on Menkiddoc, the trees were unlike any Gwenna had ever seen. From a distance they looked like pines, but up close the strangeness was obvious—black bark peeling in scales, green-black needles, cones hard and sharp as shells. The creatures in the boughs proved as alien as the trees themselves, little beasts that might have been squirrels save for their vicious, scythelike claws. They watched with dark eyes as the column passed, shrieked their small furies, raked those claws across the scaly bark.

At first the soldiers found them amusing. A few of the men tossed scraps of food on the ground in an effort to entice them closer. The squirrels, however, showed no interest in the bread. Instead, they followed the column, leaping from branch to branch, pausing when they got too far ahead to sharpen their claws and stare down at the humans with those inscrutable black eyes. As their numbers grew—five, then fifty, then five hundred—the amusement of the soldiers rusted into disgust, then wariness. The sound—the rasping, the inhuman screams—harried them from all directions until one of the legionaries cursed, drew his bow, dropped one of the creatures from a branch overhead.

That only made things worse. Instead of retreating, the animals pressed in closer. A few dozen darted down the trunks to rip apart the motionless carcass while the rest began to hurl twigs and sticks down on the party below.

Pattick, walking a few paces ahead of Gwenna and Rat, turned to Kiel.

"Are those . . ." He hesitated.

"*Gabhya?*" The historian shook his head. "No. Just a creature native to this portion of the world."

As they spoke, the squirrels redoubled their clamor, then, between one heartbeat and next, went perfectly silent. Gwenna glanced up to find them moving, darting through the branches, scattering into the depths of the forest.

"What . . . ?" Pattick breathed.

Before anyone could reply, Rat's *avesh* swung into view. It moved through the treetops with a jerking, spasmodic motion, awkward and horribly fast at the same time. In just a few heartbeats it had reached the column, then passed it, then snatched one of the fleeing squirrels out of the air. The thing writhed, screamed, tried pointlessly to free itself. The *avesh* settled on a branch, took the creature's leg in that nightmare of a mouth, and began chewing, ignoring the noise and writhing.

Gwenna stared.

The beast had been shadowing them since that first sighting, sometimes loping along just outside of the range of the column's archers, sometimes disappearing for days at a time. It seemed to have no trouble hunting—Gwenna had seen it once with some kind of bird mangled in its jaws, once atop a bloody mound of flesh it had savaged beyond all recognition—but this was the first time she'd watched it make a kill. Not that the squirrel was dead yet. The *avesh* looked down with those huge, guileless eyes while it went to work on the next leg, rows of razor teeth crunching straight through the bone, splintering it.

"*That*," Kiel said, pointing up into the trees with a gnarled finger, "is a *gabhya*."

He sounded like a bureaucrat giving a particularly dull lecture.

Pattick looked like he might be sick.

✝

Eventually the river narrowed to a gorge, and Jonon led them out of the tortuous valley up onto the shoulder of the mountain flanking it. From the high ground, Gwenna could just make out the head of the valley, maybe ten miles distant and five thousand feet above them. It looked like a plausible kettral nesting ground—a rough horseshoe of limestone cliffs, the bands stacked one atop the other, broken by less-vertical sections where a dusting of snow clung to the precipitous slopes. Dangerous terrain, even without the possibility of predators riding the thermals above.

Jonon halted the soldiers, studied the cliffs through his long lens, then gestured for Gwenna and Kiel to join him.

The men watched her with silent contempt as she made her way up to the front of the column. She kept her gaze on the ground, but out of the corner of her eye she could see Rat—following a pace away at the end of her chain— glaring at the legionaries.

Don't do anything stupid, Gwenna prayed silently. As though she were some judge of what was stupid.

"This is the place," Jonon was saying to the historian as Gwenna reached them. The admiral pointed to the map, to the peaks inked across the parchment, then to the mountains looming to the north.

Kiel simply nodded.

When it was clear he had nothing to add, Jonon's expression hardened. "I don't see any birds."

"That's a good thing," Gwenna put in.

Jonon turned that green gaze on her. "If there are no birds, this expedition is a failure, a failure dear in both time and treasure, and while you may have accustomed yourself to failure, I assure you that I have not."

"I think what Commander Sharpe is suggesting—" Kiel began.

The admiral cut him off. "She is not a commander."

The historian bowed his head in acquiescence.

Jonon's eyes bored into Gwenna, as though daring her to disagree. When she did not, he nodded. "I am waiting for you to explain why I should be delighted by this absence of kettral."

"They have good eyes," Gwenna replied. "If we could see them, they could see us. Down below, in the trees, we were safe. Up here . . ." She gestured to the bare slope, the steep, broken, rocky ground between them and the head of the valley, then shook her head. "Up here we're not."

"I did not voyage to the other side of the world out of a desire to remain safe."

"Dead soldiers," Kiel observed quietly, "are unlikely to return with eggs."

Jonon ignored the man, passed the long lens to Gwenna. "Do you see nests?"

She hesitated, then put the tube to her eye. The cliffs leapt into focus, so close it seemed she could run her fingers along the coarse stone. Slowly she scanned that stone. Caves pockmarked the cliff's base, some so small Rat would have had a hard time squirming inside, others large enough to fit the entire column. The birds back on the Islands didn't nest in caves, but who knew? Maybe at this end of the globe the kettral did things differently. No way to be sure without getting closer, without actually going inside.

She slid her focus up the cliffs, scanned along a low ledge, shifted her gaze a few paces higher, then . . .

There.

Someone who'd never seen a kettral nest would never have recognized it—a tangle of branches perched on a stone shelf forty or fifty paces up. A *neat* tangle of branches. No trees grew on the mountain above. There was only stone, and ice, and snow. The forest ended thousands of feet below. The branches hadn't climbed to the ledge themselves. Something had carried them. Something huge.

"They're here," she murmured.

"Kettral?" Jonon demanded.

She nodded. "Kettral."

The word tasted false on her tongue, like a promise she had no intention of keeping. She realized, standing there, glacial wind scything through her blacks, that she'd never expected the expedition to succeed. She'd gone because the Emperor had ordered her to, and because she had nowhere else to be. She'd nodded when Kiel talked about his maps or Jonon discussed strategy because that was what they wanted her to do: nod, then be silent. And silence had proven easy because the whole thing, the entire expedition, had seemed useless, pointless, hopeless. The historian's Csestriim treatise was what—more than ten thousand years out of date? Menkiddoc was an unexplored wasteland. A single unexpected storm could have wrecked them or drowned them, and that would have been that—the last chance to restore the kettral vanished like yesterday's wind.

Except Kiel's maps *had* proven correct—even if they were missing a major city. Storms hadn't wrecked the *Daybreak*. Jonon had managed to skirt the sickness plaguing the center of Menkiddoc. Against all likelihood, they'd reached the peaks, and there, stacked on the limestone ledges in the distance, were the nests of the creatures they'd traveled thousands of miles to find.

After seeing the first one, the others were easy to spot—two, four, a dozen, an entire eyrie built across the cliff face. The sight should have kindled in her a whole range of emotions: relief, anticipation, excitement, triumph.

Instead, she felt a blank, unreasoning despair.

She'd told herself, during the long passage south, that it didn't matter if she gave up. If there weren't any birds waiting at the end of the journey, there was no reason for her to be on the ship, no use or purpose to her presence. The brig had seemed as good a place as any for a tool with no use, and so she'd let herself rust. Day after day, week after week, slumped against the bulkhead or lying flat on her back, staring up into the dark, hiding from the panic that stalked her, from the grief, hiding from everything. And then to be dragged out into the light to see that the kettral were alive, against all odds alive and nesting just where Kiel had said they would be, in the high peaks of southern Menkiddoc. To realize that she *was* going to be needed after all, but that she was no longer equal to that need . . .

Jonon took the long lens back, gazed through it awhile, then nodded. "I can make out the nests. Where are the birds?"

Gwenna shook her head. "Hunting, probably. Or just flying."

The admiral scanned the sky. "If they were flying, we would see them."

"They could be over the saddle to the north," Kiel pointed out. "Somewhere in the next valley."

"They could be five days' march away from here," Gwenna said. "Their hunting grounds are enormous."

"When will they come back?"

She shook her head. "Dusk. Maybe later. They can hunt almost as well by night as they can by day." She stared north, over the glaciated pass between the mountains. The sky was so empty it hurt. "Whenever they *do* come back, though, we need to not be out here in the open."

It took Jonon only moments to split his force. A long-faced, gap-toothed man named Lemmer—company commander after Aron Dough's death—was given orders to take most of the men back to the shelter of the forest, to establish a camp just below the tree line, and wait.

"Watch us through the long lens," Jonon said. "If we are attacked, do not send aid. Learn from our mistakes. If we are all killed, proceed with the mission, collect the eggs, and return to the *Daybreak*."

Lemmer nodded, extended a hand. "Good luck, sir."

"Luck?" Jonon shook his head grimly. "No, soldier. No luck. It is by our merits and our faults that we thrive or die."

The legionary ducked his head. "As you say, sir."

Jonon turned away from the man without another word. "Vessik, Lurie, Chent, Pattick, Cho Lu, Raban—with me." Gwenna caught a whiff of disgust as he turned to her and Kiel. "And the two of you."

"What about Rat?" Gwenna asked.

"I gave you one task. You cannot handle even that?"

"There's no need to bring her. She can't help with this."

"Of course she can't. But she is a liability, like you, and I choose to keep my liabilities in one place, where I can see them."

Before Gwenna could reply, he turned, started off across the steep slope toward the distant cliffs.

"Quickly," he barked over his shoulder, not bothering to look back. "Those caves are our only shelter. I want to be inside them by noon."

Noon proved an impossible goal. By the time the sun hung directly overhead, they'd covered barely more than half the distance. The thin mountain air took a toll, causing all of them to pant and gasp, but the real problem was the terrain itself, which proved far more treacherous than any of them had realized. A narrow slope of broken rubble cut between the bands of cliffs, one looming over them, one dropping away below. Rock clattered down from the gullies above, shattered on the boulders, exploded into pieces, started miniature avalanches that slid for a pace or two before coming to a precarious rest above the abyss. Sometimes it took nothing more than a foot in the wrong place to start a portion of the slope sliding, and while the lip of the cliff was more than a hundred paces below, every time the ground shifted Gwenna had a vision of the whole mountainside sloughing off, carrying them with it right over the edge. She tried to hold up the chain linking her to Rat, but it kept snagging on boulders, tripping her, or the girl, or both, cutting into their ankles until Rat began limping and blood soaked through Gwenna's boot. At one point the chain snagged and Gwenna fell, splitting her knee open on a point of stone. The gash went so deep that when she spread it apart, she could see the white of the kneecap between the welling blood.

After so many weeks lying in the brig, she felt as though her bones had turned to lead, her muscles to so much suet. Her extra weight hung on her, dragging her down, but the weight was nothing compared to the fear. She imagined the birds coming back, swooping in through the saddle that loomed closer and closer above them. She imagined the stones beneath her feet giving way, sliding down toward the drop as she clawed to stay on top of them. Worst of all, she imagined herself breaking under the strain, passing out, tumbling down the slope, dragging Rat behind her, the rocks gashing the girl, gouging and slashing her, snapping the small bones of her legs or arms, fracturing her skull. Overlaid on the sun-bright day, Gwenna saw the child still chained to her, but limp and blood-soaked, eyes vacant.

"Wait," Gwenna said.

Her breath rasped in her throat. Despite the cold air she was soaked with sweat.

Pattick—just a couple paces ahead—paused in climbing over a boulder, turned to her, his brow creasing with confusion.

"Are you all right?"

"Admiral," Gwenna said, then louder still. "*Admiral.*"

Jonon turned. "By your own assessment," he growled, "every delay is a danger."

"The chain . . ." she replied, then trailed off, too winded to finish.

The admiral looked like a man who expected a trick. His gaze bored into her.

"Where are we going to run?" Gwenna managed wearily.

He ran an eye over the terrain, then nodded, motioned to one of the soldiers. "Lurie. Get these chains off. If either of them attempt to flee, shoot them."

"Yes, sir," the legionary replied. "A pleasure, sir."

That pleasure, it seemed, would come more from the shooting than the removal of the shackles.

Rat moved more easily without all that steel, and Gwenna felt her own steps quicken as well. A simple matter of weight, partly, but not only weight. There was a relief in being unlinked from the girl, in knowing that if she herself slipped and fell, she wouldn't drag Rat with her over the edge of the cliff. The child was quick, smart, nimble, preternaturally strong, even in the thin air. She was better off unchained from this old, slow woman.

For a while Gwenna was able to force back the rising panic, to strangle the visions of disaster that prowled the edges of her thoughts and to focus on one thing only: moving upward across the slope. She breathed in with each step of the right foot, out with each step of the left, refused to look down, or up, or across, kept her eyes on the few rocks in front of her, her mind on her breathing.

In. Out. In. Out.

A far cry from the days she'd spent racing through the Romsdals during training, leaping from boulder to boulder, darting along the knife-line ridges, shouting taunts at Valyn and Gent, at whoever would listen, whooping as the wind ripped at her hair. She stared back at the girl she'd been, found her nearly unrecognizable. She had carried with her, since the Purple Baths, the leaden guilt of living when Jak and Talal had died, but it occurred to her as she labored up the slope that maybe she hadn't survived after all.

Sure, a woman named Gwenna Sharpe was dragging her aching body up a mountain, sucking in breath after knife-sharp breath, staggering forward into her fear like a soldier on an open plain fighting to make headway in a vicious wind, but *this* Gwenna Sharpe, what did she have to do with the warrior who once defied orders to rescue the Emperor of Annur? What did she have to do with the woman who commanded the defense of Andt-Kyl against the whole Urghul nation? What did she have to do, for that matter, with the Gwenna Sharpe who'd been able to sit with her friends, drink a mug of ale, and gaze out into the world without seeing her own doubt, and fear, and shame reflected back?

Better to have died in the Baths. Better the spears or the fire than this sick, slow, inevitable corrosion.

A brave woman might have thrown herself from the cliff, but evidently she had forgotten how to be brave, and so she clenched her hands into fists to fight the trembling, kept her eyes on the ground, and kept going.

†

They almost made it.

They were maybe two hundred paces from the head of the valley, from the horseshoe of cliffs and the caves at their base, when Rat tripped.

"Careful," Gwenna said.

The girl looked back at her. "Careful?"

Gwenna tried to think how to explain it, then shook her head. It probably said something about her parenting that Rat knew the words for *kill* and *stab,* but not the word for *careful.*

"Just keep moving," she said instead, pointing blearily toward the caves. "We're almost—" The words withered in her throat.

Overhead, just above the saddle, silent, dark, and swift, a new shape sliced across the sky. Gwenna couldn't make out the details, but she didn't need to. She could imagine the talons tucked up beneath the bird's body, the hook of the beak, the inhumanity of those eyes as they scoured the ground below.

"Admiral. Halt the column. Now."

The words didn't sound like her own. Or rather, they sounded like an order she might have given a year earlier, in a different life. A part of her marveled at the note of command, wondered where it had come from. A very small part. The rest of her was bent toward a single, simple end—escape. With an effort of will, she forced herself not to run. The caves were so close she could almost hit them with a stone.

Not close enough.

Up at the head of the column, Jonon turned.

"What?" he demanded, but before she could reply, the shadow passed over them—a scrap of night occluding the sun. "Kettral," he said quietly, half reverently. He didn't sound frightened. Didn't look or smell frightened. Unlike Gwenna, he'd been readying himself for this. And unlike Gwenna, he'd never seen one of the birds take apart a one-ton bull like it was yesterday's table scraps. "The caves—" he began.

She shook her head. "We won't make it."

That sent a ripple of disquiet through the soldiers. A few of the men had drawn swords, or nocked arrows to their bows. This would have been the first time most of them had ever encountered one of the birds. One or two might have been in Annur when the Urghul attacked the capital. They might have caught a glimpse of the Dawn King streaking across the sky, but they hadn't had to *fight* him.

"Those caves are barely a bowshot away," Jonon observed.

"We won't make it," she said again.

The admiral straightened. For all that he loathed her, he was smart enough not to argue. "Then we make a stand. Here."

"Don't stand." She lowered herself slowly to her knees, bending forward until her face was pressed against the rough, cold stone. "Kneel. Slowly."

She didn't need to look up to smell Jonon's disgust. "You expect my men to grovel? To *let* the bird take them?"

"The bird," she replied, "hunts mostly by movement. If you want to survive, make yourself small, still. Make yourself a stone. Make yourself into nothing at all."

For a few heartbeats Jonon was silent. The men smelled of fear now, fear mixed with confusion. In most situations—preparing to defend a ship's castle or board an opposing vessel—they would have dismissed her opinion out of hand. But this was not most situations. None of them had been to the mountains of Menkiddoc. None of them had stood on an open hillside while a predator plucked from their most violent fantasies swept down upon them.

"Do it," Jonon said at last.

The command was followed, a moment later, by the creak of leather, the dull grinding of armor against stone. She could hear the mutters of the soldiers, some cursing, a few praying.

"This doesn't feel right," Pattick murmured.

"No," Cho Lu replied, voice wound tight. "It doesn't."

Gwenna disagreed. Kneeling felt *exactly* right. Giving her whole fate over to the bird felt right. It felt right to press her forehead against the cold stone, to close her eyes, and wait. No wonder so many people in the world refused to fight. It was as easy as breathing. All you had to do was nothing.

32

The night was cool, but the roof tiles beneath baked off the last of the day's heat, warming Akiil's bare soles. Smoke rose from the crooked chimneys of brick and clay surrounding him, stinging his eyes, filling the sky, smudging out all but the brightest stars. The streets below smelled of mud, shit, rotting trash, piss, and the hot, clinging scent of beggar's broth: horse hoofs and crab claws, shells, innards, offal all simmering away in a thousand pots. One street over a woman screamed—high voice half fear, half fury. As she fell abruptly silent, a baby began crying, then another. A dog joined in, barking over and over and over until finally someone kicked it, twisting the bark into a high, baffled yelp. For a heartbeat, the streets were almost quiet. Then the baby started sobbing once more.

It wasn't where Akiil had intended to go.

When he'd slipped out of the inn's garret hours earlier, his robe heavy with Adare's gold, he'd meant to get clear of the city, find a spot on the outskirts where he could lie low for a few weeks and then, after coming back for Yerrin, head south into Kresh or Aragat. His hair and complexion would blend in down there. According to stories he'd heard in the markets, there were plenty of remote farms and fishing villages, and shit, if those got boring after a while, he could always hit one of the cities—Olon, Sia, Chubolo, Sarai Pol. . . . Really, he could have gone any one of a thousand places without returning to the Perfumed Quarter of Annur.

And yet there he was.

He crouched at the edge of the roof, gazing down into the alley below.

Behind him, the baby's cries had escalated into a high, desperate wail. A man's voice—heavy, sloppy with drink—roared at the child for quiet while a woman sobbed. Akiil's chest tightened. His palms went suddenly greasy. For a moment his body took over and he was five again, or six, hungry, and angry, and frightened.

Except, he reminded himself silently, *you're not.*

He lowered himself to sit cross-legged at the edge of the roof, then closed his eyes, turned his attention inward, went about untangling the knots of thought and emotion. Babies cried—it was what they did. Drunks bellowed. Shit stank. None of it was because of him. None of it had anything to do with him. The frightened orphan who'd survived the alleys below was gone, vanished as last year's wind. He took a breath, then another, then another until his pulse slowed and his mind went smooth. When he finally opened his eyes once more, the alley could have been any alley in any city in the world.

Across the way, a door swung open and two men tumbled out into the night. Music and light and raucous voices spilled out around them, then the door swung shut, tossing the alley back into darkness.

"Fuck the Captain," one of the men snarled, "and *fuck* his *motherfucking* cards. I'm going *back* in . . ."

The Captain.

So. That bastard was still alive, still lording it over his corners of piss and misery. *These* corners, evidently. Akiil hadn't realized just precisely *where* in the Quarter he'd come until the men spoke, but now that he considered the building opposite him he recognized the place. It looked smaller than it had when he was a child. Filthier, if that was possible. Strange, that his feet had brought him here of all places. Even stranger that he lingered, listening to the conversation below.

The drunk from the tavern half turned—moving with the slowness of a man underwater—before his companion seized him by the arm, dragging him away from the door.

"I'm going *back*," he insisted. "Getting my motherfucking *money*."

"*Leave* the money, Andraz," the other insisted. "You go back in there, you're not coming out."

"Fuck that. *Fuck* that. Spent twenty years in the legions, didn't I? And this Captain. What's he the fucking captain *of*? Just some pretty son of a bitch with a club and a lot of dogs. I'm going back in and I'm gonna get right up in his face, and I'm gonna say to him—"

The man's friend hauled him back around.

"You're not going to say anything to him, Raz. You know why? Because he'll fucking *kill* you."

Andraz wavered on his feet.

"Come on," his friend said. "You'll win it back tomorrow."

It was the wrong argument.

"*Fuck* tomorrow," Andraz growled, tearing his arm free and turning back toward the doorway. "Fuck—"

Akiil dropped down from the rooftop a few paces away. The two men stared at him for a moment, then stumbled apart, reaching drunkenly for their hidden knives.

"No need," Akiil said, waving away the violence, showing his hands in the process. "I don't want to rob you. Besides—I heard you already lost your coin."

Andraz had fumbled a long, ugly dagger from a sheath at his back, thrust it out before him. The blade weaved back and forth, but remained pointed more or less at Akiil's chest.

"The fuck are you?" he demanded. He squinted. "And what the fuck're you wearing?"

"A robe," Akiil replied, careful to keep his hands visible, his voice mild.

"A *motherfucking* robe."

"A motherfucking robe," Akiil agreed.

Andraz grunted, as though that settled the robe question.

"You one of the Captain's men?" demanded the friend. His eyes skipped past Akiil toward the shadows beyond.

For a moment, Akiil heard Butt Boy's screams in the greater chaos of the night. It wasn't a quick death, being eaten by pigs.

"Hardly."

"What're you doing up on the roofs?"

Akiil smiled. "Safer up there. Cleaner. No shit to step in." He nodded toward the wavering knife. "No one to stab you . . ."

"What'd'you want?" Andraz growled.

"What do I want?" Akiil pondered the words even as he spoke them. He could have been all the way to the southern edge of the city already, could have been free and clear of Adare's goons and the Quarter both. Instead, he'd come here, like some stupid dog returning to the man who beat it. "What I want," he replied finally, a smile carving apart his lips, "is to know whether or not you gentlemen would like to become partners."

The Dead Horse smelled more or less like its name. The air inside the hall was so heavy with the heat and sweat of close-pressed bodies that Akiil pulled up short as the door swung shut behind him, fighting down the sudden urge to gag. Long trestle tables ran down both sides, but almost no one sat. Atop the nearest of them, a trio of Ghannan legionaries stumbled through some sort of dance, crouching low, hopping, whooping madly with each step, then slamming their boots into the splintered wood. Mugs and wooden trenchers rattled the length of the board, and after a particularly violent stomp one of them slipped over the edge, splashing something brown and chunky across the floor.

Behind the dancers, a man had a woman pressed up against the wall, her skirts hitched up around her waist as he thrust into her over and over. As Akiil watched, she grimaced, leaned back, then slapped the man across the face.

"If you can't fuck it right, there's plenty of others will do the job."

Cheers erupted from a small knot of onlookers. Akiil couldn't hear the man's response, but he redoubled his thrusting. An impressive athletic display, although it didn't seem to be giving the woman much pleasure.

Akiil had gone to Ashk'lan a virgin and left it the same way. After his first few cons down in the Bend, he'd spent a handful of coppers on one of the dockside whores. She made a great show of screaming and bucking and scratching his chest, but he didn't need to have spent ten years with the Shin monks to see that it was just that—a show. In the moment, some animal frenzy kept him going, but when it was finished, after she'd taken the coin, patted him on the head, and scooted out into the night, he felt a vague disgust with himself. Which was strange. Stealing the coin in the first place hadn't bothered him at all. He'd stared at the ceiling of the tiny rented room and blamed the Shin. Something about all those years sitting, fasting, denying the basic urges of the body had broken him.

He tried again the next night, this time with two whores, and this time, instead of diving right in, he left his robe on. They took it more or less in stride. Evidently there were plenty of men who weren't interested in participating—weren't interested or weren't able—men who would pay good coin just to watch. For the better part of the night he sat cross-legged at the base of the bed, committing the entire scene to memory. At first it was just a show—all exaggerated writhing and moaning—but as the candle burned down and the bottle of rum ran dry, the artifice dropped away.

The two had worked together before—that much was obvious—but it was more than a working relationship. They knew each other, where to touch, how and for how long, when to speak, when to stay silent. He'd hired them expecting to find the cheat, the right series of physical tricks that would transform him from a celibate monk into a legendary lover. He'd been ready to memorize a set of techniques, only to discover that there was nothing to memorize. The intricate positions of hands, lips, fingers, tongues—it all mattered, but only because of something else that mattered more, something deeper, something he couldn't see, even with his Shin-trained eyes. When they fell asleep tangled in each other's arms, he left the coin on the mantel above the fire and slipped out without waking them. In the long years since, he hadn't hired another whore.

"We come here to fuck?" Andraz demanded. "Or to play cards?"

Akiil pulled his attention from the grunting pair, turned to face his drunken

companion. After a last, futile effort, the man's friend had given up and retreated into the night, too smart or too sober to go along with any plan aimed
at cheating the Captain. It was obvious from his eyes that he'd already given
Andraz and the strange man in the robe up for dead. Akiil glanced over his
shoulder. The half-open door was only a few paces distant. Easy to walk out,
still. He could tell Andraz that his friend had been right after all, that trying
to cheat at the Captain's tables was suicide, that they'd find another tavern.
He'd buy the man a drink, and they could part ways still enjoying the under-
valued luxuries of unbroken bones and unsevered necks.

"You remember what to do?" he asked instead.

Andraz gave him a glassy stare.

Akiil put a hand on his shoulder. "You need to tell me you know what
to do."

"You blink, I bet." The man shrugged off the hand, started bulling his way
toward the back of the hall.

Hardly the ideal accomplice, but then, that was the point. Andraz was obviously an idiot, and he was obviously, spectacularly drunk. Whoever was at
the card table would know both things—he'd left the tavern barely a quarter
of an hour earlier—which meant none of them would suspect him of cheating. *Akiil* they would suspect, but then, Akiil wasn't planning to win. Hence
the need for the drunken idiot.

At the back of the hall, a tight spiral staircase ran up to a loft overlooking
the madness below. A pair of guards with crossbows stood at the railing,
looking down into the crowd with grim faces. Given the angle, Akiil couldn't
see the card game or the players, which made sense. The Captain hadn't survived twenty years in the Quarter by giving his enemies a lot of clear shots at
his back. Anyone who wanted to attack the man would have to fight past the
two guards at the base of the stairs—a pair of bald, scarred, muscle-bound
twins—and rush up the tight, circular staircase straight into the fire of the
crossbowmen above.

Fortunately, Akiil hadn't come to attack him.

As Andraz approached the base of the staircase, one of the guards frowned,
shook his head, put a hand on the man's chest. "You're done, Raz."

Andraz plastered on a smile. "You sure of that, Fori? The Captain doesn't
want another chance at my coin?"

"Captain *has* your coin."

Andraz fished inside his shirt for his purse, newly replenished by Akiil.
"Not this."

Fori frowned, took the leather satchel, dumped it out into his palm: a dozen silvers and some scattered copper. Not a bad sum for a game in the Quarter, even the Captain's.

The guard grunted, raised his scarred brows. "Who'd you stab for this then?"

"Found someone," Andraz replied vaguely. "Someone who owed me money."

Fori studied Andraz a moment, then looked past him, brow furrowed, as though he expected to see a dead body tossed across one of the tables. After a moment, he shrugged, dumped the coin back in the purse, handed it back.

Andraz made to move past him, but the big man pressed that meaty hand into his chest.

"You think about kicking up a fuss up there, you remember—the Captain's hogs ain't eaten yet tonight."

"Not good business, Fori, threatening the patrons."

"No threats. You take your losses like a man, you'll walk out of here like one."

Andraz winked at him. "Not planning to lose."

Akiil smoothed away any hint of a smile. *That,* that idiotic confidence, was what made the soldier perfect for the job.

Fori snorted, cracked his knuckles in a way that suggested he expected to use them before too long, then turned his attention to Akiil, eyes narrowing.

"You want something?"

Akiil nodded. "I want to play cards."

As he spoke, he undercut the words with his expression, his posture. He wanted Fori to see someone who desperately *didn't* want to play cards, someone who had been driven there by a need or compulsion almost beyond his will. With both hands, he clutched his purse, as though he expected it to be snatched from his belt. When the guard reached for him, he cringed.

"Not gonna hurt you," Fori said, shaking his head. "Not yet, anyway."

"No," Akiil said, refusing to raise his eyes. "No, I know."

The man took him by the front of the robe, testing the rough fabric between his fingers as though he were some kind of merchant. "What's this? A *robe*?"

Akiil nodded. "It's a robe."

"What're you wearing a robe for?"

"It's what I have."

"Who wears a robe?"

"Monks. I'm a monk."

Fori frowned. "This ain't really a place for monks."

Akiil nodded, held close his body's heat, poured it into his face until he felt sweat stippling his brow.

"I know that," he said. "But I heard there was a card game. . . ."

"Never heard of a monk playin' cards."

"I'm not," Akiil said. "Not anymore."

"Not playin' cards?"

"Not a monk. I was . . . expelled."

"Expelled." Fori's brows climbed. "What's a monk do to get expelled?"

Akiil kept sweating, took a deep, unsteady breath. "Fornication."

"Fornication!" Fori said, repeating the word for the benefit of his twin.

The twin, who had been surveying the crowd beyond, finally turned, cracked a yellow smile. "Means fucking."

"I know what it means," the guard replied. He turned back to Akiil.

"Who'd you fornicate?"

"What? No one."

"No one?" Fori shook his head. "Tough break, getting kicked out of the monk house for fornicating when you didn't fornicate no one."

"No. I mean. I did. She just . . . she was just this woman."

The guard narrowed his eyes, peered at Akiil's brow.

"You sick?"

"No. No, I'm not sick."

"You're sweatin' like you're sick."

The twin shook his head. "Scared is what he is, Fori. Scared out of his skinny monk bones."

Fori nodded as though that made sense. "Best find a different game. Ain't never busted up a monk before. Seems like bad luck."

Akiil leaned on his heart, made it beat faster. He doubted the two thugs would notice, but that was no reason to get sloppy.

"You won't . . ." He trailed off, shaking his head. "You won't have to . . . bust me up."

"Yeah," Fori replied. "Yeah. That's the thing. Everyone says that. Then they lose too much coin. Owe the Captain. *Then* Fari and I," he gestured to the other man, "have to go find 'em. Break 'em. Feed 'em to the hogs."

"You won't have to feed me to the hogs," Akiil said. "I need this. I need the coin. Please."

"Ah, fuck it," Fari said, obviously bored by the conversation. "Just let him up."

Fori frowned. "We have to break him, you're doing the breaking. Bad luck, busting up a monk."

"I'll do the breaking," Fari agreed. "Let him up."

Fori shrugged finally, took his time patting down Akiil, checking every hem of the robe for hidden weapons, then stepped aside.

Akiil gathered himself, made sure to clutch his purse until his knuckles ached, then climbed the winding stairs.

A single table, wide and heavy enough to hold a slaughtered hog, dominated the loft. Andraz had taken a seat, splashed the contents of his purse out in front of him, not bothering to sort or stack the coins. To his right a short-haired woman—keen eyes, crooked nose, maybe in her forties—pursed her lips, raised her brows. Past her, a massively fat man—down to his last handful of silvers—scowled. Two seats to his right sat the Captain.

Akiil let himself stare. As a child, he'd never come near the man, never closer than a stone's throw. And he'd never thrown the stone.

The Captain wasn't from Annur, not originally. He'd been born in the south, sold into slavery shortly thereafter, and raised—if that was the right word—to work on one of the vast Ghannan horse ranches. When he was twelve or thirteen—according to the story most people seemed to believe, anyway—he'd been bucked off by a horse he was exercising. The fall broke his leg, but he managed to drag himself up by the bridle, then stab the horse in the neck with his belt knife, over and over and over, until it collapsed. The head trainer came after him, naturally—a Ghannan mare was worth more than a slave boy—began viciously whipping him until that slave boy dragged the man off his horse and stabbed him to death, too. He stole the living horse and rode for the hills, somehow eluding pursuit, even with his broken leg, rode the horse all the way to Annur, where he sold it and used the coin to open the first of his many taverns.

He didn't look like the type of man to stab a horse to death. He was smiling mildly as he watched Andraz pile up his coin, then turned his attention to Akiil. One of his hounds—a massive beast with teeth like knives—gave a low growl, but the Captain rubbed it affectionately behind the ears and the creature settled back down.

"A new player," the Captain said, his smile widening. "Welcome."

He gestured to an open seat.

Akiil hesitated, let his eyes track past the man's face to the truncheon hanging on a leather thong from the chair's post, just over his shoulder. It looked like some kind of pale wood, but Akiil knew better. Everyone in the Quarter knew better. The club had once been a relatively important piece of Vicious Ryk—his femur, to be precise. According to the story, when Ryk refused to pay tribute, the Captain dressed as a whore and bribed his way into Ryk's favorite brothel. When they were alone, he drugged the man, cut his leg off, then stripped the meat from the bone. According to the story, Ryk was still sobbing when the Captain beat him to death with it.

"I think . . ." Akiil shook his head. "I didn't mean to come here."

He turned back toward the stairs.

"Don't be foolish."

The words weren't loud, but they stopped him in his tracks. He made sure his heart was pounding, poured a little more heat into his face, then turned back.

The Captain smiled. "You came for a card game, no?"

Akiil shuddered a nod.

"Fori and Fari must have checked you for coin or you wouldn't be here."

Another nod.

"Then sit down. Play cards. Are you some kind of priest?"

"Monk," Akiil replied, lowering himself into a chair beside the short-haired woman. She wore no jewelry but smelled, unexpectedly, of expensive perfume.

"A monk!"

"I used to be a monk. I'm not . . ." He trailed off, shaking his head.

"Where does a monk get a purse filled with silver and gold?"

Akiil pulled shame down over his face like a mask.

The Captain laughed. "A *thieving* monk." He waggled a finger. The ruby in his ring glittered in the lamplight. "I'll have to be careful of you!"

"No," Akiil replied. "I mean, I would never . . ."

"Of course you wouldn't," the Captain replied smoothly. "Of course you wouldn't. Do you have a name, monk?"

"Cham," Akiil replied.

"Well, Cham"—his eyes twinkled, as though the false name were a joke that they shared—"meet Veva, Harbon, and Andraz."

Akiil nodded to the table without meeting anyone's eyes.

"Now," the Captain went on, "we're just waiting for our dealer. Great with the cards that woman, but a mouse-sized bladder. Two cups of tea and . . . ah! Here she is."

A door at the back of the loft opened.

A young woman stepped out.

Akiil almost fell out of his chair.

As a child, Skinny Quinn could fit into spaces Akiil wouldn't have dreamed of attempting—storm drains, half barrels, the hole cut into the shitter of some fancy stone privy. Once, when they were six or seven, she'd gone down a chimney. Akiil could barely fit his head inside the thing—Horan *couldn't* fit his head—but Quinn insisted she could make it.

"Turn around," she said.

Horan leered. "Why? Not like you got any tits to look at."

"If you don't turn around," she replied, using that tight, clipped voice of hers, "I'm going to kick you off the roof."

It wasn't an idle threat. She'd shoved Runt off the Spring Bridge once, just for telling her she smelled bad.

Horan turned around. So did Akiil.

It took her just a few moments to strip off her rags, then slather herself with the pig fat they'd pilfered for the purpose, and then she was gone, speaking from inside the chimney.

"It's fine," she whispered. "I'll be down in a few heartbeats. Meet me at the back door."

Akiil risked a glance down into the dark. He could just make out her soot-smeared face, contorted with the effort of forcing herself deeper. She had both arms above her head, though there was nothing to grasp, nothing but the pressure of her body against the rough walls to hold her up. It made his chest ache, just looking at her suspended like that.

"You sure you're all right?"

"I'm fine," she said. "See?" She slipped abruptly deeper, so far he couldn't make out her face anymore. Then, a moment later. "Shit."

That was a bad sign. Quinn almost never swore. *Being born in a ditch,* she always said, *is no excuse for bad manners.*

"What do you mean, shit?" he hissed, heart kicking at his ribs.

"I'm . . ." She trailed off, made a sound like someone struggling to breathe, then cursed again. "I'm stuck, Akiil."

The words came out level, quiet, calmer than he could have managed, but he'd known her long enough to hear the fear behind them.

"That's all right. I'll get the rope." He fumbled for a moment with the coil, thanking a random handful of gods that they'd remembered to bring it. "I'll get you out, Skinny. Me and Horan."

Only, they couldn't.

It would have been hard enough for Akiil to manage as a grown man. Skinny she might have been, but she still weighed as much as two sacks of grain, and she was *stuck* there, lodged in the brickwork. For half the night they kept at it, lowering the rope, letting her get a grip on the loop, crouching at the lip of the chimney, pulling and pulling, ripping it from her greasy grip, then starting over again. Akiil refused to let himself consider what would happen if she were discovered there, or worse, if someone lit the fire below. He didn't let himself think of anything beyond coiling the rope again and again, lowering it down over and over, whispering the same useless encouragement as his heart shriveled inside his chest. He probably would have kept doing that all night, probably would have kept at it forever. It was Quinn, finally, who told them to stop.

"It's not working," she gasped.

Her voice had gone weak, as though the brick walls had squeezed all the air from her lungs.

"We can try again," Akiil insisted.

"There's no *point*. Go down the back wall. Get that rake we saw. Bring it up."

Horan stared at her, baffled. "What we gonna do with a rake?"

"Just *get* it."

What she wanted them to do, as it turned out, was to shove her *deeper* into the chimney.

"That's crazy, Skinny," Akiil protested.

"It is not," she said, voice level. "This is just a tight spot. I can feel it opening up again below. I can squeeze past it if you just push down on me."

"Or," Horan pointed out, "you get more stuck."

She stared up, eyes lambent in her soot-smeared face.

"We have to try," she whispered. "There's no other way."

It felt like they were killing her. Akiil and Horan leaned down on the fat end of the rake, driving the handle into her shoulder. She'd tried holding it, but the angle was all wrong for her to get a good grip, which left them forcing the thing into her bony joint while she squirmed and bit down on her pain.

"We can't," Akiil said, pulling back finally, gasping.

"You can," she said grimly, "and you will. Push harder."

"We're *hurting* you," Horan protested.

"I don't care. Push *harder*!"

Hot tears burning in his eyes, Akiil took the rake in both hands, positioned the head to be perfectly level, took a deep breath, then leapt onto it, landing with his full weight.

Quinn's choked scream exploded from the chimney, but, like a broken cork shoved down through a bottle's neck, she popped through the constriction. The rake plunged down, head catching on the edges of the chimney. Akiil lay atop it, the air knocked from his lungs.

Down below he could hear Quinn's quiet sobbing.

"Oh shit," he muttered, dragging the rake back up. "Oh shit. Oh shit. Oh shit. Skinny. *Skinny!*"

The quiet sobbing went on until he realized it wasn't sobbing at all, but laughter. After all that, after almost *dying* inside the chimney, she was *laughing*.

"I'm fine," she whispered up finally. "All scratched up, but fine. I *told* you I could make it."

Akiil still remembered that laughter all the long years later, the way the girl's relief had mingled with her triumph.

Skinny Quinn—he had no doubt that it *was* her emerging from the door— wasn't a girl anymore, and she wasn't laughing. It was hard to believe, as her eyes met his, that she'd *ever* laughed. The fierce, determined girl from his childhood, the one who came up with all the best plans, who made sure that Runt got his fair share of the spoils, who kept the little gang together even after their branding—she was gone, replaced by this slender woman with the scar down her cheek and the dead eyes.

Akiil had always believed that she *was* dead. After the Captain had scooped her up—her and Runt—he'd seen her a few times on the corners, always watched over by a hulking thug with a knife, her spindly frame draped in a ragged dress. He'd tried to get her attention once, but she'd only gazed at him blankly, given a tiny shake of her head, then turned away. When she stopped appearing on the corners, he'd assumed the worst. People died in the Quarter all the time, especially whores, especially kids. He'd done his grieving alone, on the long walk to Ashk'lan, and if he'd never quite stopped hating himself, he'd managed to put that hatred away, at least, somewhere he didn't have to look at it every single day.

Only she wasn't dead.

She looked healthy, in fact. Certainly she was better fed than she had been as a child. Her dark, curly hair—pulled back tight and tied behind her head— was clean, even lustrous. She wore unstitched, unripped trousers and a sleeveless shirt that might have been laundered that very morning. Skinny Quinn the child had been covered with bruises, scrapes, and half-healed cuts; the woman's brown skin was smooth, unbroken. She could have been the very painting of health and prosperity, except for those eyes.

For just a moment, as they slid over him, something flickered there. Surprise? Anger? Confusion? Whatever it was, it vanished almost immediately, replaced by the blank gaze of a woman in a painting. Akiil ached to call it back, to hold the *saama'an* of her vanished expression in his mind until he'd plumbed its depths, but there was no time. She was already taking her seat at the table behind the deck of cards.

"Quinn will deal," the Captain announced. "Her fingers are far more nimble than my own."

She didn't reply. Didn't even look up. Instead, she poured the cards between her hands as though they were water, shuffled faster than Akiil could follow, then poured them back and forth once more.

"You look nervous," the Captain said, a smile playing at the corner of his mouth as he studied Akiil. "Don't be nervous. You want a drink?"

Not the best idea, drinking while robbing one of the most dangerous men in the Quarter. He hadn't come in planning to drink, but then, he hadn't exactly *planned* on any of it, least of all discovering Skinny Quinn alive and shuffling cards for the Captain.

"Black rum?" he replied. "Do you have black rum?"

The Captain raised a hand and a young man raced from the shadows at the back of the loft with a bottle and a clay cup.

"Don't mind if I join him," Andraz announced, gesturing that the serving man should pour for him, too.

The short-haired woman—Veva—raised her brows, but didn't say anything. Harbon just snorted.

"And you, Andraz," the Captain said, swirling the wine in his goblet of blown glass without raising it to his lips. "I'll admit that I did not expect you back here so soon, and your purse magnificently replenished. Did you murder a man for this money?"

Andraz laughed. "Would you care if I did?"

"Well . . ." The Captain pursed his lips. "I suppose not. Providing he wasn't a friend of mine."

"Do you *have* friends?" Veva asked.

The Captain raised his glass to her. "A fair point."

"Are we playing?" Harbon demanded. "Or are we talking?"

"*You,*" Veva said, "have been losing. You should savor the respite from your misfortune."

The man scowled, but the banter between the two suggested this wasn't the first time they'd sat at the table together.

Akiil took a swallow of rum, then another, let it burn on his tongue a moment, then followed that burn down the back of his throat. He peered into the clay cup—half full—then tossed the remainder back in a single gulp. The heat spread through his chest. His body threatened to relax. When he raised his eyes he found the Captain watching him, an inscrutable smile on his lips.

"It would seem that you appreciate my liquor."

"Yes," Akiil replied. "Thank you."

The Captain nodded, waved to the man in the corner. He poured again, then set the bottle down in front of Akiil, next to the cup.

Akiil stared at it, then let his gaze shift back to the Captain. "How much . . ."

The man waved the question away. "Consider it a thanks for enlivening my table. I don't believe I've ever played cards against a monk before."

"If we keep talking," Harbon groused, "you might not get around to it."

Veva laughed. "I like this kid. Shows up in a robe, pisses off Harbon, swigs rum like a sailor. . . ." She tossed an arm around his shoulders, then wrinkled her nose in distaste, reclaimed her arm. "Although you *are* sweating like a pig."

"Just nervous is all," Akiil muttered.

"You played this game before?"

"I've watched some," he replied. "One of my brothers had a deck of cards. They used to play for dried beans."

"Dried fucking beans," Harbon said, shaking his head.

"So you know how the hands go?" the woman asked.

Akiil nodded. "Pair. Two pair." He paused for a moment, considered getting it wrong, felt the Captain watching him, decided that might be laying it on a little thick. "Three. Intarra's Sword. Intarra's Crown . . ."

The woman laughed. "In here they're just called the Prick and the Peach."

"The Prick . . ." Akiil repeated uncertainly.

"You have one of those beneath your robe, don't you?"

"'Shael on a stick," Harbon muttered, "can we play the 'Kent-kissing game?"

The Captain raised a single finger, and Skinny Quinn swept the cards into a wide fan across the table, collected them with an equally graceful gesture, passed the deck to Harbon, who cut it and handed it back.

"Place your bets," she murmured.

It was the same voice, the same precise diction, but all the edges had been sanded away.

Akiil rummaged in his purse, pushed a copper onto the wooden table.

"It's a silver," Quinn said, her face expressionless. "A silver to play."

"A silver . . ." Akiil replied.

"Did you think we were going to be playing for beans?" Harbon demanded.

"Go ahead," the Captain said, studying Akiil as he spoke. "You can't win if you don't bet."

Akiil filled his cup with rum, tossed back a long swallow, then clawed his copper off the table and replaced it with silver.

Veva had already bet, along with Harbon and the Captain. Andraz made a show of splashing around in his pile, then shoved a coin out before him.

Akiil watched the cards as Quinn flicked them across the table—three face-down to every player, followed by two faceup.

The deck was in good condition, but good didn't mean perfect. Cards were expensive—all that paper, all that printing—which meant they tended to get used until they were used up. Savvy players could pick up an advantage by noting a frayed corner here, a splotch of wine there. Learning even a few cards could pay off.

Akiil wasn't going to learn a few.

He was going to learn them all.

With an effort of will he put his questions about Quinn aside, stepped clear of his own bafflement and guilt to focus on the *saama'an*. As each card dropped into place, he carved the tiny details on his mind—that nick, that smudge, that fleck in the fiber, that darker pigment. . . . When he picked up his own cards, he matched them to their backs. The eight of flames had a stain on the corner, the two of moons, a minuscule dent in the backing. . . .

"Well," Andraz announced, smiling unsteadily. "I'm feeling lucky."

He shoved a small pile of coin—uncounted—out in front of him.

Instead of rolling his eyes, Akiil took another swig of rum. The man was an idiot. Even a monk with perfect memory couldn't learn the cards before they'd been played. Of course, it wouldn't be a bad thing for Andraz to lose spectacularly on one or two hands. That was, clearly, what everyone expected.

Akiil folded, shoving his cards back toward the center of the table as though they'd burned him. The Captain studied Andraz for a moment, then also folded. Harbon muttered something about fools being fed to the hogs, tossed his cards toward the center of the table, and waved over the serving man for a cup of wine. Only Veva took the bet.

Quinn swept up the discarded cards, dealt two to Andraz, one to Veva, her hands quick as hummingbirds.

Veva studied Andraz. Andraz glanced drunkenly across the table at Akiil. Akiil didn't blink.

Andraz looked back down at his cards, as though noticing them for the first time, then tossed them aside.

"Fuck this hand," he spat.

"Why fuck your hand," Veva said, raking the coins from the center of the table, "when I could offer you something so much more appealing?" She nodded to the pile remaining in front of him. "With that much, you could have a very pleasant night ahead of you."

"With this much," Andraz said, "I could buy every whore in your shed."

Veva smiled. "Indeed. Indeed you could."

A drunken leer crept onto the soldier's face as he considered that prospect, and for a few moments Akiil thought he might take the offer. The trouble with rash, drunken, stupid accomplices was, of course, that they were rash, drunken, and stupid. Akiil took a long drink, let the rum soak into him, then poured the cup full once more. The motion caught Andraz's eye. He glanced over at Akiil, then shook his head.

"Maybe later." He winked at Veva. "Feeling lucky tonight. Maybe so lucky I'll skip your whores and buy you instead."

If Veva was offended by the notion, she didn't show it. Instead, she laughed, patted him on the arm, then placed her next bet.

Akiil folded again. The Captain won the hand. But by the time it was done, he knew twenty of the cards.

At the end of the next hand he knew thirty-two.

Six hands in he knew them all.

He was also feeling more than a little drunk, not that that was a bad thing. A savvy gambler, one planning to cheat the Captain out of his coin, wouldn't allow himself to drink an entire bottle of rum, and so he kept drinking, kept losing, all while the Captain watched.

Good, Akiil thought. *Go ahead and watch, you son of a bitch. First I'm going to take your money, and then I'm going to find a way to free Skinny Quinn.*

Quinn, for her part, paid no attention to him at all. She might have been dealing to a circle of tree stumps.

Akiil shackled his eagerness, focused on the cards as they spun across the table, rotating them in his mind where necessary, matching the nicks and wine spots, smudges and misprints with suits and numbers. Andraz had a pair of eights. Veva held the Raven, which would have been strong except for the Eye, which canceled it out. Harbon had nothing, and Akiil's own hand wasn't much better. He rearranged the cards from low to high. Looked across at the Captain.

The man smiled. Lamplight glittered in his rings. He was sitting on a Broken Throne—not the best hand in the game, but a lot better than Andraz's eights. On the other hand, the next undealt card in the deck was also an eight. . . .

"Place your bets," Quinn murmured.

Veva tossed her cards.

Akiil blinked twice.

Andraz grinned blearily and doubled his bet.

"That," the Captain said, pursing his lips as he considered the glittering pot, "is a lot of money to risk."

"You don't win if you don't bet," Andraz declared.

Akiil took a swig of rum, polishing off the cup. Veva was watching him with a bland, inscrutable smile. He hefted the bottle—about half empty—poured himself another drink.

"All right," the Captain said finally, placing a neat tower of silver coin in the center of the table. "You have piqued my curiosity."

With a neat gesture, he flipped his cards—the Broken Throne.

Akiil made his eyes go wide.

Andraz just laughed. "Shit luck!" One by one he turned over his eights, then clawed the pile of coin to his side of the table. "*Shit* luck."

If the Captain was vexed at the loss, it didn't show. He smiled genially, shifted a new ante into the pot. "The truth of cards is the truth of life—sometimes you can do everything right and still lose."

The next several hours provided a spectacular illustration of that point. Andraz cleaned out Harbon first. A dozen hands later, Veva pushed back from the table, protesting her fatigue as she retreated with less than half her coin. And then it was just Akiil, Andraz, and the Captain. Akiil kept his own play understated, never wagering much, winning a little here, losing a little there, maintaining enough to stay in the game. He was careful not to let Andraz win too often or too obviously, though the man's fury when he folded with a winning hand threatened to scuttle the whole con.

Time to get out, Akiil thought as the midnight gongs began to toll. *Time to take the money and walk away.*

On the other hand, they were *winning.* The rum was running hot in his veins. He'd finished most of the bottle, but there were still a few cups remaining. Another dozen hands wouldn't hurt anything. This was the bastard, after all, who'd sold Skinny Quinn and Runt on the street corners, who'd fed Butt Boy to his fucking pigs. Aside from the thrill of the game—following the cards, managing Andraz, deciding when to press and when to step back, acting his own part—there was a savage satisfaction to the whole affair. He imagined Skinny Quinn watching him from behind that expressionless mask, cheering him silently on. After all these years he'd come back, an avenging spirit in a monk's robe, a drunk avatar of justice, or whatever passed for justice in the gambling dens of the Perfumed Quarter.

The thought kept him at the table. It kept him at the table too long.

Andraz had just shoved another small hill of coin into the center of the table when the Captain frowned, raised a single finger, as though a new thought had just occurred to him.

"I think," he mused mildly, "that you are cheating."

Akiil's stomach clenched. It took all of his Shin training to make his face do the correct things: a blink of confusion; a drunken look from the Captain to Andraz then back; a slight gaping of the mouth; more sweat pouring from his brow. The Captain hadn't accused *him* of cheating, not yet, but that didn't mean he shouldn't appear alarmed. Everyone knew what happened to people who tried to cheat at this particular table.

Andraz, however, in a testament to the power of strong drink, just waved away the accusation. He looked like a man trying to swat a troublesome fly.

"Good luck is what it is. Good luck and the blessing of the gods."

The Captain nodded, as though he were considering that line of argument. His face was still mild. He hadn't called his guards or reached for Vicious Ryk's femur. Instead, he pointed toward the pile of coin glittering in the lamplight.

"That is a lot of silver."

"Don't win if you don't bet," Andraz replied. The words sounded less confident this time around.

"And yet," the Captain said, "to bet *that* much, you must have very strong cards." He paused, then gestured. "Show me."

Andraz's face darkened. He pushed back from the table. "We're in the middle of a hand!"

Over his shoulder, Akiil caught a glimpse of Fori's impressive bulk. Maybe he'd been summoned by the Captain, or maybe he'd just heard Andraz's raised voice. Either way, he put a huge hand on the drunk man's shoulder. The gesture was slow, almost gentle, but there was plenty of violence folded inside it.

"Show me," the Captain said again.

Reluctantly, Andraz flipped his cards. The Locust. The Flood. The Plague. The Bloody Blade. It was not a good hand. It was nothing. Not yet.

"If I were you," the Captain said. "I would have folded. After all, unless this next card," he reached over to tap lightly at the top of the deck, "is the Comet, you are out of all manner of luck."

I am a monk, Akiil reminded himself. *A confused, horrified spectator.* He pulled the identity down over his face like a hood.

The Captain turned to Skinny Quinn. "What is the next card?"

She kept her eyes down. Instead of turning the card over, she spoke, her voice almost inaudible over the clatter from the tavern below.

"The Comet."

Akiil choked down his surprise. It wasn't entirely impossible. Quinn had always been smart, a lot fucking smarter than him. She'd always had an amazing memory. She might have taken the time to learn the deck, doing exactly the same thing he had done. It wasn't *impossible,* but Akiil had never encountered anyone who'd memorized an entire deck. He stared at the woman—staring was the appropriate response, even for a drunk, befuddled, frightened monk—but she refused to meet his eyes, refused to do anything at all but study an empty patch of the table in front of her.

Andraz, on the other hand, was purpling.

"And you accuse *me* of cheating! When this little *slut* has been . . . has been *feeding* you *cards.*"

"You will apologize," the Captain said, "to Quinn for the slur. I elevated her from *slut* to *dealer* years ago."

Andraz opened his mouth to object, then winced as Fori's hand tightened on his shoulder.

"You will apologize," the Captain said again.

The drunk gambler gaped like a fish ripped from the water. Fori, with his free hand, smashed Andraz across the back of the head, a blow so violent it almost knocked his teeth into the table.

"You will apologize to Quinn," the Captain said for a third time. He nodded encouragingly.

The drunk fog shifted in Andraz's eyes. For the first time, he seemed to understand his own peril.

He glanced at the woman—a look of pure, thwarted rage—then choked up something that might have been an apology.

Quinn didn't nod. Didn't even twitch. Akiil tried to read her face, but there was nothing to read. She might as well have been furniture. Dangerous, dangerous furniture, he realized.

"And, while I understand your suspicion," the Captain continued, "I should tell you that I never cheat at cards." He spread his hands. "It removes the sport from the game."

"But . . ." Andraz pointed at Quinn, then after a glance over his shoulder at Fori, trailed off before impugning her again.

The Captain nodded. "In addition to her capable service as my dealer, Quinn also—" He pursed his lips, as though searching for the word. "—observes things. She makes sure that the other players at the table share my appreciation of the game's purity."

He looked over at the woman. "What do you make of our drunken friends, Quinn? Are they lucky? Or are they liars? I love to watch a player ride a lucky streak, but I cannot abide a liar." He shook his head, acting out his disappointment at the thought. "Fortunately, my pigs are always hungry."

At the mention of pigs, Andraz snapped like a twig.

He hurled an arm out, stabbing his finger at Akiil.

"It was *him*. He staked me the coin. He convinced me . . . he *tricked* me into it. It was his plan. His fucking idea. I wanted to go home—"

The Captain put a finger to his lips, and Fori wrapped two massive hands around Andraz's neck. His eyes bulged, then he fell silent, his terrified gaze flicking from the Captain to Akiil.

"I was speaking to Quinn," the Captain said. He turned to the woman. "Quinn?"

"They're working together." Her words were quiet, precise. They reminded Akiil, for some inane reason, of little grains of salt. She stared right at him as she spoke. No, he realized, not at him, *through* him. As though he wasn't even there. As though he never had been. "The monk is drunk, but not as drunk as he claims. He blinks when it's time for the other one to bet."

The Captain turned his attention from Andraz to Akiil, nodded appraisingly.

"And how does he know when to bet?"

"He's learned the cards."

Akiil leaned forward. "Honestly, I haven't learned anything. I don't know why he's accusing me. I've never met him before in my life."

"One thing I've learned over the years," the Captain replied, "is to distrust men who begin their sentences with the word *honestly*." He shook his head. "It's a shame. I might have had a use for a mind like yours." He shrugged. "On the other hand, I already have Quinn." He glanced up at Fori, made a gesture with the back of his hand, like a man sweeping lint off a table, and between one heartbeat and the next, the burlap sack came down over Akiil's head.

33

"The spears need barbs," Gwenna said. "Large barbs. Like harpoons."

Torchlight slicked the polished steel heads of the weapons, reflecting onto the walls of the surrounding cave.

Jonon glowered. "You did not think to mention this back on the ship, where we had a forge?"

"I was in the brig," she replied, not meeting his eyes.

It was only partly the truth. She *had* been in the brig for most of the voyage south, but there had been ample time after dropping anchor in the harbor, after Jonon had ordered her released, to instruct him on the tools they might need if they ever encountered the birds. He would have bristled at the instruction, might well have ignored her entirely, but that didn't change the fact that she'd never even tried.

"I can manage it, sir," Lurie said. He glanced over at Gwenna, face flat, eyes dead. He was less aggressive than Chent or Vessik, didn't reek of violence and lust in the same way, but he frightened her more than the other two.

He smiled at her—no emotion in the expression—then turned back to the admiral.

"I've got a handful of files in my pack."

"Why barbs?" Jonon asked, studying her by the shifting light of the torches.

"You're not going to bring a kettral down with arrows or spears. The birds are just too big."

Annick had managed it, back in the Purple Baths, but Annick was somewhere on the far side of the world.

"We aren't trying to bring down a kettral," the admiral observed. "We are here for the eggs."

Gwenna nodded. "And if you get lucky, you can climb the cliffs, steal those eggs, then disappear, all while the birds are out hunting."

"So the spears are for . . ."

"If you don't get lucky."

"What happened to kneeling?" Jonon demanded. "What happened to cowering and praying?"

With the words, Gwenna felt again the shadow of the bird passing over them, the broken stone jagged beneath her knees, the cold on her brow as she pressed her forehead to the scree; she knew all over again the frozen panic of a defenseless animal caught out in the open, waiting to die.

She hadn't died, of course. None of them had. Maybe the bird failed to spot them. Maybe it just wasn't hungry. Whatever the case, it had swept past, so low she could feel the wind of it tugging at her hair, then disappeared down the valley, leaving the short column to half run, half stumble up the steep slope to the chilly shelter of the cave at the cliff's base. As long as they remained inside that cave, they'd be safe, but, of course, there was no way to get the eggs if they spent the whole time cowering in the cave.

"If a bird comes back while your men are up on the cliffs," Gwenna said, "you're going to need to distract it while they get down."

She hadn't raised her voice, but the cave was small. The soldiers had heard her well enough. A day earlier they'd been ready to face down the kettral with little more than their swords and bows. Now that they'd seen one, however, now that they understood the size and speed of the creatures, they reeked of wariness.

The admiral smelled only of resolve. He nodded slowly.

"Turn the spears into harpoons. They'll encumber the beast."

"Especially," Gwenna added, "if those harpoons are tethered to boulders."

"It can't rip free?"

"It might. If you only sink one or two it could probably tear them right out. Bury a dozen in the creature, though . . ." She shrugged.

Jonon narrowed his eyes. "This has been tested?"

She shook her head. "No. Back on the Islands, the harpoon idea was just . . . theoretical."

Theoretical was a stretch. She and the other cadets had enjoyed arguing the question down at the tavern, usually after too much rum. It was possible the whole plan would fail miserably, that the barbs would tear out just as Jonon suggested, that the enraged bird would shred its attackers with its beak and claws. It was more than fucking *possible*. On the other hand, whalers harpooned whales, and a whale was about as large as a kettral. There weren't a lot of other options. Besides, as Jonon said, the plan wasn't to fight the birds. The plan was to climb the cliff face while they were off hunting. Get into the nest, get the eggs—provided there *were*, in fact, eggs—and escape before they returned. If everything went according to plan, there'd be no need for the harpoons.

Gwenna tried to remember the last time something had gone according to plan.

✝

In a silent nod to her pessimism, the next day the weather turned foul.

Just after dawn, clouds poured over the northern peaks, choking out the sunlight, filling the valley until it was impossible to see more than a dozen paces from the mouth of the cave. Then the rain came—fat, ice-cold drops just at the edge of freezing, only a few of them at first, splattering across the shattered stone, then a deluge, loud enough to drown out any conversation that wasn't half-shouted. It rained all morning, and kept raining for three days, while Gwenna and the others shivered inside the dark cave. There was no wood for fires, which meant no light at night, no heat, no food but cold salt cod and hardtack, washed down with frigid water gathered from the storm.

Despite it all, Gwenna found herself grateful for the delay. It afforded both her and Rat the badly needed chance to rest and recover from the brutal march. Gwenna healed faster, of course. By the end of the first day, the bruises to her legs—from the chain, from stumbling over the chain—had begun to fade; by the morning of the second, the worst of the pain was gone. None of the soldiers seemed to notice, but on that second morning Rat sat up, peered at her own battered shins, then at Gwenna's, traced her own jagged red scabs with a finger, then shifted aside the ripped blacks over Gwenna's knee to study the wound beneath. The girl frowned at it, then looked up at the older woman.

"*Rashkta-bhura?*" she asked after a long pause.

Gwenna shook her head. "I don't know what that means."

Rat watched her awhile longer, pointed to the largest of Gwenna's scabs again, the one on the knee, then, with a quick, vicious little twist, scratched it free with her fingernail. Gwenna swatted the hand away, but the girl hadn't actually hurt her. The new skin beneath was slick, pink, sensitive, but the wound had stitched closed. Over the years since Hull's Trial, she'd grown so accustomed to the speed of her body's healing that she often forgot about it entirely. Rat, however, narrowed her eyes, then turned to her own leg and ripped free a scab. Blood welled into the gap. Not as much as Gwenna would have expected, but blood all the same.

The girl pointed an accusing finger at Gwenna's knee, then at her face.

"*Rashkta-bhura.*"

This time it was not a question.

Gwenna shook her head wearily. "Whatever that means."

"Blood, maybe," Pattick suggested.

Gwenna turned to find the legionary watching them from his post by the entrance to the cave.

"Or wound? Or scab?" he went on.

"Who fucking knows."

The legionary frowned. "But she's learned some of our words, right?"

"The bad ones, mostly."

"Gwenna Sharpe body . . ." Rat said, pointing at her, face intent. "Gwenna Sharpe body fuck quit."

She raised her eyebrows. "My body won't quit?"

The girl nodded.

Gwenna let her head drop back against the wall of the cave, closed her eyes. "Gwenna Sharpe quit before she ever met you, kid."

Instead of Rat, it was Pattick who replied. "What you did during that battle . . . against the Manjari . . ." He kept his voice low, as though he didn't want the others to hear. "That didn't look like quitting."

"You spend any time on farms, Pattick?" Gwenna asked, not bothering to open her eyes.

"I grew up on a farm."

"Then you've slaughtered chickens. You've seen how they keep running around, even after you take the heads off."

Pattick shifted. To her surprise, he smelled angry. When she looked over at him, he was glaring at her, pointing.

"Your head is still on."

"Lots of ways to kill a thing, Pattick, without chopping off its head."

"You're not fucking dead."

She met his eyes. "Why do you care?"

"I care because . . ." His mouth hung open for a moment, then he clamped it shut. "Never mind."

"You're the one who started talking."

"Forget it."

"How can I forget it when you're sitting right there staring at me?" Somehow, his anger had kindled her own. Or maybe not his anger, but the disappointment looming behind it. "How can I forget it when you, and fucking Cho Lu, and Kiel, and this miserable little bitch"—she stabbed a finger toward Rat—"keep looking at me like you think I'll grow wings and fly us all out of here?" She twisted around, half lifted her shirt. "No wings. See? Plenty of scars. No fucking wings."

A few of the other men, those close enough to hear above the pounding of the rain, had turned. She could smell the hot spike of Chent's eagerness, Vessik's slick hunger.

"Put your shirt down," Pattick muttered.

"Why? So you're not too *distracted* by a glimpse of tit?" She shook her head. "Maybe *that's* why you're so disappointed all the time. Pretty tough to fuck a woman who's locked in the brig or chained to this vagabond. 'Course there are plenty of soldiers I've known who wouldn't let a little thing like that get in the way. Is that the problem, Pattick?"

His pale face was flushed an awful red. It wasn't fair what she was doing, but then, what in the world was fair? It wasn't fair that she was alive while half her Wing was dead. Wasn't fair that Rat had lost her parents, or been abandoned by them, or whatever had happened. Wasn't fair that an entire empire, millions and millions of people, were forced to rely without even realizing it on a washed-up, busted ex-Kettral commander who let her men die and her body go to shit. *None* of that was fair, but then, welcome to the fucking world.

The legionary stared at her a moment, then shook his head, rose from the stony ground, stepped out into the driving rain to retrieve the tin pans filling with rainwater.

Gwenna turned away to find Vessik, Lurie, and Chent watching her with dark, glittering eyes.

Chent sucked at his teeth, spat onto the floor of the cave, offered her a brown-toothed grin.

"Don't let the boy get you down. Plenty of men in this cave wouldn't let those chains of yours get in the way of a little romance."

Vessik offered up an eager chuckle. Lurie just studied her, unblinking, until she looked away.

Despite the leering, they wouldn't come after her there, in the cave, not with Jonon due to return from his scouting any moment, not with Pattick and Cho Lu just outside, retrieving the pans and pails. The three of them were scavengers; if they were going to come after her, they'd wait until she and Rat were alone, and since no one on Jonon's expedition was ever alone, that ought to mean she was safe.

She tried to remember what safety felt like. If she closed her eyes, she could summon up moments from back on the Islands—lying on the beach after a long day of training, letting the sand's heat soak into her exhausted muscles, listening to the crashing of the waves; working by lamplight in her Wing's gear room, sharpening blades, stitching rips, oiling bows; even flying, hanging in her harness beneath the massive bird as the cool air washed over her. All the scenes were there—the sounds and scents, people and places—but how she'd *felt* . . . peaceful, calm, sure. That was gone. The words remained, but drained of their meaning. She tried to imagine feeling safe again someday. It was like picturing herself breathing water or sleeping on clouds. Whatever she was made for, that wasn't it.

†

After three days in the cave, the rain broke.

Gwenna shivered herself awake in the hour before dawn, sat up, pulled her knees to her chest, looked outside to see a furious wind shredding the last remnants of cloud, scraping the gray from the vast, bottomless black.

"Moon," Rat said.

The girl looked tiny with the blanket wrapped around her, even smaller than she actually was. She was shaking beneath the wool.

"Come here," Gwenna said, opening her own blanket, extending her arm.

Rat stared at her a moment, then shifted closer, leaning her meager weight against Gwenna's side.

"Moon," she said again, staring out into the night.

Gwenna nodded. The moon hung like a pale sickle above the valley.

Don't rely on the moon. Those had been the first words out of Daveen Shaleel's mouth when she began her course on celestial navigation. *The moon offers no fixed reference. This is why we will be studying the stars.*

Except, as the *Daybreak* voyaged south, those stars *had* changed, the old familiar constellations slipping beneath the northern horizon while new shapes emerged glistening from the sea. This far south, all the familiar markers were gone, as though someone had shattered the night sky, then pieced it back together wrong. All that remained was the moon. Unreliable, as Shaleel had said, nothing you could set a course by, but there all the same, when everything else was gone.

Gwenna felt Rat twitch beneath the blankets. She thought the girl was asleep, but looked down to find her large eyes on her.

"What rat?" she asked quietly.

"You," Gwenna replied. "You're Rat."

Rat shook her head. "No." She scrunched her brow in concentration. "Not girl rat. Other rat."

"Oh." Gwenna felt a weight settle on her chest. "Why did I name you that, you mean? What is a rat?"

Rat nodded.

"It's a good thing," Gwenna said. "Bright." She pointed up in the sky. "Like the moon." She hesitated. "What's your real name? The name your parents gave you?"

Rat stared at her, put a small finger to her own chest, as though trying to find herself in the darkness, then shook her head. "Rat is like moon?"

"Yes," Gwenna said, the lie bitter on her tongue. "Like the moon."

The girl smiled, snuggled her head into Gwenna's side. The next time Gwenna looked down, she really was asleep, that small smile still there at the corner of her lip. Barely there, but there.

†

"Raban and Cho Lu will climb the cliffs," Jonon said, pointing up at the craggy limestone above, then turning to the two men. "If you find eggs, you will lower them in these slings. According to our ex-Kettral,"—he didn't even bother to look over at Gwenna—"the eggs are large—each one about the size of a human head—but you should be able to fit two or three in one sling. I will not need to remind you that each of these eggs is worth more than your life or mine. When handling them, you will err always on the side of caution."

"Caution," Cho Lu repeated, staring up at the cliffs. "Of course."

In another place, at another time, Gwenna might have laughed. The rain had stopped, but the ledges were soaked. Waterfalls thundered down the crag in half a dozen different places, misting whole sections of the wall almost to invisibility. It would be miserable climbing—wet, cold, precarious—and that was without the threat of returning kettral. Ordering a soldier to be cautious up there was like telling him to drive a knife carefully into his own eye.

Cho Lu didn't object, however, nor did Raban. They knew as well as everyone else that they were the best climbers in the crew, that if the moment ever came, Jonon would choose them for this part of the mission. That was what it was to be a soldier. You followed orders, usually dangerous ones; sometimes you lived, sometimes you didn't.

Gwenna recognized Cho Lu's bravado when he grinned at the crew and said, "We'll bring back a few extra for breakfast—an egg that size ought to scramble up nice. . . ."

Jonon did not smile. "The survival of Annur may hinge on these eggs."

"Yes, sir," the legionary replied, sobering instantly. "Of course, sir. Raban and I—we'll get the job done, sir."

He set his jaw, saluted, and then the two of them turned toward the cliff and began to climb.

Rat stared at the men as they worked their way up a broken seam at the base of the crag.

"Cho Lu?" she asked after a time, then pointed up the cliff, her eyes wide.

Gwenna nodded. "He's going up."

"Why?"

She looked down at the girl. "I didn't know you knew that word."

"Why?" Rat asked again, not taking her eyes from the soldiers.

"There's something up there that we need."

"Need?"

"Yeah," Gwenna replied. "We need . . ." She tried to think of a way to explain the word. "You need to breathe," she said, taking in an exaggerated breath, then blowing it out. She fished the last of her hardtack out of her belt pouch, held it up, offered it to Rat. "You need to eat. You need to sleep. You need . . ." She trailed off, at a sudden loss.

"Need water," Rat said, pointing to the flask at Gwenna's hip.

"Yes. You need water."

The girl hesitated. "Need knife."

Gwenna shook her head. "A knife is useful, you might *want* a knife, but you don't *need* it. A person can survive without a knife."

Rat repeated the words slowly, awkwardly, as though they were some kind of prayer. "A person . . . can survive . . . without knife."

It occurred to Gwenna, not for the first time, that she was probably the world's worst tutor. Back on the Islands they had a way of teaching languages that began with short sentences, two or three verbs, a smattering of important terms. You could pass a proficiency test in Antheran or Manjari without ever learning to parse the tricky difference between need and desire. Rat, however, seemed to have a knack for piecing together the various names and phrases that she'd heard along the march. She was smarter than Gwenna, at least— that much was plenty obvious.

"Need hand-to-hand," the girl went on, pantomiming one of the defensive postures Gwenna had taught her.

Gwenna shook her head. "Nobody *needs* to fight."

Rat's eyes narrowed. Her jaw tightened.

"Need to fight," she said. It was not a question.

Gwenna exhaled wearily. "I guess," she said. "Sometimes. If someone doesn't give you a choice."

That was why she'd joined the Kettral, after all, wasn't it? Because there were situations in which fighting was the only choice. Or battle. Or war. She stared back through the scratched lens of her life into the mind of the child who'd first made that decision.

"You don't have to go," her father told her.

How old had she been at the time? Seven? Eight? Around Rat's age, anyway.

"Just because they chose you," he went on, "doesn't mean you have to go."

It was a strange thing for him—a soldier, and a father to soldiers—to say. When word came that Kettral would be testing children in the next town over, Gwenna had joined her older brothers because . . . well . . . it had never occurred to her *not* to join them. She didn't expect to be chosen. She was the youngest of them, and the weakest, with a short lifetime behind her of losing at running, at wrestling, at stick fighting, at tree climbing, at pretty much *everything,* but still, they were getting in the wagon and she had no intention of spending three days alone at the farm, and so she went.

When the trainers told her she'd passed the test, she didn't believe them. She'd spent most of those two days getting punched and kicked, bloody and bruised, and just generally having her ass handed to her by children larger and older and stronger. She'd managed to twist one boy's fingers until he screamed, and to get in a good bite on another one's ear, but that was about it. Hardly the stuff legendary warriors were made of. And yet, when it came time to say the names, there was only one name: Gwenna Sharpe.

"I'll be out of the legions soon," her father told her that night. "Two more years, and I'll be back here, on the farm. They'll offer me another post, but I'm not going to take it."

She remembered staring at him. "Why not?"

Her whole life, he'd been away—half a year, sometimes a year at a time. Her oldest brothers were in the legions, too, but they managed to stagger their service so that one of them was usually home to look after the farm and the younger kids. Usually. There were enough of them to keep the place from burning down even when the adults were away. It had never occurred to Gwenna that any of that might change.

"You want to *leave* the legions?" she asked, baffled.

Her father looked at her, then past her, into the shifting embers of the fire. "You get tired after a while," he said. "Tired of fighting other people's wars."

Tired was a word she'd never thought to apply to her father.

"But someone's got to do it, right?" she asked.

That was what he'd always told her on the nights before he left: *The empire won't defend itself. Someone's got to do it.*

Now, though, by the red, shifting light, he didn't look convinced.

"I reckon."

She watched him awhile longer. "Then *I* will," she said.

"Gwen . . ."

She shook her head, sure of what she had to do. "The empire's like a farm, right? Everyone has to pitch in. You've been fighting *forever.* And Alex. And Wullum. And Perce is off this fall. It's time for me to pitch in."

"The Kettral, though. The Islands . . ."

"They're the only ones who will *take* a girl!"

He put a heavy, scarred hand on her arm. "You don't need to do it, Gwen."

"Yes I do, Pa. Yes. I do."

A few pebbles clattered to the rocks beside her, yanking her back to the present. She looked up to find Raban gazing down from far above.

He offered an apologetic wave. "Sorry!"

The wind ripped the word from his mouth.

Despite the conditions, the two of them climbed quickly. It was hard to be sure from her foreshortened vantage, but it looked as though they'd almost reached the first broad ledge.

Jonon gazed up at them, expressionless. He'd already grilled Gwenna half a dozen times about the eggs: How big were they? How many per nest? How brittle? How sensitive to changes in heat and moisture? She'd answered as best she could, drawing on half-remembered ten-year-old lessons. Back on the Islands, the fliers had been the ones to care for the birds, to raise them and train them. Gwenna had spent most of her time learning to blow things up or cut them apart.

Up above, Cho Lu hauled himself onto the ledge and out of sight. Raban followed a moment later.

The men below smelled of anticipation, even eagerness, but there was something else there, too—fainter, sharper. . . .

Gwenna looked over to where Pattick stood—as far from her as he could get and still be a part of the group. They hadn't spoken since that morning at the mouth of the cave, when Gwenna tore into him. She couldn't have said, even in the moment, why she was doing it, and so she had no idea how to apologize. She'd never been much good with apologies and anyway it was probably better for Pattick and Cho Lu if they kept their distance. Jonon loathed her, was obviously planning to toss her back in the brig as soon as they returned to the *Daybreak*. Chent, Vessik, and Lurie were just waiting for the right time to rape her. No need to put the two good legionaries in the way of all that. Safer for Pattick if he hated her.

A shout drifted down from above.

Gwenna looked up to find Cho Lu leaning over the edge of the ledge, a broad smile splitting his face.

"What's he saying?" Jonon growled.

"He's saying they found them," Gwenna replied. "They found the eggs."

Up above, the young legionary raised his fingers.

"Seven nests," the admiral murmured. "Fifteen eggs."

"Congratulations, sir," Chent said, saluting. "An outstanding success."

Jonon shook his head. "Not a success yet. Those soldiers are a long way from us, we're a long way from the *Daybreak,* and the *Daybreak* is a long way from Annur."

All true enough, but Gwenna still couldn't help but stare as the first sling descended the cliff, then as Jonon removed the first egg from that sling. Aside from the size, it didn't look like much—gray speckled with white and brown. If you didn't look too closely, it might have been a stone lifted from the bed of a mountain stream. Only it was not a stone.

It was a weapon.

How many deaths, Gwenna wondered, curled inside that smooth shell, waiting to be born into the world? What people now walking on the far side of the globe would one day be torn apart by that unhatched beak, those unseen talons? What lines of battle would be shattered, what kings defeated, what new order forced upon the conquered?

For a heartbeat, she had the mad thought that she should destroy the thing, seize it from Jonon and smash it on the jagged rocks. If the Dawn King had never hatched there would have been no bird to bear Talal and Quick Jak to the Purple Baths. If the Csestriim had never brought the birds back in the first place, the Kettral themselves would never have existed. No trainers would have come to a small town at the foot of the Romsdals looking for recruits, and a stubborn girl with hair the color of flame would have found some other way to live in the world, a way that didn't involve killing and getting people killed.

The egg in Jonon's hands seemed too small to carry such a vast weight, but then, that was the way of all things. She could destroy that egg, but the future would still happen, some future. Locked in an ash tree somewhere was the arrow shaft that would one day orphan a family. A broken plowshare rusting quietly in some Katalan barn would one day be dragged out, hammered into a new shape, polished and sharpened, then driven through a human heart. The next month, next year, next century—it was built already, all of it. The violence that would ruin empires was already stitched into the dark, quiet, unnoticed places of the world.

"That's the last of them," Cho Lu shouted.

At Jonon's feet, nestled carefully into the hollows of the rocks, lay fourteen kettral eggs. He held the fifteenth in his hands, was gazing at it so intently that he seemed not to have heard the soldier's voice.

"Should we come down, sir?" Cho Lu called.

Chent and Vessik traded a glance.

"Sir?" Chent asked finally. "Should they descend?"

Jonon looked up finally, noticed the eyes upon him, glanced up the cliff, then nodded.

"The rest of you," he said. "Get these eggs to the cave."

Gwenna turned to help, but the admiral shook his head disdainfully. "Not you."

She started to object, then shrugged, let the others shoulder the burden while she gazed idly up into the hard blue sky.

And so she was the first one to see the kettral when it swept back over the top of the cliffs, painting the ground black with its shadow.

Rat saw it next. "Bird," she said, stabbing a finger at the sky. "Bird. *Bird. Fucking bird!*"

Jonon looked, his face hardening.

"Everyone to the cave."

Lurie and Vessik were already there. Chent, halfway across the open space, glanced up into the sky, saw the bird, and ran. Pattick, however, froze.

"They're still up there," he said, pointing up the cliff toward Cho Lu and Raban.

Gwenna couldn't see either of the men on the ledge. Maybe they were scavenging one final nest, or fixing a rope for the descent. Whether they'd noticed the kettral she had no idea.

"They're still up there," Pattick said again.

Jonon nodded, put a hand on his shoulder. "We can't help them. I'm sorry, but we can't help them."

The young legionary cast around the broken mountainside. "There has to be . . . We could . . ." When his gaze found Gwenna, a desperate hope leapt into his eyes. "What about those spears? You said . . ."

She shook her head. She knew what she'd said, and she didn't want to hear it again.

In order to fight the bird she would need to go back to the cave, take up one of the makeshift harpoons, and return. Two hundred heartbeats at the very least, and already she could feel her own fear coiling tighter and tighter around her chest, her vision narrowing, the strength draining from her legs. The Gwenna Sharpe who had spent all those nights back in the taverns on Hook arguing about the best way to take down a kettral was gone. Another woman had stolen her body and that woman was shouting at Pattick, screaming at him.

"You can't fight them!"

He stared at her. "But the harpoons . . ."

"They're just something to hold on to while you die!" she snarled. She was stumbling backward toward the cave, half dragging Rat in her wake. "Jonon's *right*. We need to get under cover *now*."

Overhead, the bird screamed.

Gwenna risked a glance up. It had swept down the valley, turned, and begun to wing back toward them. Her mind whimpered like a whipped dog.

"It's time," Jonon said, shifting his grip from Pattick's shoulder to his elbow.

Pattick twisted free.

"No." He reeked of terror, but his voice was steady. "I can distract it." He raised his spear—a brave, sad, useless gesture. "I won't leave them."

The admiral's face hardened. "So be it."

Before Pattick could reply, he turned on his heel and strode toward the cave.

The young legionary turned to Gwenna, ugly face twisted with anguish, eyes pleading. She shook her head, took Rat by the waist, lifted her over her shoulder, and ran.

Pattick made the smartest stand that he was able.

Gwenna watched, trembling, from the mouth of the cave as he climbed atop a chest-high boulder, spread wide his arms, waved his spear at the sky.

"I'm here!" he bellowed. "I'm here, you miserable fucking buzzard! Look at me, I'm here!"

The bird responded. Whether it had spotted the men on the cliff, Gwenna couldn't say, but at the sound of Pattick's cries, it cocked its head, altered course, and stooped.

"So long, Pattick," Chent said, offering up a mock salute.

Rat's ragged fingernails dug into Gwenna's arm.

The bird screamed, Pattick screamed in response, pointed his slender spear, and then, at the very last moment, stepped backward off the boulder.

The bird's talons raked over the stone. It hovered for a moment, wings furiously scraping the air, then screamed again and rose into the blue.

"Kid's quick," Lurie observed.

"The kid is stupid," Chent replied.

Gwenna just stared as Pattick emerged from behind the boulder, then climbed back atop it. Instead of following the bird, which had looped off to the east, he was staring up at the cliff, shouting, motioning furiously. "Get down! I'll keep it busy, just *get down*!"

The wind shredded Cho Lu's reply before it reached the cave, but Pattick nodded, turned to find the bird, and brandished his spear once more.

"Come on!" he bellowed. "I'm *right here*!"

"Bird kill Pattick," Rat said quietly.

Gwenna glanced down to find the girl staring out of the cave with too-wide eyes.

"Yeah," she replied. "The bird's going to kill Pattick."

Rat looked up at her. "Gwenna kill bird."

"No, Rat. I can't kill the bird."

"Gwenna *rashkta-bhura*," the girl insisted. "Or *shava-bhura*. Gwenna kill bird."

"I'm not . . . whatever that is, Rat."

Outside, the kettral was circling, studying the legionary with one black, inhuman eye. Kettral were smart, smarter than their smaller brethren. It understood now that the boulder would provide Pattick with cover and was searching for a way to get at him. The legionary pivoted with it. Slowly, the kettral tightened the gyre.

"Why?" Rat asked. "Why Gwenna Sharpe doesn't fight?"

"Because Gwenna Sharpe is a coward."

She could feel the truth of the word seared into her weak, trembling flesh.

"Coward?" Rat asked.

Without a shriek, the kettral twisted, flicked its tail, and tucked. Either it was faster, or closer, or Pattick was slower. Either way, as he threw himself from the boulder, the tip of a talon raked across his back, tearing open his tunic, slicing the flesh beneath. Gwenna could smell the blood.

"Not to be crass, sir," Chent said, "but I earnestly hope you're not going to ask us to carry his carcass back to the ship."

Jonon stared from the cave's shadow into the light, his hands clasped behind his back. "The bird is hunting him. When it is done, there will be no carcass left."

"Coward?" Rat pressed. She hadn't taken her eyes from Gwenna's.

Gwenna held up a hand. It shook.

"Coward," she said.

Rat watched the trembling fingers for a moment, then shifted her gaze back to Gwenna's face, shook her head gravely.

"No coward."

"Yes, Rat," Gwenna said. "I am."

"Why?"

Gwenna stared at her. "What do you mean, *why?*"

It was a question that, in all the days since the disaster at the Purple Baths, she had never quite asked herself. She'd wondered *how* it had happened, of course; she'd spent countless hours trying to retrace the path that led her from commanding the last Kettral Wing in the world to cowering in the darkness of Jonon's brig, and what she'd concluded was that it wasn't a path at all. A path unfolded slowly. If you followed a path too far in the wrong direction all you had to do was turn around, start walking back the other way. What had happened to her felt more like a breakage. The right force had been applied at the right time in the right way, and something inside her had snapped, something that could not be put back.

Those, though, were questions of the past. Rat was asking something else.

"*Why?*" the girl demanded again, huge eyes bright beneath the mop of her hair.

Gwenna gazed into those eyes.

Why was she broken? It was an unanswerable question. Like asking why water was wet, or pain hurt.

"There's no *why* to it," she said wearily. "You're a little girl. Jonon's an asshole. Gwenna Sharpe is . . ."

She shook her head.

Outside, Pattick had hauled himself back up onto the boulder. He was less steady now, his pale face ashen.

Gwenna closed her eyes. He could die if he wanted to; didn't mean she had to watch.

"Gwenna Sharpe is *rashkta-bhura.*"

"I'm not whatever the fuck that is."

"Yes," the girl insisted. "*Is* the fuck. Not coward. *Rashkta-bhura. Axochlin.*"

"Maybe those are their warriors." Gwenna turned to find the historian standing half a pace behind her. "Like the Kettral."

"*I'm not fucking Kettral!*"

The words exploded out of her, half shout, half scream. Jonon and the others turned, but she didn't give a shit about them. *They,* at least, understood the truth—that whatever she'd been she wasn't anymore. It was Kiel, and fucking Pattick, and Rat who refused to see it, who, no matter how many times she fucked up, wouldn't stop looking at her as though she were some kind of salvation, as though she was just waiting for the situation to get bad enough to step forward and take matters casually, easily, firmly in hand. Jonon's disdain she could live with. The disgusting looks from Chent and Lurie and Vessik she could live with. It was the stubborn, stupid, idiotic fucking *hope* she kept finding in Rat's eyes, and Cho Lu's, that she couldn't endure.

"What does it take," she demanded, spreading her arms, "for you to understand?"

Rat nodded, as though this was what she'd expected all along, as though this was what she'd been waiting for. Kiel pursed his lips, but said nothing.

"You want to see what I am?" She snatched one of the harpoons from the wall of the cave. Raban had drilled a hole through the butt of it, looped through a long coil of rope, and made it fast. All at her direction, of course, all based on some horseshit plan she'd dreamed up years earlier half-drunk in a tavern. For all his disdain, even Jonon had believed her, believed her enough, anyway, to order the things made.

"You want to see the truth?" She lifted the spear. "*This?* This is useless. No one's ever taken down a bird with a harpoon. But you idiots believed me because I used to be Kettral. Well, I'm not Kettral. I'm not your rasha basha. I'm not *anything,* you stupid pieces of shit. What do you need to see to believe that? *I'm not anything.*"

But she knew, of course, what they needed to see.

Back on the Islands, the trainers had a saying: *Death is the last lesson.*

Harpoon in one hand, coiled rope in the other, flames of rage and shame and desperation blazing in her heart, she stepped from the cave's darkness into the sunlight.

Pattick turned, saw her. Hope unfolded in his gaze.

"No," she growled. "No. *No. No.*"

"Commander—" he began. Still, after everything, with the commander.

"Get off the fucking rock," she growled.

He hesitated.

"Get. Down. Now."

The words might as well have been stones striking him in the chest, each one driving him back a half step until he offered up a half-assed salute and stumbled backward into the boulder's shadow.

Somehow, Gwenna covered the intervening space.

The leaden heaviness had lifted from her legs. The pain and fear were gone, scoured away by the need—the coruscating molten *need*—to have them finally *see.*

She turned to face the bird. It had wheeled up and around, maybe twenty paces above, circling in a tight arc, watching her with one black, unblinking eye.

"Come on," Gwenna whispered. She cocked back the spear in one hand, held the coiled rope loosely in the other. "I'm ready."

There was a grisly game the cadets used to play back on the Islands called *How Do You Die?* The annals of the Kettral were filled with tales of last stands. Blue-Haired Su holding the door of the castle keep at Last Pine, fighting an entire garrison with a kitchen pot and a paring knife, buying time for the rest of her Wing. Georg the Butcher on the Antheran flagship, unlimbing men as the burning vessel sank beneath them. Rim Fair at the Rift, holding the slot canyon. Commander Selin on the bridge over the Leva, punched through with arrows but still crying her defiance as the last of the Annurian settlers retreated to the west. The names changed, and the weapons and settings, but one thing remained the same—the nobility of the sacrifice. Every man and woman in those stories went to their deaths proudly, for a purpose larger than themselves. That was how Gwenna had always imagined her own end—she'd be saving someone, defending something, giving her life for her Wingmates, for Annur, for something good and right and true.

Turned out, she'd imagined it wrong.

She hadn't left the safety of the cave to save Pattick. A kettral could eat a full-grown cow in a single meal; after the bird was finished with her it would devour him, then the men on the cliffs, and that would be that.

She'd left the cave, finally, because she was tired. Tired of Pattick's hopeful gaze, tired of Rat's growing trust, tired of whatever inexplicable game Kiel was trying to play, tired of waking up frightened, and stumbling through the day frightened, of falling asleep frightened into nightmares of failure, of fucking up, of getting her soldiers killed, tired of picking through the detritus of her own decisions, of trying to find the precise point at which she'd gone wrong, tired of wondering what she could have done to change things, tired of the ache in her bones and in her brain, tired of the weakness that had settled in her limbs, tired, most of all, of the memories of that other Gwenna Sharpe, the one who had been able to face danger without shaking, to make decisions between one heartbeat and the next, the one who'd been able to save the people who needed saving and kill the ones who needed killing, tired of knowing in her bones that *that* was the woman she should have been, that she could never be her again, tired of knowing that whatever she became would only be a shadow of that other person, a whisper, a pitiful broken whimper.

She left the fucking cave because it was time to finally be done with it, because it was time to die.

After so many months hunched under the grim weight of herself, she felt suddenly light, painless, felt the *rightness* of her own approaching annihilation.

The icy wind shredded her hair across her face.

"Come on!" she screamed, opening her arms to the kettral. *"Come on!"*

And the bird came on.

Talons spread wide, beak split with a scream of its own, it dropped toward her.

"Yes," Gwenna shouted as she hurled the spear, "yes," as the line spooled out through her hand, "yes," as the barbed point sank deep in the creature's breast, just beneath the wing, "yes, yes, yes," as she looped the spare rope around her forearm once, twice, three times, "yes," as the bird, shocked by the stabbing pain, broke off, dragging her from the boulder up into the endless emptiness of the sky.

For a long time she was spinning, spinning wildly, the ice-capped peaks, bright sun, jagged cliff bands scribbled across her vision. She waited for the spear to tear free, to feel the rope go slack in her hands, her heart go light in her chest as she tumbled to her death. But the spear held, as did the rope, and gradually the spinning slowed. The pain was back, a vicious stabbing where her shoulder threatened to rip from its socket, but this pain, at least, was honest, clean. Unlike the vague malaise she'd struggled through for the past months, there was an explanation, a way to fight back. She tensed her arm to take the strain off the joint, reached up and caught the rope with her other hand, hauled herself up, and then, without really meaning to, she was climbing.

So was the bird.

With every wingbeat it circled higher, trying to fly free of the stabbing in its breast. The harpoon had hurt it, certainly—especially with Gwenna's whole weight dangling off of the thing—but hurt wasn't the same thing as injured, certainly not injured enough to stop it from flying, and when Gwenna glanced down she saw that the ground had fallen far, far below. At the base of the cliffs she caught a smear of color and motion—Pattick, probably, and Jonon, and maybe a few of the others, come out from the cave to watch her die.

"Good," she growled, dragging herself another arm's length up the rope.

The closer she drew to the bird, the tougher the climbing became. Each wingbeat threatened to strip her from the rope, and at every motion the rope itself jerked and twisted violently in her hands. Twice she nearly lost hold of it, found herself sliding down the braided length toward her own oblivion. Unlike the Eyrie-trained birds, the wild kettral flew with its legs tucked back up behind it, which meant there was nothing to latch onto, nothing to stabilize her wild, swinging spins until she'd climbed all the way up to where the spear was buried in the bird's breast.

Her hands were wrecked. Blood oozed from her palms, slicking her grip on the spear's wooden shaft. The muscles of her forearms throbbed. Something was wrong with her upper back—torn or spasming so violently she felt as though she were being stabbed over and over and over.

"What'd you expect, you dumb bitch?" she muttered to herself. "You came up here to die. It's *supposed* to hurt."

She could feel the heat baking off the bird as it beat its wings furiously, trying to free itself of the pain, the weight.

"We didn't have to do this," she said. "You could have left those kids alone, and I could have stayed in the fucking cave."

But she realized as she hung there, face pressed into the feathers, body ready to give out, to give up, that she couldn't have stayed in the cave. Sure, that cold hole in the mountain rock she might have endured indefinitely, but the other cave, the fathomless cavern in the belly of which she'd been lost since that night at the Purple Baths—*that* she could not abide for one more day. If the only way out was to die, then fine. Not just fine—*good*. It felt *good* to be flying again, good to be trying to do something, good to be alive, even if only for a few final moments.

Maybe Rat was right after all.

Need to fight.

Not against the bird, obviously. The kettral was just a great, savage beast following its own instincts. Gwenna bore it no more malice than she did the stones below on which she would splatter when she fell. The fight was against the woman who had spent all those days lying motionless in the brig, the one who had almost watched from the safety of the cave while the kettral tore Pattick in half, the woman who had taken her face, her body, her name, who for months had been moving through the world as though *she* was Gwenna Sharpe.

Whatever else happened, *that* bitch needed to die.

Holding the shaft of the spear with one hand, she twisted the rope high around her thigh—once, twice, five times, shoved a bight of it down through the last loop, then settled her weight into the makeshift harness. Wind buffeted her against the bird's breast, battering her into the creature, then tearing her away, until finally she managed to snatch hold of one of the quills. The spine of the feather was thick as a small branch, and she used it to drag herself in tight against the straining muscle. Then, with her free hand, she slid the belt knife from her sheath and went grimly to work.

She'd been telling no more than the simple truth when she insisted to Jonon that no one could kill a kettral with a sword, let alone a 'Kent-kissing knife. On the other hand, she'd been imagining a situation in which the bird was free to attack with its beak and talons, free to fly, retreat, circle back. No one in the history of the Eyrie—no one in the history of the 'Kent-kissing *world*— had ever been mad enough to strap herself to a bird's breast.

The knife's blade was barely the length of Gwenna's hand—far too short to reach any of the vital organs—but she didn't need to get to the organs. The first slice slit the skin, the second parted a thick layer of yellow-white fat beneath it. The third cut reached the muscle. With long strokes she carved across the straining fibers, with each slash opening the wound deeper and still deeper, until she found herself drenched in blood, plunged to the elbow in the bird's breast.

The kettral screamed at each stroke of the blade, strained with its beak to pry her free. It came close, so close she could see the hook of the beak rake the feathers off to her right, the huge black eye filled with fury, but she was in just the wrong place—a little too high, a little too far off to the side, and each time the bird's attacks fell short. Then, gradually, almost imperceptibly at first, she felt the creature begin to weaken. Muscle was just cable, after all, cable twisted out of meat. Cut partway through, and it would weaken. Keep cutting, and it would snap. And when that happened, they would drop, both of them, onto the mountainside below.

The kettral didn't understand that, but it knew in the ancient way of all beasts that it was wounded. It understood that somehow the pitiful, unfeathered thing clinging to its chest was dangerous, even deadly, that its very survival depended on getting that thing *off*, and so, instead of climbing, instead of trying to pry her free with its beak, it stooped.

The world turned abruptly on its end. Gwenna fell back, lost her grip on the blood-soaked feathers, slipped out into the void, tumbled upside down, hanging from the half-tied loop around her thigh as they plunged. Her stomach lurched. The onrush of wind ripped the breath from her throat. Something in her hip twisted almost to the point of breaking. The ground rushed up at her—cliffs, ice, shattered rock. Somehow, in the spinning madness, she caught a glimpse of soldiers, of Cho Lu and Raban down from the cliffside, standing just outside the cave, staring up at her, mouths agape.

Then the wind caught her, stripping them from her sight.

Just paces above the ground, the bird spread wide its wings, tried to pull up the way it might have if it had just taken an ibex or mountain goat. The rope cinched viciously tight around Gwenna's thigh, tighter then tighter still as the bird strained skyward, until she felt her hip had to give way. Then, with a snap like an overladen pine branch breaking in the dead of winter, the bird's wing ripped backward at a sickening, unnatural angle. Blood spattered from the gash in the creature's breast, and, still roped together, they fell the final two or three paces to the stones.

Gwenna managed to get an arm behind her head, but the blow stunned her. For half a dozen heartbeats she couldn't breathe. Her vision pinched into a tight, vertiginous tunnel, one she felt herself sliding down toward unconsciousness. Then the bird thrashed, yanking the rope around her leg, and the pain brought her back. Desperately she hacked at the line—how she'd managed to hold on to her knife she had no idea—hacked at it blindly until she felt the strands part, her thigh slip free of the awful noose.

She forced herself to her knees.

Barely a pace away, the bird struggled to rise. The broken wing, unstrung from the muscle meant to move it, flopped uselessly. It fixed her with one eye as she staggered to her feet, lashed out with its beak, lost its balance, struck wide. Gwenna stumbled forward into the opening, slipped on the blood-soaked rocks, smashed a knee, rolled to her side, just avoided another blow of the beak, and then she was right up against the blood-drenched feathers of the creature's breast. It took a moment to find the wound, and then she went to work again, hacking, stabbing, slicing the striated muscle with her blade, driving deeper and deeper as the animal screamed and lurched, until her arm was plunged well past the elbow.

For a woman of twenty-four years, she'd done her share of killing—various beasts back on the farm, people later, lots of people—Urghul, Annurian, Manjari, Dombângan. Some of them had it coming, some of them probably not. Killing was something you had to do sometimes to finish the mission, and so she'd learned to do it. This, though—there was no mission. Never in her life had she attacked a living thing with the blind, maniac frenzy she unleashed upon the kettral. Past reason, past thought, driven only by the ache to have it be *over* she hacked and hacked and hacked, fat and ribbons of flesh spattering her face, pain lancing up her arm and through her chest at each savage blow until she didn't know whether the screaming she heard came from the bird's beak or her own throat, whether, when the knife's point finally found the throbbing core and everything went hot and dark, it was the bird's great heart exploding, or her own.

34

As a kid, Akiil had sometimes listened to the legionary recruiters who came through the Quarter. They tended to promise the same things: food and clothing, a small purse of coin each month, the chance to go somewhere beyond the shit-reeking alleys and canals of the Quarter. It was an appealing proposition on the merits, but there was always someone in the crowd who pointed out that the price of that nice uniform and shiny shield was often a bloody and violent death. The recruiters were prepared for this objection. *All men die,* they pointed out. *Usually miserably, usually in pain. A death in the legions, however, is a glorious death, a proud death in defense of one's land and family. A death of honor.*

The whole notion had always struck Akiil as nonsense. He'd never come within a hundred miles of a battlefield, true, but he'd seen what a rusty knife could do to a person's guts and he wasn't buying the idea that it felt any better to have your life hacked out of you just because you were wearing a uniform. No. The idea of a good death seemed rotten at the root. On the other hand, he believed wholeheartedly that there was a whole range of *bad* deaths, from the disappointing to the truly revolting.

Being fed alive to a dozen five-hundred-pound blood hogs had to be one of the worst.

"Andraz will go first," the Captain said. He gave the man a benign smile.

Andraz gaped in drunken terror. He'd already pissed himself—the whole front of his pants was a dark, spreading stain. Maybe shit himself, too, although it was impossible to tell over the stench of the pig yard. The place reeked of feces, mud, and half-rotten slops. Greenheads buzzed over pools of stagnant water. Old eggshells and rinds were shoved up against the wooden walls in festering embankments. Something grayish white poked up from the mire—it might have been a broken stick or a fragment of bone.

"Why me?" Andraz managed finally. He stabbed a finger at Akiil. "It was his idea. *He* wanted to do it. He . . . he *made* me cheat. . . ."

In the stories and songs, grave danger had the ability to sober a man. Akiil had been drunk enough times to know that wasn't true. The approach of the city watch might take the edge off of two or three drinks, bring things back into focus that were starting to blur, but once you'd reached the bottom of the bottle nothing was going to haul you back. Not the city watch. Not a few tons of slavering hog. Over the course of the card game Akiil had tossed back enough black rum that he felt slightly numb, a little adrift, but he'd drunk nothing close to what Andraz had. The other man was lost in the liquor, tangled like a fly in the web of his own drunken mind.

Maybe that was a mercy. He was obviously terrified, but not as terrified as he would have been if he'd been able to see clearly the full tableau of his own approaching death.

The Captain put a hand on the man's shoulder. "I understand that it wasn't your idea. You are not smart enough to *have* ideas like this."

Andraz nodded furiously.

"I'm not. I'm *not*."

"That's why you are going first. This is a favor to you. A courtesy."

The drunken man gaped, speechless.

"It is not a pretty sight," the Captain explained, almost apologetically, "seeing a man consumed by pigs. You might think that you can imagine the horror, but I promise you, however vivid your imagination, the sight of the thing is worse. By throwing you into the pen first, I am sparing you this sight. At the same time"—he turned to smile at Akiil—"I am giving your friend the opportunity to dwell fully on the consequences of his actions."

Akiil took a deep breath. Even drunk, even faced with the hogs—which had begun to grind themselves hungrily against the wooden walls of the pen—the old monastic habits remained. When his heart began to pound, his body went to work slowing it down.

There is a way out, he thought. *There is always a way out.*

He started to turn, to look over his shoulder, then stopped himself. No need to tip his hand before it was time to make the play. He closed his eyes and, with an effort, summoned up the *saama'an* of the Captain's compound. The pig yard comprised half of an open courtyard closed in on all sides by the wooden walls of the buildings surrounding it. They'd come in through the only door—a heavy, triple-hinged wooden monster more appropriate to a fortress. Two guards stood at that door, one with a flatbow, one with a spear. Akiil could feel their eyes boring through his robe into his back. Getting past them would be almost impossible, and they weren't the only problem.

Directly behind him, thick hand heavy as an anvil on his shoulder, stood Fari. As he'd promised his brother earlier, he didn't seem to have any compunction about feeding a monk to the pigs. Fori had Andraz by the arm, the sharp point of a knife pressed to the man's back just behind his liver. The Captain himself twirled the club that had been Vicious Ryk's femur casually in his hand. Of Skinny Quinn there was no sign.

Akiil found himself obscurely glad of that last fact. She'd shown no compunction about betraying him, maybe because he'd betrayed her first, maybe because he'd been betraying her every day since the Captain took her. He wanted to ask her if she was all right, but the question would have been both stupid and self-serving. Despite the clean clothes and freshly washed hair, she wasn't all right. He didn't know the exact facts of what had happened to her, but the outlines were obvious enough. Ugly things had been done to her and in front of her. At least when he died she wouldn't be there to witness one more.

"Because I am in a charitable mood," the Captain continued, turning back to Andraz, "I will show you another mercy."

He pivoted with a dancer's grace, swung his arm in a wide arc, smashing the club into the side of Andraz's knee. With a sound like the limb of a snowbound tree snapping, the leg buckled. Andraz screamed. Fori caught him beneath the armpits, hauled him back up, slammed him against the wooden wall of the pen.

"Strong men," the Captain explained, "will struggle against the hogs. Sick Pyt actually survived half a morning in there. He'd ripped a board from the top of the pen, used it to defend himself until Bess got inside his guard and opened his gut with a tusk." He shrugged. "Anyway, the outcome's always the same, and I don't want to prolong your suffering. The broken leg will make things go faster."

Andraz puked, choked on it, leaned over the wall, hacked out a desperate sound somewhere between a moan and a sob, whatever human language he'd had obliterated by his terror. Death could do that to people, transform them into something other than themselves, strip away the last bits of dignity. For just a moment the memory of the slaughter at Ashk'lan washed over Akiil. At the time, he'd despised the monks for not fighting, for sitting cross-legged on the rocky ledge while the soldiers ran them through. Now, though, watching Andraz piss himself, shit himself, drool out the last of his horror, he found himself admiring the Shin. They hadn't fought, but they hadn't lost themselves either.

Andraz struggled, but Fori was twice his size and held the man pinned to the wall as though he were a child.

"You will want to watch this," the Captain said, turning back to Akiil. Which meant, of course, *You will not be able to watch this.*

Akiil felt himself sink deeper into some kind of calm. He took it, at first, for an effect of the rum, but it was deeper than drunkenness, colder. Finally, for once in his life, he hadn't escaped. Like everyone else, like Skinny Quinn and Horan and Butt Boy and Runt and Scial Nin, he'd been caught.

He met the Captain's gaze.

"You killed one of my friends here," he said.

His own voice sounded far away.

The Captain raised his brows. "Certainly possible. The hogs are always hungry."

"He was just a kid. We called him Butt Boy."

"Usually I would have other uses for a butt boy. A boy without obvious blemishes—not lame, no rotten teeth—can fetch good coin on the street."

"We called him Butt Boy because he was always saying 'But . . . But . . .' He refused to accept how things were. If you told him we were going to starve, he'd say, 'But . . .' and come up with a way to steal just a little more food."

The Captain pursed his lips. "Resourceful."

"When you took my other friends for your corners, I chalked them up as lost. Butt Boy, though, he said, 'But we can get them back. But we can save them. . . .'"

"Ah. Resourceful, but unwise."

"Your men caught him, beat him. I watched them drag him through the door just outside—I was hiding behind a barrel—but I didn't try to get to him. I only heard what happened later."

"And that," the Captain said, clapping him on the shoulder, "is why you remained alive."

"I'm good at that," Akiil said. "Remaining alive."

He found himself laughing.

He hadn't come back to the Quarter to die, certainly he hadn't planned on being caught, but now that the Captain had him, now that he was finally facing his own end, *really* facing it—nowhere to run, no more lies to tell—there was a shocking lightness to the moment, a *rightness* that he realized he'd been striving for his entire life.

"You shouldn't have come back," the Captain said.

"Actually," Akiil replied, "I never really left."

The man watched him awhile, his brow furrowed, then shrugged, turned back to Fori. "In he goes."

Andraz went over the fence like a straw doll, landed on his head and shoulder, slumped to the side, and the hogs were on him.

Akiil felt Fari's hand tighten on his shoulder; the man expected him to try to run. Instead, he stepped forward, right up to the edge of the wooden fence. All those years in the cold of the Bone Mountains the monks had trained him to watch, to observe, to *see,* and so, as a man was unmade in the mud by half-feral pigs, he saw.

They didn't go for the throat, the way a true predator might have. The goal—to the extent that beasts had goals at all—wasn't to make a quick, clean kill, but to *feast.* And so, as Andraz rolled to his side, tried to get his feet beneath him, they went for his belly. Their tusks weren't particularly sharp, but with all that weight behind them, they sank through the skin like hot iron into ice. Andraz groaned, folded in on himself, threw useless arms around the nearest hog. He looked like a man trying to hold on to something, to keep it near, though his fingers, nerveless, refused to fully close. With a quick snap of the neck, one of the hogs ripped open his stomach. Intestine slipped, slick and glistening, out into the mud. Two animals fell on it with a greedy grunting, rending it with their teeth, slurping it down with their rough pink tongues, while the first continued to gore the man, savaging his gut over and over, burying its snout in the ragged wound. Andraz jerked, twitched, hacked up blood. It was impossible to tell whether the motion was his own, or a result of the pig's savagery, whether he was still a man, or just a puppet for the beast.

A fourth pig shouldered in, buried its nose in the trough of the opened chest, ripped free something that looked like a liver, dragged it away from the scrum. Andraz opened his mouth, but no sound came out. Another hog—this one smaller than the rest and so shoved away from the tenderest meat—went to work on his face, ripping into the cheek, tearing free the flesh in ragged flaps. Another attacked the leg, worrying it like a dog, bolting down the gobbets of flesh, then shouldering its way back in for more.

And all the while Akiil watched.

This is how Butt Boy died.

The thought was true, but it didn't go far enough.

He stared, watched the pigs strip away the skin, the viscera, the muscle, until the bloody bone shone in the torchlight.

This is the way everyone dies.

That was more correct. Not at the jaws of feral hogs, obviously, but how much did it matter, really? In battle or in bed, sick or slipping beneath the sea, the results were the same. In the end, every person—every thief, every monk, every emperor, every gambler, every infant who'd barely drawn breath—died the same way. The human thing was unmade. Hogs gobbled the flesh, or ravens, or maggots, or it all just rotted in the hot sun. Whatever thoughts had lived in the body were gone, whatever fears and fury and dreams, gone, until in the end there was only blood and meat and bone and then, after enough time, enough years or centuries or millennia, not even that. Just dust. Just nothing.

Nothing.

The word closed over him like a whole empty ocean.

He floated inside it as the hogs feasted, buoyed up and plummeting at the same time, unmoored, untethered. He was aware, vaguely, of rage and horror somewhere, of a man who'd been an orphan, then a thief, then a monk who'd once felt such things, but that man was a stranger. He might as well have been a ghost.

"Are you ready?"

It took him a moment to find the source of the words—the Captain, studying him warily.

Was it so obvious that Akiil was gone? That he'd stepped free?

"Yes," he said, turning from the Captain back to the pigs, to those great agents of unmaking. "I'm ready."

Fari gave a grunt that Akiil took for surprise.

Then he felt the man's hand slip from his shoulder. A moment later, the huge man stumbled forward, collapsed against the wooden wall.

The Captain's head snapped around, eyes finding someone past and behind Akiil. He half raised his club, hesitated a moment, then lowered it.

Something is happening, Akiil thought.

He tried to remember why he should care.

"It has been a long time," the Captain said, "since anyone dared attack my men inside my home."

"We're not here for you," a voice replied. A familiar voice. "We're here for the monk."

Hugel, Akiil realized vaguely. The Aedolian guardsman.

The Captain hesitated, then spread his hands. "Take him, then. But deliver a message for me when you go, a message to your employer. Tell them, whoever they are, that I'll look forward to hosting them here, in this very courtyard, and soon."

Akiil turned in time to see Hugel shake his head. Instead of his Aedolian armor, the man was wearing a filthy tabard and shabby cloak, a half-decent disguise for someone wanting to walk the streets of the Quarter unnoticed. The bright steel in his hand, however, was unmistakable.

"I'm not your messenger, scum," he replied. "And my employer is Adare hui'Malkeenian, prophet of Intarra and Emperor of Annur, bright be the days of her life. If you threaten her again, I will open your throat where you stand."

The Captain frowned. "What does the Emperor want with a thieving monk?"

The question sounded like a riddle, one to which Akiil had long ago forgotten the answer.

35

Pain.

Then sunlight spangled across that pain.

She had no idea where she was or, for the space of many long breaths, *who*.

There was the sun like the head of a bronze spike hammered into the sky.

There, in the corner of her eye, the shard of a mountain peak.

There the ghost of the crescent moon in the bottomless blue.

And wrapped around her like a heavy cloak—agony.

She tried to form a word but had no mouth. For a moment, panic took her. Then she felt her lips peel apart, heard her moan drain out into the wind.

Blood.

She gagged on the taste of it.

It was dried blood that had sealed her mouth, blood plastering shut one of her eyes, blood sticking her clothes to her skin.

She forced herself to her knees. Pain threatened to fold her mind back in on itself, to toss her into darkness once more, but she closed her eyes and fought it down. When it had dimmed to a low scream, she opened her eyes once more and saw the bird, the kettral, dead—not just dead, *slaughtered*—the great bulk of its body slumped across the broken stone. She stared at it awhile, numb, dumb, lost.

Impossible.

The thought rose like a glimmering bubble through the murk.

Nothing could kill kettral.

Except . . .

She glanced down at her hands. One of them still clutched the bloody knife.

Oh Hull. The memory washed over her. *Holy Hull.*

The god of darkness did not respond. No one responded. When she twisted her head to look around, she found the mountains empty. There was only the dead kettral and, hunched over it, a half-dead woman.

She remembered her name at last, the name and the life that went along with it.

Gwenna Sharpe.

✝

By nightfall, she'd managed to drag herself down from the scree into the fringes of the forest. It was, she told herself, a warmer place to die, if nothing else. Already, though, she knew she wouldn't die. Her body throbbed, but she could feel her injuries knitting painfully closed, the bruise fading from her brain, the strength seeping back into her battered flesh. It struck her, somehow, as unfair. When she left the cave to go after the bird she hadn't expected to survive, to make it, to have to keep going, but there she was, huddled beneath the low-hanging boughs, still breathing. Worse, the fire that had consumed her higher on the mountain seemed to have burned itself out. When she searched inside for all that rage and loathing, she found only a great gulf, one she had no idea how to fill.

"You could start with food, you idiot," she muttered.

Though she could see well enough by the starlight filtering down through the branches, could hear small things scuttling through the brush, she had no strength to hunt, not even to set a snare, and so she leaned back against the rough bark of the tree, pulled her knees to her chest, heaped the brown needles around her as high as she could, wrapped her arms around her legs, then tucked her face down into the warm pocket of air. As shelter went, it wasn't much—barely more than nothing—but it would be enough.

At dawn, stiff from her injuries and the night's cold, she forced herself upright, then climbed back up the mountainside to the carcass of the dead bird. Grimly, she set to work. Without her rage and shame to propel her, the labor seemed to take ages, but at last she reached the liver, cut free a dozen long strips, laid them across a nearby boulder to dry, then sat down to eat one. The raw, bitter meat threatened to gag her, but she forced herself to keep eating. It would keep her alive, though what, exactly, was the point of that she had no idea.

From her seat on the boulder, she could see back up to the high peaks where the kettral nested—maybe a dozen miles away—and down the valley. Past the mouth of that valley, far beyond what she could see, lay the hills, the flatlands, and finally the strange abandoned city with its ziggurat, its empty homes and markets, its prisons carved from the rock, and its harbor, where the *Daybreak* swung at anchor, waiting.

She wondered briefly if Jonon and his men were searching for her, then discarded the thought. Now that the admiral had the eggs in hand, Gwenna herself added no more value to the expedition. Besides, anyone who saw the struggle between her and the kettral, anyone who watched the two of them plummet out of the sky, would have assumed her dead. A more sentimental captain might have ordered a search for her body, but Jonon wouldn't waste days hacking around the primeval woods of southern Menkiddoc, even for someone he didn't hate.

It was a strange relief to know she was alone and would be left alone. From her perch on the boulder, she gazed out over the valley. Despite Kiel's dire stories, the land at this southern end of the continent was healthy, if strange. She had her belt knife and a fire-striker, not to mention a whole kettral carcass full of bones from which she could fashion spears and bows. The forest below was filled with life. It had been years since her wilderness survival training, but she remembered some, enough. Within a month, she could have a snug cabin built—she studied the contours of the valley—*there,* where the grade gentled and the river slowed, deepening into pools.

As she sat, gazing out over that uninhabited world, the future blossomed inside her. Forget wilderness survival—her goal wouldn't be simply to survive. She'd left her family farm for the Kettral when she was a child, but she remembered enough to grow crops, to raise livestock. The people who'd lived in the farmsteads out on the plains would have left behind seeds, grain, plants suited to the place and climate. It would be a matter of a week or two to trek down there, scour the homes, and return. She could, of course, simply move into one of those cottages, but no. She'd grown up on a farm in a valley at the foot of the mountains, and returning to one felt . . . right. Clearing the fields would be a bitch, of course, she'd need to scavenge or fashion a decent ax, but as she imagined the labor she found herself smiling.

No one to kill. Better yet, no one to save. No one relying on her but herself. It would be dangerous, obviously. Plenty of ways to die on a farm, especially all alone out as the ass end of the world, but so what? If she died, she died. The fate of empires didn't hang on the lives of solitary farmers. . . .

"Don't get ahead of yourself, idiot," she muttered, shaking her head.

The first thing—before clearing fields or raising stock or building a cabin— was taking everything she could from the body of the kettral.

The talons were longer than her arm and strong as steel, the light bones of the wings made the best bows in the world, and the bird had enough down to stuff a dozen mattresses. Before going to work, however, she made her way up to the creature's head, laid a hand on its beak, gazed into the sightless eye.

"I'm sorry," she said quietly. "Thank you."

†

By nightfall, she'd stripped away as much as she could carry—two spans of bone, two talons, a dozen lengths of long, ropy tendon, and the rest of the liver. It would be enough to get her out of the mountains, at least. A small start on a new life.

She lashed the lot of it together, hefted the bundle onto her shoulder to test the weight, then, satisfied that she'd be able to carry it, set it down, leaned back against the boulder. Her breath steamed in the cold night air. Her body ached in a thousand places. It was different work from her Kettral training—all bending, and kneeling, and cutting. Peasant work. Farmer's work. It felt good.

Her stomach rumbled, and she took one of the strips of liver. It would be nice to get a fire going once she was back down in the trees, to start cooking the 'Kent-kissing stuff before shoving it in her mouth, but for now the liver was giving her strength, despite the bitter iron taste.

As she chewed, she studied the stars. Those would take some time to get used to. Already, though, she found herself sorting them into shapes. There was something that might have been a plow. And over there, a sickle, the star at its tip glinting wickedly. And then, if she tilted her head back, a pair of crossed swords, a fortress tower, a warship. . . .

A glimmer down near the head of the valley caught her eye, a faint light maybe fifteen miles distant, shifting, flaring, falling with some wind Gwenna didn't feel.

That would be Jonon, headed back to the ship. Making decent time, actually, considering they had the eggs to carry, not to mention Rat. Something inside Gwenna twisted uneasily at the thought of the girl. Who would be minding her on the trek back to the ship? Cho Lu or Pattick would be the best choice; she trusted them—as much as she trusted anyone, at least. Rat might even learn some more Annurian, start to confide in them. If Jonon had given her to Vessik, however, or Chent, or Lurie . . .

Gwenna put the liver down. It was too bitter, suddenly, to continue.

"Not for me to decide," she reminded herself.

In a week or so, they would be back on the ship—Jonon, Pattick, Chent, Rat, all of them. They'd weigh anchor, set the sails, and disappear over the horizon. It was sad what had happened to the girl—first abandoned by her people, then taken prisoner—but sad shit happened every fucking day. Even as Gwenna sat there, someone was dying somewhere, probably thousands of someones. While the liver churned in her stomach, orphans back in Annur were starving, girls and boys not much older than Rat were selling themselves to sailors for a few filthy coppers, someone was getting murdered, someone else was getting raped. At that very moment, somewhere in the world, some drunk son of a bitch was thrashing his wife, getting ready to start in on his son. While those strange stars swept silently overhead, people with the yellow pox were choking on their own phlegm, soldiers were burning down some miserable town or other, people were screaming, sobbing, begging, dying.

You couldn't think about it, all the world's suffering, or it would choke you. If you stopped to ponder all that misery, you'd never start moving again.

But I don't have to be part of it, Gwenna reminded herself. *Not out here. Not anymore.*

She forced herself to raise the meat back to her lips, made herself tear off a chunk, chew, swallow. She'd need the strength if she was going to carry her load down the mountain, not to mention building her cabin.

She took another bite.

Trying to stop all that suffering—it was like standing in the river hoping to block the current. The only people who attempted it were the stupid, the mad, and those too puffed up with their own pride to see how small they were. Well, if the past year had taught Gwenna anything, it was her own meager measure. Even if she went after Rat, then what? She couldn't save the girl. Jonon would just toss *both* of them in the brig. Or worse, her own return would somehow make things worse. Wasn't that, after all, the lesson of the Purple Baths? Wasn't that the lesson of the sea battle against the Manjari? Wasn't that the lesson the whole world was teaching every 'Shael-spawned day to anyone with the sense to listen?

"You cannot fix it, you bitch," she said out loud.

The campfire at the valley's mouth had gone out.

"Even if you wanted to, you can't catch them now. They've got a fifteen-mile start on you. You're in no shape to walk all that way, let alone run. Even if you were, you'd have to travel at night, probably *all* night, probably several nights in a row, and for what? You don't even *like* that vicious kid, and if you did, it wouldn't matter."

Even as she was talking, however, she found herself rising painfully to her feet, stretching her knees, testing the tendons of her ankles, measuring the miles by the light of the stars. She'd run more miles in her life. A lot more miles. Not that that made it any easier.

"Fuck," she muttered as she took the first painful step. "Fuck," with the next. "Fuck, fuck, fuck, fuck, fuck," as she made her way down the steep slope toward the forest, the valley floor, toward Jonon and Rat, toward the *Daybreak,* and Annur, back again, back a-*fucking*-gain toward the whole shitty, miserable, unfixable world.

36

"I can't do it."

Bien could have been talking about anything—running up the Arena stands, Goatface's new spear form, rolling out of bed in the morning—but the mix of dread and self-loathing in her voice told Ruc everything he needed to know. She was talking about her power. Or rather, her lack of it.

"I do everything Talal tells me, but I just can't . . ."

She shook her head, frustration baking off of her.

The two of them had been at it every night for weeks. They waited until after the others were asleep, then spent hours hunched over the table, searching for Bien's well. Ruc usually took up a post at the window. In theory he was making sure they weren't observed or overheard. In truth he was trying to give them as much space as possible. Them and himself. It was strange, watching Bien offer up her secrets so completely to this man she barely knew, telling him things that she'd hidden from Ruc their entire lives. It hurt, like something inside of him had torn open and was bleeding slowly into the space between his organs. He could bear the pain, though, if it meant she learned something that could keep her safe.

Evidently she had not.

"We shouldn't talk about it out here," he said quietly.

She'd taken advantage of the afternoon break to beckon him out of the yard, into their hidden gap between the mess hall and storage shed. The deep shade gave the illusion of privacy, but Ruc could hear the other Worthy laughing and cursing beyond the walls, just a few dozen paces away.

"I know."

"If Talal can't figure it out . . ." He shook his head. "I don't know, Bien. I don't know anything about this stuff."

The disappointment in her eyes was sharp, unexpected. "I don't want you to figure it out. I just wanted to talk to you about it. I—"

He raised a hand, cutting her off.

He could just make out, through the bulk of the warehouse, two red shapes. They were hazy, but obviously human, and they were coming closer, approaching at a lazy saunter.

Bien turned.

"What—"

"The better question might be *who,*" replied Rooster, stepping around the corner. He winked at Ruc, nodded to Bien. "Hello, lovebirds."

Snakebones followed a moment later, glanced around the shadowy nook, then laughed. "Didn't we fuck someone here back in the spring?"

Rooster tapped at his lower lip thoughtfully, then nodded. "That skinny boy, I believe. Lom Nao?"

The woman hooted. "Lom! Yes! He was *so* sweaty."

"It was a warm evening."

"Whatever *happened* to Lom?" the woman asked, shaking her head.

Rooster shrugged. "I put a dent in his skull a while back."

"What'd you do that for? I *like* sweaty boys."

"Plenty more where he came from." Rooster nodded cheerfully toward Ruc and Bien.

Ruc glanced past them. They appeared to be alone, their normal entourage of thugs and sycophants abandoned back in the yard. That might have evened the scales somewhat, except that Bien, despite Goatface's training, wasn't a fighter. Worse, the pair carried weapons: a bronze knife hung from Rooster's belt while Snakebones leaned forward on a long fishing spear. In theory, those weapons should have been locked away until the high holy days, but the theory was only as solid as the guards enforcing it, and the guards were nowhere in sight.

Rooster pointed at Ruc, then made a slow spinning gesture. "Turn around, love boy. Let's see what we have to work with here."

Snakebones cocked her head to the side, waiting.

Ruc didn't move.

"We haven't harmed you," Bien said, her voice tight but steady.

"Haven't *harmed* us?" Rooster smiled as he mimicked the words. "You haven't harmed us. My sweet, doe-eyed darling, what an unbecoming standard you set for yourself. I expect so much *more* from the two of you than the absence of harm."

"Sweat," Snakebones said, her eyes narrowed to slits. "I want your sweat."

Rooster made a face. "Not everyone shares your tastes, Bones. You know I prefer a certain cleanliness in my lovers."

"We're not your lovers," Bien said.

The man nodded amiably. "Not yet, of course! But that can be remedied."

"Not ever," she growled.

Snakebones chuckled.

Rooster frowned. "And here I was given to believe that the love of the priests of Eira extended to *all*."

"The love of the heart," Bien replied grimly, "is not the love of the body."

"Ah!" He clapped his hands together like a child receiving a gift, then tossed an arm around the shoulders of the woman at his side. She was at least a head taller, but the difference didn't seem to trouble him. "You see? That's a start! Maybe we haven't got to the bodies yet, but we have their . . ." He cocked his head to the side. "How did she put it? The love of their hearts."

Snakebones bared her teeth. "It's not their hearts I'm interested in."

Rooster shrugged. "Well, the heart is inside the body. I'm sure if we open them up, rummage around enough, all that love will come gushing out."

"Ooh," she purred. "Let's make them gush."

She lingered on the last word, then laughed gaily, nipped her companion on the ear, and gave a long lick up the side of his smooth-shaven cheek.

"I'm going to start screaming now," Bien announced matter-of-factly.

Snakebones furrowed her brow in mock consternation. "And we haven't even begun."

Rooster pointed out toward the yard. "You may not have noticed, but people are *always* making noise in here—grunting, shouting, cursing, and yes, even an unseemly amount of screaming. No one seems to care much, but by all means—add your voice to the chorus!"

"There are easier targets than us," Ruc said quietly.

"Easier?" Rooster chuckled. "Who said we were looking for easy?"

"There's no way you can hold both of us at the same time."

"There's no need to hold you down," Snakebones pointed out, "if you're dead."

Ruc studied the woman. Eagerness and lust baked off of her in a red-black haze. *This* was why she'd volunteered for the Worthy—not to face the Three, or not primarily—but for the thrill of bending men and women to her wishes. He'd seen her about it dozens of times already, leaning over people in the mess hall, snapping at them, grabbing whatever she could grab. He'd watched cats play similar games with mice and small rats, batting at them, tossing them in the air, nipping at the tails as the creatures cowered or tried to flee. . . .

"You don't want us dead," he said.

Snakebones stared at him incredulously, then turned to Rooster, as though to share the hilarity.

"No one sweats when they're dead," Ruc went on. "No one cringes. No one cries. And that's the fun of it for you, isn't it? Not the sex. A woman among the Worthy? You can get sex anywhere. It's the cringing and crying you want."

Snakebones laughed, but this time anger edged her mirth.

"I won't deny that I enjoy a little light cringing."

"You're not going to get it. You don't want to kill us, at least not right away, but there's no way you can hold us."

Rooster ran a hand over his spiked comb of hair, then waggled a finger at Ruc.

"You think you're smart."

"I think I can count. There's two of you, two of us. Unless you kill us, we're walking out of here. Unmolested."

The shorter warrior sighed. "He may have a point, Snakebones. I don't know that I can hold them both while you do . . . whatever it is you're planning to do. I guess we'll have to involve a fifth in this little tryst of ours."

Ruc stole a quick glance at the storehouse. No one was approaching, despite Rooster's threats.

"Another day, maybe," Ruc said, stepping forward.

Snakebones moved faster than he would have believed, pivoting on one foot, whipping her spear at him. Ruc's body took over as his mind was still grappling with the fact, tossing up an arm to block the shaft, knocking it aside, pulling back into a defensive guard.

Rooster raised an eyebrow. For the first time since they'd met, he looked surprised.

"Not bad, love boy. Not bad. Where'd you learn that?"

Ruc ignored the question. Obviously, he'd been wrong. Snakebones really *was* willing to kill them. To kill *him*, at least. It made a bleak sort of sense. She wouldn't be able to watch him squirm, but then she and Rooster could take their time with Bien. The realization should have terrified him, but he'd learned from the delta gods themselves how to handle terror.

He could still remember Hang Loc abandoning him in the middle of a river churning with *qirna*. The fish, Ruc knew, were attracted to only two things: movement and blood. He wasn't bleeding, which meant that if he could remain perfectly still in the neck-deep water, if he could clamp down on his panic, then he would survive. All day, they left him there, watching from the bank, Kem Anh with her golden eyes, Hang Loc with his dark ones. Night fell. Ruc could feel the fish brushing against his chest, his shins, some of them even testing the dead flesh of his feet with small bites. On the sand, Hang Loc and Kem Anh coupled noisily. All night he waited, measuring out each breath so that his chest didn't rise or fall too quickly. When the morning finally came, he looked down and found the fish gone, along with his fear.

The same calm settled over him now. A mistake would doom both himself and Bien. Rooster still hadn't drawn his knife. He was watching with a mix of interest and amusement. Snakebones, however, looked deadly serious. She was fast, faster than any of the Worthy aside from maybe Rooster himself. And the spear gave her the reach.

She feinted high, feinted low.

Ruc let go of all the techniques Goatface had been trying to drill into him and let his body respond. Once, twice, three times he knocked away the spear. She was pressing him, striking at his arms and legs, but avoiding the chest, the stomach, the head. Evidently she wanted him alive after all, alive but disabled. That limited her attacks.

The next time the spear lashed out, he caught it just behind the bronze head. For a moment he and the woman stood there, frozen, each straining with the shaft as the sharp head glittered a handsbreadth from his shoulder. Her breath came in gasps between her bared teeth as she bore down. She was strong—far stronger than Ruc would have expected—and she held the spear's shaft in both hands. He shouldn't have been able to hold it back, hadn't really expected to. His muscles bunched with the strain, trembled, but refused to give way.

The woman met his eyes, her grimace turned to a grin, and, without warning, she ripped the spear back. He let go almost in time, but the barb caught his palm, ripping a shallow furrow through the skin.

Snakebones grinned even wider.

She kept her eyes on Ruc as she spoke to Rooster. "Our fifth friend should be here any moment now."

And then, between one breath and the next, it hit him.

The gash in his hand burned as though branded. Pain raged in the wound for a moment, then crawled into his veins, began to drag its agonizing way up his arm. He recognized the shape of that pain, though in his languageless days in the delta he'd had no words for either the small orange snake or its poison. He knew that its bite could paralyze a mud rat or jaguar, but it was only later, when he joined the Vuo Ton, that he realized it did the same to humans as well. Most humans, anyway. Those not suckled for years at the breast of Kem Anh.

Snakebones stepped back. She was breathing heavily, but he could see the eagerness gleaming in her eyes.

Rooster spread his hands in mock apology. "What can I say? She cheats."

"Don't worry," Snakebones cooed. "It won't kill you. It'll just make you a little more docile."

"What did you do to him?" Bien demanded, shoving her way forward, anger blotting out her fear of the warriors or their weapons.

Ruc started to lift a hand to hold her back, then stopped himself, let the limb fall.

Snakebones's smile widened.

"He's just feeling a little stiff, sweetheart," she said, stepping forward, reaching out for Bien. "Not stiff in the exciting way, I'm afraid, but Rooster and I are used to making do."

To Ruc's shock, Bien lashed out, aimed a punch directly at the other woman's face.

Snakebones caught it, twirled her around as though the two of them were dancing, then dragged her close, pressed her body against Bien's, her face to the back of her neck. Bien struggled, but the woman held her tight.

"First thing we do," she murmured into Bien's ear, "is we watch."

Ruc's heart raged. He ached to hurl himself at Snakebones, to shatter her face, to rip Bien from her grip, then keep ripping. He forced the instinct down. A predator knew when to lie still and when to lunge.

The pain in his arm had eased, whatever fortified his blood chasing the poison back until all that remained was a nasty throbbing. He ignored the strength returning to his limbs and instead let himself stiffen, then drop to the soft dirt. Rooster narrowed his eyes, as though sensing something wasn't right.

Snakebones had no such misgivings.

"Let's see what kind of lover your man really is," she said, dragging Bien down so that her face was a few inches from Ruc's own.

Her eyes brimmed with horror. "I'm sorry," she said. "Ruc, I'm *sorry*."

He met her gaze but didn't reply. The poison of the orange snake locked the jaw along with everything else.

Above and behind him, he heard Rooster approaching finally.

"One thing I appreciate about the Dombângan fashion," the man said, reaching down, flipping up Ruc's *noc* so that he was naked from the waist down, "is that we never adopted trousers."

He slid a hand up between Ruc's legs.

Bien's face was torn between disbelief and rage. Ruc had seen her frightened before, seen her angry, but never this.

He closed his eyes, pictured a jaguar motionless in the high grass as he felt the other man kneel behind him. The jaguar was the delta's most patient predator. No wasted motion. No premature haste. A jaguar would wait and wait and wait, half a day if necessary, patient as sunlight, patient as silence, patient as the sky, watching its prey draw closer and closer, smelling and hearing as much as seeing it, *feeling* the movement in its paws. Only when that prey was close enough, only when all chance of escape was gone, only when fate closed motionlessly around its victim, did it strike.

His elbow caught Rooster in the jaw.

The man's head snapped back.

Ruc rolled, tossed the weight of his body off, struck Snakebones in the temple with a vicious fist.

She bellowed—half pain, half rage—jerked back, tried to keep her hold on Bien, but Bien was already twisting away. She might not know how to fight, but she'd spent a lifetime evading groping hands, and Snakebones was rattled, half-dazed by the blow, and within moments Bien was free.

Ruc surged to his knees to find Rooster up already, though hunched over, blood draining between his teeth, reaching for the blade at his belt. Ruc lunged, caught him around the waist, bore him back to the dirt, drove his shoulder into the other man's gut, felt the air rush out of him.

"Come on," Bien was shouting. "Ruc, come *on*."

He didn't want to come on. He wanted to kill the man beneath him. He could do it, too. He could feel the ability uncoiling inside of him, but Bien was screaming.

"*Ruc!* The spear! She has the *spear*!"

He let go of Rooster, rolled to the side, saw motion out of the corner of his eye, and kept rolling. The tip of the fishing spear drove into the soft dirt, raising a furrow. Snakebones, wobbly on her feet and drooling as much blood as her companion, yanked the weapon back, lost her balance, stumbled against the storehouse wall.

A hand closed on Ruc's shoulder—Bien, dragging him up, out, away from the fight, away from his own strength and rage, back toward light, and life, and safety, toward a world where love was still just barely possible.

For a perfect, frozen moment, he hated her.

37

Gwenna caught up with the admiral and his crew just after daybreak, a few miles from the coast.

Luckily, it was Cho Lu and Pattick bringing up the rear of the column, rather than one of the others. Cho Lu and Pattick and, on a short leash between them, Rat.

So, Gwenna thought, staring at the girl's skinny back, her tattered pants, the squirrel's nest of her hair, the admiral hadn't given her to Chent or Vessik after all.

She almost coughed up a laugh. Could have skipped the whole trip. Maybe it would have been fine if she'd stayed in the mountains alone, building that cabin.

As she watched, Rat paused, sniffed at the air, then turned.

"Come on," Pattick said, not ungently. Instead of tugging on the leash, he put a hand on the girl's shoulder.

Rat, however, after a moment's shocked stare, snatched the leash from his hand.

"Hey—" Pattick exclaimed. He reached for her, but the girl was too fast. She sprinted back along the rough track, then hurled herself at Gwenna so violently she almost knocked her over, buried her face in the filthy blacks, kept growling something over and over and over. It was only when Gwenna managed to pry her away that she could make out the words.

"Need Gwenna Sharpe." There were tears in the girl's eyes, but she sounded furious. "*Need* Gwenna Sharpe."

She wrapped her arms around the girl's slender shoulders. Such strength there. Such fragility. "I'm here."

When she finally looked up, she found the two legionaries staring, frozen, as though she were one of Menkiddoc's *gabhya* come to hideous life.

"Sweet Intarra's light," Pattick breathed finally.

She shook her head. "Nope. Just me."

In fact, she felt like the opposite of the goddess of light. She'd plunged herself into the river at the valley's base, tried to scrub off the kettral's blood, pretty much failed. It remained matted in her tangled hair, soaked through her blacks, dark beneath her fingernails. The intervening days and miles had done nothing to improve the situation. Grime caked her face, her arms, her ears, her hands. . . . She might have expected the sweat to clean it away—she'd been stumbling forward more or less constantly for days—but all it did was lace the dirt with a thick salt rime. There'd been no time to forage or to hunt, and so for the first few days she ate strips of the bird's liver, ate it until she woke one morning to find it crawling with maggots. After that she lived on water from streams and the thin taste of her own exhaustion.

Slowing to a stop proved a problem, actually. Without the momentum carrying her on, she wobbled a moment on her feet.

Pattick slammed his half-drawn sword back into its sheath, darted over, took her by the elbow.

"I'm not your 'Kent-kissing grandmother," she growled.

Cho Lu was beaming. "You *lived* through that?"

She nodded. "Evidently."

Between one breath and the next, however, the legionary sobered. He and Pattick exchanged a fraught glance.

"You lived," Cho Lu said after a pause. "And we left you." He smelled of shame. "We wanted . . . Jonon ordered us to pack up and march out, said there was no time for a search."

"We should have searched," Pattick said quietly.

"Don't be stupid," she replied, unsure what to do with this unexpected emotion. "A woman tied to a kettral falls out of the sky? You can be forgiven for thinking she's dead."

"Not you," Cho Lu insisted.

"Especially me."

Pattick shook his head. "We should have looked."

"Sweet 'Shael on a stick, boys, it's not your fault. You're soldiers. You've got orders to follow."

Cho Lu frowned. "There's stuff more important than orders."

"Not to a soldier, there's not," she replied, raising her voice, shifting her gaze past the legionaries. "Wouldn't you agree, Admiral?"

For some reason, Jonon had been marching near the rear of the column. He was far enough away from Pattick and Cho Lu that Gwenna had dared to hope he'd *keep* marching, but at the sound of Cho Lu's first exuberant whoop he'd turned, a hand on the pommel of his cutlass. His gaze, as he approached, brimmed with the same irritation and disdain that she'd come to expect, but for the first time since she'd met him he smelled faintly wary. Not the wariness that one soldier reserved for another—nothing so dignified. More the guarded caution of a farmer around a dog that might have gone rabid.

"There is a rich irony," he said, "in listening to *you,* of all creatures, talk about the following of orders."

Another Gwenna in another life might have argued, but that woman was dead.

"Easier talking about it sometimes, than actually doing it," she replied.

"She killed a *kettral,*" Cho Lu put in.

The admiral shook his head. "A military is not run on the individual whims of its various soldiers, let alone by indulging the suicidal madness of women who hold no rank at all."

"She saved my life," Pattick added quietly, not daring to meet Jonon's gaze.

Jonon turned to him, face grave. "Your life."

"Yes, sir."

"Is that what you think this expedition is about?" the admiral demanded. "*Your* life?"

Pattick hesitated. "No, sir, but—"

"If I had wanted to save lives, yours or any others, I would never have weighed anchor back in Pirat. When I accepted the Emperor's charge, I did so knowing men would die, *good* men." He shook his head. "We serve a cause greater than ourselves, soldier, and in order to serve that cause we must look beyond our own lives, beyond the lives of our friends, look to the larger work. It is my job to see that we never take our eyes from that work, and when one of you disobeys me—even if the reason seems selfless, noble—you endanger the mission. Don't be seduced by stories of mad individual bravery. Trust me when I tell you that way leads only to chaos, to ruin, and to failure. The Kettral were the jewel of the Annurian military, brilliant tacticians, peerless warriors, and what did they do? They destroyed themselves."

He'd begun by speaking to Pattick and Cho Lu, but at some point during the speech he turned his attention to Gwenna.

"I will not allow you—either through your neglect or your recklessness—to endanger this expedition further. When we return to Annur, you will face trial. Until then, from the moment we reach the *Daybreak* until the moment we dock, you will remain, like any other disgraced prisoner, in the brig."

Whatever else Gwenna thought about the admiral, he kept his word.

As soon as they were back on board the ship, she and Rat were led back belowdecks and tossed into the darkness.

As the door slammed shut behind them, Rat—who'd caught a glimpse of the seated form leaning against the far bulkhead—raised her small hands in the way Gwenna had taught her, as though she expected to have to fight. Gwenna put a hand on her shoulder.

"It's all right. Captain Dhar is a friend."

"Friend?" Rat asked warily.

"Well," Gwenna amended. "He only tried to kill me once, which is more than I can say for you."

Dhar's chuckle was dry, rusty. His voice, when he spoke, sounded as though it had not been used for years.

"Welcome back, Commander Sharpe. Who have you brought with you?"

"This is . . ." Gwenna hesitated. She felt guilty, suddenly, for the name she'd given the girl. "Rat, what's your real name? The name your parents gave you?"

The girl's eyes flashed fury. She bared her teeth, then turned away.

Gwenna hesitated. "I call her Rat. We found her on shore. There's a city there. We found . . ." She shook her head, lowered herself to the deck, leaned back against the bulkhead. She might be a prisoner, but it felt good to finally sit. "We found a lot of things we didn't expect to find," she concluded finally. "I'll tell you about it, but first, I'm going to sleep."

She woke to the gentle motion of a ship under way. Rat was still snoring, her gangly arms wrapped around Gwenna like a snare. Gradually, gently, Gwenna disentangled herself. Across the brig, Dhar was awake—she could tell by his breathing—but his head was bowed, eyes closed. Praying, maybe, or just waiting.

"A long time in here alone," she said finally. "I'm glad to see you haven't gone mad."

He stared into the darkness for a while before replying.

"The solitude plays tricks on the mind, but my *davi* is not yet complete."

"Your duty."

He nodded.

"How is it not complete? Your ship is at the bottom of the ocean, along with your men. What's the duty of a commander who has nothing and no one to command?"

"Are you asking this question of me?" Dhar replied. "Or of yourself?"

"Does it matter?"

"Naturally it matters. Your *davi* is not the same as my own."

"Is it your *davi* to sit in the fucking brig until Jonon decides to kill you?"

"Right now, my *davi* is to endure."

She shook her head. *"Why?"*

"Because there is work still to do."

"What work?"

"When the time comes, it will be revealed."

"It will be revealed." She let her head fall back against the bulkhead. "So it's all some kind of mystical bullshit."

Dhar studied the darkness where she sat.

"You are changed from when you left."

"That happens, right?" she asked wearily. "People change?"

"Tell me, Commander Sharpe—in what do you believe?"

"No." She closed her eyes. She'd met religious fanatics before—there had been more than a few back on the Islands—but she hadn't figured Dhar for one. "Just—forget it."

"You are locked in this space with me. We have weeks if not months before our return to your empire. Yet you would prefer silence over honest conversation."

"If I want conversation, I'll talk to Rat," Gwenna said. The girl shifted in her sleep without waking. "At least she doesn't know enough Annurian to make shit up."

The captain cocked his head to the side. "Why does it frighten you, the thought of your unfinished duty?"

"What bothers me isn't the unfinishedness of it. What bothers me is the thought that it's knowable in the first place. What bothers me is that I used to think I knew it."

She exhaled slowly, steadily. Since killing the kettral, the worst of her fear had dissipated. The stabbing panic was gone. She could still feel the dread, like a weight settled on her shoulders, but it had slumped into something she could bear, something she could carry. Hesitation threaded every thought, but it was now the hesitation of a woman who didn't trust her own growing health. *Better* wasn't a word she dared think, let alone speak aloud. She didn't know if she would ever be better, but something was . . . different.

That difference, however, left her baffled. Relieved as she was to have climbed free of her mind's abyss, she didn't recognize the land where she'd arrived. She wasn't the useless wreck from the voyage south—she'd proved that to herself—but she wasn't Kettral either. She wasn't the Gwenna Sharpe who'd quit on everything, who'd been ready to give up and die, but she wasn't the Gwenna Sharpe who'd commanded the defense of Andt-Kyl, not the woman who'd stormed into fights never quite thinking she could fail. That woman had known things, believed in things, trusted things. As she sat there, wrapped in Rat's arms and the darkness of the brig, she had no idea *what* to believe.

Finally, she tipped her head toward the vessel's stern. "There was a city back there, a *huge* city, where people worshipped monsters, where they fed their own families to them. What about them?"

"What about them?" Dhar replied.

"They probably thought they were doing the right thing, right? When they listened to the screams of their parents, of their children, did they think they were just following their *davi*?"

"People err. It is not uncommon."

"And how do you know," Gwenna demanded, "that we're not the ones in error? All these years, I went where they told me. I fought the people I was told to fight, saved the people I was told to save, killed the people I was told to kill. . . ."

As she spoke, her own father's words floated back to her: *I got tired of fighting other people's wars.*

"When you first spotted the *Daybreak* on the horizon," she went on, "you attacked us. We attacked you back. We can't *both* have been right."

"I told you already that I was wrong. I have accepted it."

"You have *accepted* it?" The boldness of the notion stole her breath. "What about all the people who *died*? Have *they* accepted it?"

"Perhaps a few. For most, no. It is for this," he said, ducking his head between his spread hands, "that I carry my shame."

"And do you ever think that instead of carrying it, you should just . . . do something else?" In the darkness she saw again her farm at the valley's mouth, saw herself harvesting crops, feeding livestock, living a clean, quiet, decent life. No chance of that now, not anymore. "Don't you ever think you should get out before you make another mistake, before you get more people killed?"

Dhar pursed his lips. "If I were visiting my brother, and, in trying to cook a chicken, I burned down his house, should I walk away? Or should I help him to rebuild?"

"It wasn't a house, it was a ship. And they weren't your brothers, they were your men. And they're not irritated. They're dead."

"No, Commander Sharpe. The whole world is my brother's house."

She stared at him. "The world's a big place. And it's pretty fucking broken."

"All the more need, then, for the people who would rebuild it."

"I'm not one of those people."

"You will pardon me if I do not believe this."

"Why wouldn't you believe it, you stubborn prick? Do you know what Kettral *do*? They don't rebuild houses. They stab people, and they shoot people, and they poison people. They tear things down and blow things up, they burn what's left, and then they salt the fucking ground. *That's* what Kettral do. That's what they *are*."

The words hung there a moment, trembling in the air, then fell away. Rat muttered something in her sleep that might have been a plea or a curse.

"And yet," Dhar replied gravely, "as you have never tired of reminding me, you are not Kettral."

†

Sometime in the middle of the watch on the fourth or fifth day after leaving port, the small slot at the bottom of the door—the space where the guard delivered and removed the food and water—darkened. Something black and furred squirmed its way through the gap.

The creature smelled of piss and bilge water, scuttled boldly across the decking, confident in the darkness, sniffing out a few fishbones that Gwenna had set aside, brushing up against Rat in the darkness. The girl jerked away, then lashed out with her heel, hammering the creature on the hindquarters so hard that it squealed.

"Thing!" she shouted, kicking out blindly again and again. "Fucking *thing*!"

The creature hissed, snapped at the girl, snatched a bone, then fled back through the slot beneath the door.

"Just a rat," Gwenna said. She felt the word as it left her mouth, the barb of it, the regret welling like blood.

She could smell the child's anger bleeding into the soft, too-sweet smell of confusion.

"Rat?"

She shook her head. "It's nothing."

"Rat?" the girl pressed.

"Just a little animal. What we call that kind of animal."

The girl stared into darkness. "Lives on ships? Eats trash?"

"Some of them, I guess. There's all kinds—"

"Ugly. Filthy."

Gwenna shook her head, tried to take the helm of the conversation. "What's your real name?"

Rat closed her eyes, turned her face away. All her laughter had evaporated.

"What's your name?" Gwenna asked again. She tried to make her voice gentle, found she had no idea how.

"Rat," the girl replied. "Real name is Rat."

38

The light of the fish-scale lantern washed Bien's face a bloody red. She was finishing up the stitching on a leather bracer. She looked, Ruc thought, almost nothing like the priestess of Eira who had fled the burning temple months earlier. The scars were the most obvious change—she'd picked up a gash over her right eye that carved a puckered hook down through the brow, along with a split lower lip that had healed a little crooked. She was leaner, too, more muscled, like a woman who'd spent her life tossing nets in the delta or rowing loads of reeds and timber up and down Dombâng's canals. Her hands were callused, her black hair hacked short, one of her front teeth chipped. It was her eyes, though, that he had the most trouble recognizing. They were still that same, rich brown, but her gaze, which had once been earnest and open, had grown hard, guarded, wary.

"That was my fault," she said.

"It was Rooster's fault, and Snakebones's," Ruc replied. "They're the ones who attacked us."

Monster, Mouse, and Stupid, along with Talal, were over at the mess hall, listening to the latest gossip. Apparently some fishers had seen monsters out in the delta. Not the usual crocs and jaguars, but something stranger, something worse. On another night, Ruc would have stayed, too. After the afternoon's assault, though, it seemed safer to stay out of sight for a while. Besides, he already knew there were monsters in the delta. He'd seen them. He could get the details later.

"They attacked us because I gave them the chance." She stared into the lantern's flame. "I was the one who insisted we go back there."

"Doesn't mean you should blame yourself. Besides, we survived."

She made a sound like a hacked-up laugh. "That's what we're down to, isn't it? Survival."

"It's a start."

"More like an end."

Hot night air, thick with the scent of mud and shit, stirred the canvas covering the window. She pulled another stitch through the leather.

"Do you ever think about the temple?" he asked. "About the goddess?"

She glanced over at him. "All the time."

"What do you think about?"

"How I've failed her."

"You're alive. That's not a failure. You can't spread Eira's truth if you die in here."

"What truth?" Her voice was quiet, but the tendons in her wrists stood rigid with the strain of trying to force the needle through the thick leather. "That love is a flame? That it can light a way for the lost, warm the weary, prepare a forge for the sword, or a pyre for the impious?"

"Sure, if you want to quote directly from the Teachings."

She shook her head. "What does any of it mean?"

Ruc hesitated. There was an answer to the question. Dozens of answers, actually. For centuries priests had written commentaries, and sermons, and treatises on the Teachings, elucidating every paragraph, every line, every word. Bien, however, knew those writings even better than he did. She wasn't asking him to trot out the old exegetical certainties. He wasn't sure, in fact, that she was really asking *him* anything at all. The short distance between them felt almost unbridgeable. He wanted to comfort her, to hold her, could have dealt with some comfort of his own, in fact, but they were like two people who shared a horrible secret. Each of them knew—knew in a way that none of the other Worthy could ever understand—what the other had betrayed in order to stay alive. In the early days, Ruc thought that knowledge might draw them closer. It had not.

She glanced up from her work. "Why are you looking at me like that?"

"Like what?"

"You're staring at me the same way you did back in the temple, when I first used my power. Like I'm a stranger, someone you've never even seen before."

"You're not a stranger," he said, wondering, even as he spoke the words, if they were true.

"I'm glad *you* recognize me," she replied wearily, "because I don't. I don't recognize these hands," she said, raising them. "I don't recognize my face when I stare in a scrub bucket. I don't recognize my dreams—they're all just spear thrusts and fire and screaming and killing."

"A lot has changed."

It was such a preposterous understatement he half expected her to laugh. Instead she picked up the bracer once more, went back to her stitching as she spoke.

"It's when things change that we need most to keep the faith."

"Have you lost it?"

"I don't know. I know that I used to be filled with love, filled to overflowing. I loved the beggars and bakers and the young brides with flowers in their hair. Now"—she punched the needle through the leather, drew it out the other side—"that's almost impossible for me to imagine. I certainly don't love Rooster. Or fucking Snakebones. That bitch."

"Rooster and Snakebones tried to rape us."

She shook her head. *"Love those who come bearing bread in their hands and those who bear only burdens.*

"Love the cruel with the kind, the beautiful with the beasts, your foes alongside your friends."

"Easy to say," Ruc replied, "when those foes aren't burning down your temple, murdering everyone you know, trying to feed you to the creatures of the delta."

"And is that the kind of priestess I was? One who believed things only when they were easy?"

"You're still a priestess. They can force you to fight, but they can't take that from you."

"They didn't take it," she replied grimly. "I gave it up."

Suddenly, the needle punched through the leather, stabbed into her hand. Instead of yelping, or cursing, or dropping the bracer, she just stared numbly at that length of steel protruding from her skin. When she pulled it out, a drop of blood welled from the puncture. Gently, she laid the leather on the table, then looked at him.

"I thought we would have kids together."

The world seemed to spin around him the way it had years before, when he dove too deep, held his breath too long.

"Me too."

"I'm glad we didn't."

The words landed like a slap, but he forced himself to nod. "Dombâng is broken. It's no place to raise a family."

"The problem isn't the city, Ruc. Or not only that. It's us. We're not what we thought we were."

"What did we think we were?"

"Priests. Heralds of a goddess of mercy and light."

"I was never much of a herald."

"You were my herald," she replied quietly. "If someone can love me like that, I thought, someone like *him* . . ."

"Like him?" he asked quietly.

She met his eyes. "You weren't . . . a typical priest."

"Neither were you."

"But we *were* priests." Tears stood in her eyes. "And it wasn't just the Teachings and the prayers. Whenever I doubted, I just needed to look at you, to see your strength, your love—"

"You have it backward," he said, cupping her cheek in his hand. "I was the one who stumbled out of the delta. Eira found me eventually, but *you* found me first."

She shifted away from his touch.

"It's not the same now."

"Of course it's not the same. Our friends were burned to death. Our home was destroyed. We were dragged here—"

"I mean between us." Bien's gaze was a snare. "I saw how you looked at me when I killed those men, back in the temple. I see how you look at me now, whenever Talal and I work on finding my well."

"No."

"Yes."

"Maybe we've failed the goddess, but we haven't failed each other."

"Haven't we?" She bit her lip so hard it looked ready to burst. "I'm a fuck-ing *leach,* Ruc. I told myself that I'd learn to use my power so we could escape, but we haven't escaped. All I've used it to do is *murder* people. There's a reason people hate leaches. There's a *reason* they think we're polluted."

He wanted to gather her in his arms, but there was something about the way she was sitting—at an angle to him, as though she were hiding something, or preparing to flee.

"I don't hate you. I don't think you're polluted."

She smiled an exhausted smile. "But that's not the same as loving me, or thinking I'm beautiful."

Ruc stared at her. "There's nothing I can say, is there?"

"Love's not just a matter of saying the right words."

"What about the feeling underneath the words?"

"What feeling is that?"

"That you are brilliant, and beautiful, and brave."

She looked at him awhile, then turned away. "I didn't understand."

"Didn't understand what?"

"Right up until the temple burned, I believed all of that, too—that I *was* brave, that I was beautiful, that I was a capable servant who *deserved* the favor of the goddess."

"You are."

She picked up the needle once more, prodded at a scab across the back of her fingers. "There is so much hate in my heart now, so much rage. . . ."

He reached out, gently withdrew the needle from her grip. She let it go without complaint.

"Even Eira has a dark side," he said. "Think of the *avesh*." If there was a way to reach her, to draw her back, maybe this was it. "Even the goddess of love has a line she will not cross. The *avesh* is a monster; it devours its own children. All the statues, all the paintings show Eira and her faithful creatures fighting the thing, defeating it. Sometimes she's impaling it with her sword. Sometimes the wolves have it in their teeth. . . ."

"What if the wolves aren't going to kill it?"

He stared at her.

"What if," she continued, "they're not eating it, but carrying it? The way they carry their pups."

"Why would Eira help an *avesh*? And if the wolves are helping it, what about the paintings where she's running it through with a sword? Or the ones where she's burning it with the hand that holds the fire?"

"What does that sword represent, Ruc? What does the fire represent?"

The truth went through him like a blade. Like a flame. "Love," he said quietly. "Love."

"She's not slaughtering the *avesh*. . . ."

"She loves it," he concluded.

Bien nodded wearily. "She loves it. Eira's grace extends even to the filthiest creatures, even to the most monstrous."

"This isn't from the sermons. I've never read anything like this in the commentaries."

"So?" She shrugged. "The priests who wrote those commentaries were just people. They weren't prophets."

"Neither are we."

"But you see it now. The *avesh* is there to show there is no limit to the breadth of Eira's love." She withdrew her hand gently from his, put it to his cheek. "You and I though—we have limits. We don't know how to love what isn't good."

He watched her awhile, savored the feel of her hand against his skin. The Arena afforded almost no privacy. It had been weeks since they'd been alone. He shifted in his chair, lifted the bracer from her grasp, set it down on the table. She let it go without protest.

"What are you doing?" she asked.

"I'm going to kiss you."

"That's not going to fix anything."

"Maybe not," he said, then leaned forward.

Her lips were chapped, ragged from too much sun and too little water. For a moment, she didn't move. Then, with a cry deep in her throat, the half sob of a dying creature, she pulled him into her. Her mouth opened to the kiss—the urgency was almost violent—then she was climbing out of her chair and into his lap, straddling him, thighs pressed tight around his hips, one hand reaching down to pull up his *noc*.

He felt himself harden. For all that people talked about sex and love in the same breath, the needs of the body were older than love or language, bred in the bones. A growl rose in his throat. The weariness in his legs forgotten, he rose, Bien still clutching him, crossed the room in three strides, tossed her onto the bunk. Her eyes were shut tight, lower lip caught between her teeth. He watched her a moment, then lifted her *noc,* slid down her body, nipping at her breasts as he passed, buried his face between her legs. She took her head in his hands, pressed her hips up into him, shuddered once, then twisted violently, shoving him away.

"I can't," she gasped. "I can't."

He took a deep, ragged breath, tried to find his way back.

Before he could reply, she rose, turned away.

"They were going to rape us," she said.

He sat up slowly, straightened his *noc.* The sight of his own body seemed suddenly obscene.

"They were."

"I thought . . ." When she turned back to him, he saw that she was shaking. "I thought this might be a way to, to erase it. To put something good in its place."

"Maybe we can. Not this." He gestured to the bed. "Not now, but something."

She shook her head, eyes bleak. "No. There's no erasing it, Ruc. There's no erasing anything."

39

In the darkness of the brig, Rat's conversation improved almost as rapidly as her grappling skills. Despite the cramped space, she insisted each day on drilling her technique, all the chokes, wrist locks, and arm bars that Gwenna could teach her. At night, the two of them talked with Bhuma Dhar.

Without a world to point at—*that* is a mountain; *that* is a tree; *that* is a sword—it was hard going, but the girl was indefatigable. Faster than Gwenna would have imagined she could speak basic, broken sentences: *The food is shit. The admiral is shit. This ship is shit.* Gwenna's fault, probably, that every sentence seemed to contain at least one curse, but after a month aboard the *Daybreak* she could communicate, there was no denying that. It might have been something to celebrate, a little light in the unbroken darkness, except for the fact that her growing vocabulary put her in danger.

Every few days Jonon came down to the brig to demand an update on the girl's progress. Another commander might have congratulated himself on finding the eggs and returning. Jonon, however, had grown convinced that Rat's compatriots had abandoned their city, left behind their entire homeland, in order to invade Annur. It didn't matter that the city lay thousands of miles from the empire. It didn't matter that to transport the whole population of the city would require hundreds of ships, maybe thousands. It didn't matter that no one at the ass end of Menkiddoc would have any reason to *know* about Annur.

"I will have answers for the Emperor when we return," he told Gwenna grimly, "if I have to crack them out of her savage skull myself."

Of course, cracking Rat's skull would ensure that he never *got* his answers. Twisting off a few fingers, however, or flaying a patch of skin . . . Gwenna could well imagine the admiral ordering such things if he believed the security of the empire was at stake.

Which left her walking a knife edge. When she claimed that the girl had made no progress, Jonon threatened to remove her from the brig and undertake the tutelage himself. If she admitted, on the other hand, just how much Rat had truly learned, confessed that the girl could speak and understand, she would almost be inviting him to begin his torture. The only way forward seemed to be a vague, constant delay: *She's trusting me more. She said something about the leader of the city, about his goals. Said something about where they're going. I just need to learn a few more of her words. We just need a little more time.*

All of which was utter fucking horseshit.

Despite her fascination with language, Rat refused to talk about any aspect of her life before she came creeping into the Annurian camp trying to steal food. If Gwenna so much as asked her name she clamped her jaw shut, retreated to the corner of the brig, and turned her face to the wall.

The only exception to this rule was the *avesh*.

The fourth or fifth night out to sea, Gwenna woke to the voices of sailors shouting. With her Kettral-keen hearing, there were always at least half a dozen conversations she could make out at any given time, but usually she ignored the constant wash of sound. She didn't care about the carpenter's gout, the cook's filthy dreams, or the superstitions of the soldiers. The urgency of *these* voices, however, hooked her attention, and she closed her eyes to focus on them.

". . . Just *shoot* the 'Kent-kissing thing!"

"Already loosed two dozen arrows at it. It's *too fast.*"

"Shit. *Shit!*"

Then Rahood's deep voice cutting into the conversation. "Two of you will go up there with a net and bring it down."

Gwenna shook her head. Somehow, for some reason, that wide-eyed, bloody-fanged monster had come aboard the *Daybreak*. Judging from the curses that followed, the men sent into the rigging to fetch it down had failed. Not surprising, given how nimbly the creature had moved through the trees. It could probably survive up in the ratlines for weeks, maybe the whole voyage, provided it found something to eat. Gwenna couldn't decide whether the idea was funny or worrying. Maybe both.

When Rat awoke, Gwenna pointed up through the deck above.

"Your monster. She's on the ship."

The girl's eyes went wide. "Yutaka?"

"What's a yutaka?"

"Yutaka," Rat said again. "Her name. Yutaka."

Across the brig, Bhuma Dhar had come awake—Gwenna could hear the shift in his breathing—but he didn't speak.

"Is she your . . . pet?" Gwenna asked.

"Pet?"

"Yutaka belongs to Rat? Rat owns Yutaka?"

"We hunt. Rat and Yutaka hunt."

Gwenna considered her next question. "Do all the people from your city have hunters?"

Rat opened her mouth to reply, then scowled. "Fuck all the people."

And that was the end of that conversation.

"You're sure," Gwenna asked Bhuma Dhar one night, after the girl had fallen asleep, "that those people from up in the northwest—Solengo and them, all those little towns—you're sure they didn't explore any farther south? That they didn't establish that city we found?"

The captain shook his head. "No. I am not sure. Those whaling villages have stood on that coast for over a thousand years. They were part of a larger—going out, an abandonment of our coast during the Time of Hunger. It is possible that some ships went south, established colonies, built an entire city. A thousand years is a long time. But the girl does not look like a child from my portion of the world—her hair is pale, like yours. And her skin. Nor is her speech the same as my own."

"What about the *gabhya*?" Gwenna pressed. "You said that the Manjari elites are obsessed with them. The lion with the wings? The one that's buried beneath the palace?"

"They are a sign of status, yes. Of prestige."

"Seems like Rat's people felt the same way. All those statues. And she talks about that toothy beast like it's her 'Kent-kissing *pet.*"

"People keep pets the whole world over. It seems to me the *gabhya* are less striking than the claims of your historian."

Gwenna blew out a frustrated breath. She'd avoided thinking about those claims, first because she wasn't thinking about *anything,* then later because they were too large, too outlandish to know what to do with. On the other hand, Kiel had been right about the birds, right about the maps. . . .

"The Nevariim," she said, shaking her head. The historian had made it sound like a simple matter of fact—*These are my fingers; that is an oak tree; this is the work of the Nevariim.* In her own mouth, the word sounded ridiculous. "It's crazy."

"The historian does not strike me as a madman."

"Don't have to go mad to be wrong."

"What tales do the people of Annur tell of the Nevariim?"

Gwenna snorted. "Probably the same as on your side of the Ancaz. They're a fantasy—something from the darkest days of the Csestriim wars, hope for the hopeless, a final salvation, all that shit."

"I would not be so dismissive of hope."

"Hope is fine. Hope is great. But hope doesn't sharpen any swords or lug any loads. The best way to get saved is not to fuck up in the first place."

"Sooner or later everyone errs."

"Doesn't mean someone else is going to come fix it. Certainly not some mythical race of gorgeous, naked saviors."

Of course, according to Kiel, they *weren't* saviors. What was it he'd said? The Nevariim were beasts. They lived to fuck and to hunt.

She wished, now, that she'd taken the opportunity afforded by the march into the mountains to ask him more. Jonon had called the historian to his tent nearly every night, but Gwenna had been too lost in herself or too busy with Rat to listen. It was hard to say why she hadn't been more curious, not just about Kiel's crazy Nevariim claims, but about *everything*—what happened in Solengo, the abandoned city, the ziggurat, the missing people, Rat, Rat's family. . . .

Those days, like the days on the journey south, felt like something she'd dreamed. She could remember the events, but none of those events made sense, certainly not her own thoughts and actions. She felt like a woman who had wakened finally after months of sweating fever. The irony, of course, was that just as she began to come alive she was locked once more in the brig.

"Let us entertain, for the moment, the ideas of the historian," Dhar said.

Gwenna shrugged. "Plenty of time to entertain all kinds of ideas."

He nodded, smoothed his ragged mustache into his ragged beard.

"We've got a city," Gwenna said, "ruled by Nevariim. The Nevariim like to hunt stuff. Judging from the piles of skulls, they hunt monsters and people with equal glee. Or maybe the people hunt the monsters and give them to the Nevariim. Or the monsters hunt the people." She shook her head. "Sounds like a shitty place to live, however you figure it."

Rat didn't move, but as Gwenna spoke, she heard the shift in the girl's breathing, the quickening of her heartbeat. She was awake, awake and listening. How much she'd heard, Gwenna couldn't say, let alone how much she'd understood, but something in the conversation had frightened her. Gwenna could smell the fear.

"So much hinges," Dhar said, "on the nature of the Nevariim."

As Dhar said the name, the girl tensed.

It made no sense. *Nevariim* was hardly a word she'd learned from Gwenna or Dhar. They'd been more focused on practicalities, like *Piss in the bucket,* and *There are maggots in the bread.* There'd been no reason to introduce the name of a long-dead race. Gwenna tried to imagine the explanation: *They were people, but not real people, who lived in a story, but not now—thousands and thousands of years ago. . . .*

No. Rat hadn't learned the word from her.

Maybe the Annurian word just *sounded* like something in the girl's own language, some other word that was frightening but utterly unrelated, like *murder* or *torture*. She tried to sift back through her memories of Rat's babble. There hadn't been much of it. The girl had spent much of the march into the mountains in stubborn silence. When she'd spoken, it was mostly to pester Gwenna to teach her some new fighting technique, always in Annurian. Really, the only words she'd used . . .

"*Rashkta-bhura,*" Gwenna said quietly.

Rat jerked upright, shedding instantly all pretense of sleep.

She couldn't see Gwenna in the darkness, that much was obvious, but Gwenna could see her, those large eyes boring into her.

"What's a *rashkta-bhura?*" Gwenna asked quietly.

Rat stabbed a finger at Gwenna's chest.

Gwenna shook her head. "I don't know what that is."

Dhar couldn't see what was happening, but made no move to interrupt.

"Something about my body, right?" Gwenna pressed. The girl had said it first back in the cave, looking at Gwenna's wounds. "Something about how it heals quickly. *Gwenna Sharpe body fuck quit.* That's what you said, right?"

Rat nodded. "*Axochlin* body fast. Faster. *Axochlin* body stronger." The girl reached out, questing in the darkness for Gwenna's shoulder, then her neck. "But no . . ." She searched for the word in Annurian, then gave up. "*Axoch. Rashkta-bhura* has *axoch.* Gwenna Sharpe has no *axoch.*"

"*Axochlin.*" Gwenna tested the strange syllables. "Is that the same thing as *rashkta-bhura?*"

The girl's frustration smelled like rusted iron. "*Rashkta-bhura* is *kind* of *axochlin.*"

Gwenna glanced over at Dhar. "Does any of this mean anything to you?"

The captain shook his head.

"Did they hurt you?" Gwenna asked, turning back to the child. "The *rashkta-bhura?* Did they hurt your family?"

Rat hissed, bared her teeth. She smelled momentarily of sour bafflement and grief. "*Axochlin want* Rat. Want put . . . *axoch* on Rat. *Axochlin* want make Rat *shava-bhura.*"

The main words remained vexingly unclear, but Gwenna didn't need the words to understand the story. "They wanted to make you into one of them," she said. "They wanted to put a . . ." She shook her head in confusion. "Collar? Is an *axoch* a collar?"

Rat stared at her blankly.

Gwenna unbuckled her belt, slid it in a loop around her own neck, brought Rat's hand up to feel it.

"Collar?"

The girl hesitated. "*Axoch* is collar. *Axoch* is . . . alive."

"A living collar . . ." Dhar mused.

Gwenna shook her head. "Or she has the word wrong. There's something we're not understanding."

"*Not* wrong," Rat insisted.

Gwenna started to reply, then broke off as something shifted just on the far side of the door. No, she realized, fear flaring inside her, not something. Some*one*. If she strained, she could hear the heartbeat through the wood. With all the other sounds on the ship—the shouting and creaking and shifting of ballast—she hadn't noticed it before.

Someone listening.

Wood creaked as whoever it was retreated down the passageway, bare feet light on the decking. The sailors went barefoot, of course, but a grim suspicion was mounting inside her that this had been no sailor. They'd been waiting out there, patient as a stone, listening at the door. Now that they'd heard what they needed to hear, they were leaving, going to get . . .

It wasn't long before the tramp of boots shook the deck—three people, judging by the sound. A key rattled in the lock, the door swung open, and there was the admiral, flanked by Vessik and Chent.

"Get her out of there," Jonon said, gesturing.

The men peered into the gloom, blind.

"Get who out?" Gwenna asked.

"You have been lying to me," Jonon replied. "Not only does the girl know more of our language than you have admitted, but she has been conveying to you information about her land and her people. Information that you have withheld."

Gwenna got to her feet. "I haven't been withholding anything. . . ."

Jonon raised a hand. "Enough. I will handle the questioning from here."

"You're going to torture her."

"I am going to take whatever steps are necessary to protect the empire."

"She is a *child*," Gwenna snarled.

"A savage child with knowledge of a savage people. I will have that knowledge. If she relays it freely, there will be no need to summon the surgeon."

It was impossible to know how much of the conversation Rat understood, but like Gwenna she had scrambled to her feet.

"No," the girl growled.

Chent ducked in through the low door, seized her by the wrist. "Come on, sweetie. No need to throw a fit."

"*No!*" Rat screamed, twisting away, catching his little finger in her own grasp, then wrenching it viciously backward.

You didn't need Kettral ears to hear the bone snap.

Chent stared at his own mangled digit for a moment, then shattered Rat's nose with his other fist.

He *would* have shattered her nose, that was, if Gwenna hadn't caught the blow. The soldier's eyes widened as she wrenched his arm behind him, then slammed him face-first into the wall.

"*Stop!*" Jonon ordered, but Vessik had already surged into the tiny brig.

"You bitch," he snarled, reaching for Gwenna. "Put your hands on an Annurian legionary . . ."

A stiff-fingered blow to the throat dropped him. He gagged on his own pain, choked for air.

Gwenna kicked the legs out from beneath Chent, then turned. Jonon stood framed in the doorway, a hand on the pommel of his cutlass. Despite the fate of his soldiers, he smelled of rage, not fear. He stared at Gwenna, green eyes black in the shadow.

"You forget that you were sent on this expedition for your knowledge of the kettral," he said, voice dangerously calm. "That knowledge was your shield. It protected you even when you disobeyed my orders and endangered my men. Now that we have the eggs, however, I am finally free to teach you the full measure of Annurian obedience."

"Teach me whatever you want," Gwenna growled. "Just leave the girl alone."

Jonon ignored her, turned to the fallen soldiers. "Get up. Get out."

Chent stumbled to his feet, followed by Vessik.

The admiral watched them stagger from the brig, then turned back to Gwenna. "Generally I do not enjoy the necessity of discipline." He gave her a thin smile. "Today I may make an exception."

†

"Gwenna Sharpe," Jonon announced, raising his voice so that he could be heard the length of the deck. "For insubordination, for endangering the crew of this vessel, for reckless incitement, and for an unwarranted attack on two Annurian soldiers, I sentence you to be hauled beneath the keel five times."

The ship sailed through a moment of stunned silence. Sunlight splintered on the waves. After weeks in the brig the world seemed too large, too bright.

Gwenna stared out over the assembled faces. Shock twisted their features. Some stared at her, others at the admiral. A few frowned, as though certain they'd misheard. Chent nodded with the satisfaction of a man who'd been in on the secret, while Vessik gave a little chuckle—"*Five!*" Lurie just watched her, his eyes like glass. Pattick, suddenly ashen, opened his mouth, started forward until Cho Lu put a firm hand on his shoulder to draw him back. Even at the distance, Gwenna could hear their whispered conversation.

"There's nothing you can do."

Pattick didn't take his eyes from Gwenna. "She saved me. She saved us both."

"I know that." The legionary's voice was tight with the strain. "I know it, Pattick, but if you cross Jonon on this he'll just kill you, too."

That was the heart of it. Jonon hadn't spoken of killing anyone, but the sentence wasn't lost on any of them, least of all Gwenna.

Keelhauling offered a variety of ways to die. Drowning was the most obvious—it took a while to drag a human beneath even a modest-sized ship, and no one would describe the *Daybreak* as modest. Then there was the possibility of blunt impact offered by the hull or the keel itself. Gwenna had heard of men dragged out of the water with their skulls or faces split open. Deadliest were probably the barnacles. After a few months in the water, a crust of seaweed and barnacles accreted over the ship's smoothly joined planks, and those shells were like a thousand tiny razors. It was possible to survive the hauling itself and die later from blood loss or infection. And of course, the blood would attract sharks.

As a result, keelhauling was used only rarely. If a captain wanted a man dead, it was easier to hang him, or lop off his head, or just toss him over the side. The punishment was usually reserved for only the gravest crimes: mutiny or treason topping the list. It was possible to survive, of course. There were stories of sailors enduring one, even two haulings. It took three to kill Gren the Traitor, after the battle of Lampent. Gwenna had never heard of anyone sentenced to five.

Jonon turned to her, his eyes green as the sea.

Despite his words earlier, there was no satisfaction in that gaze. He smelled like a man tending to an unpleasant task too long delayed.

"Bind her," he said, nodding to Chent and Vessik.

As Chent reached for her hands, she considered fighting. After a month grappling with Rat, she'd regained some measure of her former fitness. She'd dropped both legionaries down in the brig; she could do it again.

And then what?

Fight Lurie? Kill him? Kill the rest of the legionaries? Kill the sailors who came to their aid? Kill Rahood? Kill Jonon? Kill everyone?

The thought was as wrong as it was impossible. She stared out over the men as Chent, grinning, cinched the rope tight around her wrists. Most wouldn't meet her eyes. A few looked sick. They weren't bad people. They'd been chosen, in fact, because they were capable, brave, loyal, and if they'd never interrogated the reasons for their loyalty, well, Gwenna could hardly blame them for that. How many people, after all, had *she* killed in the name of the Emperor, bright be the days of her life? The faces of the dead flashed through her mind—Urghul, mostly, but Annurian too, Dombângan, Antheran. . . . Some of them had deserved it probably; some of them probably not. *Deserved* just wasn't a word that applied to war. For all she knew, Jonon was doing the right thing. She *had* defied him, *had* attacked his appointed officers, *had* made mistakes that led to the deaths of his men.

On the other hand, if she died, Rat died, most likely in hideous pain. It wasn't at all obvious what she could do to protect the girl if she stayed alive, but there was a passage from Hendran that she'd always liked: *First, don't die. The dead are useless, but the living are full of surprises.*

Chent leaned close as he looped a second rope around her wrists, so close she could smell the salt fish on his breath.

"This is going to hurt," he cooed in her ear.

She'd thought for months that he wanted to rape her, but judging from the lust wafting off of him, watching her suffer would be more than good enough.

"Oh, sweet Intarra's light," he went on, pulling the rope lovingly tight, "it is going to *hurt*."

It might have been those words that saved her. Whatever shame still flooded her veins, whatever guilt and self-loathing still lurked in her gut, there was something else, too, something older and harder, a part of her real as any organ, something she'd thought annihilated months earlier, something she'd only rediscovered in the days after killing the kettral, an old friend or enemy— she had no idea which—prodded awake by the soldier's words. There was a time she would have called it anger, but it wasn't anger. She understood that now. Anger was a useful tool, but one that had shattered when she needed it most. This was something else—she had no name to give it—something that, when everything else had fallen apart, somehow, inexplicably, remained.

She raised her eyes to meet Chent's gaze.

"I'm not going to die down there."

He smiled. "Oh yes you are, sweetheart. You're going to die. But first you're going to scream."

"You don't know me," she replied quietly.

"I certainly do. You're the bitch from the brig. The one with the tits." He shook his head. "I'll be sad to see those shredded."

She ignored the words, looked past him, searched through the assembled crowd for the oldest sailor she could find, settled on a man with a bald head, salt in his beard, lines beside his eyes.

"You," she said.

His eyes widened. He glanced over his shoulder.

"No," Gwenna went on, "I'm talking to you."

Jonon shifted. "You will keep silent—"

She raised her eyebrows. "Or what? You'll have me killed twice?"

She turned back to the sailor. "Old guy, I'm talking to you. What's the record?"

He blinked. "The record?"

"For a hauling. What's the longest anyone's stayed under?"

The man licked his lips, refused to meet her eyes.

"I know there's a record," she said. "The eastern fleet's got one. The southern fleet's got one. I know the western fleet has one, and I know you know it."

His eyes flickered to Jonon.

"The condemned get a final request," she said. "Even traitors. And what I'm requesting is to know the western fleet's longest recorded keelhauling."

"Two hundred twelve by the count," the man replied finally, hunching his shoulders as though he expected someone to split open his skull.

"Two hundred twelve." Higher than she'd expected. A lot higher. "Counting fast or slow?"

"Middling," the sailor said. "Middling slow."

She took a deep breath, held it a moment, exhaled. Then another. Then another.

"Two hundred twelve," she said again. It was a target at least, something to aim for while she was down there in the dark trying not to die.

Despite the time it took to set, the rigging was relatively simple. A rope ran through a pulley hanging from the end of the main yard, passed beneath the hull, up to another pulley at the other end of the main yard, and down to Gwenna's wrists. The sailors hoisted her up and out. Then, as she hung dangling above the waves, they looped the other end of the rope around her ankles and made it fast. The whole thing was now a single long loop, running from one side of the ship to the other.

She was the human link holding it together.

While they were tying her, Jonon had mounted once again to the sterncastle, well above the proceedings. The rest of the men—sailors and soldiers both—remained assembled amidships to witness the punishment. Kiel stood among their number, but alone among the men there was no emotion on his face. Instead of disgust or satisfaction, he watched her with an expression of mild interest, the look of a man watching a game of stones unfold, an intriguing game, but one in which he had no particular stake in the outcome.

"Begin," Jonon said, when the ropes were made fast.

The men tasked with the work hesitated.

"Begin," the admiral said again.

This time, they hauled on the rope, and Gwenna began to sink toward the water.

"Two hundred twelve," she said, nodding to the crew as she dropped below the rail.

When her feet touched the water, she dragged in a deep breath, let her muscles go slack, tried to slow her heart. The waves lapped at her legs, then her waist, her neck, and then she was under, shuddering along the rough hull. At first she took it for a small blessing that the water was warm; sailors hauled beneath the keel up north often died from exposure. Then the first of the barnacles bit into her skin. She'd expected them to feel like knives. They were worse. Instead of a series of clean slices, the jagged shells gouged, plunging in, dragging ragged tracks over her flesh. It hurt so bad that for a moment her plan went straight out of her head. She let herself be dragged along haphazardly, the shells ripping her to ribbons.

Then, with an excruciating effort she twisted around to face the hull. It was dangerous—she was more likely to lose an eye or split her forehead open on the keel—but with her belly toward the ship she was able to pull her body tight, into a half crouch, just her elbows and knees between her and the hull, and then, with a sort of slithering, crawling motion, walk her way along the planking. It felt a little like bellying through the dirt on a sniper mission, except she couldn't see shit, her wrists and ankles were tied together, the barnacles hurt a lot more than dirt, and she couldn't breathe. Her chest ached. With each motion, she could feel the shells grinding against the bones of her knees and elbows, but grinding against bone was a lot better than tearing long gashes in her back, legs, and sides. As long as she could localize the damage to a few spots, she shouldn't bleed out.

By the time she reached the ship's keel, the breath in her lungs was a blaze. Judging time was impossible. There was no way to know if they were going slow or if she was just wasting too much energy trying to keep her body separate from the ship. Not that it really mattered. As long as she was under, she had to keep holding her breath, and if there was one thing she'd spent a lot of time doing with the Kettral, it was holding her fucking breath. She sang a Kettral drinking song in her mind as she grated up the other side of the hull.

> Rum for the women,
> And rum for the men,
> Rum for the soldiers
> Who won't fly again.

Rum for the fliers,
And rum for the leaches,
Rum for the bastards
Who died on the beaches.

Rum for the snipers
And rum for commanders,
Rum for all stubborn
Lost-cause last-standers.

Rum for retreat,
And rum for attack,
And rum for us dumb
Sons of bitches in black!

Because of the way she was rigged up, her feet emerged from the water first, then her hips, then finally, with agonizing slowness, her head. She dragged a desperate, ragged breath into her lungs, caught a wave in the face, choked, puked up the water, tried to breathe through her coughing. Wet hair plastered her face, draining into her nose and mouth, covering her eyes. When she had the strength, she shook it free.

She was dangling upside down on the far side of the ship, her head just below the level of the rail. Kiel stood there, and Pattick and Cho Lu, and everyone else on the 'Kent-kissing ship. She took another unsteady breath, searched for the old sailor with the salt in his beard. She found him at the edge of the crowd, gnawing at his lip.

"How long?" she called out.

Or tried to call out. The words drained from her throat waterlogged and weak, but he heard her all the same.

"One hundred ninety-nine," he replied.

"One hundred ninety-nine," she protested. That came out a little bit stronger. "Who's doing the fucking counting?"

"I am," the man replied.

"What's your name?" she demanded.

Everything about her hurt. Her shoulders and wrists, her lungs, her knees, her elbows, her elbows, her bloody, battered *elbows.* Talking was a way to take her mind off the pain.

"Genir," he replied.

"Well, Genir, you old bastard," she said. "Count slower this time."

He gaped. "Slower?"

"I'm trying to break a record here, and I won't have you assholes saying later that it didn't count because you went too fast."

Genir stared at her, confusion scrawled across his face. Someone else, though, someone she couldn't see because of the way she was hanging, let out a quick shocked grunt of a laugh.

"Intarra's light," another voice muttered, "that bitch is tough."

She took that phrase with her as she went back beneath the waves, holding it close, repeating it over and over like a prayer, saying the words in her mind as though they had the power to save her, as though that simple phrase could be stronger than the rope, and the water, and the sharp knives of the hull: *That bitch is tough. That bitch is tough. That bitch is tough.*

When she emerged on the other side, she wanted to sob, but that would ruin the image. Instead, she coughed up half a gallon of seawater, spat into the waves, and found Genir.

"How'd we do?"

This time, half a dozen voices called out.

"Two hundred!"

"One ninety-nine!"

"Two oh four!"

"Silence!" Jonon bellowed from his post on the sterncastle.

"Admiral," Pattick called. *"Admiral!"*

All faces turned to him.

"Aw shit," Cho Lu muttered, but even as he said it, he stepped up beside his friend.

"Stand down, soldier," Jonon said.

Pattick did not stand down. "Please, sir. Mercy on her."

"I don't *need* his mercy," Gwenna shouted. Or tried to shout. It came out more like a moan.

The legionaries ignored her. "Mercy," Cho Lu said, echoing his friend. "Mercy."

A long silence stretched over the deck. Had it been a story, the other soldiers and sailors, overcome with emotion, might have added their voices, one by one, until the whole deck became a single chorus pleading for her life. Unfortunately, it wasn't a fucking story. Aside from the creaking of the rigging and the splash of the waves, the silence reigned. Jonon gazed down at the pair of legionaries, then shook his head grimly. "Abetting a known traitor is, itself, treason. Take them below and lock them up."

In any other situation, Gwenna might have worried more about the two soldiers, but as they were led away her own ropes were already in motion, dropping her toward the water once more. As her head slipped beneath the sea, a line from Hendran bubbled up in her mind: *Just because you're dying doesn't mean you're losing.*

It had been an easier line to appreciate when she wasn't actually dying.

By the time she emerged from the fifth haul, the final haul, her eyesight had narrowed to a dim, hazy tunnel. The pain was a blanket swaddling her so close she couldn't breathe. Blood roared in her ears, like the surf on the shore; she couldn't hear anything else. It was only after she'd managed a few shallow, gulping breaths that her vision cleared enough for her to make out Genir standing at the rail. Everyone else was there, too, silent, absolutely silent, standing the way people stood at a funeral.

Thanks, Hendran, she thought. *You fucking asshole.*

"How long?" she croaked. "And I swear to Hull, if I didn't break it, I am going down there again."

Genir stared at her.

No one said anything.

"How *long?*"

"Three hundred and twelve," he replied, his voice ragged with awe.

No one said anything.

Every fiber of her was pain, and beneath the pain, exhaustion, and beneath the exhaustion, terror, and beneath the terror all the old shame and sorrow and regret. But beneath the regret, like a smooth stone plucked from a river, that other thing, worn down but still hard, still there, still refusing to let her die. She had no idea, as she hung from the rope, dripping blood and water into the endless sea, whether or not she should be thankful that she had a stone lodged in the center of her beating heart.

Pain is a gift.

Another line from Hendran.

It keeps the weary soldier awake. It reminds the irresolute warrior that there is work still to finish. It whispers in the ear of all who feel it something they might otherwise forget: You are not dead.

Back in the darkness of the brig, huddled in a heap against the bulkhead, knees drawn up to her chest, eyes squeezed shut, Gwenna half wished she *were* dead. Rat and Bhuma Dhar were there, leaning over her, saying something, but she couldn't hear the words past the roar of the agony.

She wouldn't have believed a person could hurt so bad without passing out. With each desperate breath she expected her vision to pinch in, then go dark as she tumbled into oblivion. Unfortunately, oblivion didn't seem to want her. Breath after breath she remained stubbornly awake until the grave realization dawned that there would be no escape. The pain had her. It was crushing her. Which meant it was her job not to be crushed. Grimly, she turned her attention inward. Instead of trying to blot out the agony, she opened herself to it.

Pain was a foe like any other foe; in order to fight it she had to know it.

Her shoulders felt as though they'd been wrenched from their sockets, her ankles and wrists throbbed, her head ached where she'd smashed it against the keel, her lungs burned, and her elbows and knees felt flayed to the bone. Blood from a hundred cuts and slashes soaked her blacks, so much blood she wondered if she'd survived after all. If she stayed perfectly still, the agony was just bearable, but it was impossible to stay perfectly still on a ship shouldering its way through the swells. Every time the *Daybreak* pitched or rolled, she felt half a dozen knives driving into her. Every time, the scream boiled up in her throat, and every time she choked it back.

Crying, she could do silently, and in the darkness of the brig neither Rat nor Dhar could see her, and so she cried. For a long time she cried, hours maybe, maybe a day, huddled against the bulkhead, her body shaking with the silent sobs. The shaking hurt and the tears burned her lacerated cheeks, but she made no effort to stop. Those sobs had been locked inside her, she realized, since Talal and Quick Jak died in the Purple Baths. No—longer. Far longer. Since the day she'd learned that the Kettral had destroyed themselves. Since Laith died trying to hold the bridge in Andt-Kyl. Since the Urghul forced Gwenna to murder that lost legionary up on the steppe. Since the day she decided to leave her father and her brothers behind. Since she was a child learning that her mother was dead . . .

In all those years, she'd never cried, not once. Grief was useless to a soldier, after all, and so she'd turned all that grief into rage, an armor hammered from a thousand layers, and now, after all these years, the rage had finally broken. Wave after wave, her grief washed over her, blotting out thought, scrubbing away even the agony in her limbs, until finally, after what seemed like a lifetime, the waves slowed, then slackened. Her body stopped shuddering. There were no more tears. She opened her eyes, woke again to the present, found Dhar sitting beside her, his hand on her shoulder, Rat gently stroking her hair. They might almost have been a family, her family.

Almost.

40

For a gate fashioned by the most powerful magics of an ancient race, a doorway that led, literally, through nothingness, for a strategic weapon that had nearly destroyed humanity itself, the *kenta* didn't look like much—just a slender arch standing at the center of a round, vaulted chamber, the kind of architectural flourish you could find in any of a hundred temples around the city, except that this arch was part of no wall. The longer Akiil looked at it, the stranger it became. For one thing, he couldn't quite decide what it was made of; from one angle it appeared to be metal, from another, polished stone. And the light reflected strangely off of it, as though the flames burning in the surrounding lanterns weren't the source of its illumination. There was a vague sense of something wrong, something unnatural.

"Leave us," Adare said.

Hugel, the larger of the two Aedolians, shot Akiil a warning glance—he was always shooting warning glances—before withdrawing.

"He's still not very friendly," Akiil observed.

Adare ignored him, waited until both men were gone, crossed to the heavy steel door, checked that it was firmly shut, then turned to Akiil.

"So," she said, the syllable a gauntlet tossed down between them.

Akiil met her eyes, smiled, used the time to calm his kicking heart, to slow his breath.

Stop trying.

Yerrin's advice. For whatever the fuck it was worth.

"You said you've been studying it," he said. "How?"

"We have sent animals through—chickens, dogs, monkeys."

"I take it they didn't come back?"

Adare crossed to one of the torches, removed it from its sconce, then walked to the *kenta*. "We sent them in with leashes on. It didn't work." She held the torch out toward the gate. When the flame passed beneath the arch, it vanished.

The scene reminded him, strangely, of fishing the small ponds below Ashk'lan on summer nights, the way the line dropped into the black water and seemed to simply cease. This was like that, except vertically, and without the water. He could see straight through the *kenta* to the far side of the room—the walls, the floor of the cavern, the torches in their sconces, everything where it should be. Everything except the fire at the end of Adare's brand. When she withdrew it, the entire top of the torch was gone, the wooden stump smooth, as though sheared off by some beautifully honed blade. The Emperor ran a finger over it, shook her head, then tossed the whole thing through the gate. It disappeared into the air without a shiver or splash.

"No," she said. "They didn't come back."

Her jaw tightened fractionally. Her eyes dilated.

Akiil considered her face.

"You didn't just send animals," he said finally. "You sent humans through, too."

The Emperor studied him. "You have Kaden's knack for reading people. It's vexing."

"Only if you're trying to keep secrets."

"An emperor's job is keeping secrets." She seemed about to say more on that subject, then shook her head. "I didn't order them through."

Akiil raised a skeptical eyebrow.

"Two of my Aedolians, good men who had been down here with me dozens of times, insisted on testing it." She turned away to stare through the *kenta*. "*Dogs can't report back,* they said. I explained to them the danger. I even read them passages from some of the earliest human histories, accounts of people destroyed by the gates. They understood the risk and they insisted."

"That happen often to emperors? People insist, and you have to do what they say?"

She rounded on him. "People die because of my decisions every day. So many people die that it's tempting to stop making decisions, except do you know what would happen then? People would keep dying, only faster." She shook her head. "The men who went through that gate were soldiers. They died the way any soldier would choose to die."

"Snuffed into nothingness on an emperor's pointless whim?"

Adare had him by the neck before he realized what was happening. He reached up to grab her wrist, to shove her away, then crushed the instinct. He wasn't a child anymore. This wasn't a tavern in the Quarter. The woman holding him didn't want to use him or sell him. All his old methods of survival were useless here. If he punched her, he died. If he tried to run, he died. An old Shin saying bloomed in his mind: *If you are fighting, you have already lost.*

He relaxed his shoulders, his gut, his chest. The Emperor's grip was stronger than he'd have expected, but she wasn't actually choking him. The *kenta* might kill him, but this woman wasn't going to.

Her eyes burned inches from his face, but her voice was cold when she spoke. "I had a general once. The man mocked me at every turn, betrayed me, lied to my face. I hated him, but I refused to see him executed. I kept him at his post. Do you know why?"

Akiil managed to speak, despite the fingers gouging into his neck. "Tell me."

"Because I thought I needed him." The Emperor's eyes remained on Akiil, but she was looking at something else, some fragment of memory. "I thought that without his battlefield brilliance I would be lost, that *Annur* would be lost. By the time I realized my mistake, he had taken my son and nearly destroyed my empire."

Akiil shook his head incrementally. "I didn't come here to destroy Annur. I came to help you."

"Do you have any idea how many people present themselves at this palace claiming to want to help?"

"I can do something they can't."

"No one is indispensable."

"If you need the *kenta,* I am."

"I would *like* to use the *kenta,*" she replied grimly. "I would find the gates useful in all manner of ways, but I made a point, after I finally killed my general, to stop believing I needed things. So if you hope to play on whatever it is you claim to know, if you think, because you are the last of the Shin, that you are safe, if you believe you can do or say whatever you want because I *need* you . . ." She shook her head grimly, dropped her hand from his throat, but kept him fixed with her eyes. "I don't."

Akiil resisted the urge to rub his neck.

"Spoken," he said evenly, "like a Shin monk. Teaching you might not be impossible after all."

"Enough talk about teaching." Adare gestured to the *kenta.* "The time has arrived for a demonstration."

Fear dragged a cold fingernail down Akiil's spine.

He turned away from the Emperor to consider the gate.

Know less, Yerrin murmured. *Know nothing.*

He closed his eyes.

The calm that had enveloped him in the Captain's pig yard was gone, vanished, trampled by a stampede of emotions. Fear seethed in his gut, restless and sharp-clawed. His whole life, that fear had helped to keep him alive, to run faster when he needed to run, to fight harder when he had to fight. Suddenly, it felt wrong to let it go, like abandoning the only piece of flotsam while stranded in the open ocean.

He didn't have to do it. The Emperor would be furious, but what did he care about the Emperor? She wasn't *really* going to have him executed for changing his mind. A month earlier, she hadn't even known he existed. She already suspected he was a fraud. If he told the truth and walked out, he'd end up penniless, but he'd been penniless before. There were other ways to get coin, better cons to run, more reliable cons, cons that weren't going to end up with, well, the *end* of him.

And there was Skinny Quinn to consider.

Her betrayal didn't bother him—she'd done what she needed to do to stay alive. What bothered him was the fact that the Captain still *had* her. If she was only dealing cards, then fine, but those empty eyes, that blank face, suggested more and worse. Not that he had any idea how to fix it. Obviously she didn't want him to try. And yet the fact that she was alive tugged at him, as though someone had tied a slender thread around some organ to which he could not put a name. Staring down the Captain's pigs he'd been ready to die, convinced of the rightness of his own annihilation. Now, though, a new thought nagged at him, the possibility that death, too, might be just another kind of escape, that if he failed he might just be running away again.

He turned back to the *kenta*.

What did it feel like if it went wrong? Those men who'd tried it—what had they experienced in the slender moment when they were only partway through—the front leg, the hand and arm. Did they know they'd failed? Could they sense their bodies, half-undone, hemorrhaging blood into nothingness? He imagined yanking his arm back, finding the hand gone, watching the blood gush from the stump. . . .

Knock it off, you asshole, he told himself.

His heart was hammering, but he knew how to calm it. His breath came hot and ragged through his nose, but that, too, he could manage. He was Akiil from the Perfumed Quarter, but he was also a Shin monk. He'd had the same training as Kaden, and Kaden had learned to use the gates. Passing beneath the gate was a gamble, but then, life was a gamble.

The trick to gambling was not caring if you won or lost.

That was the lesson of the hog pen.

He wasn't sure what had happened to him, as he watched Andraz torn apart by the animals, but it felt like the way the Shin described the *vaniate*. No fear. No hope. No emotion at all.

No self.

Of course, Shin meditation had never involved watching men rent into gobbets of flesh, but maybe there were other ways, other paths. That frigid emptiness from the Captain's courtyard was, in the end, what he had, and so, while the Emperor of Annur watched him, he called to mind the memory of Andraz's final moments, watched the club come down against the man's knee, watched Fori topple him over the wall, watched the hogs close in and open his stomach with their tusks, watched the guts spill.

This is all he was, he reminded himself.

Blood. Bone. Meat. Piss. Shit.

That is all anyone is.

That is all I am.

In his perfect memory, he watched Andraz's eyes go wide with horror, then glaze over as everything he'd loved and hated and hoped for drained away. He shifted the image, imagined himself among the hogs, imagined their teeth tearing at him, ripping, rending, tearing him away in layers, felt himself coming apart, ceasing to be.

I am nothing.

The thought rose natural and unbidden as breath. He could picture Skinny Quinn watching him as he died, that pretty face of hers blank as the sky.

I am not.

There was no satisfaction in the words. He tried to remember what satisfaction felt like, failed. What was satisfaction to a bag of meat?

Between one breath and the next, he opened his eyes.

The world remained: the vaulted stone chamber, the torches burning in their sconces, the Emperor studying him with those eyes of flame, the *kenta* standing in the center of space. He felt nothing about any of it. He could remember his fear of the gate, but the emotion might as well have been something he'd heard about thirdhand. There was no urgency to it, no color, no life.

"Is this . . ." Adare asked. "Did it work?"

"You want me to go through?"

She studied him warily for a moment, then nodded. "Go through, come back, and tell me what's on the other side."

He shrugged, turned away from her, and stepped through the gate.

†

A small island, maybe a hundred paces across, surrounded by sea.

Two dozen *kenta* ringed the perimeter. Beyond them cliffs dropped away seventy or eighty feet into the waves. The bright sun hurt his eyes, but the pain didn't bother him. It was hard to be sure why pain had ever bothered him. Like the wind, like the waves, like the ring of gates, like the tent of sky stretched overhead, it was just a fact of the world.

Graven into the apex of each *kenta* were words in a script he didn't recognize. Place names, probably. He walked in a slow circle around the island's edge, memorizing the shapes of that script; perhaps the Emperor or one of her historians would recognize it. Halfway through his circuit, he stepped on something hard hidden by the high grass. When he knelt, his fingers closed around the wooden shaft of a spear. A few feet away he found a skull and other bones half-sunken in the dry dirt. It took him only moments to excavate the entire skeleton, a large man, judging by the size of the legs and arms. Csestriim? One of the Shin? The remains could have been lying there for one year or a thousand, although the wooden shaft of the spear remained relatively unrotten. Akiil sifted the dirt until he found one of the small bones of the hand, tucked it into a pocket in his robe, then straightened.

More skeletons lay near the first. One of the skulls was half-crushed. A flat-bow bolt nestled among the ribs of another. It was impossible to know who had killed them, or why. Outside the *vaniate,* the thought of people fighting and dying on this island in the middle of the ocean would have been unsettling. Inside the vast hall of his calm, he felt only a mild curiosity.

When he had traveled halfway around the island, he paused, turned, looked back at the gate through which he had come. It would be easy for someone else, someone without the Shin trick of committing images to memory, to lose track of the way home.

Home. He tried to make sense of the notion.

He'd always thought of Annur as his home, even during the years at Ashk'lan—but what did that mean, really? What was the thought of home, but a kind of mad attachment to one place instead of all the rest? He stared out through the gate to Annur, found only the sea, the sky hazed by distant cloud, dozens of some kind of bird he didn't recognize diving into the waves. For a moment, it felt as though his whole life—everything from his first memories in the Perfumed Quarter to the slaughter of the monks to Skinny Quinn's empty face as she gave him to the Captain—had been nothing more than a febrile hallucination, as though only the island was real, as though all those empty gates led, not back to actual places, but to a useless dream world of suffering and stupidity, of madness, of grasping, of endless bright-hued ludicrous human delusion.

41

Storms had a smell. Some reeked of wet stone, others of rust, still others of salt and hot seaweed. There had been Kettral back on the Islands who could tell you what kind of weather was coming just by closing their eyes and taking a deep breath. *Thunder,* they'd say. Or, *high seas.* Gwenna never quite got the knack. The most she'd ever managed was to tell good weather from bad, which was how she knew, even buried in the darkness of the brig, that some truly nasty shit was headed their way.

Three days since the keelhauling, and each day the ocean had grown rougher. That roughness, most likely, was the only thing preventing Jonon from returning for Rat. It was possible to torture a person in the middle of a storm, but not all that smart. One wrong pitch of the deck, one unexpected roll, one slip of the knife, and there was your irreplaceable prisoner, bleeding out all over the table.

On the fourth day, a sudden lurch tossed Gwenna and Rat clear across the brig, slamming them into the far bulkhead beside Dhar.

"It grows worse," the Manjari captain observed.

"No shit," Gwenna muttered.

She slipped the belt from her waist, looped it around Rat's, and lashed the girl to one of the steel rings set into the floor. The tingling air pricked at the hair on her arms. She could hear, muffled through the thick hull of the ship, the growl of thunder, far-off but approaching.

"Hold on," she said, guiding Rat's hand to the ring, then taking a firm grip herself.

The strain hurt. She was still bleeding from a dozen gashes, and the muscles of her ribs and shoulders felt ready to tear. Those injuries weren't going to kill her, though. The growing storm, on the other hand . . .

"Hamaksha," Dhar said. His face was grim.

"Does that mean *oh shit* in Manjari?"

"It is a kind of storm."

"Just feels to me like we're being rolled downhill in a barrel."

"There is a rhythm."

Gwenna sure as shit couldn't feel any rhythm. She'd also never heard of a *hamaksha*.

"I thought the Manjari didn't sail this far south."

"We do not, but sometimes the storms come to us."

"How do your captains handle them?"

"In the same way that a wise captain handles any storm."

"Which is?"

"By avoiding it."

Gwenna coughed up a laugh as another violent roll tried to hurl her across the brig. "Yeah. Well. Doesn't seem like Jonon agrees with the Manjari wisdom."

She meant it as a joke, but Dhar shook his head. "Since the Treaty of Gosha, the Annurian fleet has not left the Ghost Sea. Your admiral has never encountered the *hamaksha*."

"He's seen storms."

"None like this."

She raised her brows. "That bad?"

Dhar looked toward her from across the brig. "Do you pray, Gwenna Sharpe?"

The question caught her off guard. "More swearing than prayer, I guess."

"You think this pleases the gods?"

"I think the gods have better things to do than worry about my language."

The captain nodded as though that settled the matter, closed his eyes, placed his palms together in the manner of Manjari worship, and began to pray. At least, that's what it looked like he was doing—Gwenna could see his lips moving, but she couldn't read the words. Maybe he was doing some cursing of his own.

"Bad?" Rat asked, staring blindly at Gwenna in the darkness.

Gwenna put her free arm around the girl's shoulders, tried to hold her against the worst of the ship's rolling. She was shaking.

"It's just a storm," she said. "Just a storm."

As the day wore on, however, the storm grew steadily worse.

Up above, the wind screamed through the rigging, thrumming the lines, making the whole boat shiver and moan like some discordant instrument. Toward the stern something had come loose—a crate or chest or barrel—and was sliding back and forth, battering into the bulkheads with each shift of the sea. Gwenna was growing exhausted from trying to hold on to both Rat and the steel ring, but letting go would mean disaster. As the *Daybreak* climbed each swell, she and the girl were pinned against the stern bulkhead; then, as the ship tipped over the top and careened down the far side, she found herself sliding down a deck grown steep as a Romsdal roof. On the other side of the brig, Bhuma Dhar endured the same battering, clinging to his own ring as he rode out the swells. He seemed to have stopped praying. Whether that was a good thing or not, Gwenna had no idea.

If she bothered to, she could sort the individual voices clattering down from the deck above.

. . . Fix that line . . .

. . . Sweet Intarra's light . . .

. . . Jessik, get over here. Jessik . . .

. . . Man overboard! . . .

That last hit her like a fist in the gut. She had no idea *who* had gone overboard, but she had a sudden vision of a single sailor thrashing in the vast, foamy black of the sea. She'd heard people say that drowning was a peaceful way to die. They were wrong. Every Kettral cadet was half-drowned in training. It fucking hurt.

As Gwenna shifted, trying to get a better grip around Rat's waist, a spray of warm water splattered across her face. She spat it out, stared across the brig to where Dhar was wiping his own soaked hair back from his eyes. Water was leaking in from half a dozen places. Leaking *down*.

"Bad luck," the captain observed quietly.

That was a massive understatement. The brig was three decks down, so deep in the hull it was almost sitting on the keel. For that much water to be draining onto them, the upper deck had to be completely awash. As Gwenna stared at the ceiling, she could feel the ship crest another swell, tip, then race down the back of the wave. When it plowed into the trough, the whole hull shuddered, then rose slowly to the surface again.

"The waves are too steep," Dhar said. "If he buries the bow enough times, she will come apart."

"It's bury the bow or breech."

The captain shook his head. "He needs to ride the swells at an angle. Too sharp and he drives her beneath. Too shallow and she will roll. It is an art, feeling this angle."

"Jonon is an arrogant ass, but he knows his work."

"Not this work."

"You can't even see what he's doing."

"I can feel it. He is making mistakes." He gazed into the darkness where she sat. His position hadn't changed—he was still braced against the bulkhead, one hand wrapped around the steel ring, one planted against the bare deck—but there was a new readiness to him, as though some moment long awaited had finally arrived. "I can save this ship."

"What? From the brig?"

"If you get me out of the brig. If you put me at the helm."

Gwenna barked a laugh. "Get you *out*? You think I'd still be in here if I had a way out?"

The Manjari captain nodded. "Before, there was no reason to leave. Now there is."

"Doesn't change the fact that we're on the wrong side of a locked door."

"You killed a kettral. You were hauled beneath the keel five times and survived. I do not believe the door is an impediment."

Gwenna started to object, then stopped, closed her eyes, forced herself to listen. She could hear Pattick and Cho Lu in the makeshift second brig down the corridor, their voices low, tight, frightened. Up on deck the sailors were still shouting to one another, though wind played havoc with the words. At the very edge of hearing she could even make out the shape of Jonon's commands, though not their content. Directly outside the door to the brig, however—no one. They were unguarded.

She opened her eyes, stared at that door. Heavy strap hinges ran across vertically joined boards. Each board was as wide as her two hands held side by side. During the daytime, she could make out a faint light in the narrow gaps between them, gaps wide enough to shove a dagger through. If she'd had a dagger. Without tools, the only way past the door was to batter it down, kick the planking and keep kicking it until it split. Dhar was right. She could do it. Normally, of course, the racket would have brought a dozen sailors running, but in the madness of the storm she could probably hack a hole in the hull and no one would notice until the ship began to sink. She could break out, fight her way up to the helm, put Dhar in charge. She trusted him more than Jonon lem Jonon, that was for sure. Somehow, during the long days locked inside the brig, she'd come to believe in both the decency and judgment of the Manjari captain. With him steering the ship, they'd have a chance. . . .

"No," she said, driving the word like a knife into the space between them.

Dhar pursed his lips, then nodded. "I understand. I am a foreign captain, your enemy. . . ."

She shook her head. "It's not a question of enemies."

"Then what?"

The ship slammed into the base of a wave, hurling them all into the bulk-head.

Rat cursed, Gwenna wrapped her arm tighter around the girl, waited for the *Daybreak* to split apart. Only when it started climbing the next swell did she answer.

"Back in Annur, before we left, the Emperor told me something I didn't want to hear. She said I was a gambler."

"Sailors and soldiers—sometimes we all must throw the dice."

"Sometimes," Gwenna agreed. "But I was throwing them *all* the time. I was throwing them when I didn't need to. I was throwing them because I'd won so many times I'd stopped believing I could lose. And what I was gambling for—it wasn't just my own life. I gambled with the lives of my soldiers, with the lives of my friends, and you know what? I fucking lost."

"Eventually," Dhar replied, his face grave, "everyone loses."

"Fine. But it doesn't have to happen on my watch." She stabbed a finger up toward the sterncastle. "Jonon's the captain of this ship. He's an asshole, but he's not incompetent. What happens now, it's not my call to make."

The *Daybreak* pitched, sending more water down through the gaps in the decking overhead. Bhuma Dhar wiped it from his eyes. He smelled angry. Strange. He'd been in the brig for months on end, the captain of a Manjari throne ship made the prisoner of a foreign navy, shitting in a bucket, eating slops, locked in the darkness, and this was the first time he'd smelled angry.

"This," he said quietly, "is the coward's path."

"No. It is the sensible path."

"There are over a hundred men on this ship. . . ."

"Yes, *Jonon's* men. They swore allegiance to *him,* not me. They're counting on *him* to get them through this, not me."

"He is not going to succeed."

"That's not my call to make."

She'd come back for Rat, sure, because there was no one else to take care of the girl. She hadn't come back for the whole 'Kent-kissing ship. Just because she'd survived up there in the mountains, that didn't make her Kettral. It didn't make her *anything.*

"You want to break out," she said, gesturing to the door, "I won't stop you. Maybe it's your *davi.* I don't know. What I do know is that there's enough on my head already without the sinking of the *Daybreak* added to it."

"Refusing to act is also an act. If this ship sinks when you could have prevented it . . ."

"I *can't. Fucking. Prevent it.*"

"You are wrong."

Gwenna shook her head grimly. "Not the first time, won't be the last."

†

It was another day and a half before the cry came to abandon ship.

Even buried deep in the hull, Gwenna could hear it, the admiral's horn followed by the shouts of the sailors, the stampede of soldiers racing above-decks to board the boats.

By that point, the water in the brig was five or six fingers deep, and instead of draining down into the hold below, it had started rising.

"She is foundering," Dhar observed.

After the one brief argument he had spoken no more of breaking out of the brig or taking the ship. Like Gwenna and Rat, he held tight to the metal rings in the walls and tried his best not to be battered to death with every pitch and roll.

"A breach?" Gwenna asked.

He shook his head. "No. Or maybe many small breaches. She's taken on more water than the pumps can handle. Or the pumps are broken. Or the men who should be working them have quit. It is impossible to know, from down here."

"How much longer can she stay afloat?"

"I don't know."

"*Guess.*"

Dhar shook his head again. "Perhaps an hour. Perhaps a day, as long as someone remains at the helm to keep her pointed into the swells."

"Jonon just gave the order to abandon ship."

The captain didn't look surprised. "Is your admiral the kind of man to remain at his post as long as there are souls on board?"

"He'll get everyone off that he can, but his devotion is to the mission."

"Then we are doomed. When he leaves the helm she will swing broadside to the swells and the sea will swamp her."

Gwenna had seen ships sink. She'd been the one to sink some of them. When the Dombângans tried to run the Annurian blockade, she'd watched half a dozen vessels go down, desperate men scrambling over the decking like termites, trying first to work the pumps, then, as the ships listed and dipped, as the first waves washed over the rails, leaping into the water, even those who couldn't swim, clinging to whatever they could cling to—broken spars, barrels, even things that obviously wouldn't float like spears and coils of rope—made stupid by their terror. It would be worse for anyone trapped below. She imagined the *Daybreak* wallowing between hill-sized swells, the water pounding down, grinding it under. How long would the hull hold? A hundred heartbeats? Two hundred? Long enough, anyway, to hear the water snapping the timbers. She glanced down at Rat. The girl was ghost pale in the near-perfect darkness, clutching the steel ring with one hand, clinging to Gwenna's blacks with the other.

"Jonon will send someone for us," she said.

Dhar raised an eyebrow. "For the Manjari dog, the woman who crossed him, and a girl? I do not think so."

"Maybe not for us," Gwenna said. "But for Rat. She knows things that he needs."

Outside the brig, across the corridor, Cho Lu had begun hammering on the bulkhead.

"Let us out, you assholes! We can help. *Let us out!*"

From above, the slow groan, then awful crack, as when a tree collapsed under the weight of too much snow. The hull shuddered, then yawed violently to the side. Water sloshed into the angle between the bulkhead and floor, dragging Gwenna with it.

"The foremast has snapped," Dhar said. "It is dragging in the sea to port. Soon, the weight will capsize the boat." He cocked his head to the side.

Gwenna looked away from him, found herself staring into Rat's eyes.

"Gwenna Sharpe," the girl whispered, her words almost lost in the general cacophony.

In that moment, Rat didn't look fierce or furious or defiant. She didn't look preternaturally strong or fast. She looked like a small child far from her home, far from everyone and everything she'd known, lost and filled with fear. Her gaze was heavier than the weight of the whole ocean pressing in around them.

Gwenna cursed, turned away from the captain and the child both, rose unsteadily to her feet. It took her a moment to find her balance, but she'd spent days, weeks, half a lifetime balancing on the pitching decks of ships. After a few breaths she steadied herself, measured the distance, then lashed out with her heel at the center of the door. It shuddered, but held firm. As she stepped back up the slanting deck, the ship pitched, tossing her into the bulkhead. She caught herself, squared up against the door, kicked it again. This time a crack laced down one of the boards.

"Commander?" Pattick called, his voice tight. "Is that you?"

"Who the fuck else would it be?" she growled, lashing out at the door again.

Her heel hit wrong; pain lanced up her leg into her hip. The door barely budged. She took a deep breath, stuffed the pain down deep into herself, somewhere it wouldn't get in the way, and slammed her heel into the wooden planks again.

"Listen to me, Dhar," she said, kicking the door again, "as soon as we're through, you get Rat to the boats. You get her on board one of those boats if you have to cut your way through Jonon to do it. Do you understand?"

"I understand," the captain replied. "And you?"

"I'll be right behind you. After I free Cho Lu and Pattick."

Another blow opened a finger-width split in the planking. The water was rushing around Gwenna's shins now, threatening to drag her down.

"Swear to me that you'll get her to the boats."

"I will do everything in my power to save the girl," the Manjari captain replied. "This I vow in the names of Shava and Bhir."

"Your gods?"

He hesitated. "My children."

In all the long months, he had never once mentioned his children.

Gwenna took a deep breath. "Even better."

She cocked her leg back for a final blow when something clanked on the far side of the door. She paused, and a moment later it swung heavily outward, slamming against the bulkhead. The gloom was deep, even for her eyes, but Gwenna could make out a figure standing in the passageway beyond. At first she thought Jonon had sent someone after all, a sailor or soldier to spring them free, then she realized the figure wasn't dressed like a sailor or soldier, nor did he smell like one.

"Come," said the imperial historian, gesturing toward them. "There is not much time."

✝

No time would have been a better estimate.

When Gwenna finally shoved open the hatch and staggered out onto the deck, the second boat was already away. She caught a glimpse of men dragging desperately on the oars, of Jonon half standing at the tiller, and then it slid off behind the curtains of rain and night.

"Those bastards," Cho Lu swore, following Gwenna's gaze. It had been only a matter of moments to free the two legionaries, although it seemed she'd done so only so that they could die atop the deck rather than trapped below it.

She swept her gaze over the ship. It had been frightening below, locked in the brig, unable to see what was happening. Out in the air, it was even worse.

Black waves loomed like hills on every side, higher than the remaining masts, their crests whipped to foam by the wind. The *Daybreak* shuddered between them, a toy boat lost in the immensity. Jonon had had the sense to reef most of the sail before the storm hit, but half of the canvas still aloft hung in tatters. Worse—far worse—Dhar was right. The foremast had snapped and dropped over the side. It was dragging along, partially submerged, tethered to the ship by the riot of rigging and ratlines, like some great net threatening to drag the whole vessel down.

"They left us," Pattick said, shaking his head.

"Bastards," Cho Lu repeated.

"Fuck the admiral," Rat said. She was clinging to Gwenna's leg, hair plastered to her face, lips drawn back in a snarl.

"No *shit,* fuck the admiral," Cho Lu agreed. "He—"

Bhuma Dhar sliced through the word. "I am going to the helm."

The legionary nodded. "Good a place to die as any."

"I am not going there to die," Dhar replied. "I am going there to sail this ship."

He didn't sound like the man who'd been locked in the brig with Gwenna for months. He sounded like a captain, and when he pointed at Cho Lu, his voice cracked like a whip.

"You will cut free that mast. You, and you," this was Pattick, "and you, Sharpe."

A tiny part of her mind took note that it was not *Commander* Sharpe.

"Rat and the old man are with me," he continued. *"Move."*

Somehow, the command kindled a new life in the two legionaries. Pattick even offered half a salute before remembering Dhar was a Manjari captain. He dropped the hand, made a confused grimace, then turned to sprint across the deck, Cho Lu at his heels. To her surprise, Gwenna found herself running with them. It was pointless, obviously. Even without the dangling mast to drag her under, the ship was foundering. One swell or the next, they were going under. On the other hand, it felt better to be moving, running, *trying* to do something, than sitting in the brig waiting to be crushed. She risked a glance over her shoulder. Rat, Kiel, and Dhar had reached the sterncastle. The historian was lashing the little girl to the mast while Dhar wrestled the wheel. A flash of motion caught her eye. There, in the rigging above Rat, knifelike teeth bared to the storm, hung the *avesh,* Yutaka, howling a blood-chilling cry.

A Manjari captain, a half-savage orphan, a historian, a pair of legionaries, and a monster straight out of the sickness of Menkiddoc. Not the people Gwenna had expected to die alongside, not by a long shot. Whenever she'd imagined her death, she'd imagined Talal there, or Annick, maybe Quick Jak or even Qora. Strangely, though, it didn't feel wrong to be spending the final moments of her life with this ragtag band of semi-strangers. It felt almost right.

She reached the forecastle just a few strides behind Pattick and Cho Lu. The first problem was that none of them had knives, but there were weapon racks against the port side of the castle, and while half the spears had been washed away, they only needed three.

"Here!" Cho Lu tossed her one. She caught it, and went to work, hacking at the tangle of rope tethering the broken mast to the ship.

How long they worked she had no idea. A few minutes? Half the night? All she knew was that when the mast finally tore free, her shoulders ached and her waterlogged hands were a mass of blisters. Cho Lu let out a whoop, while Pattick stood staring as the mast crested a wave, then slid out of sight.

It wasn't the last task that Bhuma Dhar gave them.

All night, the captain picked his intricate course through the waves, fighting his way forward into a morning that wasn't worth the name, just a vague paling of the sky from black to indigo to grudging gray. Somehow, Gwenna had allowed herself to believe that if they made it through the night the worst would be past, that sunlight would bring some slackening of the storm. As usual, she was wrong. If anything, the swells raged higher in the waxen light, while the wind tore at the sails and rigging.

Each new swell half buried the forecastle. Water flooded the midships. Every time they slid into a new trough, it felt as though the ship would keep going, plunging straight down toward the ocean's bottom, but there was still air inside the hull, enough air to stop the slide, and each time the *Daybreak* quaked beneath the water's weight, shimmied like some terrified creature, then rose with awful slowness up, up, shedding water over the rails in great torrents until she broke free again to begin climbing the next swell.

The waves were killing them slowly, but when Gwenna returned to the helm after another of Dhar's orders, the captain's face was grave.

"Don't tell me," Gwenna said. "We're sinking."

"We have been sinking for days. The process may now go much faster."

He jerked his head backward, over his shoulder. Gwenna turned as the ship crested a swell, shielded her eyes with a hand, stared into the gloom. At first she could make out only spray and rain scrawled against the gray, but then, for just a moment the wind shifted and she saw it—a dark brooding shape that she took for another wave at first, looming out of the madness. Unlike the rest of the waves, however, it didn't move.

"Well, shit."

Dhar nodded. "Cliff. A mile off. Perhaps a little more. The coast of Menkiddoc."

"Can you change course?"

He shook his head. "Any other course will swamp us. I will keep her off the rocks as long as I can. The rest of you will have to swim."

"In *this*?"

Alone, with outstanding luck, at the peak of her strength, she might just have managed it. But she wasn't alone, or strong, or feeling all that fucking lucky.

"We won't make it."

"Use flotation," Dhar said. The tendons on his neck stood out as he dragged on the wheel. "Do whatever it is you must, but get my people off."

Gwenna stared at the captain. "They're not your people."

"While I am standing at the helm of this ship," he replied, not shifting his hands from the wheel, not taking his eyes from the lashing waves, "they are my people."

Gwenna glanced over at Rat. "Can you swim?" She made a motion like swimming.

The girl stared at the waves, then shook her head.

Pattick and Cho Lu clambered up the ladder. Something had opened a gash across Cho Lu's scalp; blood sheeted his face with the rain, but his eyes were clear. Pattick's jaw was clenched. He smelled frightened. Frightened but defiant.

"There's cliffs," Gwenna said, chucking her thumb toward the distant shore. "Probably reefs. We're going to wreck."

"Land!" Pattick said, a surge of hope in his eyes.

"The reefs will grind this ship to kindling," Dhar replied. "Sharpe is going to take all of you and swim for it."

"No," Gwenna said. "I am not."

Until she spoke, she hadn't realized she'd made the decision. "I'm staying."

"If you're staying on board," Cho Lu said, "then so are we."

She shook her head. "If you swim, you might make it."

"No we won't," Pattick said, eyeing the waves.

"What about you?" Gwenna asked, turning to Kiel.

"I will remain."

"Should have gotten off when you could. Should have gone with the boats." The historian shook his head. "My chances are better if I stay on the ship."

She stared at him. "The *sinking* ship?"

He nodded.

"How do you figure that?"

To her shock, he made a face that might have been a smile. "You would not understand the math."

☩

It could be tough, Gwenna had found, to distinguish between the divine hand of providence and sheer dumb luck. In the moments before they struck the reef, she'd been too busy comforting Rat to do any praying, but maybe someone else had been at it double-time, muttering exhortations to whatever god saved women and men from shipwreck and drowning. Or maybe Bhuma Dhar was right, that work *was* prayer, in which case she'd put in more than her bit of piety. Whatever the case, the ship didn't sink.

Not entirely, anyway.

Instead, with a sound like a great bone shattering, it ground up on a reef a few hundred paces from the shore. The hull lurched, threatening to toss them all into the seething waves. Gwenna could hear the water surging into the breach, boiling up through the decks below. She held Rat to her chest, ready to leap when the time came. But the time did not come.

For the remainder of the night the wind tried to grind the ship to splinters, twisting it back and forth over the coral. Waves lashed the hull, clawed at the deck, tried to drag the *Daybreak* under. Gwenna could feel planks buckling deep in the vessel's belly, but the hull held, and gradually, finally, as the day wore on, the storm began to relent.

"Done," Rat said, pointing up. "Rain done."

Gwenna glanced up and realized it was true.

"I guess we're not going to die a horrible watery death after all," Cho Lu put in.

Pattick stared at the sky, as though he didn't quite believe it.

Up in the rigging, Yutaka chittered furiously, gnashed her knifelike teeth. Her gray hair was soaked, slicked down across her body. It made her appear sleeker, even more dangerous than normal.

Gwenna turned to Bhuma Dhar. He looked like a man half-dead. Rain, sweat, and spray matted his black hair to his head, dripped from the ends of his mustache. His eyes were sunken, and when he pried his hands from the wheel, they came away as claws. Two days. For two full days he had held that post, keeping the *Daybreak* afloat.

Gwenna met his eyes, nodded. "Thank you, Captain."

The thinnest smile cracked his lips, then he shook his head. "We have not finished yet. One tide, perhaps two, will lift her from the reef and she will sink."

Kiel pursed his lips. "I suggest that we vacate the ship before that happens."

"Remind me again," Gwenna said, "who can and can't swim." Rat, she could manage. Maybe one more, if they didn't panic . . .

Pattick glanced at the water—the most punishing waves had abated, but it still looked dangerous—then raised a tentative hand.

"We'll get you a barrel," Cho Lu said. "Or something else that floats."

"Anyone else?" Kiel asked.

Gwenna had just started to breathe a sigh of relief when Rat tugged at her. The girl was staring toward the shore, eyes bleak.

"Not safe," she said, gesturing.

At first Gwenna misunderstood. "The swim will be tricky, but now that the storm's settled down, I can manage it—"

Rat cut her off. "Not swim. Land." She hesitated. "Monsters."

From above, Yutaka let out a shriek, part challenge, part delight. Then, between one blink and the next, she hurled herself into the waves, began paddling awkwardly but furiously toward shore.

"Your pet doesn't seem too scared," Cho Lu observed.

"Not pet," Rat replied, face grave.

"And she is not scared," Kiel added, "because this is her home. All the *gabhya* whose skulls we found in the south, all the monsters shipped up to the Manjari empire? *This* is where they come from."

42

Ruc tried not to be relieved by the failure.

Every night after a full day of training, after dragging themselves to the mess hall, then back to Goatface's meager barracks, after Monster, Mouse, and Stupid had gone to sleep, often after the tolling of the midnight gong, Bien and Talal had worked to unlock her power. They'd been at it for weeks. The Kettral seemed to have an inexhaustible list of approaches. One night he asked her to hold her breath until she felt like she was going to die. Another he blindfolded her, then battered her with a fly swatter until she finally erupted into curses, ripped off the cloth, snatched the swatter from his grip, and snapped it in half. On yet a third occasion, she got so drunk on *quey* that she puked into a bucket until morning.

None of it worked.

"I can feel it sometimes," she said, shaking her head. "Not all the time, just sometimes. But trying to grab it . . . It's like trying to hold on to the rain."

Exhaustion and frustration had rusted her voice down to a hoarse whisper. Goatface had been pushing them all hard, but Bien was the least prepared for the physical rigors of the Arena. It seemed impossible that she was still getting up every day, still enduring the running, lifting, and battering, still forcing herself to stay awake at night trying to master her power. He might have the strength of the delta gods woven through his flesh, but she was the strong one, the brave one.

"It's all right," Talal said, setting a hand on her shoulder. "Back on the Islands some leaches take years to figure this out."

"We don't *have* years."

She forced herself to her feet, stood unsteadily for a moment, then crossed to the window, drew back the canvas. Torches burned around the perimeter of the yard. Aside from a few patrolling guards, however, the space was empty. When she spoke again, she didn't turn, as though she were saying the words to herself.

"I need to be able to do it now."

Talal nodded. "You said it feels like you're trying to hold the rain. Can you describe it any other way?"

His voice was quiet, patient, but he'd been asking the same questions every night now, over and over. For all his mild manner, the man was implacable.

"She *has* described it other ways," Ruc said, shaking his head. "She's said it's like hearing voices without understanding the words. Like a smell from childhood to which she can't put a name. Like an itch that's everywhere but nowhere at the same time. We've been *over* this."

His vehemence surprised him. It wasn't *his* struggle, after all, but he hated watching it, hated seeing the exhaustion on Bien's face as she tried one more thing, then one more, then one more, hated the grief that replaced it when she failed, hated that a part of him, not a small part, was actually *relieved* when she didn't succeed. It meant that they were still trapped, of course, still prisoners. It also meant that Bien was still the woman he loved—leaner, harder, angrier, but not fundamentally altered.

"The Kettral have been around for hundreds of years," Talal said, "and they haven't figured out a good way to do this. It's always a matter of banging your head against the wall until it breaks."

"The wall?" Bien asked, the weary ghost of a smile playing over her lips. "Or the head?"

He smiled a response, but didn't let up with the questions. "How does it feel when you *do* manage to touch your well?"

She frowned, squinted at the lamp burning on the table. "Broken. Like something inside me is broken."

"There are other ways to escape," Ruc pointed out. "Ways that don't involve"—he gestured vaguely to the two of them—"this."

Talal nodded. "Almost certainly. It's a question of choosing the one most likely to succeed."

"This isn't succeeding," Ruc said. "Goatface has keys. To the armory. To the gate out of the yard."

"The armory is guarded," Bien replied, shaking her head. "And so is the gate. Everything is guarded. Even if we got his keys, it doesn't help us get past the men with the flatbows."

"Then maybe we start putting our effort into solving *that* problem. This was all worth a shot, but it's been months now, months of you trying every night, and we don't even know what your well is. I don't think—"

"Love," Bien said.

For a moment he thought she meant *him*. She called him that sometimes—*my love*—or she had, anyway, before . . . She wasn't looking at him as she said it, though. She was staring straight into the flame of the lantern, as though waiting for it to burn out her sight.

Talal shifted in his chair. "Your well is love?"

She nodded, mute.

In the silence, Ruc could hear the rats scratching just inside the wall. Trying to get out? Trying to get in? Just scratching, because that's what rats did?

"How do you know?" he asked finally.

"The same way you know you have two hands," she replied, not taking her eyes from the fire.

Talal nodded, as though that made sense. "The love of others?"

"No. My own love. The love inside me."

"How long have you known?"

"I don't know. Maybe a month. Maybe forever."

Ruc stared at her. "Why did you *hide* it? Every night we've been in here, going over the same exercises—"

She looked up finally, her face hot with anger. *"Because I didn't want it to be true."*

He struggled to make sense of the words.

"Why not? It's a connection to Eira. Something that redeems . . ."

He regretted the word as soon as it was out of his mouth.

Bien's lip twisted into something like a sick smile. "Redeems what I am?"

"That's not what I meant."

"Of course it is." She waved his excuse away wearily, the anger draining out of her as quickly as it had come. "That's what I thought when I first realized it. *Maybe I'm not so polluted after all.*"

"You're not polluted," Talal said, voice quiet but firm.

"I'm not *anything*," Bien replied, "because I can't reach my well."

The Kettral frowned. "You're a priestess of Eira. Love—"

She talked right through him as though she were all alone, speaking to herself. "I *was* a priestess of Eira. Love used to come to me as easily as breathing. Since the attack on the temple, though, since we went back to burn all those bodies . . ." She didn't shudder or sob, but tears poured down her cheeks. "It's gone. Whatever I used to love with, whatever part of me that was—it's crushed. The love is gone. All that's left, all that I'm made of now, is grief and fear and confusion and doubt and rage."

✝

Ruc didn't expect to sleep. For half the night he lay awake, sweating into his mattress, listening to the whine of the redflies, watching the shape of Bien's heat on the bunk above as she twisted and thrashed, caught in the claws of some nightmare. He considered waking her, then decided against it. Whatever violence she faced in her dream, she needed the rest.

Grief and fear and confusion and doubt and rage.

The words kindled inside him a rage all his own.

For all the horror of the attack on Eira's temple, he'd held on to the fact that at least Bien had survived. The ways of the goddess could be strange, inscrutable, but he had seen Bien's escape as a kind of grace, a small bright space of sunlight in all the world's tangled savagery. As long as she was still alive there was something good in the world, something worth striving for, a reason to be better than himself.

She is *still alive,* he thought grimly. *But we betrayed her.*

On the back of his closed lids, he saw the statue of Eira gazing down at him. She was holding her wine and her sword and her flaming torch. The fire licked upward, tasting the darkness. Her fourth hand, the severed one, dripped blood.

Why did you turn your back on her? he demanded.

The wolves prowling around Eira's feet cocked their ears, bared their teeth. The *avesh* made a sick, chewing noise.

Was it I who turned my back? the goddess replied. *Or was it you?*

She raised her torch as though to see him better.

The light gleamed in her golden eyes.

Her smile was all teeth and beauty.

There was something wrong with her. Not enough arms. No clothes.

The sword she was holding wasn't a sword at all but a snake, sliding through her grip to wrap lazily around her naked body.

You never ask questions, he said. *You don't have words.*

Words like weakness? she asked. She stalked toward him, movement so smooth it looked like stillness. *Words like* fear?

He shook his head. *I didn't leave because I was afraid. Not of the delta. Not of you.*

No?

She paused in front of him, took him by the chin, lifted his face—even as a grown man he was half a head shorter than her—considered him with that inhuman gaze.

Then why?

He struggled to step back, but her grip was iron.

I chose to be something different.

She laughed then, the sound of water flowing over stones. He went cold. In all the years he'd lived with them, he'd never heard them laugh.

You cannot be something different. A snake is a snake. A spider is a spider. You are what we raised you to be.

With a curt blow he knocked her arm aside.

I am not some beast of the delta.

Her eyes darkened, as though storm clouds had passed over the sun.

What are you?

I am a priest of the goddess of love.

It came out louder than he'd intended, almost a shout. She didn't flinch. She never flinched.

We did not teach you to lie.

I am a priest of Eira.

We did not teach you to grovel at the feet of wooden statues.

I am a priest—

We did not teach you to hide behind words.

No, he snarled. *No. All you taught me to do was kill.*

He didn't see her move, but suddenly she was behind him, wrapping him in her arms, holding him to her chest as she'd done when he was barely more than an infant. Her heat swaddled him. She smelled of sweat and skin and mud and sun. With one hand she brushed his black hair back from his eyes.

Maybe that was a mistake. Maybe we should have taught you what we teach all the others.

He twisted from her grip, turned to face her once more.

And what is that?

She bared her teeth.

How to die.

As she said the words, she plunged her hand into his chest, found his heart, wrapped her fingers around it. Then, as easily as a woman plucking a lemon from a bough, she ripped it from his ribs.

He woke to find himself drenched in a sweat that he took at first for blood.

For a desperate, baffled moment he pawed at his chest, then let his hand fall as the dream drained away.

Shuddering, he sat up, shrugged aside the rough sheet, stood, crossed to the window on bare feet. He moved aside the sailcloth, stared out into the night. In the dark hours before dawn, the world was still as some predator patiently waiting, or something already dead.

†

Vang Vo, the high priestess of the Arena herself, arrived in the yard during the morning's sparring.

At first Ruc didn't even notice her. Mouse had been battering at his shield with a bronze sword for what seemed like forever. It was supposed to be an exercise in slipping and dodging, tactical retreat. Instead, Ruc had pressed forward. The weight of the other man's attacks drove out—if only for the moment—the dread, the doubt. It wasn't until Goatface called the halt that Ruc felt the exhaustion wash over him. He bent over, head ringing, leaning on his shield. When he'd caught his breath, he unbuckled the straps with clumsy fingers, shucked the dead weight from his arm, then straightened to find the priestess watching him. She might have been a marsh hawk watching a vole.

"So," she said. "Has your goddess been watching over you?"

He'd seen her around the ring in the months since the capture, but it was the first time she'd spoken to him directly since that morning on the deck of the ship.

"We're alive," Ruc replied.

Vang Vo nodded thoughtfully, shifted her gaze to Bien. She'd been working spear forms against Stupid just a few paces away. "Like I told Gao Ji when he first dragged you in—you're survivors." She watched a moment longer, then turned to Talal. "What about you? How does this measure up against your Kettral training?"

The soldier shrugged. "Less swimming. More mud."

"How's the ball," she asked, gesturing to the iron weight resting on the ground.

"About like you'd think."

The priestess cocked her head to the side. "Are you really a leach?"

"Nope," Talal replied. "Does that mean I can take it off?"

The woman shook her head. "Nope."

"Go ahead," Monster said, glaring at Vang Vo from beneath her tangle of sweat-drenched hair. "Ask me how *I'm* doing."

The priestess raised an eyebrow. "How are you doing?"

"I want a new fucking trainer."

Goatface looked mildly affronted. Vang Vo caught the expression and let loose a rich laugh.

"You have it better than you know."

"I don't see *you* down here getting pounded to fucking pulp."

"Goats puts more Worthy in robes than anyone else but the Nun."

"The Nun," Goatface objected, "is working with more . . . refined stock."

"Don't doubt yourself, Goats," Vang Vo said, slapping him roughly across the back. "If anyone can turn a pair of love priests into vicious killers, it's you." She turned back to the others. "*Three* of his Worthy have made it to the delta and returned."

Stupid tipped back his sweat-soaked straw hat, looked pointedly around the group. "There are six of us."

Vang Vo shrugged. "Half's not bad."

Mouse pulled a long face. "Bad."

"Well," the priestess said, "bad or not, we're about to find out. You're fighting in the culling. One week from today."

For a few moments no one spoke.

"Which three?" Goatface asked finally.

"Both of them."

"Both?" The trainer blinked in confusion. "For *all* the Worthy of a single trainer to take part in the culling. It is . . . unprecedented."

"I'll go ahead and assume that means you don't like it." Vang Vo shrugged. "Too bad. One week, and they've got a date in the Arena."

"This is pig shit," Monster growled.

The priestess smiled. "Have faith."

"In your blood-hungry gods?" Bien demanded, shaking her head.

Vang Vo met her eyes. "In whatever it takes to get you through the day."

There was a long silence as the woman walked off toward the northern end of the yard. Finally, Bien broke it.

"What's the culling?"

"For fuck's sake," Monster snapped, "try to at least *pretend* like you're Dombângan."

"Not everyone in this city revels in blood."

"You don't need to revel in blood to have ears."

"I've heard of it. I thought it was part of the high holy days."

Goatface nodded. "Just before, generally. There are different numbers of Worthy every year. The culling is a way to bring those numbers down to forty-eight."

"Forty-eight?"

"Sixteen threes. Which makes for fifteen fights, five for each of the high holy days. It is also a way of ensuring the . . . integrity of the holy contests."

"Meaning no one wants to watch the assholes who die too quickly," Monster put in.

"On the contrary," the trainer replied. "The Dombângan citizenry watches the culling with almost as much zeal as they do the later fights. The culling is generally sloppier. Messier."

Bien grimaced. "Sounds like the kind of thing Vang Vo would appreciate."

The trainer shook his head. "The high priestess appreciates skill. She believes that inept performances . . . demean the sanctity of the holy days."

"So," Ruc asked grimly, "who are we going to fight?"

"That," Goatface said, "we will not learn until the morning of the culling."

Bien glanced at Ruc, then back to the trainer. "Rooster and Snakebones?"

"Certainly not. The point of the culling is to test the threes of more . . . questionable viability."

"It makes me uneasy," Stupid put in, "when people question my viability."

"But this is good, right?" Bien said. "It means we don't have to fight anyone really dangerous."

Goatface frowned. "Perhaps your years as a servant of Eira have warped your notion of both the good and the dangerous. I can assure you, the culling is no occasion for complacency. The men and women you stand against in a week's time will be trying to kill you with no less fervor than their more accomplished peers, and their bronze blades will be no less sharp."

43

Despite Rat's fear and Kiel's warnings, the beach, at least, seemed devoid of monsters.

Gwenna dragged the last of the barrels up onto the sand, then allowed herself to collapse. She and Cho Lu—the strongest other swimmer in the group—had made six trips to the *Daybreak* and back, first ferrying barrels filled with food and fresh water, then bringing those with the remaining kettral eggs packed inside—Jonon had managed to carry all but two of the eggs with him when he quit the ship—shepherding them through the surf, then passing them to the others to be dragged up the rocky shingle. Dhar had questioned that last decision.

"We are wrecked on a remote and dangerous coast," he said, dark eyes sunken with exhaustion. "Are these eggs truly necessary?"

"These eggs," Gwenna replied, "are why we came."

"They help no one if we die trying to haul them."

"Each one's the size of a loaf of bread. I think we can manage it."

"The difference between living and dying." Dhar held up his finger and thumb a hairsbreadth apart. "Often it is this small. You understand this better than most. Often, it is not what we lack that dooms us, but what we cling to."

Gwenna started to say something cutting and dismissive, then stopped herself.

"This is my job," she said quietly. "My *davi*."

He studied her awhile, then nodded. "We will bring the eggs."

A few paces away Cho Lu coughed up an exhausted laugh. "I'm glad that's settled. I didn't climb all the way up that cliff just to leave these little bastards on some foreign beach."

When it was done, when all the supplies were piled up on shore above the high tide line, exhaustion washed over her. Every tendon, every muscle, every fiber of her flesh felt strained to breaking. The keelhauling had been brutal enough, and then to endure the battering of the storm . . .

But she *had* endured it. She stared down at her body with a kind of dumb surprise. She'd survived the hauling and *hamaksha* both. Somehow, somewhere, she'd rediscovered her old strength, except . . . it didn't *feel* like the old strength. Not quite. Gingerly she turned her attention inward, terrified to find the panic still there, shoved aside in some corner of her mind, fuse lit and ready to explode. Her thoughts, like her body, were raw, red, ravaged. When she allowed herself to remember the Purple Baths or the battle against Dhar's ship, the old fear and shame blazed through her veins, twisted her guts, and for a moment the old vertigo took her. She felt as though she were falling, despite the hard sand at her back, plummeting into the abyss of herself. It was like those final moments roped to the wild kettral, how she'd known, *known,* she was going to die, but this time, instead of struggling or screaming as she fell, she let the awful weightlessness take her, let the fear close over her. All those weeks and months in the brig she'd been trying to run from it, hide from it, deny it, but the grim truth was that the fear had become a part of her, like her stubbornness, and her striving, and her strength. To run from the fear was to run from herself, and she was done running.

There'd been a trainer back on the Islands, Ugly Darren, who taught the advanced demolitions classes.

"The secret to explosives," he said once, "is the secret to life."

He was called Ugly Darren because at some point, many years earlier, he'd misgauged the charge on a flickwick and blown himself up. The mistake left him with a half-melted face and a body that looked like it had been flayed, then boiled alive. The whole episode struck Gwenna as an inauspicious background for the demo trainer, but then, as Darren liked to say, *You don't know where the edge is until you step off of it.*

He said a lot of things like that. Gwenna—only eight years old at the time— had never been quite sure if they were wisdom or pig shit.

"What *is* that secret?" Darren went on, raising the livid wrinkle of flesh that should have been an eyebrow, then lifting the scored, cast-iron tube of a modified starshatter.

All the cadets, Gwenna very much included, leaned back slightly in their seats. As though that could save them if he accidentally blew the place up.

"The secret," Darren said, tapping the starshatter lightly against his forehead, "is that the world wants to be unmade."

In the row ahead of her, Valyn glanced over at Gent. "Whatever that means," he muttered.

Somehow, even given the withered state of his ears, the instructor heard. "It means, Valyn hui'Malkeenian, that whatever order you see—this building"—he gestured up at the roof of the pole barn—"that ship"—out through the open walls toward the harbor—"the elegant proportions of the human form"—he glanced down at himself with the barest hint of a smile. "It is all constantly under siege.

"Given enough time, the beams will snap, the ship will sink, your muscles will grow slack, your brain dull, and eventually it will all turn back to so much dirt. This is the only way that the world moves. Buildings do not assemble themselves, driftwood does not accumulate into ships, old bodies never grow young again. You look at a fortress wall and see something strong, perhaps impregnable, but the truth is this: that wall *wants* to crumble. It is not your explosive"—he gave a little wave with the starshatter—"that brings down the fortress. The explosive makes the barest crack; the *world* does the rest. That is why the work of demolitions is so much faster, so much more certain than the work of making and building. To destroy is to swim with the current of reality. Once a thing is shattered—and this applies to people"—he glanced down at his withered hands—"as well as to castle walls—once a thing is broken, the world rarely allows for it to be put back together. Not the same way, at least."

Ugly Darren, as it turned out, was right.

Something inside of Gwenna had broken after the Purple Baths. Something else had broken in the mountains. She'd attacked the kettral fully expecting to die, and when she didn't . . . well, the woman who woke up battered and blood-soaked on the side of the mountain wasn't the same one who'd gone after the bird in the first place. She sure as shit wasn't the Kettral soldier who'd once commanded a Wing.

The question was, who had she become?

She had no answer to that question, but when she opened her eyes she realized the fear had rolled through her, through and away, just like the storm.

Slowly, gingerly, she leaned back against the barrels.

Rat was already asleep, a small, sodden ball curled beside her in the sand. The two legionaries lay sprawled out a few paces away. Bhuma Dhar sat, eyes closed, mouth moving in what must have been prayer. Even Kiel had his eyes closed, though the man was sitting cross-legged in the sand.

"Set a guard," Gwenna muttered to herself. "We need to set a guard."

She recognized the impossibility even as she spoke the words. The others were well past any kind of guarding. None of them could stay awake; even if they did, they'd be useless if something actually attacked. The best she could do was to stay awake a little longer, watch while they slept. She shifted, sat up straighter, found a long, ragged splinter of wood, pressed it into the flesh of her leg until the pain forced away the weariness. In training, she'd stayed awake for five days once. It seemed impossible, thinking back on it, but then, it had seemed impossible even when she was doing it. She prodded herself with the splinter again, turned away from the sea, from the waves, from the listing wreck of the *Daybreak,* to face the interior of the cursed continent.

They'd made landfall on a tiny crescent beach tucked between high cliffs. It was hotter here than it had been in the south—far hotter—which meant they'd sailed back north to somewhere near the equator.

Only half a world away now, she thought, picturing Kiel's map.

Greenery spilled from the lip of the cliff above, palms overhanging the drop, something that looked like ferns, and a riot of dangling vines. Brilliantly colored birds flitted from perch to perch, cocked their heads at the newcomers, pierced the frog chirp and thrum of unseen insects with volleys of staccato song. The breeze had shifted offshore, carrying with it the tangled scents of life, and rot, and green, struggling heat.

Bad luck to have landed on the edge of a fucking jungle.

On the other hand, they *had* landed. Wrecked slowly, anyway. Managed to swim ashore. Strange, how good luck and bad came all tangled up, so that you couldn't sort the one from the other without destroying both. That was the last thing Gwenna remembered thinking before sleep, despite her resolve, clamped down around her.

She woke to find the sun hanging just above the waves to the west, low, hot, and sodden. She cursed, staggered to her feet, wrenched her sword from its sheath, cast about blearily. When she found the others still asleep and nothing worth attacking, she relaxed a fraction. Sore and stiff, she stumbled down to the water, plunged her face into the waves, tried for a while to scrub the grit from her eyes, the sand from her hair, then gave up and turned back toward the beach.

The sand was strewn with debris kicked up by the storm—seaweed; driftwood; fish, their dead eyes dry and staring; and three sailors. Gwenna closed her own eyes, dragged in a weary breath, then opened them again, made her way along the sand to where the men lay sprawled. It was hardly a surprise. There would be others somewhere, probably lots of others, washed up on a different stretch of coast or dragged down and out into the deep. Maybe a few had survived, made landfall on some other forgiving scrap of shore, but most of those who slipped into the water, unable to swim, had drowned. She'd heard them screaming when she was still in the brig, voices pitched above the keening wind, pleading for help or mercy. Those screams hadn't lasted long.

She gazed out across the water. The sea was still, almost smooth as lacquer, blue-green instead of black, warm and inviting, the breaking waves barely knee-high. It was hard to imagine that same sea in a fury, strange to think that men had drowned out there, within easy reach of shore. A tough break, getting so close to safety and then not making it, but then, dying probably always seemed like a tough break to the people doing the dying.

Gwenna made herself look at the bodies. She recognized one as old Genir, who had counted for her during her keelhauling. The other two she couldn't say. The wounds were ghastly—one man's head had been smashed, lacerations from reef or rocks carved open the other—but the sea had washed away the blood, and their calm faces belied the violence of their deaths.

"We should tend to them."

Gwenna turned to find Dhar and Kiel standing a few paces away. It was the Manjari captain who had spoken.

She shook her head. "Whatever we bury the sea will dig up."

Dhar gestured. "There is driftwood. How do your people feel about the burning of the dead?"

Her people? The phrase seemed momentarily strange. Who were *her* people? These dead sailors that she barely knew? Men who had hated her, had not lifted a finger when Jonon tossed her in the brig or hauled her beneath the keel? Were *they* her people?

"Annur is big," she replied. "People worship different gods in different ways." She shrugged. "Most folks I know would rather burn than rot."

The problem, of course, was that the storm had soaked the majority of the driftwood. It took a long time to sort through the debris for the drier pieces, lengths that must have been on the beach before the *hamaksha* began. As they built the pile, the sun dropped into the waves, and one by one the others woke, blinked away sleep's oblivion, and rose slowly to help. It was nearly dark by the time they'd amassed a heap as high as Gwenna's waist and a few paces long.

Rat stared at it, her face a mask.

"Now the bodies," Gwenna said wearily.

She was always surprised by the weight of the dead. It felt as though, when life leaked out of the flesh, something else took its place, something heavy, sluggish, reluctant. She pictured tar congealed inside the veins, bones turned incrementally to lead, flesh calcified to stone. All part of death's alchemy—transforming the familiar into something troubling and strange. In a way, it made no sense to bother with any of it. The men who'd inhabited the skin were gone. There may have been other survivors somewhere, if either of the boats reached shore, living people who would need water, food, shelter. For that matter, she and the others on the beach had more pressing needs than the building of pyres. And yet there was a debt owed to the dead, something that went beyond logical considerations of water and shelter.

She lit the fire with Pattick's flint and steel, watched the sparks nip at the

tinder, catch, grow, then begin to gnaw through the stacked wood. By the time
the blaze reached the bodies, the flames were as long as her arm. The clothing
caught, then the flesh, sizzling sickeningly as the skin blackened to char. Rat
stood at Gwenna's side, staring into the fire with furious intensity.

"Should anyone . . ." Pattick began, ". . . I don't know, *say* something?"

Gwenna was about to respond when the wind shifted, tugging the smoke
across her vision, dragging with it the fragment of a far-off voice. She couldn't
make out the words, but she recognized the tone's glittering edge. She closed
her eyes, inhaled through her nose. She could smell him, too, beneath the reek
of the dead, his exhaustion, and determination, and above all, his black-red
rage.

"Jonon's alive," she said, opening her eyes.

Dhar looked at her, eyes grave.

"How do you know?"

"I can hear him, not far off." She gestured to the top of the cliff. "He's coming. And he has men with him."

Kiel cocked his head, looked up at the cliffs. "We cannot put out the fire.
He will find us."

"Not all of us," Gwenna replied, scanning the beach. She pointed to the
hollow grottoes at the base of the cliffs, little half-caves gnawed away by the
highest tides. "The rest of you could hide. He has no way to know who survived."

Cho Lu stared at her like she'd gone mad. "Why would we *hide*?"

"We broke out of the brig. The admiral will not be pleased."

"It was break out of the brig or *die*."

"He didn't leave us in there hoping we'd survive."

Dhar stroked his mustache. "It will not be the first time today I have been
prepared to die."

"What about your *davi*?"

"I am a captain of the Manjari Navy, twice decorated by the Empress herself. I will not hide in the sand like a turtle, or run, to be hunted down like
a dog."

"The rest of you—" Gwenna began, turning.

"No."

The fire shifted and flickered over Pattick's face, but his eyes were steady.
"We're staying."

Rat just took Gwenna's hand, squeezed it tight.

Before they could argue the matter further, a cry rang out from the top of
the cliff.

Gwenna looked up to find an Annurian soldier—she couldn't remember his name—pointing down at the fire, mouth agape. A moment later Jonon joined him at the cliff's edge, then more soldiers and sailors, twenty or thirty in all.

"Well, it's too late now," Gwenna muttered.

The men on the clifftop looked like shit—ripped clothes, battered faces, eyes just a little too wide. Chent had survived the storm, Gwenna noted with displeasure, along with Lurie and Vessik. It wasn't hard to imagine them shoving others into the open sea in order to secure a place on one of the boats. A grim fact of disaster: usually it was the cruel, the greedy, and the ruthless who survived. And now Jonon had them all in one collection. Almost none carried true weapons, but most hefted lengths of driftwood. Hardly an army, but they didn't need to be. They outnumbered Gwenna's group at least three to one.

Jonon studied them from the top of the cliff awhile, then pointed down at Gwenna. "Kill Sharpe and the Manjari, bind the others."

"*Kill* you?" Pattick asked, turning to her, baffled. "Why does he want to kill you?"

"He doesn't want to kill me," Gwenna replied wearily. "He just doesn't want me alive anymore."

Back on the ship, law and custom had managed to hold sway, if only barely. Jonon had been willing to keelhaul her, of course—*that* he could justify as a punishment for a crime—but the specter of Annurian justice had prevented him from executing her outright. Now the *Daybreak* was gone, destroyed, leaving them all stranded on a foreign shore where even the long arm of the empire failed to reach.

Jonon's men hesitated. Not, as far as Gwenna could see, because of any qualms about killing her or concerns they might not be able to manage it, but because the cliff itself offered its own difficulties. It took them a few moments hacking at the undergrowth to find a vertiginous path down from the top.

"How do we play this?" Cho Lu asked.

She shook her head. "Why the fuck are you looking at me?"

"I don't . . ." The legionary glanced from Gwenna to Kiel to Dhar and back.

"I'm not your commander," Gwenna said wearily. "If I were, I'd tell you to surrender, to throw yourselves on Jonon's mercy. I already *did* tell you to hide, actually. You ignored me."

"We could fight," Pattick said, fingering his sword. "I mean . . . you're—"

She cut him off. "If you say *Kettral,* I'll kill you before they get the chance."

Pattick winced. "I was going to say you're good with a sword."

"You've never seen me use a sword."

"We *have* to fight," Cho Lu said. "We have the weapons we salvaged. They just have sticks."

"Need fight," Rat agreed, eyes glittering, small hands balled into fists.

"We could," Kiel observed quietly, "negotiate."

The first of Jonon's soldiers reached the sand just as he spoke the word. They shifted nervously, hefting their driftwood as though trying to get used to the weight. Cho Lu was right—sort of. Steel against sticks did something to even the odds. Of course, Kiel was a historian, Rat was a little girl, and all of them were exhausted. Five adults against more than twenty. If Gwenna's side fought from the water it would be tough to get behind them, but the battle would be ugly, bloody. People would die. Lots of people.

Jonon descended last, made his way through the cluster of men, crossed the open beach, then stopped ten paces from her. Flame seared his face. He'd managed to keep his cutlass during the storm, though he made no move to draw it. Instead, he looked at Gwenna, then past her, to the pyre and the bodies of the dead.

"You had no right," he said quietly, "to touch my men."

"No one else was here to do the work."

Firelight glinted in his green eyes as he studied her. For a moment, she thought he was going to relent, take her prisoner, perhaps, but recall his order for her execution. They were a long way from home, after all, and if Rat and Kiel were right, in grave danger. It hardly made sense to start slaughtering people.

Unless you believed those people were *part* of the danger.

Chent stood nodding at the admiral's shoulder. Vessik fingered an ugly belt knife. She could read the hunger for justice in their eyes, or for something that looked like justice. Maybe it had been a mistake, attacking those two back on the *Daybreak,* but had there been another choice?

"Kill her," Jonon said again. "Take the others. The historian may prove useful."

Chent licked his lips. "The soldiers . . ."

"Are a disgrace." The admiral nodded. "But they can carry a load. And I'm not finished with the little girl."

To Gwenna's shock, Pattick stepped forward.

"No."

Jonon's jaw was so stiff, Gwenna wondered he was still able to speak. "I should have seen the treason in you earlier."

Pattick jerked as though slapped, but Cho Lu surged forward, his blade in his hands. Gwenna caught him by the shoulder, dragged him back.

Out of the corner of her eye, Gwenna saw Kiel watching, his face blank as the sky.

"Three hundred and eighty miles," he said.

His voice was so mild, his demeanor so at odds with the violence about to unfold, that for a moment everyone paused.

Jonon turned to regard the historian, slow as a snake fixing on new prey. "What are you talking about?"

Kiel pointed toward the cliffs. "It is three hundred and eighty miles that way, more or less, to the northern shore of Menkiddoc, at least half of that distance through the pollution that plagues this land."

The admiral narrowed his eyes. "You have no *idea* where we are."

"On the contrary," Kiel replied. "We are four hundred and ninety miles east of the fang-shaped cape marked on my map. The ship ran aground at the very northernmost extent of the bay."

"How do you know that?" Jonon demanded, a dangerous note in his voice.

The historian shrugged. "I kept track while we were at sea."

"Kept track of what?"

"Currents. Compass bearings. The height and frequency of the waves. The wind. The weight and shape of the *Daybreak*. There are calculations."

"Calculations."

Kiel nodded. "Math."

"I know what math is," the admiral snapped. "To do math, you need numbers, and I have given you none."

The historian did something that might have been a shrug. "The math suggested a number of possibilities. The geography narrowed those possibilities to one. From this point it is three hundred and eighty miles to the northern coast, difficult miles through jungle, then over mountains. The chances of survival are low. They will be far lower if you weaken your force with a needless fight here."

"Needless?" Jonon dragged out the word like a knife across steel. "*Needless*? What you have here, historian, is a group of mutineers." He leveled a finger at Gwenna. "She has defied my orders and endangered this mission at every step, not to mention becoming a whore for the Manjari."

"Whore." Gwenna shook her head. "Why does it always have to be whore? Traitor wasn't enough?"

"Who do you serve?" the historian asked, his eyes still on Jonon. "The Emperor, or yourself?"

Jonon stiffened. "I serve the Emperor, bright be the days of her life, and will serve her until my death."

"Your death won't help," Kiel said matter-of-factly. "If you fight here, you might kill Commander Sharpe and those who stand with her, but the toll will be dear. If you lose fifteen men, who will carry the eggs? What if you lose twenty?"

"Twenty men?" Jonon scoffed. "At the hands of a woman, a girl, a Manjari cur, and a pair of traitors?"

"She is Kettral," Kiel observed quietly.

"She is *nothing.*"

"Perhaps you were not paying attention when she survived your keelhauling. Or when she brought down one of the birds alone, with nothing more than a spear and a dagger."

Jonon's men shifted nervously at that.

"If you fight here, you will win," Kiel said. "But you will cripple the mission. We are far from home on a dangerous shore. There is work still to be done, and this is not it. So I will ask again, Admiral, whom do you serve? The Emperor or yourself? Your duty? Or your pride?"

Chent leaned forward to murmur in the admiral's ear. Gwenna could just hear his silky voice above the washing of the waves. "The historian is all talk, sir. We can dispense with them easily."

"Come on, you pretty bitches," Vessik said, tossing his dagger, catching it overhand. "Let's see the color of your blood."

"No."

Gwenna was staring right at the admiral when he said it, and she still didn't quite believe her ears. It was only when he continued speaking, grinding the words between his teeth, that she allowed herself a sliver of hope.

"We can slaughter them," Chent pressed.

"No," the admiral said. "We will take the eggs and we will leave these traitors to their fate."

His face was a rigid mask of rage. He reeked of fury, and contempt, and frustration, but Gwenna smelled nothing to suggest he was lying.

"With any luck," Jonon continued, "they will die on this continent without our wasting the effort."

"Given the dangers of Menkiddoc," Kiel replied evenly, "our deaths—all of them—are not simply a possibility. They are a likelihood."

44

Adare hui'Malkeenian might have made a decent emperor, but she was hopeless as an artist.

"I spent the entire night," she said, gesturing to the sheaves of parchment on the table before her, "from the midnight gong until just before dawn, painting flowers."

She did not sound pleased. She did not look pleased. She looked like someone who had spent the whole night, from the midnight gong until just before dawn, making terrible paintings of flowers.

Akiil picked up the nearest of the pieces, studied it a moment. The petals were irregular, the stem disproportioned, the shading an unconvincing mess. Back at Ashk'lan, a child of six or seven could have produced better work. Of course, back at Ashk'lan a child of six or seven would have spent whole months at a time doing nothing but painting. Well, painting, and meditating, and running, but mostly painting. According to Adare, this was the first time she'd ever held a brush.

"How many times do I have to do this?"

He could have made a guess at the actual number—five thousand paintings? Ten?—but he suspected the figure would do nothing for the Emperor's temper. "A lot. Some of the monks take longer to learn the various disciplines than others."

"I am not a monk. I am the Emperor of Annur. Most days I don't have time to piss, let alone paint."

"I didn't invent the *kenta*."

"There has to be a faster way."

After seeing Akiil emerge unscathed from the gates a couple of weeks earlier, Adare had redoubled her own efforts at the monastic training. Gone—mostly gone—was the skepticism she'd shown at first, replaced by a steely determination. If the *kenta* in the cave beneath the palace had been a brick wall, Akiil had no doubt she would have walked straight through it. Unfortunately for her, the emptiness inside that arch was far more unyielding than brick.

He shook his head. "The Csestriim built the gates to be proof against human passage. If you want to use them, you need to learn to put away the part of yourself that's human. It's not a discipline you can learn overnight."

For just a moment, he found himself sympathizing with the woman. She was an emperor and the daughter of an emperor. Of *course* she thought there was a shortcut. While he'd been scraping to survive in the Perfumed Quarter, servants had been offering up everything she needed on a golden platter. While he'd been freezing his balls off in the Bone Mountains, she'd been living in the most opulent palace in the world. The idea of something beyond her reach, something she couldn't purchase or compel, must have felt almost unimaginable. To her credit, she didn't argue further.

"What do I need to do tonight?"

Akiil gestured to the paintings. "More of these. Draw the plants upside down this time."

"Upside down?"

He nodded. "Your problem is that you think you know what these flowers look like. You've made paintings of your thoughts, which are blinding you to the world."

"So I need to hang the 'Kent-kissing things upside down?"

"You need to make the world strange again."

Unbidden, he thought of Skinny Quinn's strangeness, the way she was at once the girl he remembered and someone new, some other woman altogether. He hadn't returned to the Quarter since the card game, but the events of that night remained stuck inside him, like a fish bone lodged in his throat, something he could neither cough up nor swallow. His dreams of the girl had been bad enough when he'd believed her dead. Now that he knew she was alive, the weight of guilt followed him into the waking world, panting and whining at his heels. Not that he had any idea what to do about it. Quinn didn't want *his* help—that much was obvious. Maybe she didn't want help at all.

He forced his attention back to Adare, to her shitty painting.

"You need to see the world," he said, trying to pick up the thread of the conversation, "through strange eyes."

To his surprise, she laughed. "I've been criticized for a lot of things, but no one ever said my eyes weren't strange enough."

The fire in those irises shifted as she sat back in her chair.

"I need you to go back."

He nodded slowly. The request—if it *was,* in fact, a request—wasn't unexpected, although he wanted to hear the Emperor explain it in her own words.

"Why?"

"If you're right, it's going to take me *years* to master this. . . ."

"You do not master the emptiness. The emptiness masters you."

Those old Shin aphorisms had always made him want to strangle the older monks. Now that he was on the other side, however, he could appreciate the satisfaction in doling them out.

Adare's jaw clenched. Her irises flared.

He raised a finger before she could speak.

"Stop right there. This," he said, leveling the finger at her, "is pride." He squinted. "With a healthy dash of anger and impatience."

"I hired you for your knowledge, not your impertinence."

"You're old."

"I'm thirty."

"Some Shin monks start training before they're five. Just as bad, you're rich and you're powerful. Any one of those facts could stop you from reaching the *vaniate.* Taken together, they may prove fatal. If you're going to survive this, you *need* a little impertinence. You need someone to be rude to you. You need someone to remind you that this self you've built up—emperor, prophet, Malkeenian—it's all just words. The reason you've hired me—whether you understand it or not—is to crack open the shell."

She watched him. Even after knowing her brother for years, Akiil still half expected those burning eyes to spark and crackle like a fire, but there was only silence.

"And when you crack the shell," she asked finally, "what's inside?"

He smiled. "Nothing."

"How well do you think Annur will function with nothing on the Unhewn Throne?"

"How well does it function with you atop it?"

This time, instead of the standard suite of royal emotions, shame flashed across her face, and doubt, and regret—all three wiped away almost as soon as they arose. What would it feel like, he wondered, to hold an entire empire on his shoulders? Taking care of Yerrin was burden enough, and Yerrin was just one old monk, more mad than sane, probably not long from death. With Quinn plaguing him, too, he felt beset from all sides. He had two people to worry about. Adare had millions.

She mastered herself, set her face, nodded.

"I have failed in dozens of ways. That is why I need you to go back."

"You want me to explore. To tell you what lies beyond the gates."

"I *know* what lies beyond the gates. What I *don't* know is what is happening in those places." She shook her head. "I'd planned to do it myself, like my father, but I can't wait ten years. I need to use them now."

"Which means you need to use *me* now."

"You said there are more than twenty gates on the island. According to my understanding, they span Eridroa and Vash, if not farther. You could bring me reports of what's happening in Dombâng or Freeport or the Bend, reports I'd need to wait days or weeks to receive otherwise, reports that could save hundreds of lives. Thousands."

"I could," he said mildly.

It was dangerous, negotiating with an emperor, but what he was doing wasn't a con anymore. He had a real skill, one he'd demonstrated when he stepped through the gates, a skill that she needed. He could see that need in her face.

Her eyes narrowed.

"What do you want?"

He shrugged. "Gold."

"How much gold?"

The question hung between them like some glittering ornament.

Desire is pain, his old teachers whispered. *To have more is to want more. What is sweet will sour in your mouth.*

What had that wisdom earned the monks? A foot of sharp steel through the chest. Ravens to pick out their eyes.

"One hundred suns per trip."

Adare shook her head. "Ludicrous. I can feed a batallion for a year on a hundred suns."

"Can a batallion travel across the continent and back in an afternoon? Can a batallion tell you what's happening in Freeport, or the Bend?" He'd spent so much of his life bluffing. It felt good to be holding the right cards, for once. "I risk my life every time I step through those gates."

"My soldiers risk their lives every day. Do you know what they get paid?"

"About five silvers a month?"

"Three."

Akiil shrugged. "Any man can swing a sword. There is no one else in this empire who can use the *kenta*."

The Emperor watched him awhile in silence. "You remind me of Kaden," she said finally. When he smiled, she shook her head. "It is not a compliment. His stubbornness tore Annur in half."

"That seems unfair."

"Spare me a speech on respecting the dead."

"Not to him, to *me*. I'm trying to help you stitch the place back together."

"No," she replied. "You are trying to make yourself rich, and to 'Shael with what happens to anyone else."

"Actually," he said, raising a finger, "there is one person I'd like to see helped. She works for the Captain down in the Perfumed Quarter. Goes by the name Skinny Quinn . . ."

☩

The first gate off the strange *kenta* island nearly killed him.

He had no idea what to expect, of course—a cave like the one beneath the palace? Another island lost in a tropical sea? He wouldn't have been surprised to find himself atop a glacier or standing among swirling sands. Even in the *vaniate,* however, he felt the shock as the cold, black water clamped down around him, pressing into his eyes, flooding his nose, snaking a chill tendril down his throat. The trance shivered. Fear's sharp claws skittered on the outside of the emptiness, threatening to puncture it. In other circumstances, he would have taken a deep breath to steady himself, but there was no breath to be had. No air, no light, no sense of up or down. His soaked robe twisted around him like a serpent, pulling tighter and tighter.

For half a heartbeat his body took over, legs kicking, arms thrashing for the surface.

Then he heard Yerrin's voice, quiet and distracted in the back of his mind: *Stop trying.*

He allowed his arms to float up and out, stopped fighting against the cold soaking into him, quit kicking. Slowly, the *vaniate* steadied. It struck him as strange, suddenly, that he'd been so frightened of that vault of black water. There was a peace to the dark, weightless silence, and for a while he allowed himself to hang there, motionless. His lungs burned, but the fire felt faint and far-off, a distraction from that great, vacant purity. It was hard to remember why he'd ever valued sunlight or color, why he'd ever wanted anything but this.

He might have stayed there forever, but for the greedy imperatives of the body. When his head broke the surface, his lungs dragged in a desperate, ragged breath, then another, then another. The air was as dark as the water—a perfect, inky black—but the sensation of breathing dragged him back from the brink of abandon. He still hung in the center of the *vaniate,* but he could think once more, and with thought came that same ice-cold curiosity. The *kenta* had brought him somewhere, somewhere underground, but where? He would have to come back, obviously, bring some kind of light that would survive the underwater pool, and then he could explore. There was no sense blundering through the darkness.

He took a deep breath, flipped his body in the water, and stroked down into the darkness. He might have been swimming for a moment or an age when his hand finally brushed the top of the arch. He closed his fingers around it, pulled, swung himself down and through . . .

. . . And tumbled back into the blinding, equatorial light of the *kenta*-ringed island.

He was more cautious with the next passage.

He tested the space beneath the arch slowly, watching as the tips of his fingers passed through. After a moment, they collided with something rough, cool, solid. Even inside the *vaniate,* it felt strange to stare at those truncated fingers, to feel what must be stone with their invisible tips, but to see nothing there but the open space, ocean, spray from the waves. He stretched up as high as he could reach, then down to the ground, but something on the other side was blocking the passage. Hardly surprising, if he paused to think about it. The *kenta* had been built thousands of years earlier. The world had changed since then. Some would have been buried in landslides, or flooded when rivers shifted their beds. Judging from the texture of the stone, this one seemed to have been walled off intentionally. Also unsurprising. How many people had to disappear through one of the things before others decided to build over it? How many years had to pass before everyone forgot there had been a gate there in the first place?

He withdrew his hand, studied his fingers, then moved on to the next arch.

No water on the other side. No stone. Nothing he could feel but cool, dry air.

All around him, sun shattered off the waves.

One stride took him through that hot, glittering light into darkness.

Darkness and screaming.

He dropped into a crouch, ready to step backward onto the island, but nothing attacked. The screaming shifted to a low moan that he realized, after a few heartbeats, wasn't moaning at all, but the howling of the wind. He straightened slowly. The last shreds of that wind tugged at the sodden hem of his robe, ran chill fingers over his wet flesh. It was cold here—not frigid, but a bone-deep, grudging cold. He straightened slowly, advanced a few steps into the chamber.

It was circular, ringed with windows. Some retained their glass while others gaped, empty. Weak, silver-gray light filtered in, carving canted rectangles across the floor. Walking as quietly as he could, he crossed to the nearest of them. A gust of wind tousled his hair, tugged at his robe. Above, dark clouds scrubbed a star-studded sky. The moon hung among them like a sickle. Ice-rimed peaks rose rank after rank into the distance. From what he could tell, he was *inside* the very top of one of those peaks, although in what range or on what continent he had no idea.

The wind kicked up again, more violently, clawing at his robe, threatening to snatch him into the abyss below. He took a moment to commit the whole scene to memory—perhaps there was someone in Annur who might recognize a painting of the place—then turned back toward the cavern.

He could see almost nothing—the feeble starlight penetrated barely a few paces into the gloom—and so he made his way slowly around the perimeter, hand trailing the wall. The stone was smooth as glass, polished a thousand times over or honed by some tool he couldn't begin to understand. The *kenta* had been built by the Csestriim. It seemed more than possible that the fortress—and he was sure it was a fortress; something about the place whispered danger, vigilance, violence—was likewise Csestriim work.

Halfway around, he reached a gap in the wall. A massive slab of stone, easily a pace thick, stood at its side. To his shock, it shifted when he put a hand on it, swung silently, almost effortlessly in. He caught it before it could close. Not a slab of stone after all: a door, one built, evidently, to keep out an army. Why it was open he couldn't say. Beyond it, his eyes made out little more than shadow, dark against the darkness, but air flowed up out of the gap, a slight warm breeze, and when he extended a foot, he found a stairway leading down. Carefully, pausing on each step, he descended. There was no railing or banister, but the steps were dead level, smooth without being slick, utterly unworn, a straight shaft boring down into the mountain. He followed them for hundreds of paces before they leveled off at what felt like a landing. The stairs continued, but he turned instead toward a vague, diffuse light emanating from a doorway.

Fear skittered along the surface of his calm. He ignored it, stepping through the door and into . . .

For a moment he struggled to find the word. *Room* was too small. Ludicrously so. Even *hall* and *chamber* failed to capture the vast size of the space, and while the whole thing was entirely underground, no one could have taken the graceful, smooth dome arching overhead for the roof of a cave. If anything, the place reminded him of a temple, although it was large enough to shelter half the people in the Quarter if they stood shoulder to shoulder. A delicate tracery of pale blue . . . something—crystal? Glass? Quartz?— spread in a web across the ceiling, glowing faintly, shedding just enough light for him to make out the walls, which were punctuated every few paces by shallow alcoves. Inside those alcoves hung all manner of weapons—one per niche—spears, swords, daggers, silently reflecting the light.

Akiil stepped forward onto that vast floor, then froze, narrowed his eyes,

realized that the floor was not a floor at all, not polished stone, but water, reflecting back the illumination from above. As he watched, a drop of water—
condensation, maybe, or leakage from some seam far above—struck the water
with a barely audible *plip*. The surface trembled. The tiny wave spread out and
away. Far out in the center of the lake, maybe a hundred paces away, stood
a single, solid, solitary plinth or table, some kind of rubble scattered across
its surface. Inside the *vaniate* there was no scope for true *awe*, but he stared
anyway, mind awash with the impossibility of the space. He no longer had any
doubt that the place was Csestriim, and if the massive chamber was Csestriim,
then the artifacts in the niches along the wall had to be as well.

He turned away from the lake, found a walkway two paces wide ringing
the chamber, and followed it to the nearest alcove. A dagger hung there, suspended by a delicate chain from a hook set into the stone. The black blade
seemed to bleed shadow into the space around it, but the handle was fashioned from something that looked like pale bone, carved with a single word
in a script that reminded him of the writing over the *kenta*. When he closed
his fingers around it, cold jolted up his arm, as though he'd seized a handful
of ice. Outside the *vaniate,* he might have dropped it, yelped and tossed the
thing away. Inside the trance, the frigid numbness was no more than a fact,
like the darkness, like his own heartbeat. It was a small blade, but heavy, far
heavier than he'd expected, as though fashioned from lead. As he passed it
back and forth through the air, shadow trailed behind it, like inky mist, and
when the ring, hanging from the chain, swung up to hit the blade, it struck,
not with a metallic clink, but a deep, reverberating *thrum,* like a huge ringing
gong. Akiil put his hand to the blade to still the sound.

The dark dagger was far from the only mysterious object in the room.
Something that looked like a porcelain platter hung from a set of brackets
set into the next alcove. When he paused in front of it, the surface seemed to
swirl, as though he weren't looking at a surface at all, but into a deep mist. He
watched it awhile, thought for just a moment that some shape might resolve,
then turned away. A flute as long as his arm hung in the next niche, and in
the next, what looked like a collar and leash. Akiil ran his fingers over it. The
material was smoother than leather, light and supple. Maybe it wasn't a collar
at all, but something else entirely.

As he made the circuit of the room, he passed spears and swords, two
bows, each with a single arrow. He hadn't spent much time around beautiful
weapons—most people back in the Quarter fought with nicked-up daggers,
clubs, or their bare hands—but he knew that these were no ordinary weapons. There were no gems set into the pommels, no golden scrollwork laid into
the hilts, and yet there was something eternal in the sweep of those curved

blades, an inevitability that reminded him of the arc of the stars through the night sky. He was just reaching out for a double-ended spear when a sound echoed through the open doorway—the scuff of footsteps, ascending the stairs from below.

Urgency skated across the surface of his calm.

The only place to hide in the whole vast chamber was behind that table out in the middle of the lake.

The lake.

Still holding the dagger, Akiil crossed to the water, sat at the edge, then lowered himself in as smoothly as he could. The chill folded around him, soaking into his flesh, numbing his fingers and toes. He ignored it, watched as the ripples expanded. They were larger than the waves created by the drop of water, but not too much larger. Slowly, he let himself sink until only his eyes and nose were above the surface. He tightened his freezing fingers around the handle of the dagger. The future was a forking path. Either the person would come in, or they would not. They would see the ripples, or they would not. They would attack him, or they would not. If they did, he would stab them, just as he'd stabbed the abbot back in Ashk'lan.

Inside the *vaniate,* the memory no longer haunted him.

The tiny waves caused by his passage were almost smoothed away by the time the woman stepped through the stone doorway. If she was one of the Csestriim, she didn't look like it. Not that he knew what the Csestriim looked like, but aside from the sword she wore strapped across her back she might have been a fisher, or a shopkeeper, or a scribe, any one of the thousands of people he'd passed over the course of his life without looking twice.

She didn't spare a glance for the larger chamber. Instead, she followed the walkway around the perimeter to one of the alcoves, where she lifted a long spear from the bracket that held it. Then, for just a few heartbeats, she paused, seemed to weigh the thing in her grip. The motion was familiar. Akiil had seen the same measuring from thieves, the hesitation in that delicate moment when the gold or jewels were finally in hand, when there was no stepping back from the act. Of course, a normal thief would have spent at least a moment marveling at the domed roof spread overhead, at the expanse of the subterranean lake. This woman, after that brief pause, turned on her heel and departed the way she had come.

Akiil counted to one hundred, ignoring the cold clamped down around him, then dragged himself back up onto the walkway. His limbs were stiff, his robe soaked. He'd be leaving a sodden trail all the way back up the stairs, but there was no way to avoid that. He couldn't stay submerged in the water forever, and there was no telling how many other people—*or Csestriim?*—inhabited the strange fortress. The most important thing was to get out, to get away, before anyone came back. He ached from the lake's cold, but the dagger was worse. Carefully, he slit open a seam inside his robe, then slipped the blade inside, between the layers of wool. It slid down to the bottom, came to rest against the hem. He tested his hand. The fingers still curled open and closed, but he couldn't feel them. A problem for later, when he was safe.

Moving as quietly as possible, he climbed on leaden legs through the heart of the mountain toward the outpost above, and the gate, and Annur.

†

The Emperor stared at him with her burning irises.

"You're still in the trance."

He nodded.

"Let it go."

He considered the demand. Inside the *vaniate* he felt nothing—no fear, no anger, no guilt. For the first time in his life he found no impulse to fake anything, no temptation to fight or to flee. What would it be like, he wondered, living inside this freedom forever?

"Let it go," Adare said again.

He breathed in through his nose slowly, evenly. The chamber smelled of stone and smoke. He let the *vaniate* go.

The emptiness didn't slip away so much as it shattered. The wreckage threatened to bury him. The voyage to the Csestriim fortress was by far the longest he'd remained inside the *vaniate,* and between one heartbeat and the next he felt everything he'd avoided: the fear of the *kenta,* the relief to have passed through and survived, the shock of the cold water, the bafflement at the strange fortress, the horror at being discovered. . . .

For a moment, his vision went strange. The torches on the walls seemed to multiply. The Emperor ramified, stared at him with six, eight, a dozen burning eyes. The floor beneath his feet canted precipitously. He stumbled sideways, threw out a hand to catch himself, found the upright of the *kenta* arch, leaned against it panting until the dizziness ebbed out of him. He felt the Emperor's hand on his elbow, her grip urgent, though for a moment he couldn't make out her words. Only when he raised his head did he realize how close he'd come to stumbling back through the gate into his own annihilation.

"Akiil." This time he understood.

"I'm all right." He straightened, moved away from the *kenta.*

The Emperor studied him. He met her gaze, focused on the shifting fire, cobbled together his most winning grin.

"I have returned in a single stride from the far side of the world."

"I was starting to think the journey killed you."

He waved away her concern.

"It takes more than a Csestriim gate of inestimable power to kill me."

Adare didn't move, didn't lean in or step forward, but he felt the need on her, the eagerness.

"What did you find?"

He explained about the first two gates—the stone wall, the flooded chamber.

She nodded as though she'd expected as much. "What else?"

"Some kind of fortress beyond the third. Old, I think. Very old."

"Fortress?"

Judging from the dilation of her pupils, the leap in her pulse, this was something new, something she *hadn't* heard of.

"More like the carved-out top of a mountain." He cocked his head to the side. "I guess your records didn't mention that one?"

"They did not. What did you find there?"

He opened his mouth to tell her about the massive domed chamber with the lake inside, the cache of weapons, the dagger he'd slipped into the fabric of his robe, the woman who'd come for the spear, all of it . . . and then stopped. His childhood opened like a flower inside him. As a kid in the Quarter, you learned early and always to hold your secrets close. He had no good reason to deceive the Emperor, nothing he could articulate, just some stupid animal instinct. Instincts, though, were hard things to escape. This one had tracked him, evidently, all the way to the Bone Mountains and back, waiting through the decades in his blood and his bones for this moment to whisper all the old lessons back to him: *lie, flee, hide.*

He shook his head ruefully, tried not to think of the weapons, all those beautiful weapons, standing silent vigil in their alcoves. "Nothing. It was dark, and I didn't want to loiter. I'll go back with a torch. For now, I'm just sorry I don't have anything more interesting to report."

45

The admiral stole much of what they'd salvaged from the *Daybreak*—rations, water, packs, the best weapons, the two remaining kettral eggs, Kiel's map of Menkiddoc—which left Gwenna and Cho Lu swimming out to the ship again by moonlight, picking over the wreck once more, dragging back barrels of water and weapons and salt cod. There was hardly a shortage. The *Daybreak* had been provisioned for over one hundred men, most of whom were dead. Of course, those provisions were meant to be carried in the ship's hold, not lugged on human backs through a trackless jungle.

"Three hundred eighty miles," Gwenna said, staring at the pile after she'd rolled the last of the barrels up out of the surf. "How sure are you about that number?"

Kiel closed his eyes for a moment, in the way of a man making calculations, then opened them once more. "It may be off by one or two percent."

"We did thirty-mile days sometimes in the legion," Pattick said.

Gwenna glanced over at him. "Over what kind of terrain?"

"Open," he admitted. "Mostly flat."

The historian shook his head. "The land here is neither open nor flat. We will be moving through jungle until we climb free of it, into the mountains. On the far side of the mountains the vegetation should be more forgiving. Perhaps we will be able to move faster."

"So, say, with no road, no trail, with all this weight, over unfamiliar terrain, we make ten miles a day. That puts us out there for more than a month. If nothing goes wrong."

Rat, staring up at the verdant lip of the cliffs, echoed the word. "Wrong."

Dhar frowned, followed the girl's gaze up toward the jungle. "We have been here one day and nothing has attacked."

"Doesn't *feel* . . ." Cho Lu groped for the word. ". . . polluted."

Kiel nodded. "There are pockets along the coast free of infection."

"Then why don't we follow the coast?" Pattick asked. He looked from Kiel to Gwenna and back. "If the middle of Menkiddoc is so bad, why don't we just stay on the shore?"

"The whole length of the shoreline is not safe," the historian replied. "Only isolated places where the wind and currents have conspired to scour away the infection."

"Besides," Gwenna added, studying her memory of Kiel's map, "we're at the northern end of a huge bay here. The coastline leads southwest for hundreds of miles before it hooks back north. We'd have to cover at least, what? A thousand miles just to get to Solengo?"

Kiel nodded. "More."

Pattick's shoulders slumped.

"So," Gwenna said, turning her attention to the historian. "How do we stay alive in there?"

The historian whistled tunelessly as he considered the question. "There are accounts," he replied finally, "of trappers and explorers who ventured into Menkiddoc and survived. Many of them are nearly incoherent, little more than the ravings of madmen, but they agree on a few particulars: the fringes of the continent are safer than the interior; the danger increases with each day spent in the diseased terrain; all water and food must be packed in."

"Great," Gwenna said, "so there are three rules—don't go in, don't stay long, don't eat anything—and we're about to break all of them."

"The first two, at the very least."

Pattick was shaking his head. "There's no way we can hump a month's worth of water."

"Not a month," Kiel said. "Twelve days."

Dhar shook his head. "I am a sailor, not accustomed to marching, but even I know we cannot make three hundred and eighty miles in twelve days."

"We don't need to," the historian replied. "The infection drains from the high ground into the valleys. The wind and cold keep the peaks clean, and the land north of the range is uninfected. If we reach the mountains, we can restock our water, begin to hunt once more." He paused. "There is also a fortress."

Gwenna stared at him. "A fortress? *Whose* fortress?"

"No one's. Not now. Not for a very long time. It was built by the Csestriim."

A hot breeze knifed between them.

"The Csestriim," Dhar echoed finally.

"Meaning it's a ruin," Gwenna spat, shaking her head.

"Csestriim engineering was superior to our own."

"I don't care how superior it was—thousands of years have a way of taking things apart, grinding them down to dirt."

"Nonetheless, those peaks are our goal. They mark the northern boundary of the sickness. Fortress or no."

Gwenna shook her head. "So we go straight through the 'Kent-kissing continent. You realize that going straight through is the opposite of sticking to the edges."

Kiel shrugged. "There is no path without risk."

"About that risk," Cho Lu put in. "What is it, exactly, that we're expecting to kill us?"

"Monsters," Rat said. *"Gabhya."* She twisted her small face into a snarl, bared her teeth.

"Yutaka doesn't seem so bad," the legionary replied.

Gwenna hadn't seen the creature since the storm. Perhaps it had drowned trying to swim ashore. Somehow, though, she doubted that.

"Not so bad?" Pattick asked, raising a crooked eyebrow.

Cho Lu laughed. "I mean, she's a wild animal who likes to rip apart other wild animals, but she hasn't tried to kill any of *us* yet."

Rat shook her head gravely. "Yutaka is not like other monsters."

"We all saw the skulls," Pattick said. "Some of them were huge."

"The *gabhya,*" Kiel said, "are not the only danger. Nor perhaps are they the greatest."

Cho Lu stared at him. "There are things in there *worse* than monsters with fangs the length of my arm?"

"Madness," Gwenna said quietly.

There'd been a time when she would have scoffed at the notion. Sure, she'd always understood that people went crazy. There'd been a madman two farms over from her father's who spent every night sitting at the grave of his dead son, talking to the boy as though he were alive. Half the Kettral cadets never made it past Hull's Trial, some because they were physically broken, others because their minds buckled under the strain. And yet, everyone who *did* make it, everyone who joined the ranks of the fabled warriors, had been trained, tested, vetted. They were the ones who *hadn't* gone mad, who wouldn't. That's what she'd thought, anyway.

"How does it come on?" she asked.

Kiel considered the question. "As I have explained to you, it manifests first as a kind of euphoria, a wild, irrational strength. You will feel good—"

"What's good," Cho Lu cut in, "about some hideous disease?"

"At first? Everything. Moving. Seeing. Hearing. You will notice patterns you never noticed. You will understand truths that have always eluded you. You will discover an unknown strength in your bones and in your veins. You will be able to run for days if you want, go for weeks without sleeping. At first this will play to our favor."

Gwenna shifted uncomfortably. It sounded a little bit like what happened after drinking from the egg of the slarn—only more.

"Doesn't seem so bad," the legionary replied.

"These," Kiel said, "are only the initial symptoms."

"What's the bad part?" Pattick asked warily.

"With that strength comes the madness, the inability to sort truth from delusion, the loss of the self."

Pattick shook his head. "How do you lose your *self*?"

The same way you lose anything, Gwenna didn't reply. *One moment you're there. The next you're just . . . gone.* Like a woman spying on her own past, she peered back at the memory of her own body huddled listlessly in the corner of the *Daybreak*'s brig. The filthy woman cringed when the door slammed open, shied away from the bucket filled with food. The sight terrified her more than a whole jungle writhing with *gabbya*.

When she spoke, it was more to escape the memory than anything else.

"But you're saying if we pack enough water, make it to the mountains, we could survive."

Kiel nodded. "This is what I am saying."

"All right, Commander," Cho Lu said, turning to Gwenna. "What's the call?"

"I'm not your commander," she replied quietly.

Kiel gazed at her with those gray, unreadable eyes. "With Jonon gone, someone must command."

"Great," Gwenna replied. She pointed at Kiel. "You know all about this place. How about you?"

He shook his head gravely. "I am only a historian."

"Dhar saved us in the storm. He can be in charge."

Pattick and Cho Lu exchanged a glance.

A gust of despair swept through her chest. "I am not Kettral," she said.

"None of us are Kettral," Bhuma Dhar said quietly.

"I haven't prepared for this command."

Cho Lu stared at her like she was already crazy. "Look at this place. *None* of us are prepared."

Gwenna locked gazes with him for a moment, then stabbed a finger up toward the jungle. "The only thing I know about Menkiddoc is that people are going to fucking *die* up there."

She expected Kiel to respond, or Bhuma Dhar, or Cho Lu, but it was Pattick who stepped forward.

"Do you think we don't know that?"

She searched for an answer, found she had none.

"It's dangerous," the soldier went on after a pause. "We get that. There are monsters. We get that. We could all go mad. We get that. You can't keep us alive, we *get* that. We're not *asking* you to keep us alive. We're asking you to lead us because even though you don't know what you're doing here, the rest of us know even less and we're fucking scared. *I'm* fucking scared.

"I don't want to go up there. I want to turn around, dive into the ocean, and start swimming. Or curl into a small fucking ball and just—I don't know— give up. And I'm not doing that because I'm waiting, *waiting,* for someone, for *you,* to say, 'Soldier, cinch up your shit and start marching. We're going in, we're going through, we're going to finish the mission. If we run into any monsters, we're going to kill them. If we run out of food, we'll go hungry. It's going to be a miserable goat fuck up there, but we're going to stay sharp, watch each other's backs, and we are going to make it through this.'"

He was panting with the effort of the words.

"*That's* what you're supposed to say. I'll know it's a lie. We'll all know it's a lie. But you're supposed to fucking say it *anyway.*"

He trailed off, his face red, splotchy. Tears stood in his eyes. She could smell the shame on him, the anger and the confusion, his tangled scent an echo of her own.

Years ago, on a training rotation to the Kreshkan Hills, she'd learned to trap. They were at it for better than a month, laying snares every afternoon, checking them every morning, learning to clean the carcasses, dry the meat, tan the hides. One day, just after dawn, she found a blue fox in her deadfall, not killed, but near enough, hindquarters crushed beneath a large rock. Blood soaked the ground around it, but somehow it was still alive, scrabbling with its front paws, fighting blindly to drag itself free.

Hopeless, she'd told the Flea later that night, roasting the creature over the campfire. *It was never going to make it.*

Her trainer sat a long time, firelight playing over his scarred face, before replying: *None of us make it, Gwenna.*

As the memory washed through her, Rat slipped her thin fingers into Gwenna's hand. The touch dragged her back to the beach. She glanced down at the girl, then raised her eyes to meet Pattick's.

"Soldier," she said, "cinch up your shit and start marching." She held his gaze as he nodded, then she turned to run her eyes over the others. "Listen to me, and listen good. We are going in, we are going through, we are going to finish the mission. If we run into any monsters, we're going to kill them. If we run out of food, we'll go hungry. It's going to be a miserable goat fuck up there, but we're going to stay sharp, we're going to watch each other's backs, and I promise you this—we are going to make it through."

It was a lie, of course, a promise she had no business making.

None of us make it, Gwenna, the Flea murmured in her ear. *The only question is how you finally go down.*

✝

The historian was right.

It did feel good.

Gwenna couldn't pinpoint the precise moment she'd walked into the sickness, but holy *Hull* did it feel good.

They'd climbed the steep trail up from the beach, then followed Jonon's track north into the jungle. It wasn't hard to see which direction the admiral had gone. His men had left a passage of hacked vines and churned-up mud that even a blind person could have followed. Of course, Gwenna had no intention of catching up. The admiral had warned them about following, and she didn't plan to test him.

"I thought we were trying to hurry," Cho Lu said, halfway through the first morning.

Gwenna shook her head. "Sometimes slow is fast. With Jonon's men clearing the path, we're using less energy than we would otherwise. Eating less food. Drinking less water."

And so, for the first part of the morning, they moved at a leisurely pace, stopping once when Rat had to piss, another time for Kiel to examine some kind of strange, oblong seeds.

"It's not so bad," Cho Lu said, peering up into the green. "I was expecting something . . . stranger."

Despite the dire predictions of Rat and the historian, Gwenna had to agree. She'd spent a fair bit of time down in the Waist, and this jungle looked more or less like that one—green everywhere, plants cascading from the trunks of massive trees, vines draped across the limbs, sunlight wan and watery, trickling down from so far above it might have been imagined. There were flashes of color and movement. Small birds darting through the understory. A yellow snake sliding into a rotten stump. A spider the size of Gwenna's fist skittering across her web. It was probably all dangerous, maybe even deadly, but hardly the land of horrors Kiel had described.

When a small blue lizard darted across her path, she found herself laughing.

"Did you see that?" she asked no one in particular. "Did you *see* that? I swear he looked back at me as he went by. He looked *guilty.*"

"Fast," Rat said, dropping to all fours to imitate the lizard's scuttling. "Fast little dog."

"Not a dog," Cho Lu said. "Lizard. *Li. Zard.*"

That got Pattick laughing, and within a few moments the whole march had come to a halt.

"Dog! Dog! Dog!" Rat chanted, still pretending to be the lizard.

Cho Lu chased after her, arms spread wide in the manner of a bumbling drunk.

Gwenna started to call them back, then doubled over with laughter, unable to breathe.

It was a relief to be laughing, a *joy,* a delight just to be alive and outside, breathing fresh air after so long locked in the brig. She found herself wanting to run ahead, to race along the path that Jonon's men had carved, and . . .

"Wait," she said. The word felt wrong in her mouth, awkward, even cruel. She made herself say it again. "Wait."

Rat ignored her, continued her frantic dance, spurred on by the laughter of the legionaries. Gwenna felt the laughter bubbling up inside her all over again at the sight of the little girl, the same girl who had been so grim, so guarded, actually *playing.*

She forced down the thought and the laughter both, turned to face Kiel.

The historian was not smiling.

"This is it, isn't it?" Gwenna asked.

He nodded.

"This is what?" Pattick asked, clapping her on the back. His hand lingered on the base of her spine. It was the kind of casual intimacy that, in other circumstances, might have earned him a broken wrist. Instead, she found herself leaning into the touch.

"What is this?" he asked again, shifting his hand around to squeeze her waist.

Gwenna moved the hand deliberately away. It felt like a loss.

"This is the sickness," she replied. "We're in it."

Pattick blinked.

Cho Lu laughed out loud.

"*This* is what you warned us about?" He shook his head. "I should have been sick all my life!"

"The euphoria," Kiel said gravely, "is only the beginning."

Dhar frowned. "Like rum."

Cho Lu shook his head. "I've had rum. Plenty of rum. This is *way* better than rum."

"I shipped with a sailor once," the captain replied, "who took a fall from the mast. His pain was very bad and so his friends, against the orders of my surgeons, brought him rum. When I went to visit him he was very drunk, very happy, claimed the pain was gone. The next morning, he was dead."

"We're not going to die," Pattick said, shaking his head.

Gwenna turned to the soldier. "Do you remember how we felt back on the beach?"

He stared at her like a man lost. "I mean . . . sure. Scared and all that, but—"

"Scared," she said. "Exhausted. Confused."

Even as she said the words, she doubted them. It was a strange sensation. She remembered the horror of staring up the cliffs into the overflowing jungle, remembered her own doubt, remembered the dread at being asked to lead the small, doomed group, but none of it felt real. All the emotions might have been something she'd dreamed, a strong but passing phantasm. Nothing more.

Of course, that was exactly what Kiel had said would happen.

She could still hear his warning, but like her old emotions it was slippery, almost impossible to hold.

"No monsters yet," Cho Lu said cheerfully.

"Still," Gwenna replied. "No one drinks from the streams. No one eats from the trees. If we didn't pack it in, don't touch it. Watch each other. Watch yourselves."

They looked like a group of children chastised by an adult for playing too noisily, but their chagrin didn't last. As soon as they were moving again Cho Lu started singing old drinking songs under his breath. Gwenna recognized a few of them. They were the same songs her father used to sing late at night in front of the fire, when he'd had a little too much ale. As Cho Lu tapped the rhythm against his leg, Pattick snuck in a dance step here and there, to Rat's unending delight. They were lost, of course, faced with a difficult march across dangerous terrain, but despite it all Gwenna couldn't help feeling hopeful, even happy as they forged ahead into the jungle.

Yutaka's screaming saved them.

One moment Gwenna was stepping over a downed, mossy tree, wondering why she'd never noticed how *attractive* Cho Lu was, how attractive *Pattick* was—even Pattick, who she'd always considered pasty and ugly—the next the *avesh* was swinging through the vines directly overhead, screeching as though she'd been scalded or stabbed.

"What—" Cho Lu began, brow creasing.

Gwenna reached for one of her swords, but Kiel proved somehow faster, spinning and leveling his spear just as . . . *something*—Gwenna caught a glimpse of teeth, claws, bloodred eyes—erupted snarling from the underbrush.

The historian's spear turned it aside, but the beast roared, twisted, ripped the spear from his hands, then roared again.

It moved like some kind of cat—a jaguar or tiger—but it was larger than either, and, Gwenna realized with a delicious shudder of horror, covered with scales instead of hair. It bared its teeth, lowered its head, hissed, slid a pace closer, then leapt off into the shadows of the forest.

"Sweet Intarra's light," Pattick said, staring at the place where the creature had disappeared. "Was that . . ."

"*That*," Kiel said, reclaiming his spear, "was a *gabhya*."

"Not so tough," Cho Lu proclaimed. "One thrust sent it running, tail between its legs."

Rat, eyes wide, shook her head. "*Is* so tough."

Gwenna dragged in a deep breath. Beneath the green, and the mud, and the heat she found another smell, one she hadn't noticed before, almost like rotten meat or dried blood.

"I'm not sure it's gone," she said, sliding her second sword from its sheath.

Yutaka yammered in the branches above. So the creature hadn't drowned after all.

Rat glanced up at the *avesh*, then out into the trees once more. "Not gone," she agreed.

Pattick and Cho Lu exchanged a glance. Kiel set aside his spear, and nocked an arrow.

The next attack came from the other side. Somehow the beast had looped around them, moving through the thick jungle silently as a breeze.

Gwenna heard the twang of the historian's bowstring as the cat erupted from the shadows, then, a fragment of a heartbeat later, the wet *thwack* as the arrow slammed into the back of the thing's snarling maw. It was a nearly impossible shot but it barely slowed the creature. Instead of dying, as any decent animal would have, it snapped the wooden shaft between its jaws and came on so quickly there was no time for Gwenna to think. No time to decide or doubt. In the fragment of a heartbeat her training took over.

Kiel stepped aside smoothly, the jaguar lunged for him, and she swung both her blades in a great, sweeping overhand arc down into the creature's neck. The shock of the impact shuddered up her arm, jarring her shoulder. She dropped one of the swords when the animal jerked, twisting toward her, bloody teeth bared, but that was why the Kettral carried two. How the thing was still alive, she had no idea, and she didn't plan to leave it that way.

As it snarled, she drove the steel of her second blade directly into its eye.

Hot blood showered her. The cat seemed to lean into the sword, as though it were still trying to get at her. Then it spasmed once, twice, and fell over.

She wrenched the sword free and stepped back.

For a moment no one spoke.

Then Cho Lu let out a high, delighted cheer. "You *slaughtered* that thing!" He whooped again. "You carved that fucker *apart*!"

Pattick was more subdued. He stared, wide-eyed, at the corpse. "What is it?"

The historian knelt beside the huge cat, peeled open one of the eyes with his fingertips. Clotted red streaked the yellow irises, as though the blood vessels inside them had hemorrhaged.

"This is what happens," the historian replied, "when the sickness seeps into something mortal."

"No," Cho Lu said, grinning, shaking his head. "This is what happens when Gwenna Sharpe gets *pissed off*." He bared his teeth at her, hefted his sword, as though planning to take another stab at the dead beast. "You killed the *shit* out of it."

Gwenna shook her head. "Not just me." She turned to study the historian. "I've spent my whole life with warriors, women and men who were very good at killing things. Most of them would have missed that spear thrust."

Kiel did something that might have been a shrug. "As a younger man, I spent some time hunting."

"Hunting."

He nodded.

She narrowed her eyes. "Before you became a historian."

"Yes. Before I became a historian."

†

It was nearly dark when they finished digging the circular ditch, then building a short palisade with stakes cut from a small copse of trees. Not much of a defense, but it might slow another creature like the one they'd killed that afternoon. For a while, Gwenna stood at the edge of the rough wooden wall, staring out into the night. Even with her eyes, she couldn't make out much—just a scrawl of branches and vines across the darkness.

What else, she wondered, *am I not seeing?*

Behind her, the others were finishing a cold dinner of salt cod and water. Not enough water. She'd started them all on strict rations and could already feel the thirst gnawing at the back of her throat. She could hear the trickle of a stream somewhere off through the trees, the sound of the water urging her to drink, *drink. . . .*

She forced it away.

"I'll take the first watch," she said, turning back to the camp.

Rat pointed up into the trees. "Yutaka watches."

The girl seemed to find that a comfort; Gwenna wasn't about to trust her life to a fanged creature born in the throes of Menkiddoc's disease.

"I'll sit up."

"You can wake me for the second watch," Pattick put in. "Me and Cho Lu."

Cho Lu groaned. "You heard Rat. The hideous little monster bear is taking care of it."

"Bear?" Rat asked.

"Like Yutaka," the soldier explained. "Except a lot less scary."

Gwenna expected all of them to sleep, but when she settled herself against the broad trunk of a tree, Kiel joined her.

"I will watch with you awhile," he said.

She blinked. "You're not tired?"

"There are things more important than sleep."

As usual, she had no idea what he was talking about.

For a long time the two of them sat in silence, gazing out into the alien night, Kiel's bow strung at his side, one of Gwenna's swords naked across her knees. Finally, the historian looked over at her.

"You have a question," he said.

Gwenna frowned. "I have a thousand."

"Perhaps you could begin with one."

"What *is* the sickness?"

The historian pursed his lips.

"The better question might be, what does it do?"

"Fine. What does it do?"

He glanced down at his own hands, studied the lines of them, then looked out into the night. Gwenna was on the verge of asking the same question again and louder when he finally replied.

"It affects all living things differently, unpredictably. One tree will rot while the trunk beside it grows to enormous proportions. A third, just ten paces away, might sprout tails instead of limbs."

"That's the kind of horseshit I expect to hear from drunks at the tavern, not from Annur's imperial historian."

"You saw the scales of the cat you killed earlier. You saw the eyes."

"Not the first time I've killed something with weird eyes."

Kiel performed a shrug. "Here, there are plants that feed on blood. Molds that grow nearly as fast as a man can run. House-high fungi. Swarms of flies that burrow into the eyes. Spiders the size of dogs that weave webs across canyons . . ."

"Sounds pretty far-fetched."

"It is the nature of this land's disease to realize the implausible."

"How?"

"By increasing capacity."

"Would you please try to make sense."

"It is difficult to explain in terms that you would understand."

"I'm no historian, but on a good day I can rub two thoughts together."

He nodded. "We are carrying food with us—rice, barley, dried fish. Without it, we would die. Even the most ravenous creature, however, even a woman on the verge of starvation, can only eat so much. The body cannot handle more. A plant, likewise, requires sunlight, but provide too much and it dies."

"What does this have to do with Menkiddoc? With the monsters?"

"The disease allows creatures to . . . take in more."

Gwenna tried to make sense of that. "The plague crippling an entire continent comes down to the ability to eat larger meals?"

"The plague allows plants, animals, people to feed off any source of energy—sunlight, the vibrations of the earth, the wind."

"Living off the wind doesn't sound so bad."

"It is not the ability to do so that is the curse, but the inability to stop. The disease strips all limits. Or, at the very least, it raises them beyond comprehension. Nothing here is ever full. You could devour half a pig tonight and keep eating. The land cannibalizes itself."

"So, why the monsters?"

Kiel lifted an arm, studied it a moment, then let it drop. "This frame was not made to accommodate so much. You and I eat and we stop eating. We do not absorb the power of the wind. Sunlight does not make us grow."

"But in the sickness . . ." Gwenna said, understanding burrowing like a slick worm into her brain.

The historian nodded again. "Everything is hungry, and nothing ever stops eating—eating sunlight, eating blood, eating the earth itself. Power floods through flesh and bud, twists it, corrupts it . . ."

"Makes spiders the size of dogs."

"Or trees that walk. Or any of a thousand other things that should not be."

Gwenna forced down a shudder. Spider dogs she could stab. Walking trees she could burn. "What about people?"

Kiel nodded thoughtfully. "With time, it will warp a human body to some degree, as it does with animals. The bulk of the energy, however, it pours into the mind."

"And that's what drives you mad."

"Among other things."

"What other things?"

"Perhaps you have heard stories."

Gwenna thought back to those ale-sodden nights in the tavern, listening to the tall tales of smugglers and pirates.

"Visions and voices, mostly. The usual crazy shit."

"There is nothing usual," Kiel replied, "about the visions and voices that arise from this disease. They are real."

She blinked, wondered if she'd heard correctly. "Real *what*?"

"Real phenomena."

"I don't understand."

"The diseased have visions sometimes, visions they are not equipped to endure, but that does not mean the visions are false. Those visions depict the truth, in this world or another."

"Another?"

"Surely, you do not believe that *this*"—he gestured with a hand—"is everything."

Gwenna stared at him, then out into the darkness. Something off in the trees cried out, then fell silent. The historian didn't *look* crazy. He didn't smell it. He looked like a man seated beneath an apple tree in his garden, pontificating blandly on the progress of his green beans.

"This," she replied finally, "being not just *this* tree and *this* dirt and those vines over there, but all of the world?"

He nodded.

"Yeah," she replied guardedly. "I sort of assumed this was it."

"And the gods?" Kiel asked. "Where do they abide?"

"I'm not sure what you know about the Kettral, but I spent more time learning to cut people in half and blow them up than I did philosophizing about the abodes of the gods."

"An oversight, perhaps, in your training."

She shook her head, trying to clear it, to get back to something that made sense. "What the fuck kind of historian *are* you?"

"Like any other—one who seeks to understand the world."

"And your *understanding* is that the sickness of this continent gives people . . . powers."

The thought might have struck her as ridiculous if she didn't already have powers of her own. Ever since she'd been bitten by the slarn, ever since she went down into the caves, she'd wondered whether there was something wrong with her, something broken. There were advantages, of course, to being stronger, healing faster, seeing farther—but no gift came without cost.

"Giving," the historian replied, echoing her thoughts, "suggests a gift. What

the disease drives into the mind is something else, something excessive, like a barrel of water forced down the throat of a thirsty man."

"A few of the explorers survived it," Gwenna pointed out. "Some of them came back all right. Some of them are only . . . slightly insane."

"There are ways to resist."

"Don't eat," Gwenna said, echoing the earlier injunctions. "Don't drink. And if we do that we'll be all right?"

A hot wind gusted, bending the branches, then fell still. The whole continent waited, as though the land were holding its breath.

"Partially," Kiel replied. "For a time. Eventually, the sickness will corrupt whatever you bring into it."

"Anything else we can do to level the odds?"

"Breathe slowly."

She turned to stare at him. "You have got to be fucking kidding."

"There are ways," he replied evenly, "to regulate breathing, to slow heart rate and other bodily processes. Some believe that avoiding thought helps to hold off any infection."

She shook her head. "I'm going to learn the truth about you before this is over."

"What is it about truth that you have such a strong desire for it?"

"When I'm sent on a mission to the far side of the world with some asshole, I want to know who he is. Especially when he claims to be a historian but handles a bow and spear as well as most Kettral. Especially when he talks casually about not breathing."

"Breathing more slowly," Kiel corrected her.

"Right," she muttered. "Breathing more slowly."

She turned her attention back to the jungle pressing in around them. Somewhere off to the north, maybe a mile distant, a creature was making a noise halfway between sobbing and laughter. The sound rose and fell, then spiked to a shriek and went silent. She scratched her leg absently, glanced down to find some kind of slender worm half burrowed into the skin of her calf. Gritting her teeth, she ripped it free, held it writhing in the meager moonlight, then tossed it down, crushed it with the heel of her boot.

"What about the Nevariim?" she asked finally.

Kiel nodded slowly. "I was wondering when you would ask about them."

"Back in that city you called them monsters."

"They fit the definition of the word: strong, fast, vicious, utterly lacking in pity."

"Are they . . ." Gwenna gestured toward the surrounding dark. "Were they infected? With this sickness? Is that what made them what they were?"

Almost, for the barest splinter of a heartbeat, she thought she saw something that might have been emotion flit across the historian's face. Then the branches above shifted, groaning against each other like fevered sleepers; starlight slid across his face, and whatever it was she thought she saw was gone.

"No," he replied. "They predated the infection of this place. Predated it by many millennia."

"So what made them monstrous?"

He pursed his lips at the question. "What makes any of us what we are?"

She stared down at her hands, traced the fine lace of scar webbed across her knuckles. "Choices. Teachers. Dumb fucking luck."

He nodded. "Indeed. And yet some monsters come into this world already monstrous."

"In all the stories, the Csestriim killed them."

"The stories are correct."

"So . . ." She gestured to the south, where somewhere many leagues distant the empty city lay, filled with its awful statuary and piles of empty skulls. "You said that place was the work of the Nevariim. Seems unlikely."

"Unlikely." He set the syllables between them one by one, as though they were objects of study. "Live long enough, and you will discover that *unlikely* and *impossible* are entirely different lands."

"I've got two and a half decades under my belt. They've taught me not to invent complicated stories where simple ones will do the job."

Kiel raised his brows. "And what simple story would you tell about that city?"

"People landed there a long time ago—colonists maybe, or refugees from whatever Dhar called it—the Time of Hunger. They lived the way people live, farmed, fought, built shit. . . ."

"And the enclosure?" Kiel asked mildly. "The stacks of skulls?"

"Doesn't take Nevariim to stack skulls. Maybe these people worshipped the *gabbya* in some fucked-up way. Maybe the human skulls were the bones of their greatest warriors."

"Maybe," the historian replied. He studied Gwenna awhile, then turned back toward the jungle around them. "Maybe."

46

Stepping from the training yard into the shadowed space beneath the stands of the Arena was like walking into a giant drum. Ten thousand feet hammered on the boards overhead, raining down dust and debris so thick it was difficult to breathe. Bien doubled over coughing, but Ruc couldn't hear her above the tumult, a din so great he could feel it pressing into his skin and rumbling inside his chest like thunder. A few paces ahead, one of the Worthy stumbled to the side, knelt, vomited into the dirt, was prodded roughly back into motion by one of the guardsmen.

Dozens of those guards flanked the shadowy passage; according to Goatface, there would be dozens more ringing the pit. *On the actual day,* the trainer had explained, *even the most devout warriors have been known to suffer . . . crises of faith. The guards will ensure that you remain steadfast in your purpose.*

Ruc's purpose, of course, differed from that of the Worthy who had come to the Arena willingly. Not that he intended to remind Goatface of that. For all the trainer's good-natured advice, for all the fondness he showed his warriors, he was a part of the same grim religious machine as the guards, the high priests, the Greenshirts, and the rest of the murderous fanatics crammed into the stands above. Goatface wouldn't countenance an escape attempt any more than Vang Vo herself, not that Ruc expected to escape from inside the pit. It was the only part of the Arena more heavily guarded than the yard, and that was on the days when there *weren't* ten thousand spectators staring down from on high.

It was a grim situation, made only slightly less grim by the fact that Ruc and Bien and Talal weren't scheduled to fight for another two days. The high priests' obsession with groupings of three extended to the culling, which meant that the contests were spread over three days. All of the Worthy attended—it was a chance for the crowd to lay eyes on them and for the warriors themselves to study their foes—but on that day at least Ruc wouldn't be expected to do anything more strenuous than sit in Goatface's box while out on the hot sand other people battled for survival.

Despite that, his heart was hammering as he emerged from beneath the stands into the bronze-hot sun. He paused, raised a hand to shade his eyes. When he was a priest, he had sometimes worked down at the temple docks, unloading full barrels from barges, then loading those same barges with empty barrels to be refilled. From time to time, he'd find something dead inside—a mouse, a frog—some creature that had hopped or stumbled to its wooden doom, then expired by slow degrees of heat and dehydration. The Arena had always reminded him of one of those barrels. It was bad enough when it was empty, and today it was far from empty.

The stands couldn't hold the whole population of Dombâng—not remotely close—but it *felt* as though the entire city had gathered to watch the Worthy hack one another into nonexistence. Men, women, and children packed the Arena, the small sitting on laps or perched on the shoulders of their parents. People had made flags—hundreds of flags—some with the three bronze slashes of the city itself, others with the names of favorite Worthy painted across them in jagged letters. They were screaming those names as the warriors entered the Arena, roaring encouragement to some, raining down jeers and curses on others. It was almost impossible to unthread the individual voices, but there was no mistaking the glee in those straining, open-mouthed faces, the elation, the hot, red need.

"A fine day," Goatface announced merrily, leaning in toward his warriors, pitching his voice above the crowd, "for a . . . contest of wills."

"A hot day," Monster muttered, "to get stabbed in the gut."

"So don't get stabbed," Stupid replied.

Mouse shook his head gravely. "Don't."

By this point, Ruc was used to their banter. Monster complained, Stupid needled her into complaining more, then Mouse soothed the whole thing over with his deep-voiced monosyllables. Beneath the cursing and casual mockery there was a rhythm to their disagreements, a choreographed give and take that was almost like music once you got used to the notes. To his surprise, he had come to find it comforting. Today, however, an unusual brittleness marred their voices. It reminded him of a blade sharpened obsessively against the stone, honed and honed until the bronze was too thin to hold an edge.

Which made sense, given that they might well be the first of the Worthy to die. Ruc had no idea how Vang Vo created the schedule, but the three of them would be fighting before the day was done.

"This way," Goatface said, gesturing them to follow the other Worthy, who were walking a semicircle around the perimeter of the pit. He might have been inviting them for a stroll in the garden.

Up in the stands, people had noticed Talal. Unsurprising. His black skin in a sea of so much brown was impossible to miss, and, of course, he was still carrying the steel ball chained to his ankle. According to Goatface, it would be removed when the time came for him to fight. For now, however, it was just another thing marking him out from the rest. No one knew him for Kettral, of course—as far as the official story went, the Kettral captured after the attack on the Purple Baths had been executed on the steps of the Shipwreck. Still, Talal was far darker than most Dombângans, different, and that was enough. Taunts and screams of derision fell on him like rain.

"You're not very popular," Monster observed.

The soldier shrugged.

An overripe firefruit splattered on the earth near Talal's feet.

Ruc looked up in time to see two of the Greenshirts posted in the stands dragging away a screaming woman.

"At least the guards are looking out for me," Talal said.

Goatface shook his head. "They are not looking out for you. They are guarding the sanctity of the Arena and the contests held here. This place is sacred, as are all of you."

"In my religion," Bien said, "we don't kill what we hold sacred."

"Yes," Goatface said, nodding. "Well. I'm sure you've noticed before now that your beliefs . . . diverge from those of most Dombângans in a number of particulars." He smiled benignly, then motioned them toward one of the wooden boxes at the edge of the ring. "Here we are!"

There was no door, but even the short trainer was able to swing himself over the low partition. The wall behind them was eight feet high—the same wall over which they'd hauled the funeral skiff what felt like years earlier. Today, however, climbing it would be impossible. Guards patrolled the top, and though they were mostly facing upward into the crowd, there was no way to sneak past them.

There was a long bench inside the box, but no one—no one aside from Goatface, who plopped his lopsided body down immediately, then spread his parasol above him—seemed to feel like sitting. Monster cracked her knuckles, rolled her neck, clenched and unclenched her fists, as though she were crushing some small, helpless creature. Even Stupid seemed more agitated than usual, if agitated was the right word; he'd tipped back his straw hat so he could look out from beneath the brim, studying the surroundings.

Ruc barely recognized the fighters or the trainer in the box to their left. He wondered if that was a bad sign, if they should have spent more time studying the other combatants. There was, however, no mistaking Small Cao, who occupied the box immediately to their right. After raising his arms to accept the praise of the mob, the trainer sauntered over, planted his hands on the low divider between the two boxes, ran his eyes disdainfully over Ruc, Bien, and the rest, then smiled at Goatface.

"Not your year, is it?"

Goatface, shaded beneath his red parasol, glanced up at the other man, looked to his own Worthy, raised his own eyebrows as though noticing them for the first time, then turned back to Cao.

"I have worked with . . . less promising warriors."

Cao belted out a laugh. "Like the three the Rooster took apart?"

Goatface frowned. "That was . . . unfortunate."

"How are your new pair of idiots?" He nodded toward Ruc and Bien.

"Eager."

"Eager to roll into the culling with barely a few months of training?" The trainer shifted his gaze from Goatface to Ruc, grinned even wider. "There's a word for that kind of eager: stupid."

"I resent your taking my name in vain," Stupid said mildly. He'd pulled the straw hat back down, letting it settle so far over his eyes that he couldn't have seen much more than his own feet. He busied himself with a length of reed, splitting it, then going to work cleaning his teeth with one of the slivers.

Small Cao laughed again. "I forgot your colorfully named trio. What is it? Stupid, Fat, and Nasty?"

"Fat?" murmured Mouse ruefully.

"As long as I get to be Nasty," Monster growled.

"Call yourself whatever you want, baby," Cao replied, winking before he turned away.

The stands, which had seemed strained to bursting before, continued to fill. People balanced on the wall all the way at the top, sat on the rails of the silted-up ships, or perched in whatever was left of the masts and yards far above. In the boxes ringing the pit the fighters went about their own private rituals—stretching, working forms, boasting, meditating. It seemed there were almost as many different ways to face death as there were people to do the dying.

The shadow of the eastern stands shrank across the dirt of the pit by incremental degrees until at last, atop the deck of the highest ship, Vang Vo emerged to take her accustomed place.

A great roar erupted from the crowd. The stamping of feet mounted to a frenzy. The screaming felt like a weight of water pressing down from every direction.

When the high priestess raised a hand, however, the Arena went so silent that Ruc could hear the wind tugging at the flags, the creaking of the wooden boards, and somewhere outside the Arena, not too far off, the shriek of a marsh hawk as it fell upon its prey.

"People of Dombâng," she began, her voice carrying easily on the light breeze. "You know me, and you know I'm not a speaker."

It was only partly a lie. While Vang Vo had risen to her station almost as much on the strength of her sermons as on her heroics during the war, she made no effort to embroider her words. In fact, it seemed to be her plain talk, coming after so many generations of affected Annurian bureaucrats, that endeared her to the crowd.

"I was a croc wrangler before I was a priest," she went on, "so I know what it's like to fight, to kill, to almost die. It is pure in the way nothing else in life is pure. Brewers water their beer. Shopkeepers cheat. Laborers lie and slaves shirk. It's the world's way. But there is no lying or no shirking here.

"Our gods taught us this. They taught us that to be great we must face our own annihilation. We forgot the lesson for centuries. Even now we are in daily danger of forgetting it. The men and women gathered below"—she gestured to the Worthy—"have taken it upon themselves to remind us.

"There are no words to measure what they will do here today, so I won't say anything else—to you or to them—other than thank you, fight hard, die well."

With three fingers, she made the ancient salute of Dombâng.

As she stepped back from the ship's railing, a door opened in the far wall of the pit. Half a dozen men entered at a half trot, carrying a long teak table between them. Six more followed, each bearing one of the traditional weapons of the Worthy. Last came the crier, the massive bull of a man charged with bellowing out the order of the fights and the names of the fighters.

He waited for the table and weapons to be settled, for the laborers to withdraw, then raised his hand and began to declaim:

"The first contest of the culling!"

He waited for the cheering and hollering to die down, then continued.

"Trained by Small Cao, and fighting from the western end of the Arena: Danh Fau, Sang Tam, and Chinh Ti Tro, known also as Blue Chinh."

Ruc glanced over at the neighboring box. He recognized Blue Chinh from the yard, but wasn't sure which of the two others swinging over the low wall was which. There wasn't much to choose between them—all were men, all large and heavily muscled, although slightly lighter, slightly leaner, slightly younger than Cao himself. They wore the stiff, contemptuous faces of men getting ready to do a job they considered beneath them, an attitude that Small Cao seemed eager to encourage.

The trainer had leapt out of the box along with them.

"I said it before," Cao declared, clapping them roughly on the shoulders, raising his voice so the crowd could hear, "but I'll say it again. It's an outrage that you're fighting today. You're going to take apart whoever Vo throws against you. You're going to turn them into fucking chum."

The Worthy growled their agreement.

"Take your places," ordered the crier.

The four of them strode out into the Arena. While the fighters crossed to the table, Small Cao went to the western edge where he climbed a short ladder to a wooden platform cantilevered out over the pit. The opposing trainer would occupy an identical platform on the opposite side. In theory, the position allowed the trainers to coach their warriors through the fight, but Ruc couldn't imagine anyone hearing anything above the howl of the crowd. Most likely, all the perch afforded was a better vantage from which to witness the victory or death.

"Fighting from the eastern side of the Arena," the crier continued, "under the training of Lao Nan, the Worthy known as Monster, Mouse, and Stupid."

Monster twitched.

Mouse shook his head. "Fighting."

Stupid turned to the trainer with a raised eyebrow. "Lao Nan, eh? Forgot you had a real name."

"Goatface *is* my real name," the trainer replied. "The other is just what my parents called me."

"Fuck," Monster said.

There was an edge to the curse that made Ruc look over. Her face was twisted with indecision.

"Fuck?" Mouse asked.

"I've gotta piss again," she muttered.

Goatface gestured toward a clay pot at the back of the box. "It is not uncommon," the trainer said. "Take the time to relieve yourself. You will fight better."

"With all these fuckers watching?" she demanded, gesturing to the mob packing the stands.

"They are going to watch you kill," the trainer replied. "They may well watch you die. This is considerably less intimate."

All the same, he handed her his red parasol, which she held awkwardly as she squatted over the pot.

Only when she'd straightened up, handed back the parasol, and readjusted her *noc* did the trainer speak again.

"It would appear that it is time."

"Any advice?" Monster asked as she stepped out of the box.

Goatface blinked, as though he'd never heard this question before, gazed up at the sky. "Move," he said finally.

"Move?" Mouse asked.

"Move *where*?" Monster demanded.

Stupid lifted off his hat, tossed it onto the bench, squinted out into the ring. "I'd imagine that, against those three, any movement is good movement."

"Blue Chinh has a bad knee," Ruc offered. "Did something to it in training a few weeks back."

"Useful to know," Stupid replied. "Thanks."

Monster shot a baleful glance at Goatface. "More useful than *move,* anyway."

The eyes of ten thousand Dombângans followed them as they strode out onto the sand, but Ruc turned away from the spectacle, toward the clay pot in the back corner of the box. A thought scratched inside his mind, like a chick trying to hatch. For Monster, the prospect of pissing while the world watched offered nothing but humiliation. There was, however, another possibility.

Like the rest of the Arena, the wall at the back of Goatface's box was made of wood, broad planks almost as wide as Ruc's torso. Those planks were nailed—judging from the pattern of the nail heads—into the framing behind. As the crowd screamed and Goatface mounted his platform, as Monster, Mouse, and Stupid crossed to the table at the center of the pit, Ruc moved to lean against the back of the box. To anyone in the stands, it would have looked as though he were shifting out of the sun into the narrow rim of shade. Not that anyone was looking at him. The action, after all, was unfolding at the center of the pit, a good twenty paces away.

As he leaned against the wall, he let a foot swing back. He couldn't hear the thud over the din, but he felt the board vibrate. Hope sliced into him, the blade so sharp he didn't feel the pain until a moment later. There was a way out. A dangerous way, maybe an insane way, but what was crazier—attempting an escape or waiting day after day for their turn to fight in the Arena?

He tested the wall three more times, searching for the weakest spot, then rejoined Talal and Bien at the edge of the box.

Out at the center of the pit, the Worthy were choosing their weapons. Monster had the spear, which seemed good, and Mouse was holding the dagger and shield, but Stupid had ended up with the grapple and line. Which meant Cao's men had the sickles, the net, and the ring dogs.

"Stupid doesn't know how to use the grapple," Bien said.

She was gripping the edge of the box so hard Ruc wondered if she meant to rip it off.

Talal nodded. "But that big bastard doesn't know how to use the net."

Bien glanced over at him. "How do you know?"

"The way he's holding it." He frowned. "I'd say they came out even with the weapons."

"There's a way out," Ruc said.

Bien turned to him, confusion scribbled across her face. Talal just raised an eyebrow.

"We rip out one of the planks at the back of the box," Ruc went on. "Squeeze through the gap. Almost all the guards are *inside* the Arena, making sure the Worthy don't bolt, making sure the crowd stays under control. Once we're underneath the stands, we find our way to a boat. Or swim."

"What about the part," Bien asked grimly, "where all the guards are in here. *Making sure*—to repeat your words—*that the Worthy don't bolt.*"

Ruc shook his head. "They'll be watching for people trying to climb over the wall, not go through it."

"You have no idea what they'll be watching for," Bien countered.

"When Monster pissed," he said, "she went behind Goatface's parasol." He gestured toward the edge of the box where it was leaning, neatly folded. "*That* parasol."

Talal pursed his lips. "Interesting."

"You're the smallest," Ruc went on, his eyes on Bien. "No one would be able to see you behind the parasol, even if they were looking, and they won't be looking." He gestured out toward the sand, where Monster, Mouse, and Stupid were returning to the eastern edge of the pit, about fifteen paces distant. "Every eye in the place is going to be on them."

Bien shot a quick glance at the low wall. "How am I supposed to get through? If I were on the other side, I could kick the nails out, but they're set in the wrong way. We don't have any tools."

Talal smiled, hefted the steel ball he'd been holding in the crook of his arm. "I do."

She eyed the ball skeptically. "You're going to smash it? That seems incredibly stupid."

"Not smash it. Just put a crack in it."

"Too risky," Ruc said, gnawing back his own frustration. "If we don't all get out and Goatface returns to find a huge hole in his wall . . ."

Bien shook her head. "That's not how wood cracks." This time she did rip a long wooden strip off the edge of the box, held it up, snapped it between her fingers. Then she narrowed her eyes, slid the splintered ends back together until it appeared whole once more.

Ruc nodded slowly. "All right."

He had no idea if it was all right, but there wasn't time to consider.

Bien turned to Talal. "You're the Kettral. Is this stupid. Insane?"

The soldier shrugged. "Doing stupid, insane things was more or less the heart of my job."

"Fuck it," Bien said. "Let's go."

Out in the pit the table had been whisked away, and the two groups of Worthy were closing warily on each other. As Ruc watched, Monster and Mouse fell back while Stupid continued forward. When he was far enough away from them, he began whirling the grapple in wide loops above his head, the hooked bronze inscribing a glittering circle on the air. The move required him to separate from his three, but it also forced Cao's men back toward the far wall. Blue Chinh took a few swipes at the grapple with his sword, but Stupid tugged it back just out of range.

The Arena throbbed with the pounding of the crowd.

Talal dropped to the back of the box, measured out a length of chain, tossed the iron ball out in front of him, then let it swing back past him into the wall. Just a pace away Ruc couldn't hear the impact over the rest of the chaos. He glanced up at the guards but they, like everyone else, had their eyes on the fight. Casually as a fisher hauling in his net, Talal hoisted in the ball, hefted it in his hands, threw it in front of him, let it thud into the wooden planking once more.

Bien leaned over toward Ruc, her face twisted with worry. "He's too obvious!"

Ruc was tempted to agree. The Kettral made no effort to disguise what he was doing. He was standing in the shade, sure, which would obscure the ball hitting the actual boards. But anyone who bothered to look would see him hefting it, measuring out the chain, tossing it. How was it possible that no one had sounded the alarm?

Ruc forced himself to look out over the Arena instead of back at Talal. Most of the other Worthy were at the edges of their own boxes, some screaming taunts or advice, others watching the fight in grim silence. At least a dozen of the warriors, however, seemed oblivious to the violence unfolding at the center of the pit. One man was bent over at the back of his box retching into the pot. Across the way, a woman helped her companion strap on a leather breastplate. A few boxes down, some of Other Dao's Worthy were caught up in what seemed to be a vicious argument, stabbing their fingers in one another's faces. Against that backdrop Talal's hoisting and dropping of the ball seemed less suspicious. Some people paced before a fight, some prayed. It wouldn't seem that strange for one of the prisoners to be worrying at his restraints.

And, of course, there was the violence unfolding at the center of the pit.

Stupid had managed to force a wedge between Blue Chinh and the other two with the spinning grapple. It was growing obvious, however, that he couldn't do much more with it than whirl the thing in circles above his head. For the moment, that was keeping his opponents at bay, but they were already testing the defense, ducking beneath it, trying to snag it from the air.

"It's cracked," Talal said.

Ruc hadn't even heard the Kettral approach. When he glanced over, however, he found the man at his shoulder, gazing out over the Arena as though he had no interest in the world but the fight.

"Get the parasol," Bien growled.

Ruc nodded, took it from where it leaned against the wall, unfolded it, crossed to the back of the box. Bien made a show of lifting her *noc* before he lowered the parasol into place. It seemed a weak shield—just a layer of waxed canvas and some finger-thin wooden stays—but it was large enough to cover her almost entirely, especially when he held it at an angle. He felt her bump up against it as she shifted to get in position, then felt it jump. He risked a glance.

She was on her back, kicking at the wooden plank with her heels. Each blow folded it inward a little further on itself. Ruc thought he could hear the shriek of the nails tearing free of the framing, but maybe that was the screaming up in the stands. Talal stood at the edge of the box, leaning casually on the rail. Bien slammed her heel into the board again and this time it cracked, both halves folding back into the shadows.

The look she gave Ruc was one part triumph, one part horror. They were committed now. For a moment, Ruc wondered what would happen if the guards saw them, or Goatface returned before they'd escaped, or one of the Worthy in Small Cao's box happened to sneak a glance past the edge of the parasol. They were all at the rail, however, screaming meaningless advice at their companions out on the hot sand.

By the time Ruc looked back, Bien had turned around and shoved the bottom of the broken board all the way into the gap.

"I'll see what's on the other side," she said. "Wait here."

A mad laugh bubbled up in Ruc's chest. He forced it down. It seemed like there should be something to say, but there wasn't. Either there would be a path to freedom or there would not. He nodded. She nodded. Then, as she wriggled through the gap, he turned back to the battle.

Things had taken a bad turn for Goatface's Worthy. One of Cao's men had finally managed to rip the grapple out of Stupid's hands, which left him weaponless. He fell back behind Monster and Mouse, giving the other three a chance to regroup. Blue Chinh was grinning, and the other two looked almost as pleased. They had good reason. Three against two. Monster's spear and Mouse's dagger and shield against the sickles, the ring dogs, and the net.

Mouse passed his dagger to Stupid, which gave the smaller man a weapon but left Mouse holding nothing but the shield.

Talal nodded, as though that made sense.

Ruc leaned over, spoke directly into his ear. "She's through. Checking the other side."

The soldier nodded again.

"One of us could follow," Ruc said. "If there are guards she might need help."

"If there are guards," Talal replied, not taking his eyes from the fight, "we're dead. Either way, we can't *all* disappear from the box until we know we can get all the way out."

It made sense. The parasol provided plausible privacy for one person pissing in a pot, but there was no way two would fit behind it. Fight or no fight, there were ten thousand people in the stands. Sooner or later someone would look over at Goatface's box and notice the strangely dwindling number of Worthy. Until they were sure of a way out beyond the wall, the best course was patience. That knowledge, of course, didn't stop the patience from aching like poison in Ruc's veins. Every breath seemed to stretch on forever. Every heartbeat felt loud as a gong.

He schooled himself to stillness, kept his eyes away from the guards patrolling the wall above, away from the parasol leaning up against the wall, made himself watch the other Worthy as they battled for their lives.

Small Cao's men kept trying to close, but Goatface's warriors refused to let them. Every time they got close Monster would trade a few blows with her spear while Stupid and Mouse fell back. Then she'd retreat to join them. It didn't make for a very interesting fight—the crowd was bellowing its derision— nor did it seem vigorous enough to wear down Small Cao's three. Monster was quite obviously frustrated with the progress. Ruc could see her shouting, though he couldn't hear the words.

"Patience," Talal murmured. "Patience, Monster."

Ruc shook his head. "What's she being patient *for*?"

"For someone to make a mistake."

"They're not likely to trip over their own feet."

"But they *are* likely to rush. You heard Small Cao. They believe this fight is beneath them. Every moment it goes on is an embarrassment."

An embarrassment for Cao's fighters, maybe, but an opportunity for Ruc and Bien and Talal. They didn't need to just slip through the gap before the fight finished—they needed to be *gone*. With the noise and the madness of the Arena, it would take Goatface some time from the moment he noticed them missing to alert the guards, but once those guards were alerted, things would get bleak and fast. The Arena, after all, sat in the center of Old Harbor. Mudflats surrounded it for hundreds of paces on every side. They might hide in one of the piles of trash dotting the flats, but eventually those would be searched. They would need to get clear of the flats entirely before they reached anything resembling safety. Stealing a boat was probably the best option, especially given that Talal still had an iron ball shackled to his leg, but stealing a boat would take time. If they were going to make it, Bien needed to get back. When he stole a look at the parasol, however, it was still where he'd left it, leaning against the wooden wall.

Images crowded Ruc's mind, lightning flashes in a storm. Bien captured by guards on the far side of the wall. Bien stuck trying to squeeze through some crawlspace. Bien turned around in the darkness, disoriented, lost. . . . The space beneath the stands was a labyrinth, some sections open and cavernous, others a warren of hallways and locked storage. There was no way to guess what was happening back there, though the guesses kept coming, bloody and relentless.

"There," Talal said.

Ruc looked back to the ring.

Nothing seemed to have changed. Cao's men were still prowling forward, forcing back the other three.

The Kettral shook his head. "They missed it."

"Missed what?"

Talal narrowed his eyes, dragged in a slow breath, then nodded. *"That."*

It took Ruc a moment to see. Blue Chinh was out in front by a pace or two, obviously impatient. The next man held the net. He was clearly uncomfortable with it, letting the end drag in the dust. The last of Cao's Worthy, the one with the ring dogs, followed another pace back, his face creased with concentration.

"The netsman's out of place," Ruc said.

Talal nodded. "He's in the way. If Mouse rushes Blue Chinh, the one with the ring dogs can't cover his flank. Not for at least a few heartbeats, which is when Monster . . ."

As he was saying it, it happened.

Mouse, who had been slowly retreating since the fight began, reversed direction, hurling himself forward. Blue Chinh lashed out with a sickle, but he was unprepared for the sudden attack, and the curved bronze shrieked harmlessly off Mouse's shield. The man with the ring dogs started toward Chinh, found the netsman in his way, stumbled to a stop. The whole thing took just a moment, but Monster was already in motion, driving in from the side with her spear, plunging it into Blue Chinh's ribs while the man was tied up trying to force back Mouse's bulk.

Ruc couldn't hear Chinh's cry, but the crowd bellowed his pain for him, until it seemed the great roar of all Dombâng was pouring from his open mouth. Then came the blood, a hot gush of it, splattering across the bronze rim of Mouse's shield.

Monster twisted the spear, Mouse shoved, and Blue Chinh collapsed.

Ruc's eyes, however, were on Stupid. "Throw," he shouted, dragged into the violence in spite of himself.

When the dagger had been the only weapon available to the man, throwing it made little sense. Now, however, with the sickles lying in the dust to be scooped up, there was no reason not to.

Stupid cocked his arm, then hurled.

The bronze blade darted like a bright delta bird flitting to its nest, soaring one moment, then buried in the netsman's neck.

As the man dropped, Stupid trotted forward, lifted the sickles from the sand.

Blue Chinh twitched out the last of his life.

And just like that, it was three against one.

"We don't have much time," Talal observed. His voice was calm. He didn't take his eyes from the pit but Ruc could see the tension in his neck. "We should go now."

Ruc shook his head. "We don't know what's on the other side."

"We know what's on this side, and we know we don't want to be here."

"If there's not a way out, we're finished." It was almost impossible to make himself say the words but they needed to be said. It was, in fact, exactly the argument Talal had made when Bien first disappeared through the gap. He imagined them trapped inside a locked storeroom. Goatface would call the guards. The guards would pen, then slaughter them at their leisure. Or, more likely, they would drag them back out onto the sand to be tortured slowly before the assembled mob. "This isn't our only chance. There are two more days of the culling. . . ."

"We're going," Talal said, moving back toward the parasol. "We'll fight our way free if we have to."

"With what?" Ruc demanded.

Before the Kettral could reply, the parasol twitched.

Ruc turned to the back of the box, glanced behind the red canvas to find Bien crouched there, face streaked with grime, sweat matting her hair to her brow, eyes bleak.

"It's locked," she said. "We can't get out."

The soldier didn't object, didn't ask more questions. "Get the board back into place."

Out on the sand, Monster was finishing off the last of Cao's fighters, driving her spear into him over and over, her face twisted in an awful howl.

"As soon as they start back this way," Ruc said, "all eyes are going to be on this box."

"I *know* that," Bien growled.

Both halves of the broken board were still attached to the framing beneath. The bent nails served as a kind of rough hinges—the top of the board had folded in and up while the bottom folded down. Bien fished around the darkness for a moment, managed to drag the bottom half back to vertical, then pulled it through until it jutted out slightly into the box. She shifted to the side, reached back in, strained on the top half.

Out at the center of the pit, Monster, Mouse, and Stupid had their bloody weapons in the air to accept the congratulations of the crowd. Goatface beamed down at his warriors from his seat on the platform. The crier had emerged from the northern door, and was making his way over to them.

"It's stuck," Bien hissed.

In her effort to pull the board back into place, she kicked the handle of the parasol. For a moment, only a thin strip of shadow cloaked her from the eyes of ten thousand blood-hungry spectators. Pulse hammering in his veins, Ruc shifted the parasol back into place.

"Not much time," Talal said.

The crier announced the victors, not that anyone could have been too confused. Three of the Worthy had their weapons hoisted in the hot air while three had been tossed to the sand, their bodies torn open. When the time came, Goatface accepted his acclaim with a raised hand, then began to descend from the trainer's perch. Monster started jogging a victory lap around the edge of the Arena. Mouse and Stupid took a more direct path toward the box.

"Got it," Bien said.

A moment later, she shoved the parasol side, emerged once more into the light.

Ruc glanced past her. The work wasn't perfect. The broken board didn't sit quite even with the others. The nails, wrenched by the violence of the entrance, stood out a finger's width from the wood. The crack itself was almost invisible, but some of the splinters around the edges had broken off. Looking at it, the breakage seemed preposterously obvious. Which was why he forced himself to stop looking at it. For all its sanctity, the whole Arena was ramshackle, a mishmash of boards hammered together between the hulls of rotting ships. Better yet, there were dead bodies out on the sand and more fights to come. No one in the stands was going to notice a few nails out of place. Now that Bien was out, the only danger was from Goatface himself.

The trainer, however, was focused on Monster, Mouse, and Stupid, who had just reached the edge of the box.

"An exemplary performance," he said over the din of the crowd, clapping Stupid on the back. "Admirable discipline. Admirable timing."

"Exemplary?" Mouse looked over his shoulder to where slaves were busy dragging the dead from the pit. The bodies left long red streaks across the sand.

"Fucking right, exemplary," Monster crowed. "Whatever that means! Where's the fucking *quey*?" She looked at Bien, frowned. "How the fuck'd you get so dirty?"

"I fainted," Bien replied, gesturing toward the dirt. "Fainted, then spent the whole fight puking into the pot."

"Well"—Monster tossed an arm around her shoulders—"that's a fucking shame, because I'll tell you what—I was *amazing*."

Small Cao crossed to the side of the box. He didn't look particularly bothered by the slaughter of his Worthy.

"Not a bad fight," he said, extending a hand to Goatface.

Goatface took it. "They died bravely," he said. "That's all any of us can hope for in the end."

"The end?" Small Cao raised an eyebrow, ran his eyes over Ruc, Bien, the rest of Goatface's Worthy, spat onto the ground, then shook his head. "You know as well as I do this isn't even close to the end."

"Yes," Goatface began. "Well—"

He didn't get to finish whatever he'd been about to say because at that moment a roar erupted from the crowd. Ruc turned, expecting to see Vang Vo atop her ship. Instead, he found a single figure approaching the center of the pit—pale skinned, light haired, sculpturally muscled, almost impossibly beautiful, and entirely naked save for the collar at his throat.

No, he realized a moment later as Bien's fingers dug into his arm. Not a collar—an *axoch*.

"Well hello, gorgeous," Monster crowed. She nudged Goatface in the ribs. "Tell me he's my reward for fighting so well."

Goatface frowned. "I am . . . unacquainted with the gentleman."

Monster cackled. "All that ass and a *gentleman,* too?"

"Where did he come from?" Stupid asked.

"He's *mine,*" Monster growled. "You want a naked gentleman, you find your own."

"He was in the crowd," Talal said. "He dropped his robe, then jumped down into the pit."

The man appeared untroubled by his nakedness. In fact, he didn't look as though he'd ever been troubled by anything. He wore a proud, aloof expression as he sauntered across the sand. When he reached the center of the pit he paused, turned in a slow circle, not so much showing off as taking the measure of the place, waiting for a tattered silence to settle over the Arena. When it had, he turned, raised his chin until he was staring directly at the gallery atop the largest ship, the silk-shaded pavilion where the high priests and Dombân-gan aristocracy sat. His eyes looked like nails pounded into his head. His smile was a fishhook.

"I am come among you," he began, "with another message from my master."

His accent was strange, sinuous, impossible to place. The same accent as the messenger from the bridge.

"You ignored my brothers and my sisters. You mocked them and cast them down. That was a mistake. They came to warn you, as have I. After today, there will be no more warnings."

Ruc waited for the mob to scream at him, to shout him down, to pelt him with the remnants of their morning food. There was something in his voice, however, or maybe in his stance, that seemed to compel their silence. When no one spoke for a dozen heartbeats, he went on.

"You are a broken people, but my Lord will make you whole. You are a low people, but he will raise you up. You are a weak people, but he will make you strong. You are a homely people, but he will bathe you in beauty. You need do only one thing." He paused, turned in a slow circle once more, then pointed his finger directly at the high priests. "Submit.

"He is coming even now, garbed in his glory and his might. Even now he is approaching. Like my brothers and sisters before me, I have been sent to make you ready. When he strides into this city you will bend your knees, you will press your faces to the dirt, you will learn the truth of life and death and rebirth, and you will serve."

Far above, one of the high priests—Ho Anh—had risen from his seat. He stood at the rail of the ship, glaring down into the pit.

"Who are you?" he demanded.

"I am no one."

"Who is your master?"

"He is the First."

"Another imperial meddler? Some Annurian general?"

The man laughed. "Annur will bow, just as Dombâng will bow. This is my message."

"Well this is *our* message," Ho Anh declared. "Dombâng is home to a free people. We are guarded by the delta, by our own strength, and by our gods."

The messenger smiled wider. "Your gods will crawl. Even now, he hunts them. Even now he—"

The arrow sprouted from his chest like a flower.

The man raised his hands to it. He seemed surprised, but unafraid. There was no pain in his face as he raised his eyes and found Vang Vo standing on the rail of the ship far above, the bow still in her hands.

"Someone get this idiot out of my arena," she said.

And as though her words had finally loosed them, the guards poured into the pit with their swords and their spears.

The messenger made no effort to resist as they seized him, no effort to protect himself when they hurled him to the ground and began punching and kicking. Ruc caught just a glimpse of his face through the press of bodies. His nose was broken, his skin streaming with blood, one of his purpled eyes already beginning to close, but instead of cringing or crying out, he seemed to be laughing.

47

"I have to say," Cho Lu announced, peering around in the twilight gloom, "I don't love this spot."

As the last light drained from the sky, they'd climbed a low, small hill—not much more than a knoll, really—hoping to camp above the marshy ground through which they'd been slogging for hours. The dirt *was* slightly firmer, less sodden, but the trees made Gwenna's skin crawl.

Instead of leaves, they had hair, hair in lengths as long as her arm, *human* hair, or so it seemed.

She hacked a few strands from the nearest branch—black, straight, lustrous in the fading light—the kind of hair you might see on a Dombângan courtesan. Not all the trees were alike. Curling brown locks tumbled from a limb a pace away, and beyond that, a crooked tree, its trunk split and weeping sap, trailing long, wispy strands of gold. Rain beaded on it, slid the flaxen length, then dripped in a syncopated rhythm on the wet ground.

"They're just trees," Gwenna said, tossing aside the hairs she'd chopped free. They curled when it struck the dirt, as though singed by fire. "Unless you want to sleep in knee-deep water."

The legionary frowned down the slope. "I didn't say I liked it down there any better."

"We're marching across a poisoned continent. I wouldn't plan on liking very much."

The exhilaration that had seized them all when they first stepped into the sickness was fading. Gwenna still felt moments of unexpected strength, even elation, but those feelings were molting into something new—an alertness so keen it almost hurt, prickling her skin, prying her eyes too wide. She felt a little drunk, and a little like she'd chewed too much *yaga* root. The sensation reminded her of the rush at the start of battle, the fire and ice coursing through her blood—only there was no battle, nothing but the hot, wet wind fingering the hair of the trees.

They pitched camp, built a low, tight palisade around it, ate a cold dinner of dried fish, seaweed, and lukewarm water, all mostly in silence. Everyone volunteered to take the first watch—evidently none of them felt any more capable of sleep than she did. Bhuma Dhar ended up with the duty. Gwenna was just turning toward her tent when Rat seized her by the sleeve.

"Fight," the girl said.

"You want to train?"

Rat nodded.

"No. We've been pushing all day, and there are harder days ahead. You need to save your strength."

"No saving." Her eyes were huge in the darkness. "Train."

Gwenna started to object, then stopped herself. The girl was obviously infected with the same agitation plaguing the rest of them. At best, a little training might tire them both out. If not, well, Rat would be a little bit less likely to die the next time some monster tried to tear her apart.

"All right," she said. "Let's talk about tendons."

Rat blinked. "Ten. Dons?"

Gwenna flipped her arm over to show the cords running beneath the skin of her wrist. "Tendons." She took Ruc's hand, placed it on the skin. "They connect your muscle"—she flexed, demonstrating muscle—"to your bone."

"Bone," Rat repeated, nodding. "Like skull. Like ribs. Like"—she tapped her skinny chest, searching for the word—"sternum."

Gwenna Sharpe's school of language: all cursing, weapons, and human anatomy.

"Exactly," she replied. "And why are tendons important in a fight?"

"Cut them," Rat declared without hesitation, baring her teeth as though she meant to gnaw through Gwenna's flesh.

"Yes. Cut them, snap them, break them, and that part of the body stops working. If you sliced these"—she drew a fingernail across the tendons of her inner wrist—"I wouldn't be able to close my hand. Or here"—she bent, slipped up the leg of her pants, showed the thick tendon running down the back of her heel—"I wouldn't be able to walk. Animals have tendons, too. And *gabhya,* regardless of how fucked up they are."

"Attack tendon," Rat announced.

"Not always. Sometimes there are better choices, but it's good to remember there are other things to stab than the face and the chest."

Rat slipped her knife from the sheath at her belt. "Attack Gwenna Sharpe tendon?"

When Gwenna grinned, her teeth felt sharp against her lips. "You're welcome to try."

For hours they went at it beneath the dangling sodden locks of the trees, Rat feinting and lunging, hacking and slashing, dodging, rolling through the mud, dragging herself back up, and coming on again, eyes slicked with star-light. Gwenna fought with a short green branch she'd sliced from one of the trees, punishing Rat for each mistake with a blow across the shoulders or knees. Rat hissed each time the wood struck home, but she rarely made the same mistake twice. And the girl was fast—fast as any cadet back on the Islands—strong for her size, indefatigable. It was tempting to see Menkiddoc's poison behind that strength and speed, but the truth was, Rat had been good even from those first nights when they were chained together. Not Kettral good, but far better than any nine-year-old orphan had any business being.

In a lull between attacks, Gwenna studied the girl.

"Tell me about the *rashkta-bhura*," she said finally.

Rat stiffened.

There had been no time between the keelhauling and storm, the shipwreck, and the mutiny, to follow up on the conversation from the brig. No time until now.

"Some kind of warriors, right?" Gwenna pressed. "They were training you to be one of them? That's why you have Yutaka? That's why you're already such a good fighter."

Instead of replying, Rat launched into a vicious attack, slashing high to drive Gwenna back, lashing out for a knee with a foot, rolling into the empty space when Gwenna jerked her leg back, coming around with the knife in a sweep that should have left Gwenna with only one working foot. She blocked the blow with her stick, knocked the knife aside, dropped onto Rat, pinning the girl to the ground. Rat struggled, tried to find a point of leverage. Her grappling had improved during the long days in the brig, but not enough to sweep the larger woman. She strained anyway, twisted and writhed, and only after a long time, when it was obvious she couldn't slip free, did she let her head drop back against the wet dirt.

"Fuck," she muttered.

Gwenna pulled back slightly, cautiously, stared down into the girl's eyes.

"Why won't you talk to me about this?"

"Why?" Rat echoed.

"That's what I'm asking you."

The girl shook her head. "*Axochlin* are gone. Everyone are gone."

"But what *were* they?"

Rat rolled her head away. For a few heartbeats, Gwenna thought the girl had gone silent for good. Then she spoke in a small, quiet voice.

"Prisoners. *Axochlin* were prisoners."

"I thought you said they were warriors." Gwenna shook her head. Teaching prisoners to fight. Giving them *gabhya*—none of that made any sense.

"Prisoner warriors. Happy prisoners still prisoners."

"That's why they wore that—what did you call it? That collar."

"Axoch," the girl said, the word rough in her mouth as though she were hacking up a gob of phlegm.

"But you didn't want to join them."

Rat turned back to her. *"No."*

"Why not?"

"No collar. No feasts. Rat is . . ." She searched desperately for the word. "Rat is *wild* person."

Gwenna coughed up a laugh at that. "Yes," she said. "Yes you are."

She rolled off the girl, sat up, passed back the knife. Rat took it, cleaned the blade on her pants, then slid it into the sheath. The hair of the trees twisted in the hot night wind. A few paces away, Pattick thrashed in his sleep, as though trying to throw off invisible bonds.

"Whose prisoners?" Gwenna asked finally.

Rat turned to her, brow knit with confusion.

"You said the *axochlin* and those others were prisoners. Who were they prisoners *of*?"

Confusion twisted into rage. "Of fucking *Nevariim*."

✝

Three days into the march they broke from the jungle into a broad, rolling expanse of knee-high grass. It stretched only two or three miles before the jungle closed back in around it, but for the first time since the beach Gwenna was able to see more than a few paces in front of her. The land rose slowly into hills, and beyond those hills, far beyond, hazed by heat and distance, mountains like a jagged line chalked across the horizon.

She turned to Kiel.

"That's where we're going?"

He nodded. "To those mountains, then over."

"And where, exactly, are the ruins of your Csestriim fortress?"

"You cannot see the pass from here."

For a moment no one spoke. It was one thing to talk about walking for hundreds of miles, another to see every inch of that distance sprawled out in front of you.

"There's a river," Pattick said. He pointed off at an angle toward a gentle valley meandering through the hills. "It'll lead to those peaks. Might be easier than charging straight ahead."

"Looks like Jonon had the same idea," Cho Lu observed.

The tracks that they'd been following turned to cut across the grassland toward the valley.

"It would seem," Dhar said slowly, "that we will be following the admiral for a while longer."

Gwenna, however, found herself frowning as she studied the tracks. She turned to Kiel. "Why hasn't anything hit us yet?"

The historian raised his brows. "Hit us?"

"*Gabhya.* Monsters."

Pattick looked baffled. "Did you forget about that scaled cat?"

"Sure," she replied, "but that was it. According to the stories this place is *crawling* with *gabhya*. You're not supposed to be able to take two steps without having something bite your foot off. We've been marching for days."

Pattick didn't look convinced, but Kiel nodded. "We have had an easier passage than I expected. Far easier."

"Easy makes me nervous," Gwenna said. She glanced at Jonon's tracks once more, then shook her head. "We're done following the admiral."

Bhuma Dhar raised his brows. "The admiral's route is not the most direct, but it may be the fastest. He took the compasses. Without them or his trail to follow, we will be lost when the jungle closes down around us once more."

Gwenna turned to Kiel. "Will we be lost?"

After a sliver of a pause, he replied: "I can help with the navigation. There are ways to hold a straight course through the forest, even when there is no sun."

"Another trick from your hunting days?"

He made an expression like a smile. "Precisely."

"What's wrong with following the valley?" Pattick asked.

She shook her head. "There's a river at the bottom of that valley. Rivers are where things go to drink."

"You mean *gabhya*."

She nodded.

Nothing had attacked them since the scaled cat. According to Kiel, that was probably because they were still close to the fringe of the sickness. As they went deeper, he said, they'd encounter larger monsters, and worse. Still, the living things that they'd encountered already—the hair trees, lizards with two heads, vines with flowers red as human tongues that lapped and lapped at the air, some spiky blue-gray plant with steel-sharp leaves, biting moths in clouds so dense they made it difficult to breathe—were enough to put Gwenna's teeth on edge. If there were worse things in the sick, she didn't want to see them.

"Fighting our way up and down those hills," Cho Lu said, eyeing the terrain. "It's going to be brutal."

Gwenna still felt that strange, preternatural strength, but it had transformed from a physical delight into a shifting, restless urgency, a need with no apparent source or object.

"You know what's brutal?" she asked. "Being fucking eaten."

Pattick stared down toward the valley. "So the admiral. He and the men—they're in trouble."

Rat scowled. "Monsters can chew the admiral."

"Monsters can chew the admiral," Gwenna agreed. She checked her blades, shouldered her pack once more, pointed toward the mountains. "At least we can see where we're going."

Walking through the grass was like wading through a shallow sea. The blades were blue-green, almost translucent, beautiful and mesmerizing. With each gust of the breeze, they bent, then straightened in slow, undulating waves.

Except, Gwenna realized, when they were maybe a mile into the grass, there was no breeze.

She stopped short.

"What—" Cho Lu asked, half drawing his sword.

She didn't reply.

The air was dead still but the grass kept moving, as though the ground beneath were convulsing silently. At first she thought the motion was random, but as she turned in a slow circle she saw the pattern: the waves centered on *them,* the grass leaning toward the small group, reaching, drawing back, then reaching once again, whispering as it shifted. Gwenna looked down to find a long blade winding slowly around her leg. She kicked viciously free—the thing wasn't hard to break—and for a moment the grass beneath her feet looked just like any other grass. Then another blade bent toward her and began to twine around her ankle.

"Intarra's light," Pattick breathed.

"Bad grass . . ." Rat said.

Kiel nodded. "It is the kind of thing that happens here."

"Dangerous?" Dhar asked.

"Not yet."

Gwenna looked up. There were still at least two miles before they reached the jungle once more.

"Will it stay like this, or get worse?"

"It is impossible to say."

"Can't you do some math?"

The historian did something with his face. "There are aspects of the

sickness that resist all calculation. The grass could grow fiercer, more dangerous, or it might not."

"I'll take my chances with the grass," Cho Lu said, slashing his sword
through the nearest blades. "At least out here we can see things coming at us."

"Well," Gwenna said, shooting a significant glance across the knee-high
grass, "very *tall* things, at least."

It was hardly an ideal situation, but she had long ago quit hoping for ideal.
Menkiddoc was brimming with dangerous shit. If they turned back every
time they encountered something strange, they'd die of starvation before ever
reaching the peaks.

"We keep going," she said. "Eyes up. Blades out."

They were less than half a mile from the jungle when Cho Lu, who was
leading the group, let out a yelp, his voice rising through surprise into sudden
pain.

Gwenna dropped into a defensive crouch, turned in a quick circle, but the
only thing to see was Cho Lu, dancing in place as though he were standing
in a fire.

Her gut shifted uneasily inside her. Had he gone mad already? So suddenly?
If people were losing their minds after three days, what were the odds of any
of them making it up into the mountains and down the other side?

As the legionary stumbled back toward the group, however, he stopped
dancing, stopped shouting.

"The grass," he said, pointing. "The motherfucking *grass*."

Gwenna narrowed her eyes. It looked like the same stuff they'd been walking through all day, but when she knelt she could see that they'd come to the
verge of something new. These stalks were sharp, serrated, like the saw blades
of a fine cabinetmaker, only more slender, more hungry, more . . . alive. As she
crouched, one of them flicked out for her, fast as a frog's tongue. It came up
short just inches from her face.

"It tried to eat me," Cho Lu declared.

The bottoms of his pants hung in tatters. Blood from a dozen lacerations
soaked into the leather of his boots. None of the cuts were grave—Gwenna
had had worse hundreds of times over—but this was just *grass*. She looked
up at the jungle blanketing the slopes of the hills ahead. As Kiel said, it was
impossible to know what waited for them there.

"We can cut through it," Pattick announced.

He was already swinging his cutlass with a frenzied, maniacal energy, scything through the blades, forging ahead almost blindly.

"Stop," she said.

He didn't stop. If anything, he went faster. "We can mow it down!"

He reeked suddenly of triumph, as though the grass were an ancient foe he had defeated for the first time.

She put an edge into her voice. "*Stand down,* soldier."

Reluctantly Pattick slowed, then turned, raising his blade.

"It's *bleeding,*" he said, pointing to the steel.

Blood smeared the weapon, the same red blood that oozed from the cut stalks at his feet. It would have been obvious when Cho Lu first stumbled into the grasses except for the fact that he was bleeding himself.

"Interesting," Kiel murmured. "A hybrid circulatory system."

"We could go around," Cho Lu suggested.

"We could go *through,*" Pattick insisted, raising his blade again. "Cut a swath from here to the trees."

Gwenna gazed out over the sea of green for a while. The grass shifted, whispering sounds just on the wrong side of sense. She was tempted to lean closer, to let the not-words wash over her. There was a meaning there, she was sure of it. . . .

She jerked when Kiel put a hand on her shoulder, spun to find him studying her.

"Commander Sharpe?"

She shook herself free of the grass's spell.

"We're not cutting it," she said. "We're burning it."

It was Cho Lu who'd found her kit back on the *Daybreak*—Kettral knives and blades, a short bow, extra blacks, and her explosives. Evidently Jonon had been keeping everything in his cabin.

As she spoke, she drew a flickwick from the holster at her belt.

"A fire will draw attention," Dhar observed.

"Normal animals would flee a fire," Gwenna replied. She turned to Kiel. "What about the *gabhya*?"

"Impossible to say. Most will likely flee. It may draw a few closer. Fire is energy, after all. There will be those that feed on it."

She weighed the odds, feeling like a blind merchant with broken scales. Some of the monsters would flee, some might come running. If something attacked, maybe they could kill it, maybe not. There was no way to know about any of it. She found herself thinking about the crippled fox in her trap, about the Flea's words: *None of us make it, Gwenna.*

"Fuck it," she said. "I'm burning it."

She checked over the munition, then waited while the others finished digging out a wide circle in the grass, enough space that the fire wouldn't sweep over them. The waiting was hard. She'd always been interested in the work of demolitions, but this was different. She was eager to see the grass burn, she realized, hungry for the conflagration.

A flickwick wasn't a starshatter. It didn't explode. Instead, it burned in a hot, wide arc, hot enough to melt steel, more than hot enough to set damp grass ablaze. Normally, she'd have shielded her eyes. Not this time. This time she watched, let the light etch onto her retina as the grass took fire. The men erupted into cheers as the wind whipped the flame into a low wall. They were too close, all of them, despite their digging. She could see the heat in their faces, feel it in her own, but she didn't step back. Instead, she added her own voice to the chorus as the fire grew and grew, chewing through the grass, mounting, raging, spreading, until it looked as though it might devour the whole world.

✝

They camped that night at the edge of the scorched earth, crossed the smoldering ground in the morning, then entered the jungle once more. Gwenna had half expected the grasslands to ignite the forest, but due to some trick of the wind only the southernmost trees were scorched. Beyond them, ash settled on the leaves, turning the green to gray. A hundred paces beyond that, deep beneath the canopy, there was no sign of the blaze.

Without Jonon's trail to follow, they were left to hack their own way through the tangle of branches and vine. It was hard, sweaty work. Gwenna still felt the strange strength coursing through her, but it was accompanied by something else, too, something new, almost an itch, although she couldn't point to any part of her body she wanted to scratch. The sensation reminded her of having drunk too much *ta* when she needed to pull an all-night patrol, an alertness so acute it felt uncomfortable.

Not that a little discomfort was a bad thing. If she'd been worried about creatures lurking in the knee-high grass behind them, entering the jungle once more had her wound to the point of breaking. It was impossible to see more than a dozen paces in any direction. On the miraculous chance that they *did* see something, it would be too late; it wasn't as though she could count on Kiel to manage another impossible shot. The trees, thank Hull, were nothing like the grass, but the vines had a way of reaching out, tangling arms and legs, tripping even the most vigilant over and over and over until the others were cursing, hacking at roots with their blades, their faces painted not with the exhaustion she might have expected, but with fury.

That fury only mounted when they found the corpse trees.

Gwenna had taken point for the afternoon, and so she was the first one to stumble across them. At first glance she took the forms beneath the branches for some kind of foe, a group of soldiers, Jonon's men probably, lurking in ambush. As she pulled up, however, she realized that the people weren't standing in the trees' shadows—they were hanged from the branches by vines.

"Sweet Intarra's light," Pattick breathed when he reached her. His eyes were wide as saucers. "Did it . . . How did those people . . ."

Gwenna studied the trees for a while, then stepped forward, sword held before her. "I don't think they *are* people."

By the time the others reached them she had hacked down one of the grisly forms. It was fruit. Or some twisted version of whatever Menkiddoc considered fruit. They were shaped uncannily like naked human corpses and ranged in color from pale to dark. The rind had the look and texture of weathered skin. When she split one open, bloodred juice splattered across the ground.

"Just vegetation," Kiel observed quietly.

"Right," Cho Lu said, "but something we've learned about the vegetation here? Sometimes it *eats* you."

"These aren't eating anyone," Gwenna replied. Compared to the grass and the clinging vines, the corpse trees seemed benign, and yet walking through them hour after hour began to wear on a person. It felt like marching through a forest laden with the dead.

By the time they finally trekked beyond the grove she was spending so much time looking before and behind her that she felt as though her head might come unscrewed from her shoulders. At one point, a flock of screaming songbirds—feathers an awful, unnatural blue—erupted into cacophonous flight. A little later, something large and ponderous, roused by the sound of their approach, lumbered off through the darkness. Both cases drew shouts of alarm from the others. The legionaries brandished blades, Rat bared her belt knife, snarling, Kiel raised his bow, though he had nothing to shoot at.

Still no large *gabhya*. Still nothing like the monsters she'd feared.

For two days they went on like that, leaping at shadows, every one of them wound tight as the string on a flatbow. By the middle of the third day after the fire, Gwenna began to think she might be sick. It was rare for Kettral to fall ill, but though strength and urgency still blazed in her veins, there was a new feeling now as well, a gnawing in her gut that didn't feel quite like hunger, as though some organ were too tight or too loose or just twisted the wrong way inside her. She could see just fine, better than normal, actually—beads of water on the leaves, translucent ants crawling up the trunks of trees—but the new acuity meant that nothing she looked at felt real. She might have been lost in a painting. More and more she found herself touching things as she passed—branches, flowers, trunks of trees, the half-eaten corpse of a huge bird. She saw the others doing the same, as though everyone were losing faith in the world, as though they all needed to convince themselves that it was actually real.

When they made camp that night, after clearing away the brush, building a rough perimeter of sharpened sticks, starting a fire, and eating, she found Kiel.

"It's happening to us," she said, careful to keep her voice low.

The historian took a bite of dried fish, chewed it for a while, then nodded.

"But all of our food and water has come from our supplies. I've been watching. No one has touched any of the streams."

"That helps," he replied. "It slows the spread of the pollution, but even our precautions cannot stop it. Eventually the mind breaks and you will destroy yourselves."

She shook her head. "You sure know how to comfort a girl."

"I am not trying to be comforting."

"No shit. How long do we have?"

"It grows dangerous after a week. There are tales of explorers spending longer in the sickness and surviving, but they are unreliable. It is difficult to extrapolate from such scant information."

"I thought that's what you were good at. Extrapolating."

"There are limits."

She glanced down at the hardtack in her hand, then stared off into the shadows between the trees. "I don't feel hungry," she said. "Not even for regular food."

The historian kept chewing on his fish, swallowed after a while, then nodded again. "Not yet."

✝

The next day was worse.

The land's sickness pressed down as they marched. In some ways, she felt as though she were moving underwater, as though all of reality were a shifting, invisible weight. Where the weight of water felt natural, however, even comfortable for someone like Gwenna who'd spent her whole life in it, this was an oily, strange sensation, impossible to get used to.

It didn't actually slow them, of course. The air was still air. The ground was still ground. The weight they felt didn't settle on the limbs, but in the mind. Every so often one of the men would raise an arm, stare at it a moment, confused, then let it drop. Gwenna felt the urge, too, the need to check to see that she was still all there, that the parts of herself had not come unbuckled. She would not have been surprised, when she looked down, to find a leg missing, or all her skin gone, or her intestines trailing along over the stones behind her, glistening but insensate. It was a momentary relief each time to find her body still present—pale skin sunburned, all the old scars still closed, legs and arms where they belonged, doing the work they'd been trained to do. The relief lasted only as long as she was looking, however. Each time she raised her head she felt all over again that she was drifting away.

And it wasn't just the physical sensations that proved unnerving. The forest grew stranger the deeper they penetrated. The birds, for instance. At first she didn't think anything of the brilliant, elaborate plumage—she'd seen plenty of tropical birds before; they were always bright, always preposterously gaudy. These birds, however, were different. Sprays of feathers exploded from heads and tails, some of them as long as Gwenna was tall. Dark beaks curved like sickles. One had twin feathers standing feet above its head, each widening to a fan emblazoned with a feverish-looking eye. Another seemed to be bleeding from the breast until she realized the thick, dripping strands were also some kind of feather. It cried over and over in a voice that was eerily human, but wordless.

Obscene.

The word kept boiling up in Gwenna's mind. She couldn't say whether it was the colors or the wailing songs or the way they followed the party with too-bold eyes, but the creatures were obscene. She felt a need deep in her gut to go after them, to cut them to pieces, to make them *not be.* Halfway through the afternoon she found herself stopping, sliding a blade carefully from its sheath. The steel was almost free when Kiel put a firm hand on her shoulder.

"Just birds," he said quietly.

"They're *not* just birds," she hissed, but saying the words aloud broke, if only for a few moments, the compulsion to see them destroyed.

"Just birds," the historian said again.

She let go of the sword.

A little later, Pattick sat down abruptly on a rock and began sobbing. By the time Gwenna caught up, Cho Lu was already there, kneeling beside him.

"Pattick," the legionary said. *"Pattick."*

"I need to wake up," Pattick whispered. "This is a dream. I need to wake up."

Cho Lu shook his head. "You're not dreaming. You're all right. We're all all right."

Pattick looked at him with wide, desperate eyes. "I need to wake up," he whispered again.

Kiel squatted down. "If this is a dream," he asked quietly, "what will happen?"

Pattick stared at him. He looked as though he was staring at a ghost. "I don't know."

"Nothing," Kiel replied. "Nothing will happen. A dream is a game the mind plays with itself. Nothing inside it is real. Nothing can hurt you."

The soldier stared at the stony ground, the canopy of the trees above. He stared for a while at his own hands.

"Nothing is real," he said. "Nothing can hurt me." Then he stood up abruptly. Mania fringed his laugh. *"Nothing is real!"* he screamed into the wind. *"Nothing can hurt me!"* Before anyone could stop him, he raced ahead, stabbing a finger north, struck the jaunty pose of a general before battle. "Onward, everyone!" he declared. "To victory!"

As he strode deeper into the trees, the others followed. Cho Lu seemed to catch his enthusiasm. Rat, however, kept glancing over her shoulder, gnawing at the inside of her cheek.

"Was that wise?" Gwenna asked, when she and Kiel were alone once more.

"He needs to keep moving," the historian replied. "I told him what he needed to hear."

"Maybe he needed to hear the truth."

"Which truth?"

"That there *are* things here that can hurt us."

She gestured vaguely to the rocks, the trees that seemed to be reaching for them with withered branches. The wind had teeth. The sunlight was fire on her skin. There were a hundred ways to die in the forest, a thousand. Pattick had been right to be frightened. If anything, he hadn't been frightened *enough*.

Kiel, however, just shook his head. "The most dangerous thing to him right now is his own mind." He met Gwenna's eyes. "As yours is to you."

He said those last words in the same tone that he said everything: indifferent, academic. It was a tone she'd been hearing from him since they weighed anchor back in Pirat, but this time it dredged up a sudden, violent hatred inside her, a hatred for his smugness, his certainty, the vague way he looked past her when he spoke, as though she didn't matter at all. She ached to cave in his face with her fist, to visit some kind of terrible suffering upon him. She wanted to see some fear for once in that keen gaze. She needed to take him by the throat and devour him. . . .

"No," she said. The word was an anchor, steadying her in the storm, and so she said it again. "No."

Kiel watched her. His eyes were shaped like human eyes, but there was nothing human in them.

"You feel it," he said.

She nodded. The hatred drained away as quickly as it had come. At least, it seemed that way at first. After a moment she realized it wasn't gone at all, but suspended, as though the emotion were a great pendulum that had swept through her mind, missed her by inches, carried on past, and hung now at the far end of its arc, motionless, poised to plunge once more.

"Someone is going to get killed in here," she said grimly.

Kiel nodded.

She shook her head. "You don't understand. *I* might be the one doing the killing."

Again he nodded. "You will, if we do not reach the mountains in time."

"How do I hold it off?" She narrowed her eyes. "How do *you* hold it off? And don't tell me to fucking breathe slower."

So far, he had shown none of the nervy twitching, none of the giddiness or despair that plagued the rest of them.

Instead of replying, the historian knelt, sifted through the dirt, picked up a stone. Unlike most things in the jungle, it was unremarkable—smooth, black, almost round, about the size of Gwenna's thumbnail. He brushed it clean, rolled it in his hand a moment as though testing the weight, then handed it to her.

"What is this?" she asked, suddenly wary.

"You tell me."

"It's a rock."

He nodded. "Indeed. And what will it be tomorrow?"

She stared at him, studied the rock a moment, then looked back up. "The fact that you're asking makes me think this is a trap."

"No trap."

"Really?" She tossed the stone in the air, caught it overhand. "Because there's some pretty strange shit in Menkiddoc."

"There is. But the sickness affects only living things."

"In that case . . ." She rolled the stone across the backs of her fingers. It was a trick she'd learned back on the Islands. "I'm guessing tomorrow, just like today, it will be a little black rock."

"Your guess would be correct. Eventually, of course, after enough millennia, the world will break it, then break it again, grind it down to sand so fine you could not feel it between your fingers. And still, those pieces of sand will share the same nature. They will be smaller, but they will not have changed, not fundamentally."

"And this is useful to me how?"

"You must understand something, Commander Sharpe, if you are to survive our passage through Menkiddoc: you are not like that stone."

"No shit. I'm paler, less durable, hopefully a little smarter. . . ."

"You are a different order of being entirely. As am I. As are our companions."

The pendulum of rage swung back toward her. They were surrounded by jungle, a jungle infested with monstrous beasts, many days' hike from even the most dubious safety, and the historian was taunting her with riddles. She clenched her hands into fists in order not to reach for her swords.

"I'm going to ask you one more time," she growled, "how to hold on to myself when the madness comes."

Kiel shook his head. "You don't."

For a moment, confusion shoved aside the anger.

"What the fuck does that mean?"

"You think that Gwenna Sharpe is a thing, like that stone, that you can hold on to. You believe she is composed of various elements—her rage and regret, her training and terror, the memories of her family and friends and foes. You think that what you must do is keep those elements in place, maintain the balance and proportion, resist all change."

"If the change means madness, then yeah, I sure as shit intend to resist it."

"You cannot."

She leaned forward, shifting into his space. "You have no idea what I can do."

"On the contrary, I have very precise ideas regarding your abilities. This is not an attack, Gwenna, it is a fact, one the world has been trying to teach you ever since the Purple Baths."

"All I learned in the Purple Baths is that there are consequences to fucking up. That people die when you make mistakes."

Kiel nodded. "You were one of those people."

She opened her mouth to object, but he forestalled her with a raised, crooked finger.

"Gwenna Sharpe died that night. She died again when Frome imprisoned her, and again when the Emperor stripped her of her rank. She died during the fight against the Manjari, died in the darkness of the brig afterward, died when she rushed out of the cave to kill the kettral. This is what it is to be . . ." He hesitated for half a heartbeat. ". . . to be human."

"If she died so many times, then what am I still doing here?"

He smiled. "You were reborn."

"Save the religious pig shit."

"Not reborn in the way of the prophets with their promises and their paradise. It is difficult to explain." He furrowed his brow. "Human minds are built to see a world of objects, but you are not an object, Gwenna. You are a process. You are the change taking place inside you. The woman at the end of this conversation will not be the woman who began it. The Gwenna who wakes up in the morning will not be the same Gwenna who went to sleep. It is impossible to fix a person in time. I could not pin you like a butterfly to a board any more than I could pin down a piece of music. Your essence lies in your unfolding."

She stared at him, her mind teetering on a brink. Whether it was the brink of understanding or madness, she couldn't say.

"People resist this idea," the historian continued. "They look at their passions and say, *Those are me*. They stare inward at their beliefs, and tell themselves, *That is what I am*." He shook his head. "Before the Purple Baths you looked at your strength, your rage, your string of victories and told yourself that they were you. When they were taken away, you nearly shattered. You stared into your well of fear and shame and you thought, *This is what I have become*."

"It *was*," she snarled. Or tried to snarl. The words came out a whisper.

"It was," he agreed. "But you were not done becoming. Not then, not now. Your joy is not you, Gwenna. Your sorrow is not you. Your strength is not you. Your failure and your flaws are not you. Your heart and your hopes are not you." He gestured to the jungle around them. "And when the madness comes, that is not you either. That is what you must remember."

His gray eyes were wide as the sky before a storm.

The question lifted itself from her lips as though it had been waiting there her entire life, begging to be asked. "Then what am I?"

He smiled. "You are the unfolding, Gwenna. You are the change. You are whatever it is that, in the face of misery and bliss and bafflement, keeps going."

She studied him awhile, then stared down at her hands. Broken fingers mended not quite straight, a lace of white scar carved into the tan, calluses on the inner thumb, across the palm. Not the same hands she'd had as a child. Her hands, all the same.

She looked up finally, gestured to the men resting on the rocks ahead.

"This isn't what you told Pattick. You didn't tell any of them this."

Distrust bloomed inside her like a too-sweet-smelling flower. She studied it. Her distrust, certainly, but not *her*. There was something beneath it or beyond it, something wider than the feeling flooding her.

"They are not like you," the historian replied. "The sickness will gnaw at them. It is gnawing at them already, but it will work on them more slowly."

"Why?"

"They were not bitten by the slarn. They did not drink from the egg."

Gwenna shook her head. "How do you know about that?"

"It is a historian's work to learn about the world and its people."

"That is a Kettral secret."

"It is a historian's work to learn the secrets."

As he spoke, the pendulum of rage swung back through Gwenna's mind.

He knew. He *knew* about the Kettral. He knew about everything. He was a danger to her, to the men, to Rat, to the mission, a danger to the whole world. Her hand tightened on the handle of her sword. She wanted to see him opened, bleeding. . . .

"Who are you?" Kiel asked calmly.

She ached to plunge the steel through his body, but instead she took a shuddering breath, closed her eyes.

There was the fury, but she was not the fury. There was the fear, but she was not the fear.

"Wrong question," she murmured.

The historian cocked his head, birdlike, to one side.

"What is the right question?"

"Can you go on?"

"Ah." He studied her. "And can you go on?"

She bared her teeth. "Let's find out."

✝

She called a halt at dusk.

For the second half of the day they'd been struggling forward through muddy bogs, following knee-deep channels between the trees, hacking their way through the overhanging vines. She would have preferred to keep moving—the work of marching forward gave her something to focus on, something to distract her from whatever was happening in her mind—but the thickening night was too dark for the eyes of the others, and the rise where she ordered them to set up camp was the first dry land they'd come across in hours. A single tree grew near its center, a tree with leaves the size and shape of human hands.

She loathed it.

As she went about her share of the work—pitching a tent, checking Rat's feet for blisters, then kindling a fire—those hands, dangling from vinelike branches, had a way of caressing her face, her neck, always just the slightest brush, as though they'd been lifted there naturally by the wind. After the twentieth or thirtieth touch, Gwenna whirled around, drew both swords, and began slicing away. When she thought she'd cleared the worst of it, she sheathed her blades, but then, when she bent over her pack, she felt them once more, on her cheek, in her hair. . . .

"Rest," Kiel said, gesturing to her tent.

She shook her head. "I don't need to rest."

"You don't *feel* as though you need to rest, but your body is tired. When it is tired, it will draw more sustenance from the air, from the ground, and the air and ground are tainted."

"The watch . . ."

"Pattick and Cho Lu have the first watch."

She hated the idea of lying down, of listening to those leaves fingering the canvas of the tent. She didn't feel as though she needed to sleep, but the historian was right. She *should* have been tired. And so, after another meal of hard biscuits, dried fish, dried fruit, she unrolled her blanket, closed her eyes, and tried to sleep.

She dreamed of Talal. He was alive in her dream, his ankle chained to an iron ball that he carried in his hands as he strode out onto an expanse of hot, shadeless sand. She wanted to tell him to stop, to rest, to put down the ball, but she had no body, no voice. At one point, he looked right at her. For half a heartbeat she thought that he saw her.

"Talal," she said. "I'm sorry I left you. I'm sorry I didn't go back for you."

He walked right through her, as though she were nothing but air.

"Talal!"

He didn't turn, just kept on over the sand, carrying that awful ball.

"Talal!"

This time she shouted his name, shouted it over and over until she woke to find herself sitting up, hands stretched out before her, pressing on the dark wall of the tent as though she were trying to escape. Her own mouth was closed, but the shouting was still going on, not in the dream, but in the real world, in the forest just beyond that scrap of canvas—Cho Lu, his voice edged with rage.

"I said *stand down*. The first man comes near me, I swear to Intarra I'll cut him in half and eat his fucking heart."

Gwenna struggled from the tent—Rat like a shadow behind her—staggered out into the night, tore a sword from its sheath. Cho Lu and Pattick stood a few paces away, their own blades drawn. Beyond them, half a dozen figures loomed in the night. It was too dark for the legionaries to make out the faces, but Gwenna could see them clearly enough—the faces and the blood and the lines of exhaustion scrawled across them.

"Jonon," she said, stepping forward, unsheathing her other blade. "Decided you wanted to kill us after all?"

She wanted him to try it, she realized. Eagerness raced like fire beneath her skin. After months of the man's scorn and contempt, she could finally carve him apart, drink in his screams as he died. . . .

"Look at him," Kiel murmured. The historian stood just behind her.

Gwenna looked. Jonon had his cutlass out, but he hadn't deployed his men to attack. If he'd wanted to ambush them he would have surrounded the small camp first, come in from every side.

She could taste her own disappointment, bitter on the back of her tongue.

From the other side of the rise, Bhuma Dhar approached. He held his own blade low but ready.

"Why are you here?" Gwenna asked quietly. "Where are the rest of your men?"

She dragged a long breath through her nose, searching for the scents of the others, finding nothing but mud and the vague rot of the swamp.

The admiral shook his head. "They are dead."

"*Dead?*"

"Something has been stalking us. Killing us, one or two every night, ripping them right out of camp whatever guard we set, and eating them alive."

48

Gelta Yuel kept her shop of antiquities in a quiet poplar-shaded square just north of the Dawn Palace. The building looked like the others to either side— gray stone stitched with ivy, narrow windows, flowering shrubs growing out of a skirt of crushed gravel flanking the door. No sign hung above the entrance. Gelta—in all the dozens of stories told about her, she was always Gelta, never Yuel—had no need of a sign. As a child in the Perfumed Quarter, several miles distant, Akiil had heard of the place and the woman who owned it. Every petty thief in the city had a plan to break into Gelta's, make off with a fortune in ancient relics, live like a Malkeenian prince off the profits for the rest of their lives. As far as Akiil knew, no one had ever succeeded.

Studying it from the square, it wasn't hard to see why. There may not have been a sign, but four massive men stood guard outside the door. According to the stories, Gelta employed only former legionaries, all of whom had held at least a commander's rank. The men certainly looked like soldiers—iron-straight, muscle-bound, carved with scar. Unlike most guards, however, who passed the time at their posts smoking or chatting, these men were obviously alert, scanning the placid square for threats. Two of them had already noticed Akiil. He smiled, nodded, gave a genial wave. Rumor had it that, in addition to the guards, the woman kept two or three soldiers with flatbows hidden on the surrounding roofs. Hard to blame her, really. If Akiil had presided over a shop packed with enough wealth to buy a small city, he'd probably have a few guards, too.

Of course, Gelta's guards weren't the only problem.

He glanced over his shoulder, back the way he'd come. It had been sloppy, allowing Adare's spies to follow him back to the Quarter all those weeks earlier, the kind of mistake he wouldn't have made if he'd been paying closer attention. This time, instead of climbing out his window, he'd walked straight out the door of the inn, just the way he would any other day, nodded at the soldiers with their spears, then headed for the Wool Market. The men followed as they always did, eyes alert, maybe a dozen paces behind. It was enough distance to be respectful, but after the Quarter, they'd all dispensed with the charade of his freedom.

Halfway to the market, however, Akiil turned abruptly south, rounded a corner, and then, just under the wide span of the Bridge of Bulls, climbed nimbly up the stone pier supporting the arch overhead. It was an escape route they'd used as kids, though the holds had felt larger back then, his body lighter. He reached the narrow ledge, rolled onto it, pressed himself back into the shadow, just as the first of the guardsmen rounded the corner below. The man gave a start, stood on his toes a moment, bellowed an order to the others, then shoved ahead through the crowd. Akiil lay back on the stone, allowed himself a smile. The Bull Bridge escape had always been one of Butt Boy's favorites, the ideal vanishing act for a thief fleeing the Wool Market. He would have been thrilled to know it still worked. Would have been, if he hadn't been fed to the Captain's hogs.

The thought scoured away Akiil's smile.

At his request—actually more like a demand than a request—Adare had sent men back to the Dead Horse. According to the Emperor, they'd interrupted a card game in order to make Skinny Quinn the offer: Come with us. You'll be fed, protected, provided with gold, provided with a safe escort out of the Quarter, out of Annur entirely, if you want.

"Why?" Adare had asked. "Who is this woman?"

"Just someone I used to know. Someone who deserves better than counting the Captain's cards."

He'd imagined Quinn on the coast somewhere. The girl had spent whole days down at the harbor, gazing out over the Broken Bay. With the gold—gold from Akiil's own negotiated wages for exploring the gates—she could buy a house in Katal. Maybe even a boat. Not that Skinny Quinn knew how to sail a boat, but if anyone could learn, it was her. The vision of her sitting on her own dock, feet dangling in the waves, had filled and warmed him, like mulled wine on a winter night. It had, anyway, until Adare's men came back with word she'd refused.

When he asked why, the sergeant just shook his head. "Said she was happy where she was."

The narrow ledge beneath the bridge felt suddenly cramped, hard, cold. With Adare's soldiers nowhere in sight, Akiil had climbed down, made his way across the city to Gelta Yuel's shop.

When he'd approached to within five or six paces of the door, one of the guards raised a hand.

"Please stop there, sir."

It was probably the only time in Akiil's life that he'd been referred to as "sir."

He stopped, smiled, held up his empty hands. "I'm here to see Gelta."

"Madame Yuel works by appointment only."

"Then I'd like to make an appointment."

The soldier flicked an eye over Akiil's tattered robe. "You may do so with me. My name is Lors. I handle her appointments."

He did an admirable job keeping the skepticism from his voice, but there was a tightening to his eyes, a slight downturn of the lip which, if magnified a thousandfold, could have turned into a sneer. Still, it was more courtesy than Akiil had expected. He'd planned, in fact, to be threatened and chased off—maybe at the point of a sword—before he could make his pitch. It was surprising to find that one of the city's richest merchants would even consider a meeting with a nameless monk in a shitty robe, but of course, Gelta *herself* was considering no such thing. One of the benefits of being rich: the ability to pay people to be courteous on your behalf.

"I should inform you," Lors continued, "that Madame Yuel is a very busy woman. The soonest available appointment is in the spring."

"It's spring now."

"The spring of next year."

Akiil smiled wider, reached into his robe, then froze as the men to either side of the door drew their blades.

"My apologies," said Lors. He did not sound remotely apologetic. "My men are sometimes overly zealous."

In Akiil's experience, people whipped out swords for one of two reasons: to frighten, or to kill. The soldiers didn't look as though they cared if he was frightened.

"I notice you're not asking them to put away those blades."

Lors smiled thinly. "Sometimes I, too, am overly zealous. Please remove your hand from your robe slowly."

"I have a dagger," Akiil said.

"If you think to threaten me . . ."

"To *sell*."

Slowly, his back itching as he waited for the crossbow bolt to bury itself between his shoulders, Akiil withdrew his hand, the pommel of the dagger held between his finger and thumb. Cold seeped into his skin where he touched the thing. The world looked darker around the night-black blade.

"A year is a long time," he said, raising the small weapon slightly. "If Gelta isn't interested in what I have to sell, I'd be happy to take it elsewhere."

It didn't take a Shin monk trained in the arts of observation to see that at some point in her life something terrible had happened to Gelta Yuel. She couldn't have been much older than forty, but an elegant cane leaned beside her chair, easily within reach.

Within reach of her remaining arm, to be precise.

Where the other should have been, the silk of her shirt ran sheer from the shoulder to her waist.

Scarred, smooth skin marred half her face, from the temple down into the collar of her shirt. It looked as though someone had held her head in a fire. She wore her black hair shaved on that side of her scalp, though on the other it cascaded down well past her shoulders. The eye on the ruined side was glass, but the other studied him with a shrewd intelligence. To his surprise, she was smiling.

"Well," she said. "I did not expect a . . . what are you? Mendicant? Ascetic?"

"Monk," he replied.

"A monk! This ought to be fun!"

Her voice was rich, joyful, beautiful, the kind of voice a person could listen to all day without growing bored.

"I hope," Akiil replied, "that it might prove profitable for both of us."

She made a face, waved a dismissive hand. "Profit. Boring. You think I do this for the coin?"

"Most merchants appreciate being paid."

"Sure. Fine. I like drinking good wine and spending my winters outside the city, but those are side benefits. The reason I do this, the reason I have all this stuff in the first place?" She winked at him with her good eye. "It's for the stories."

Akiil raised his brows. "Stories?"

"Of course, stories! Don't monks have stories?" She lifted her cane, pointed.

The room was unlike any shop he'd ever been in in his life, unlike any shop he'd ever imagined. There were no cases, no counters, no drawers or bins, no shelves stacked with goods. It was, he realized, almost like the trove of treasure Adare kept inside Intarra's Spear. The walls were white marble, as was the floor, although in most places that floor was covered in intricately woven carpets. A massive bloodwood bookshelf covered one wall, packed with leather-bound codices that looked old as the world itself. Time-stained scrolls hung from the walls, this one painted with a branch and spray of blossoms, that one with a warrior in some kind of ceremonial dress Akiil didn't recognize, a third with a waterfall cascading down a mountain slope. The largest glass bowl he'd ever seen sat on a table near the center of the room. Inside, a pair of resplendent blue-red fish, each about the size of his hand, finned in lazy circles. It took Akiil a moment to find what Yuel was pointing at—a tiny, pitted knife in a wooden cradle atop a fluted column.

"That," the woman said, "is the blade that opened the throat of the Wolf King of Anthera."

"I didn't know Anthera *had* a Wolf King."

Her laugh was a chime. "Not anymore!"

"Doesn't look like much."

"That's the point. No one was allowed armed in the presence of the Wolf King. The knife was small enough that the assassin could hide it in her hair." The woman pointed toward Akiil's feet, where an unsightly burn marred the carpet. "And here's something. That's the burn from Rishinira's first kenning. She was only a child—didn't realize she was a leach until her brother made her angry enough to set the rug ablaze. There are stories in everything." She pointed at him. "Your robe has a story. At least one, I'd imagine."

For just a moment, Akiil felt all over again the heat of Ashk'lan burning, the blood of his wounds soaking into the coarse cloth.

"I'm willing to sell it."

"Maybe someday. If you conquer the world, or found a new branch of the faith, build a famous fortress or destroy one. For now, I'm more interested in this." She gestured to his dagger, which sat at the center of the table before her. "What is it?"

Akiil shook his head. "I don't know."

"Where did you get it?"

He'd expected that particular question, had put a lot of thought into how to answer it. "I found it in the abbot's quarters of my monastery."

"Found it? Or stole it?" She waved away his expression. "Spare me the wounded face. I may only have one eye, but I can see your brand. You might be a monk, or you might not, but you are *definitely* a thief."

"People change."

"Not in my experience."

He put on an expression of dismay.

"The monastery was destroyed. Burned to the ground. All the monks slaughtered. I don't think it's stealing if the owner is dead."

"There are men and women lying in graves all over this world who might disagree with you."

Akiil shrugged. "I'm happy to hear them out."

Yuel laughed again. "Do you know how I lost my arm and my eye?"

"A really tough card game?"

"Looting the Tomb of the Hakti Concubines."

"Never underestimate a concubine."

"Or the eunuchs charged with guarding her tomb." She grimaced, touched a hand to the side of her face. "The point is, I don't care if your knife is stolen, but I need to know. There are certain . . . precautions I've learned to take if I think a former owner might come calling."

Akiil thought of the chamber ringed with Csestriim artifacts, of those in-humanly smooth walls, of the inexplicable light filtering in from the ceiling, of the strange woman who moved through the place as though she owned it. . . .

"Not to worry. No one is coming."

Gelta watched him awhile, silent. When she blinked, her glass eye remained open, staring.

"All right," she said, "so here we are."

"I thought *you* might know what it is."

"A dagger, obviously."

"I don't think you would have invited me in if it were *only* a dagger."

"Nothing is only one thing."

"But this," Akiil said, tipping his hand just a little, "is Csestriim."

She raised her remaining brow.

"A monk familiar with Csestriim script. Intriguing."

He smiled at her. "Nothing is only one thing."

Gelta studied the blade without touching it.

"Strange item for an abbot."

"It was a strange place."

"Is it warm or cold to the touch?"

He could still feel the glacial chill soaking his skin.

"The monks have an expression," he replied. *"Learn with your hands."*

She smiled. "The thing is, I only have the one hand left. I'd prefer to keep it."

"I don't think it's going to leap up and cut you."

"An optimistic position, but not a very intelligent one."

That sent a new chill through him.

"So it's dangerous?"

"Csestriim weapons are often dangerous, especially to those who don't un-derstand what they are."

She lifted a stylus from the table, nudged the blade. It rotated on the wooden surface, like any other knife.

"I carried it all the way here, and I still have my arm," he said. "And both my eyes."

"Show me."

Akiil hesitated, then shrugged and took up the dagger, marveling all over again at how heavy it was.

"It's cold," he replied. "Like ice. But I'm still alive."

"I'm glad. I'm starting to like you."

"What does it come from," he asked cautiously, "that cold?"

Gelta frowned. "No telling with these things. The fact that you're still here and in one piece is a good sign." She watched him. "Do you see anything when you touch it? Hear anything?"

"Just you."

For a while, far longer than seemed necessary, they sat in silence. Finally, the tightness faded from around Gelta's eyes, from the muscles in her neck. She'd been ready, he realized, despite her outward calm, for something awful to happen.

"So," he said, "it's just a cold, normal knife?"

"Nothing Csestriim is normal. There's not a person living who knows how to forge this metal." She squinted at the black blade. "If it *is* metal."

"But it's not . . . some kind of leach thing?"

She shrugged. "Maybe. Or it might only work . . ."

"Work?"

"Do whatever it is that it does. It might only function on a full moon, or if you say the correct words, or if it comes in contact with blood. Items like this aren't horseshoes. Each one is different. That's what makes them so dangerous." She winked. "And so fun."

"Fun isn't exactly the word I would have chosen."

"People keep telling me I have a strange notion of fun."

Akiil ran a finger over the script. "What does it mean?"

Gelta frowned. "It's a hard word to translate, especially out of context. *Necessity* might be closest. Something that has to happen. It's the *will* in our phrase 'Winter will come,' or 'You will die someday.' Maybe *inevitability* is a better word, but it's not a noun."

"Seems strangely sentimental, naming weapons, especially for a race devoid of emotion."

"When all weapons work more or less the same, they don't need names. When some of them wield unnatural powers, it's a good idea to have them clearly labeled."

Akiil pondered that. Despite Adare's earlier warnings, he'd never taken seriously the idea that the most dangerous thing about looting an ancient fortress might be the loot itself.

"So," Gelta continued, "I assume you brought this to me because you hope to sell it."

He nodded. Finally, they were moving toward the sort of discussion that he understood.

"How much?"

"I trust you'll pay me what's fair."

She raised an eyebrow. "No wonder your robe looks like that."

Akiil just smiled. In truth, he had no idea what the dagger was worth. Gelta knew he didn't know. But she also knew she wasn't the only antiquities dealer in the city. She had the muscle, of course, to simply steal the blade, but that wasn't her reputation—she might loot tombs, but she wasn't known for robbing actual living humans. If she wanted the knife, she'd pay for it. The question was, how much?

"A unique artifact," Akiil observed, "of unknown age, provenance, and power."

"One hundred golden suns."

It was a massive sum, but he wasn't listening to the number. Instead, he was watching Gelta's face, the angle of her head, the rate of her breathing, the pulse at her neck. He watched just as the Shin had trained him to watch, then he slid out of his own mind into a model of hers. She was eager, and keen to hide her eagerness.

He shook his head. "One thousand."

She laughed out loud at the insanity of his offer. "Not a chance, I'm afraid."

But Akiil could read her face, her posture. She was good at hiding her emotions, but she wasn't used to sitting across the table from a monk.

He stood, slid the dagger back toward him. "It was a pleasure meeting you."

She held up her hand. "All right. Five hundred."

He shook his head again. "Let's be honest with each other. I could have asked for more than a thousand, and you would have paid. But the Shin trained all the greed out of me."

Gelta snorted, sat back in her chair, whistled ruefully. "Who are you?"

"Just a simple monk with simple needs."

"So the thousand is all for robes?"

He smiled at her. "And a healthy diet of vegetables."

"Did he have anything else squirreled away, this dead abbot of yours?"

"If I remember anything else," Akiil replied, thinking of that vast room packed with weapons, "you'll be the first to know."

†

Akiil's garret in the Wolf's Head was loud, filthy, dim, and cramped. All day and half the night, noise echoed up from the common room below, and in the few hours when the inn finally fell quiet, Yerrin was usually up, prowling around, muttering to himself as he counted the spiders or watched bats from the tiny window. The air hung hot and still, even on cooler days, the blankets itched, lumps filled the mattress. Still, Akiil felt safer there than anywhere else in the city, safe enough to take the heavy purse from inside his robes and scatter the gold across the blanket.

He hadn't brought back most of the coin, of course. Hadn't even seen it, truth be told. Gelta had provided him with a sealed letter, which he presented to a stone-faced man inside the stone-faced citadel that was the Bank of the Twin Lions. The letter allowed him to draw the full sum of a thousand gold suns, but Akiil had taken just fifty, to make sure it worked.

Just fifty.

The sum was astronomical. He might as well have talked about pocketing fifty stars. His childhood self would have choked with awe at the sight of so much gold. At that moment, though, looking down at it, he felt only cold. After a while, he swept it up, deposited it back in the leather purse, dropped heavily onto the bed.

Yerrin sat cross-legged a few paces away, staring down into the floorboards.

"What's down there?" Akiil asked finally.

"Everything," the monk replied.

"Sort of a small space for everything."

Yerrin didn't glance over. "Time grinds everything to dust. The dust gathers between the boards."

A sudden irritation flared inside Akiil. It wasn't that he didn't want the old man to be content, but the sources of Yerrin's contentment were so strange and implausible. Was it really possible that anyone could enjoy pressing his eyeball to the floorboards for hour after hour, studying dust? What did he see that Akiil had been missing all his life?

"What do you want, Yerrin?"

"I don't," the monk replied mildly.

"Everyone wants things. Even Shin want things."

"Oh, there is a wanting that goes on inside here." Yerrin gestured vaguely to himself. "But I have nothing to do with it."

"Then who's doing the wanting?"

"No one. Wanting is wanting. It doesn't need me."

"A stone doesn't want," Akiil pointed out. "Dust doesn't want. Only people want."

Yerrin shook his head. "Desire sticks to people, like leeches. But the leech is not the person."

That made more sense than most things Yerrin said. Which was to say, it didn't make much sense at all.

Akiil rose laboriously from the bed. Sitting still for too long made him itchy, twitchy. He took a swig of water from the pitcher by the bedside, glanced out the window at the street below. Adare's thugs were there, as usual. They'd berated him about his disappearance until he pointed out that it wasn't his fault they'd lost him in the crowd, that it wasn't his ass that would end up caned if the Emperor found out.

"I'm stepping out for a while," he said. "To clear my head."

"Bring back peaches," Yerrin replied.

Akiil rolled his eyes. He had the coin to afford fruit now, enough coin for wagons upon wagons piled with it, enough coin to buy an entire orchard of peach trees, but Yerrin didn't know that. As usual, he seemed oblivious to the fact that outside of Ashk'lan people had to pay for things. Including peaches.

"Weren't you just telling me you don't want anything?"

The monk shrugged. "I don't. But the wanting is the wanting."

49

Jonon was thinner than he had been when Gwenna first met him on the deck of the *Daybreak*. Thinner, sharper, keener, like a knife honed too many times. His eyes were bright, almost feverish, glistening by the light of the fire. He refused to sit, stalking back and forth across the low rise where Gwenna's group had camped, fingering the handle of his cutlass over and over, whipping his head around at every snapped twig and bird call to stare intently into the trees.

His men—those that were left, anyway—seemed almost as taut. Chent had survived, and Vessik, and Lurie, along with a legionary named Hevel, and two sailors, brothers, Bult and Rummel. Hevel was obviously broken. The moment he stepped into camp, he collapsed, weeping silently into his beard even as the others went about adding stakes to the meager palisade. Gwenna's small crew watched them warily, but Jonon's men seemed to have no appetite for fighting. They were looking back the way they had come, and they reeked of terror.

"We still have the eggs," the admiral said. He gestured toward the packs they'd been carrying. The canvas bulged with the weight of the unhatched birds. "We can still complete the mission."

Gwenna shook her head. "Forget the mission for half a heartbeat. What happened to the rest of your *men*?"

Jonon bared his teeth, stared at her, seemed to speak against his will. "Eigen disappeared the first night." His eyes flitted from Gwenna to Kiel to Dhar, then skittered away. "He was on guard, but never made a sound. I thought he'd deserted, but once we started marching we found his helmet. Good Raaltan steel, crushed like an eggshell."

"What about tracks?" Gwenna asked.

Jonon gritted his teeth. "Eigen was our tracker."

"Anything large enough to haul off an entire human leaves tracks."

"I have spent my life in the service of the western fleet. Not grubbing about in the mud of foreign jungles examining paw prints."

Gwenna shook her head. "Probably not paws. Probably something a lot fucking nastier than paws."

She found, to her surprise, that Jonon's arrival made things easier. Being stalked by a deadly *gabbya* was obviously less than ideal, but it distracted her from the beasts wandering her own mind, from the anger, and the hunger, and the lust for blood. This—murdered soldiers, uncertain terrain, limited supplies—was the kind of problem she'd been trained to face.

Jonon had frozen, his eyes locked on her. Suddenly he reeked of suspicion. "You know what did this."

"How in Hull's name would I know?"

"You're not surprised."

Gwenna shook her head. "I've been hearing for almost half a year that Menkiddoc is a miserable shitpool of madness and monsters from which no one emerges alive. Why the fuck would I be surprised?"

She felt her hand creeping up toward the handle of her sword, forced it back down.

Kiel shifted slightly at her side.

"Have you seen it?" he asked quietly.

Jonon held Gwenna's glare. For a moment, she thought he was going to bare that cutlass of his, but then he shivered, turned to the historian.

"Only glimpses. It doesn't always come at night. It ripped Berin straight out of the column in the middle of the day. Two sailors saw it. Sorn described something like a spider; Ji said it was a squid."

"Are they here?" Gwenna asked, casting her eye over the diminished group.

Jonon ground his teeth. "They almost came to blows over the question. That night Sorn murdered Ji in his sleep. Strangled him, then tore out his eyes. When we found him he was laughing, yammering on about how Ji didn't need the eyes because he couldn't see anyway."

"What happened to Sorn?" Gwenna asked.

"I executed him."

"Diseased," Kiel said.

Jonon clenched his fist. "What is this place doing to my men?"

"The same thing," the historian replied, "that it is doing to you, to all of us. It is . . . expanding them."

Jonon shook his head, glanced over his shoulder to where the pitiful remnant of his crew hunched by the fire, blades drawn, staring out into the dark. "It is breaking them."

Kiel nodded. "Fill a waterskin too much, and it will burst."

"How did you find us?" Gwenna demanded.

"After the . . . thing took Handaf we left the river. This would have been four nights ago. I was searching for high ground, a hill, something defensible. Instead we saw the remnants of your fire."

It made sense. The blazing grass would have bathed the sky pink and orange for miles, left a burned scar obvious to anyone who stumbled across it.

"So you saw the fire," she said. "Why did you follow us?"

Jonon blinked, stiffened, looked around him as though he were only just waking to the moment. His voice was ice when he replied. "I am not bound to answer a traitor's questions. Count yourself fortunate that I have not already carved you open."

His fingers tightened around the handle of his cutlass.

"Go on." Gwenna realized she was smiling—a terrible, joyless smile. "Draw it. Let's see how fast you are."

A vision flashed across her mind of Jonon's head lopped off and rolling in the mud, of his neck fountaining blood as the dead body stumbled to its knees before her.

"This," Kiel said, interposing his own body between the two of them, "is the land's sickness speaking."

"You want to die too, historian?" Jonon asked, his eyes wide, gleaming. "That can be arranged."

The rest of the group had been drifting gradually closer, drawn by the raised voices, until Chent stood at Jonon's shoulder, Vessik and Lurie just behind him, all their blades naked. Back on the beach the admiral had had the numbers. Not anymore. Cho Lu and Pattick loomed behind Gwenna, reeking of violence. Bhuma Dhar smelled more cautious, but he, too, had risen to his feet and stripped his steel. Even Rat was ready, small knife clutched in her right hand.

Gwenna's smile widened until she thought her face might split.

She could feel muscle and bone shuddering beneath her sword blows, hot blood spraying across her face. She could taste that blood, feel the still-warm flesh in her mouth, the stringy heart, the liver's bitter meat. . . .

Someone screamed.

She found herself staring down at her own empty hands. Where were her swords? Had she already hacked Jonon apart? She looked up. No. He was standing there, barely a pace away, his face a mad mask of rage. The others were standing as well. No one had killed anyone, not yet. So who . . .

"Hevel," Kiel said, pointing toward the fire.

Somewhere off in the trees, already too far away to reach, the scream came again—long, desperate, lost.

"What . . ." Cho Lu asked, staring about like a man waking from a dream.

"The *gabhya,*" the historian replied. "It came from the trees and took him."

They found the sailor a hundred paces from the camp. Found what was left of him, at least—boots, belt, sword, a rib cage gnawed open, the organs gone, an eyeless, brainless skull ripped off, slurped dry, tossed aside.

Kiel knelt by the body, held up a rib to the torchlight, studied the grooves carved across it, turned to the skull, excavated one of the gaping eye sockets, then let it drop.

"Ah," he said quietly.

Gwenna shook her head. "Ah?"

"This explains why we have not been attacked already."

"Not attacked?" Cho Lu said. He gestured toward the ribbons of flesh. "Tell it to that poor bastard."

Kiel shook his head. "As Commander Sharpe observed earlier, the *gabhya* should have been crawling all over us for days. There would have been more and worse the deeper we pressed into the continent's interior. Those we have faced, however, have been relatively benign."

Gwenna could hear Jonon's teeth grinding. "You would call this benign?"

"No," Kiel agreed, straightening. "Whatever did this is large, fast, deadly. It is also the reason there are no *other gabhya* around. It is scaring them off."

"You present this as a blessing," Dhar said warily.

"It all depends," the historian replied, "on how you measure your blessings."

✝

For three days they fought their way higher into the mountains. Gwenna couldn't quite bring herself to believe in Kiel's promised fortress, but even a high pile of rubble, even a wind-scoured mountain peak would offer better lines of sight and opportunity for defense than the tangle of dripping trees. All of them pressed hard, working their bodies to exhaustion and beyond, and for three days, the thing did not attack. In other circumstances, that might have seemed like a reprieve. Not in Menkiddoc. With nothing to fight, nothing to hunt or defend against, Gwenna was forced to contend once more with the violence of her own mind. The farther they fought into the hills, the harder the struggle became.

Sometimes, when she glanced down, she wondered why she was wearing all black. Sometimes she forgot where she'd sheathed her swords, or that she had swords at all. Memory turned eel-slick. She had more and more trouble holding it, more trouble recalling why she would want to.

Worse than the gaps in her memory was what bubbled up to fill them. Sometimes she felt just a raw hunger; not the desire to eat, exactly—it had nothing to do with chewing or savoring or swallowing—but the need to *consume*. The morning after Hevel's death a long-toothed creature the size of a marmot or a large rat skittered across her path. It had four eyes, all of which appeared to be weeping. She lashed out with a blade, slashing it in two, was reaching for the still-twitching carcass when Kiel paused beside her.

"You don't want that," he murmured.

She stared, first at him, then at the bloody pulp she was about to devour.

"Why the fuck would I want it?" she snapped, though she could still feel the gnawing inside of her, the need.

She closed her eyes sometimes when the world grew too close, too enticing, trying to blot it all out. That was when the visions happened. Sometimes she saw just a face, a scrap of an image, someone she knew or didn't know, people screaming or laughing or just staring blankly at a scene outside the field of her vision. She saw Valyn once, her old Wing commander, stared into his scarred, black eyes for three or four heartbeats until he turned away, called out a few words in a strange harsh language she didn't quite recognize. Once, she thought she saw Talal again, just as she had in her dream, only this time his iron ball was gone and he was fighting back-to-back in an arena with a young man she didn't recognize.

No, she told herself.

No.

No.

No.

The real people, the ones trekking through the jungle with her, were even worse than the visions.

The last time she'd spoken to Jonon had been a day earlier, when they'd argued briefly about which valley to follow up toward the mountains. For the dozenth time he had called her a traitor and a whore, and for the dozenth time she'd seen herself, *felt* herself, leaping atop him, seizing his shoulders, burying her teeth into his throat. It felt so real. She could taste his blood, hot and coppery. Or no. Not his blood; *her* blood. She'd bitten through the side of her cheek. Despite the pain, she wanted to keep biting. Instead, she spat a gob of bloody phlegm onto the rocks. Gray lichen writhed at the touch of the blood, swelled, spread another handsbreadth across the stone. Gwenna stared at it, then turned away.

Jonon's men never stopped staring. Chent was the most open, leering at her constantly, sometimes winking, sometimes licking his lips. Lurie, however, was worse. Instead of a man wanting to rape a woman, he looked like a starving farmer getting ready to carve into a side of seared, seasoned beef. Somewhere else, *anywhere* else, those looks wouldn't have troubled her much. She could take care of herself if they came after her. The problem was that *taking care of herself* meant something different here than it did in the rest of the world. She could feel her own eagerness lurking. If she started taking care of herself she wouldn't stop at breaking a wrist or shattering a nose. If one of them started something with her she might not ever stop.

Even the men on her own side were starting to feel dangerous. For days, as they worked their way into the foothills, she'd caught them stealing looks at her, feral, hungry looks, as though they wanted to fuck her or devour her or both.

The air grew colder, the leaves on the trees turned to needles, and then one morning, well before dawn, she woke to find a thin rime of ice on the tent, a few inches of snow on the broken ground. Her own heart, her own mind, still felt dark, and hot, and tangled as the jungle below, a violent trackless madness in which the only choices were to hide or to kill. Of the twelve survivors, Rat was the only one remaining that Gwenna felt no urge to eviscerate, and so she took to walking just behind the girl, focusing on the child's breath as they labored higher and higher, listening to her heartbeat, quick and small as a bird's.

For three days nothing killed them, but on the fourth morning after Jonon's sudden appearance, they woke to find tracks in the snow, thousands of tracks, the kind of print that squirrels might leave, but with sharp, vicious claws. Gwenna realized, with a sick dread, that those tracks centered around the meager pile of supplies. When she threw aside the tarp she found two of the sacks of rations slashed open, one small barrel of dried fish splintered and pillaged.

She was still standing there, grappling silently with her rage, when she heard Kiel approaching.

"A setback," he said quietly.

Gwenna stared at the empty barrel, the strips of burlap. For a moment she felt like a creature that had never learned the value of words.

"More food remains," the historian continued. "And water."

"We can't survive on water," Gwenna hissed. "If we don't climb out of the sickness soon, we'll have to start hunting."

"That would be a mistake."

"What about starving? Is *that* a mistake?"

"Starving is natural. What the pollution will do to you is not."

"You said it didn't extend into the mountains, but we're in the mountains and I can still fucking feel it."

"We are not yet high enough." He gestured. "The soil, the trees, the vegetal matter—it is all diseased. We must climb above them."

Gwenna shook her head. They'd been climbing into the high hills for days, but the true mountains, the height of the range, still lay beyond, elusive.

"How much farther?"

"Four or five days," the historian replied. "Maybe a week. Once clear, we will be able to hunt once more, and drink from the runoff."

"A week," Gwenna breathed.

Talal had had an expression: *You can do anything for a day.*

There'd been a time when she'd agreed with him. Swimming. Fighting. Running. She could do anything for a day. But Kiel hadn't said a day. He'd said a week. She tried to imagine surviving for a full week, found that she couldn't. She tried to remember why she would want to.

The camp began to stir. Soon everyone would be up. Soon they'd all know what had happened to the stores.

"I saw Talal," she said. "First in a dream. Then in a . . . hallucination while I was walking."

Kiel nodded slowly, but didn't respond.

"First he was walking over sand, shackled to a metal ball." She had no idea why she was telling him this, but she found herself unable to stop. "Then he was fighting in an arena somewhere, fighting beside someone I've never seen. It felt real. *He* felt real, like he wasn't even dead."

"Perhaps he is not."

Gwenna wanted to sob, wanted to slash the man across the throat. "Why would you say that?"

"Because it may be true."

"He *died*. They killed him. They opened him up on the steps of the Ship-wreck."

"Did you see him die?"

She hesitated, then shook her head. "Frome's spies saw it."

"And what is your opinion of the quality of Frome's spies?"

Her hands were clenched into fists so tight the knuckles felt ready to snap. There was a scream building inside her like a storm.

"*Dreams aren't real.* Everything in this place is a lie."

"Not everything."

She closed her eyes, watched Talal fight for a moment, then shifted her gaze to the structure behind him. She recognized those rickety wooden stairs. They were part of the Arena in Old Harbor, where the high priests held their blood sport rituals. If Talal had survived, if they *hadn't* killed him, it was just possi-ble that he'd ended up there, forced to fight as some sick glorification of their gods. Of course he'd be shackled—they knew he was dangerous. Of course she wouldn't recognize the people fighting at his back. Hope burned like a sickness, like a fever accompanying a plague.

"He could be alive."

She opened her eyes to find Kiel nodding.

"Or it could all be a fucking trick, a new twist of the sickness."

He nodded again, as though the answer didn't make any difference.

She gritted her teeth.

"Well, I'll be shipped to 'Shael if I die out here before I find out which it is."

†

The next day they lost Bult; one moment they were hacking their way through the jungle, the next, a vicious snapping echoed through the trees. By the time Gwenna turned, he'd been ripped in half. The torso was gone. The legs remained, still twitching as they gouted blood out into the dirt. There was nothing to fight, nothing to chase, nothing to flee from or defy—just half a body, a few scraps of meat that had once been a man.

No one made any move to sleep that night, even after the sun had long set. Ostensibly they were all watching the forest, on guard against another attack, but the grim truth of the matter was that they spent just as much time eyeing one another, as though the gravest threat was already inside the makeshift camp. Some of the crew whispered that they'd seen eyes glittering in the dark. Others insisted it wasn't one monster but a pack of them. Toward midnight they almost came to blows again, screaming about the nature of a beast that no one still living had seen until Gwenna intervened, yanking them apart. Cho Lu and Pattick sat back to back, staring into the darkness, while Chent, Vessik, and Lurie prowled around like a pack of feral dogs.

Gwenna tried to get Rat to sleep, but the girl refused to go inside the tent.

"Stay," she said. "Stay with Gwenna Sharpe."

And so Gwenna forced herself to sit, Rat settled in beside her.

"Watch," she hissed, staring at Chent. "Watch the bastards."

Gwenna nodded. "I will, Rat. I will."

The girl's furious vigilance quickly faded. Her eyes slid closed and she slumped over, exhausted, half in, half out of Gwenna's lap. Gwenna started to shift her aside—the position looked horrifically uncomfortable—then stopped. Somehow, unlike everything else in the 'Shael-spawned sick, the weight of the girl felt real. As everything else unraveled, Rat's shallow, steady breaths were a tether. Gwenna drew a short sword and set it on the ground beside them. It wasn't a good position to fight from, sitting pinned beneath a kid's weight, but then, fighting hadn't done anyone any good so far.

She put a tentative hand on Rat's shoulder. The girl was thin, even thinner than she had been back on the boat—the toll of the jungle, the endless walking, and the rations. If she'd looked like a wild thing when they first found her, back in the abandoned city, now she looked even worse. Gwenna picked a twig from the tangled mat of her hair, then a burr, then a crushed bug that she must have mashed against her scalp. It was a hopeless task—the head was a snarl of sweat and mud—but Gwenna kept at it. It was, she realized, something she'd never done before. She'd *seen* people do it, back when she was a child, on feast days maybe, parents smoothing or braiding their children's hair, but her own father was bald, and while her older brothers had shown her a million things—how to put an edge on a knife, shoe a horse, slaughter a hog—none of them had ever touched her hair. Hour by hour, strand by strand, Gwenna worked at the tangles and twigs until the moon was staring down through a gap in the branches overhead. She paused, bathed in the cool light, stared down at Rat's face. For the first time in days, she felt almost human.

Then she heard the footsteps approaching.

She tensed, shifted her hand from the girl's hair to the handle of her sword. It took barely a moment for the sickness to bury its talons in her gut all over again. She was about to shove Rat aside and rise to her feet when Jonon spoke.

"I'm not going to murder you."

Judging from his voice, from the smell of him, he was a few paces behind her.

The word *murder* bred inside Gwenna a strange kind of excitement. She wanted him to try it, wanted him to come after her, to give her even the slenderest excuse. . . .

Rat muttered something in her sleep, shifted, cinched an arm around Gwenna's knee, and the feeling faded.

"Then maybe don't stand directly behind me."

Jonon grunted, moved forward to where she could see him. He was holding a waterskin, but his other hand kept straying to his cutlass, as though itching to draw it.

"What do you want?" she asked.

He blinked, looked down at her, stared for a moment, as though he hadn't expected to find her there, then shook his head, wiped the sweat from his brow, took a long swig from the skin.

"It's killing us," he said. "The *gabhya*."

She nodded.

When she didn't speak, he shook his head again and went on.

"More than a dozen men, *my* men, ripped to pieces." He stared at his hands, as though he were the one who'd done the ripping.

"Kiel says it will be better," Gwenna replied finally, "when we get to the mountains."

Jonon took another drink from the skin. "When we get to the mountains."

"Another two days. Maybe three."

"We'll all be *dead* in another three days. We'll all be bloody fucking ribbons decorating the trees."

It was, she realized, the first time she'd ever heard him curse. As quickly as his voice had risen, however, it dropped to a skeletal whisper.

"I can't let that happen."

"Sometimes shit happens," Gwenna said quietly, "and there's nothing you can do to stop it."

The admiral stared at her. "Is that what you tell yourself? About why you lost your bird? About why you got your soldiers killed? That *shit happens*? That there was nothing you could do to stop it?"

She half expected the rage to rise up inside her. Instead, there was only a vast emptiness.

"It doesn't matter what I tell myself. They're dead."

"I do not accept that." His teeth were bared, the half snarl of a trapped animal. "I do not *accept* it." He glared out into the darkness surrounding them. "If you could go back," he murmured, "sacrifice yourself in order to save your men, would you do it?"

"We can't go back."

"Would you do it?"

"Yes."

He nodded, took a long pull on the waterskin, then another, then another, and then, like a blow to the gut, the horror hit her.

"You're drinking the water."

Jonon nodded, not taking his eyes from the jungle.

"It will kill you. It will drive you mad."

"I am already going mad. We *all* are. This, though . . ." He hoisted the skin, stared at it, then laughed. "It's making me stronger. Faster. I can feel it already."

"It will make you into a monster."

The admiral whirled to face her. "Good! *Good!*" Tears streamed down his face. "Because the man I am?" He plucked at the chest of his filthy uniform, held up a trembling hand, shook his head. "The man I am can't defeat that thing. My men are dying and I can't save them."

Gwenna shook her head, gathered Rat in close. "Sometimes you can't save people."

Jonon stared at her, then drew himself up, scrubbed away the tears, twisted his face into a sneer. "Spoken like a coward." He spat onto the ground. "I should have known."

✝

They burst from the trees without warning. One moment, the forest crowded in around them, close and oppressive; the next, the branches gave way to a wide, cold, blue sky and the diamond-bright peaks. At first, relief flooded Gwenna's veins. After the confinement of the trees and vines she could finally see where she was going, take stock of the terrain and the dangers that might lurk there. That relief soured instantly, however, when she realized that the sickness was still with her, crawling beneath her skin, burrowing into her brain.

"So," Jonon murmured. "These are the mountains."

It had been half a week since he first drank the polluted water, and the admiral had grown positively gaunt, the muscles of his arms, shoulders, and chest withered to desiccated strips beneath his skin. His head looked like a skull. His hands twisted into claws. For all that, there was an awful vigor in his voice when he spoke, a knife-bright keenness to his eyes as he studied the terrain, as though he were a predator come face-to-face finally with his prey.

"We need to get up there," Gwenna said. "Free of the disease."

"Such a hurry!" Jonon laughed, a dry, delighted sound. "What happened to the fearless Kettral?"

Gwenna shook her head. "I was never fearless, even when I was Kettral."

"How disappointing."

"It was," Gwenna replied. "It certainly was."

Jonon arched an eyebrow. "Not anymore?"

"I've gotten used to it."

"The fear, or the disappointment?"

"Both."

The admiral lifted the waterskin from his belt. "You could drink. I can't explain to you the . . . the *strength*. Fear, disappointment . . ." He waved them away with a dismissive hand. "You never need to deal with them again."

Gwenna studied the skin, studied her own eagerness to reach for it, the thirst that was more than human thirst.

"Yes," she said finally. "Yes, I do." She turned away. "We keep moving until we're up in the mountains."

A few days earlier, Jonon would have bristled at her command. With the land's sickness breeding in his veins, he just laughed. The sound was too loud. "There are so *many* mountains! Which one to choose?"

"There." Kiel raised a finger, pointing toward a notch in the peaks miles distant and thousands of feet above. "That valley will take us through. There should be no sickness near the summit or on the northern slope of the range."

"Through," Rat murmured, gazing up. The word came out half a curse, half a prayer.

The historian fixed Gwenna with those gray eyes. "There may be artifacts inside the fortress, one in particular that could help the admiral."

"Artifacts." She shook her head. "You mean there might be a *cure* up there?"

"I would not call it a cure."

"You could have mentioned this earlier. You could have mentioned it when we left the 'Kent-kissing ship."

"Mentioning it would have weakened your resolve." He shook his head. "Besides. It cannot help the entire group—only one or two."

"And that's if it's there at all, if any of this ten-thousand-year-old shit is still standing."

"Indeed."

They climbed all day, working their way up through the steepening scree, weaving between blocks of granite the size of houses as the air went from cool to chill, chill to cold. An icy wind grated over them, blowing down from the peaks flanking the pass, forcing the men to walk faster or freeze inside their jerkins and breeches. Even worse than the cold was the thirst. They'd drained the last of the barrels a day earlier. It didn't seem a long time to go without water, but that day had left them all in agony: parched, cracked-lipped, swollen-tongued.

Cold and thirst, however, were foes that Gwenna understood. She'd trained in mountains; she'd run miles under a desert sun. In a way, the suffering was a friend walking beside her, a companion she recognized even when everything about the world had grown strange. She took hold of that cold, buried herself in it, and carried on. As long as she concentrated on the cold, she wasn't thinking about the hunger mounting inside her.

And then, almost between one footstep and the next, the hunger vanished.

She felt it first as confusion, a disorientation similar to the kind she'd experienced sometimes deep underwater, when she lost track of up and down. She could still see the sun, still feel the ground beneath her feet, but they seemed wrong, misplaced, dangerous. Next came the feeling of loss, like the pain when Jak died, or the awful laceration of her heart when she'd believed Talal, too, was dead—only this was even stronger, a hundred times stronger, so violent she almost turned and raced back down the slopes. Then came the deep, creeping horror when she saw clearly for the first time what she'd become, when she remembered the things that she'd done and almost done, when she understood how close she'd been to losing the last shreds of herself.

That was what it felt like, leaving the sickness of Menkiddoc.

She stumbled ahead for a hundred paces or so before bending over, retching up her guts. For a while, her whole focus narrowed to the scattering of stone and snow directly before her. Her body trembled, spasmed, burned. Back on the Islands, there was a class on poisons and their antidotes. She remembered drinking nightwort, being forced to sit with it curdling in her gut for half a day, then drinking the bitter antidote, remembered how her body shook with the struggle to be clean again, how she'd half wanted to just die and be done with it. This was like that, but worse.

She had no idea how much time had passed before she finally straightened up.

Sunlight gleamed on the ice, warmed the clean white granite.

She felt wrung out, weak-kneed, feeble as something just born. The others were grappling with the shift in their different ways. Some puked up phlegm and blood. Others lay on their backs, eyes blank as the eyes of the dead, staring into the sky as they shook. Kiel sat cross-legged atop a wide boulder. He appeared no different than usual, but when she looked closer she could see the tremor in his fingers, in one eyelid that kept twitching over and over.

Jonon lem Jonon seemed to have recovered the most quickly. The First Admiral and his trio of thugs—Chent, Vessik, and Lurie—stood a few dozen paces away, staring back down the valley. It bothered her that she'd been insensible while they were already up and about, but there was nothing to be done about it. Kiel had warned her that the disease would affect them all differently.

"Sweet Intarra's light," Pattick breathed. He was sitting beside a small, ice-blue tarn a few paces away, his head cradled between his knees. "What happened to us?"

"We survived," Gwenna said, forcing herself upright.

A harsh, jarring laugher rattled the cold air. She turned to find Jonon staring at her. "You think so?" he asked. "That thing—that beautiful thing that's been killing us—it's coming."

"How do you know?"

"I can smell it," Jonon hissed. "I can *feel* it."

Gwenna closed her eyes, half expecting to find Talal there, still struggling or sprawled out dead, but found only darkness. She could smell the filth on the men, the sweat-drenched leather, the fungus. And blood—everyone had nicks, cuts, scrapes. Not long ago she'd wanted to taste that blood, to drink it. Now, the thought turned her stomach. She could smell the fear on some of them, the horror of what they'd done mingled with the eagerness of Jonon lem Jonon for more blood. Beneath all of it lay the smell of stone and a coming storm, and then there, for just a second, something else, awful, rotten, wrong.

She opened her eyes, studied Jonon. "What do you mean," she asked quietly, "you can smell it?"

She'd almost missed the odor herself, and she was Kettral.

Jonon just smiled that rictus smile.

"We should keep moving," Kiel said, descending from the boulder.

She turned to the historian. "Can the *gabbya* follow us out of the sick?"

He nodded silently.

"It's coming," Jonon crooned. "It's co-ming!"

Chent belted out a laugh. Vessik just nodded silently, his face a mask.

"Come," Kiel said. "We may reach the fortress before nightfall. We can mount a defense there."

"Oh," Jonon replied. "Oh, oh, ohhhh. There's no defending against it. If we could defend against it, Hevel wouldn't have been ripped up, or Sorn, or Handalf." He shook his head, slid his palm along the handle of his cutlass, caressing it. "What we need to do is fight it, face to beautiful face."

"Not here," Gwenna said.

"Here." Jonon shrugged. "There. It doesn't matter."

50

A greenfly circled the lamp over and over, turning lazy gyres through the hot air until Monster shot out a hand, caught it in her fist, and crushed it. She'd been drinking *quey* most of the night—celebration of her victory, relief at being alive, or just a plain old hankering for the stuff—but that hadn't slowed her down any.

"All I'm *saying,*" she announced irritably, "is that sometimes it's a good idea to ask the questions *before* you murder the fucking messenger."

"The guards exceeded their mandate," Stupid agreed. He was reclined on the bench by the door of the common room, his hat pulled down over his eyes.

The woman belted out a half-drunk laugh. "*Exceeded their mandate!* They turned his face into meat!"

"Meat," Mouse said, frowning at his leg of chicken. He took a tentative bite, grimaced, then set it down.

Ruc understood the large man's queasiness. The guards had more than killed the messenger. They'd hit him so many times that when they finally peeled away, what was left at the center of the pit hadn't looked like anything human.

Bien shook her head. "He had to know he was going to die. Coming here was suicide."

"So why come?" Talal asked.

"He had a message," Stupid pointed out.

"Bow down." Monster rolled her eyes. "Crawl. Cower. Whatever."

"Well," Ruc said, "message delivered, I guess, but what was the *point*? He didn't ask for anything. Didn't offer anything. Didn't negotiate anything. Just came, made a speech, got shot, then had the guards rip apart what was left of his body."

"What a body it was, though," Monster lamented, raising her glass to the memory.

"It would seem likely that he was Annurian," Stupid suggested from beneath his hat.

"He was *obviously* fucking Annurian," Monster said. "The son of a bitch was whiter than milk."

"We *do* have an Annurian here." Bien nodded across the table toward Talal. "Someone who might have some insight."

"I don't think he was imperial," the soldier said, shaking his head.

Monster rolled her eyes. "You know everyone in the empire?"

"The empire doesn't send messages before it starts killing people."

"I guarantee you the good citizens of Dombâng believe he came from Annur," Ruc said.

"It's easy to blame Annur for things. That doesn't make it correct."

Bien squinted. "Is the First a title in the Annurian army?"

Another shake of the head. "Not in the army. Not the navy. Not the Kettral. I've never heard of it before."

"What about someone else?" Ruc ransacked his memory. "Urghul? Aren't they sort of milk-colored?"

"They are," Talal replied, "but the Urghul all have ritual scarring. He didn't. And he had the wrong accent for the Urghul." He frowned. "Sounded . . . vaguely Manjari."

Monster snorted. "I've met Manjari. They're browner than I am."

"Maybe not all of them," Ruc said. "Not every place in the world murders people for having different skin."

Talal shook his head. "Most Manjari are brown, but that's not the point. There's no way that a non-Annurian army could *get* here in the first place. If they were coming from the west or the north, they'd have to cover a thousand miles of Annurian territory, subdue dozens of fortresses and garrisons, protect supply lines from the local population. . . ."

"What if they're coming by sea?" Stupid asked. "From the east?"

"Makes a little more sense," the soldier conceded, "but the Annurian Navy is as dominant in the Channarian Gulf as its army is in central Eridroa. Not to mention the fact that any naval force would need to get from the ocean into the delta. Dombâng has blockaded all the main channels."

Bien had been picking at a large scab across her knuckles. As Ruc watched, she bit her lip, then ripped the scab clean off. "What about from the south?" she asked quietly.

"The messengers *have* been naked," Stupid observed.

Talal shook his head. "The Waist tribes don't go entirely naked. And they're brown-skinned, just like you. And tattooed."

"And they're fucking *savages*," Monster added. "They'd never be able to *find* Dombâng, let alone attack it."

"I wasn't talking about the Waist tribes," Bien said. She hesitated. "I meant farther south."

All eyes turned to her. A moth fluttered into the lantern flame, caught fire, fell twitching to the table.

"What?" Ruc asked after a moment. *"Menkiddoc?"*

"Menkiddoc," Mouse said, his voice filled with foreboding.

Silence stretched, then Monster burst out laughing.

"Listen to you idiots!" She tossed back a gulp of *quey,* swallowed noisily, then started laughing again. "There's no one *in* Menkiddoc."

Bien turned to her, arched an eyebrow. "I didn't realize you'd been."

"I don't *need* to go there, bitch. I spent enough time drinking with sailors to know the stories. The whole place is a wasteland."

Ruc ignored her. He was watching Talal instead. The soldier traced the curve of his iron ball with a finger as he pondered the suggestion.

"The coast is barren," he said finally. "The northeastern coast, at least. We don't know about the rest of the continent."

Stupid grunted from beneath his hat. "There's something the Kettral don't know?"

"They tried to map it," Talal replied. "A few times, actually."

"What happened?" Bien asked.

"No one came back."

Ruc stared at him. "Even with the birds . . ."

The soldier shook his head. "The birds can't cross the equator. Something about their physiology. Even here in Dombâng it's almost too hot for them."

"What about taking a fucking ship?" Monster asked. "You know, like normal people?"

"They did," Talal said. "The first mission was more than a hundred years back. The most recent maybe a generation ago. Like I said—no one returned."

Monster rolled her eyes. "Next thing you're going to tell me all those sailors' stories are true—all that pig shit about curses and monsters and madness."

Ruc frowned. "A little madness would explain walking naked into an arena of people and pissing on their gods."

"We're pretty far out on a very slim limb," Talal said. "I've read reports of a few small settlements clinging to the northwestern coast of Menkiddoc—fishing villages, whaling towns—but those have to be a couple thousand miles from here, all the way on the other side of the continent. There's been no contact or commerce out of the heart of Menkiddoc, no one coming or going up through the Waist in . . ." He paused, shook his head. "Ever. At least as far as I know. Annur keeps a garrison in the Waist itself, but the only people who attack them are the Waist tribes."

"And *wherever* he's coming from," Monster said, "why attack Dombâng? There are easier places. Cities not built in the middle of the Shirvian fucking delta."

"Dombâng's all alone," Bien pointed out.

Ruc nodded. "Since splitting from Annur, there's no empire to save it, no armies to pull in from other parts of the globe."

"Still," Talal said, "not an easy target."

"Your gods will crawl," Bien put in quietly. *"Even now he hunts them."*

"Meaning . . . what?" Monster asked. "That that gorgeous dead idiot worked for a group of god-hunters?"

Mouse let out a low whistle. "God-hunters."

"Yeah," Ruc said. "It does have sort of an unnerving ring to it, doesn't it?"

"Wherever he was from," Bien said, shaking her head, "why would he warn us?"

"Make people uncertain," Ruc suggested. "Make them scared."

Talal frowned. "If you want to frighten people, you do something more spectacular. Blow something up. Burn something down. More fire and blood. You don't just show up and die."

"The First didn't die," Bien pointed out. "Whoever he is. Wherever he is. The poor fool in the Arena today was only a messenger."

Monster rolled her eyes. "Yeah. We've been over this. Try to keep the fuck up. What soldier boy is saying is that he'd've been a more fucking *effective* messenger if he'd stomped some people."

"Maybe not." Memory rose inside Ruc, inevitable as a flood. "Maybe the First is like a dawn adder."

Stupid raised his head incrementally, tipped back his hat to peer at Ruc out of the gap.

"Dawn adder?" Mouse asked.

"And just what the fuck," Monster inquired finally, "is a dawn adder?"

"A delta snake. You don't see them close to the city—I don't know why. They're orange and pink—like sunrise."

"How poetic."

Ruc ignored her. "They're venomous, but the venom doesn't paralyze or kill, at least not immediately, not from a single bite. If it's hungry, it will bite several times in a row, make a quick end of the thing, but often it bites only once, then withdraws. The venom makes whatever's been bitten thrash, roll around, scream if it's a thing that screams. You can hear a jaguar that's been bitten by a dawn adder for miles on a calm day. Scavengers come, wait, then clean up the carcass."

"Why kill a thing," Stupid asked, "that it never gets to eat?"

"Eating isn't the point," Ruc replied. "The adder isn't hungry. It uses the screams of the dying creature to attract a mate."

"I don't think," Monster said skeptically, "that the general of some foreign army is coming here looking for a hot fuck."

"Neither do I," Ruc agreed, "but principle is the same."

Talal frowned. "Remind us of the principle again."

"Most creatures," Ruc said, "snakes, jaguars, people—they're all fighting all the time just to survive. A jaguar doesn't waste a kill, because it needs the food. Generals don't throw away soldiers, because they *need* those soldiers." He shook his head. "For the dawn adder, though—it doesn't matter. It can kill at will. The snake wears these wasted lives, the pointlessness of their wreckage, the way a bird wears its plumage."

It was Monster, finally, who broke the long silence. "Makes a fucked-up kind of sense." She glanced over at Mouse. "You remember how we'd decide which houses to rob?"

"Trash," he replied, nodding his huge head slowly.

"Measure a person not by what they keep," Stupid said from beneath the hat, "but by what they can afford to throw away."

"The First is certainly tossing these fools away like trash," Talal said.

"Which would mean," Bien added grimly, "that he doesn't care whether we're scared. He doesn't care that we know he's coming. He doesn't care if we prepare. He doesn't care if he destroys his own army before he even arrives. He's so strong it just doesn't matter."

Ruc had killed a dozen flies, snatched them out of the air and smashed them into the table, but others kept coming, attracted to the heat, the light, the scent of skin. In Dombâng, there were always more flies. They buzzed around the lantern, the drone of their wings the only sound in the small bunk room. Monster, Mouse, and Stupid had retired to their bunks an hour earlier, the exhaustion of their fight finally catching up to them. Ruc, Talal, and Bien stayed up. The three of them hadn't been alone since the morning, which meant there'd been no chance to discuss their aborted attempt at escape. Ruc had a dozen burning questions, but he could hear Monster muttering to herself in the other room, tossing back and forth while she waited for sleep, and so he waited. Bien picked her scabs. Talal traced the grain of the rough table as though he were following a path on a map.

Eventually the midnight gong broke the silence. The shivering bronze sounded like a portent or a warning, but it didn't wake the other three. Ruc could see their heat through the wooden wall, all lost to exhaustion.

He shifted his gaze to Bien. "We're going to have to fight," he said quietly.

She nodded, stared into the lamp's shifting flame. "It was obvious the day we came here. But all this time I still thought . . . I thought we'd discover a way out."

"What did you find back there?" Talal asked.

She shrugged. "Like I said. A storeroom. Dark. Locked."

"Can we break through the door?"

"Maybe. I kicked it a bunch of times. It didn't break, but you're both stronger than me."

"Sounds like we're close," Talal said.

Bien shook her head. "Close isn't good enough. We'll be back in the pit tomorrow, but none of us are fighting. Which means Goatface will be in the box the whole time. And then, the day *after* tomorrow, we fight."

The day after tomorrow, we fight.

The revelation held no horror for Ruc. That absence of that horror, however, was a horror all its own. Half a lifetime devoted to Eira, to love and compassion, to the helping of his fellows, even the helping of his foes, and for what? All the Teachings, all the pieties, all the worship—worthless. His years as a priest had been nothing more than an elaborate mask. He was still the same blood-soaked creature who had happily stalked jaguars through the reeds. Everything he'd tried to escape—the cruelty, the eager heat, the sheer brute joy of the hunt—it had been with him all along, waiting. He was right back where he began, faced with the same ancient, fundamental choice: kill or die.

"We need to tell the others," Bien said quietly.

It took Ruc a moment to return to the conversation. Talal was frowning at her.

"Which others?"

"Monster, Mouse, and Stupid."

"Why would we tell them?" Ruc asked.

"Because," Bien replied, "while we're fighting, they'll have a chance to go through the wall. The same way I did. They were thieves before they came here. Breaking into houses and all that. They'll be able to find a way out."

Ruc shook his head. "As soon as Goatface comes back to the box to find them gone, we're done."

"He won't *find* them gone," Bien insisted. "We can tell them to find a way out—unlock the door, explore what needs to be explored—then to come back."

Talal grimaced. "One thing I've found about people—they don't always do what they're told."

"Especially," Ruc added, "when their lives are at stake. We'd be offering them a way out and the perfect opportunity to take it."

To his surprise, Bien smiled. For just a moment she looked almost predatory. "They don't have anywhere to *go*."

"Dombâng is a city of a hundred thousand people," Talal said. "There's always somewhere to go."

"Not for escaped Worthy. No one will help them. No one ever does. They might survive a week, two, but then what? There are no ships in or out. All the main channels are patrolled by the Greenshirts. The causeway is crawling with soldiers. Anyone who gets out of here has two choices—hide or flee. Both are death sentences."

Talal raised an eyebrow. "Remind me again why we're so eager to get out."

"Because," Bien replied, "we have the two of you." She leveled a finger at Ruc. "He knows the world of the delta, and you know the world outside it. Anyone who escapes with one of the Vuo Ton and the Kettral actually has a chance. . . ."

"I'm not Vuo Ton," Ruc said.

"Close enough."

The soldier sucked at something in his teeth, then shook his head. "So. Let's say we tell them. Let's say they agree. And let's also say, since we're having such good luck in this scenario, that while we're fighting, one of them is able to find a way out. Then what? When will we use it?"

"The high holy days."

Ruc studied her, then shook his head. "It doesn't work. We always fight in threes. There's no time when we're all in the box without Goatface."

"There are ways," Talal said, frowning, "of dealing with Goatface."

"Ways that work in front of ten thousand people?" Ruc asked. He shook his head. "It was touch and go just getting Bien through that gap and back. If Monster, Mouse, *and* Stupid disappear, someone's going to notice, and then if you kill Goatface in the box—"

"Not kill," Bien said, her voice hard, angry.

"He's the enemy, Bien," Talal replied.

She shook her head. *"The only foe is the hate in your heart."*

She must have recited the words a thousand times, but now, her features shifting in the light of the lantern, she sounded desperate, as though the ancient Teaching were the flimsiest shield held up against what had to come, as though she expected it to shatter at the first blow.

"That hasn't been my experience," Talal said quietly.

"It doesn't matter," Ruc cut in. "It's just not feasible. If the people in the stands don't notice you killing one of the most famous trainers in broad daylight . . ." He paused, a new thought unfolding slowly inside him. He glanced over at Bien, and nodded. She'd seen it all along.

She shot him a worried smile. "Except the fights of the high holy days don't take place during the daylight. They happen at night."

The soldier frowned. "Sounds like the high holy days were misnamed."

Ruc shook his head. "During the day there are feasts and sermons and games and all the rest. The killing is the crux of it, and so the killing comes last. After dark."

"How well lit is the Arena?"

"There are hundreds of torches," Ruc replied. "But no torch is as bright as the sun. Not to mention the fact that everyone is drunk by that point."

Talal nodded slowly. "It could work."

"It *has* to work," Bien insisted. "In two days, Stupid or Monster clears a way out. Then we wait. We wait for the high holy days, subdue Goatface— *Can* you subdue him without killing him?"

Talal nodded again.

"That's it then. When he's down, we go."

The look on her face was half defiant, half pleading. As Ruc watched, however, the pleading seemed to drain away, leaving only defiance.

"It's a pretty big risk," Talal said at last.

She rounded on him. "This from the idiot who flew a giant bird into a burning building, then tried to fight his way out."

"I wasn't on the bird—"

"It doesn't matter. The point is, you're Kettral. You do stuff like this all the time."

"Not when I have other options."

She arched an eyebrow at him. "And do you have other options?" When he didn't respond, she shook her head. "It's this, then. The first thing we have to figure out is which way we're going when we get clear of the Arena."

"No," Ruc said.

Her face hardened.

He held up his hands. "I'm in. But in two days, while Stupid or whoever is finding a way out, we're going to be in the pit fighting. Which means the first thing we need to figure out is how we want to do our killing."

51

"You should walk with Pattick," Gwenna said for what had to be the hundredth time, pointing up the defile. The legionaries were maybe fifty paces ahead, climbing toward the saddle above, followed by Kiel and Bhuma Dhar. There was no way of knowing what waited up there, but it had to be better than what followed.

The *gabhya* was still behind them. Whenever the wind shifted, Gwenna caught a whiff of it, that sick, rotten smell, though the monster remained hidden in the labyrinth of scree, massive boulders, and steep ravines. Almost as worrying as the *gabhya* were Jonon and his men. She glanced over her shoulder to find the admiral's too-bright eyes fixed on her. He should have been exhausted from the climb, 'Shael knew that Gwenna herself was, but Jonon—it was growing harder and harder to think of him as an admiral—and his men trotted up the mountainside like goats. Chent had clambered atop a boulder to sketch a few manic dance steps. Their strength was obviously unnatural, a twisted vitality that refused to flag, despite the rigors of the climb. Gwenna didn't want Rat anywhere near them.

"Go ahead," she said, gesturing up the ravine. "I'll be right behind you."

"No." It was one of the first words the girl had mastered, and remained a favorite. "Not leaving you."

"You're not *leaving*. You're just moving up the column a little. Pattick and Cho Lu are up there." She pointed to the soldiers picking their way between the boulders. "You like them."

Rat shook her head again. "No."

Gwenna blew out a frustrated breath. "I'm not always going to be around, you know. You need to learn to be independent."

"Independent?" The girl reeked of suspicion.

"Alone. By yourself."

Rat stopped short, rounded on Gwenna, fixed her with a furious glare. "*Was* alone. *Was* with self."

Guilt pricked at Gwenna. She thought again of the empty city with its monstrous statuary, all those neat stacks of skulls, the heaps of bones discovered by Jonon's soldiers. Rat had lived there alone—alone save for Yutaka's dubious company. She'd survived when plenty of other children, plenty of other *adults* would have panicked, fucked up, starved, died. The last thing she needed was a lecture about the value of independence, and yet . . .

"If something happens to me—"

Rat cut her off. "Something?"

"There's a monster behind us. I might have to fight it."

Despite Kiel's assurances, there was still no sign of any Csestriim ruins, let alone an intact fortification.

"Me too," Rat declared.

"No." Gwenna shook her head. "If it attacks, you get away, get somewhere safe. You can trust Cho Lu and Pattick, or Bhuma Dhar, or . . ." She hesitated. "Probably Kiel. If I don't survive—"

"Not leaving you."

Gwenna marshaled her patience. "Rat, I know you think I can keep you safe, and I promise you I'll do everything I can, but . . ." She put a hand on the girl's shoulder. She'd intended it as a comfort. Instead, it felt like she was leaning on the child. "People fuck up, Rat. *I* fuck up."

"Yes." Rat nodded as though she'd just explained that water was wet. "Gwenna fucks up. Rat saves her."

Gwenna stared at the girl, half choked on her own laugh. "You're worried about *me*?"

"Yes."

"Rat, I'm a soldier. I'm a . . . a grown woman. I've spent my whole life learning to fight."

"Me too. *Shava-bhura* teachings, then Gwenna Sharpe teachings. I learned."

"It's not the same."

Gwenna was still talking when Rat stripped the knife from its sheath, the movement so fast it happened between one syllable and the next. She lunged for Gwenna's gut. The right play was to catch the wrist, twist it, break it, but Gwenna wasn't about to break the girl's arm to make a point. Instead, she knocked the attack aside just the way she had hundreds of times before.

Just the way Rat expected.

The heel of Gwenna's hand caught Rat on the wrist, but not before the girl had tossed the knife to her other hand. As Gwenna's block knocked Rat's right hand aside, the girl snatched the dagger out of the air with her left, fast as a striking snake, laid the cold blade against Gwenna's throat. She had to stand on her toes to reach, but the knife was steady.

Gwenna blinked.

"I am a fighter," Rat said quietly. "Like Gwenna."

Half a dozen objections rose up in Gwenna's throat. The girl had won, sure, but that was only because she knew how Gwenna would respond. It wasn't a real fight. In a real fight, Gwenna would have cut her apart. Going against a trainer wasn't the same thing as standing against a mortal foe. And yet, there was an expression back on the Islands—*The steel doesn't lie*—and the steel was pressing against the artery in her neck, just as she'd shown the girl a thousand times before.

"I am a fighter," Rat said again, lowering the blade at last.

"The thing about fighters, Rat—they die."

The thought of the girl's small body broken open and bleeding flooded her mind. She had a vision of the *gabbya* burrowing in the child's guts, making the dead limbs dance with the violence of its feeding. The awful possibility was like a stone lodged in her throat, heavy and cold, choking her. She felt a physical compulsion to wrap her arms around the girl, cinch her close, guard that too-slender form with the weight of her own body. Not that it would do any good. The *gabbya* would just devour them both.

"All people die," Rat said.

"Yeah, well, children shouldn't have to."

"*Should.*" She wrinkled her nose in disgust. "*Shouldn't.* Stupid words. I *am* alive. I *am* a fighter."

Gwenna stared at her, at the pale, filthy skin, tangle of hair, gritted teeth, defiant eyes. She might as well have been looking at herself two decades earlier. She tried to imagine telling that furious, red-haired girl that she didn't have a choice, that she should stay on the farm while her father and brothers went off to war, that she shouldn't have to suffer the brutality of Kettral training, that she shouldn't have to die or watch her friends die. The laugh rising in her throat felt heavy as lead. That kid wouldn't have listened either.

Still, she could try.

"Don't you want to be something else?"

Rat studied her, baffled. "What else?"

"I don't know . . ." She trailed off, scouring her mind for an answer. A young girl, nine years old, all alone, no family, no friends, no *anyone* except, now, Gwenna—whatever the fuck *she* was. What *could* Rat be? Farmer? Seamstress? Shipwright? Merchant? Carpenter? From where they stood, all the possibilities seemed ludicrous. To get to any of them meant fighting, to get *anywhere* meant fighting. Maybe there were other people, other places, whose lives weren't stitched out of blood and struggle. Hopefully there were. Rat, though, wasn't one of them.

"All right," Gwenna said finally.

Rat's face was wary. "All right?"

"You're a fighter."

The wariness bloomed into a smile. "Like Gwenna Sharpe."

"No. You're smaller, and weaker, and slower than Gwenna Sharpe. If you had to fight Gwenna Sharpe for real, Gwenna Sharpe would kill you ten times out of ten—"

Rat bared her teeth. Gwenna put a soothing hand on her shoulder.

"But," she went on, "you're faster than most people I've fought, and you're tough, and if you survive, you might even be better than Gwenna Sharpe one day."

To Gwenna's shock, the girl hurled her arms around her. Those skinny limbs pulled tight as a vise, squeezing the air from her chest.

Gwenna struggled to keep her heart closed. The girl was a fighter, after all, and she'd seen too many fighters die.

⸸

The monster hit them at dusk, halfway up a steep, rocky defile from which there was no retreat. The only escapes were up over the shifting, precarious scree, or back down, the way they had come.

If there'd been time to ponder the question, Gwenna might have wondered if the creature had chosen the spot on purpose, or if it was all just shitty luck, but there was no time for pondering. The only warning was a whiff of something necrotic, the sound of claws skittering over the cliff above, and then, by the time she looked up, it was on them.

Back in the jungle, despite the outlandish descriptions from Jonon's men, she'd imagined the thing stalking them might be something like a tiger or a bear. Worse, certainly—larger and uglier, strange in ways that made the skin twitch, but still just a natural predator made unnatural by the pollution of Menkiddoc. Twisted but fundamentally familiar. The carcasses it left behind were ample evidence of its savagery, but its unwillingness to face the entire group had convinced Gwenna that it was wary. That thought had been a relief. Creatures were wary because they had vulnerabilities, because they understood, at some deep, bestial level, that they could be killed.

As the monster hurled itself from the lip of the cliff above, she realized just how wrong she'd been.

The *gabhya* wasn't afraid.

It had never been afraid.

And it looked nothing like a fucking bear.

For a few awful moments, her mind scrambled to make sense of the size and shape.

Centipede, she thought. *It's a centipede.* It had a long, sinuous, scaled, segmented body, so that made sense. It was also more than half a dozen paces long and as thick as her waist, so that did not.

It had no head, just a bristle of thrashing antennae, each as long as a whip, while at the other end a vicious, hooked scorpion's tail wove back and forth through the air. If the ends of the thing were horrid, what happened in between was worse. Half of the hundred legs—every other one—were grotesquely large versions of a centipede's legs—red-black, gracile, sharp tipped. The other half, however, weren't legs at all but arms, hairless and almost human in their contours, though they had too many joints. Muscles flexed and bulged beneath the too-tight skin. Some of those arms ended in horribly human hands, others in blind, thrashing, razor-toothed mouths, dozens of mouths, all gaping, all slavering.

It landed on Vessik.

The sailor opened his mouth to scream, but before the sound could pour out, one of those mouths closed over his, biting through his lips, his cheeks, his face. In the time it took for Gwenna to slide free her blades, it seized the sailor in a dozen places, some of the mouths holding him fast while the others fed, tearing gobbets of flesh off his chest, his legs, his back, splattering blood and slick yellow fat over the sun-bleached stone. His body jerked desperately. With one hand he tried to pry away the mouth feasting on his face, then another of the creature's mouths ripped that arm free at the shoulder. The man had to be dead, but his corpse kept dancing with the savagery of the attack.

Rummel bellowed, then hurled himself at the monster, sword gleaming red with the late-day sun. He swept it down in a savage chop, hacking into the nearest leg.

The thing screamed from a dozen mouths, an awful, glass-pitched, child-like scream, then whipped its body around and impaled the sailor through the chest with its tail. Rummel dropped his blade, scrabbled at his chest as the beast lifted him from the ground. Shock glazed his eyes.

"Admiral . . ." he managed, then went slack.

With half a dozen mouths, the creature ripped him apart—the arm from the shoulder, the head from the neck, the leg from the hip. Some of those mouths began feeding, snapping at each other over the scraps. The others rose up, twisting and writhing, dark tongues flicking forth as though tasting the air.

Gwenna had stripped her swords the moment the monster attacked, but as it devoured the ribbons of meat that had been Vessik and Rummel, she found she had no idea what to do with them. It was obvious, just looking at most creatures, where you needed to stab them. There was usually a heart in the chest, a brain in the head, lungs and guts somewhere in the middle. This abomination, though—it didn't even *have* a head, and getting to that segmented body looked impossible.

Tendons, she reminded herself. *Go for the tendons.*

Although how it would help to hamstring a creature with a hundred legs, she had no idea.

It tossed aside the last of the sodden, ruined carcasses, then turned toward her, antennae thrashing.

Out of the corner of her eye she caught a glimpse of Rat. The girl's naked dagger was out, steel winking in the last of the daylight. It looked pathetically small.

"Get back," Gwenna growled. "Retreat up the gully."

"Fight—" the girl began.

"Retreating *is* fighting. We make it climb to get at us. Hit it from above."

That was the theory, anyway. Every treatise on tactics ever written agreed on the value of high ground—having it, holding it. Hendran's advice was simple: *Get high. Stay high.* Gwenna was willing to bet, however, that Hendran had never faced anything like the monster below. It flowed over the stone like water, almost as fast moving uphill as it had been going down.

"Go," she said, shifting to put Rat behind her, then retreating up the gully slowly, blades in a split guard, stones shifting dangerously beneath her feet.

From somewhere close behind, a bowstring twanged.

The arrow licked past, barely a pace from her head, buried itself in a joint of the scaly carapace.

The *gabhya* stopped, reared up, lifted the front half of its body until it swayed like a snake. Some of those too-human mouths howled. Others hissed. Some just licked bloody tongues over bloody teeth.

Kiel got off three more shots in the space of as many heartbeats. All hit home. None seemed to matter. The monster twitched, danced, screamed, but aside from a few drops of ichor—yellow-brown and reeking of infection—it didn't seem hurt.

"Where in Hull's name are you supposed to hit it?" Gwenna growled.

"A question I have posed to myself as well," Kiel replied mildly, letting fly another arrow.

The monster had divided the small force. Dhar, Kiel, Rat, and the two legionaries were retreating up the defile behind and above Gwenna; without looking back, she could hear their panting, smell the ripeness of their fear. Jonon, Lurie, and Chent comprised the other group, maybe twenty paces down the gully, the two sailors half hidden behind blocks of scree while the admiral had vaulted atop a chest-high boulder—as good a place as anywhere else to fight from. If they could come at the creature from two different sides, attack it from above and below simultaneously . . . Gwenna opened her mouth to call down to Jonon, but before she could form the words, the *gabhya* was moving again, slithering up the defile after her, lapping the air with those ragged tongues.

She took a careful step back, then another, then stumbled into Rat.

"Shit," the girl cursed. "Shit. Oh *shit*."

"Keep climbing, Rat," Gwenna hissed.

"Can't!" the girl half sobbed. *"Stuck!"*

Gwenna risked a glance backward, saw that the loose scree had shifted around the girl's leg, pinning her ankle. Blood trickled from the gash, staining the pale stone, but the blood wasn't the problem. A little blood wouldn't kill the girl. A centipede the size of a whale, on the other hand . . .

"I'm coming," Pattick shouted. Small stones clattered past as he stumbled back down the slope.

"Bastard leg," Rat snarled.

The smell of the girl's blood bloomed in the air.

The *gabhya* hesitated, twitching, licking the flavor.

"I'm here," Pattick gasped. "I'm here."

"Hurry," Gwenna growled.

Blood hammered in her ears. Every muscle in her body felt too tight and somehow, at the same time, water-weak. The thought of her own death she could stomach. The idea that she'd still be alive when the horror tore Rat to shreds, though, that she'd have to watch as the girl screamed and danced beneath those mouths, *that* thought flooded her with rage and dread in equal measures, a desperate strength so terrible she felt it pressing out, out, threatening to rip her open.

She took a step back down the ravine, back toward the monster.

A stone almost the size of her head sailed above, smashed into one of the *gabhya*'s limbs. Then another. Then another.

"Plenty of rocks up here!" Cho Lu shouted.

"Stop!" Gwenna shouted.

The stones weren't hurting the thing, not badly enough to stop it, anyway. Mostly, it seemed, they were just infuriating it.

"Is Rat clear yet?" she demanded, not daring to turn.

Pattick was panting with exertion. *"Almost."*

"Here." Bhuma Dhar's voice. Evidently he'd descended as well. "Tip, then *pull . . .*"

Stone ground against stone, Rat screamed, then a large boulder crashed down the slope, a few paces to Gwenna's right.

"Got her," Pattick shouted.

Too late.

The *gabhya,* goaded on either by the sound of its escaping prey or by its own ravenous appetites, surged up the defile. Gwenna could hear the others struggling to retreat, but there was no time to join them, no time to do anything but shift her stance, ready her swords, and prepare to die.

The first of the creature's arms came at her fast as a spear strike, razor teeth eager and gleaming. She ducked beneath it—no chance of rolling on the jagged stone—pivoted, hacked down with a blade, and lopped it off. Kiel's arrows might not have done much damage, but her smoke steel carved into the too-human flesh as though it was already rotten. The stump pumped ichor while the severed arm dropped, teeth still gnashing. It might have felt like a victory, she thought grimly, if there hadn't been another ninety-nine arms already grasping for her.

"Get high," she shouted over her shoulder. "Get to the top of the ravine. Try to start a slide."

It was a mad hope, partly because the slope seemed too stable for a true avalanche, partly because even if they managed one, she'd be caught up in it along with the monster. Ugly way to go—crushed beneath a few hundred tons of rock—but a lot prettier than the alternative.

"I'm coming," Pattick gasped.

"No." Her own voice echoed off the stone walls. "Get Rat and *go.*"

She could hear Rat cursing behind her, struggling. "Help Gwenna Sharpe," the girl snarled. "We *must.*"

"Pattick," Gwenna growled, knocking aside another mouth, ducking under a third, then burying her sword down the gullet of a fourth. "You get that girl clear, or I will skin you and feed you to this fucking thing myself."

If Pattick responded, she didn't hear it because the *gabhya* began screaming again. The sound felt like a rusty knife dragged over her skull, along the ridges of her spine.

She slipped to the side as it lashed out for her face, lopped the lower jaw from the mouth, then felt the teeth tear into her calf. Only a lifetime of training kept her from losing the leg. She hacked down with her free sword, sliced halfway through the creature's limb, felt the hot ichor splatter across her face, almost lost the blade when the thing yanked back.

It hissed from a dozen mouths, reared up once more.

Gwenna gritted her teeth, tested the leg. The muscle felt weak, compromised, but she could stand on it. Poison like fire snaked up her veins, but the tendon was intact—that was the important thing. The venom—if it *was* venom—might kill her later, but the moment that mattered was *now*.

Two more arrows flickered past—Kiel had shifted his focus from the body to the limbs—but after another heartbeat the bowstring fell silent. Either the historian was out of arrows or he'd decided to move to a different position. Not that it mattered.

She raised her swords, tried to see some new way to fight the monster, something that might actually work.

The whole miserable situation came down to a simple problem of arms. She had two. The thing before her had dozens. No matter how fast she was with the sword, she couldn't keep them all back. The starshatter at her belt might slow it, might even kill it, but there'd been no time to reach for it earlier, not to get it free, light a striker, and set it to the fuse. Certainly there was no time now. She grappled with the thought as the monster came on again, lashing out at her with half a dozen arms, all their mouths gnashing.

She battered two aside, dove behind a boulder, landed hard on her shoulder, twisted around to find the sick bug looming over her. She gritted her teeth, dropped her blades, and reached for the starshatter. Too slow—she *knew* she was too slow—but if she could just light the fucking thing, could just hold on to it while those mouths shredded her, maybe the explosion would take it down, or start a slide, or do something that gave the others a chance. Her blood-slick fingers closed over the munition; she yanked it from her belt. Before she could light it, however, a howl, half pain, half ecstasy, blotted out all other sound.

She thought, at first, that it was the beast keening its delight before finishing her.

Then she realized that the thing was twitching, antennae thrashing the air, rising up yet again, eyeless mouths agape, turning back down the slope.

Starshatter in her hand, Gwenna stumbled to her feet.

The howl came again, louder this time—if that was possible—a mad shriek of such awful eagerness that some animal part of her wanted to dive back behind the boulder, bury her head in her arms, blot out all sound, all vibration. Instead, she forced herself to scour the ravine below.

There.

Still standing on the boulder, his filthy uniform half ripped away, naked cutlass in one hand, Vessik's bloody sword in the other, head tipped back, throat heaving as though the sound pouring out of it were thick as half-clotted blood: Jonon lem Jonon, once First Admiral of the Western Fleet of Annur.

"Here!" he screamed. "Come *here,* my beauty. *Come to me!*"

The *gabbya* turned, quivered, hesitated. Then, like darkness flooding down over the stone, poured itself downhill at the solitary man.

"Sweet Intarra's light," Pattick gasped, somewhere above and behind her.

An old Annurian curse, one she'd heard from the soldier a hundred times, but there was nothing sweet or light about what was about to happen. The *gabbya* was going to kill Jonon. It was going to swarm down the gully, fall on him, and take him apart limb by limb. There was no way to help him, no chance of getting there in time, not that he looked like he wanted to be helped. As the monster advanced, he stared at it with glittering green eyes, his arms spread as though opening for an embrace. He was going to die, die horribly, but his dying might save the rest of them.

Her hands steady with the focus of the fight, Gwenna slipped a striker from her belt. She tried striking it on the stone before her, but it was wet with blood—her own?—and the flame sparked, then died.

Slowly, she reminded herself as she reached for a second striker.

Down below the *gabbya* spread its dozens of arms, a grotesque echo of Jonon's embrace, then reached for the man.

Gwenna ran the striker over the stone. This time the flame held. Carefully, she touched it to the fuse of the starshatter, which hissed to life.

"He's going to die," Cho Lu whispered.

Jonon lem Jonon, however, did not die.

As those awful arms closed around him, he shifted, moving faster than Gwenna had ever seen him move, faster than she herself could fight, hacking and whirling and slicing with a speed she'd never witnessed, not even from the Flea or Ran il Tornja. The only thing like it had been Valyn fighting at the height of his powers, but Jonon had none of Valyn's training, none of the slarn's blood running through his own. It should have been impossible for him to stand against the monster, but stand he did in a rain of yellow ichor, his mouth pried wide in a smile of delight, his cutlass a dream in his hands as he carved the thing apart.

The sickness, Gwenna realized with horror. The same pollution that had created the *gabbya* throbbed in the admiral's veins. What was it he'd said? *The water is making me stronger. Faster. I can feel it already.* At the time she'd thought that was just the madness talking. How wrong she'd been. Not about the madness, but about the strength, the speed.

For the first time, the monster fell back.

Instead of pausing, taking stock, Jonon leapt from atop the boulder, landed square in the center of its back, then drove his blade down between the over-lapping scales. It screamed, thrashed, tried to toss him off, but it had begun to slow. Its balance was all wrong. It had lost too many arms and legs. Ichor poured from a dozen ghastly wounds. What arms were left strained for the admiral, teeth gnashing empty air, but he was out of reach. As the monster writhed, he kept driving, driving, shoving that blade deeper and deeper between the segments of the body until at last the whole thing dropped, shuddered, and fell still.

Gwenna took a deep breath, steadied herself.

A cold wind knifed down out of the mountains.

The world reeked of piss, and shit, and rot, and blood.

"He did it," Pattick murmured.

It should have been a relief. The thing that had been stalking them lay dead on the cold stones. They'd made it—come through the jungle and survived. They were already free of the sickness. If they could just reach the pass it was downhill, a clear shot all the way to the coast.

All Gwenna could see, however, was Jonon lem Jonon's face, his bared teeth grinning through the slick muck, his hands twisting the sword in the open wound, driving it still deeper, though the fight was already over. Behind her, Pattick and the others panted their relief, but all Gwenna could hear was the sound of the admiral's laughter—delighted, crazed, only barely human.

He stopped grinding away at the wound finally, raised his eyes, found hers.

"You see?" he whispered.

The wick of the starshatter hissed wickedly.

Jonon grinned. "This. *This* is what we were meant to be." He let out a great, mad whoop of laughter. "Not groveling little creatures, but *gods*!" A negligent wave of the hand. "Put out your candle. The beast is dead."

Gwenna reached for the wick, ready to snuff it, then paused.

Jonon's eyes narrowed.

"Put it out, you foolish bitch."

For an endless heartbeat she studied him, the man who'd once been an Annurian admiral. Maybe he could still be saved. Kiel had mentioned some artifact in the fortress above. She had no idea how Menkiddoc's sickness worked. They'd won free of the pollution, after all. Maybe if he stopped drinking the diseased water, stopped eating the rancid meat, found whatever Csestriim remedy had survived all the long centuries . . .

He bared his teeth as though reading her thoughts. They were bloody as the teeth of the creature he'd slain.

"Put it out," he said again.

Instead of replying, Gwenna threw the munition.

"Down," she shouted, rolling behind the boulder. "Get down!"

The explosion came a moment later. The explosion, then the grinding rumble of rockslide, louder and louder as the gully below collapsed in on itself, stones smashing against one another, filling the air with dust and a noise so great Gwenna could feel her own heart trembling. When it finally subsided, she dragged herself to her feet, stared down the slope.

Jonon was gone. The *gabhya* was gone. Lurie was gone.

"You killed him," Pattick murmured.

"Killed *gabhya*," Rat hissed.

"Not the *gabhya*," Pattick said. "The admiral. She killed the admiral."

"Stupid," the girl replied. "Admiral *was gabhya*."

52

Adare was desperate—though she hid that desperation well—for news out of Dombâng, or the garrisons along the White River, or Mo'ir, or any of the dozens of other places that Annur was slowly crumbling. She had riders and runners, soldiers who reported to the Dawn Palace daily, ships' captains who bore sealed missives in their hands. The trouble was that their reports were always days or weeks out of date. If the currents and winds weren't right, word from Anthera and the Bend could take over a month to arrive. Which meant she needed Akiil. He—an orphaned thief from the Quarter—was the single link that could hold together the whole sprawling empire, and so when she sent him back through the *kenta* he'd nodded his obedience, repeated back his orders, promised to explore the other gates as quickly and safely as possible.

And then went straight back to the Csestriim fortress in the mountain.

Fixing the Annurian Empire was hardly *his* job.

This time, as he stepped through the *kenta* into the mountain stronghold, he let the *vaniate* go. Fear and eagerness, guilt and greed—all the old emotions shivered through him like a fever as they returned. It was tempting to build the trance once more, to climb into that endless empty shell, but if he was going to do this right, if he was going to survive, he needed his emotions. He felt safer inside the *vaniate,* but that safety was an illusion. Nothing within the hollowed-out mountain was safe—if he knew nothing else about the place, he knew that. He needed his fear, needed all the old instincts of stealth and flight that he'd honed as a child.

Heart thudding, he made his way down the staircase, pausing every few steps to listen. For a while, he could hear the wind moaning through the broken windows above. Then, when he'd descended far enough, even that sound was lost in the cavernous silence, a stillness so deep it seemed to reach into him, spread through his flesh, until he felt only half real, half alive. The place might have been a crypt. All the weapons and artifacts below might have been the grave goods of some long-dead Csestriim prince, except, if he remembered the stories right, the Csestriim didn't *have* princes. And they didn't usually die.

When he reached the landing, he stopped once more.

Argent light filtered through the open door, spilling across the stone.

The air smelled faintly acrid, like steel heated too long in a forge. It hadn't smelled that way the last time. Which meant . . . what? Impossible to know.

"Slow is stupid," he muttered to himself.

It was something Skinny Quinn used to say when they were robbing houses up in the Graves.

He'd never quite agreed. There was a value to planning, to patience, to choosing the best moment. On the other hand, once you were *in*—through the window, or the busted back door, or the dormer—that was the time to take what you'd come for and get the fuck out. Quinn understood that better than some of the other kids, who liked to hang around, try on clothes, eat the fruit, smear shit on the paintings and scrolls.

A hundred heartbeats.

That was how long Quinn always gave herself, and he'd already been in the Csestriim fortress at least ten times that.

He stole a quick glance through the door. The room was just as he'd remembered. . . .

No. Not quite. While the silver-blue veins still streaked the ceiling, reflecting off the flat black water, more of the alcoves along the wall were empty. He closed his eyes, compared the memory with the present moment. Three swords were missing, and something that might have been a vase, and the flute thing. Rods and spears, some inexplicable leaf-shaped thing, a breastplate, a gauntlet that might have been carved from ivory . . . So much treasure, gone. Removed by the woman he'd seen before? By someone else? Were they being taken someplace else to be used? Or simply stolen? It didn't much matter. If he intended to pry more money out of Gelta Yuel, he'd need to work fast, take what he could get while there was still something left.

He chose the smallest items he could find, something that looked like a shark's tooth—although the surface swirled as though coated in oil—and a segmented thing halfway between a necklace and a collar. He could have carried more, but greed was almost as dangerous to a thief as moving too slowly. The trick to staying free, to staying alive, was stealing no more than you could carry at a dead run over uneven rooftops. Not that there were any rooftops in the Csestriim fortress, but the principle applied. Plus, there was the not insignificant matter of smuggling the shit back into Annur. The swords were gorgeous, but Adare would have questions if he returned lugging a Csestriim sword.

He'd climbed halfway back up from the great domed room to the watchtower, was just congratulating himself on his discipline, when he heard the noise.

His stomach lurched. Fear spiked his blood.

He ached to run, but forced himself to stop, to draw a long breath through his nose, hold it, and listen.

Footsteps, just as before, but this time they were coming from above, from between him and the *kenta*.

And this time, they weren't alone.

Something else—not the leather soles of boots or the slapping of bare feet—was skittering and scratching over the stone. It sounded like someone dragging a dagger across the steps or walls, dragging a dozen daggers, hacking and stabbing at the stairs. Or maybe like some creature trying to claw its way free. Both the footsteps and that other, awful sound were coming toward him, coming fast.

He turned, started back down the steps.

As he ran, his fear molted into a clear, cold focus. It was a gift, one he'd had even as a young child; no matter how frightened he was in the days or hours leading up to a job, no matter the dread lacing his veins as he forced the window and climbed through, if the time came to flee, some older, surer instinct took over. He'd heard priests talk about being inhabited by a god, and while there was no god of thievery—none that he knew of, anyway—he recognized the sensation, the feeling of being guided by something wiser and more confident than his own mind.

On the other hand, he could only run so fucking fast.

He flew down the steps like falling but whatever was behind him gained.

Two hundred more steps to the chamber. One hundred fifty.

He considered darting past it, following the stairwell down into the unexplored portion of the fortress, then decided against it. Someone was being chased—that much seemed clear—someone in *addition* to him. If that person knew the layout of the place, which seemed likely, they'd know that the domed chamber was a dead end. Hopefully they'd continue on past, drawing along whatever 'Kent-kissing thing followed. He'd be able, then, to double back safely to the *kenta*. Maybe this time when he escaped he'd be smart enough not to come back.

He hit the landing, slid on the bare stone, then ducked through the doorway. For a moment he thought about diving into the water as he had the last time, but the footsteps following him were too close. If anyone followed him in, they'd see the waves of his passage, follow them back to his head bobbing just above the surface, and that would be that. There'd be no running away then. No fighting.

Instead, he lifted one of the Csestriim blades from the first alcove, then pressed his back against the wall just inside the doorway. It was the best defense he could think of; that didn't mean it was good. He'd held a sword maybe half a dozen times in his life. He'd killed Scial Nin with a sword, but the old abbot had been kneeling, defenseless. Quickly he hauled to mind the memory of a dock guard he'd seen back in the Bend, shifted his body into a rough imitation of the man's stance, hefted the blade into what felt like a plausible position. People fought with swords all the time. An arm's length of razor-sharp metal—if it *was,* in fact, metal. How hard could it be?

Panting echoed off the walls of the stairwell, quick human breathing, wet and irregular. Boots clattered on the stone. Judging from the sound, the person was injured, limping slightly, but still moving faster than he could believe. The awful scrabbling and scratching followed behind it, and then, laid over those sounds like some kind of twisted flute above the thudding of a drum, rose a high, eager whine.

The footsteps skidded to a halt on the landing outside the door.

Akiil flexed his grip on the sword's handle, imagined carving a cool arc through the air. Despite his ignorance, the Csestriim weapon felt right in his hands, solid.

After half a heartbeat's pause, a woman stumbled through the open door, the same woman from before, the one who had taken the spear. Her own blade dangled from a mangled arm. Her other hand pressed tight to her stomach, as though holding shut a wound. It was impossible to be sure in the watery half-light, but she looked young, younger than he'd realized before, not much older than Akiil himself. Aside from that sword—which might as well have been the mirror of his own—she was unarmed and unarmored. A poor choice, evidently, given the blood matting her dark hair, and sheeting down her face.

He checked his attack.

Whatever danger she posed couldn't be as great as that awful sound pursuing her.

She dove hard to her right, away from Akiil, collapsed, dragged herself up, twisted around so that she was sitting, back pressed against the wall on the other side of the door. Despite her wounds, despite the bloody spit slicking her chin, the woman mastered herself with astonishing speed, quieting her breathing, bringing her weapon awkwardly to bear. As she turned to face the doorway, she saw him. He expected some expression of shock, alarm, even relief, but aside from a slight dilation of the pupils she might have been expecting him all along, even counting on him.

"I will draw it this way," she said. "You kill it. Strike where the thorax meets the head."

Akiil stared at her. In the space of two heartbeats she had evidently abandoned one plan and devised another.

"Thorax?" he asked.

She gestured weakly to her torso. "Body."

Even as she spoke, she staggered weakly to her feet, moved away from him along the stone walkway ringing the lake, turning as she retreated to keep that gleaming blade between her and whatever it was that came.

Akiil opened his mouth to ask something more, then stopped. The thing was just outside, scrabbling over the stone, keening that same hungry, eager cry. There was a time for talking and a time for shutting the fuck up, and it was pretty obvious which one this was. He nodded to the woman, rehearsed in his mind again swinging the sword, feeling it bite, and then the moment was upon him.

He had no name to put to the creature that surged into the chamber other than *monster,* no way to think about those bulbous, multifaceted eyes, that clear carapace, the glowing ichor pulsing within. It might have been an insect, except it was at least twice the size of Akiil himself and its shell and quivering limbs seemed to be made of ice or glass, a substance so translucent he could see right through it. Reddish light suffused it, a light brighter than the faint blue of the chamber. He could make out organs shifting, as though digesting something. What might have been veins or nerves glowed with a slick light all their own.

"Here," the woman said. Her voice was flat, matter-of-fact.

The thing turned, quivered. Antennae like pale white ferns twitched, then went still.

The woman raised her blade into some kind of defense. She didn't look frightened or defiant. She looked like a person preparing to do a dull, complicated job, the consequences of which she cared about only in the abstract.

After a tight silence, those antennae twitched again and the thing, which had been moving horizontally, hinged at a slender wasplike joint, reared the front half of its body, and made a noise like a scream, a scream that climbed through all human registers, high and higher, as though some harpist had overtightened his instrument then dragged a knife across the string. The creature unfolded gracile limbs—each tipped with a serrated claw—and advanced slowly on the woman.

"Its tail is poison," she said calmly, never taking her eyes from the insect. "As is its venom. Stay well clear when you strike. Wait for it to come for me."

He nodded, forced himself forward one silent step. Two. Three.

When the monster lunged, he lunged with it, closing the gap from behind, sweeping the Csestriim blade up in a wide, bright arc, then bringing it down into the narrow juncture just at the back of the head.

Someone else, someone who had held a sword more than half a dozen times in his life, might have carried the blow, but Akiil felt the blade bite, then twist in his grip. Red ichor splattered his face. Instead of collapsing, the creature screamed again, spasmed, then rounded on him. Its eyes, each the size of his fist, glittered red, like thousand-faceted gems. Its mouth hung open, a huge spiral of grinding teeth. From between those teeth, it spat something slick and viscous. Only a set of mindless reflexes saved Akiil from catching the venom directly in the face. It sailed over his head as he ducked. He stumbled to the side, came up awkwardly clutching the sword.

The thing advanced on him, slender claws opening and closing greedily.

Attacking from behind had been difficult enough. From the front it looked impossible. Each of the limbs was longer than his blade, and for all its size, the creature was fast. He barely managed to knock aside one claw when another darted out, snatching the sword from his grip, tossing it into the still water with a splash.

Akiil stumbled back, barely keeping his feet. The passage to the stairwell loomed directly behind him. He'd spent half his life running up and down the mountains around the monastery. If he managed to get two steps on the thing, he might be able to beat it to the *kenta*. If he fled, it might well turn back to finish off the injured woman while he made good his escape.

He glanced past the monstrous insect to find her closing on it from behind. She'd kept hold of her sword somehow—she clearly understood how to use it far better than he did—but her steps were weaving and uneven, as though she were about to collapse. This was the time to run, but he did not run. Instead, he dropped to his knees. If he was going to distract the monster, there was no point in doing so halfway. He spread his arms wide, tilted his head back, offering up his chest and throat. The creature advanced, and for a moment he thought he'd gambled wrong, that it was about to plunge one of those serrated claws through his neck, tear out his trachea, and devour him.

Just as it loomed above, however, he heard the sick crunch of steel striking home. The thing writhed, vomited a stream of ichor onto the stone floor. It hissed and steamed, tried to wrench itself around to face its attacker, but the woman moved with it, driving the blade deeper, then deeper still. With a high whining wail, the creature fell, carapace crunching against the stone floor. The front legs spasmed, reached for Akiil, then curled in on themselves. Those fernlike antennae jerked over and over. Dark, foul-smelling ooze drooled from between razor teeth. The red light pulsing in the abdomen faded, then failed entirely, tossing the whole scene back into cool blue light.

Shaking, careful to avoid the pool of vomit, Akiil picked himself up, then circled the monster's carcass to where the woman lay panting on her back. Blood flooded the lower half of her jerkin, stained her pants all the way down her left leg. Her breath rattled in her chest, wet and ragged. She tried to rise, then fell back, the sword wrenched from her grasp, blade still lodged in the creature's shell.

Akiil hesitated, then glanced back toward the doorway. The fight had been loud. If someone else was inside the fortress—or some*thing* else—it might have heard. Even as he stood there, it might be coming. The smart thing to do was to run, to get free.

The smart thing, he thought grimly, *would have been not to come in the first place.*

After listening for a dozen heartbeats, he turned away from the silence, back toward the woman sprawled across the stone.

She looked up at him with dark eyes. There was no terror in that gaze, no rage or defiance, no obvious response at all to her body's ravages. Even up close, it was impossible to put an age to her. At first glance, she appeared young—no sign of gray in her black hair, skin unlined, unweathered—and yet there was something about her, some quality to which he couldn't put a name, that whispered age. She fixed him with a stare, tried to speak, choked, spat up blood, then tried again.

"Shin monk," she managed.

He raised his brows. "How did you know?"

"Robe." She nodded toward him weakly. "Eyes."

"Who are you?"

"Doesn't matter. Take the seed." She struggled to raise her hand, to unclench bloody fingers. Cradled in her palm was . . . something. Something dark, the diameter of a walnut, but nothing like a walnut. It looked like a hole punched out of the world straight into the night sky. Akiil could see stars spangling the far side, dozens of them sparkling in the small space. Vertigo washed over him. He closed his eyes, drew in a steady breath, then another. The feeling dissipated.

When he opened his eyes again, the woman tipped her hand, and he realized the thing he'd been looking at—the seed, she'd called it—wasn't a hole at all, but an object, like a smooth but irregular stone. She gave it a weak toss. He caught it reflexively before it hit the floor.

"What is it?" he asked, Gelta Yuel's cautions echoing in his ears.

"A weapon . . ." she replied, voice reed-thin. "A destroyer . . . The most dangerous . . . The Nevariim . . ."

A hacking cough choked off her words. She turned her head, vomited blood onto the stone, spat, tried to speak, but managed only a groan.

"What kind of weapon?" he asked, leaning closer.

He could smell the blood on her, the sweat, and something else, too, something wrong and awful, like rot.

"Winter . . ." she murmured. "Wait for winter . . ."

"Why? What happens in winter?"

She stared at him as though lost. Then her gaze swam back into focus. "Where . . . did you come from?"

He hesitated, unsure what to say, whether to lie or tell her the truth.

"Annur?" she demanded. A new urgency flooded her voice. "You are from . . . Annur?"

"I work for the Emperor," he replied at last.

"No," she whispered, gazing past him, as though she could see the whole edifice of the Dawn Palace looming behind him.

"Yes."

"She cannot . . ." The woman trailed off, hacked a glob of blood across the floor, spat to clear her mouth, then tried again. "You *cannot* give it to her."

He nodded, uncertain.

Not good enough, evidently. The woman struggled to one elbow, seized him by the front of his robe, dragged his face close enough that he could see the blood vessels ruptured across the whites of her eyes.

"Hide it," she whispered. "Keep it hidden. If the Emperor knows . . ." She choked on something deep in her throat, opened her mouth, gagged. "Over . . ." she gurgled.

"What?" he demanded. "If the Emperor knows, *what's* over?"

The woman stared at him as though baffled. "Everything," she whispered. "Everything."

Her grip on his robe slipped. She fell back, head thudding back against the floor, eyes blank and staring. He put a finger against her neck, but her pulse was gone. Akiil studied her face, carved the *saama'an* into his mind.

She was Csestriim. Like the object he cradled in his hand, the truth was both impossible and undeniable.

According to Adare, for centuries the Malkeenian emperors had effectively blocked the few surviving Csestriim from using the *kenta*. With the empire in flames, however, and no one on the throne capable of passing through the gates, the Csestriim would be free to travel them once more. The question was *why*?

He turned his attention to the stone—the *seed,* the woman had called it—rolling it in his hand. It was made of some substance that looked like coal and felt like water. Even holding it, his mind bucked at the thought that it was a real thing with solidity and weight. It looked like a lack, an absence. Only when he closed his fingers, blotted out the sight of it, did it feel real.

A weapon . . . A destroyer . . .

If the Emperor knows, everything is over. . . .

The words were cool razor dragged down his spine.

He hesitated, then tucked the object into a pouch hidden inside the stitching of his robe. It nestled beside the tooth and the necklace. Straightening, he tested the fabric between his fingers. It had been thick and rough enough to hide the dagger on his last trip, and these items were so much smaller. Adare hadn't patted him down yet; she shouldn't have any reason to start now. She would, however, be expecting him back, and soon. The longer he remained, the more questions she would ask, and he had no answers to any questions.

The dead woman, the dead Csestriim, gazed into the darkness. As a child, he'd been able to rifle a body in less than a dozen heartbeats. It didn't take him much longer now. All he found, however, were a belt knife—ordinary steel, not the strange metal of the sword—and what looked like a bird's bone on a leather thong around her neck. It seemed strange for a creature with no emotion to wear jewelry or adornment, but this wasn't the time to consider it. With a sharp tug, he ripped the thong free, tucked it into the secret pocket alongside everything else.

He briefly considered doing something with her body, but what was there to do? He couldn't bury her, couldn't burn her. He might have rolled her into the lake, but he'd seen too many sodden, half-rotten bodies in the canals of the Quarter. And anyway, what was the point? She must have walked the world for thousands of years, thousands upon thousands, piling up experiences, thoughts, memories. The monstrous insect had hacked all of that out of her with its claws. What was left of the immortal creature was what would be left of any of them in the end—bone and blood, sightless eyes, an unbeating heart, everything else vanished, evaporated, stolen, drained away, a whole life reduced to rotting meat between one breath and the next.

53

The wound burned.

The teeth of the *gabhya* hadn't severed the tendon or the muscle, which, though torn, bore up readily enough under Gwenna's weight. The blood had already clotted to scab, and by the morning following the fight she could feel the flesh stitching itself back together. It should have been reassuring—her body healing itself the way it always had. Except for that ice-hot burning.

Gwenna studied the wound, flexed her ankle, stretched the injured muscle.

Vague predawn light washed the sky above the peaks to the east, but the ravine they'd been ascending remained plunged in chilly darkness. The others still slept wrapped in their blankets: Pattick curled in on himself, one arm between his knees like a small child; Bhuma Dhar slumped in a corner between two boulders; Cho Lu huddled beneath a shelf of stone; Kiel sitting cross-legged in that unnerving way he had, breathing slowly, steadily; Rat a tangle of skinny limbs half a pace away.

Gwenna had pushed them hard after the battle with the *gabhya,* driving them up the defile toward the safety of Kiel's promised fortress. Jonon was dead. Chent and Lurie were dead. The hideous creature that had been preying upon them for weeks was dead, and yet something inside her refused to let them rest. Even if they didn't reach the fortress, the more distance they put between themselves and the diseased forest below, the safer they'd be. That, at least, was what she'd told herself. Studying the flaming, tender flesh of the *gabhya* bite, however, a sick worry settled in her gut. What if she was running from the wrong thing? What if she'd carried the danger along with them?

"It is infected."

Gwenna jerked her head up to find Kiel—still cross-legged, still motionless—gazing at her with those gray, illegible eyes.

"Kettral don't usually get infections."

"This is not a normal infection."

The words were a cold hand gripping her by the throat. For a few moments she didn't move, didn't breathe, as though if she remained perfectly still the danger might pass her by.

"How bad?" she asked finally.

"Bad."

"Is it going to . . ." She shied away from the words, then forced herself to say them. "Is it going to drive me mad? Turn me into . . . whatever Jonon became?"

"In time."

"How *much* time?"

"You are stronger than the admiral, more stubborn."

"I'm also not stupid. Poison kills strong people, too. And stubborn people."

"The etiology of the sickness is variable, inconsistent."

"Which means?"

"Blood is a more direct vector than water. The change may take a day. Two. Likely no more than three." He cocked his head to the side. "How do you feel now?"

She stared at the historian for a moment, then studied the scabbed-over skin, then turned her attention inward, to the tangled mess of her own thought and feeling. She found none of the euphoria she remembered from the jungle, none of the feverish heat or hunger. But *there,* like a dark vine twisting around all the rest—something strange, foreign, wrong.

"It's inside me," she said quietly.

He nodded.

"But there's a . . . a cure, right? Up at the fortress? Some Csestriim potion that can fix it?"

"It is not a potion, and it is not a cure. If the artifact is there, however, it can hold the sickness at bay."

She dragged herself abruptly to her feet. "Then let's get moving."

With the sudden motion a wave of dizziness washed over her, followed by nausea, then a stab of hunger. For a moment, the scents of the others eclipsed all thought—the dried sweat on their skin, the reek of unwashed flesh, the blood crusted over their wounds. . . .

"The hunger is not you," Kiel said quietly.

Gwenna blinked, turned her attention back to the historian, nodded.

"You must hold it at bay until we reach the pass, the fortress."

"Jonon didn't."

"Jonon didn't try. He chose the sickness. He embraced it."

"So . . ." She trailed off. "What am I supposed to do?" Her voice sounded like ash.

"You already know the answer to that question."

"Fight," she said wearily. "Keep fighting."

Kiel nodded.

"Is that ever *not* going to be the answer?"

"Perhaps someday."

"But not today."

"No," the historian replied. "Not today."

"Come on," Gwenna said, hoisting Rat up onto her shoulders. "Stop arguing and ride on my shoulders."

"Can walk," Rat protested, but that was just the last dregs of the girl's stubbornness talking. She'd been stumbling most of the afternoon, tripping over stones, muttering what must have been curses in her own language.

"You can walk later," Gwenna said, shifting the weight, starting up the slope once more.

It should have felt terrible. The ravine had only grown steeper. Massive boulders choked the defile—some the size of dogs, horses, hay carts—forcing Gwenna and the others to scramble rather than hike. Rat weighed as much as a bushel of grain, and Gwenna had her own pack to deal with as well. They were almost out of food, but the kettral eggs were heavier than they looked, each one like a smooth granite stone. The added burden should have turned every step into agony, but she had grown stronger since the bite of the *gabhya*. Her body hungered to hurl itself against the world. She was still aware, in a vague way, that her lower back ached, that her thighs and calves throbbed with every step, that the thin, frigid mountain air left her gasping like a fish plucked from the river, but she found herself enjoying that pain, seeking it out, devouring it.

Better to devour that than something else. Better attacking her own exhaustion than the people around her.

The burning in her calf had subsided, dispersing through her body until she felt it everywhere, an almost-itch just beneath the skin. It reminded her of a terrible rash she'd had as a child. For almost a week she'd scratched herself raw, bloody, despite the admonitions of her brothers, had soaked her sheets in blood, and sweat, and pus. This was like that, except there was nothing to scratch. Her skin looked normal—tan after so many days in the sun, freckled. Nothing to indicate the infection coursing beneath.

Fight it, Kiel said, but she had no idea how to fight it, and so she just kept doing what she knew how to do: moving forward, moving up, carrying Rat on her back, laboring on, pouring herself into the work, as though by climbing she might drag herself out of the sickness, the madness, the past.

Kiel's voice broke into her thoughts.

"It was here."

She stopped, scrubbed the sweat from her brow with one hand, steadied herself against the side of the canyon, looked up.

She'd been so intent on her footing that she hadn't realized that they'd climbed nearly to the saddle. The ground had begun to level off. Another few hundred paces and they'd be up and over the mountain pass, over the spine of the continent.

There was no fortress.

Despair stabbed through her. She'd never really expected to find some Csestriim ruin. Too much time had passed. Too many millennia. And yet, the historian had seemed so confident. He'd been right so many times before that she'd dared to hope. . . .

She slipped Rat roughly from her shoulders, rounded on Kiel.

"Where is it?" she hissed.

She was vaguely aware of the others eyeing her warily. She'd spoken to none of them about the bite, about the infection consuming her, but they'd been there for the fight, they could see the blood bathing her ankle.

"Where is the cure?" she demanded once more.

Pattick's face was a mask of confusion. Cho Lu had dropped back, the way one might in front of a rabid dog. Everything about their postures screamed concern. Despite the breeze, the mountain air stank with their newly kindled fear.

"Gwenna Sharpe?" Rat asked.

"You are sick," Dhar said, his weathered face grave. "The bite of the *gabhya*."

She strangled the impulse to lash out at him, to cut him down before he could warn the others.

"Yes."

Pattick staggered back half a step, as though he'd been struck.

"There may be a remedy inside the fortress," Kiel interjected quietly.

Gwenna turned in a slow circle, her arms outstretched. To either side of the canyon the stone walls climbed up and up in sweeps of white-gray limestone smoothed by the weather and water, soaring to peaks hundreds of paces above their heads. A formidable spot for a fortress. A dozen good soldiers would have been able to hold a wall built across the narrow gorge. If anyone had thought to build a wall. Which they had not.

"No fortress," Bhuma Dhar said, frowning through his mustache.

"Could be the wrong pass," Cho Lu suggested. He had his hand on his sword.

The posture made Gwenna itch. For a moment she closed her eyes, listened to the blood throbbing in the soldier's veins. When she opened them, she stared for a while at the artery just beneath the dirty curve of his neck. Did he actually think he could fight her? She half choked on a laugh.

"You need to go," she whispered. "All of you."

"Go where?" Pattick asked. He pointed back the way they had come. "There's a storm rolling up on us."

She'd been so focused on herself that she hadn't noticed the clouds piling up the canyon below.

"I don't give a limp fuck *where,*" she snarled. "But you need to get away from me."

"No," Rat declared, taking her by the hand.

Gwenna ripped free of the girl's grip. "Don't touch me." A shudder ran through her, awful and delicious. With an effort of will she harnessed her rage, forced herself to speak slowly, enunciating the words. "Do not touch me."

Cho Lu put a protective arm around Rat's shoulders, but the girl shook him off. Tears stood in her eyes.

"Gwenna. Sharpe."

"Here," Kiel said.

Gwenna spun to find him standing at the canyon wall, his palm pressed to the stone. After a moment, he shifted his hand a few inches, nodded, then closed his eyes and began to sing.

It sounded like a song, at least, until Gwenna realized it was just a single note, low and wide, held far longer than she would have thought possible, rasping over the rock, echoing back off the canyon walls. Then, just when she thought he must be about to run out of breath, he laid another note atop the first. She stared. She'd never heard anyone sing two notes at the same time, but Kiel was already adding a third, high and strange, well above the other two. The chord stretched on and on, grating against the sky and stone, longer than any breath Gwenna had ever held.

And then, with the satisfying click of something falling neatly into place, a section of stone swung open on silent hinges.

Pattick recoiled, sketched the circle of the Annurian sun with one hand while he fumbled for his blade with the other. "You're a leach."

Kiel shook his head. "No."

"That's some kind of kenning," the legionary insisted. "I saw it."

"Not magic," the historian replied. "Technology." He gestured.

The door was thick as Gwenna's arm was long, hung from hinges that seemed too slight to support its weight. They gleamed like just-polished silver. A complex mechanism—all gears and rods—was built into the door's back.

"It is a harmonic lock," Kiel said.

Cho Lu stared into the darkened doorway. "Which means what?"

"It responds to a very specific set of frequencies. Notes."

Bhuma Dhar studied him. "How do you know these things?"

Kiel smiled. "It is a historian's business to know."

Hope lurched to its feet in Gwenna's heart, a sick animal stumbling dumbly forward.

She ran a hand over the inside of the doorway. She'd studied a lot of masonry in her life—a big part of blowing things up involved understanding how they'd been made in the first place. She'd gone over towers and turrets, curtain walls and keeps, bridges and buttresses everywhere from Freeport to the Waist, but she'd never encountered work like this. The cut stone was smooth as glass, beveled to fit flush with the frame. As rock went, limestone was soft. After ten thousand years there should have been some erosion where water seeped into the crack, staining where it ate away at the minerals. The door and its frame, however, might have been cut by a jeweler only the day before.

She gazed up at the cliff towering above them.

"The mountain *is* the fortress."

Kiel nodded.

"Why?" Dhar asked.

"It was once a place of learning, then, later, a bulwark against great danger."

"Yeah," Gwenna said. "Well. I guess that didn't work out."

"Why do you guess that?"

A vision of the Csestriim swept through her, bodies shattered across the rock of the pass, broken open, ropes of intestine gleaming in the sunlight. . . .

"Because everyone who built it is dead."

Cho Lu peered into the darkness of the narrow passageway. "How do we know there's nothing in there?"

"As Commander Sharpe observed, the inhabitants of this place died long, long ago," Kiel replied.

"Yeah, but I mean, *new* inhabitants. More stuff with too many faces and not enough eyes."

The historian gestured to the lock. "Unless the *gabbya* have learned to sing, it should be safe enough."

"Safe enough." Bhuma Dhar frowned. "This is a phrase I have come to distrust."

As they moved down the corridor, Gwenna imagined the weight of the mountain pressing down from above, squeezing, crushing. Her breath felt heavy in her lungs. She could hear the others half panting, still winded from the long climb up the mountain.

This is a place where people die.

The thought didn't feel like her own, but no one had spoken.

After maybe a dozen paces, the passage opened into a large, circular room, domed, maybe a dozen paces across. She had expected darkness inside, an absolute tomb-blackness. Instead, she found the air suffused with a cool, weak, watery light. Motes of dust floated silent and weightless in the chill space. It felt almost as though she'd stepped underwater. It took her a few moments to locate the source of the light: glowing stones, each one a pace across, set into the ceiling of the antechamber in which they stood.

"This *has* to be a kenning," Pattick murmured, following her gaze.

"Just daylight," Kiel replied, "filtered and focused from high above through lenses and shafts of something like glass."

"Something like glass," Dhar repeated quietly.

Gwenna squinted, tried to imagine the artificial veins built into the heart of the mountain, the engineering that would require. The science. The patience.

"How the fuck did we ever defeat them?" she muttered.

"The Csestriim?" Pattick asked.

Kiel stared up into the blue-gray light. "That," he replied after a long pause, "is one of the great questions of history."

The soldier followed the historian's gaze. "This is from those wars?" Awe hushed his voice. "From the wars between the humans and the Csestriim?"

"It is older. Far older."

"If it wasn't built to fight humans, then what?"

"Initially it was not built for fighting at all."

Pattick shook his head. "Then why the hidden door? Why carve it into a *mountain*?"

"You have been hunting?" Kiel asked.

"We used to go for ducks. Take them on the wing with short bows."

"Did you hunt from a blind?"

Pattick nodded. "My sister and brother built one at the edge of the marsh. Not much of a thing, just some reeds tacked up over the timber, enough to hide us from . . ." He trailed off, eyes going wide.

"This place was called Oztoc in the Csestriim tongue. It means *the Blind*."

"This is no structure of reeds and timber," Dhar observed. "What were they hunting?"

"*Gabhya?*" Pattick whispered.

Kiel shook his head. "Something a good deal deadlier than *gabhya*. The Csestriim who built the Blind had come here to hunt Nevariim."

Rat half flinched at the word. When Gwenna glanced down, she found the girl's small face twisted into a snarl.

Cho Lu forced a laugh. "Not the same skull-collectors from Rat's hometown."

"I would not have thought so," the historian replied. He shook his head. "And yet . . ."

The words hung there, light as the dust motes. For a few heartbeats no one spoke. Then Gwenna unshouldered her pack.

"The rest of you stay here," she said, moving toward a door in the far wall. The discovery of the Blind had distracted her for a few moments from the fire blazing in her blood, but now that they were inside she could feel it once more, the heat raising blisters in her brain. "The historian and I will go on."

"Here?" Pattick asked, turning in a slow circle. There was no wood for a fire, and no chimney to vent it, but the room was warmish—not frigid, at least—as though the stone itself radiated a faint, unflagging heat. "Should we close the door?"

Outside, the storm was shredding itself through the mountain pass. With the greatest gusts, a few flakes drifted the length of the corridor, landed on the floor, melted.

"No," Gwenna replied, too loudly, too quickly. "That door is your only way out."

She imagined them trapped, scrabbling at the slab of stone while she took them apart piece by piece.

Cho Lu pointed at Kiel. "He knows the tune. He can sing us out whenever we want."

"He can," Bhuma Dhar agreed quietly, his dark eyes on Gwenna, "if he is still alive."

"The door stays open," Gwenna said again.

Pattick looked past her, toward the other side of the chamber, where a second passage bored deeper into the mountain.

"What about *that* doorway?" he asked warily.

"If anything you don't recognize comes through *either* door—"

"We kill it," Cho Lu replied.

She nodded. "I don't care if it looks like a kitten. I don't care if it's the world's meekest mouse. I don't care if it's . . ." She shook her head. "If it comes through that door and it looks wrong, you slaughter the living shit out of it."

The words echoed strangely off the bare stone of the chamber. Pattick shot her a worried glance. Gwenna realized she'd started reaching up for her own blades, as though the time for slaughter had already arrived. Slowly, deliberately, she lowered her hands.

The Manjari captain didn't take his eyes from Gwenna. "And if you do not find your cure?"

"Follow your *davi,*" Gwenna ground out grimly.

Pattick shook his head. "*Davi*? What does that mean, follow the *davi*?"

"We will guard both doors," Dhar said, ignoring the legionary, leaning slightly on the word *both*.

"And Rat."

Rat shook her head furiously. "I go with you."

"No."

The girl's face hardened.

"Gwenna Sharpe—"

"We're going to keep her safe," Pattick cut in. At first, Gwenna thought he was talking about Rat. After a moment, however, she realized he had spoken *to* the girl. "We have to stay here," Pattick said, "in order to keep Gwenna safe."

Rat turned to him, suspicion scribbled across her face.

"Here?"

The legionary nodded. "We have to watch her back. Make sure nothing goes in after her. Make sure nothing sneaks up on her."

The girl bit her lip, turned from Gwenna to the open door, then back.

"We will not be very long," Kiel said. "We should return before dusk."

"Return," Rat said.

Gwenna smoothed her hair. "It will be all right."

Rat swatted the hand away. "Nothing is all right." She pointed a skinny, filthy finger directly at Gwenna's chest. "*Return.*"

"You have a job to do," Gwenna said. "You watch the doors. Can you do that?"

Rat straightened, put a hand on her knife, nodded gravely. "Something comes through, kill it to shit."

"Kill it to shit," Gwenna agreed.

✝

Csestriim or not, the layout of the fortress was simple. A short passage led from the antechamber to a spiral staircase, which wound up and up through the stone, a hundred paces, then two with no landings or doorways. It felt like trudging up out of the bottom of a very deep well, only there was no light at the top, no air, no freedom, no apparent end of any kind.

As they climbed, Gwenna wrestled with the poison inside her.

It was like the sickness back in the jungle—the same eagerness, the same hunger, the same feeling that the world wasn't quite real—but worse. Where the other had seeped into her gradually over the course of days, drifting in with every breath, soaking her skin with each touch, this coursed through her like fire, devouring her bones, her blood, the fevered workings of her brain.

Fight, she told herself. *Keep fighting.*

The words had seemed sane when Kiel first spoke them, outside, under the wide bowl of the sky. In the cramped space of the stairwell, however, she began to forget what she was supposed to be fighting. There were people below. She could still hear their voices, echoing faintly off the stone. They claimed to be her friends, but people claimed all kinds of things. There were four of them, all armed, but none of them were Kettral, none of them were . . . whatever she was becoming.

She pictured them one at a time.

Cho Lu was strong, fast, but reckless. Pattick would hesitate at the wrong moment. Dhar was old. Rat just a child . . .

The girl's face filled her mind—wide eyes, bared teeth, riot of filthy hair.

The vision dragged her momentarily back to herself.

"You have to kill me," she said quietly.

Kiel didn't pause in his ascent.

She could feel the sweat bathing her face, feel herself shaking as though with fever. Her hands had ached first for her blades, then to take the historian's throat, to squeeze it until his lips purpled and eyes bulged, until he stopped breathing.

"If we don't find it," she rasped. "If the cure's not here, you have to kill me."

He nodded. "I will do what needs doing."

She seized him by the shoulder. She hadn't meant to do that. Slowly, painfully, she loosened her fingers. "You don't understand. If you don't kill me soon, you won't be *able* to kill me."

"I do understand," the historian replied. He gestured up the stairs. "It is not far now."

They reached a landing after what seemed like an age.

Kiel sang their way through a second door—new notes this time, but the same, strange, tripartite structure, the same breath that seemed to extend beyond all mortal possibility.

The corridor beyond was wider than the one far below, and opened on either side into rooms. Gwenna slipped her belt knife free of its sheath, then
glanced over at the historian. He nodded, hefted his spear, and side by side
they proceeded down the passageway.

When they reached the first door—gleaming metal, bright as new-polished
steel—Gwenna paused just outside, back to the wall.

"Not here," Kiel murmured, pointing down the passage. "Farther on."

She hesitated. The smart move would be to clear the rooms as they passed
them, to make sure nothing was lurking inside, waiting to strike them from
behind. The only smells, though—aside from the stone and something that
might have been polished steel—were her and Kiel. All she heard were their
two hearts, his slow, measured, hers hammering out a mad, galloping beat.
Whatever might be lying in wait, it wasn't as dangerous as the thing she was
becoming.

They passed five more doors, all the same bright metal, all closed and windowless. It felt like exploring a prison, only prisons tended to be darker,
damper, filled with rust and filth. This place—the Blind, Kiel had called it—
was perfectly empty, scrupulously clean, as though someone had swept and
dusted and polished the long corridor that very morning. The same silver-blue
light filtered down through the not-glass panes set into the ceiling above, illuminating the hallway. It should have been a relief, not having to carry torches
or jump at every shadow. Instead, Gwenna found herself baring her teeth,
overgripping her sword.

Finally Kiel paused before another door, slid his fingers into a gearlike
mechanism set flush into the metal.

"A lock?" she asked.

He nodded, turning it slowly. There was a sound of metal sliding over stone,
then a faint puff of air. The door swung fractionally out.

She took a deep, ragged breath. "All right."

He nodded. "All right."

Sword in one hand, belt knife in the other, she slipped into the room.

Her first thought, exploding like a starshatter in her mind, was that she'd
been wrong. Wrong about what she'd smelled. Wrong about what she'd heard.
Wrong in her assessment of the Blind's security. The place wasn't empty at all.
It wasn't safe. It was crawling with spiderlike horrors. They crouched on the
rows of gleaming metal tables, their slender, awfully jointed arms as long as
her own. Some looked ready to spring. Others seemed to be reaching for her
already, legs tipped with razor claws.

She retreated a step, blades raised, blood blazing in her veins. Instead of
giving chase, however, they remained perched there, motionless, as though

frozen in the moment of their unfolding. And then, a moment later, she saw that they weren't *gabhya* at all. The long articulated legs weren't made of chitin, but steel—or whatever passed for steel inside the Blind—and they weren't sitting atop those shining tables, they were a *part* of them, each arm curling up from beneath the flat surface.

"They are harmless," Kiel said, stepping into the room behind her. "Just old tools."

They didn't look old and they sure as shit didn't look like any tools she'd ever seen, although some of the arms were tipped with knives, others with what looked to be pliers or pins or lenses.

"Tools for what?" Gwenna growled, trying to calm her heart's mad gallop as she stared.

The tables were all bolted to the floor, each about waist-height and large enough for a very tall man to lie down comfortably on top. Comfortably, that was, provided the tall man in question didn't mind lying on cold metal.

"For research," the historian replied.

He crossed to a wall of glass-and-steel cabinets, shelves, drawers. Some of those shelves were empty, others held delicate vessels of strange shapes, too small to bother drinking from. More tools hung from rows of hooks—shears, razors, metal rules, incremental markings scribed on their surface.

Kiel ignored it all. Instead, he flipped the latch of a cabinet with gnarled fingers. More drawers, each one just a few fingers deep, stood inside. They whispered as he pulled them out, then replaced them, one after the next. Gwenna caught a glimpse of a bundle of something that looked like silk or muslin; some feathered instrument, or perhaps an actual feather; a pair of golden frames, each as large as her hand; more lenses; a slender glass tube, closed on both ends, with a silver liquid flashing inside. She recognized none of it. The strangeness made her wary, then angry.

Trembling with the effort, she placed her sword and knife on one of the metal tables, then stepped carefully away. She didn't want to be holding them when the full weight of her rage swept over her.

Kiel's voice broke into her thoughts. "Here," he said, lifting something from the lowest drawer.

She squinted. "A ring?"

He nodded, then tossed it to her.

Her hand snatched it reflexively from the air. It was cold, freezing cold, like a shard of ice carved from a glacier. The cold drained into her fingers, spread through her palm. She expected numbness to come with it, but there was no numbness, only a deep bleeding ache.

"Put it on."

"*This* is the cure?" she asked, studying the ring. It was black, lacquer-smooth, twisted in a way that hurt the brain to look at, as though it had too many sides, too many curves.

Half of her didn't *want* a cure. Maybe more than half.

"For Rat's sake," the historian said quietly, "put it on."

Gwenna slid it over the middle finger of her left hand.

Then she collapsed.

In a vague, distant way, she could feel the stone floor pressed against her cheek, her hair in her face, the edge of her belt digging into her side. Eclipsing those sensations, however, blotting them out almost entirely, was the polar cold sweeping through her flesh, pouring through her veins, crashing like a great wave into the poison's fire. That fire blazed at the touch, flared into perfect, excruciating pain. Screams flooded her ears, furious, horrible screams that she recognized only after a very long time as her own. She tried to writhe free, to escape, but the violence was inside her, a war between the poison of the *gabhya* and the awful cold of the Csestriim ring.

A vision swept over her. She was standing on a high mountain, thigh-deep in snow. Wind carved into her skin, but she was standing inside a fire, a fire high as any tower. The roar of it filled her ears. She could feel her skin melting, her eyes turning to slag in their sockets as her bones cracked with the cold. She was dying, that much was obvious, but whether it was the fire killing her or the ice, she couldn't say. The world dropped away in cliffs on every side. There was nowhere to flee, nothing to do but feel her frozen flesh slough off, feel all the strong bones of her body turn to ice, listen to the wind keening across the sky, stare blindly into the heart of her own annihilation. It seemed the battle between ice and fire would last forever, but slowly, *slowly* the flames flickered, guttered, fell, then went out.

She stood alone, naked, on the mountain's top.

The ice in her veins faded from a razor purity to a deep, awful ache.

She opened her eyes. Kiel knelt beside her, studying her with that gray gaze.

"That was a near thing," he said, putting a hand on her shoulder.

"This . . ." she began, trailed off shuddering, then tried again. "This is supposed to be a fucking *cure*?"

He shook his head. "There is no cure for the poison inside you. Think of this as . . . a counterweight."

She stared at him a moment, then let her head drop back against the stone. "I have no idea what that means."

"It balances the toxin."

"It fucking *hurts*."

He nodded.

"When does that part stop?"

"Never."

She stared at the gray stone of the ceiling, the perfect angles, the light draining down through the Csestriim substance that wasn't glass.

"Never," she repeated. Her voice sounded distant, dull.

"There is no driving out the poison of the *gabhya*'s bite. It is only with great force that the *matzcel* holds it at bay."

Gwenna raised her hand weakly, studied the ring. The black had shifted to deep, shadowy red, but it still looked . . . *wrong*.

"The *matzcel*? You couldn't just call it a ring?"

"It is not a ring, not any more than a mask is a face."

"A face is alive."

"As is the *matzcel,* at least in a manner of speaking. The poison inside you will shift and change. This"—he touched the ring with a single, gnarled finger—"will change with it. It will protect you."

"If it's protecting me, why does it hurt so much?"

Her body felt carved out, her limbs unstrung.

"A violence is unfolding inside you. A war. All wars have a cost." The historian studied her. "Can you bear it?"

She shoved herself up to her elbows, then rose slowly to her feet. Her body hurt, but not with the pain of any actual injury. Gingerly, she tested her range of motion—uncompromised. The truth was, she'd had worse after a nasty training session, but that pain had always been temporary. . . .

"It never goes away?" she asked.

"It will ebb and flood. Some days will be better than others, but no. As long as you wear that ring, the pain will be with you."

"And if I take it off?"

He met her gaze without responding.

She straightened her back, cracked her knuckles, nodded. "I guess I'd better get used to it, then." Before the historian could reply, she turned away, reclaimed her knife and blades from the table.

"What is this place?" she asked.

"It is a laboratory."

The answer twisted something in her gut. Or maybe that was the ring. Or the poison. She had no idea, but looking around, talking—it gave her something to focus on other than the pain.

"What's a laboratory doing inside a fortress? Or a hunter's blind, for that matter?"

"To hunt a creature, to defeat it," Kiel replied, "one must first understand it."

The room was long and wide. To Gwenna's surprise, a bank of windows—angled halfway between vertical and horizontal—lined the wall.

"Didn't see those from outside."

"The angle keeps them invisible from below."

"And what keeps them from breaking? If this place is as old as you say, they should have shattered ten thousand times over."

"Science," Kiel replied vaguely.

She turned her attention back to the nearest table, ran a finger along the smooth metal. It remained utterly unspotted by rust.

"You're telling me these are thousands of years old, too?"

"Many thousands."

"I guess the Csestriim knew how to make better steel than we do."

"They did. But this is not steel."

Beneath the tables hung racks with various glass jars and vials, trays of instruments made for plying, cutting, sawing, all forged of the same unspotted metal. Gwenna picked up a short knife, found it almost feather-light in her fingers.

"I take it the Csestriim posted here weren't just soldiers."

"The youngest of the Csestriim lived thousands of years. None of them devoted all those millennia exclusively to war." He paused. "Almost none."

"So the ones at this fort spent half their time outside hunting Nevariim. And half of it down here—" Understanding settled over her like a cold, leaden coat. "Cutting them apart."

"They had a hunger for knowledge."

Gwenna spun the short knife between her fingers, then set it on the nearest table. Grooves ran down the center and the edges of the surface, as though to drain some liquid through a series of small holes set in the end. "And not," she concluded grimly, "the kind of knowledge you find only in books."

"Where do you think the knowledge in the books comes from?"

"You talk as though you admire them."

The historian didn't respond. Gwenna turned to find him gazing once more across the empty space. His eyes, though not so reflective, were almost the same color as the steel. It wasn't clear what he was looking at, if anything.

"They were an interesting race," he said finally.

"If you think genocidal monsters are interesting."

"All creatures have the capacity to become monsters."

"I suppose we didn't hold back when it was our turn to slaughter them."

"No," the historian replied, still staring at nothing. "We did not."

Gwenna watched him a moment longer through narrowed eyes, then turned away, stomach churning. She crossed to the metal cabinets.

"What else is in here?"

"I'm not certain."

"You knew about the . . ." She glanced down at the ring. "The *matzcel*."

"Deduction. Extrapolation."

"Care to extrapolate some more?"

"There is no need when we can look."

"If I open the others, is something going to leap out at me or explode in my face?"

"Unlikely."

She stepped well to one side anyway, flicked open the nearest latch with the tip of her knife.

The door swung slowly open, hinges so silent they might have been oiled that morning.

Nothing exploded.

Nothing leapt into her face.

Inside, more shelves. More flasks and bottles. More very sharp implements, a truly baffling array of shapes and sizes. She could probably have sold any one of them for a small fortune in an Annurian market. None were longer than her hand. She gazed at the cutting tools a moment, tried to imagine what each was for—flaying back the skin? Sawing through bone?—then turned to the next cabinet.

She opened the door to find a skull staring back at her.

She studied it for a few heartbeats, then reached in, hooked a finger through an eye socket, and lifted it out. She'd spent months learning human anatomy as a cadet. She'd handled dozens of skulls. This one, however, seemed heavier, sturdier. The teeth set into the jaw showed no sign of chipping, decay, or discoloration. They were sharper, too, as though for tearing and rending meat. It didn't feel so much like a real skull as it did the sculpture of a skull, carved from some material whiter, harder, cleaner, *better* than mere bone.

"A model?"

"Nevariim."

She shook her head. "Not a chance. I've handled old bones. They're brown and brittle. This"—she rapped it across the crown with her knife—"is strong as steel."

"As I have told you, the Nevariim looked like us but they were not us. They were faster and stronger. Their frames were made to accommodate that strength." He extended a hand.

Gwenna passed him the skull. The historian held it in his palm a moment, gazing into the eyes, then turned and hurled it against the wall. Gwenna took a step back, half raised a hand to shield her eyes, but instead of shattering, the skull bounced off the stone with a solid, hollow clunk, rebounded, and landed half a dozen paces away, where it spun on a wobbly axis then came slowly to rest.

She picked it up, studied it for cracks, nicks, any sign of damage at all, but the dome remained smooth as marble.

"You want me to believe this is real," she said, looking from the empty eyes to the historian.

"My desires are beside the point. The skull is real, as were the Nevariim. That is why the Csestriim built this place."

In the next chamber, instead of long metal tables, they found a single stone slab at waist-height, the whole surface polished to a high sheen. When bent over the thing, she could see her face reflected—filthy, haggard, sunburned, flecked with blood. She stepped back. Chains were set into the stone every few feet. From some of those hung manacles.

"I guess this is where they took care of the torture."

"The Csestriim did not torture, not in the way humans practice it."

"Then why bother with all the chains?"

"They were trying to understand their foe. They needed to know what would harm the Nevariim, what would slow or confuse them."

"So they experimented on the live ones in here," she said, then jerked a thumb back the way they had come, "and when they experimented a little too hard, they took apart the bodies back there." She shook her head. "This place isn't a blind. It's a slaughterhouse."

"It did not happen the way you think."

Gwenna started to respond, then pulled up short, her thoughts spinning. She turned slowly to stare at the historian.

The truth was a cold blade sliding silently between her ribs.

"You're one of them," she said. "You're Csestriim."

Kiel nodded, as though the revelation were an afterthought.

She moved instantly, instinctively to put space between them, ripped a blade from its sheath, dropped into a low guard. She could kill him. . . .

No, she corrected herself, she *thought* she could kill him. That broken form looked so vulnerable, so unthreatening, but that was because he wanted it to look that way. He'd survived the battle with the Manjari. He'd survived the *hamaksha*. He'd kept pace with Gwenna herself, despite his limp, as she climbed into the mountains. She realized with a shock of horror that, in truth, she had no idea what the immortal historian was capable of.

He looked straight past her unwavering blade into her eyes. "I am not your enemy."

Kill him, whispered a voice inside her. *Kill him now, before it is too late.*

She didn't know if it was wisdom or the sickness talking.

"Not my enemy?" She shifted to the side, tried to create an angle. "Is that what you told the Nevariim before you strapped them to the table?"

"I was never posted here."

"You know a lot about the place, for someone who was never here."

"I know a lot about a lot of things."

He moved with her casually, almost indifferently, but she could see it now, see what she'd missed all the many long weeks they'd spent together—the way he always left himself either a parry or a way to slip free, the way he matched his movements to her own so effortlessly that she'd never even noticed.

"Why did you let me find out?"

He'd *allowed* her to see the truth. That much was obvious. He'd been dangling it in front of her for weeks, even months. If she hadn't been so stupid, so lost in herself, she would have realized it earlier.

"It will be easier to collaborate," he replied, "if you understand who I am, if you understand the source of my knowledge and abilities."

"Then why didn't you tell me? Why didn't *Adare* fucking tell me?"

"It would have destroyed the foundation of your trust."

"I don't *have* any trust in you."

"Yes, you do," the historian replied evenly. "Over the past months I have helped you time and again. Before you learned that I was Csestriim, you learned that I was strong, resourceful, reliable."

"A reliable person wouldn't have spent all this time lying."

"Reliable people lie all the time. None of my omissions endangered you, the ship, the men, or the mission."

Slowly, methodically, she forced herself to go over every statement he'd made, every action taken since the moment they left Annur. So far, the things he'd said about Menkiddoc and the sickness had all turned out to be true. When the Manjari ships attacked, he had been there on deck, loosing his arrows into the fray. During the storm, he'd helped Bhuma Dhar keep the *Daybreak* on course. If he'd wanted to scuttle the mission, he'd had plenty of chances to do so. He'd saved her from the poison of the *gabhya*'s bite.

None of which meant she had to trust him. She'd be insane to consider him an ally. But she had to reckon with the fact that he hadn't behaved as a foe.

"You're not here," she said slowly, "not on this expedition, out of idle, historical curiosity."

"Curiosity is never idle."

"I'll be sure to have that carved on your tombstone."

"People have been waiting for me to die for a very long time."

He seemed to take no satisfaction from the fact.

"Let me put it more directly," she said. "*Why* are you here? Why did you come on this mission? You sure as shit don't care about the Kettral."

He looked at her with those gray eyes. "On the contrary. I care a great deal about the Kettral. But you are correct that the Kettral are not the *only* thing I care about."

"I can't wait for you to elaborate."

"In the histories—"

She cut him off. "History is over. Whatever this place was in the past, it's not anymore."

Kiel regarded her gravely. "History is never over. Sometimes it sleeps for a while, that is all."

"Whatever the fuck that means."

"It means that something is amiss in Menkiddoc."

She stared at him. "No shit."

"Something beyond the sickness. The city we found in the south—it should not have been there. The bodies in Solengo." Kiel shook his head. "The world is out of joint."

"That's the way the world is. You ought to know that; you're the historian. Something's always fucked up somewhere."

"This time, there is a pattern."

"What pattern?"

"I have yet to see all the pieces."

"That's what you're doing here? Looking for more pieces?"

"As well as preparing for various contingencies."

"What contingencies?"

He regarded her with those stone-gray eyes a long time. When he finally replied, his voice was cold as the vault around them. "War." He raised a finger that had been broken and healed Hull knew how many times. "Famine." Another finger. "Plague. Madness. Chaos." When all his fingers were spread before him, he stared at his palm as though he didn't recognize it, then clenched his fist shut. "Annihilation."

54

The morning of the third day of the culling was split in half. To the north, cloud blackened the sky. Lightning stabbed into the delta. Thunder grumbled along the horizon, rivaling the clamor of the gathered crowd. Directly overhead, however, the sun blazed, hot and unyielding. Ruc reached for the water, though he'd been drinking steadily all morning.

His body, like the day itself, felt cloven in two. At the thought of the slaughter to come, his gut had clenched down into a sick, furious fist. After the months of running, lifting, and training, the time had finally come to kill. Kill or end up dead. When he imagined his hand wrapped around the shaft of a spear, imagined burying it in another body, the urge to vomit swamped him. He could see Eira with her huge eyes witnessing his failure. And yet the nausea was not all. Beneath it, like the hot crackle of a summer storm, coursed an almost convulsive eagerness, as though, once the vomiting and regret had run their course, he would be free and clean to pursue his hunting unencumbered.

He took another swig of water, hauled his attention back to the moment, reminded himself that the fight wasn't the end. It was just a passage they needed to go through to reach the true goal: escape.

Monster, Mouse, and Stupid had reacted to the revelation of the plan with a mixture of disbelief and glee.

"This is some stupid fucking shit," Monster cackled. "Stupid, stupid, stupid. Of course I've been running with stupid for a long time—no reason to quit now." She'd narrowed her eyes. "You've got to know it's gonna be tempting, once that door's open, to just keep going without you."

"Going where?" Ruc asked quietly.

She gave an elaborate shrug. "Lots of places to hide in a city the size of Dombâng."

"Is that what you want to do? Spend the rest of your life hiding?" He shook his head. "Getting out of the Arena means nothing. If you want to escape, you need to get out of the city entirely. And to do that, you need me."

Her face soured. "You sure know how to shit on a girl's dreams."

He patted her on the shoulder. "I don't mind you having your dreams. I just want to make sure that Bien, Talal, and I are *in* them."

In the end, the woman had agreed to go through the wall, see if she could pick the storeroom lock, then report back. Whether she'd stick to the agreement was another question altogether, one that—with the fight almost upon them—there was no time left to consider.

Talal was leaning against the wall of the box, gazing out over the sand. After a while, he shook his head.

"Hundreds of people die in this city every day—spider bites, drowning, old age—but still they need to do this."

"Sacrifice," Mouse said with a shrug, then glanced back toward the piss pot and the cracked board behind it.

"A false sacrifice," Bien growled, "to false gods." She had gnawed her fingernail down to the quick; blood filled the nail bed. She stared at it a moment, as though surprised to see it there, then wiped it on her *noc* and turned to Talal. "What's it like, growing up somewhere no one's ever heard of the Three?"

"People are people."

"Whatever the fuck that means," Monster said.

"It means," Talal replied, "that people like watching things die. They come up with different reasons for the killing—for the gods, for the Emperor, for their children, for honor—and they come up with different *ways* to do it—war, slavery, a little light genocide somewhere out at the edge of the empire. . . ." He trailed off, gave a half shake of his head. "The killing, though, is mandatory. There's always killing."

Bien stared at him. "I don't believe that. There has to be a better way."

He turned to her at last. "Sure. But no one *wants* a better way."

He gestured to the thousands of Dombângans filling the Arena. They were hanging from the framing, leaning out over the stands, hammering with their heels on the planks, filling the air with a noise so great it felt like a weight leaning on everything.

Ruc forced himself to look up into the crowd, to peruse the individual faces.

After a moment, he fixed on a man with thinning hair and a boil on his cheek. His brown arms were almost purple to the elbows. A dyer, then. Any other day he'd be at his vats, probably working quietly, coloring cloth, doing his small part to make the world more bright. Now, as he bellowed in the face of his neighbor, spittle flew from his mouth.

A few seats to the right, a little girl, no more than six or seven, had fashioned a doll from sweet-reed husks. It was dressed with rags to look more or less like one of the Worthy—a scrap of net in one hand, a stick standing in for a spear in the other. As he watched, she began to dismember it slowly, deliberately, with obvious glee, tossing the limbs into the people gathered below.

"Eira offers a better way," he said.

The words sounded false, like poorly fired clay, ready to crumble beneath the slightest weight.

Talal met his eyes. "There's no place for Eira in what we have to do today."

Stupid chuckled from beneath the broad brim of his hat. "Just to remind you—you're here to fight, not compose a treatise on the theological underpinning of human ethics."

He gestured toward the pit, where the slaves were carrying the weapons table out onto the sand.

"When do we find out who we're fighting?" Bien asked, turning to Goatface.

"Soon," the trainer replied. "First, the high priestess will . . . favor us with some words."

Monster spat onto the sand. She, however, seemed to be alone in her contempt. As Vang Vo stepped to the rail of the ship high above, a quiet slid over the space, as though simply by standing and showing her face the woman had transformed the raucous mob into something different, something almost holy.

She took a moment to run her eyes over the throng, then spoke.

"Chum."

She paused after that one word. Then, to Ruc's surprise, grinned.

"That's right: chum. Two days ago, a man walked into this arena to spit on our gods. . . ."

She paused as a murmur of disquiet rippled through the crowd, then made a motion with her hand as though she were shooing away a fly.

"He talked and talked and talked about his lord and his army, how strong they were, how terrifying. And then what happened?" Ruc could hear the smile in her voice. "We turned him into chum."

A cheer erupted from the stands, but she raised her hand to quell it.

"His death in the Arena was only the start. That night, I took his body, tossed it in a swallowtail, and paddled out into the delta. I cut him up—first the fingers, then the joints of the wrist, elbow, shoulder. Nothing special. Just like taking apart a pig or a goat or a chicken. Piece by piece, I tossed the meat into the water for the crocs. They came to take communion at my boat and do you know what this fool's master—this First, whoever he is—did to defend the mutilated body?"

She shook her head. "Nothing.

"When I was done, I cleaned my hands and came home, just the way I would after slaughtering an animal.

"That idiot wasn't the first person to deny the Three or taunt our belief. The most powerful empire in the world tried for two hundred years to crush the spirit of Dombâng. It failed. You can bet your last copper coin that anyone else who comes here, to our home, spouting nonsense about submission is going to meet the same fate."

She shook her head once more.

"Dombâng does not submit."

She pointed a finger down into the Arena.

"These Worthy are our reminder. A reminder that our gods are gods of struggle and defiance.

"Whoever the First is, I *hope* he comes, and I hope he comes soon. I look forward to teaching him that the delta is always hungry."

A roar erupted from the crowd. Waves of sound rolled over the hot sand, shook the sky.

Despite himself, Ruc found an obscure pride surging in his own heart.

He'd tried to leave Kem Anh and Hang Loc, tried to forsake their bloody path of struggle and death, and yet they were the closest thing to parents that he had. Beasts, yes, but beautiful beasts, and a part of him bristled at the thought of some foreign tyrant having the nerve to threaten them. He realized to his chagrin that he agreed with Vang Vo; he *wanted* someone to attack the delta, to march an entire army into the reeds. He wanted to be there when the bastards died. Ruc Lakatur Lan Lac, priest of the goddess of love, wanted to take part in the killing.

"Some of the Worthy are going to die today," Vang Vo continued when the noise settled back to silence. "But we don't worship death."

"Pig shit," Bien muttered.

"We worship in these Worthy the traits of the Three themselves: beauty, bravery, skill, strength. It is *this* that makes us great. It is *this* that keeps us free."

Stupid grunted when she was finished. "Eloquent, for a croc wrangler."

"Ex–croc wrangler," Goatface observed. He stood just to their side, shaded, as usual, by his parasol. "Never forget that those who succeed in the Arena are . . . elevated."

Monster spat. "Putting on different clothes doesn't make you a different thing."

She looked like she had something else to say on the matter, but the fight crier was already striding into the pit. Today, the barrel-chested man wore a resplendent purple vest with his black *noc*. When he reached the center of the sand, he held out his arms, spoke in a bellow that had to reach all the way to Drowned Horse Island.

"In the first contest of this day, fighting from the eastern side of the Arena, under the training of Lao Nan: the Worthy known as Ruc Lakatur, Bien Qui Nai, and Talal the Annurian."

Not *Kettral*, Ruc noticed. Vang Vo hadn't revealed that little piece of the truth. Not that it mattered. No one seemed to wonder where Talal had come from—maybe he was a merchant who'd been hiding in an attic, maybe a soldier captured prowling around the far end of the causeway. Whatever the case, at the mention of Annur the crowd went rabid. The stands shook until Ruc thought they might collapse. Directly above and behind Goatface's box, the Arena guards were cursing, holding their spears sideways, using them to shove back the surge of bodies.

Monster clapped Talal on the shoulder. "They *really* fucking hate you," she said cheerfully.

The soldier nodded. He didn't look particularly tense, but then, he never looked all that tense. Instead of glancing up into the stands he turned to Goatface, held out the iron ball that was still chained to his ankle.

"Do I have to fight with this?"

The trainer tutted. "Of course not. Such an impediment would be . . . anathema to the fair contest of the culling."

He fished inside his shirt for the leather thong, pulled out a key, then knelt to unfasten the cuff around the Kettral's ankle. Talal watched silently, then glanced up to meet Ruc's gaze. A single blow of that iron ball to the back of the trainer's skull, and that would be the end of him. It was amazing that most people survived so long when they were so fragile, so easily broken. For a mad moment, Ruc was tempted to do it himself, snatch the iron from Talal's hands, kill the trainer, and break through the wall behind them. Everyone would see, of course. The guards would be after them in moments, but at least they'd be doing something. They'd die, but they'd die trying to escape rather than out on the hot sand, dancing for the delight of the Dombângan mob.

He ground out the thought as though it were an ember.

He'd watched birds caught in traps, the way they'd flap and flap endlessly, pointlessly, striving against the cruel cord until they were too exhausted to twitch when they were finally lifted from the snare. It was an animal failure not to imagine a moment beyond the present, a failure he could not afford.

He would fight—he, and Bien, and Talal. Monster would go through the wall and find a way out. They would escape from the Arena, but not today.

The voice of the crier cut into his thoughts.

"Fighting from the western side of the Arena, under the training of Goc Lo: Yon To, Nung the Fisher, and Sang the Ox."

Goatface nodded approvingly. "A winnable fight."

"I like to think that all the fights are winnable," Ruc replied.

The trainer shrugged. "Some wins are more . . . conceivable than others."

"I feel like shit," Monster announced to no one in particular.

Ruc winced. The transition was too abrupt. A moment before she'd been laughing and joking. Now she was bending over, her face twisted with a grimace that looked obviously forced, her voice unnaturally loud.

Goatface, however, didn't spare her a glance. He was busy studying Bien.

"You will want to approach this contest with some . . . tact," he suggested.

"You mean stay out of the way so I don't get killed." Her voice sounded already dead.

He spread his hands in a loose apology. "Your skills have waxed more rapidly than the moon. . . ."

"But I'm still terrible."

"It doesn't matter," Talal said. "You're going to have a weapon. Hopefully the spear. You might not be a born warrior, but you can put the point through someone's throat easily enough. They'll have to respect that. One of them will have to square off against you."

Bien was worrying the inside of her cheek. "Which one?"

Ruc gazed out across the sand, tried to take the measure of the other three. He'd seen them all in the yard, of course, although he'd never had the chance to study them closely. The woman—Sang the Ox—was aptly named. She was huge, a hand taller than Ruc himself, with shoulders like her namesake and a broad, flat, angry face. He'd watched her smash through stacks of clay tiles with her bare hands, but she moved slowly, awkwardly.

"If you're facing the Ox . . ." he began.

"I know," Bien growled. "Keep my distance."

"Good advice for all of you," Goatface observed. "People become . . . unpredictable when fighting for their lives. Cowards are filled with desperate bravery. The weak find reservoirs of unexpected strength. . . ."

"The fisher's not weak," Talal said.

Ruc shifted his gaze to Nung. The man was smaller than Sang the Ox— *everyone* was smaller than Sang the Ox—wiry rather than brutish. He had, however, the sinew of someone who'd spent most of his days rowing a boat and tossing nets.

Only the last of the Worthy appeared at all uncertain. Yon To was barely more than a kid, eighteen or nineteen, his face a riot of pimples. He didn't look like the type to have volunteered his life to the worship of his gods, but

Dombâng was a strange place. It wouldn't be the first time a skinny kid had dreamed of glory. He would have signed up when the high holy days were still a year off. He would have imagined the fame, the cheers, the adoration of the crowd, would have convinced himself that a year was enough time to grow into the role. . . . Judging from his expression, he regretted his decision.

"I'll take the boy," Bien said. The words were firm, even bold, but it was easy to note what she didn't say: *I'll fight the boy* or *I'll kill the boy.*

"You take the boy," Monster replied. "I'm going to be taking a *shit*. Fucking sweet-reed last night was crawling with weevils. Stupid," she said, gesturing to Goatface's folded parasol, "a little privacy would be nice."

Goatface glanced over at her, frowning. Ruc's stomach clenched. If the trainer suspected . . .

But evidently he did not suspect.

"It is not the sweet-reed," he replied. "It is your nerves. It is not uncommon for the Arena to have this effect."

"My nerves are just fucking fine, thank you very much," Monster snapped.

Goatface shrugged, then vaulted over the low wall of the box. Again, Ruc was surprised by the man's agility—his body had all the shape of an ill-stuffed sack, but his movements reminded Ruc of a delta cat. He waited for Talal, Ruc, and Bien to join him on the sand, then smiled.

"In a fight like this, you have no greater friends than your own patience and the haste of your foes."

He patted Talal genially on the shoulder, as though the soldier were a small puppy, then headed off toward his perch at the eastern side of the pit.

The two groups of Worthy met in the center of the open space, on opposite sides of the weapons table.

Sang the Ox ran her eyes over them, spat into the sand, shook her head. She kept clenching and unclenching her massive fists, as though her hands itched to hold a weapon. The fisher kept his eyes on the sand. The kid—Yon To—stared at them, but he looked dazed, as though he'd just awoken, as though he didn't quite believe that he was there.

The crier lifted the bronze dagger, held it up for the crowd to see, then laid it flat on the table once more and spun it. For a few heartbeats it turned into a flashing disk of sunlight, then slowed, slowed, and came to rest pointing to the east, to the space between Ruc and Bien.

"The first choice of weapon," the crier said, nodding to them, "is yours."

It was a stroke of good luck, and Bien wasted no time stepping forward to claim the spear.

The fisher grunted, but his face betrayed nothing.

Ruc expected the Ox to claim the dagger and shield. Bigger, stronger warriors could use the heavy bronze disk for both defense and attack. To his surprise, she picked the ring dogs. The bronze hooks looked slender, almost delicate in her broad hands. She swept them, one after the other, in vicious, whistling arcs, then bared her brown teeth in something that might have been a smile.

That left the sickles, the net, the grapple and line, and the shield and dagger. Ruc was tempted by the sickles. He wasn't strong enough to toss the shield around as readily as he'd have liked, and the sickles offered better reach and more speed. But the shield could prove useful, even crucial, especially if the kid was more dangerous than he seemed. Ruc could use the shield to cover both himself and Bien while she thrust from behind or overhead with the spear. He stepped forward, lifted the bronze circle from the table, took up the dagger.

Nung took the net. That was a dangerous development. Most of the Worthy couldn't do much with the knotted rope, but Nung handled it like what he was—a fisher who'd spend a lifetime plying the delta.

Ruc was tempted to ask him why he'd given it up to come here. Boredom? A lust for blood? Some inchoate hunger for power? Whatever the case, the time for asking questions was long past.

The kid claimed the sickles, staring tat them as though he'd never seen then before.

Talal shrugged, took the grapple and line from the table, and the choosing was done.

Half a dozen slaves scuttled in from the pit's perimeter, lifted the heavy table, and carried it off toward the open gate. Bien looked after them longingly, as though tempted to follow. Ruc risked a glance over his shoulder toward Goatface's box. Mouse leaned against the back wall, arms folded across his chest. Stupid chatted with him as he held the parasol obscuring Monster and the wooden bucket. The two men looked surprisingly casual—like old friends chatting at a market. Almost too casual, Ruc thought, given the fight that was about to unfold. He wondered if Monster was through the wall yet. It felt like she had to be, but time was difficult to judge out on the sand. He might have been standing there for half the morning or only a handful of heartbeats.

"To your sides," announced the crier, pointing to opposite walls of the Arena.

"So?" Bien said as they retreated across the open space.

"I can kill them all," Talal said, voice matter-of-fact. "But it'll be over too fast."

Ruc blinked. "You sound pretty confident."

The Kettral just nodded.

Bien was staring at him, her face twisted between amazement and horror. "You say it so casually. *Kill them all.*"

Talal shook his head. "It's never casual, killing a person."

"Casual or not," Ruc said, "you can't do it. Not right away. Like you said—Monster needs time. Which means we need to stall."

"I can keep Sang and the kid away from me," Bien said. "Goatface taught me that much. I'm worried about the net, though."

"The net's a problem," Talal agreed.

"We have the right weapons to draw this out," Ruc said. "Your grapple can hold them at a distance. So can Bien's spear. I'll cover with the shield if the kid throws one of those sickles. We just keep retreating until we see Monster again."

"Won't be popular with the crowd," the soldier pointed out.

"Fuck the crowd," Bien growled. There was fear in her voice, but anger too, in equal measure.

And that exhausted all the time they had for strategy. Up on the ship's deck, a bare-chested man was hammering out a heartbeat on a huge bronze disk. Ruc glanced up to see Goatface on his raised platform. The trainer waved merrily.

The first fight of the third day of the culling had begun.

The Ox stepped forward, still spinning the ring dogs, the fisher and the boy at her shoulders. They moved well together, staying close enough that it would be tough to force a wedge between them, but not so close that they couldn't use their weapons.

It was only when Ruc felt Bien's hand on his shoulder, pulling him back, that he realized he'd stepped forward to meet the attack.

"What about stalling?" she hissed.

He nodded, forced himself to retreat a step, then another. It felt strange. Everything about his bright, wordless childhood had trained him to hunt, not to run. Kem Anh would have snapped at him, swatted him into the water for giving ground before such a shabby collection of mortals, but Kem Anh only ever wanted one thing—the bright, hot blood. Even if she'd had words, the notions of *delay* or *escape* would never have occurred to her.

Even as Ruc stepped back, Talal shifted forward. Unlike Stupid, he didn't whirl the grapple in a circle around his head. Instead, as the other three closed, he hurled it, glittering, toward the ankles of the Ox. *Toward,* Ruc realized, but not exactly *at*. The woman shifted to the side, but the movement wasn't necessary. The grapple thudded into the sand to her right. Talal yanked it back. If he'd landed it a little closer, the hooked bronze would have taken the woman in the back of the leg, tripping her, maybe ripping through the muscle or tendon. As it was, it missed her entirely, whistling back through the empty air.

Talal cursed.

Ruc risked a glance over at him.

The soldier looked worried—furrowed brow, nasty grimace—but when Ruc shifted his perspective to look beneath the skin, to read the language of the body's heat, he found Talal's heart beating slowly, steadily. He might as well not have been fighting at all. He reeled in the grapple, reclaimed it, and took another step back.

The failed attack had the necessary effect. The other three slowed, alert to this new danger. The Ox dropped one of her ring dogs into a kind of low guard, ready to block the grapple when Talal threw it again. Nung moved forward in a wary crouch. The kid followed half a step behind, the sickles held up before him as though they weren't weapons, but some kind of talisman that could ward off danger, even death.

Sang took a cautious step forward. Ruc and the others fell back.

The fight had opened in the middle of a wide, expectant hush, but it didn't take long for the taunts to come. People didn't flock to the Arena for a patient dance of pace and retreat. They came, as Talal had said earlier, because they wanted to see something die. None of the Worthy were obliging. Sang, for all her spitting and scowling, was proving more cautious than Ruc expected, and she seemed to be setting the pace for the others.

Curses fell like rain. Ruc backed up and backed up, one cautious step and then another, until he'd made a half circuit of the pit. He could see Goatface's box now without turning his head. Mouse and Stupid were still there, which was good. Monster was still missing, which wasn't. According to Bien, the storeroom beyond the wall had a single door, and that door would open barely a handsbreadth—just enough to show a few links of the chain and padlock holding it shut. Monster boasted that there was no lock she couldn't pick with the right tools and a little bit of time, but Monster was always boasting. If she failed to open the lock, or worse yet, opened it but decided to escape on her own . . .

The attack came faster than Ruc would have guessed.

One moment the other three was moving forward at the same steady, grudging pace, the next the kid screamed, darted up, hurled one of those glittering sickles.

Ruc moved without thinking, lunging between Bien and the deadly bronze, stretching out with his shield. . . . The great roar of the crowd struck at the same moment as the sickle, the one pounding down from above, the other skittering off the shield's rim to drop into the sand.

Blocking the attack had forced Ruc to bring his left arm, his shield arm, all the way across his body, which meant that he landed sprawled on the ground with his back half turned to the attackers. Out of the corner of his eye he saw Talal throw the grapple, an underhand snap almost too fast to follow. At the same moment, Nung the Fisher attacked. He might have been twice as old as Ruc, but he moved easily, fluidly. That was what a life balancing on the rails of a swallowtail would get you. Balance was balance—in the boat or the pit; speed was speed, spearing fish or men. The net dropped over Ruc's head, then tightened around his neck and shoulder as Nung yanked back on the cinch cord.

His shield hopelessly fouled, Ruc gave himself over to instinct. Instead of trying to pull back against the netting—a move that would only leave him snared and immobile—he surged forward, felt the rope go slack, saw the bronze hook of a ring dog shred the air, managed to slip just inside the swing. The Ox's forearm caught him across the head. The blow almost knocked him down, but it was better than a length of bronze to the skull. The woman swore, tried to shove him back, but Ruc pivoted against her body—she might as well have been a pillar for all the ground she gave—leaning against her as he rolled around to her side, ensnaring her in the net.

With a quick, vicious thrust, he drove the dagger up into her ribs. The shock of the blow stiffened her. She dropped one of the ring dogs. He ground the blade deeper, grimly willing her to collapse. She did not. Instead, with a roar that threatened to dislodge the knife from inside her, she seized the net, twisted it, began to haul.

It was a desperate gambit. In the madness of the moment, she couldn't have known that the cinch line had snagged Ruc around the throat, couldn't have known that he didn't have an arm up blocking it, couldn't have known that by dragging on the rope she was choking him. The Vuo Ton had an expression, though—*Bad luck kills quicker than poison.*

He could feel her straining against the cord, the rough fibers cutting into his neck. His vision dimmed, as though a bank of clouds had slid across the sun. Strength fled his legs. Was that roaring in his ears, or silence? He tore free the dagger—the motion felt slow, as though they were both underwater— then plunged it into her again. Bronze grated on bone; hot blood soaked his hand, his arm, everything. The woman groaned, faltered. The rope around his neck slipped a fraction. Ruc dragged the dagger out, then stabbed her again, then again, searching for a lung, a heart, anything, really, that would make her drop.

At last she shuddered, lost her grasp on the rope, stumbled forward, dragging him with her, and collapsed. Blood flooded his brain once more. The world brightened to sun and screaming. Ruc rolled, pulled the blade free of the body, hacked at the rope still wrapped around him.

A few paces away, the fisher was on his knees, clutching at his neck. He seemed unbloodied, but his face was turning from brown to a sick purple. A crushed throat? Talal rolled to his feet a pace beyond the man. Whatever happened, Nung was finished, gasping out the last of his life into the sand.

Two down . . .

The rope parted beneath the knife, and Ruc yanked himself free, stumbled up to a knee, searched desperately for Bien, found her five paces off, her spear held before her as the kid with his sickle closed in. She lunged—the same lunge Goatface had made them practice ten thousand times. Yon To made an awkward parry. There was an opening, but Bien didn't press home the attack. The boy, Ruc realized, was sobbing. He couldn't hear the sound over the clamor of the mob, but he could see the kid's shoulders shaking, the bronze of the sickle flashing as his hands trembled.

It was over. The boy knew it was over. The only question was how it would finish.

Ruc had just regained his feet when the kid gave a horrible, desperate cry, and lunged at Bien.

As it turned out, Goatface was right. In a real fight, a life-and-death fight, sometimes all you needed were the basics. Yon To came on, and Bien extended her spear, an action so simple, so plain, so utterly unadorned that it was almost boring. The boy ran right onto it. She held him there a moment, her brown eyes wide. The sickle dropped. Yon To peered tearfully at the shaft buried in his gut, reached down to touch it.

"No," the boy said, sobs twisting his face.

Bien tossed aside the shaft of the spear as though she'd found herself holding a snake, then dropped to her knees. "I'm sorry," she gasped. "I'm sorry. Oh sweet Eira, I'm sorry."

"No," the kid said again. "Please . . ."

Whatever he was about to ask for, he didn't get it. Talal, who'd picked up the other sickle on his way across the sand, slid behind him and slit his throat.

It was the kind thing, the merciful thing, the necessary thing, the thing they had trained to do. For a moment, though, all Ruc could see was an Annurian soldier killing a boy who couldn't fight back.

The crowd was frothing.

Bien, on her knees, stared at the body.

"What did we do?" she groaned. "What did we do?"

"We did what we had to," Ruc said.

He had no idea if that was true.

He tried to help her up, but she refused to rise. Her gaze was fixed on Yon To. He looked even younger, dead. Even thinner. What the fuck had he been thinking, joining the Worthy?

A few paces away, the Ox was still struggling to breathe. She had a hand pressed to her side. Blood dribbled from her lips.

Ruc walked over, knelt at her side.

"Done," she managed, turning her head to face him. Her face was ugly, but her eyes were beautiful, brown flecked with green, like the delta at dawn. "Done."

He nodded, wiped her sweaty hair back from her forehead, opened her throat with the knife.

She offered up a great sigh, half breath, half blood, before her beautiful eyes went glassy.

The noise of the crowd fell like a rain, like a storm, like a monsoon that threatened to drown them. For a moment he was twenty years and as many miles away, out in some clearing in the reeds, heart pounding, skin slicked with sweat, body impossibly light. It had been a long time since he'd killed anything other than a snake. Too long . . .

From somewhere, the crier appeared. He stood over the fallen bodies and announced their victory to the Arena, as though anyone with eyes could have missed the slaughter.

By the time Ruc rose from Sang's body, Goatface was striding toward them across the sand, his ugly face split by a wide grin.

"Alive!" he declared, standing on his toes and straining to throw one arm around Talal's shoulders, the other around Bien's. That arm seemed to be the only thing holding her up.

"I won't deny that I felt a few moments of . . . apprehension, even dismay. There is room to improve, but the most important thing is that you are *alive*. The dead, after all, face grave impediments in the bettering of their skills. Come, let's get you back to the box."

The box.

In the final spasm of violence, Ruc had all but forgotten that they'd gone out on the sand not just to fight, not just to survive, but to buy time for Monster. He squinted toward the perimeter of the pit. Mouse was still there, and Stupid. The parasol was still leaning against the wooden wall. Of Monster, there was no sign.

As Goatface started herding the others, Ruc dropped to a knee, pressed a hand against the side of his leg, forced out a curse.

The trainer turned, furrowed his brow.

"Are you wounded?"

"I . . ." Ruc scrambled for something plausible. "No, but I twisted something in my leg. It won't hold my weight."

Talal shrugged free of Goatface's genial embrace.

"I'll help him."

The soldier took his time getting an arm around Ruc, then hoisting him to his feet. Ruc put on a grimace, made a show of testing the leg, winced, ignored the gibes of the crowd. Their derision was far better than what awaited if Monster were discovered on the wrong side of the wall.

"Slowly," Ruc muttered, leaning on Talal as they began to move toward the box.

"Slowly," the soldier agreed.

Goatface and Bien waited until they drew even, then the four of them made their laborious way back toward the wooden box and their waiting fate. The red parasol was large, preposterously so. It was possible, more than possible, that Goatface wouldn't notice anything amiss. He'd think Monster was pissing out her nerves, or puking them up, behind the privacy of the waxed canvas. On the other hand, if he tried to talk to her, if she didn't talk back, he would know something was amiss; one thing about Monster—she *always* talked back.

If it came to it, if the trainer peeked behind the screen and found a hole in the wall and one of his Worthy gone, there would be only moments to silence him.

Ruc glanced at Talal.

There was no way to talk, not without Goatface noticing, but the soldier nodded almost imperceptibly.

They were going to have to kill him.

Not subdue him, as they'd planned. Not under cover of night, as they'd planned. Not with the distraction of another fight unfolding on the sand, as they'd planned. They were going to have to kill him right now, in the bright light of the sun, fresh from their own fight with all eyes on them. It was madness, but there was no alternative. They were going to have to murder the man, then flee through the gap, pray that Monster had forced open a way from inside the warehouse, pray that they could get to the water before the guards caught up.

Goddess . . . Ruc began silently, then let go of the rest.

Murder and flight were no work for Eira. The Three were more likely patrons for the ugly business to come, but he had abandoned them long ago, and anyway, despite the furious faith of Dombâng, Kem Anh and her consort had never been answerers of prayers.

By the time they reached the box, the concern was evident on Mouse's face. Stupid managed to look more relaxed, but he was tapping nervously on the wooden rail.

"I return to you," Goatface announced as he helped Bien over the barrier, "your most intrepid companions."

Stupid made a show of clapping them all on the back as they entered. "Well," he said, "you certainly made it exciting."

"Exciting," Mouse agreed. He licked his lips, then shot a glance at the parasol.

Goatface followed his look. "And yet our dear friend Monster missed all the excitement."

He paused, obviously waiting for the rejoinder, frowned when no response was forthcoming, turned to Stupid.

"She's not taken seriously ill, is she? Two years ago, the yellow sickness struck the yard." He shook his head. "A most . . . macabre development. Monster," he said, crossing to the parasol, "have you been afflicted with any blood in your vomiting?"

Talal shifted behind the trainer. He had no weapon, but he'd killed the fisher out in the pit with nothing more than his fist. Most likely, he'd take the man by the back of the head, smash him once into the wall, and that would be that. When it happened, it would happen fast. Heart hammering inside him, Ruc readied himself. Bien seemed shattered after the fight, distracted by her own violence. He needed to make sure she got through the gap before the others. . . .

"Monster," Goatface said again.

Just to his side, Bien cried out, then doubled over, retching.

The trainer turned as puke splattered up against his boots. For a moment he looked genuinely alarmed, then squatted beside her, trailed a finger through the slime.

"No trace of the sickness," he said, shaking his head. "You wouldn't be the first to . . . abandon your breakfast after a fight. It is your companion that has me worried."

He straightened, turned back to the parasol.

Talal moved forward, face grim. He raised a hand, fingers curling into a fist . . .

. . . then subsided as Monster staggered clear.

"Sweet 'Shael on a fucking stick," she spat, glaring first at Goatface, then at everyone else.

Ruc shot a glance past her. The broken board was back in place, the fracture almost invisible, the wooden bucket set directly in front of it, a slop of piss and vomit in the bottom.

Monster wiped her chin.

"Can't a bitch get a moment of fucking privacy in here without some old bastard wanting to paddle through her puke?" She sounded genuinely incensed.

"The yellow sickness . . ." Goatface began.

"My parents died of the yellow fucking sickness," she spat. "I know what it looks like, and I don't have it."

Talal eased back a step, let go of his fist.

Bien, still kneeling inside the box, closed her eyes.

"So," Monster said, glancing out into the pit. Slaves were dragging away the bodies. "Looks like you fuckers got lucky."

55

Like swimming, and swords, and sneaking around in the dark, pain was central to the life of the Kettral. Gwenna had spent the better part of two decades getting to know its many faces: the hard cramp of a gut sick on its own hunger; the blinding wash of a blow to the head; the burn of blisters; the crazy-making scrape of half-dried cloth after a long swim in salt water; the red-ragged agony of torn-open flesh; the slow explosion after a hard blow to the ribs. Like any soldier worth her blacks, she knew how to face each one, ride it out, keep going until—after a moment, a day, a week—it finally faded.

A pain that never went away, though—that was something new.

As she followed the historian up the spiral stairs, higher and higher into the mountain, she studied the feeling unfolding inside her. It felt like the ache and itch of frozen muscles coming back to life, only her muscles weren't frozen. Despite the strain of the climb, she moved as fluidly as ever, found none of the fumbling numbness she would have expected to accompany the sensation. And yet the pain persisted—hot-cold, throbbing, stitched through every vein, hammered into every bone.

It threatened to overwhelm her. Not the sensation itself—which was tolerable—but the thought that she would never be free of it. If she let herself, she could see a whole life stretched out before her, hundreds of days, thousands, the long, silent nights, the meals, the conversations, the fucking hours shitting in the outhouse—all scribbled with that pain.

One day at a time, she told herself grimly. *One step at a time.*

She forced her attention back to those steps. They'd been climbing since leaving the laboratory. She'd been counting until the pain distracted her.

"A lot of work not to get anywhere," she muttered.

"That is the point," Kiel replied.

She shook her head. "You want to build a defensive staircase, there ought to be some way to defend it. Doors to close. Murder holes. Landings for soldiers to fight from."

"Fighting the Nevariim was a losing proposition. They were faster than the Csestriim, stronger, more durable."

"So the idea was what? Make them climb so many stairs they got bored and went home?"

"The idea was to flood this entire column." He pointed up. "There are vast cisterns above to collect glacial melt. In the event of a breach at the laboratory level or of the lower door, the staircase would be flushed."

Gwenna pulled up short, imagined the sound of water crashing down from above, the weight of it hammering into her, driving her back, smashing her into stone walls, crushing her.

"Not very sporting, were you?"

"The Csestriim?" Kiel shook his head. "No. We were not."

All over again it hit her, the brute fact that this man, this quiet historian with whom she'd shared meals and conversation for month after month was, in fact, immortal, a member of a race that had once tried to wipe out her own.

"Why did you hate the Nevariim so much?"

"We did not hate them. The Csestriim lacked the capacity for hate. Or for love. For any human emotion. Those are the province of the young gods."

"A lot of work," Gwenna said, "wiping out an entire race. Hard to imagine bothering if you didn't hate them at least a little bit."

"It did not begin in that way. In the first centuries those who worked here were interested only in study, in learning." He gazed past her. "Think of a human breeder of horses or dogs."

"But they weren't horses."

"No. As we learned about them, they learned, too. Learned enough to fight back, to make war."

As though it were all so simple—a little study, a little learning, a little war.

"And so you decided to annihilate them?"

"The war with the Nevariim was a war for survival."

"Everyone says that about every war."

"In some cases it is true."

She started to reply, then found she had no words. She herself had killed plenty of people, and for what? In the heart of the Csestriim fortress, the glory of Annur felt dim and distant. She turned away from the historian and began climbing once more.

Gwenna had been in old buildings before—dilapidated castles, crumbling fortresses, some in good repair, others little more than rubble. This place reminded her of none of them. Though it was carved from stone—like every other defensive structure worth the name—something alien pervaded the space. It wasn't until they reached the next landing that she was able to put her finger on the strangeness: all the angles were too perfect, the lines too sharp. The stone looked carved by a razor, not some mason's hammer and chisel. Even the hallways of the Dawn Palace had imperfections, spots of discolored tile, tiny places where the wood had warped or the stone chipped away. There were no imperfections here. There was hardly even any dust.

"Who were the last people to hold this?" she asked.

Kiel shook his head. "The records end with the Csestriim."

"Meaning you're not sure."

"No," he agreed. "I am not."

"Was it ever taken? By the Nevariim?"

"They tried. Several times. Each attack was thrown back."

Gwenna frowned. "If the Csestriim needed a fortress built out of a mountain just to survive, how did they ever win the war?"

At first, the historian didn't reply. He kept climbing, the measured tread of his boots on the stones unbroken, his breathing quick but even. He held his peace so long that she started to wonder if she'd actually spoken the question aloud. There was a new weight to their mutual silence, though, a heaviness that had not been there before, as though the chill air were turning slowly to water. Two more turns of the staircase, and the steps stopped, finally, leveling out into a small room just a few paces across. A gleaming metallic door was set into one wall, but Kiel didn't turn to the door. Instead he looked at Gwenna.

"If you were losing a war," he asked, "losing badly, what would you do?"

She blinked. It wasn't clear whether this was an answer to her question or some new line of conversation altogether.

"Fight harder," she replied, after a pause.

Kiel shook his head. "All creatures have limits, even the Csestriim. After hundreds of years of war, they had reached those limits."

"Fight smarter, then. Change strategy. Shift tactics."

"The best minds had deployed such strategies, only to see them fail."

"Then I guess you put on a good face, kick back the last of the black rum, and get ready to die."

The historian gazed blankly at the wall. "They considered this, considered accepting their own extinction. Some even argued in favor of it."

Gwenna tried to wrap her mind around the idea. She'd fought in wars before, wars for the fate of entire civilizations. The stakes had seemed overwhelming at the time, but those stakes paled beside the survival of an entire people—if you could call the Csestriim people—women and men, young and old, all the living and all that would ever be born.

"Things must have been pretty fucking bleak," she said, shaking her head, "if they were ready to call it quits."

"Some insisted that the alternative was yet bleaker."

"Survival?"

"Obliteration."

"Of the Nevariim."

"Of an entire continent. Maybe an entire world, if the necessary weapon could not be controlled."

Gwenna stared at him, the words echoing in her skull.

The annihilation of an entire continent.

All over again she felt the hungry grass of the southern jungle wrapping around her ankles, heard the awful, human screaming of the bright-plumed birds, smelled the fetid rot of things that should have died under the weight of their own disease but kept moving anyway, scrambling forward on twisted claws, felt the jaws of the *gabbya* sink into the meat of her calf. . . .

"They did this," she whispered. "*You* did this. The Csestriim destroyed Menkiddoc."

Kiel nodded. "And the Nevariim with it."

Back on the Islands, fifth-year cadets took a class on poisons. They learned to mix nightwine into a barrel of red, to smear green-scale toxin on a blade, to foul whole wells with human corpses. Gwenna had hated the class. Blowing someone up was vicious work, but at least the targets she'd been trained to take down were all military—walls, bridges, castles. The poisoning work, on the other hand, seemed focused on villages and civilians. There was something disgusting about polluting an entire river just to break the will of the local population.

The thought of doing the same thing to an entire continent made her sick and furious in equal measures. And tired. Very, very tired.

"Did it work?"

"You saw the results for yourself."

"Did it work on the *Nevariim?*"

He nodded. "They were destroyed. The Csestriim enjoyed another three millennia of dominion over this globe until humanity arrived—humanity and the young gods—to finish the work the Nevariim began."

She shook her head. "If the Nevariim are gone then what was all that horse-shit down south, in Rat's city? Nevariim, you said."

"You grew up on a farm," Kiel replied.

"I grew up on the Qirin Islands, but sure, before that I was a little kid on my father's farm."

"Did you ever struggle with rats?"

"Every few years, when the winter wasn't cold enough to knock their numbers down. We'd spend weeks in the spring killing them."

Kiel raised an eyebrow. "Did you ever kill them all?"

"Of course not . . ." Gwenna paused, stared at him. "The Nevariim weren't rats."

"No. They were far smarter, far stronger, far deadlier than rats."

"You think some survived."

"At this point, I am certain of it."

She shook her head. "How?"

"In any population, there are always a few that are faster than the others, more cunning, more ruthless. These are the ones that live. These are the ones that learn from their mistakes. These are the ones that return eventually—in a month, in a year, in ten thousand years—to plague you."

Gwenna climbed a long time in silence and pain, her thoughts a tangle of twisting thorn.

The Csestriim were killers.

No. That wasn't right. The word was too small. They had destroyed an entire *continent*—every insect, every animal, every tree and blade of grass—to eradicate their foes. According to the historian, they'd been willing to risk blighting the whole world. The historian, who was himself one of the Csestriim.

She started to ask him what side he'd been on, all those thousands of years earlier, when his people debated deploying a weapon that might have ended everything. Before she could frame the words, however, she felt something high in her sinuses, just behind her eyes—a faint itch, the whiff of something that wasn't stone or metal. She took a longer breath, deeper.

"Rot," she murmured grimly.

The historian paused. "My senses are not as keen as yours."

"Like something died in here."

"Let us hope that it is dead."

"I thought you said the *gabhya* couldn't get through the doors."

"I said," he replied, "that it was unlikely."

Gwenna drew her second blade. "Not comforting."

Kiel arched an eyebrow. "Were you looking for comfort?"

She ignored him, closed her eyes, listened hard.

"I don't hear anything. No footsteps, no heartbeats. Are there other ways in than this passage?"

"The conduits for flushing the staircases. And above, far above . . . yes."

"Could something have climbed in?"

"Something capable of climbing several hundred paces of smoothed limestone."

"*Gabhya,*" Gwenna spat.

"Possibly. There are limits to inductive logic. Some things must be seen."

"Meaning you want us to go up there to check if it's a man-slaughtering monster or a batch of dead bodies."

"Can you think of another way?"

"I was hoping for something more from one of the Csestriim than *Let's look at it and see if it tries to kill us.*"

"I've always found hope to be an intriguing emotion."

Gwenna growled a curse, then, blades held before her, advanced up the spiral stairs once more.

By the time they reached the next landing they might as well have stepped into a charnel house. The thick stench flooded her throat, choking her, gagging her. She'd spent plenty of time around the dead—in training and later—but the dead were usually outside, on battlefields mostly, or ships. In the closed space of the Blind, the smell had nowhere to go.

A stone doorway opened off the staircase. She glanced through it, then over at Kiel.

"Still no heartbeat," she whispered. "No breathing."

He nodded.

She gestured with her blades. "Doesn't mean I want to go first."

"You are faster than me," the historian pointed out.

She lowered the tip of a sword to his chest. "So don't test me."

Kiel studied the length of steel for a moment, then nodded, readied his spear, and stepped through.

Gwenna counted to five—long enough for the man to spring any traps or trigger any ambushes—then followed.

The first thing that struck her was the size of the chamber. It had to be a hundred paces across at the very least, easily large enough to contain a small village and still race horses around the perimeter. The ceiling swept into a graceful dome overhead, so high she might have tested a working trebuchet in the massive space. Into that dome, the Csestriim had embedded a graceful pattern of their strange, unbreakable glass through which a blue-gray glacial light filtered down, quiet and cold. That light reflected off the floor, which was utterly empty—save for a chest-high table or altar off in the center—the stone polished to a perfect, lacquer-black sheen. . . .

No, she realized. *Not stone. Water.*

Enough water to sail a boat on, had there been any wind. Enough to fill a small lake.

She paused, then spat onto the surface. Ripples rose silently, widened out and away.

"There," Kiel said.

She turned to find the historian pointing with his spear.

Around the perimeter of the chamber ran a stone walkway, just two paces wide and a hairsbreadth above the level of the water itself. Sprawled across that walkway, barely a stone's throw distant, lay two carcasses. Gwenna studied them, heart thudding dully in her chest.

The first was obviously a product of Menkiddoc's sickness, some kind of massive, clear-shelled insectile monstrosity with faceted eyes, serrated wings, far too many teeth. Blackened ichor had leaked from a slash across its back, staining the stone. The sword that made the cut lay nearby, just a few feet from the hand of the woman who had wielded it.

She wasn't dressed like a soldier. Instead of armor, she wore slim, simple trousers and a close-fitting shirt. The garb of a sailor, maybe, though Gwenna smelled nothing of the sea on her. Her hair was short, tucked back behind her ears, revealing the smooth, dark skin of her face. Her eyes were empty, fixed on the light-spangled ceiling arching above them. The wound that felled her wasn't immediately obvious.

Gwenna followed as Kiel crossed to the body.

He knelt, rolled the woman from her side onto her back, then paused, his hand on her shoulder.

Gwenna caught the hint of a scent wafting off the man, something at once soft and astringent. She stared. Just when she'd finally understood why the historian never smelled of emotion he went and scrambled her understanding. The scent was faint—the echo of a whisper—but unmistakable all the same: *regret*.

"You knew her."

Kiel nodded. "A long time ago."

"Which for you means what? Hundreds of years?"

"Thousands. Many thousands." He fell silent for a while, then: "She was the mother of my only child."

Gwenna blinked. "She was your *wife*?"

"The Csestriim did not share human notions of matrimony or pair bonding. We always found them inexplicable."

"Well you must have spent some time with her, anyway."

"She was the mother of my child," he said again, as though there were no more to explain.

"Where's your kid?"

It seemed ludicrous to use the word *kid* for a being that had been alive for millennia.

"Long dead. Killed in the wars with the humans."

He said the words without a hint of sorrow or anger. Indeed, aside from that single whiff of regret, he seemed to feel nothing but a mild surprise at finding the body. He didn't close her eyes or touch her face or do any of the things a human might have done, but he didn't move either, just knelt there studying her.

"What was she doing here?"

"The same thing we are, I suspect."

"And just what the fuck is it," Gwenna asked, "that *we're* doing?"

"Searching for weapons."

"For one weapon in particular," she said, understanding backhanding her across the face. It was from this place that the Csestriim had destroyed Menkiddoc. "You want to find the source of the sickness. The thing that created it."

"There were other weapons here as well," the historian replied without looking up. "Many others." He had begun at last to search the woman's clothing, running the fabric carefully between his fingers. "Do you see these niches ringing the chamber?"

Gwenna turned. She'd been so focused on the bodies when she first entered that she hadn't noticed the slim alcoves carved from the wall. They stood at even intervals a few paces apart, each one taller than her and as deep as her forearm. Most held empty pedestals; a few contained weapons, a few, strange items of unknown purpose or provenance.

"This was the armory," Kiel said. "All manner of weapons were kept here. Some of them leach-forged. Some very dangerous."

"An armory?" The armories back on the Islands had been low, functional buildings packed tight with racks and racks of weapons. "Looks more like a temple."

"There is what you might call a holiness to the dealing of death and the preservation of life."

"Holy or not, most of it's gone."

"Evidently."

"So someone came in here, stole a whole batch of deadly shit, and disappeared."

"Indeed."

Gwenna turned back toward the body of the dead Csestriim, the fine hairs at the nape of her neck prickling.

"Her?"

"Perhaps."

"How did she get in? The doors below were closed."

"She did not come from below."

"Spare me the riddles."

Kiel straightened finally, his hands empty. Whatever he'd been looking for in her clothing, he hadn't found it.

"You have heard of the *kenta*?" he asked.

Gwenna nodded slowly. "Some kind of Csestriim leach gates. Came across one years back in northeastern Vash."

Kiel nodded. "There is one here." He pointed toward the stairs. "Above."

Instead of moving toward the doorway, however, he turned to the center of the chamber, gazed out across the glass-still water to the small stone table at the center. Not a table, Gwenna realized as she followed his eyes. More like a crypt, or a bier. Before she could frame the question, Kiel started out once more, following the stone walkway around the perimeter. Roughly a quarter of the way around the arc he turned toward the center once more, then strode off across the water, walking on its surface as confidently as a man moving over stone.

Two steps behind him, Gwenna pulled up short, stared down into the ink-black water. Her own reflection stared back. She was leaner than she remembered, lips thin, cheeks almost gaunt. No more than she'd expect after a hard march on meager rations, but that thinness wasn't the only change. Her eyes gleamed in the faint, otherworldly light of the cavern. Swollen pupils nearly eclipsed her irises. Her teeth, when she drew back her lips, looked like the teeth of some feral, predatory creature. She couldn't tell if they were actually longer, sharper, or if her mind was playing some kind of vicious trick.

With an effort of will, she hauled herself away from her reflection. Kiel was halfway to the center of the room, striding across what she saw now wasn't water at all, but a stone path polished perfectly black, set dead level with the water's surface. She could make it out only at the edge, where the light reflected differently.

"Come," Kiel said, not bothering to look back.

And like a woman walking across the night sky, she followed.

The island at the center was a hand higher than the path. The altar occupied most of the space. It reminded her vaguely of the tables in the laboratory below, but where those were clean and exact, polished as fine tools, the stone of the altar was rough, heavy, solid, the sort of thing that, in a human space, would have been consecrated to some kind of ceremony. Also, unlike the tables below, it was not empty.

Bones sprawled across the pitted surface—femur, pelvis, a scattering of ribs, vertebrae lined up like a child's blocks. A skull. All the flesh had long since rotted away along with the ligaments and tendons, but with no animals to disturb the site, with no wind or water to work at it, the skeleton lay almost perfectly intact, as though someone had reassembled it only that very morning. The arms were bent at the elbows, the small bones of the hands scattered through the rib cage, as though the person had died with their hands folded across their stomach. A peaceful death, if there was such a thing.

"Another Nevariim?" she asked.

He shook his head. "She was one of my kind."

"What's she doing"—Gwenna gestured to the stone bier—"here."

"It was her task to deploy the seed."

"The seed?"

"The weapon that destroyed Menkiddoc. Many millennia have passed since the event."

"The *event*?"

Kiel met her glare. "The attack. The victory."

"How about the *slaughter*."

He nodded. "Most victories involve an element of slaughter."

She frowned. "Seems tough to deploy a weapon from inside a mountain."

"This was a weapon like none you have encountered." Kiel regarded the tableau for a moment, then shifted the ribs aside, sifted through the finger-bones, the carpals and metacarpals. "And it is gone."

"Gone?" Gwenna glanced down at her newly acquired ring, the *matzcel*. "Was it . . ."

Kiel shook his head. "The seed was an even more intimate instrument. It was not worn by the wielder. It was consumed."

Gwenna looked back at the stone surface. "So where did it go?"

He followed her gaze, as though he could scry the future in the bones' scattered angles. "A great deal may rest on the answer to that question."

"But you don't know the answer, do you?"

"No," he replied, still not looking up. "I do not."

"You exterminated a race—"

"I was not stationed here—"

She talked right over him. "You poisoned a continent. And then you *lost* the fucking poison."

Finally he turned to meet her eyes. "Lost is the wrong word. A ring slipped from a finger and tumbled into a river is lost. A ship crushed by a storm and dragged to the sea's bottom is lost. A glass shattered on stones, an ancient tome consumed by fire, some boundary oak felled by lightning and devoured by rot—these are lost. What should terrify you about the seed, what should terrify the entire world, is not that it is lost, but that now, after so many years lying silent and still, locked away at the heart of a mountain behind doors of stone and song, it has been found."

⸸

As they climbed, the air went from chill to cold, cold to frigid. The faint scrape of wind over stone began to break the tomb-silence of the lower levels.

"Feels like someone left a window open," Gwenna muttered.

Kiel shook his head. "A door, more likely."

They rounded the final curve of the staircase to find just that—another heavy stone door hanging open on gleaming hinges. A few flakes of snow spun in from beyond. A faint breeze caught Gwenna's hair, tossing it back from her face.

The historian glanced over at her. "What do you smell?"

She inhaled, tested the air for any hints of flesh or rot, shook her head. "Stone. Ice. Snow. The only poisoned thing up here is me."

Beyond the door, the wind howled and screamed. After the still, silent reek of the dead pervading the spaces below, it was almost a relief to feel the knife-sharp gusts slicing through her blacks, the cold air filling her lungs. Despite her assurances to Kiel, she turned in a quick circle, blades half raised, scanning the space for anything monstrous—for anything at *all*.

The fortress watchtower wasn't really a tower, of course. Instead, the Csestriim had cored out the very summit of the mountain, hollowing the stone peak, carving massive windows into the rock. The strange non-glass from the chambers below filled two or three, but most stood empty, gaping wide onto the blizzard scribbled across the sky beyond.

"I guess the glass breaks after all."

"Not the glass," Kiel said, nodding to the crumbling sills. "The weather finally wore down the stone holding it."

That was how long the historian had been alive—long enough for wind and snow to erode a fucking mountain.

She crossed to one of those windows, let the snow burn her cheeks, gazed out into the crazed white beyond. "So this is how the *gabbya* got in. And when it did, it found the door already open for it."

"So things would appear."

She turned to him. "Seems like a dumb mistake for a Csestriim, not closing the door behind her."

"We left the door open below," Kiel pointed out. "As you have seen, the song locks are not quick to open. Axta would have had—"

"Axta?"

"The woman we found slaughtered below. The mother of my child. She couldn't know if the Blind was compromised. She would have left herself an escape."

"Escape," Gwenna said, turning back to the inside of the chamber, "through *that*."

Like the ring Gwenna wore on her finger, the *kenta* looked . . . wrong. Warped. Turned in on itself in some way she couldn't quite articulate. She could trace its lines with her eyes, follow the arc of the gate from base to base, but the effort left her feeling disoriented and vaguely nauseous.

"Where does it go?"

"To any number of places," Kiel replied, crossing to the *kenta,* kneeling just a few paces away from it. "For one who knows the way."

"So, your girlfriend came through. She opened the door. The *gabhya* followed her down and killed her."

"That much seems clear."

"Doesn't explain where all the weapons went."

"She could have been removing them if she thought the Blind was no longer secure. Or she could have arrived here only to discover the armory already emptied."

"So who else knows the way?" She gestured to the *kenta.* "Who can go through that thing?"

"The Shin monks."

"Thought they were all dead."

"Most of them. And those remaining likely know nothing of the *kenta.*"

"So, not them then. Who else?"

"The Ishien. The emperors of Annur."

"The *emperors* . . ."

He nodded. "It was for this purpose that Kaden and his father trained with the Shin in the first place—in order to be able to use these gates."

"And *they* never came here?" Her head ached just thinking about it, but according to the historian, Annur was just a handful of steps away. "Why didn't some Malkeenian clean out your hoard centuries ago?"

Kiel gestured toward the door leading down into the fortress. "They would not have been able to pass the door. They would not even have *seen* it. They did come here, but they believed it a single chamber set into the mountain's peak. Some kind of watchtower, nothing more."

"What about Adare?"

"She did not train with the Shin. She could no more pass through the *kenta* than you can."

Gwenna frowned, made herself look at the gate.

"What would happen if I tried to go through?"

"You would cease to be."

"I'd die?"

"Something considerably more thorough than that."

She tried to imagine something more thorough than death. No blood or corpse, nothing to bury or burn, a perfect scrubbing out, as though she'd never even been born. The thought fascinated and horrified her in equal measures. She didn't want to die anymore—she'd understood that after fighting the kettral—but there was something so clean, so unsullied, about just . . . ceasing to be. A shiver ran through her, whether from the storm's cold or her own emotion, she couldn't say.

"So we're back to your girlfriend. She was the only one who could pass both the *kenta* and the song lock."

The historian nodded. "She is the most likely source of the breach."

"Maybe she got all the weapons somewhere safe and just came back for one last sentimental look at the place."

"Or another party followed her here, found her and the *gabbya* dead, took the weapons and the seed."

"What other party? You just got done telling me that almost no one can go through that fucking thing."

"Almost no one is not no one." He looked past her toward the gate. "And the centuries have taught me to distrust my own convictions."

Gwenna bared her teeth in frustration. The pain inside her flared, then subsided.

"Whatever the case, all that shit is gone. The seed, the weapons, all of it, and we don't know a 'Kent-kissing thing about whoever took it."

"We know one thing," Kiel replied gravely. "We know they are preparing for war."

Gwenna narrowed her eyes. "Wait. You're Csestriim. Adare *knows* you're Csestriim. You can sing your way through all these locks. If you're so concerned about this seed, about all these weapons, why didn't *you* just come check on them? Move them somewhere safe?"

"This *was* somewhere safe. An armory guarded by Csestriim locks. An empty fortress in the center of an abandoned continent. It was only on this expedition that I realized something is wrong here."

She stared at him. "Something has been wrong here since you assholes poisoned the whole fucking place."

"Not that. Something more. Something worse."

"Looks like your girlfriend understood."

"She was always adept at seeing patterns." For a few heartbeats he stared out into the snow. Then: "I must return to Annur. To warn the Emperor."

"We've been working on that for a couple months, right? Just a jaunt down the northern slope of the mountains, through the foothills, an overland trek through land we hope is still unpolluted, then start looking for someone with a boat—"

"I must go now." He turned, stared through the *kenta*. "Here."

"Ah." Stupid. She should have seen it earlier. Immediately. "You can bring the eggs." The words blurting out of her even as the idea occurred. "The rest of us might not make it, but the eggs will get back."

The historian shook his head. "No."

"What do you mean, *no*?"

"I could no more carry the eggs through the *kenta* than I could carry you."

"Then how did, what's her name? Axta. How did she get in? How'd she bring the sword with her? Why isn't she naked?"

"The *kenta* allow clothing to pass, small objects, even weapons. Not other living creatures. The gate would annihilate the eggs."

She considered that. It sounded like bullshit, but no more bullshit than the idea that, on the other side of that slender arch, waited other continents.

For a long time they stood in silence, staring through the empty space circumscribed by the *kenta*. Gwenna felt a stab of envy at the man—*no,* she reminded herself, *not a man*—for his ability to go free. The rest of them faced an overland voyage of hundreds of miles only to arrive on an alien coastline that was hopefully still untainted. Kiel could just step through the arch and be home.

If Annur *was* even home.

She turned the thought over in her mind. It had felt like exile when Adare sent her south with the expedition, a banishment from everywhere and everything she understood. After months at sea, however, months wandering the blighted wilderness of Menkiddoc, months trying to survive the tangled jungle of her own mind, when she looked back at the place she'd left she found it difficult to recognize. Even if she was allowed back to the Islands, what would she find? A home? No. The woman who had lived there, who had inhabited that world, that life—she was gone.

She stared at the *kenta*. If she could step through the gate, if it could take her anywhere she chose, where would she go?

It seemed a simple question; she had no answer.

Grimly, she turned away. "Do me a favor. When you get back to Annur, send a fucking ship to meet us."

The historian didn't answer right away. He traced a finger down the side of the arch, seemed about to reach through, then drew his hand back.

"You going?" she demanded roughly.

"I'm no longer certain I can use it."

She frowned. "They're a Csestriim creation. I thought *all* the Csestriim could use them."

"We could. *I* could. And yet, the last time I went through I felt myself . . . waver."

"Waver?"

He nodded. "I've spent so much time around humans, I've lived so many centuries in a world touched by your gods of fear and love, hatred and courage, that some of those emotions have taken root inside of me."

"Love?" Gwenna asked incredulously. "Fear? I've met stones with more emotion than you."

"Only the roots," Kiel replied. "The slenderest tubers."

"And those stop you from using the gate?"

"I don't know."

"Will you come back? After you've warned Adare?"

"I will try."

He held her eyes for two heartbeats, three, four, then turned, stepped forward, and vanished.

Gwenna studied the empty space beneath the arch. Kiel was gone—that much was obvious—but the two possibilities about *where* he'd gone seemed equally impossible. Either he'd traveled to Annur between one step and the next, or the *kenta* had obliterated him.

She turned away, crossed the snow-crusted chamber, gazed out one of the open windows.

The wind howled and tore at her, tried to yank her into the void.

Something is amiss. . . .

When had that ever *not* been true? She was no historian, but you didn't need to be in order to see that the chronicle of the world was a chronicle of things going wrong, of plague and famine, slaughter, rebellion, greed and cowardice, human misery wide as the sea. And yet, when she thought about the pollution of the seed, the awful twisting of Menkiddoc, the fact that it could happen somewhere else, maybe *everywhere* else, she couldn't suppress a shudder. She'd come on the expedition because she had nowhere else to go, because she thought that by finding the kettral eggs and bringing them back she might redeem herself, but what did it matter, one woman's redemption, in the face of what she'd seen in the jungles below?

The poison ached inside her.

She closed her eyes, watched again as Jonon drank from the tainted water, that miserable, arrogant bastard sacrificing himself to save the tattered remnants of his crew. Had he understood what he was doing? Had he seen what he would become?

Outside the window, the storm screamed in a voice almost human, high and furious, like Rat's voice. . . .

Gwenna's eyes slammed open. Her heart bucked inside her chest.

Not *like* Rat's voice; it *was* Rat's voice, stabbing up from far below where the door of the fortress opened into the saddle, screaming the same two syllables over and over:

Gwenna! Gwenna! Gwenna!

56

They spent the rest of the day watching people die.

There was no way to ask Monster if she'd managed to pick the lock, no way to ask her what she'd found on the other side, no way to ask her anything at all. Her smirk suggested success, but Ruc wanted more than a smirk. He wanted to hear the words: *It's open. We can get out.* Instead, the six of them had been stuck in Goatface's box, the blood of the fight drying on their skin, the aches and twinges blooming beneath it while overhead the sun traced its blazing path across the sky. Ruc kept stealing glances at Monster, and he wasn't the only one. Even Talal, with all his vaunted Kettral discipline, looked at her more often than was truly warranted.

The only one who seemed indifferent to the success of Monster's mission was Bien. She didn't look at the woman, or anything else for that matter, just stared with blank eyes out over the sand as the Worthy screamed and swore and fought and bled and died. When Ruc offered her water, she took the crock, drank, handed it back, all without saying a word. At one point, Talal sat beside her on the bench, leaned over to ask something Ruc couldn't quite hear. She shook her head slightly, refused to meet his eye.

The last of the bodies weren't dragged from the pit until the sun had dipped below the western wall of the Arena. Then there was the procession of the Worthy back to the yard, the trip to the mess hall, which meant talking to the other warriors, and *then,* back at the barracks, Goatface's seemingly interminable analysis of the fight, the ways in which they'd both succeeded and failed, opportunities for improvement, pitfalls to be avoided. Finally, in the dark stretch of time between sunset and the midnight gongs, the trainer retired, and at last there was a chance to learn what had happened in the dusty shadows beneath the Arena.

Monster, of course, was in no hurry to rush the revelation.

"It was *dark* back there," she said.

"Dark," Mouse said mournfully.

She nodded. "Dark as *fuck*."

"As a simile," Stupid opined, "I'm not sure that makes sense." He'd taken up his customary spot, lying on the bench along the wall, although for once he didn't have the straw hat pulled down over his eyes.

"You want me to tell you where you can shove your simile?" Monster demanded.

Stupid furrowed his brow, then shook his head. "Also doesn't make sense."

"Did you pick the lock?" Ruc asked.

Monster turned back to him, waggled a finger. "Look who's so impatient! This is what's wrong with men—always in such a rush to get to the end that they don't enjoy the ins and outs along the way."

"According to Bien," he replied, "the ins and outs are just finding your way through a few rows of crates to the door."

Bien said nothing, just stared into the lantern flame.

"Fine, you fucking killjoys," Monster said. "I found the door. I picked the lock. We're free." She spread her hands, glared at Ruc. "See. Every story's boring if you tell it too fast."

"Or too slowly," Stupid observed.

"We're not here for the story," Ruc said. "What's *beyond* the door?"

Monster glared at him, took another swig of her *quey,* then shrugged. "A long corridor. More storerooms on either side. It doubles back around beneath the stands, probably makes a huge loop all the way back to the Arena." She winked. "But there's a back door. Little dock about opposite the main gates where barges bring in supplies."

"Guarded?" Talal asked.

"'Course it's fucking guarded."

"Did anyone see you?"

Monster offered a derisive snort in response.

"She is a constant vexation of the spirit," Stupid offered from over on the bench, "but there's no one in the city better at sneaking around in the shadows."

"So that's our path out," Ruc said.

"What about the lock?" Talal asked.

Monster glowered at him. "I'm not a fucking idiot. Door's closed but not locked."

"What if someone checks it?" Ruc asked.

"Then they'll fucking lock it." She tapped her temple. "I know the trick of the little bastard now, though. I'll be able to pick it in a tenth the time if it comes to that."

A silence settled over the room. Ruc looked at Bien. She didn't look back.

"Well," Monster said, glaring around the table. "Don't everyone thank me at once."

"We're not out yet," Talal observed.

"Obviously fucking not, but we will be. You can bet your Annurian ass on that."

Ruc nodded slowly. Now that the dangers of the day were behind them, it seemed suddenly, almost suspiciously easy. He reminded himself that they'd almost failed. If the fight had finished a few beats earlier, if Goatface had been more suspicious, if Monster hadn't managed to fit the wooden board back into place—they would all be dead, executed before the setting sun.

"Easy," Stupid said.

"Easy?" Mouse asked.

Ruc shook his head. "Things are always easy until they're not."

He was lying in his bunk when the midnight gong finally tolled. He could hear Talal's even breathing from across the room, Bien tossing and turning in the bunk above him. He thought she was struggling with some nightmare until she spoke.

"This isn't how it was supposed to be."

He paused a moment before replying. "The escape?"

"The fight," she replied, voice thick with anguish. "We were supposed to be *gone* already. Off into the delta. Or maybe dead. We weren't supposed to *kill* anyone."

Ruc stared into the darkness. He had no answer. A priest of Eira, a *true* priest, faced with the contest of the Arena, would have tossed his weapon into the sand and accepted death, would have gone to his foe with open arms and an open heart, absolved the killer even as the bronze slid between his ribs. It was a hard thing, realizing half your life had been a lie.

In the end, however, it was Talal who replied.

Evidently none of them could sleep.

"When we stepped into that pit, someone had to die."

His voice was calm, serious but conversational.

"They weren't even good," Ruc said, shaking his head.

That, he realized, was the crux of it. It was one thing to stalk a jaguar, to struggle with it in the prime of its strength. There was something beautiful in that, something noble. Try as he might, though, he could find nothing beautiful or noble about what had happened out on the sand.

"They weren't good," Talal said, "but they were good enough."

"Good enough for what?"

"To kill us."

"But we killed *them*," Bien whispered. "That kid couldn't have been what? Seventeen? And I *murdered* him."

The quiet was a weight pressing down on Ruc's chest.

"It will get easier," Talal said at last.

"I don't *want* it to get easier."

"Sometimes," the Kettral replied, "the world doesn't care what you want."

"How many people have *you* killed?" she demanded.

"Why do you want to ask that?"

"How many?"

A pause.

"I don't know."

Bien made a sound somewhere between a sob and a gasp. "How can you not know?"

"War is ugly. Battle is messy. There's not always time to keep count."

"Doesn't it *bother* you?"

"Every day."

"Then how do you do it?"

"I consider the alternative. If we'd refused to fight, if we'd let them kill us, then what? Someone else would have killed them when the time came—"

"But it wouldn't have been *us*," Bien snarled. Her shape on the bunk above was a blaze so bright it seemed she should ignite the mattress, set the entire room aflame.

"I'm glad it was us," Talal replied quietly. "We didn't draw it out, didn't mock them, didn't make them suffer." He paused. "And when you don't see the blood on your own hands, it's too easy to forget that there's a price for every decision. Too easy to believe you're innocent."

Bien exhaled raggedly. "It's just . . . It's different for you. You've done this before. Ruc and I have never killed anyone." She flinched at her own words, then added quietly, "Not on purpose, anyway."

A fly circled in the darkness, buzzing, bumping dumbly off the wall, buzzing again. The Witness had told him once that most flies lived less than a week. Some survived barely a day. They hatched into the world in the morning and were dead by night.

Why? Ruc remembered asking the old man. *What's the point?*

The Witness shrugged. *What's the point for any of us?*

He shifted on his sweat-soaked bunk, stared up at Bien's burning shape.

"I have," he said at last.

Bien flinched, as though she'd been bitten by something. She didn't reply, however, so he kept talking.

"My early memories are all sun and blood.

"The people of Dombâng worship Kem Anh and Hang Loc like they're gods, but they're not. They're animals. Predators.

"When I couldn't even walk, they taught me to cover myself in mud and wait for the gorzles. I was snapping the birds' necks before I took my first steps. Later, they showed me how to catch snakes, twist off the heads, strip the flesh from the bones, how to take a croc's back, hold on while it thrashed and dove, how to drive a knife into the joint below the skull. I spent months stalking jaguars through the reeds, paw print after muddy paw print. By the time I was seven I had a necklace of teeth hanging halfway to my waist."

"Those were animals, Ruc," Bien said. He could hear the fear and hope tangled in her voice. "Just animals."

"Just animals to start," he replied. "Then the people started coming."

He reached back into the bright heat of his childhood, felt all over again the sun blazing on his naked skin, the joy of his own strength.

"It seems insane now, but the first time I saw people, I didn't know what they were. They wore clothes, which confused me, and they showed up in a boat. I'd spent my life swimming and running; I'd never seen a boat before. And even though they had two legs, two arms, one head, all the rest of it, they were so much . . . *less* than the creatures that raised me. Smaller. Slower. Uglier. I thought they were disgusting.

"I recognized their knives, at least. Hang Loc had given me a knife when I was almost too young to hold it. He never hunted with one. Kem Anh didn't either. Either one of them could take a croc apart with their bare hands. I thought—if I thought about it at all—that the blade was something I was allowed because I was young, that when I grew up I wouldn't need one either.

"Anyway, when the Vuo Ton came—that's who the people were: the chosen warriors of the Vuo Ton—I expected them to die, and they did. They fought bravely, ferociously even, but Hang Loc killed them anyway, crushed a chest, ripped out a throat, choked the life from the last of them. I'd seen him do the same to countless animals over the years, so it wasn't a surprise. What did surprise me was the sick misgiving I felt after, as I watched him separate the heads from the bodies.

"I couldn't figure out why I was feeling that way, had no words to put to it. Something was wrong, but I didn't know the word for *wrong* or *slaughter* or *murder*. All I knew was that my stomach ached and my head felt too light, as though it had come unmoored from the world. I made myself stand there as he scooped out the eyes, tossed them in the mud, packed the sockets with dirt, then planted the delta violets. I made myself watch as he and Kem Anh unmade the bodies, then feasted on the dark meat of the liver. When they offered me the flesh, I couldn't bring myself to eat.

"*This is not right.*

"That's what I would have told them, if they had ever taught me any language."

He fell silent awhile, listened to Bien's breath rasping between her chapped lips, to the claws of some animal or other skittering across the sunbaked tiles of the roof. It was strange to speak the story aloud after so many years, to force all that brightness and violence, the blood and flashing bronze into a handful of words. Was Bien seeing anything like what actually happened? No way to know. If he stretched out his arm he could touch the bottom of her mattress. She might as well have been on the other side of the delta. The other side of the world.

"A year later, the Vuo Ton came again," he said finally. Once he'd begun to tell the story, there was no way to stop or call it back. "This time it was my turn."

He saw it all again, the low mist shrouding the channel, the ripples where shortfins rose to feast on the striders, and then the canoe sliding out of the silence, grinding up onto the low beach where he waited, flanked by Kem Anh and Hang Loc.

"The Witness sat in the back. He told me later that he was watching me, but I had eyes only for the warriors. Like the last time, there were three of them, two men and a young woman, and like the ones who came before, they carried bronze weapons in their hands. They bowed to Hang Loc, then to Kem Anh. I could almost smell their awe.

"Kem Anh killed the first two. She tore out one man's throat with her teeth, ripped free the woman's heart. The last of them she left to me.

"I knew what I was supposed to do. I'd known it for a whole year, since the last warriors came to the beach to test themselves against their gods. The man I faced, however, was confused, then surprised, then furious to find himself fighting a child, a *human* child. He'd been prepared to lose an arm or an eye, prepared to *die,* but he wasn't prepared for the humiliation of fighting me while Kem Anh and Hang Loc looked on. That humiliation molted almost instantly into violence.

"He came at me with a long delta spear. I'd never fought a man before, let alone one with a spear, and I had only my knife. His first attack plunged past my guard, ripped open a gash along my shoulder." He ran his fingers over the scar as he spoke. The skin was smooth and cool in the darkness. "I didn't know any of the right techniques to kill a man with a weapon, but my whole life had been a lesson in survival. I'd spent endless days learning to dodge, roll, feint, attack. As the warrior attacked, I saw things that I recognized—the way his gaze betrayed him before each lunge, how he moved his weight onto the back foot before uncoiling, the breath that came heavier in his chest as the struggle dragged on.

"His best chance to kill me was right away, in the opening moments, before I understood the kind of creature I was facing. When he failed to do that, I knew. I knew at some deep, old, predatory level that I had him. It wasn't over—the fight seemed to last half the morning—but every time he tested me with that spear I learned something new. Every time he retreated, I saw his weaknesses more and more clearly, and as the sun bore down, he began to slow.

"I killed him by pieces.

"A nick to the ribs. A gash across his lower back. A kick to the outside of his knee.

"I landed a deep slash across the thigh—that hobbled him, soaked the sand with blood.

"Then a stab to the ribs that would have put down most men. It was a mortal wound. I could see it on his face, I could smell it, but he refused to fall.

"I took his spear away, stabbed him again in the gut, and then, when he tried to get his hands around my throat, I put the bronze straight into his eye.

"He died beneath me, half holding me, his hands slick with his own blood.

"I climbed off, stared at him as the heat seeped from his body, then puked into the sand."

His own stillness felt suddenly intolerable. Driven by the memory of the violence he rose from the bed, crossed to the window, pulled back the canvas flap, gazed out into the night. The rickety walls of the yard looked nothing like the delta of his childhood, but he recognized the smells drifting in on the hot night wind—mud and rot and wet green reeds. When he spoke again, he might have been addressing the night itself.

"Kem Anh came up behind me, put an arm over my shoulder, but I shrugged her off, stumbled away into the bush. I wanted to scream, but the creatures that raised me had taught me to scream only in triumph, and though I'd killed the man who stood against me, the slick sickness washing my gut felt like anything but triumph. I felt like I'd lost, not just the fight but something else, some part of myself I'd never even recognized before that moment.

"She found me later. I'd spent the afternoon staring into a still pool, studying my own reflection. When she loomed over me, I compared her face with mine. It seemed impossible that I'd never noticed the difference. *She* glowed with the heat of the late sun on the water. The lines of her face were clean as the arc of a fish leaping from the water, or the slice inscribed on the sky by a plunging marsh hawk. Even her scars she wore like adornments.

"Me though? I was lopsided. One ear was slightly higher than the other. My teeth were too blunt, like the teeth of a creature made to feast on reeds and rushes rather than raw meat. There was a dark mole low on my cheek, two more on my shoulder. They reminded me suddenly, powerfully, of some kind of mold, or the rot that spreads through sodden leaves. She didn't have any such blemishes. Neither did Hang Loc.

"I didn't have the words to frame my revelation, but it burned inside me all the same, torching my world to ash. I wasn't their child. How could I be—a crabbed, twisted thing, a stunted creature who had to fight with a knife? How had I ever believed that? No. Now that I'd seen the warriors from the boat, now that I'd fought them, I understood. There had been a mistake. It was as though a clumsy mud duck had slipped an egg into the nest of a marsh hawk. I wasn't a predator. I was something sadder and weaker, the kind of thing *they* preyed upon.

"Her reflection watched me from the water with those golden eyes. My eyes were the color of mud.

"I turned away from her gaze, pointed in the direction from which the boat had come.

"I didn't know who the people were, but I knew that I was one of them.

"Kem Anh bared her teeth, tried to slide an arm around my waist, but I forced it back, held my slender brown arm straight out, pointing, until at last she made a sound like a jaguar giving up a hunt, turned away, melted back into the brush.

"I sat up all night on the river's bank. A hot wind carved the rushes. The moon reminded me of bronze.

"I waited for her to come, or him. I wondered if they could cradle me as they always had, or kill me now that their mistake was clear. I tried to imagine the feeling of my neck snapping, or my heart being lifted from my chest. That night might have been easier—a little easier anyway—if I'd had the words for *loneliness* or *love, loss* or *hunger* or *hate*. If I'd had the words for *mother* or *father*? All I had, though, was the starlight burning my eyes, my small hands clenched into fists, and a taste like bile on my tongue.

"The next day, when the Witness appeared in his boat to carry off the bodies, I went with him."

After so many words, the silence felt tight, heavy and hot. It had seemed important to tell the truth at last, to put voice to the simple fact of his life: he was a creature raised to kill. Not murder, not exactly—the Vuo Ton who faced their gods came prepared to fight and ready to die—but not hunting either. There was no *reason* to slaughter the warriors with their bronze, no need, nothing beyond the sheer delight of blood and struggle. He'd understood the ugliness of it, even as a child, but despite fifteen years as a patient servant of the goddess of love, nothing had blotted out the beauty.

He heard Bien's feet hit the floor behind him, soft on the hard wood.

He listened as she crossed the floor.

For a crazed moment he imagined that she was Kem Anh come to kill him finally for his failure. His relief tasted like rage.

She stopped behind him, so close he could feel her breath on his back, the heat radiating from her chest.

"Thank you," she said, sliding a slim arm around his waist, resting her forehead against his spine.

He shook his head. Exhaustion washed over him, as though he hadn't just been recounting the fight, but living it all over again.

"For what?" he asked.

"For reminding me."

"Reminding you of what?"

"That we're lost."

He choked up a laugh. "You and me?"

"Yes. And Talal. And the people we killed today. Rooster and Snakebones. All the people who fought. All the people who watched."

"I wish that were true," he replied, "but some people are just hungry for blood."

He tried to free himself, but her arm was strong.

"Of course they are," she said, then kissed him lightly on the shoulder. Her lips were both warm and cold. "But I was only thinking about the blood. I hated them for all that blood, hated them in a way that severed me from myself, hated them until this moment, tonight, listening to you tell your story at last." She turned him to face her. For the first time in months, the first time since the slaughter at the temple, she looked like herself beneath the scars. "You reminded me that they're hungry, Ruc, and I learned long ago, learned at the feet of the goddess herself, how to love all those who hunger."

57

By the time Gwenna arrived in the domed antechamber of the fortress—lungs heaving, legs ablaze from the endless descent, both blades naked and eager—there was nothing left to fight.

The stone room reeked of terror and blood. A few paces distant, Pattick lay sprawled across the floor. Pattick, who had always been so frightened and so brave, his throat torn out as though by a rabid dog.

"No," Gwenna growled. *"No."*

Cho Lu had fallen just beyond him, facedown, sword dropped from his nerveless hand. The steel gleamed, bloodless; he hadn't managed to land a blow against whatever killed him.

"It was Jonon."

Gwenna whirled to find Bhuma Dhar slumped against the wall. He was struggling to stand, but his right leg sprawled in front of him, twisted sickeningly at the knee. When he tried to weight it pain flooded his features and he collapsed, sweating, gasping, his back to the stone. Like the slaughtered legionaries, he had also drawn his cutlass. Like theirs, his was unspotted with blood.

"He entered," the captain continued, grimacing through the words, "like a wind."

Gwenna stared, silent. It wasn't that she couldn't ask the questions. There was no need; she already knew the answers.

Dhar went on anyway.

"He smiled. He chided us for leaving him. He asked after you. Then he took Rat by the arm. The girl cursed at him, fought, tried to draw her knife. It was like watching a mouse struggle against a snake. A brave mouse, but still."

He closed his eyes against the memory or the pain or both, but continued speaking.

"He invited the soldiers to join him. *You will be my deputies.* These were his words. *My honored lieutenants. You will feast as I have feasted on the fruits of this land, and you will know strength and bliss and wisdom beyond your imaginings.* Cho Lu drew on him then. A bold attack, but useless." He gestured toward the body. "Jonon was still holding Rat with one arm when he took the soldier's heart."

Gwenna glanced over her shoulder. She hadn't noticed the sodden lump draining onto the stone. It lay just a few inches from Cho Lu's empty, outstretched hand, as though he were reaching for it, straining to hold it once more.

"Pattick and I attacked. . . ." The captain trailed off, gazed blankly at the wall. "Useless."

He held his hands before him, lowered his face between his palms. The same gesture he'd made months ago back on the *Daybreak,* just after the sinking of his ship, the gesture that meant *shame.*

Gwenna could taste her own shame. She was the one who'd ordered them to leave the door open. She was the one who'd insisted they stay below. It had seemed reasonable at the time, as she felt her own mind slipping away and that awful hunger rising. She'd been so consumed by the fear of what she herself might do that she'd left them open to Jonon, a creature already in Menkiddoc's clawed grip.

"What did he want?" she asked.

She said the words, but she could already see the answer to this question.

"You," Dhar replied. "He broke my knee, but left me alive to deliver the message."

"What message?" Her voice sounded dull, lifeless, but her body throbbed. Blood hammered in her veins.

"That if you want the girl you'll follow him."

"Where?"

"Back," Dhar said, gesturing toward the south. "Down. Where we faced the *gabhya.*"

"It makes no *sense,*" she snarled. "He could have killed you and taken me when I came through the door, right here in this room."

"I do not know," the captain replied, shaking his head wearily, "whether there is any sense left inside him. When he was not laughing, he was muttering to himself. Something about this place." He gestured to the walls, the ceiling. "He seemed to believe it was too small. Too small to contain him."

For the first time, Dhar looked over his shoulder, back toward the door through which Gwenna had come. "Where is the historian?"

"He had somewhere to go."

The Manjari squinted through his pain. "Go? Where?"

Gwenna tried to imagine explaining it all—Kiel's true identity, the poisoning of Menkiddoc, the seed, the *kenta*—gave up, slid down the wall beside Dhar. "He's gone, at least for now. Csestriim leach bullshit. Maybe he'll come back. Not in time to help Rat."

She clenched her teeth against a sudden flood of nausea, let her head tip back against the stone. From where she sat, she could see down the short corridor to the pass outside. The snow had begun to flag, its energy spent almost as quickly as it had come on, leaving the world beyond the fortress a rectangle of painful light. She ached to hurl herself out into that light, to go charging down the mountainside after Rat, but she hadn't forgotten the fight against the *gabhya,* the way Jonon had sliced his way past those hundred arms and buried his sword in its heart. He'd killed an unkillable monster. He'd survived an explosion and a rockslide. If she went after him without a plan, she would die. And then Rat would die.

"You found your cure," Dhar said.

For a few heartbeats she didn't reply. She didn't *feel* fucking cured. Her body ached like she'd been beaten with bricks, like she'd just swum a hundred miles.

"Yeah," she said finally, lifting her hand to show him the ring.

Dhar studied the artifact, but made no effort to touch it. "This is what?"

"Fucked if I know. Something the Csestriim made to hold the horror of this place at bay."

"Does it succeed?"

"Does it succeed," she repeated blankly. A strange way to ask the question. "I guess. I haven't started tearing out people's hearts."

She let her eyes rest on the bodies of the two legionaries. She should have found their deaths easier than Quick Jak's or Laith's or Talal's—provided the leach *was* dead, that she hadn't abandoned him back in Dombâng. She hadn't spent a lifetime training and fighting beside the two soldiers, hadn't shared all the experiences—the barrel drops, endless swimming, sunset training fights, all that memorization of maps and languages—that bound the Kettral together. She knew nothing about Pattick's family, or Cho Lu's favorite foods, or why they'd enrolled in the legions in the first place. To her surprise, none of that seemed to matter. They'd sailed beside her, marched beside her, fought beside her. She'd heard them muttering in their sleep and watched them stumble when they were exhausted. She remembered the sound of Cho Lu's laugh and the shape of Pattick's frown. She knew that when Jonon lem Jonon came for Rat, when the man who'd been their admiral tried to take away an orphan girl, they'd drawn their swords.

What else did she need to know?

It hurt that they were dead, hurt like a weight of gravel stitched into her chest, and that hurt added to the other, deeper hurt of the poison and whatever was fighting it.

"I lost them," she said.

Dhar shook his head. "They were not yours to lose."

"I lost *her.*"

"People are not things, Gwenna Sharpe."

Not *Commander.* Not *Gwenna. Gwenna Sharpe.* The way Rat always said her name.

"No. She's *not* a thing. She's a girl. A brave, smart, stupid little girl, and I let Jonon take her."

"*You lost . . . You let . . .*" The captain shook his head. "You speak about the world as though everything in it were yours to command."

"I *was* in command," she snarled. "Back on the beach, right after the wreck, you all *put* me in command."

And back in Dombâng, she didn't add. *Back in the Purple Baths . . .*

"And what does it mean to you," Dhar asked, "to be in command?"

"That the decisions are mine. The responsibility is mine. The fucking mistakes are *mine.*"

"And those that you command? What are they?" She could feel him studying her from beyond the gulf of his own agony. "What are we?"

She stared back, wordless.

"Are we stones on a board?" he pressed after a time. "Pieces to be moved around?"

"If you were stones, you wouldn't keep *dying.*"

He nodded. "So. Not stones. What, then? Slaves?"

"That's horseshit, and you know it."

"I am asking about what *you* know." Dhar closed his eyes, leaned his head back against the wall. "There was a time before you rose to command, yes? When you were just a student, or a common soldier?"

"Of course."

She leafed through the memories: Adaman Fane screaming in her face for swimming too slowly; Daveen Shaleel twisting every limb in her body to the breaking point, just to show how it was done; the Flea sending them out on yet another barrel drop; Valyn ordering them to fight the Flea. . . . They were all her memories, though they didn't feel like hers. They felt like something she'd overheard in a tavern somewhere, or witnessed from a distance. She tried to remember what it *felt* like, not to be in command, not to be personally responsible for another life, or two, or five.

"What were you then?" Dhar asked quietly.

"Just a person."

"You are still just a person."

"It's a commander's job—"

"To command. To make decisions."

"To make the *right* fucking decisions."

"No." Dhar shook his head weakly. "This is a *davi* too great for anyone to carry."

She turned to stare at him. "Doing a good job? That's too much? Making the right call?"

"Yes. This is too much. There is no life without error, without failure."

She laid her swords gently on the stone floor, stared down at her hands.

"It was this vision of his *davi,*" Dhar went on, "that broke your admiral."

"The poison of Menkiddoc broke him," Gwenna replied, but she could find no heat for the words. Instead, she remembered Jonon standing a pace away from her in the poisoned jungle, the fury of his own failure carved into his face. What was it he'd said? *My men are dying, and I can't save them.*

The memory shimmered, shivered, and she saw herself standing in Jonon's place, clutching the skin of polluted water, raising it to her lips, drinking it down.

The captain cut into her thoughts. "Your *davi* has nothing to do with victory or defeat. Nothing to do with life or death. Not yours. Not those of the men and women you command." He shifted, winced, took a deep, unsteady breath.

"What then?"

"Do what you are able to do. Do *everything* you are able to do. The rest . . ." He made the gesture of a person holding something loosely, then letting it go.

She gazed out into the light.

"He's going to kill me," she said. "He's going to kill me, and then he's going to kill Rat, and there's nothing I can do to stop him."

To her surprise, the Manjari captain nodded. "He will destroy you, as a vicious boy rips the wings from a fly."

Gwenna almost choked on her laugh. "Thanks for that."

"Does it change anything to know it?"

"The people who trained me would say it changes everything. There's even a passage from Hendran: *Heroic last stands and suicidal charges make for excellent stories and terrible strategy. Only a fool goes into an unwinnable fight.*"

"Life is an unwinnable fight, Gwenna Sharpe. If ends are all that matter, then we are all fools and failures."

She closed her eyes once more. The smell of the dead legionaries filled the chamber, thick, wet, red. Had they known, when they drew their blades, that

Jonon would take them apart? Probably. They were bright boys. They had been. Now they were . . . what? No one. Nothing.

"I'm going after her."

"I know."

She shook her head. "No. You don't. I'm going after her, and I am going to kill Jonon."

She could feel the captain's eyes on her, but she didn't look over. Instead she found herself staring at the Csestriim ring, those not-quite-possible curves and whorls, the light reflecting off it. Inside of her, the war raged, the poison of Menkiddoc straining against whatever it was that held it at bay, whatever it was that kept her human.

Slowly, deliberately, she twisted the ring from her finger.

The moment it slipped free, relief washed over her, cool as a light rain. Between one breath and the next her pain vanished. She could feel the blood coursing in her veins, the strength coiled in her legs and shoulders, each breath filling her with light and air and eagerness. She shut her eyes and shuddered with something approaching delight.

"Gwenna." Dhar's voice sounded far-off, as though he were speaking to her from a distant mountain peak. "Gwenna."

"Don't," she said. She didn't want to hear her name.

"This is not the way."

"It is the *only* way." Bliss rippled up her skin, trembled on her tongue. She slid the ring into a pocket of her blacks. "If I'm going to kill him, I need this strength."

"It is no true strength."

She shook her head. "You saw what he did to the *gabhya*. You *saw*. . . ."

"I saw a soldier who lost himself, who could not face his own failure."

Gwenna rose to her feet. Dhar followed her with his eyes, but made no attempt to stand up. It felt good, standing above him like that. It felt *right*.

"I won't abandon Rat. I won't leave her to him."

The captain scrubbed his brow with a filthy hand. "And what will happen to her, after you kill your admiral?"

"He's not my admiral. He was never my fucking admiral."

"What will happen to the child," Dhar pressed, "when you are done killing the man?"

"I'm going to send her here, to you."

"And what will we do when you come for us?"

"I'm not going to come for you. I'm going to kill Jonon—" The word *kill* sent a shiver down her spine. "And then I'm going to put the ring back on."

Dhar watched her. "You know this is not the case."

"I put it on once already. I can do it again."

"And if you cannot? If you choose not to?"

She took a deep breath, pointed toward the massive slab of stone. "Then close the door."

Dhar shook his head wearily. "This would transform the fortress into a crypt."

"No. Kiel will return. He can bring you both food and water, enough to keep you alive while you heal, while you figure out a way to escape."

"To escape from you."

She swept her swords from the floor, slammed them into their sheaths.

"Yes. To escape from me." She stabbed a finger toward the door. "You wait for Rat. Watch from the pass. If you see me coming, and I'm not . . . not myself, you get her inside and close that fucking door, and you do not let me in until you are certain, absolutely *certain,* that you can kill me."

58

Night had a way of unmaking the world. As a child Ruc had marveled at this, at the way the delta, by sunlight so bright and green and sharp, seemed to dissolve as the sun drained into the western reeds. The far lines faded first, the sharp slash of the rushes hazing to a vague wall of green, then gray. The sky flamed awhile, orange and red; then the clouds lost their shapes in the gulf of gathering dark. Water gave up reflecting anything but the stars. You could never see far in the delta, but after dark the whole world shrank to the scrap of dirt on which you sat, those stones, that swaying branch.

The world shrank at night, and at the same time, strangely, it seemed to grow.

Darkness ground down the boundaries between land and water, water and sky. The night was larger than the world it had replaced. The scrap of sandbar—delimited by day—became infinite. The channels stretched on forever.

It was the same way, Ruc realized, inside the Arena.

Lanterns ringed the pit, hundreds of them, while hundreds more hung from poles above the carefully raked sand. The place where the Worthy would be doing their fighting, their dying, was bright as a comfortable room, and yet beyond and above that ring of fire he could see nearly nothing, just the vague red heat of innumerable bodies pressed tight together. The lack of lanterns in the stands made sense—it would take only one lantern knocked askew to set the entire structure alight—but the effect was almost dizzying. There was no visible limit to the great crucible of the Arena. It stretched up and away into darkness on all sides, a cage as tall as the sky, a theater without end.

Night in the delta, however, was quiet. The air inside the Arena trembled with sound. The pit was loud by day, sometimes deafeningly so, but at noon you could look into the ranked seats and see the thousands of mouths from which the screaming poured. Now, as he gazed up, he could make out only the faces of the spectators in the lowest rows, maybe a few hundred of them, ruddy with the torchlight. The rest were swallowed by the emptiness. It felt as though the night itself was bellowing its heat and rage and eagerness, and for a moment the sound stopped him short. Like the first sheets of a monsoon rain, it felt almost solid, impenetrable.

"Looks different," Monster muttered.

Her habitual scorn seemed, for the moment, to have abandoned her. Ruc glanced over. She looked younger than her thirty years, eyes wide, the incipient lines of age smoothed away by the shifting torchlight. For half a heartbeat he saw what she might have looked like as a child, an orphan lost on the streets of Dombâng.

Goatface turned. "It is the same Arena you have fought and trained in all these months. The same size. The same sand. The rest"—he gestured to the torches, to the red and bronze drapery hanging from the walls—"is but pomp and ostentation."

Monster furrowed her brow, spat into the sand, and the thief and murderer swallowed up the little girl once more. "No fucking shit."

Ruc glanced over at Bien. Her expression was a new language, one he hadn't had a chance to learn. Or maybe an old one that he'd forgotten. Whatever the case, since the last day of the culling she seemed . . . changed. Stiller, calmer. Whether it was the stillness of resignation he couldn't say. While the rest of them went over and over the details of the escape, she held herself apart, listening to the discussions, nodding sometimes, but adding little. She'd kissed him that night. He could still feel the press of her lips on his shoulder, the tightness of her arm around his waist as he stared out the window, but that contact hadn't bloomed into anything more. Her distance reminded him of the distance in the eyes of the Vuo Ton warriors in the days before they went to face their gods. The approach of death affected everyone differently.

"Come," Goatface said, gesturing toward the center of the pit. "The good people of Dombâng are eager to welcome you."

A low, wide wooden dais stood at the center of the sand. Ruc had never seen it before—not during training, nor the three days of the culling. He did, however, recognize the crier who waited just at its side. For the first of the high holy days, the man wore a bloodred leather vest and a black *noc*. The bronze hoops in his ears reflected the torchlight. He offered a toothy smile as they approached, threw wide his arms as though to welcome old friends, then pivoted to the crowd.

"Next . . ." he announced as they mounted onto the platform, "fighting under the tutelage of Lao Nan, also known as the Goatface . . ."

Goatface frowned. "Goatface," he muttered. "Just Goatface. No *the*."

"The Worthy known as Monster, Mouse, and Stupid."

Stupid didn't bother glancing up from beneath the brim of his straw hat as a roar erupted from the crowd. Mouse hunched slightly, as though to make himself smaller. Monster made a series of rude gestures that earned her jeers and cheers in about equal measure.

Goatface frowned at her. "Hardly the behavior of a holy warrior."

"Not feeling all that fucking holy tonight," she replied.

"And a second three," the crier went on, "also trained by the Goatface: two priests of Eira . . ."

Ruc looked up sharply. During the culling, the crier had given only their names. Vang Vo knew their history, of course, but she'd made no indication that she intended to share it.

At the mention of the goddess, the crowd erupted into a frenzy. Ruc could make out individual voices stitched into the larger tapestry of sound:

. . . Unbelievers . . .

Annurian puppets!

Traitors! Traitors! Traitors!

Beside him, Bien raised her chin slightly. Ruc gazed up, past the torchlit faces at the rim of the pit, into the faceless dark beyond. Up there somewhere stood people that he or Bien had helped. The porter with the broken leg, maybe. Or the mother of triplets whose milk never dropped. The young man with the monsoon cough? The scabrous orphan? The boy who sold his body beneath the Bridge of Flowers? The brokenhearted fisher? The merchant who'd lost her daughter to the pox?

In his mind, they packed the stands, shoulder to shoulder, staring down at priests at the center of the pit. Did they remember the gifts of food and clothes? The offer of a warm room beneath Eira's roof? The hours of shared prayer and conversation? When the rest of Dombâng chanted for Ruc's blood, for Bien's, what would they do? Stand silently by or join their neighbors?

He could see no faces, but the weight of sound hammering down was all the answer he needed. Tonight was not a night for the remembering of kindnesses.

If possible, that hammering grew even louder with the announcement of Talal.

The Kettral didn't bother looking up, just held that iron ball patiently in the crook of his arm and waited for the crier to wave them off the dais toward the box.

The box.

The wooden bucket sat in the corner, as it always had, and no one seemed to have noticed the cracked board behind it, but whatever luck Ruc might have hoped for ended there. Four torches blazed overhead, one at each corner, chasing away the last sliver of darkness. Above and behind them, atop the high wall of the pit, stood both Arena guards and Greenshirts—there were hundreds more guards than usual in the Arena—some carrying spears, others flatbows. Those closest to Goatface's booth studied Ruc and the others with a mix of interest and contempt. The contempt didn't matter, but the interest was disastrous.

"We may be fucked," Monster said, not bothering to lower her voice.

"Fucked," Mouse agreed bleakly.

"Nonsense," Goatface replied, mistaking the source of their concern. "While you may not be . . . virtuosos of death, you are better trained than most of those you'll face."

"Who will we face?" Bien asked, staring out across the sand as the other Worthy and their trainers filed to their booths.

"That," Goatface said, "is a truth known only to Vang Vo."

He gestured.

Ruc had grown accustomed to finding the high priestess far above, perched like some carrion bird on the rail of her ship. For the first of the high holy days, however, she had descended to the pit itself. Even as he watched, she crossed the sand toward the wooden dais.

"I wouldn't mind fighting that bitch," Monster muttered.

"Yes, you would," Talal replied. He was studying the priestess with that hooded gaze of his.

Monster shot him a glance. "What do you know about it?"

"I know she's more dangerous than most of the Worthy."

"You've never seen her fight."

"I don't need to."

Ruc shook his head. "It doesn't matter. No one's fighting Vang Vo."

"Maybe no one has to fight anyone," Bien murmured, too quietly for Goatface to hear.

Ruc snuck a glance behind him. The crack in the board looked obvious, wide enough to slide a knife through. It seemed amazing that no one else had noticed—none of the guards, none of the trainers—but then, who would have thought that any of the Worthy would attempt to escape from the center of the pit in the middle of a fight? It was the very madness of the plan that had given it a chance of success.

"When do we do this?" Monster demanded.

She wasn't even bothering to be subtle, but then, Goatface was as unlikely to understand her question as he was to notice the crack at the back of his box.

"You will fight," he replied, "in the order Vang Vo decrees."

"Let's wait for the fights to start," Talal said.

That was the plan they'd settled on. It wasn't a good plan. They'd still need to deal with Goatface, and the Worthy in the neighboring boxes were still likely to notice the six of them disappearing behind the parasol one by one. Still, they'd have a better chance when everyone was distracted by people dying out in the middle of the pit.

Stupid tipped back his straw hat, sucked at something between his teeth. "Hope we don't fight first. Or against each other."

Bien shook her head. "I won't fight you."

Monster laughed. "That's the best news I've heard all fucking night. Wish I could promise the same."

Goatface tutted, interposed himself between them. "It is . . . highly improbable that the six of you will fight. In the early bouts, Vang Vo pits the Worthy of the *different* trainers against one another. With any luck you will not be forced to cross blades."

"And by luck," Stupid noted drily, "you mean that at least three of us will be too dead to fight."

"Yes," the trainer replied. "Well. This is a night, above all other things, of sacrifice."

While they were talking, Vang Vo had reached the center of the pit. She stepped up onto the wooden dais, waited patiently as the crier raised his hands for quiet. The din of the Arena settled like blood through water. When it was finally silent, she spoke.

"Sooner or later," she said, "we're going to forget."

Ten thousand bodies leaned in just slightly in order to hear her better.

"We'll spend enough years free, worshipping our own gods in our own city, and we'll forget that it wasn't always this way. There are kids here tonight who weren't alive when the Annurians went around knocking down doors, taking our idols, telling us what stories we could tell, what songs we could sing, which sacred names we could speak aloud."

She began to pace the perimeter of the dais.

"One of the reasons we do *this*"—she gestured to the sand, to the Worthy waiting in their boxes, to the invisible bowl of the Arena immuring them all— "is so that we *don't* forget. These warriors remind us that no one is born free. No one has a *right* to it. Freedom is something that has to be fought for, that has to be seized over and over and over, every year, every day, every moment."

She made a full circuit of the platform before continuing.

"Tonight offers another reminder, too. Most of our Worthy are Dombân-gan. Most, but not all."

She turned, pointed a finger at Goatface's box.

"Tonight, an Annurian soldier will fight on the sand beside two priests of an Annurian god."

The silence shattered into hissing and jeers. Vang Vo waited for the noise to subside, then continued.

"Some of my fellow priests tell me this was wrong. The unbelievers, they say, shouldn't be allowed to fight in such a sacred contest.

"I disagree.

"It's been so long since we've seen a foreign soldier in Dombâng that some of us have forgotten that they're out there. We've convinced ourselves that the Annurians are weak, stupid, doomed from the start." She shook her head. "Watch these warriors fight, and then tell me if they look weak or stupid. They may die, but their presence here should remind you that someone—Annur, the Waist tribes, pirates, *someone*—is always waiting to take your freedom. You can jeer at them all you want, but I'm grateful to them in the way I'm grateful to all the crocs that almost took my legs or arms over the years, in the way that I'm grateful to the gods who *did* take my hand." She paused to hold up the ruined stump. "They remind me not to forget, never to get lazy. *That* is why three Annurians will partake in the very first fight of these high holy days."

"First," Mouse murmured.

There was a heartbeat of silence before the Arena erupted in a fountain of furious sound. Ruc could make out none of the words, but he could hear the rage, the impatience, the animal hunger in the ten thousand voices. He could feel something answering inside himself, a grief transmuting to readiness.

"They do not appear," Stupid observed, "to have taken the more subtle lessons of the high priestess to heart."

"They want to watch us die," Ruc said.

"May I suggest," Goatface put in, "that you . . . disappoint them?"

"Who are we fighting?" Bien asked.

"She'll want to make an example," Talal replied. "It's one thing to have a handful of scary Annurians—"

"We're not Annurian," Ruc cut in.

The soldier met his gaze squarely. "Tonight you are. And the high priestess is putting us out there to show two things: first, that we're still dangerous, and second, that we can be killed. She'll match us against someone good."

"Oh," Bien said.

The sound was mild, the kind of exclamation she might have made seeing an old friend at the market.

Vang Vo still stood at the center of the dais, but now she was pointing west, to a box at the far side of the pit.

"Rooster," Ruc said.

A hot poison spiked his veins.

Talal nodded slowly. "Could have seen that coming."

"The high priestess," Goatface agreed, "has a . . . flair for the dramatic."

When the crowd fell still, Vang Vo spoke again.

"Against the Annurians, in the first contest of these high holy days, I have set a three trained by Lo Dao. You won't recognize the names their parents gave them, so I'll use the names you know: Rooster, Snakebones, and Toad."

Monster grunted as though someone had punched her.

"That is less than ideal," Stupid observed.

Ruc ignored them, stared across the pit instead, to where the three Worthy were stepping clear of their box.

Rooster's spiked black hair gleamed in the torchlight, as did the bells at his ankles and wrists, as did his teeth when he smiled. He was bare-chested, as usual, muscles oiled to a sheen. Unlike many of the Worthy, he looked relaxed, ready, happy. He gave a wave to the crowd, tilted back his head, and let loose with his cock's crow. Ten thousand Dombângans crowed back. At his side, Toad crunched his knuckles. Snakebones raised a hand. Ruc could just make out the mouse dangling by its tail. The small creature twitched and jerked. She brought it to her eye, then caught it between her teeth as it fell. Ruc couldn't hear the crunch, but he could imagine the small bones breaking, the organs bursting. He'd taken his own meals in the same way, once. Blood trickled from the corners of her mouth as she chewed twice, then swallowed. The crowd cheered louder for her than they had for Rooster. He didn't seem to object. While Snakebones wiped the blood from her chin with the back of her hand, the man dropped his gaze from the stands until he was staring directly across the Arena at Ruc and the others. With a single crooked finger, he beckoned.

"Bad fucking luck," Monster said.

"Bad," Mouse agreed.

They were right, of course. Of all the threes to face, Rooster, Snakebones, and Toad had to be the most dangerous. Ruc had watched them take apart other Worthy in the yard, always with insulting ease. The notion should have terrified him. When he looked inside himself, however, he found a dark, hungry craving. This fight would be nothing like the contest of the culling. Snakebones and Rooster would make no mistakes. Toad would not panic. There would be no space for second-guessing or hesitation. Ruc found that he was glad of the fact. For months, ever since the temple burned, he'd been clinging to his faith, trying to hold on to the goddess even as she slipped from his grasp. Even fighting for his life against Sang the Ox, even with the net pulled tight around his neck, there had been time—just fragments of heartbeats, but time—to doubt, to question, to hate what he was doing, what he had to do.

As he stepped onto the sand he realized how tired he had become of doubting and questioning. Maybe there had been a chance to be a priest of Eira, a *true* priest, but he had missed it. He should never have returned to the delta, never faced the men back in the burning temple, never resisted when the other Worthy came for him. The goddess had tested him, and he had failed the test. Over and over he had failed, and yet, until that moment he'd been trying to find a way back to Eira's grace, telling himself they wouldn't have to kill anyone else if they could get out of the Arena, if they could just disappear into the delta. . . .

Wrong, all of it.

Even if they *had* escaped, he carried the rot inside him. It wasn't the fault of the Arena, or of the delta, or Rooster, or the people of Dombâng. The land of blood and claw was inside him. The old hunger for violence was a part of him, like an organ he could no more live without than his lungs or his heart.

He could still refuse to take up a weapon, kneel in the center of the pit, and let Snakebones run him through, but he knew that he would not kneel. The pounding of his heart, the sweat of his palms—they didn't come from fear. After so many years praying and singing and trying to be better, he could do what the gods of the delta had raised him to do—fight to the death against something deadly. He could almost taste his own teeth.

As he watched, half a dozen laborers carried out the heavy table laden with weapons, the bronze bloody with the lamplight.

"No one," Goatface said, settling a hand on Bien's shoulder, gazing across the pit at Rooster and his three, "is invincible."

She shrugged away from the touch.

"They will make mistakes," the trainer went on. "Wait for those mistakes, then strike."

Monster shook her head. "Good fucking luck with that." She hesitated, then extended her hand to Ruc. "For a pair of priests and an Annurian, you three were all right."

For just a moment, Ruc thought he heard a hitch in her voice, then it was gone.

"We're not dead yet," he pointed out.

"Yet," Mouse agreed.

The man wrapped Talal in an enormous hug, then turned to Bien. To Ruc's surprise, she smiled, then stood on her toes to kiss him on the cheek. Mouse's eyes widened, but she was already turning away to embrace Stupid, then Monster.

"Thank you," she said simply.

Monster narrowed her eyes. "For what?"

"For being yourselves."

The woman glanced down at her body skeptically. "Not sure it's worth much thanks."

Bien just smiled wider, and then, with a surprising agility, vaulted over the rail of the box.

By the time they reached the table at the center of the pit, Rooster, Snakebones, and Toad were already waiting.

Rooster's spiked hair gleamed in the torchlight like something newly lacquered. Toad and Snakebones were also shirtless. All three of them looked as though they'd been oiled for the fight, skin slick and glistening.

"Well," Rooster said. "Well, well, well. How delightful."

Toad did not look delighted. He glowered at them from beneath heavy brows. Snakebones licked her lips.

"Unfortunately," Rooster continued, "it doesn't look as though we'll have time to continue our . . . courtship." He gestured to the stands. "They seem rather eager to watch you bleed."

"Or you," Ruc pointed out.

Rooster laughed. "Yes! Of course, or me."

Bien was gazing down at the weapons like she'd never seen them before.

Snakebones leaned in, snapped a finger in front of her face.

"Wake up, bitch. I want to hear you squeal when I stick you full of bronze."

Ruc started forward, then felt Talal's hand on his arm.

"Not yet," the Kettral murmured.

When Bien didn't respond, Snakebones shifted her gaze to Ruc, ran her tongue over her teeth. "He *is* pretty, Rooster. Shame. Maybe you can fuck him after he's dead." She flicked a glance at Bien. "Fuck both of them."

"Let's not get ahead of ourselves," Rooster replied. "Before we even think about any of that, we've got all this delicious killing to enjoy." He smiled at Ruc. "Tell you what—we'll let you take first choice of the weapons. Just to keep it sporting." He gestured to the table. "Go on."

Ruc waited for Bien to step forward, but she didn't move. Instead, she raised her eyes from the weapons, then frowned as though noticing Rooster and Snakebones for the first time, as though they were a problem she had not quite learned to solve.

"What do you want?" she asked them quietly. "What do you want out here, tonight?"

Snakebones blinked. "What we *want,* little sweet-reed, is to split you right open."

Bien cocked her head to the side. "*Why* do you want that?"

The other woman glanced at Rooster, obviously wrong-footed by the question.

Rooster shrugged. "Snakes? She just wants what she wants."

"But you didn't have to come here. You didn't have to do any of this."

A spasm of rage creased Snakebones's face. "You don't know shit about me."

Bien nodded slowly, as though working her way through the words. "You're right," she conceded finally. "I don't. And I'm sorry for that."

Snakebones stared, mouth ajar, as though something she couldn't quite bite through were stuck in her teeth.

Rooster chuckled. "This is all very sweet, but are you going to choose a weapon or not?"

Bien switched her gaze to him, held it for a moment, then nodded, took the spear from the table.

"You three," Rooster went on, squinting at them while Toad claimed the shield and dagger, "you were special. I'm going to miss you when you're dead."

Ruc ignored the man, picked up the sickles. And then Snakebones had the ring dogs. She spun them in her hands and laughed, all the emotion from moments earlier wiped away like so much sweat.

Talal took the grapple and line, which left Rooster with the net. He swept it around him in a graceful, ostentatious gesture, as though it were a cloak.

"Have you noticed," he asked, "that almost no one *likes* the net?" He shook his head. "In my opinion, it's the best weapon here. With the sickles or the spear—things are over so fast. Slash and blood, a little blubbering, and it's done. With the *net,* though, you get to watch the *struggle.* I love a good struggle."

Ruc started to respond, then stopped. He'd been so focused on Rooster and Snakebones that he hadn't noticed until that moment that the noise of the crowd had shifted. Shouts and screams still fell like a monsoon rain across the Arena, but the pitch had shifted. There was a new note of surprise and confusion, something different from the deafening clamor for blood. Talal touched Ruc's arm, pointed up toward the rim of the pit where three people stood balanced on the wall, two men and a woman. They wore knee-length cloaks, but it wasn't the sight of the cloaks that sent a frigid shiver over Ruc's skin. Around their necks, thick and fat, coiled the living collars of the *axoch.*

A knot of Greenshirts was shoving toward them through the crowd, knocking people out of the way with the butts of their spears, bellowed orders lost in the greater din.

Rooster rolled his eyes. "More messengers. Normally I wouldn't object—I like watching fools cut apart as much as the next man—but honestly, right now they are detracting from the sanctity of my night."

"No," Talal said quietly.

"Oh." Rooster waved a dismissive hand. "I know that in theory it's your night, too, but not *really.*"

"No, they're not messengers," the Kettral replied.

Up on the wall, the three had stripped their cloaks. They were naked beneath, and, like the other messengers, gorgeous as statues. Unlike them, however, these three carried spears.

The Greenshirts, almost upon them now, tried to pull up, to form into some kind of fighting unit, but it was already too late. Those spears flicked out, viper quick, opened a throat and a stomach, plunged into an eye. Two of the Greenshirts fell back into the stands, where the crowd closed over them like the sea. The third clutched his ruined belly, screamed blood, staggered forward, then toppled from the wall onto the sand.

"Well," Rooster said, speculatively twirling the end of his net. "*This,* at least, is more interesting."

"We have to go," Talal said, taking Bien by the arm.

Rooster crowed. "Go? Where are you going to go?"

Talal ignored him, shot Ruc a glance. "Now."

The collared foreigners had already leapt down onto the sand, were walking slowly toward the center of the Arena. . . .

No, Ruc thought. *Not walking. Stalking.* They moved like jaguars, ruddy flames shifting over their pale skin.

A few paces away, the Arena crier was trembling with rage. "This is a sacrilege!" he bellowed. "A profanation. It is—"

The woman, almost without breaking stride, cocked back her arm and hurled her weapon. The spear shaft carved through the air, the heat, the torchlight, bright point driving into the crier's open mouth, plunging straight through his head and out the back of his neck. He dropped like a slaughtered pig.

For a moment, shocked silence stretched like a tent over the Arena. The woman laughed, a bright, joyful sound, the sound of triumph. Then the crowd erupted. Ten thousand people lurched to their feet, hammered at the boards beneath them, screamed their fury. A dozen guards raced into the pit, clubs and swords brandished before them.

"Well, that," Rooster observed, "is the end of that."

Talal and Bien were already moving back toward Goatface's box. Ruc started to follow them, then stopped, some instinct bred deep in his flesh holding him in place.

"Stop," he shouted.

The Kettral's hand was clamped around Bien's arm. She looked utterly lost.

"The time is now, Ruc," he shouted.

The guards were halfway across the sand when the first of them dropped, an arrow sprouting from his throat. Half a heartbeat later, another stumbled to his knees, clutching a shaft in his gut. A third collapsed, then a fourth. Those still standing wheeled around, searching for their foes, but even as they searched they were slaughtered.

Toad loosed a furious growl, raised high his shield, charged at the nearest of the naked spear bearers. He managed four steps before an arrow plunged into the back of his neck, dropping him to the sand.

Talal stopped in his tracks, brought Bien up short along with him.

Snakebones was turning in a slow circle, teeth bared, ring dogs hefted before her, like a wild animal brought to bay.

"This," Rooster admitted, slicking back the side of his hair with a casual hand, "I did not expect."

Ruc glanced over at Talal.

"Annurian?"

The soldier hesitated, then shook his head.

Up in the stands, people were screaming, cursing, trying to run, trying not to be run down. Of Vang Vo there was no sign, but in the box atop the ship the other high priests had lunged to their feet, pointing, bellowing orders that none of the Greenshirts or Arena guards could hope to make out. In the space of a few dozen heartbeats, the entire space had descended into madness.

Then the *khuan* came.

Ruc had already seen one of them, of course, pinioned out in the delta by the Vuo Ton, defiant but half-dead. He'd heard the account of their attack. Neither fully prepared him for the fact of it.

The bats were almost twice as tall as Ruc himself, their wingspans the length of a swallowtail boat. Nothing that large should have been that fast, but they proved almost dizzyingly so, carving dark arcs through the air, snatching up the priests with their fangs and claws, hauling them up out of the torchlight, then dropping them. One woman thrashed as she fell, flailing her arms as though she could fly. She landed, broken, in the sand of the pit. Another tumbled, already limp as an old rag. One of the *khuan* hauled a third priest up to the top of the highest mast. Someone had thought to hang lanterns from the old broken yards, and as a result everyone could see the creature perching there, wings furled, body caught in its jaws. The priest struggled, spasmed, threw out a desperate hand. The jaws clamped down. The man shuddered and went still.

"We have to leave," Talal said calmly.

Bien shook her head. "They'll shoot us."

"Listen to wisdom when you hear it."

Ruc turned to find the woman with the *axoch* just a pace away. Sweat streaked her body, but her smile was placid, almost benign. The collar around her neck pulsed, as though it were digesting something.

"Remain here," she went on, "and you will come to no harm."

The other two messengers—that word was seeming less and less appropriate—took up positions at the other two points of a rough triangle around the pit's center.

"No harm?" Rooster asked. He cocked a thumb at the *khuan* high in the dead ship's mast. It had begun feeding on the body of the priest.

"These . . . priests"—the word sounded awkward in the woman's mouth—"refused to bow before the Lord, and so they are being removed. *You,* however . . ." She ran an eye over Rooster's gleaming body. "You are warriors. Pay him the proper obeisance, and he may even see fit to honor you with the *axoch.*"

Bien shuddered.

"I see the snipers now," Talal said. He was shielding his gaze, staring up into the stands. How he could see anything up there, Ruc had no idea.

"The people will tear them apart," Snakebones hissed.

Talal shook his head. "No. The archers are guarded by others, spears, swords. Groups of ten or twenty all over the stands."

"Who are you?" Ruc demanded, turning back to the woman.

Instead of replying, she knelt to wrench her spear from the mouth of the slaughtered crier, ran a finger along the flat of the blade, then tasted the blood. She smiled, utterly unconcerned with the chaos unfolding around her.

"We are the eternally reborn, blessed to come again into this present life as *rashkta-bhura.*"

Bien's eyes were fixed on the scaled, twisting skin of woman's *axoch.*

Ruc shot a glance at Goatface's box. Goatface's *empty* box.

The trainer himself, of course, had climbed up to his wooden platform to view the fight. He sat there now, an utterly incongruous figure, red parasol spread above him as though it were a mild afternoon and he had come to enjoy a picnic. Down in the box, however, the loose plank had been torn aside. Monster, Mouse, and Stupid were gone.

Smart, Ruc thought ruefully.

They must have made their play when the *khuan* attacked. No one would have noticed in the madness, and anyone who did notice wouldn't have cared. The guards were all fighting or dying. The three thieves could be halfway through the labyrinth beneath the stands already, halfway to freedom. He measured the distance to the box—twenty-five paces. Twenty-five paces across open sand with archers covering the pit from above. It wasn't far. It was impossible.

Even as he searched for a way out, the great gate into the pit clattered open.

Along with Talal and Bien, Snakebones and Rooster, along with everyone in the Arena, he shifted to watch the iron grate rise. A roar erupted from the darkness beneath. Ruc hefted his weapon.

Something terrible exploded into the torchlight.

"Monster," Bien murmured, shaking her head.

Ruc could think of no other word to describe it.

The creature was the size of a huge horse, but instead of a horse's legs it scuttled forward on nimble, apelike arms, six of them, grafted at odd angles to its glistening, hairless body. It had a blunt, piggish face, tusks, massive jaws, and horrible, tiny, almost human eyes. A few feet away walked another collared woman. Unlike the others, however, she carried not a spear, but a kind of goad, one she used to urge the monster out into the pit, then along the walls.

A few feet from the creature, a man dangled from the railing at the edge of the lowest stands. Ruc couldn't tell whether he'd caught himself mid-fall, or was trying to flee the crush above. If he was looking for escape, he'd made the wrong choice. The woman barked some kind of command, lashed her monster across the haunch. It turned, seized the dangling man, roared once more, then ripped free an arm. The man poured his scream silently into the rising din. When the beast tossed him aside, he began dragging himself away, blood pumping from the wound, as the thing raised the torn arm, then stuffed it into its mouth.

"What is that?" Talal asked quietly.

The woman with the *axoch* beamed. "One of the *shava*. We call it the Herald. It is what comes before."

Bien stared. "Before what?"

As if in response, soldiers began marching in through the open gate.

During his fifteen years in the city, Ruc had had plenty of time to witness both the Annurian legionaries and the Dombângan Greenshirts. He'd seen soldiers march and fight before, but never anything quite like this. The warriors pouring into the Arena moved with an uncanny precision, taking up positions around the perimeter of the pit as though they'd been training the maneuver for years. Unlike the naked messengers, they wore some kind of light armor, with gleaming, overlapping scales that made them look like insects grown to monstrous proportions. Each wore a short sword at the hip and carried a spear, spears that they used to chivvy the Worthy—those who had leaped from their boxes in the initial confusion—back up against the walls of the pit.

"SILENCE."

The word erupted inside Ruc's head. Only when he saw everyone else flinch, cringe, press hands to their ears or temples, did he realize it had been spoken aloud, far louder than should have been possible.

"THE TIME OF TRUTH HAS ARRIVED."

"There," Talal said after a moment, nodding toward one of the naked men at the center of the pit, one of the three original spear bearers. He was speaking—speaking, not shouting—but his words emerged as wide as the night sky.

"A kenning," the Kettral murmured.

Bien stared. "They're leaches?"

Talal frowned. "*Someone's* a leach. Doesn't have to be him."

The bats had begun circling once more, dipping and diving, seizing people in their claws. It looked like they were plucking randomly from the crowd, dragging the struggling figures high into the sky, then dropping them.

"HE HAS COME TO BIND YOU AND TO SET YOU FREE."

"They're only taking the people who try to run," Bien said.

Ruc stared into the stands. It was hard to make any sense in the darkness and chaos, but she seemed to be right. Slowly at first, then more and more quickly, the citizens of Dombâng appeared to be learning the same lesson. They dropped to their knees on the boards and benches, abandoned all thought of escape, and cowered in place. A few cast terrified glances at the sky, as though they were mice caught in the open.

The naked woman with the axoch turned to them, triumph bright in her eyes. "You should kneel."

Ruc stared at her a moment, glanced up at the massive bats swooping through the sky, then dropped to his knees. Out of the corner of his eye, he could see Talal and the others, even Rooster and Snakebones, doing the same.

"YOU WERE WARNED THAT THIS DAY WOULD ARRIVE," the messenger went on. "YOU WERE TOLD TO PREPARE." He shook his head. "BUT YOU HAVE NOT PREPARED."

As he spoke, more warriors trotted into the Arena carrying lengths of chain and collars, not the *axoch,* but normal collars of steel. They spread around the perimeter of the pit, to all the boxes of the Worthy, then, with vicious efficiency, began shackling the warriors, four, five, eight to a chain, steel rings clamped tight around their necks. A few tried to fight. They died, slaughtered by arrows from above.

Up in the stands someone very drunk or very stupid started screaming. "The Three will destroy you! Kem Anh will come for your abominations. Sinn will shred them limb from limb." She stumbled into the lamplight, still shouting. "The Three will have their revenge for this profanation. They will—"

An arrow punched into the woman's chest. For a moment, she spoke only blood, then collapsed.

One of the soldiers paused behind Ruc, took him by the chin, dragged back his head. He felt the cool steel close around his throat, tighten, then clank shut. A pace away, Talal and Bien were locked to the chain, and then Snakebones and Rooster, all of them bound together.

Again the messenger shook his head. "YOUR THREE WILL NOT SAVE YOU. THEY COULD NOT SAVE THEMSELVES."

His smile grew into a sickle as he swept his hand toward the gate, and then he, too, dropped to the ground, face pressed into the sand. The ranks upon ranks of the soldiers remained standing, but bowed their heads, snapped their spears to bristling attention.

Ruc tensed, waiting for some other monstrosity to emerge, some new nightmare.

Instead, two human figures crawled from the shadows beneath the gate. Aside from the bats sweeping silently through the air, the world fell still. The only sound was the hot wind and the faint sobbing of the wounded.

Ruc saw the heat of the creatures first, so much heat pouring from the bodies that they should have been delirious with fever, more heat than any human could withstand. Then he saw what lived beneath the heat.

Not human. Not human at all.

From darkness into the torchlight, collared not with *axoch* but some other glistening metal, crawled Kem Anh and Hang Loc, the gods of Dombâng, the figures that, for the first years of his life, Ruc had taken for his own mother and father. Chained. Defeated, somehow. Humiliated.

Behind them, like some perverse charioteer, holding a leash in each hand, strode the tallest man Ruc had ever seen—eight feet high if he was an inch. Ruc had studied his share of big fighters in the Arena. Most moved strangely, as though their limbs hadn't been joined together quite right. This man, however, moved like water flowing downhill, more graceful than a cat sliding through the reeds. Like the figures crawling before him, he was utterly naked. Behind him strode half a dozen gorgeous men and women. . . . *No,* Ruc thought, not men and women, but whatever *he* was, the same race as Kem Anh and Hang Loc. They, too, came into the torchlight naked, larger than life, perfect in every proportion.

When the holder of the leashes reached the center of the Arena, he smiled down at the messengers, then up at the crowd. That smile reminded Ruc of no expression he had ever seen: decadent and predatory, hungry and contemptuous, utterly, perfectly at ease. When he spoke, it was with the same liquid, alien accent as the messengers who had foretold him and his companions.

"These," he said, snapping the chains against the backs of the figures kneeling before him, "are your gods."

The wind had stopped. The sobbing had stopped. Everything had stopped. There was no air. No breath.

"Up, worms," he said, whipping them again with the chains. "Show your faces. Let these fools read the measure of your defeat."

At first, it seemed they would refuse. Neither moved. Both remained with their faces to the mud.

"It can't be," Snakebones snarled. "That's impossible."

But, of course, it was not impossible. Horror opening inside him, Ruc watched Kem Anh rise slowly to her knees, then her feet. The creature who taught him to walk, to swim, to run, to climb, to hunt gazed up into the Arena with her liquid golden eyes. Even shackled, even chained, she radiated strength. Even naked, she wore a beauty beyond all human beauty, a divine inhumanity, a perfection like that of the man holding her leash.

"He's one of them," Ruc said. "Sweet Eira's touch, he's one of *them*."

As though she'd heard his voice, Kem Anh turned. Their gazes locked.

Her eyes scrubbed away the intervening years and he was a child once more, wordless and free, afire with life. How had he ever traded her perfection for the wan teachings of a goddess he'd never seen? She bared her teeth. He waited for her to speak, to say something, then remembered—how had he forgotten?—that the goddess of the Vuo Ton lived in a world beyond words.

At her side, Hang Loc rose.

He stood almost as tall as his captor, and broader through the shoulders and chest. Ruc had watched him take fifty-year-old crocs in his embrace, snapping their spines while they thrashed, but he remembered too being held in those massive hands, rocked patiently to sleep. There was no patience now. Unlike Kem Anh, who attended on the future motionless as an idol, Hang Loc turned to face his captor.

For a long time they stood there, like some image out of myth.

Then the creature who could only be the First smiled.

Hang Loc struck, fast as a viper, so fast Ruc couldn't see the motion, only the aftermath. The First shrugged to the side as though time had no claim upon him. Hang Loc's fist swung harmlessly through the night, and his captor reached up, the motion so fast it felt slow, took him by the neck, tore out his throat.

Ruc gaped like a fish ripped from the current, held up to suck at the hot, awful air.

A man would have dropped instantly, but Hang Loc was not a man. Blood sheeted his naked chest, pumping from the ragged wound, but he was still reaching, trying to seize his foe as Ruc had once watched him seize the champions of the Vuo Ton, still moving forward, as though it were impossible for him to conceive of his own end.

The First stepped contemptuously aside, watched Hang Loc stumble to the sand, then raised high the bloody trachea.

Kem Anh did not move. Or rather, her body remained motionless, but her eyes were fixed on Hang Loc, following him as he dragged himself over the dirt, one pace, then another, then another.

"Behold your gods," the First declared, tossing his grisly trophy to the dirt.

Hang Loc spasmed, tried—amazingly, impossibly—to rise, fell again.

"You have spent your lives worshipping something weak," the holder of the chains went on. "You have made your minds small, but do not fear. I have come to make them great once more."

He gestured with a sweeping hand to the ranks of soldiers, to the bat-things circling above the Arena, to the monstrous creature with six legs that prowled the edge of the pit.

"These," he said, flicking a long finger at Hang Loc's corpse, then at Kem Anh, "led you astray. I have come to lead you back."

He gave a quick, vicious snap of the chain, slamming Kem Anh to her knees once again. She remained there, beautiful face pressed to the sand, making no effort to rise.

"These"—he pointed to the men and women holding the spears—"have already seen the truth. In time, you will see it, too."

Up in the stands, someone screamed. Ruc waited for the voice to cut off, but instead others joined it, a rising, panicked chorus. He risked a glance and realized that, in all the chaos, one of the torches had fallen. Flame licked at the wall of the pit, gnawed at the hanging fabric before igniting the wood. Tongues of fire tasted the air, devoured the old timber, combined and leaped into the night. The sound was a roar. A breeze kicked up, whipping the fire along the walls, and the stands erupted into a mad panic. People crawled over one another like ants fleeing a flooded hill. They screamed as they fell, as the heels of their countrymen crushed them to pulp. Parents tried to lift children above the fray only to fall, ground down in the press of so much flesh.

"Now," Talal said.

In one fluid movement, the Kettral had risen, turned, smashed his hand into the throat of the soldier behind him.

Yes, Ruc thought.

A part of him understood that it was madness. The five of them were chained together at the center of the pit and surrounded by the vanguard of a foreign army. Even with the distraction of the fire, fighting their way free was impossible. Talal would die, *Bien* would die. . . .

Even as the thoughts flitted, swallow-like, through his mind, he found himself staring across the corpse of Hang Loc into Kem Anh's eyes.

Violence opened inside him. The chain's weight didn't matter. The soldiers didn't matter. The snipers didn't matter. The *khuan* patrolling the skies above didn't matter. He was going to die here—he felt the truth of that in the same way he felt his heart hammering the blood through his body—but if he had learned anything in those early years in the delta, it was the beauty of a good death.

He seized the bronze sickles and surged to his feet even as the woman with the *axoch* turned to face him.

"You should have stayed on your knees," she said, eyes afire.

Ruc smiled, then shook his head. "I was not raised to kneel."

Behind him, the whole world was fire. In front of him, the spear danced in the woman's hands, darting in high, low, high again. He twisted aside from the first thrust, swept away the second with the sickle, ducked the third. He was vaguely aware of Rooster fighting, too, and Snakebones, and Talal. Then the naked woman came on again and his world narrowed to the point of her gleaming spear. She was snake-fast, smooth and unpanicked, stabbing over and over and over. There was no time to set his feet, no time to feint or weave, no time to think, no time to do anything but *react*. He fought the way a beast would fight, giving himself up to the ancient instinct of sinew and jaw. She slipped past his guard, nicked his shoulder, and he roared, hurled himself forward, battered her back, hacked through the shaft of her spear, lopping the head clean off. She tried to shift her posture, but he was already on her, hammering her down, sweeping the second blade in a clean arc through the air to split open her face. She screamed through the ruin of her lips. The *axoch* writhed. Ruc slashed her across the throat, parting the dark flesh of the living collar and the neck beneath.

For a heartbeat he stood there, panting, waiting for the shame to wash over him. Instead of shame, however, elation blazed through his veins, the white-cold excitement he'd felt as a child hunting through the rushes. The priest of Eira shuddered, but the goddess of love had no altar on the bloody sand.

He killed three more soldiers in the space of a dozen breaths. They came at him screaming or silent, wielding those spears. Their flesh opened like ripe fruit beneath his sickles. Blood erupted and the bodies started their long fade into darkness.

Ruc surged forward, searching for the next foe, when the chain at his neck snapped him back. A bronze spear tip flashed through the space where his face should have been, so close it flicked hot blood across his cheek.

"Eyes up, lover boy!" It took him a moment to recognize Snakebones's voice. The woman was laughing a few paces behind him, her savage glee cutting through the screaming and roar of the fire. "You're not allowed to die while you're on this chain with me."

He pivoted, blocked the next attack, lopped the hand from his nameless attacker, then slashed him across the face.

Somehow, impossibly, in the space of a few hundred heartbeats, Snakebones had become his ally. The world was broken. He wondered if he cared.

He opened the next spear bearer to come at him, reached into the slash he'd carved across the man's gut, ripped out the intestines. Somewhere off to the side Rooster was crowing over and over, as though he were a bird driven mad by the fire. Ruc roared in response, surged forward, indifferent to the steel dragging at his throat, killed a doe-eyed woman, and then the First loomed up before him, inevitable as death.

Silhouetted against a curtain of flame, he looked down. Off to the right, Talal was hacking at someone. To the left, Snakebones laughed maniacally. A dozen paces distant, her golden eyes ablaze, stood Kem Anh. At some point in all the violence, she had taken to her feet once more.

The First didn't deign to glance over his shoulder. Instead, he kept his eyes—blue eyes, a shocking blue webbed with black—fixed on Ruc.

"Do you think she is going to save you?" His voice was gorgeous as the dawn.

Ruc shifted his grip on the sickles. "You think I need saving?"

"You were not made to face me."

"You have no idea what I was made for."

Ruc struck as he spoke, lashing out with both sickles, one high, one low.

The First plucked them from his hands as though they were toys, glanced at them a moment, then tossed them aside.

"Your faith is misplaced. If you wish to worship, you may worship me."

"I'm just about done," Ruc growled, "with worship."

He settled his weight into his feet, prepared to attack, to die. No one could hold on to life forever. The Vuo Ton had understood that truth, at least.

Before he could strike, however, Kem Anh uncoiled. She moved like sunlight dancing across waves, searing and silent, faster than anything alive.

Her foe was faster.

He turned, stepped clear, brought his fist up then over in an awful arc, smashing it down into the back of her skull. The woman who had hunted jaguars barehanded through the rushes, who wore the blood of crocs like paint across her face, who had forever ruled all creatures of the delta, dropped to the sand, unstrung.

The First made a quick hissing sound, bared his too-sharp teeth.

"That was my mother," Ruc said quietly.

"She will serve me. I have seen it. Seen her with me atop a tower by a lake. She will serve me. As will you."

He shook his head slowly, closed his hands into fists. "She taught me a lesson when I was a child. For a long time, I forgot it."

The eyes of the huge gorgeous creature were empty as the noonday sky. "What was it, this lesson?"

"Never serve."

As the words left his tongue, Ruc hurled himself forward.

The First caught him by the throat, hoisted him into the air. The hand might have been made of stone. Heat poured from the creature's face, but the rest of the world began to fade. Ruc lashed out with a kick. Useless if he wanted to win, but he wasn't trying to win. The fight wasn't about what came next, who lived or died. What mattered was the struggle.

A scream carved the night like a blade. At first he took it for his own, but he couldn't scream, couldn't even breathe. Bien's voice, he realized, but too loud, as though the whole sky were her throat.

"Put him down."

Those blue-black eyes looked past him, narrowed. "You would beg for his life?"

"I'm not begging. I am demanding."

"It is not your place to make demands. You will learn this."

Flame fringed Ruc's vision. The world felt too huge, too tight. Out of the corner of his eye, he saw Bien move forward. Her steel collar caught the flame, but her eyes were dark.

"I am telling you this for the last time," she said. "I love that man. I love him, and those chained to him. I am a priestess of Eira, and I love all the people of this arena. They are mine. Not mine to possess and control, as you want to, but mine to love, every one of them."

"Love." The man who was no man at all smiled his teeth. "A human thing. It is a weakness."

"Not to me, you son of a bitch."

His eyes widened. Something that might have been surprise skittered across those inhuman features. Ruc felt the hand around his throat open, and then he was free, falling.

The First opened his mouth, but something, some invisible hand, took him up and hurled him the length of the pit.

Ruc struggled to his feet.

"We need to *go*," Talal declared, appearing from somewhere, swords in each hand, swords he hadn't held before.

Like a man underwater, Ruc turned slowly, found Bien standing, her eyes alight with the burning world.

The First, however, wasn't finished. Between one heartbeat and the next he was back on his feet, lips twisted in a snarl. He leaped forward, but Bien was leaning toward him, like a woman laboring into the teeth of a monsoon.

"I am a priestess of Eira," she screamed, "and you are not my lord!"

With the words, some awful force snatched him from the air, hammered him down again.

Again he rose.

Ruc could do nothing but stare. Talal was staring, too, and Rooster, and Snakebones, all of them frozen in that moment of violence.

"I am a priestess of Eira!"

The huge man staggered.

"Love is the burning of my fire!"

Each word knocked him back another step.

"Love is blood dripping from my jaws!"

He roared, lunged.

"Love is the constant ache of my loss."

Somehow he fought past whatever force she threw against him, drove himself forward, slaver sliding from his lips. Bien, though, was moving forward, too.

"I believed them," she screamed. "I believed everyone when they said my love was my weakness, but it is *not!*"

She closed her hand into a fist, strangling the air. The First rose into the sky.

"My love is my motherfucking *sword*."

With a savage gesture, she hurled him back. The creature who had humbled the gods of the delta flew, trailing a roar of rage like a flag behind him, shattered into the burning stands in a eruption of fire, then disappeared as the structure collapsed around him. Ruc stood, useless as a man transfixed by a snake's poison, gazing at Bien. The fire's light raked her face. Her eyes blazed. Tears streaked her cheeks. For a moment she looked larger than herself, greater, a being of light and shadow stepped down from the vast space of the night itself. Then she gasped, slumped, doubled over.

Talal recovered first, shifting to her side, catching her before she could fall. "Really now," he said, stabbing a finger back toward Goatface's box. "We need to go."

Rooster cocked his head to the side. "Go where?"

"No," Ruc growled.

"There is no time to decide this," Talal said. "We all go, and we go now."

"I *did* save your life, lover boy," Snakebones pointed out.

"We're not leaving," Ruc replied, "without her."

He pointed to where Kem Anh lay, splayed across the sand.

"She's dead," Rooster said. "Sexy, but dead."

Ruc shook his head. Heat poured from the still body, white-hot as the noon-day sun. "No. She is not so easy to kill."

He crossed to her in two strides, knelt, raised her up, staggered beneath the weight. He had never tried to lift her, this creature who had carried him so many times. She weighed twice, maybe three times any human body, but she had not raised him to shirk a difficult task. With an effort of will, he settled her across his shoulders.

"Are you sure—" Talal began.

"Go," Ruc snarled, hurling himself into a run.

The foreign soldiers caught up to them just at the edge of the pit. If they were frightened of the sparks raining down, or the Arena collapsing around them, or the defeat of their Lord, evidently they were more frightened by whatever happened if they retreated.

Rooster tangled two in his net, Talal dropped one, Ruc heaved Kem Anh over the low wall, followed her.

"Go!" Talal said, gesturing toward Bien. "Go!"

She nodded, then slipped through the gap.

"I'd stay to fight," Rooster said, then gestured to the chain, "but it looks like I'm next."

He and Snakebones slid through.

"Now her," Talal said, flicking a glance at Kem Anh's limp form.

Ruc nodded, knelt beside the wall, tried to pass her through. He felt hands on the other side, but the chain snagged on a jagged splinter of wood. Slowly, he drew her back out, fixed the chain.

"Faster would be better," Talal shouted.

Ruc risked a glance over his shoulder. The spear-wielders had paused, spread out. A bright, manic intensity glazed their eyes, something like what he'd seen before in the gaze of men smoking rotweed. Most fighters, even good fighters, *especially* good fighters, would have looked cautious. These people looked as though the thought of their own death hadn't occurred to them. Then, even as he watched, something tore into the soldiers from behind. One dropped, then another, a few turned to face this new foe, and then a moment later Goat-face burst through the knot. He was holding the handle of his parasol, but instead of the red waxed canvas, it ended in a slender arm-length blade.

"I will . . . detain them," he announced matter-of-factly.

Talal shook his head, adjusting to the new development. "No. You go. I'll come next."

The trainer shook his head. "I think not."

"*Go,*" the Kettral snapped.

"Do you know," Goatface asked, his voice light, almost conversational, "why I never joined the Worthy? Never went into the delta myself?"

"Now is not the time," Ruc said. Kem Anh was through, but the stands overhead roared with fire.

Goatface, however, continued as though he hadn't spoken. "I never went, because I was afraid."

He punctuated the comment with a flick of the blade, knocking away the nearest of the spearpoints, then shook his head.

"What a loss."

He stepped aside as another spear stabbed past him, hacked down, knocking the shaft from the other fighter's grip, then slid that slender blade almost gently into the man's eye.

"We can all get out," Ruc said. "You, too."

Goatface replied without turning. "You are laboring under a . . . misapprehension." He pivoted, ducked a spear thrust, impaled a woman. "No one gets out. There is no *out* to *get*. This is the beauty and the truth of the Arena: in Dombâng, in the delta, in the wide world"—he gestured grandly with his slim blade, a sweep taking in the fire and screams, the monsters and the fighting and the dying—"there is only ever this."

59

"Yerrin. Have you ever seen anything like this?"

"There is a spider here," Yerrin replied, "that I have never seen."

The old monk gazed out the window of the garret into the falling night.

Akiil picked up the stone. The seed, the Csestriim woman had called it. It felt warm in his hand, warmer than it should have, but then, the night was warm. Maybe he was imagining things.

He crossed to the window where Yerrin stood. As promised, a web stretched across the wooden frame, gossamer-thin strands catching the late-day light. A spider crouched at the edge, waiting. Whether it was an unusual spider or not, Akiil couldn't say. He hadn't made a study of the world's spiders.

"Look at this," he said, holding out the seed.

Yerrin turned slowly, took the stone, then shook his head. "Look *into* it." He tossed the stone lightly once, twice, three times, then handed it back.

"What do you make of it?" Akiil asked.

"Make of it?" The monk shook his head. "We do not make the world."

There had been no reason, really, to hope for anything more useful. Yerrin could spend all day watching an anthill without noticing an army marching around him. Once, after Akiil went to the trouble of stealing a handful of silver moons from a merchant's desk, Yerrin had tossed them into a stream. He wanted to watch the fish, and the fish were attracted to the sunlight glinting off the metal. Akiil had recovered about half of the coin—the rest was swept down current and lost. The monk was hardly an appraiser of fine gemstones or Csestriim artifacts, but Akiil didn't have anyone else, and besides, sometimes Yerrin saw things that other people missed.

"Have you ever seen anything like this before?"

"Of course!"

There was a long pause. The monk touched one of the strands of the web with the stem of a leaf. The spider scuttled out, tested the web, paused, then retreated to her corner. Yerrin smiled, but said nothing.

"Where?" Akiil asked finally.

The monk raised a gnarled finger toward the window, pointing outside, past the frame, past the bats. . . .

Akiil took a deep breath. He'd kept the old man alive this long. It would be a shame to murder him now.

"Apart from the night sky," he said slowly, "have you ever seen something like this? A stone? A gem? The . . . woman who gave it to me called it a seed."

"I've seen many seeds! Hemlock, spruce, ghost pine. I used to eat the seeds inside bruiseberries. The fruit was sweet, but the seeds were bitter. . . ."

"But you don't know what *this* is? What it does?"

The faint hope that Yerrin might provide some wisdom was rapidly fading.

"It is not a stone," the monk replied. He prodded gently at the web once more.

Akiil narrowed his eyes. "What does that mean?"

"A seed is more than itself. It is the future furled into the present. The acorn holds the oak inside it."

Akiil turned it in his hands. It took him a moment to overcome the vertigo, but once he did he was able to stare into the thing. Some of the glinting points inside seemed close, some impossibly far away. As he rotated it, others slid into view. It was one of the most beautiful things he'd ever seen, even more beautiful, somehow, than the night sky, in the way that a cut diamond could be more beautiful than a whole field of ice. When he finally pulled his eyes free, it was impossible to know how long he'd been staring at it. Yerrin still stood at the window, but now the spider was sitting in the palm of his hand, silently rubbing her front legs against each other. The old monk smiled as he watched her.

"Why would a seed be dangerous?" Akiil muttered, shaking his head.

"Thorns grow from seeds," Yerrin observed. "Poisonous plants grow from seeds."

"What do you think grows from this?"

The old monk turned slowly, glanced at the stone once more, then raised his eyes to Akiil. For once, his gaze was focused, grave.

"Something beyond us. Something too much. Something we were never meant to see."

†

Akiil was asleep when they kicked in the door of the garret, dreaming, for once, of something other than slaughter.

He sat on a narrow stone ledge high in the Bone Mountains, a spot just north of Ashk'lan. It was tricky, dangerous work reaching that ledge, a precipitous down-climb from the trail above in which one missed foot, one crumbling handhold meant death. And yet, he'd gone there over and over as a child, partly because it was a place to hide from the monks, but mostly because nowhere in the mountains offered such a spectacular sunset. In springtime, looking west from the perch, he could follow the arc of the declining sun as it settled between the peaks, then slipped below the far horizon. Out over the steppe the color lingered, rinsing the sky in blues and pinks and yellows. There'd been nothing like it back in the Quarter, where smoke from ten thousand cook fires choked the air.

He never would have admitted it to the monks, never would have admitted it to *anyone,* not even Kaden, but when he sat on the ledge, maybe *only* when he sat on that ledge, he felt like a monk. He would draw his robe around him, shut out the chill as he'd been trained, let his mind fill with the beauty of the world. More than once he'd stayed out there the entire night, as the pink drained into darkness and the stars came out in all their astounding scatter.

He used to wonder what the kids from the Quarter would make of that view. Horan would have mocked it, probably. Butt Boy would have had a thousand theories about what the stars were, where they came from, why they looked like so many chips of ice, how they stayed up there. Runt would have fallen asleep while Skinny Quinn memorized it all, the million shapes sweeping above in their great, silent arc. He would have liked to share it with them, even Horan. He would have listened to the boy making fun of him for admiring the colors and then he would have said, "Just shut up. Just look, Horan. Just look at it."

The door shattered open, ripping away the dream and the world it contained as though they'd been no more than shabby curtains.

Akiil rolled to his feet—too slow. A man in full armor—Hugel, he realized, Adare's Aedolian—was already swinging a short club, bringing it down into his temple with a bright, dazzling smash that ushered in the dark.

†

Cold water flooded his nose, forced its way between his lips.

For a moment, he thought he was drowning, but when he struggled to swim he found his arms bound at his sides, his legs shackled at the ankles. It was only when he managed to wrench open his eyes that he realized he wasn't underwater at all, but strapped—strapped naked—to a table in a small stone room. There were no windows—none that he could see, anyway, from his limited vantage—but light from a dozen lanterns turned the space bright as a market at midday. He twisted, searching for the door, discovered the

Emperor instead, gazing down on him with those Intarran eyes. Hugel stood beside her, a dripping, empty bucket dangling from one hand. Beside him hovered a small, mouse-faced balding man in a heavy leather apron, lenses of the type scribes sometimes wore balanced on a wire frame before his eyes.

"Time to wake up," Adare said, moving down into his line of vision.

He met her eyes, then glanced down at his goose-pimpled flesh. "I take it that you're displeased."

"Your gift for understatement matches your talent for treachery."

"Treachery?" He frowned. "I think you have me confused with someone else."

"Another Shin monk hopping back and forth through the *kenta*?"

"*Hopping* sort of downplays the effort involved."

The Emperor shook her head grimly. "Tell me: when someone sells a valuable antiquity, an artifact worth hundreds or even thousands of Annurian suns, who is it, do you suppose, who *purchases* that artifact?"

His stomach went sour. *More* sour, if he were being precise. He exhaled between pursed lips. "I have to say, I'm more than a little disappointed in Gelta Yuel's ideas about privacy."

"Don't blame Gelta. She tries to hide the identities of her tomb robbers, but when I lean on a person, I lean hard. Half of what she sells, she sells to me."

"So. No harm done. You got your dagger in the end."

The Emperor's eyes were an inferno, but her voice remained mild. "I did. And what I want to know now is where you got it, and what else you found there."

Beside her, the small man watched through his lenses, brow furrowed, as though he were hunched over a game of stones.

"Who is this?" Akiil asked. "I don't believe we've met."

Adare glanced down at the man. "This is Galter."

Galter nodded, as though confirming the answer, then turned away. There was a clanking as of metal rods being shifted. When Akiil twisted his neck to the breaking point, he could just make out an oven set into the wall. Galter, with a cook's fastidious precision, was arranging the rods inside the oven.

A blanket of dread settled down over him.

"And who is Galter?" he asked, though he already knew the answer.

Adare didn't bother responding; instead she stepped closer, gazed down into his eyes.

"You're a monk," she said quietly, "and so you can see things you're not supposed to see. Tell me—what do you see when you look at me?"

For a long time, he studied her in silence. Blood tattooed its rhythm inside the veins of her neck. The flames in her irises shifted. Her breath came quick but steady. She kept her eyes fixed on him, didn't look away.

"You're angry," he said.

She shook her head. "Look deeper."

Galter hummed tunelessly at the back of the room.

Akiil took a deep breath, closed his eyes, studied the image of the Emperor inscribed across his mind.

"Frightened," he said after a long time.

He opened his eyes to find her nodding. "I am frightened."

"Seems strange, given I'm the one that's strapped to the torture table."

"Oh, I'm not frightened for myself, Akiil. Or not mostly. I'm frightened for my son. I'm frightened for my soldiers. I'm frightened for the people of Olon, and Sia, and Raalte, and Katal."

"Your concern for your people is admirable," he replied. "But I'm not sure how hurting me is going to help them."

"What else did you find inside the fortress?"

"Weapons," he replied. "Artifacts." He'd known the question was coming since he woke strapped to the table, since he saw Hugel darkening his kicked-in door. "The place was packed with stuff, at least the first time I went there."

Adare pursed her lips. Evidently she hadn't expected him to be so forthcoming so quickly.

"Why did you conceal this from me?"

He tried to shrug. "I was going to sell them. Like I did with the dagger."

Not the truth—not all of it—but not entirely wrong, either. More important, it was something the Emperor would accept. For all his robes and ancient Shin sayings, he'd always been a thief to her; she'd never seen past his brands. She would believe his story because she *already* believed it.

"Where is the rest of it?"

"I don't know."

"On your first passage, this fortress was filled with weapons and artifacts, while on the second they were all simply . . . gone?"

Not simply *gone,* he thought, remembering the Csestriim woman, the huge monster, its puke boiling over the stone. Not simple at all.

"Obviously, I'm not the only one who can use the *kenta*." He cocked his head to the side. "What about those Csestriim? The ones you keep insisting don't exist?"

Her lips tightened into a thin line. He expected her to deny it again, to shake her head, then drag the conversation back to all his lies and betrayals. Instead, she gave a tight nod of her head, then gestured to Hugel.

The Aedolian left the room without a word.

"You don't need to torture me," Akiil said. The word *torture* felt like something slick and wrong slithering through his guts; a snake, maybe, or a huge worm. He couldn't see Galter, but he could hear the man quietly shifting his tools at the head of the room. He could hear the quiet crackle of the fire. "I'm not an idiot. You caught me. Good job. I'll cooperate."

Her eyes burned into him. "Why did you lie in the first place?"

"I wanted the gold."

"I *gave* you gold."

"I wanted more."

"You had enough to buy your own village. You've spent almost none of it."

He exhaled slowly. He didn't answer the question because he didn't have an answer.

Adare scrubbed her face with a hand, shook her head. "I didn't want to do this." She gestured to the room, to the table, to the shackles holding him down.

"Then let's not." He forced a brightness he didn't feel into his voice.

She ignored him. "I knew you were a liar when you first showed up, but I thought that maybe, *maybe* there was a chance I could get something out of you, something that would help me hold this fucking empire together."

"I *can* teach you to use the *kenta*."

"It doesn't matter. You told the truth about that part, at least. It would take me years, maybe decades."

"So, take the years. Take the decades. If the Shin could do it, if some stupid kid from the Quarter could manage it, then so can you."

"Annur won't *be* here in decades."

"I think you underestimate this empire of yours."

"It's not mine," she replied, staring past him at a blank expanse of stone wall. "It was never mine."

Before he could frame a reply, the door swung open. Instead of Hugel, an old man stood in the space, or maybe a middle-aged man who'd had half the bones in his body broken, then inexpertly reset.

"Your Radiance," he said, bowing slightly to the Emperor.

"This is the imperial historian," she said.

"The Csestriim," Akiil said quietly.

It was the eyes that gave the creature away, those gray, empty eyes set into that unremarkable face. The monks back at Ashk'lan, those who had mastered the teachings, had possessed something like that distance in their gaze, as though they were watching the world from far, far away. This man, though, this historian—Akiil could find nothing human at all on the other side of that gaze. Looking at him was like looking into the endless winter sky.

The historian raised an eyebrow. "Well noticed."

"That's what they taught me," Akiil replied. "To notice things."

"Tell him," Adare cut in, "what you told me."

The Csestriim nodded slowly. "I have just come from the Blind, from the fortress that you found."

"If you had *him*," Akiil said, turning to Adare, "why did you need me?"

"Because I did not trust him." The Emperor's words were flat, matter-of-fact, all the emotion sanded away. "With you, I had another set of eyes, someone who could tell me if he was lying."

The historian didn't seem bothered by the suggestion. He stood beside the Emperor, mild as a slave.

"And was he?" Akiil asked.

Her face tightened. "He . . . omitted some things. Like the fact of an ancient Csestriim fortress."

"A fortress that until only recently was sealed," the historian put in. "Irrelevant to the fortunes of Annur."

"Except it's become pretty relevant now, hasn't it?"

The man inclined his head in acquiescence. "It has."

"Tell him," she said, pointing to Akiil. "Tell him what you told me."

The Csestriim nodded again. "Among the relics contained inside the armory that you found was one in particular, a weapon of sickening power." The word *sickening* sounded strange on his lips, as though he'd learned the syllables without ever plumbing their meaning. Akiil felt his own stomach go sick. Dread opened inside him like an abyss. The dead Csestriim woman whispered in his ear, *You cannot give it to her.*

"It is the size of a peach pit or perhaps a walnut," the historian went on, "though the surface is dark, smooth. Inside are what appear to be stars. It would be unlike anything you have ever encountered."

"Have you seen it?" Adare asked, stepping forward. "Do you have it?"

Akiil harnessed his pulse, his breath, every instinct of his flesh. He had no reason to believe the slaughtered Csestriim woman, but her words crashed in his mind like waves in a sea-wracked storm. *If the Emperor knows, it's over. Everything is over.* A weapon of power, given to the most powerful woman in the world . . .

He shook his head. "No."

Adare glanced over at the historian. The man considered him, then did something that might have been a shrug. "The monks taught him well. I cannot read his face."

"I am going to ask you again, Akiil," she murmured, "did you find it?"

"Why ask the question when you've said you don't trust me?"

"Because if you have it, and you tell me where it is, I will let you go."

"Just like that?"

"Just like that."

"Even though I lied to you."

"Everyone lies to me, Akiil. If I had them all tortured, the bodies would be spilling over the red walls." Exhaustion washed over her face. "This thing, this weapon, it's dangerous. *Beyond* dangerous."

"I do not have it."

Carefully, like a man moving a delicate structure carved from ice, one that the slightest nudge would shatter, he shifted the memory of the seed from his mind, locked away the thought of it lying silent and hidden among the other Csestriim treasures he'd pilfered from the fortress. If he was going to survive what happened next, if he was going to keep the weapon from the Emperor, if he was going to hide from the historian the truth of his knowledge, he needed to step clear of the memory entirely, to become someone who had never been inside that fortress, who had never held the strange, ancient object in his hands.

Adare exhaled slowly.

"Galter."

Akiil shook his head. "You don't have to do this."

"Yes," she replied. "I do. I need to know."

The small man came forward. At some point he'd put on thick leather gloves. He held a glowing iron in his hand. The red-orange tip reflected in his lenses, as though he, too, possessed the eyes of the goddess of light.

Akiil felt his bowels turning to water. He almost reached for the *vaniate*. He would feel the pain inside the trance, of course, but the terror blazing through his blood would vanish. So would all his confusion, anger, sorrow, bafflement . . . From within the emptiness he would be able to watch his torture as though it were some kind of performance acted out in all its anatomical horror by someone else. He wouldn't shit himself, at least, the way he had as a child.

It was that thought, strangely, that decided him.

Instead of reaching for the void, he locked eyes with the Emperor.

"This isn't the first time I've been burned on Malkeenian orders."

His flesh began to tremble, but he took a long breath, stilling it.

Adare just shook her head, whether denying the statement or absolving herself, he had no idea. Not that it mattered.

Galter, with the precision of an artisan—a woodworker or stone carver, perhaps—leaned close, brought the tip of the glowing rod down into the flesh of Akiil's chest, just above his heart. The agony was perfect, blossoming out from that single point until he felt his whole body was turning to char. The wet reek of burning meat filled the air, and the crackle of his blackening skin. It felt as though the torturer were folding an entire lifetime of anguish into the space between the heartbeats.

When it was over, when he finally pulled the iron away, Adare leaned over him. He stared up at her through the red haze of his pain. She was sweating, but he could read the resolve on her face.

This is why, he thought, understanding hatching inside him. This *is why she cannot be given a weapon of inestimable power.*

"I am going to keep burning you," she said.

He nodded. "I know."

"I need that weapon."

He shook his head. "I don't have it."

He considered the possibility that he'd lost his mind. With a few words, he could reveal the truth. Adare might set him free, or she might not, but there wouldn't be any point in torturing him further. What was he doing this for? The half-mangled insistence of a dying woman he'd never even met? Because of Yerrin's mutterings of poisonous seeds and things people were never meant to see? Out of some warped sense that it had somehow become *his* job to save the world?

No.

He realized the truth even as Galter pressed the iron back into his flesh.

Maybe those things mattered, but it was all so much simpler than that.

He was doing it for himself, for the kid he'd been, the child who'd sobbed and begged and shat himself in front of the only friends he knew. Adare could keep burning him. Emperors would always burn thieves. It was the way the world was built. She could char the skin from his body, break his bones, strip the life right out of him. But this time, at least, he wouldn't beg. As the historian said, the Shin had taught him well. This time they wouldn't hear him scream.

60

She should have been miserable.

The sudden storm had dropped at least two feet of snow on the pass, enough that Gwenna had to wade through it step after laborious step. As she descended the ravine to the south—the same ravine they had climbed almost a day earlier—that snow turned to slush, making the shifting stones beneath even more slick and treacherous. Over and over again she slipped, bashed a knee or a foot, bloodied both palms trying to stay upright while the last daylight leaked from the sky and night came on. By the time the slush turned to runoff—a raging stream fat with meltwater and moonlight—she was bruised and soaked through. She *should* have been cold and tired and utterly fucking miserable.

She felt fantastic.

Menkiddoc sang in her blood.

It's dangerous, she reminded herself over and over. *It's not true. It is making you into something different, something awful.*

A part of her knew that.

Remember what it did to Jonon, that part insisted. *Remember what it did to* everything *on this continent.*

Another part of her, though, a voice in her mind that was strong and growing ever stronger, just laughed. As the snow gave way to stone she found herself jogging down the slope, then running, then bounding, leaping from rock to rock, boulder to boulder, reveling in her own lightness and strength. It seemed impossible to believe that she was the same woman who had spent so many weeks crouched in the darkness of a ship's brig, broken, defeated. The thought of that creature made her sick, but the sickness didn't last. It evaporated off of her like steam from a hot skillet.

She should have been working on some kind of plan, but Dhar hadn't known exactly where Jonon was going or how far. She could spend the whole night creeping down the canyon, darting from one shadow to the next, only to find she'd arrived too late, that he'd lost his patience and done something unspeakable to Rat. Better to move quickly, to use the speed and strength and surprise to her advantage. With any luck, she might even overtake him before he got where he was going, strike while his back was turned, carve him apart before he even understood what was happening. . . .

No.

She wanted him to see. She wanted him to *understand*. She needed him to know that it wasn't *right* to take children, to use them as stones in whatever game he thought he was playing. He'd always been so proud, so rigid. Dhar was right about that, at least. The admiral's rigidity had shattered him. She needed him to know that before she drove the blade home.

And then . . .

The Csestriim ring hung in her pocket, small but heavy as lead. Fire-cold as ice. She brushed her fingers over it.

"Once Jonon's dead, I'll put it back on."

She forced herself to say the words aloud, to imagine removing the ring from her blacks, then forcing it down over her finger once more. It would be hard—hard to go back to the pain, weight, and weariness—but she'd done plenty of hard things. This would be just one more to add to the list.

"Kill Jonon," she said, "and it's done."

"Kill Jonon?"

The man's voice reverberated off the walls of the canyon, rich and delighted, as though she'd made a particularly clever joke.

Gwenna pulled up short, slid on the crumbling stone, ripped her swords from their sheaths. Clouds scudded across the moon, shifting shadows over the massive boulders. The broken defile offered dozens of places to hide, but Jonon wasn't hiding.

He sat atop a wagon-sized stone eight or ten paces distant, naked cutlass lying within easy reach on the rock. Moonlight gleamed on the steel and in his eyes. With one hand, he tossed her a lopsided salute. In the other, he was holding something that looked like a lamb shank. While she watched, he lifted it to his teeth, ripped free a ribbon of flesh, and started chewing. The lineaments of his old beauty remained—the cut of his jaw, the angle of his shoulders—but the sickness of Menkiddoc had twisted it to a new and awful purpose.

The urge to attack rolled over her, but the sight of Rat brought her up short.

The girl lay huddled in the shadows at the boulder's base. Jonon had tied her at the wrists and ankles. Blood leaked over her face from a wound hidden somewhere in her hair. At the sight of Gwenna she let out a cry, then struggled to sit up, straining forward against her bonds.

"Gwenna Sharpe!"

"I'm here," Gwenna replied. "I'm here now."

Jonon nodded encouragingly. "She *is* here. You *are* here." He sucked something from between his teeth, swallowed it down, then smiled. "I knew you'd come."

This time, the need to hurl herself at the man was so visceral it dragged her forward a couple steps before she managed to stop herself.

If Jonon had survived the avalanche, Lurie and Chent might have survived as well. It seemed unlikely, almost impossible, but then, there was the admiral, perched atop the rock, still smiling at her. He nodded some kind of vague encouragement, then took another bite. Blood dripped into the grisly mess of his matted beard. He glanced down, made a vague effort to wipe his fingers on his uniform, then shrugged.

"Where's Lurie?" Gwenna demanded, glancing behind her. If it was an ambush, Jonon would want to draw her attention while the other two struck. "Where's Chent?"

As though summoned by her words, a shadow slunk out from behind the rock. It took her a moment to recognize it as a man, let alone the sailor who had once been Chent. At some point, despite the cold, he had stripped away his clothes, retaining only the cutlass on the leather belt around his waist. He crouched there like a beast, gazing at her with glassy eyes while a thin line of spit dribbled from his lips. When the wind dropped, she could smell the hunger on him. He shifted his stare from Gwenna to Rat, then back again.

"He's right here," Jonon announced cheerfully, lifting his chin to indicate the broken creature.

Talk, Gwenna told herself, choking down the urge to fight, cut, kill. *Talk until you have a plan.*

"We thought you'd been killed in the rockslide."

"You thought we'd *been killed*?" Jonon laughed again. His voice brimmed with joy. "Clever use of the passive construction. I think what you mean is that *you thought you'd killed us.*" He winked at her. "Right?"

Gwenna scanned the stones to either side.

"What about Lurie?"

Jonon spread his hands. "Poor Lurie. Chent, why don't you tell Commander Sharpe what happened to Lurie?"

Chent blinked as though dazed by the question, then narrowed his eyes. "Crunched." The word was barely intelligible.

The admiral smiled benignly. "I believe the word you're looking for, sailor, is *crushed.*" He turned his gaze back to Gwenna, nodded regretfully as a man at a funeral. "As it turns out, you *did* manage to kill Lurie."

"Lurie got slow," Chent muttered. "Got dumb." He began chewing his own lip, chewing it so violently it bled.

"Yes." Jonon nodded. "Well. It's poor form to speak disparagingly of the dead, but Lurie did prove less nimble when you brought all that rock down on top of us." He shrugged, then brandished the bone in his right hand. "So we ate him!"

Chent turned to his admiral, straightened up somewhat, fumbled a salute, then stretched for something like his old military bearing. "If it please you, sir, a man could stand to eat some more."

Gwenna's stomach lurched inside her.

"Greed," Jonon said, shaking his head ruefully, "is unbecoming in an Annurian sailor, Chent."

"Let the girl go," Gwenna demanded, cutting through their gruesome conversation.

Jonon frowned, leaned forward to peer over the edge of the rock. "Oh yes. The girl."

Rat twisted away from him with a snarl.

"Sure. She can go."

Gwenna hesitated. "Her legs are tied."

The admiral made a dismissive gesture. "Easily solved. Easily solved. Chent, cut the rope tying the child's legs."

For a moment the sailor looked baffled by the command. He patted his bare chest, then his legs, fumbled with his flaccid cock, as though he expected to find some kind of weapon there. Only when the heel of his hand brushed the pommel of his cutlass did he pause, then smile.

"No," Gwenna snapped. "He doesn't get any closer to her."

Jonon furrowed his brow. "Come now, Commander Sharpe. Be reasonable. If the girl is to go free, *someone* must free her."

"Not. Him."

"Ah." The admiral nodded sagely. "You don't trust old Chent." He chuckled. "Can't say that I blame you. Look. Let me do something, call it a . . . gesture of good faith. Chent," he said, waving at the man with a bloody hand, "come up here."

Chent, still fingering the handle of his cutlass, eyed Rat once more, then reluctantly turned away, leaping with surprising agility onto the boulder's top.

"Give me your hand," Jonon commanded.

Chent stretched out his hand.

The man who had once been the First Admiral of the Western Fleet took the sailor's hand almost tenderly, closed his fingers slowly around it, then, with a movement too fast to follow, ripped it off at the wrist.

Chent staggered backward, stared as the wound gouted dark blood down the stump of his arm. Gwenna's stomach shifted with something that might have been nausea or hunger.

This is wrong, she reminded herself.

Chent made a confused mewling sound.

Jonon ignored him, held the hand out to Gwenna. "This was his right hand. His good hand. He's not as dangerous with the left."

When Gwenna didn't move, he frowned, tossed the hand aside.

"You are sick," Gwenna murmured.

Jonon rolled his eyes. "Sickness. Disease. Pollution. The historian has been stuffing your head with all these *words.*" He frowned. "Where *is* the broken old man, anyway? I expected him to come with you."

"Maybe he did," she replied. "Maybe he's up the canyon right now, lining up his shot."

The notion didn't seem to trouble Jonon. "You shouldn't trust him, you know. There are things he hasn't told you. Secrets. Secrets he never told *any* of us."

"At least he's not eating his own crew."

Chent made an incoherent sound, lapped at his bloody stump.

Jonon shook his head, as though frustrated with a wayward child. "Gwenna. Come on. You were bitten by the *gabhya.* I was there. I saw it. This place is inside you now, just the way it is with me."

She could *feel* it inside her, eating like acid through her weakness and uncertainty.

"It is," she agreed, then fished the ring from her pocket. The whorls inside it seemed to shift, form and re-form, but when she fixed her eyes upon them they went still. "It is," she said again, "but I found a way to fight it."

For the first time something other than benign amusement flicked through Jonon's green eyes. Rage, maybe. Revulsion.

"That *thing,*" he said, gesturing to the ring, "is disgusting. It is *obscene.*"

"It is a cure."

"You don't *need* a cure, Gwenna." He gestured toward his body, then to her. "This is not something to be cured."

"It is a plague."

"A plague?" He snorted. "Certainly it proves too much for more . . . limited minds." He gestured furtively to Chent. She could smell the amusement on him. "But for you? For me? For soldiers with the discipline to resist the more unfortunate effects while welcoming the vision and strength . . . For *us* it is a blessing. A *gift.*"

"Not one I want," Gwenna replied, trying to believe the words. "When this is done, I am putting this back on."

She raised the ring, then set it carefully on the shelf of a boulder to her side. It felt better to have it out of her pocket, not dragging at her with its weight. She lifted her right sword into a high guard.

"I'm coming for the girl now. I am going to cut her loose."

Four paces from Rat, three, two . . .

The admiral nodded his encouragement, made no move for his cutlass. Smart. If he was going to attack, he'd wait until Gwenna was distracted trying to carry the girl or free her.

Rat made a sound in her throat, half growl, half moan, and hurled herself forward. She landed awkwardly, her forearms bashing against the rough stones.

Gwenna lashed out with her blade. The movement shocked her. She'd meant to wait, to grab Rat by the arms and drag her backward toward whatever passed for safety in the narrow space of the ravine. Instead, she saw her sword slice down, faster than any attack she'd ever managed, moonlight licking the dark steel. For an awful heartbeat, she thought she'd killed the child, but no. . . . The blade slit the rope binding Rat's legs without even nicking the skin.

Jonon clapped. "Well *done*." He sounded genuinely pleased. "You've seen disease before, Gwenna. It's horrible—all sweating, and bleeding, and weakness. It's not *this*."

Rat staggered to her feet, stumbled forward into Gwenna, who wrapped an arm around her shoulders. The girl was shaking, her breath ripped into ragged gasps. She felt like a bird, all hollow bones ready to shatter, but the warmth of her steadied something inside Gwenna, a humanity that had begun to slip.

"You came back," Rat whispered.

Gwenna didn't take her eyes from Jonon. "Of course I came back."

"But you came back," she said again.

"Quickly now." Gwenna lowered her sword, blade up.

The girl understood, laid the rope binding her wrists to the steel, and she was free.

Too easy. The whole thing had been too easy.

Gwenna glanced over her shoulder once more, but nothing moved between the stones. When she returned her gaze to Jonon, he hadn't shifted.

"Why'd you take her?" she demanded. "Why'd you take her if you didn't intend to keep her?"

"Keep her?" Jonon looked genuinely confused. "What would I want with a half-rabid orphan? I wanted you, Gwenna. *You.*"

The words filled her with a blood-black rage.

"Then you should have come for *me.* You didn't need to murder Cho Lu and Pattick."

"Well, they *did* attack me."

She shackled the maelstrom grinding inside her. When she spoke again, her voice was cold, far off. "What do you want?"

Chent made an incoherent sound.

"Want?" Jonon pursed his lips. "Well, there was some disagreement there. Lurie wanted to fuck you to death, but Lurie is, well . . ." He gestured to the discarded femur. "*Chent,* on the other hand, thought we should eat you. Isn't that right, Chent?"

The sailor looked up from his bloody stump, nodded, his eyes bright.

"But I told him *no,* that he had it backward." Jonon shook his head gravely. He might have been a filthy masker play-acting an Annurian admiral. "What I *want,* Gwenna, is to complete the mission." He gestured up the ravine. "No one else has kettral eggs. No one but us."

"We *were* finishing the mission. You just slaughtered two of the last soldiers carrying those eggs north."

"North." He made a face as though he'd tasted something vaguely rotten. "No."

Gwenna shifted to put Rat behind her. Jonon had made no effort to attack, but that didn't mean he wouldn't. Even if he stayed perched on his boulder, she intended to kill the man, to butcher him down to his bones, to take from him what he'd stolen from Cho Lu and Pattick, and when that happened— she could taste her own anticipation—when that *happened,* she didn't want Rat anywhere near.

"Run," she growled. "Up the canyon to the fort. Get . . ." She almost said *Get inside, get safe,* but Rat would never agree to that, not while Gwenna herself was outside, staring down the admiral. "Get help," she said instead. "Kiel and Dhar, go find them."

The girl reeked of anger and confusion.

"I won't leave. . . ."

"I need them, Rat. I need Kiel. *Please.*"

All a lie. What she needed was to be alone with Jonon, to see to the necessary justice.

Justice?

An unsteady laugh welled up in her throat.

"Hurry," she murmured.

"I *will* come back," Rat said finally, her voice just on the edge of breaking.

"Good," Gwenna replied. "Go fast now. Go as fast as you can."

"I will come back."

"I know you will."

Don't, she thought.

Dhar would see to that. If Rat made it up the canyon, the captain would get her inside the fortress. If necessary he'd drag the door closed behind them both, broken knee or no. She wouldn't be safe, but she'd be *safer.* Kiel was Csestriim. He'd find some way to get the two of them free. They had kettral eggs, after all. Adare would send another whole expedition if she had to, a dozen 'Kent-kissing ships.

The clatter of pebbles over stone marked the sound of Rat's retreat. The girl was fast, scampering up the canyon like a mountain goat. As the sound faded, something slipped inside Gwenna, some constraint—invisible but strong as any leash or ligament—that had held her in check. Her flesh ached strength.

Wait, she reminded herself. *Let Rat get away.*

Jonon watched her. He smelled of bemusement.

"I was wrong about you," he said.

"Yes." Her voice sounded dead, even to her own ears.

He went on as though she hadn't spoken. "I thought you were weak—"

"I *was* weak."

Memory rolled over her, disgust at what she'd been, at what she'd allowed herself to become.

"You were not at your best," Jonon acknowledged with a smile. "But then, neither was I." His eyes went distant. "We were weak in different ways. I was like glass, like some gem—hard but brittle. You, on the other hand, were a rotten, rotting thing."

"Not anymore."

"Oh, I know you're not. I *know*!"

"And it's not because of the *gabhya.* I killed the kettral before I ever set foot in that jungle. I survived your little keelhauling."

She donned the facts as though they were armor. Against Jonon? Against the poison raging inside her? Against her own desire to rip and rend?

He laughed. "And no one was more surprised than me! You're right—you were finding yourself again, even then, but *this* . . ." He gestured to her. "This is something new."

"New . . ." Chent drooled.

Jonon frowned, turned to the sailor. "Chent, show this woman the truth."

Chent stared at her with wide, uncomprehending eyes while he lapped at his bloody stump. The wound should have already killed him, drained away his consciousness at the very least, but it had clotted faster than a normal wound. The strange strength of Menkiddoc at work, even there.

"Go ahead, Chent," Jonon said. "You can have her."

Gwenna felt a growl rising in her throat. "I will cut him apart."

Jonon smiled, spread his hands. "Would it not be a mercy?"

Mercy.

Gwenna turned the word over in her mind.

"It is murder," she replied finally.

"You're a soldier, Gwenna. Soldiers kill people. That's your job."

There was something wrong with the idea, but she couldn't quite put her finger on it. She *had* killed people, killed them by the dozens, by the scores, killed so many people she couldn't remember all the faces anymore, people far better than Chent. It was what she'd trained to do, what she'd spent her entire life practicing. Not only had she killed them, but she'd felt satisfaction in the act, the well-being of having done a difficult, dangerous job and done it well.

She turned her attention from Jonon to the sailor. He looked up at her with glazed eyes, half-dead already.

"Chent," Jonon said mildly. "Bring me Gwenna's heart."

The man's face lurched into a smile and he stumbled down off the boulder.

"You want to know what he said to me back on the *Daybreak*?" Jonon asked. "Tell her, Chent, tell her what you kept telling me."

"Give," the man murmured, his lips bubbling with his own blood.

Jonon nodded. "That's right. *Give her to me.* That's what he said. If I gave you to him—him, and Vessik, and Lurie—they'd teach you a lesson. You'd never disrespect me again. That's what he promised."

Gwenna stepped forward, put the point of her sword to the sailor's neck.

"What lesson?" she asked, her voice quiet.

Chent stared at the blade, baffled. He seemed to have forgotten he had a weapon of his own.

Gwenna leaned into the blade. *"What lesson?"*

"Teach you," he mumbled. "Teach you and that Rat girl . . ."

The steel slid through his throat, cutting off the words.

Blood splattered her face.

Breath rattled out through the gash.

Before he could fall, Gwenna shot out a hand, drove two fingers into the wound, held him up like a fish through the gills while he gaped and struggled to breathe, while his eyes went wide and glassy and the strength ebbed from his flesh. A shiver of satisfaction ran through her, the silent, wordless thrill of watching a bad man die a bad death at her own hands.

Justice.

And something older. Something worse.

She let Chent drop, wiped her fingers over her cheeks. His blood was still hot. It smelled sweet. A blissful dizziness swept her up.

"See?" Jonon said cheerfully.

"See what?"

"You were frightened once, weak and pathetic. Not anymore."

She tried to remember being frightened, tried to remember the endless days she'd spent crouching in the brig, found them thin as last week's dreams. Strength raged inside her. It felt wonderful.

Finish it, she hissed to herself, *then put the ring back on.*

For a moment she couldn't remember where she'd put it.

She shifted her gaze to Jonon, opened her mouth to speak, found she had nothing to say. The words they'd been trading back and forth felt like so much rubble—the wreckage left behind after the crumbling of a proud structure. There'd been a point to it all once, a meaning, a purpose. She couldn't say what.

The man who had been admiral sighed expansively. "You're not going to join me, are you?"

She didn't bother replying. Moonlight blazed bright as the sun. Wind honed the edges of everything, until the world looked carved from crystal. She could see each pore on Jonon's face, every clot of blood in his black beard, every vessel in the whites of his eyes. If she bothered, she could hear his heart beating, the pulse throbbing in his veins. When he took up his cutlass and rose to his feet—less the motion of a man standing than a snake uncoiling for the strike—a thrill surged through her. No more words, not even words like *justice* or *revenge*. Speech was for the weak, and she was finished being weak.

Jonon dropped down from the boulder, relinquishing the high ground with the confidence of a man who could not imagine his own annihilation.

Gwenna felt herself smiling, the flesh of her cheeks terribly tight.

Back on the Islands, even the worst warriors had been savagely fast. You learned early to hurt people and break things, how to be hurt and be broken in turn, and then keep going. You learned, or you washed out. Gwenna had cut her opponents, fractured bones, bitten arms and shoulders and ears, clawed for eyes or lips. She'd had her own skin busted open Hull only knew how many times. Once, Gent had hit her so hard on the head that she'd been dizzy for weeks. By the time she went down into the Hole for the Trial, she'd seen more violence than most legionaries four times her age, and the years since had only been more brutal.

None of it prepared her for the fight against Jonon lem Jonon.

The man didn't move like anything human. His attacks weren't versions of any of the two dozen sword styles she'd studied. If anything, the way he came at her reminded her of the *gabbya*. It should have been impossible—the monster had been ten times the admiral's size, with scores of writhing arms and teeth—and yet there was a bonelessness to Jonon's movements, a sickening whip-snap to every attack that left her baffled and off-balance, knocking aside his cutlass at the very last moment over and over and over, gasping like a puckered trout in the thin mountain air. When she lashed out, he bent at the lower back, flowed beneath her blades, straightened at the wrong angle, caught her with a nick across the shoulder, smiled.

She managed a half step back, tested the arm. Everything still worked. The wound wasn't deep, but she could feel the blood soaking her blacks, could smell it on the cool night breeze. Jonon ran a tongue over his teeth, and for a moment she wondered if he would eat her, too, carve her apart the way he had Lurie and feast on her still-warm flesh.

"You're too slow, Gwenna," he crooned. "Far too slow."

She attacked again, battering down his guard with her right, then lunging with the left, giving herself to the motion. She had his cutlass trapped, if only for a moment, but Jonon writhed away, moving like smoke, struck her across the face with a casual fist. It *looked* casual; it landed like a sledgehammer, snapping her neck around, blotting out the moonlight. She stumbled forward and away, managed to keep her feet on the uneven ground, turned, blocked a half-dozen of the admiral's attacks before he paused, face split with a smile.

Her teeth had sliced through the inside of her cheek. She spat blood onto the stones, but she could still taste it on her tongue, feel it sliding down the back of her throat.

Jonon watched her with a mixture of curiosity and contempt.

"I thought you'd be better than this. You *should* be better. After that bite from the *gabbya* . . ." He narrowed his eyes. "You're fighting it, aren't you?"

"Fuck you."

"You're still trying to resist the gift."

As he spoke the words she could feel the truth. The vicious bliss of Menkiddoc's sickness burned in her blood, but she had braced herself against the fire. The poison was a wave grinding her down, lifting her up, but she kept trying to swim. Unlike Jonon, she was bound to her old bladework, all the forms she'd spent a lifetime mastering, because she was still bound to herself. Whatever had happened to the admiral, it wasn't happening to her. Not yet. Not fast enough.

Her conversation with Kiel floated back to her:

Jonon chose the sickness. He embraced it.

At the time, that choice had seemed insane.

"You understand now," he said, nodding. "You understand why I had to drink the water."

"You didn't have to."

"I did if I wanted to defeat the *gabhya*."

She licked the inside of her cheek. The blood was warm, slicker than spit, strangely delicious. She felt the same hunger she felt back in the jungle, only stronger, angrier, stalking back and forth inside her like a ravenous creature trapped behind bars. More than Jonon or the *gabhya,* it was this monster that had terrified her since she first set foot in the sickness of Menkiddoc, this monster she'd been fighting every step of the march. It seemed suddenly terribly unfair. After months of fear and darkness in the brig of the *Daybreak,* after being ready to fucking *die,* she'd finally clawed back some measure of her self, her soldier's spirit, her old stubbornness, only to discover it was all ugly, wrong, rotten at the heart.

"It's a sad fact of life, Gwenna," Jonon said, "that strength and goodness don't go hand in hand."

The struggle inside her almost blotted out his words. She could fight the poison, keep fighting, just as Kiel had said, but for what? In order to be weaker? She'd spent months wallowing in her own weakness, all those days she hadn't even bothered counting lying half-insensate in the dark. The old fear, as though summoned by the memory, traced a frigid tickle down her spine.

"I'm not going back."

Menkiddoc's poison bared its eager teeth.

Jonon nodded as though he understood, as though he'd seen straight into her soul. "Of course not. Back doesn't *exist,* Gwenna. There's only forward. Onward."

His next attack came like a spasm—all perfect stillness, then motion too fast to follow. The tip of his cutlass licked past her guard, punched a ragged hole in her side.

She lunged out in a desperate riposte—too slow. He was already out of reach. Her sword sliced nothing.

Rage and regret closed over her. The litany of her failures rose, thousand-handed, to choke her—Cho Lu, reaching for his heart on the floor of the fortress; Pattick's empty eyes; Quick Jak's slaughter; the loss of the Dawn King; the shredded men on the deck of the *Daybreak;* Laith dying at Andt-Kyl out beyond the barricades; Valyn losing his sight up on the tower because she didn't even know he was there; the washouts she'd sent down into Hull's Hole to die at the teeth of the slarn; the too-hastily-trained Kettral she'd thrown to their deaths against Balendin. In a terrible eyeblink she saw all the bodies piled up, all the lives she'd had the chance to save but hadn't, all the people she'd failed, and why?

Hesitation. Weakness. Stupidity. Fear.

That broken girl in the brig was the truth of her, the deep disgusting truth. Adare was right. When people relied on her, they died, some sooner, some later, all because she'd been pretending so long to be something she wasn't, pretending to be Annick, or the Flea, or *anyone* but Gwenna Sharpe.

Only now she didn't need to pretend any longer.

Slowly, deliberately, she closed her eyes.

She could hear Jonon, the blood throbbing inside him, the breath rasping up through his throat, the crunch of the gravel when he shifted his weight, the quick *snick* of his cutlass as it swept out. Her own steel caught it a handsbreadth from her throat. The blades trembled there, sword against sword, weight against weight, will against will. He leaned in, shoving her back an unsteady step, forcing her toward failure once more.

"No." Her voice came out strangled, half sob, half howl.

"Yes," Jonon whispered, sweet as any suitor.

At the sound of his voice, the poison inside her surged, hurling itself against all the bulwarks she'd thrown up, all the walls she'd tried to hold, all the battlements of her crumbling human castle. She stood for a suspended moment, a lone woman, the final defender of her own doomed outpost, and then, with a cry like a lover giving the last of herself up, she let it all collapse.

The laws went first, all those stale military statutes crafted to hold the world's soldiers in check.

Then the mission.

Then the lessons she'd learned at the feet of her trainers, crooked notions about *honor,* and *pride,* and *justice.*

Then her private qualms and misgivings.

Then the bonds she thought she'd shared—with Annick, with Talal, with Rat or her father. They were all dead anyway, or would be before long. She felt the lines of her loyalty snap like the cords in a broken snare.

Then her human notions of right and wrong, ideas she'd carried with her so long they felt like her own bones.

All of it and utterly, she let it fall before the onslaught, fold beneath the weight of this old and awful thing that flooded through her, gorging her veins, rising in her throat until she could hold it no longer, until it erupted into the mountain night as a scream.

No, she thought, giddy with the hot-bright strength. *Not a scream.*

Screams were for the fearful and the weak. What she felt was the opposite of that, the opposite of guilt and worry and shame. It was what she'd always imagined real Kettral felt when they went into battle—people like the Flea, and Daveen Shaleel, and Adaman Fane—not just confidence, but *certainty.* Certainty and the strength undergirding it, strength as wide and deep and indifferent as the sea.

She opened her eyes at last, found Jonon gazing at her with something like wonder.

"You . . ." he began.

She didn't let him finish.

It was so simple, the barest twist of a wrist to shrug free of his cutlass. It sliced down across her body, carving her thigh. That didn't matter. The pain was nothing, an ember quenched in the darkness. . . . Or was the pain the darkness and that sun-bright sky-wide fire her strength? The bliss of the moment obliterated the rest of the thought.

Jonon's mouth was open, searching for words as she bulled into him, driving him back and down, carrying them both to the ground, abandoning her blades as they fell, closing her hands around his wrists. He thrashed with the cutlass, pounded the pommel against her shoulders, her spine. Her own laughter echoed off the walls of the ravine, laughter at the sheer joy of the fight, at being tested and for once—for fucking *once*—not struggling, finding herself equal, *more* than equal.

Jonon dropped his blade, tried to bring his hands to bear on her throat, tried to get his knees between them, to make space. She twisted past them, came down across his chest, one elbow crooked behind his head, hands locked, shoulder driving into his chin, cranking his neck savagely to the side. His chest heaved beneath her. His breath raged hot in her ear.

"Do you want to get up?" she whispered.

He made a strangled sound.

"No?"

Quick as a trap snapping shut she shifted, throwing a leg on top of him, straddling his chest, bringing her full weight to bear as he scrambled to get free. She looked down into his eyes. They should have been green. In the moonlight, they were black.

"Maybe you were right," she said. "Maybe we could have accomplished great things together."

He reached for her throat again. A mistake.

She caught the wrist, drew it to her chest, coiled her legs around the arm, rolled off of him, unfurling the arm out straight, arching her back, driving her shoulders down into the ground, her hips up into the joint, felt it strain, felt

Jonon try to curl into the attack, forced him back down with her legs, squeezed her thighs, let her head fall back, closed her eyes as the elbow snapped beneath the force.

She laughed.

Tossed the limp arm aside.

Like a fool, like a fucking fool, Jonon tried to roll away. In half a breath, she was on his back, legs around him, heels locked in his groin. He tried to rip them free, but one arm was useless and the other wasn't nearly strong enough. Slowly, she wrapped an elbow around his throat, flexed her arm, felt the lock go tight.

He managed to speak one word, his voice a mangled, broken thing. "No."

She smiled, laid the side of her head against his. "Yes, First Admiral," she murmured as his body spasmed. "Yes." He raised a hand, as though reaching for the moon. "Yes." The hand dropped, the body shuddered in her grasp, shuddered again, a third time, then went still.

For a while she lay holding him, savoring the feel of the life draining from his limbs.

Cold wind yawned down out of the peaks. It felt hot on her skin. She breathed in deep, held the scents of blood, and sweat, and mangled flesh in her lungs, exhaled, inhaled again. Jonon's smell was sharp and sweet—all sweat and leather and death—but even as she lay there, it was already going stale.

Growling, she shoved the body away, kicked it aside, rose to her feet.

The exultation of the fight, so bright only moments before, was fading, slipping away, leaving a hole in its place where hunger gnawed. She glanced down at the body, considered tearing out Jonon's heart the way he'd ripped Cho Lu's from his body, then turned aside. It wasn't that the idea disgusted her; almost exactly the opposite—it wasn't *enough*. The man was dead. He was nothing. If only she hadn't killed Chent so quickly. A sword through the throat after everything he'd done? It was too good for him, too easy. If only Cho Lu or Pattick were still alive. . . .

Something inside her twitched at the thought. They'd been her friends. . . .

No. That wasn't right. They'd fought on the same side because they, like her, had been trying to stay alive. They just hadn't been as good at it.

She laughed, knelt to retrieve her blades, felt her leg almost buckle beneath her.

So. Jonon's cutlass had bitten deeper than she realized. She reached down, peeled back the wet cloth, tested the edges of the wound, then sunk a finger knuckle-keep into the rent. Pain blazed like a beacon. She kept the finger there awhile, exploring the contours of the hurt, then pulled it free, wiped it on the shirt of her blacks, offered up a bloody salute to the admiral's corpse.

The wound would slow her, but she could still reach the Csestriim fortress before Bhuma Dhar shut the door.

Again, the ghost of a misgiving shifted inside her. She was supposed to do something first, something important before she went back. She turned the thought over in her mind. Chent was dead. He lay a few paces away, gaping at the stars. Lurie was dead. Jonon was dead. Everyone was dead.

"No," she murmured. "Not everyone."

Bhuma Dhar was still up at the fortress. Bhuma Dhar, who had attacked the *Daybreak,* who was responsible for all that slaughter on the ships.

The man wouldn't put up much of a fight with that shattered leg, but he was alive, which meant she could kill him, which was more than she could say for the useless corpses at her feet. After months of listening to the Manjari captain prattle on about *davi,* after enduring all those righteous lectures, she could finally teach *him* something. And Kiel, if he'd returned to the fortress, the Csestriim who had been lying to her since that very first moment in the Emperor's study, choosing his words, hiding the truth, leading them all along as though they were fucking sheep. The son of a bitch was responsible for an entire genocide, the poisoning. . . .

She stumbled over the word.

Her hand, obeying some alien imperative, reached for her pocket.

The ring. The matzcel.

That's what she was supposed to do—*put the ring back on.*

The pocket was empty.

And then she heard the voice.

"Gwenna. *Gwenna Sharpe!*"

The voice was small but strident, echoing off the walls of the ravine.

Gwenna had drowned once, in the wide salt sound back between the Islands. She'd gone down into a wreck on a training mission, slipped inside the scuttled ship, and then, trying to hurry, kicked up too much silt, turning the dim water to a thick, muddy murk. She'd tried to retrace her path, the route she'd taken down belowdecks, but in the swirling dark she lost all direction. Twice she smashed her face against bulkheads where she'd remembered clear passage, breaking her nose, bruising her eye. That pain was nothing, though, compared to the dull leaden fire growing in her lungs. She'd never forgotten the way the dumb muscles struggled for control, trying to drag in air in a world fashioned all of water.

Seeing Rat standing a few paces away, sweating, limned in moonlight, was like that, like drowning. Something in her body—something beyond all thought—tried to respond, tried again and again, tried so hard it hurt, her spirit as dumb as her lungs, searching for something like love or mercy where there was no longer any to be had. She had become both the flooded ship and the woman trapped inside it, the prison and the prisoner, and though she'd once moved through a world of light and space and air, that world was gone, replaced by a flood that should have filled her up, filled her utterly, but left only hunger.

"I'm sorry," Rat gasped. "I'm sorry I left you."

"Don't . . ." Gwenna managed before losing the end of the sentence.

Don't be sorry?

Don't leave again?

Don't—please, you brave, stupid child—don't come near me.

Rat slid a few paces on loose stone, came to an unsteady stop, raised her eyes and stared. Not at Gwenna, but past her, at the bodies of Chent and Jonon splayed out across the stone. For a moment she swayed, as though sickened by the slaughter. For just a moment, Gwenna saw the lost child she'd found in an empty city at the southern tip of a cursed continent, the girl who'd managed to survive all on her own. Then a snarl crept onto Rat's face and she leapt forward, crossing the broken slope with surprising speed to hammer her foot into Jonon's side, screaming as she did so.

"Dead," she shrieked, kicking him again. "Dead."

As Gwenna watched, Rat fell on the man, ripped her dagger from its sheath, and slammed it into his gut. "Dead!" she screamed. The thick scent of ruptured bowels opened on the air. "Dead!" Gore slicked her arms, splattered her face. She didn't stop. "Dead. Dead. Dead. Fucking. Dead."

Finally she wore down, like a fish left too long on the shore, stared at the mangled corpse, then shoved herself up, rounded on Gwenna, eyes wide, chest heaving, teeth bared, not a frightened child, not anymore, just another monster like all the rest. She lunged forward, dagger still clutched in her hands. . . .

Not an attack, sobbed something deep in Gwenna's chest. *She's in shock. She forgot she's holding the knife!*

But words were slow, weak things. For months the girl had been hurling herself at Gwenna, trying to bury a blade in her, and here she was again, coming on, bloody as any nightmare. There was no need for words, no need for thought at all. Gwenna stepped aside easily as breathing, caught the knife hand at the wrist and twisted.

"Fuck!" Rat shouted.

Her breath reeked rage.

Gwenna twisted harder, bent the shoulder up toward breaking, the memory of Jonon's ruptured elbow hot in her mind. If Rat had stayed still, she would have split like a roast chicken, parted bone from bone, snapped at the ligament. But the girl did not stay still. Instead, she hurled herself into a flip, rotating with the motion of Gwenna's own attack, landed awkwardly—one foot, one knee—and ripped her arm—still slick with Jonon's viscera—clear of Gwenna's grip.

For a moment she crouched there like a rabid animal, like a fucking rat, eyes bleeding moonlight, staring.

Good. Gwenna smiled. *A real fight, then.*

"This is not . . . You are not . . ." The girl groped for the words. Fluency eluded her.

"You don't know what I am."

The girl bared her teeth, hissed the words. "Gwenna Sharpe."

The name tugged at something inside her, something painful. She shoved it aside, moved forward, forcing Rat back into a corner between two boulders. Her own right leg lagged slightly but the pain was distant, blotted out by the fear-smell on the feral girl, her charred odor of defiance. Gwenna raised her hands. Empty, she realized. She hadn't bothered picking up her swords. It didn't matter. She'd slaughtered the admiral with her bare hands. Actually, it would be better that way. More real.

"Why you're doing this?" Rat demanded. "Gwenna. *Why?*"

Some remote part of her considered the question.

Because you attacked me.

Because you're a killer, just like the rest of us.

Because you made me weak.

Instead of answering, she dropped her guard, opened her arms.

"Come here, Rat. It's all right." She twisted her lips into a smile. "I'm sorry. Come here."

The child studied her warily, kept the dagger up just as Gwenna had taught her.

"No."

The disobedience lit a flare of rage in Gwenna's heart. She'd kept the girl safe for how long? Defended her against Jonon, the crew, the *gabhya, every-thing . . .*

"Get over here, you little bitch."

"No." Tears stood moon bright in the child's eyes. "You are not . . ." Rat shook her head, as though trying to rid it of some awful ringing, some voice she couldn't bring herself to believe. "Not Gwenna Sharpe."

The words forced her back on her heels.

"The thing is, Rat?" She shook her head, smiled between clenched teeth. "I was never Gwenna Sharpe."

"Were!" the girl insisted. "Fucking *were*."

"No. Gwenna Sharpe was just someone I made up. She was a fiction. Do you know what a fiction is?"

Rat stared at her, baffled, terrified.

"It means a story. Gwenna Sharpe was just a *story* I told to everyone. She was a story I told to *myself*. Gwenna Sharpe, the cadet. Gwenna Sharpe, the Kettral. Gwenna Sharpe, the warrior who never quit. Gwenna Sharpe, who always managed to get the job done. . . ."

"Killed the huge bird," Rat whispered. "Killed the admiral."

"*That*," Gwenna said, wagging a finger at her, "is the truth. Gwenna Sharpe is someone who kills things. She's killed *hundreds* of things, and do you know why? I'll tell you. She did all that killing because Gwenna Sharpe was a coward, and killing things made her feel brave. She—"

Give it to the girl, she'd learned at some point between their first sparring sessions and that moon-drenched moment how to keep her eyes flat, her body still, how to hide her attack until the very moment it happened. While Gwenna was still talking, Rat unfolded, shoving off from the rock behind her, hurling herself across the space, slashing at Gwenna's face at an angle that forced her to block with her forearm instead of grabbing the wrist.

The knife bit down to the bone.

Gwenna shrugged aside the pain, reached out, grabbed the child in both arms, pulled her close.

Rat didn't even try to resist. Her thin ribs flexed. Her chest heaved, struggling for breath. To crush a full-grown man, Gwenna would have had to use her legs, but Rat was no full-grown man, and the strength of Menkiddoc howled in Gwenna like the wind of the *hamaksha*. Inch by inch she pulled her tighter, closer, just as she had on those cold nights on the trek to the mountains, squeezing, squeezing, until the girl couldn't breathe anymore, until she was nothing but bone and spasm, ribs bent to snapping.

And then the daggers slashed across the back of Gwenna's skull.

That's what it felt like, anyway—long, hot knives slicing through the scalp, grinding against the bone, a scream like a splinter driven straight through her ear.

She dropped the girl, jerked back, clawed at the weight hanging from her head, found furred, furious limbs, ripped them free, felt her own skin tear with them.

Rat was screaming too, words in her own language, *something something something Yutaka*.

The fucking *gabhya*.

The world went white with rage. Gwenna swung the creature once above her head, then hurled it across the ravine.

She felt half scalped. Blood sluiced down her back. It didn't matter. Now there were two monsters to kill instead of one. All the better—

A clean, bright pain opened her ankle. She tried to spin, but the weighted leg folded beneath her.

The tendon. Rat had slit her tendon.

A howl poured from Gwenna's throat, thick as vomit. Even as she fell, however, she twisted, catching the girl by the ankle, yanking her close. A grin opened her face.

"That was a mistake," she hissed, pulling the child in. "You should have run. Should have run when you could."

Tears streaked Rat's filthy face, but her eyes were hard. "Never run."

Gwenna shook her head, twisted the girl's leg, waited for the knee to break. "Someone taught you the wrong shit, kid."

"No," Rat growled. "Gwenna Sharpe taught me." Then, fast as thought, she sliced down through the wrist of the hand holding her ankle, parting those tendons as well. "Gwenna Sharpe taught me this." The girl seized the hand, suddenly limp, then shoved the flame-cold Csestriim ring down over the joint. "Gwenna Sharpe taught me the right things, Gwenna Sharpe taught me good things, Gwenna Sharpe taught me *everything, AND I FUCKING WANT HER BACK!*"

Gwenna woke to find the moon had traveled half across the cloud-scraped sky.

Shivers wracked her. Something jagged stabbed into her back. Her scalp felt shredded. Her shoulder and leg throbbed. Her wrist felt broken, too loose, and somewhere down near her ankle a deep throbbing ache counted out her heartbeat. Those pains, however, like grains of sand, were nearly lost in the ocean of cold agony that suffused her.

She shut her eyes, took a breath, tried not to scream, held it in her chest, then exhaled.

The pain released its grip by a degree.

Another breath, another loosening, inch by horrible inch, until eventually she could leave her lungs to their work without fearing they would collapse beneath the burden. The pain remained, of course—what was it Kiel had said? It was a war raging inside her—but after a long time she found a space in all the suffering for thought, then immediately wished she had not.

Rat. She'd tried to kill Rat.

The memory was a hot stone in her throat, choking her. She rolled to the side, ignoring the lacerating rocks, ignoring the blaze in her ribs, and vomited over the stone.

Rat was a girl, nine years old, and Gwenna had tried to murder her.

When she opened her eyes, she found the child sitting a pace away. The monster, the *avesh,* crouched at her side. The girl stared at her, skin pale in the moonlight, eyes wide. She reeked of fear and defiance, rage and regret, confusion and the granitic refusal to admit that she had no idea what to do. It was a smell Gwenna knew well, one she'd been choking on her entire life, the smell of a little red-haired child—her face half mud, half freckles—on a farm at the foot of the Romsdals wondering when her father would come back; the smell of an awkward girl on the Islands who knew, who just *knew* she was slower than everyone else, and weaker, and stupider; the smell of the woman who'd gone down into Hull's Hole, gotten lost, found herself screaming as she slaughtered the slarn; the smell of the Wing leader who had no idea how to lead, of the friend watching her friends die, the smell of the woman who'd refused to drown when Jonon lem Jonon hauled her beneath the keel over and over and over and over and over.

Tears burning in her eyes, Gwenna looked at the girl. Just looked at her.

Rat bared her teeth.

"You are back?" she demanded.

Gwenna searched for words. There were none. Regret didn't matter. Regret was less than nothing. For some crimes there could be no atoning.

"You are back?" the girl asked again, voice shaking just slightly.

"Rat . . ." Gwenna said. Tears scaled her face. "Oh, Rat."

The girl shook her head slightly. "Name is not Rat."

She bit her lip, then shifted closer to Gwenna, close enough to hold. Close enough to kill.

Gwenna tried to reach out to her, but the hand wouldn't work. Rat took the limp fingers in her own, held them close.

"What is your name?" Gwenna asked.

"Alashki."

Gwenna closed her eyes. It had a beautiful sound to it. Far more beautiful than the name Gwenna had given her.

"What does it mean?"

For a long time, Rat didn't reply. Wind sloughed down through the gap, chilling Gwenna's blood-soaked blacks. The only warm thing in the world was the girl's hand, and then, when she finally spoke, her voice.

"Many storms came to my land. My city. Huge storms. Lightning. Waves as big as mountains. They crash on ships, on docks, on houses, on streets, on everywhere. After a storm there are many lost things, broken things, pieces shattered. Most are taken by the ocean. Some the ocean gives back . . . spits them on the shore. Alashki is a person . . . a job. It is this job to go along the shore after the storm, to find what is lost and broken, to bring it back. That is my name. Alashki."

Gwenna's laugh felt like something inside her breaking. "Of course it is, Alashki. Of course it fucking is."

ACKNOWLEDGMENTS

Here's a funny story—this book used to be an entirely different book, one I was all finished with and ready to publish (three hundred thousand words, a year and a half of work), until my agent, Hannah Bowman, called me up (10 P.M., Friday night), to tell me it wasn't good enough. That was a tough call to get, I'm sure it was a tough call to *make,* but she was right, and I'll be forever grateful that she had the courage to tell me to start over. The book you're holding wouldn't exist without her.

Jen Gunnels took the new product, tossed it on the anvil, and started hammering. She helped me to find strengths in my story that I didn't know were there, bringing me back again and again to the heart of the tale I wanted to tell.

Finally, Suzanne Baker, Gavin Baker, and Patrick Noyes were there as they have been every time to read, consult, challenge, and console. Their fingerprints are on all these books, back to the very beginning.